W9-ATY-475

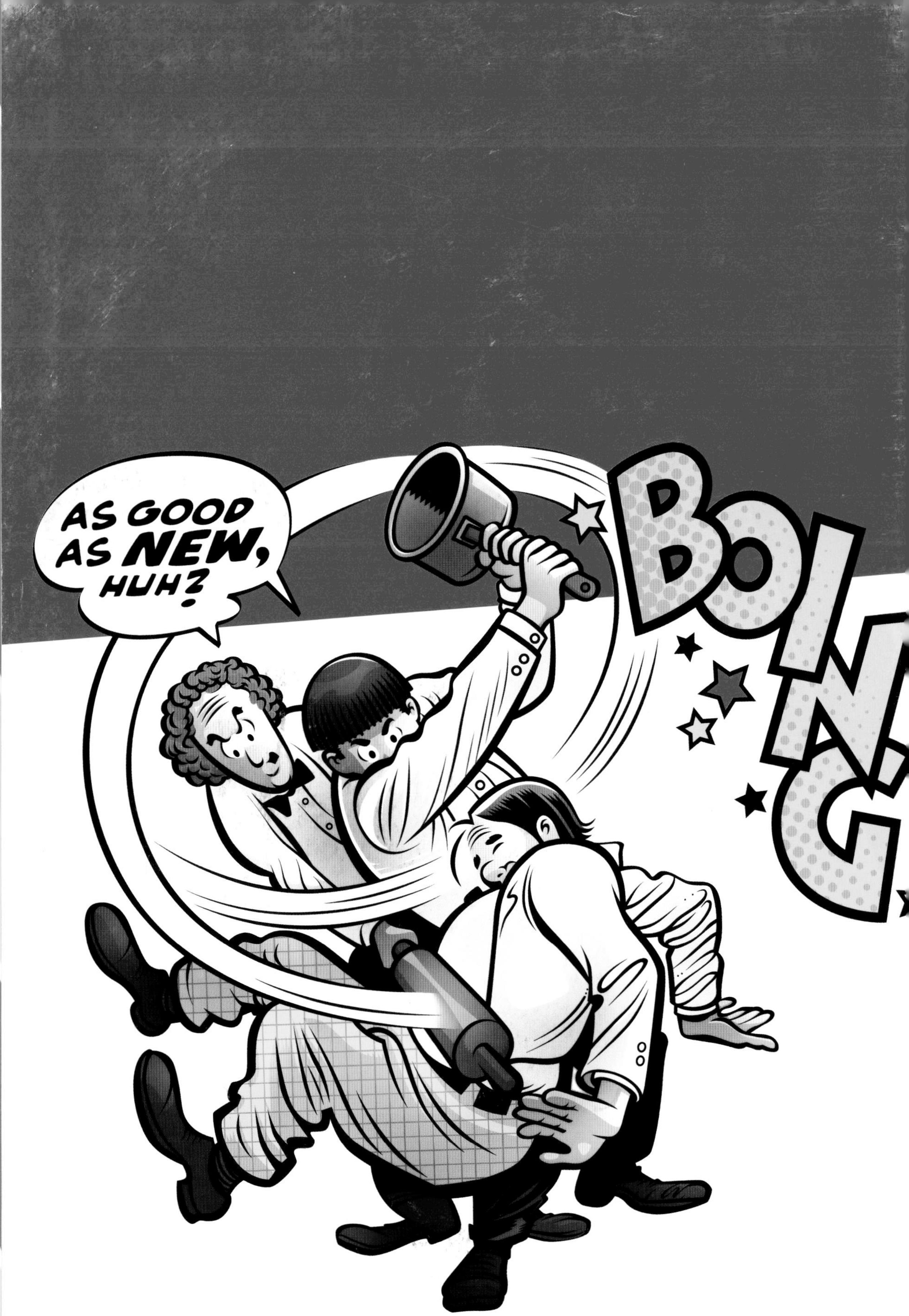
AS GOOD AS NEW, HUH?
BOING

The Best of THE THREE STOOGES® Comicbooks

Volume 1

Presented by *C3 Entertainment, Inc.*

by

NORMAN MAURER
& PETE ALVARADO

Introduction by
JOAN MAURER

PAPERCUT℞ ™
New York

THE THREE STOOGES® GRAPHIC NOVELS AVAILABLE FROM PAPERCUTZ™

ALL-NEW! FULL-COLOR GRAPHIC NOVEL!
SEE THE NEW MOVIE!
The Three Stooges
BED-BUGGED!
PAPERCUTZ

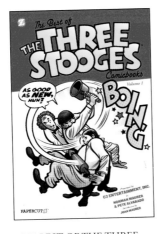

THE THREE STOOGES
#1 "Bed-Bugged"
All-new comics by
George Gladir,
Jim Salicrup, &
Stan Goldberg

The Best of THE THREE STOOGES Comicbooks
Volume 1
AS GOOD AS NEW, HUH?
BOING
PAPERCUTZ

THE BEST OF THE THREE STOOGES COMICBOOKS
Volume One
Classic Stooge comics by
Norman Maurer &
Pete Alvarado
Introduction by
Joan Maurer

THE THREE STOOGES graphic novels are available for $6.99. each in paperback, and $10.99 in hardcover. THE BEST OF THE THREE STOOGES COMICBOOKS graphic novels are only available in hardcover for $19.99 each. Available from booksellers everywhere.

Or order from Papercutz—1-800-886-1223. Please add $4.00 for postage and handling for the first book, and add $1.00 for each additional book. MC, Visa, Amex accepted. Or order by mail, make check payable to NBM Publishing, and send to: Papercutz, 40 Exchange Place, Ste. 1308, New York, NY 10005

WWW.PAPERCUTZ.COM

The Best of The Three Stooges Comicbooks
Presented by C3 Entertainment, Inc.
By Norman Maurer and Pete Alvarado

Norman Maurer and Joe Kubert – Original Editors (St. John comics)
Chase Craig – Original Editor (Western/Dell comics)
Ken Cooper – Art Restoration
Diego Jourdan – Cover/Title Page Illustration (after Norman Maurer)
Adam Grano – Design and Production
Michael T. Gilbert – Consulting Editor
Michael Petranek – Associate Editor
Jim Salicrup
Editor-in-Chief

ISBN: 978-1-59707-328-8

Printed in China
April 2012 by New Era Printing LTD
Trend Centre, 29/31 Cheugn Lee St
Rm1101-1103, 11/F, Chaiwan, Hong Kong

Distributed by Macmillan
First Papercutz Printing

TABLE OF CONTENTS

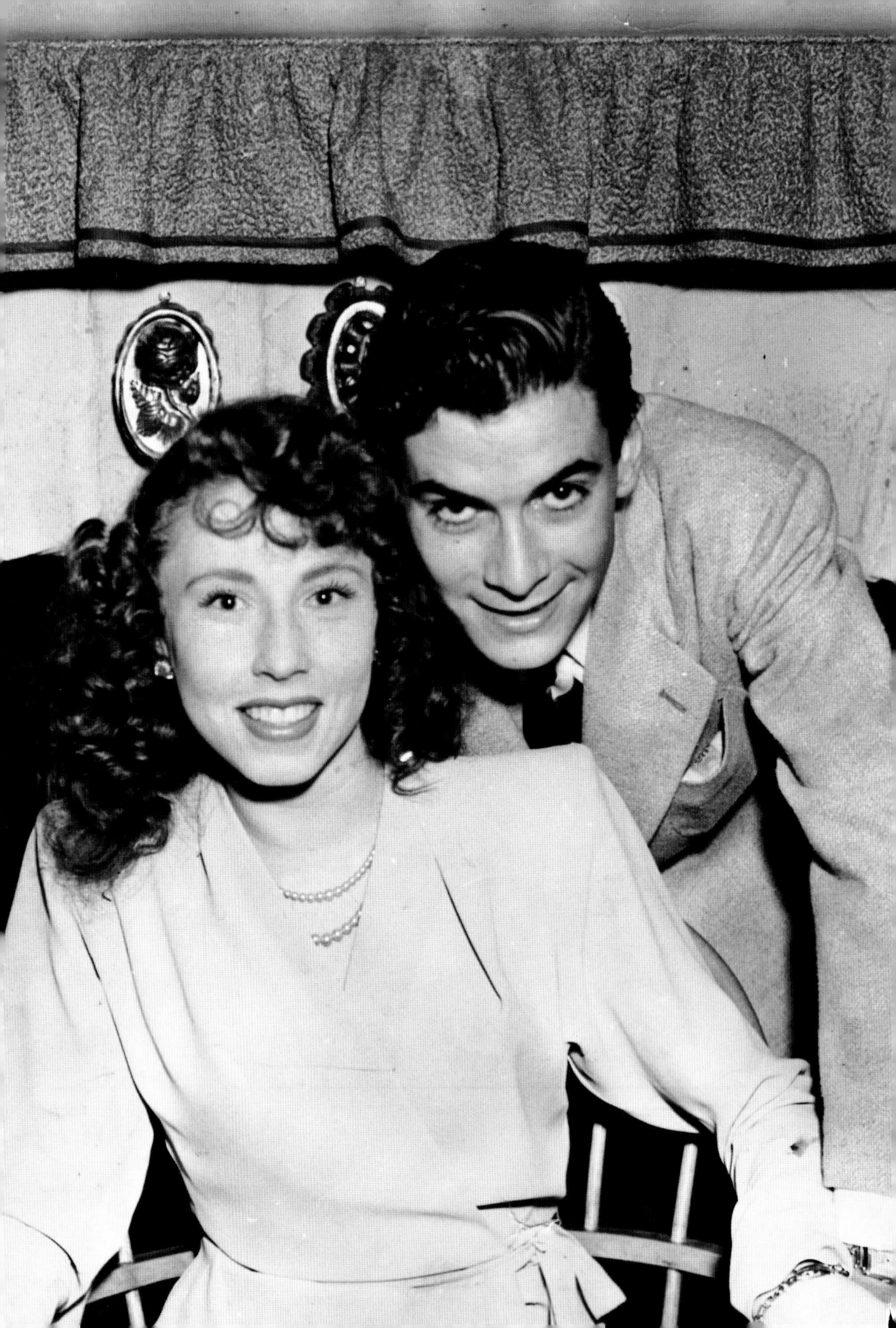

INTRODUCTION

by Joan Maurer

When I met my husband, Norman Maurer, at a party in 1945, he was still in the Navy. While we chatted he proceeded to draw his "Daredevil" character on a paper napkin. From the time I was a young child I loved creativity. So when I saw Norman's dazzling artwork I couldn't help myself; I was hooked. Little did I realize that the decision had been made; from that moment on I would live vicariously through Norman's endless creativity.

Being wary of men in uniform, I felt more comfortable bringing Norman home to meet my parents. What a shock it was for him when my dad walked in. I hadn't bothered to tell Norman that my father was "Mean Moe" of The Three Stooges fame. Fortunately for me dad didn't poke Norman in the eyes and say, "I'll moida ya!" In social situations my father was the perfect gentleman.

Realizing that Norman's comicbook know-how had given him skills in every facet of the film industry, my dad pushed Norman in the direction of Hollywood. It was 1949 when Moe told him, "Forget Daredevil! I want you to do a comicbook for the Stooges." Norman entered "Stooge-dom" with trepidation. And I held my breath. But luckily the books were a huge success.

It wasn't long before Norman's career went from Three Stooges ridiculous to 3-D sublime when he and his partner, Joe Kubert, succeeded in creating the first 3-D comicbook: MIGHTY MOUSE. And it took even less time for Norman to turn Larry, Moe and Curly's slapping, poking, and pie throwing into page-popping mayhem with a series of 3-D THREE STOOGES comicbooks.

In the late fifties, Norman took a radical step that would launch his career in a new direction. Two-reel shorts, like those

the Stooges had made for the past 25 years, were going the way of the dinosaur as TV continued to grow. When the Stooges' contract with Columbia came to an end, Moe figured his career was over. But then the Stooges shorts hit TV and soon became the hottest children's show in the nation. The Three Stooges were back on top. But my dad realized he would need help "surfing" this new tidal wave of popularity. So, he gave Norman an offer he couldn't refuse: to be manager of the Three Stooges.

The rest is Hollywood history.

Norman went on to produce The Three Stooges feature films, write the storylines and direct their last two films, "Around the World in a Daze" and "The Outlaws is Coming!" He managed the boys' live stage act, produced an animated Stooges cartoon series, and put his artistic skills to use yet again, overseeing Stooges merchandising and licensing and even illustrating their movie one-sheets.

So, turn the page and take a look at some of the ridiculous and sublime comic art that all started with a doodle on a napkin. ★

Above: Joan Maurer, Norman Maurer,
Moe Howard, and Helen Howard

Opposite: Joan and Norman Maurer

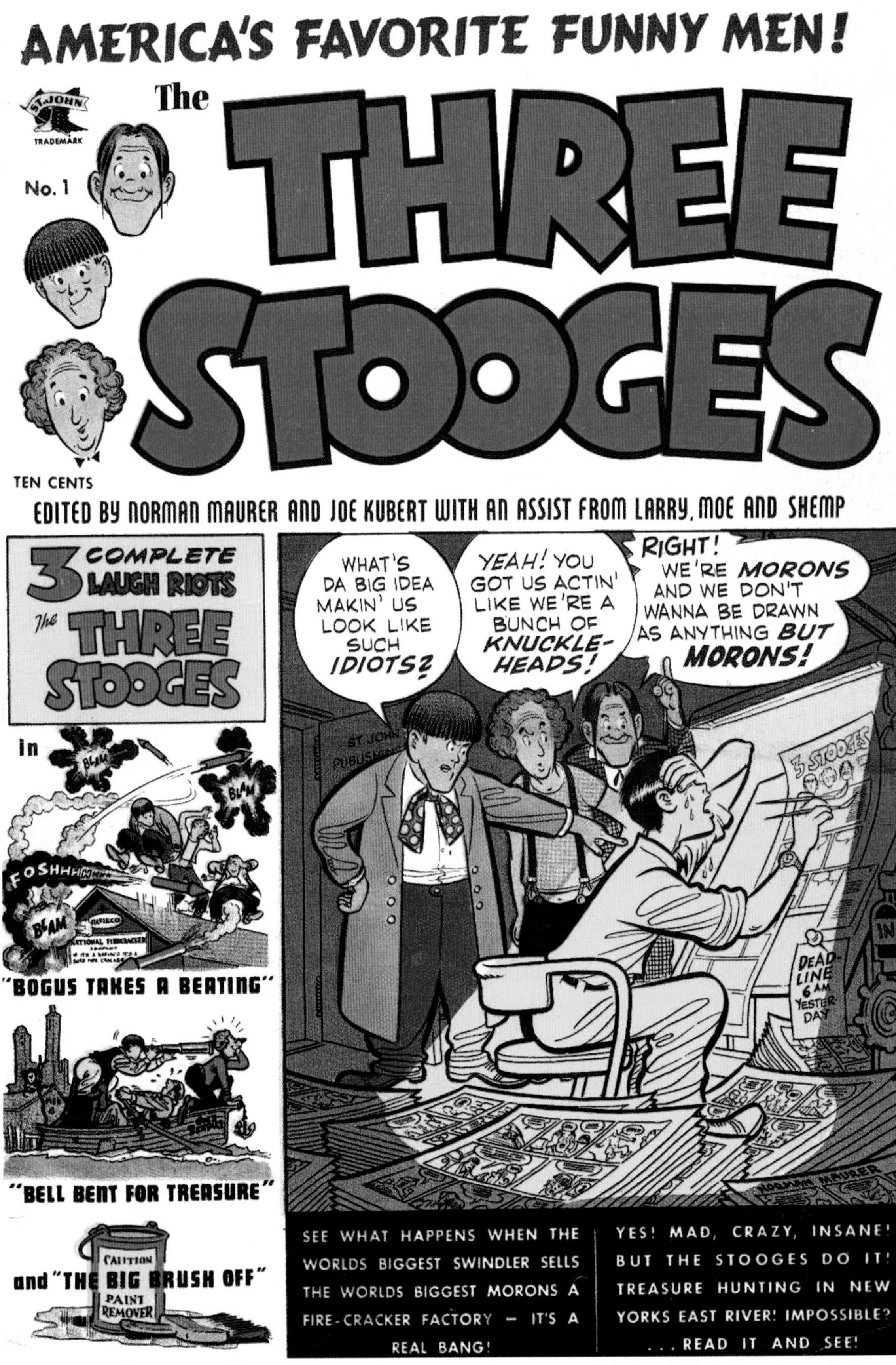
AMERICA'S FAVORITE FUNNY MEN!
ST. JOHN TRADEMARK
No. 1
The THREE STOOGES
TEN CENTS
EDITED BY NORMAN MAURER AND JOE KUBERT WITH AN ASSIST FROM LARRY, MOE AND SHEMP
3 COMPLETE LAUGH RIOTS
The THREE STOOGES
in
BLAM
BLAM
FOSHHHHHHH
BLAM
"BOGUS TAKES A BEATING"
"BELL BENT FOR TREASURE"
CAUTION PAINT REMOVER
and "THE BIG BRUSH OFF"
WHAT'S DA BIG IDEA MAKIN' US LOOK LIKE SUCH IDIOTS?
YEAH! YOU GOT US ACTIN' LIKE WE'RE A BUNCH OF KNUCKLE-HEADS!
RIGHT! WE'RE MORONS AND WE DON'T WANNA BE DRAWN AS ANYTHING BUT MORONS!
3 STOOGES
INK
DEAD-LINE 6 AM YESTER-DAY
NORMAN MAURER
SEE WHAT HAPPENS WHEN THE WORLDS BIGGEST SWINDLER SELLS THE WORLDS BIGGEST MORONS A FIRE-CRACKER FACTORY – IT'S A REAL BANG!
YES! MAD, CRAZY, INSANE! BUT THE STOOGES DO IT! TREASURE HUNTING IN NEW YORKS EAST RIVER! IMPOSSIBLE? ... READ IT AND SEE!

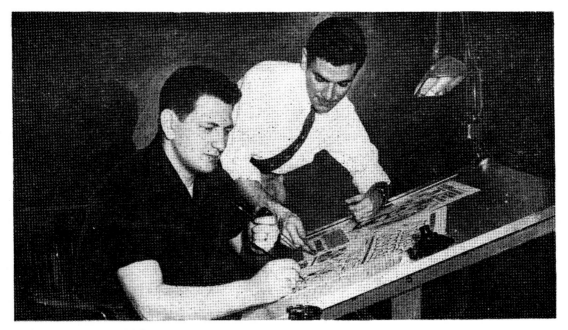

A Letter from the Publisher:

I'd like you, our readers, to meet Joe Kubert and Norman Maurer. Joe and Norm have been friends since boyhood. They first met in New York, where they attended the High School of Music and Art together, in 1940. It was here, at the age of thirteen, that they became interested in cartooning. They got their first jobs working for comic books less than a year later. Yes, Norm and Joe have been drawing for comic books for more than *thirteen years!*

When Joe was sixteen, his parents moved to New Jersey . . . and he along with them. But both boys remained in close contact with one another . . . both dreaming of the time when they could write, draw, and produce comic books themselves. They had a single goal: To create the kind of books that *you,* the *reader,* wants!

It took World War II to separate them, Norm enlisted in the U. S. Navy. While stationed in Los Angeles, California, he was able to continue his work. Norm now makes his home in Hollywood, California.

Joe, on the other hand, made his "new home" in the U. S. Army. After spending some time in Germany, he came back to take up permanent residence in New Jersey.

The 3,200 mile distance between them did not discourage their lifelong ambition. The years of experience . . . the hundreds of successful comic strips both had done . . . are paying off! Now, thirteen years after their first meeting, their aspirations have become reality.

I think that Joe and Norm have created the kind of magazine that you, the reader, will like as much as I do. This magazine is the product of the combination of almost thirty years of experience in this business! But . . . it's *still* up to *you!* The only way they can produce the kind of magazines you want, is through your letters of constructive criticisms to them. Every letter will be screened and evaluated by both Norm and Joe. Consideration as to content in future issues will be based *entirely* on letters received from you. (Some of your letters will appear in these books, answered personally by Norm and/or Joe.) Any and all questions concerning comic books, artists, or writers will be answered.

Their product is in your hands. Norm and Joe have done their work . . . now . . . it's up to *you!*

Archer St. John
Publisher

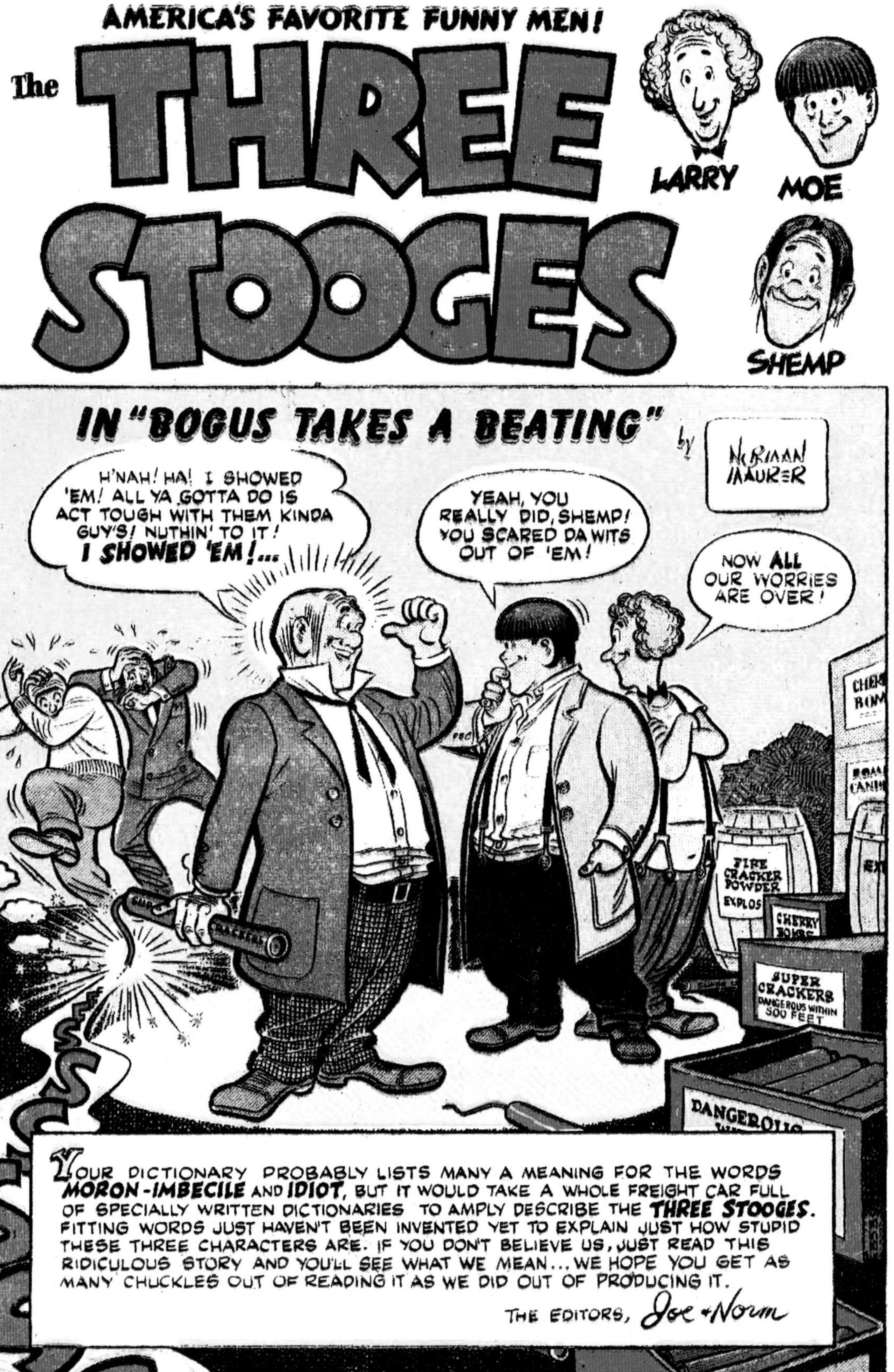

AMERICA'S FAVORITE FUNNY MEN!
The THREE STOOGES
LARRY
MOE
SHEMP
IN "BOGUS TAKES A BEATING" by NORMAN MAURER
H'NAH! HA! I SHOWED 'EM! ALL YA GOTTA DO IS ACT TOUGH WITH THEM KINDA GUY'S! NUTHIN' TO IT! I SHOWED 'EM!...
YEAH, YOU REALLY DID, SHEMP! YOU SCARED DA WITS OUT OF 'EM!
NOW ALL OUR WORRIES ARE OVER!
FIRE CRACKER POWDER
SUPER CRACKERS DANGEROUS WITHIN 500 FEET
YOUR DICTIONARY PROBABLY LISTS MANY A MEANING FOR THE WORDS MORON-IMBECILE AND IDIOT, BUT IT WOULD TAKE A WHOLE FREIGHT CAR FULL OF SPECIALLY WRITTEN DICTIONARIES TO AMPLY DESCRIBE THE THREE STOOGES. FITTING WORDS JUST HAVEN'T BEEN INVENTED YET TO EXPLAIN JUST HOW STUPID THESE THREE CHARACTERS ARE. IF YOU DON'T BELIEVE US, JUST READ THIS RIDICULOUS STORY AND YOU'LL SEE WHAT WE MEAN... WE HOPE YOU GET AS MANY CHUCKLES OUT OF READING IT AS WE DID OUT OF PRODUCING IT.
THE EDITORS, Joe + Norm

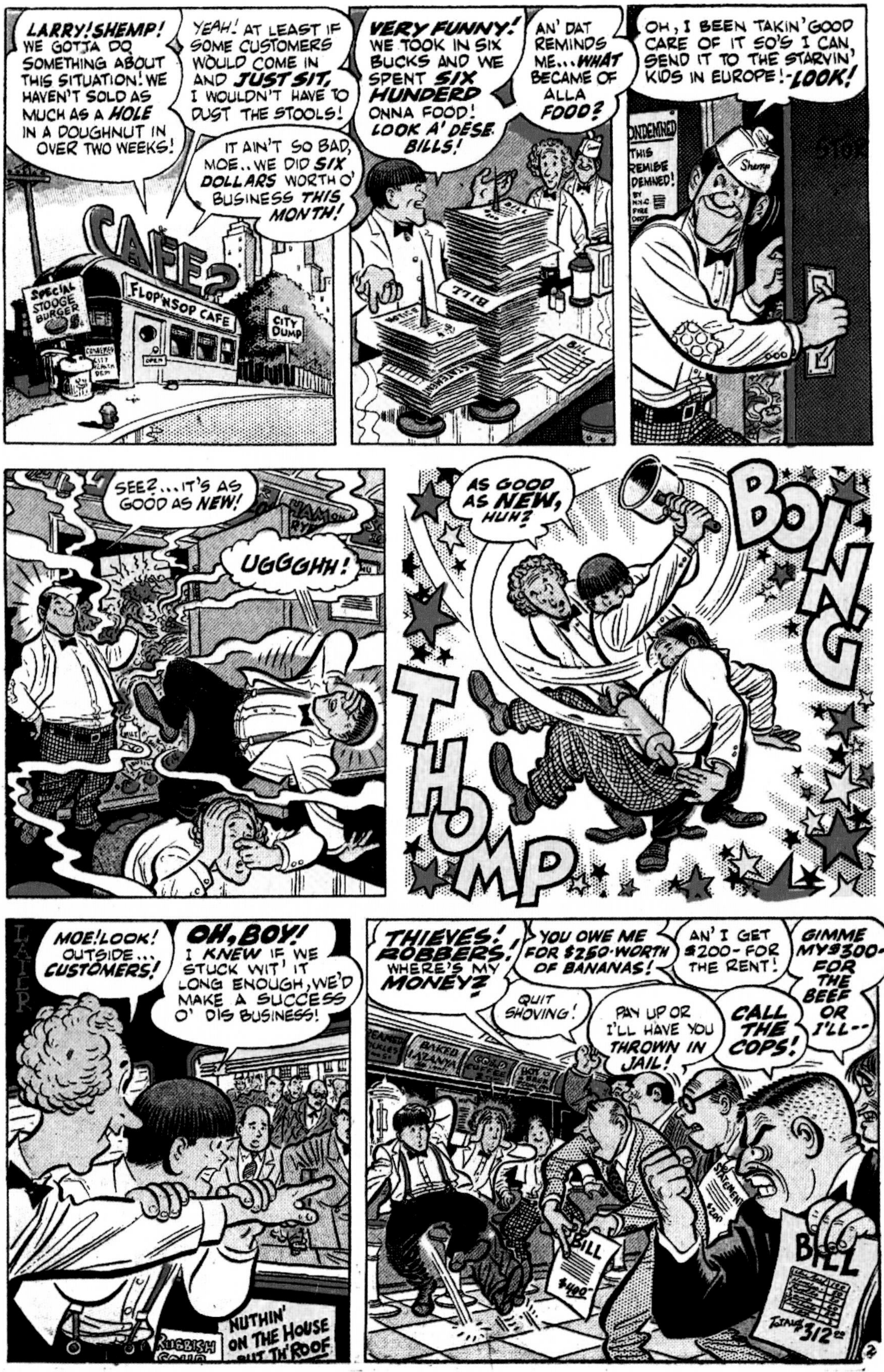

LARRY! SHEMP! WE GOTTA DO SOMETHING ABOUT THIS SITUATION! WE HAVEN'T SOLD AS MUCH AS A HOLE IN A DOUGHNUT IN OVER TWO WEEKS!
YEAH! AT LEAST IF SOME CUSTOMERS WOULD COME IN AND JUST SIT, I WOULDN'T HAVE TO DUST THE STOOLS!
IT AIN'T SO BAD, MOE.. WE DID SIX DOLLARS WORTH O' BUSINESS THIS MONTH!
CAFE?
SPECIAL STOOGE BURGER
FLOP'N SOP CAFE
CITY DUMP
VERY FUNNY! WE TOOK IN SIX BUCKS AND WE SPENT SIX HUNDERD ONNA FOOD! LOOK A' DESE BILLS!
AN' DAT REMINDS ME...WHAT BECAME OF ALLA FOOD?
BILL
OH, I BEEN TAKIN' GOOD CARE OF IT SO'S I CAN SEND IT TO THE STARVIN' KIDS IN EUROPE! -LOOK!
Shemp
SEE?...IT'S AS GOOD AS NEW!
UGGGHH!
AS GOOD AS NEW, HUH?
BOING
THOMP
LATER
MOE! LOOK! OUTSIDE... CUSTOMERS!
OH, BOY! I KNEW IF WE STUCK WIT' IT LONG ENOUGH, WE'D MAKE A SUCCESS O' DIS BUSINESS!
NUTHIN' ON THE HOUSE BUT TH' ROOF
THIEVES! ROBBERS! WHERE'S MY MONEY?
YOU OWE ME FOR $250-WORTH OF BANANAS!
AN' I GET $200- FOR THE RENT!
GIMME MY $300- FOR THE BEEF OR I'LL--
QUIT SHOVING!
PAY UP OR I'LL HAVE YOU THROWN IN JAIL!
CALL THE COPS!
STATEMENT
BILL $400
BILL
TOTAL $312

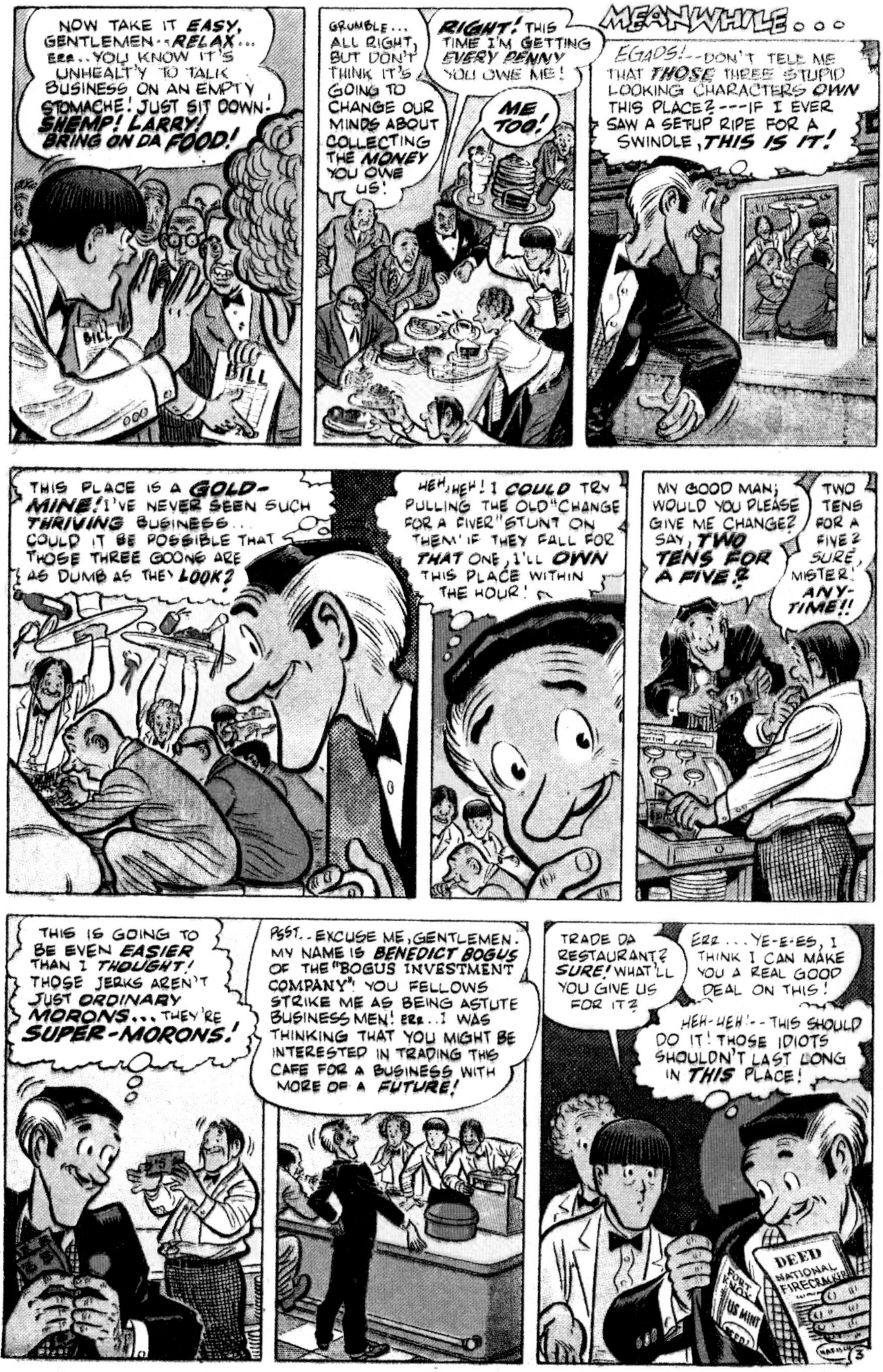
NOW TAKE IT EASY, GENTLEMEN--RELAX... ERR..YOU KNOW IT'S UNHEALT'Y TO TALK BUSINESS ON AN EMPTY STOMACHE! JUST SIT DOWN! SHEMP! LARRY! BRING ON DA FOOD!
BILL
BILL
GRUMBLE... ALL RIGHT, BUT DON'T THINK IT'S GOING TO CHANGE OUR MINDS ABOUT COLLECTING THE MONEY YOU OWE US!
RIGHT! THIS TIME I'M GETTING EVERY PENNY YOU OWE ME!
ME TOO!
MEANWHILE...
EGADS!--DON'T TELL ME THAT THOSE THREE STUPID LOOKING CHARACTERS OWN THIS PLACE?---IF I EVER SAW A SETUP RIPE FOR A SWINDLE, THIS IS IT!
THIS PLACE IS A GOLD-MINE! I'VE NEVER SEEN SUCH THRIVING BUSINESS.. COULD IT BE POSSIBLE THAT THOSE THREE GOONS ARE AS DUMB AS THEY LOOK?
HEH, HEH! I COULD TRY PULLING THE OLD "CHANGE FOR A FIVER" STUNT ON THEM! IF THEY FALL FOR THAT ONE, I'LL OWN THIS PLACE WITHIN THE HOUR!
MY GOOD MAN; WOULD YOU PLEASE GIVE ME CHANGE? SAY, TWO TENS FOR A FIVE?
TWO TENS FOR A FIVE? SURE, MISTER! ANY-TIME!!
THIS IS GOING TO BE EVEN EASIER THAN I THOUGHT! THOSE JERKS AREN'T JUST ORDINARY MORONS... THEY'RE SUPER-MORONS!
PSST..EXCUSE ME, GENTLEMEN. MY NAME IS BENEDICT BOGUS OF THE "BOGUS INVESTMENT COMPANY"! YOU FELLOWS STRIKE ME AS BEING ASTUTE BUSINESS MEN! ERR..I WAS THINKING THAT YOU MIGHT BE INTERESTED IN TRADING THIS CAFE FOR A BUSINESS WITH MORE OF A FUTURE!
TRADE DA RESTAURANT? SURE! WHAT'LL YOU GIVE US FOR IT?
ERR... YE-E-ES, I THINK I CAN MAKE YOU A REAL GOOD DEAL ON THIS!
HEH-HEH!--THIS SHOULD DO IT! THOSE IDIOTS SHOULDN'T LAST LONG IN THIS PLACE!
DEED NATIONAL FIRECRACKER
FORT KNOX
US MINT

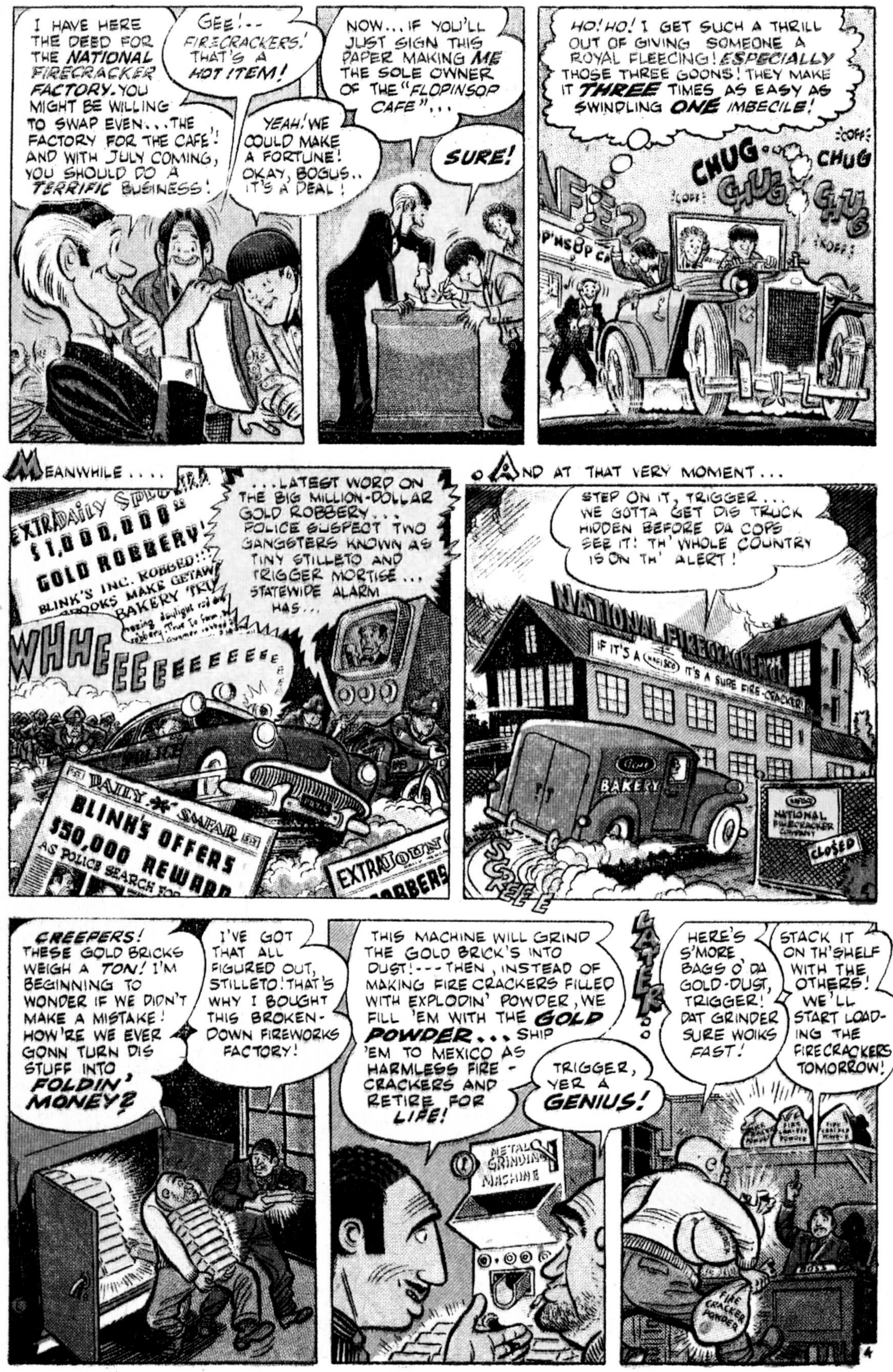
I HAVE HERE THE DEED FOR THE NATIONAL FIRECRACKER FACTORY. YOU MIGHT BE WILLING TO SWAP EVEN...THE FACTORY FOR THE CAFE! AND WITH JULY COMING, YOU SHOULD DO A TERRIFIC BUSINESS!
GEE!.. FIRECRACKERS! THAT'S A HOT ITEM!
YEAH! WE COULD MAKE A FORTUNE! OKAY, BOGUS.. IT'S A DEAL!
NOW... IF YOU'LL JUST SIGN THIS PAPER MAKING ME THE SOLE OWNER OF THE "FLOPINSOP CAFE"...
SURE!
HO! HO! I GET SUCH A THRILL OUT OF GIVING SOMEONE A ROYAL FLEECING! ESPECIALLY THOSE THREE GOONS! THEY MAKE IT THREE TIMES AS EASY AS SWINDLING ONE IMBECILE!
CHUG CHUG CHUG CHUG
COFF
MEANWHILE....
...LATEST WORD ON THE BIG MILLION-DOLLAR GOLD ROBBERY... POLICE SUSPECT TWO GANGSTERS KNOWN AS TINY STILLETO AND TRIGGER MORTISE... STATEWIDE ALARM HAS...
EXTRA DAILY SPL
$1,000,000 GOLD ROBBERY!
BLINK'S INC. ROBBED!
BAKERY TRU
WHHEEEEEEEEEE
DAILY SMEAR
BLINK'S OFFERS $50,000 REWARD
AS POLICE SEARCH FOR
EXTRA
ROBBERS
AND AT THAT VERY MOMENT...
STEP ON IT, TRIGGER... WE GOTTA GET DIS TRUCK HIDDEN BEFORE DA COPS SEE IT! TH' WHOLE COUNTRY IS ON TH' ALERT!
NATIONAL FIRECRACKER CO.
IF IT'S A NAFISCO IT'S A SURE FIRE-CRACKER!
BAKERY
NATIONAL FIRECRACKER COMPANY
CLOSED
SCREEE
CREEPERS! THESE GOLD BRICKS WEIGH A TON! I'M BEGINNING TO WONDER IF WE DIDN'T MAKE A MISTAKE! HOW'RE WE EVER GONN TURN DIS STUFF INTO FOLDIN' MONEY?
I'VE GOT THAT ALL FIGURED OUT, STILLETO! THAT'S WHY I BOUGHT THIS BROKEN-DOWN FIREWORKS FACTORY!
THIS MACHINE WILL GRIND THE GOLD BRICK'S INTO DUST!---THEN, INSTEAD OF MAKING FIRE CRACKERS FILLED WITH EXPLODIN' POWDER, WE FILL 'EM WITH THE GOLD POWDER... SHIP 'EM TO MEXICO AS HARMLESS FIRE-CRACKERS AND RETIRE FOR LIFE!
TRIGGER, YER A GENIUS!
METAL GRINDING MACHINE
LATER..
HERE'S S'MORE BAGS O' DA GOLD-DUST, TRIGGER! DAT GRINDER SURE WOIKS FAST!
STACK IT ON TH' SHELF WITH THE OTHERS! WE'LL START LOADING THE FIRECRACKERS TOMORROW!
FIRE CRACKER POWDER
4

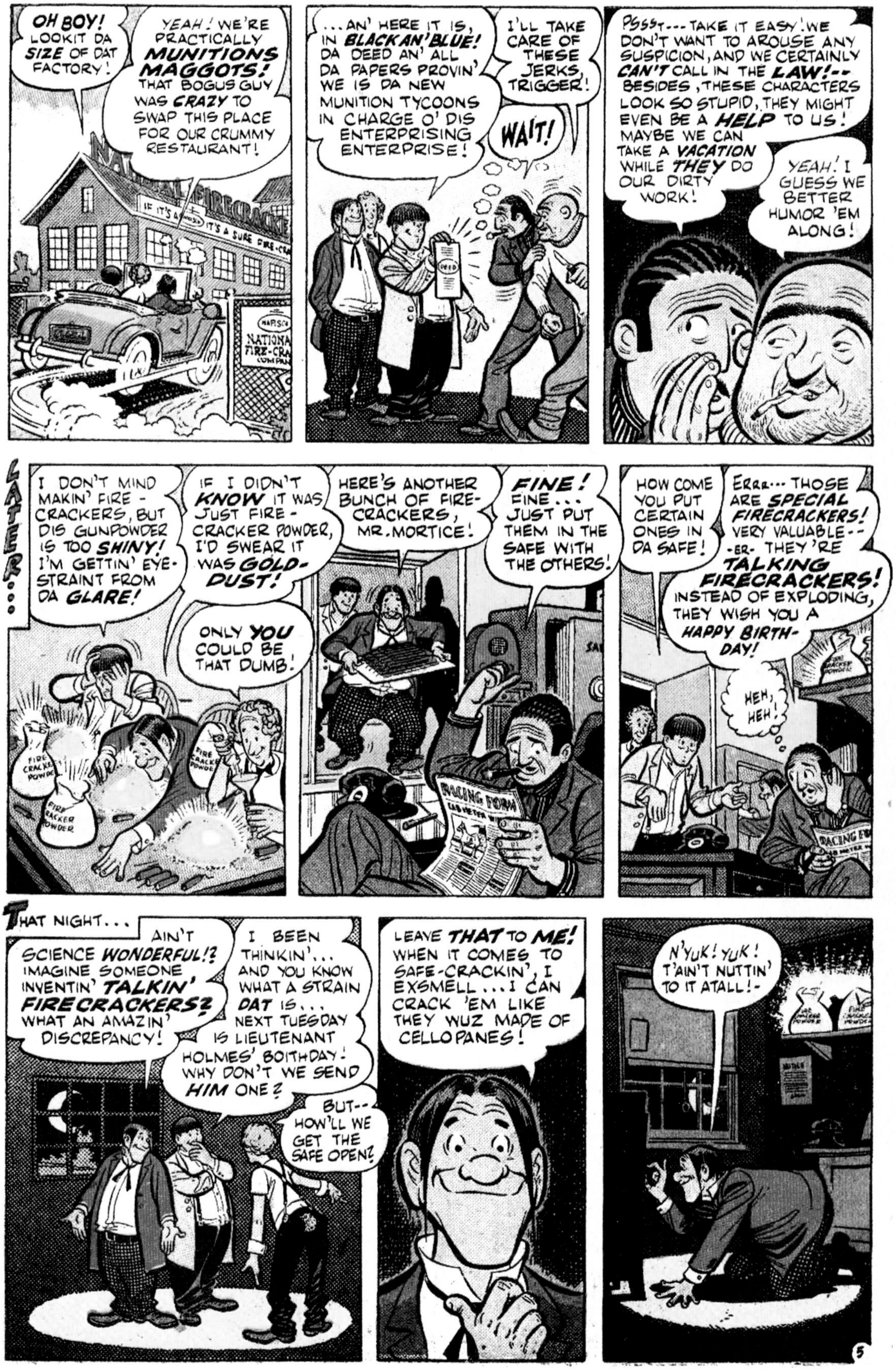

OH BOY! LOOKIT DA SIZE OF DAT FACTORY!
YEAH! WE'RE PRACTICALLY MUNITIONS MAGGOTS! THAT BOGUS GUY WAS CRAZY TO SWAP THIS PLACE FOR OUR CRUMMY RESTAURANT!
...AN' HERE IT IS, IN BLACK AN' BLUE! DA DEED AN' ALL DA PAPERS PROVIN' WE IS DA NEW MUNITION TYCOONS IN CHARGE O' DIS ENTERPRISING ENTERPRISE!
I'LL TAKE CARE OF THESE JERKS, TRIGGER!
WAIT!
PSSST--- TAKE IT EASY! WE DON'T WANT TO AROUSE ANY SUSPICION, AND WE CERTAINLY CAN'T CALL IN THE LAW!-- BESIDES, THESE CHARACTERS LOOK SO STUPID, THEY MIGHT EVEN BE A HELP TO US! MAYBE WE CAN TAKE A VACATION WHILE THEY DO OUR DIRTY WORK!
YEAH! I GUESS WE BETTER HUMOR 'EM ALONG!
LATER...
I DON'T MIND MAKIN' FIRE-CRACKERS, BUT DIS GUNPOWDER IS TOO SHINY! I'M GETTIN' EYE-STRAINT FROM DA GLARE!
IF I DIDN'T KNOW IT WAS JUST FIRE-CRACKER POWDER, I'D SWEAR IT WAS GOLD-DUST!
ONLY YOU COULD BE THAT DUMB!
FIRE CRACKER POWDER
HERE'S ANOTHER BUNCH OF FIRE-CRACKERS, MR. MORTICE!
FINE! FINE... JUST PUT THEM IN THE SAFE WITH THE OTHERS!
RACING FORM
HOW COME YOU PUT CERTAIN ONES IN DA SAFE!
ERRR... THOSE ARE SPECIAL FIRECRACKERS! VERY VALUABLE-- -ER- THEY'RE TALKING FIRECRACKERS! INSTEAD OF EXPLODING, THEY WISH YOU A HAPPY BIRTH-DAY!
HEH, HEH!
THAT NIGHT...
AIN'T SCIENCE WONDERFUL!? IMAGINE SOMEONE INVENTIN' TALKIN' FIRECRACKERS? WHAT AN AMAZIN' DISCREPANCY!
I BEEN THINKIN'... AND YOU KNOW WHAT A STRAIN DAT IS... NEXT TUESDAY IS LIEUTENANT HOLMES' BOITHDAY! WHY DON'T WE SEND HIM ONE?
BUT-- HOW'LL WE GET THE SAFE OPEN?
LEAVE THAT TO ME! WHEN IT COMES TO SAFE-CRACKIN', I EXSMELL... I CAN CRACK 'EM LIKE THEY WUZ MADE OF CELLOPANES!
N'YUK! YUK! T'AIN'T NUTTIN' TO IT ATALL!-
5

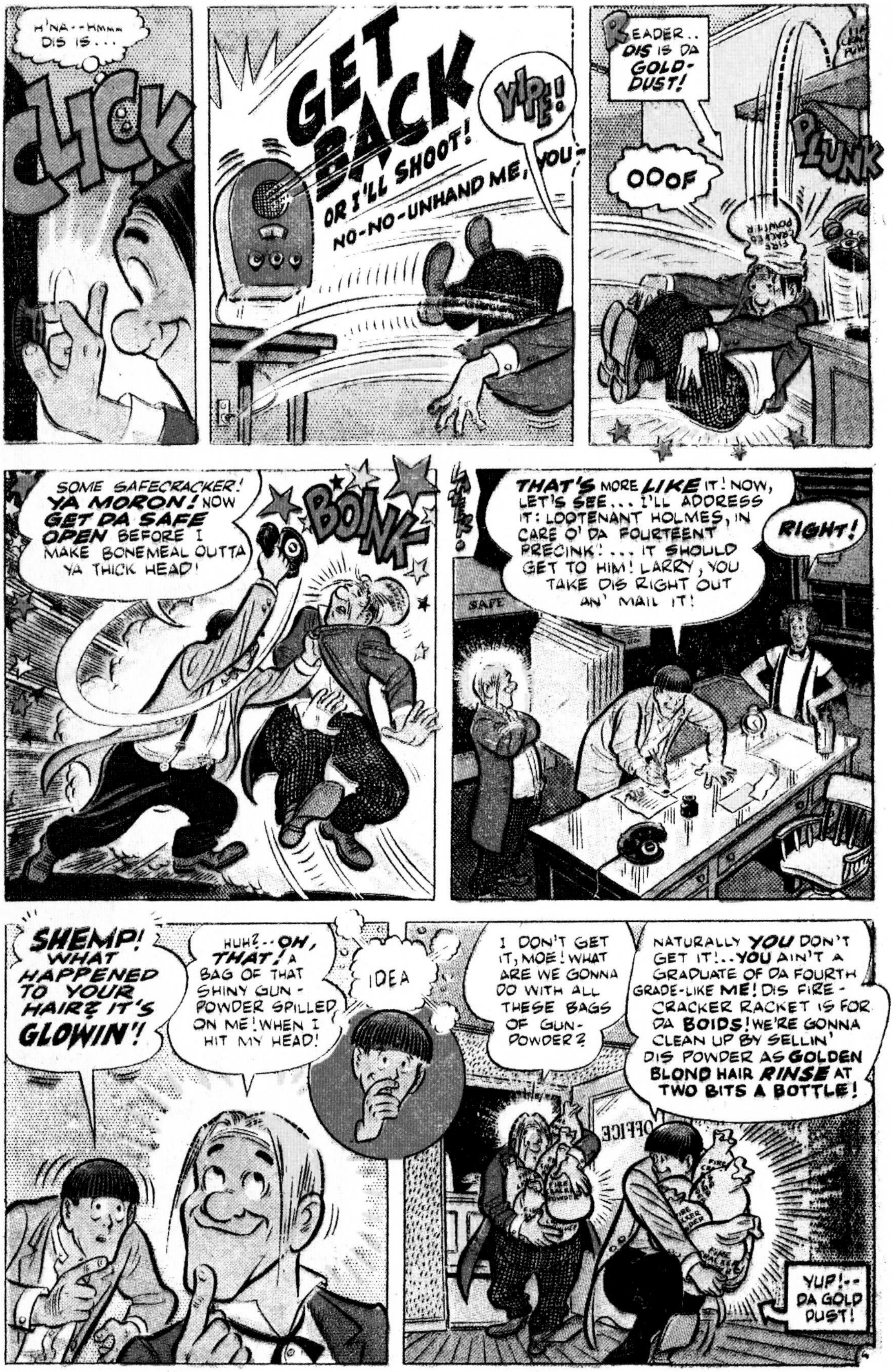
H'NA--HMMM DIS IS...
CLICK
GET BACK OR I'LL SHOOT!
YIPE!
NO-NO-UNHAND ME, YOU-
READER.. DIS IS DA GOLD-DUST!
OOOF
PLUNK
FIRE CRACKER POWDER
SOME SAFECRACKER! YA MORON! NOW GET DA SAFE OPEN BEFORE I MAKE BONEMEAL OUTTA YA THICK HEAD!
BOINK
THAT'S MORE LIKE IT! NOW, LET'S SEE... I'LL ADDRESS IT: LOOTENANT HOLMES, IN CARE O' DA FOURTEENT PRECINK! ... IT SHOULD GET TO HIM! LARRY, YOU TAKE DIS RIGHT OUT AN' MAIL IT!
RIGHT!
SAFE
SHEMP! WHAT HAPPENED TO YOUR HAIR? IT'S GLOWIN'!
HUH?--OH, THAT! A BAG OF THAT SHINY GUN-POWDER SPILLED ON ME! WHEN I HIT MY HEAD!
IDEA
I DON'T GET IT, MOE! WHAT ARE WE GONNA DO WITH ALL THESE BAGS OF GUN-POWDER?
NATURALLY YOU DON'T GET IT!..YOU AIN'T A GRADUATE OF DA FOURTH GRADE-LIKE ME! DIS FIRE-CRACKER RACKET IS FOR DA BOIDS! WE'RE GONNA CLEAN UP BY SELLIN' DIS POWDER AS GOLDEN BLOND HAIR RINSE AT TWO BITS A BOTTLE!
OFFICE
YUP!--DA GOLD DUST!

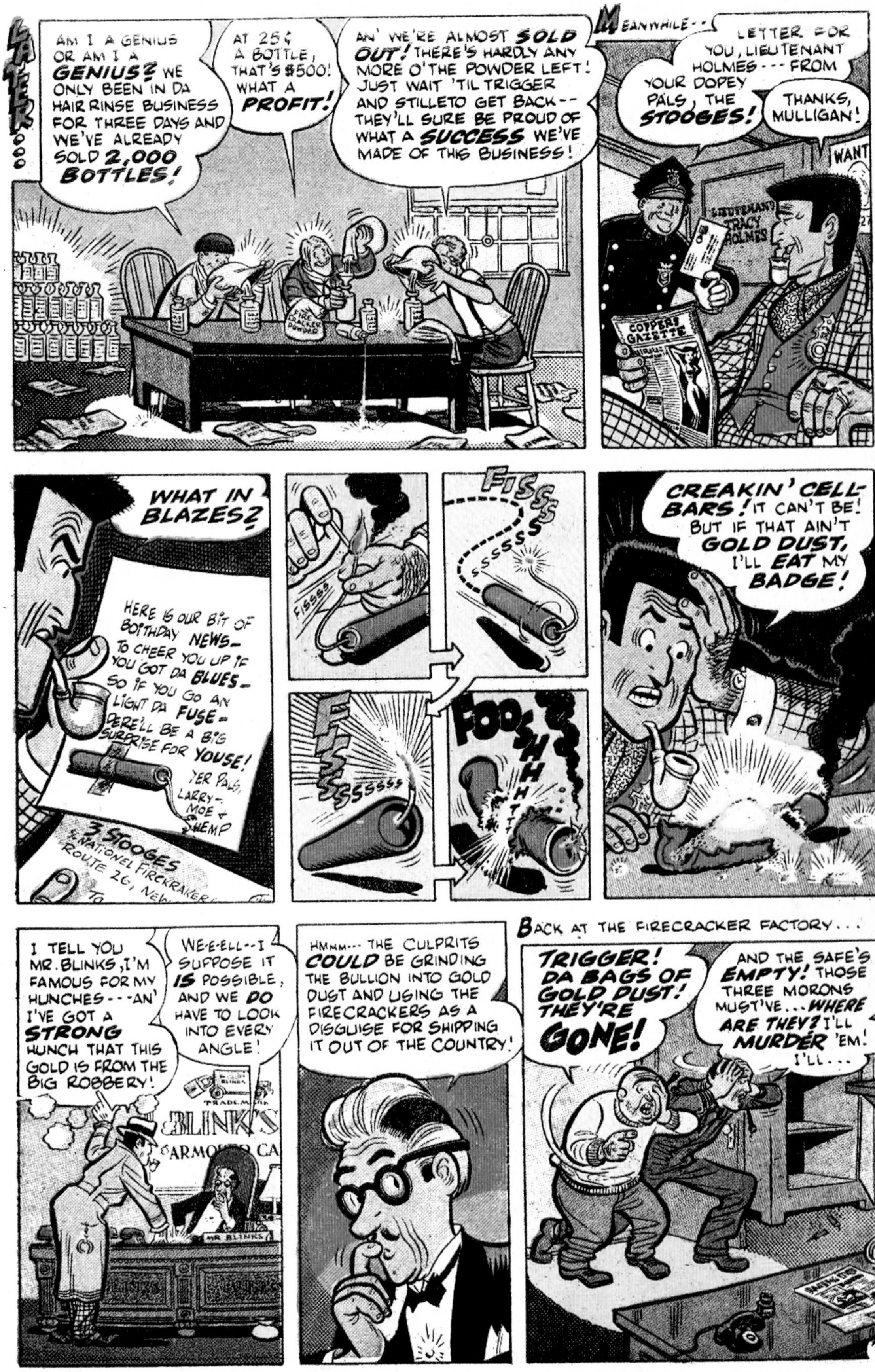
LATER...
AM I A GENIUS OR AM I A GENIUS? WE ONLY BEEN IN DA HAIR RINSE BUSINESS FOR THREE DAYS AND WE'VE ALREADY SOLD 2,000 BOTTLES!
AT 25¢ A BOTTLE, THAT'S $500! WHAT A PROFIT!
AN' WE'RE ALMOST SOLD OUT! THERE'S HARDLY ANY MORE O'THE POWDER LEFT! JUST WAIT 'TIL TRIGGER AND STILLETO GET BACK -- THEY'LL SURE BE PROUD OF WHAT A SUCCESS WE'VE MADE OF THIS BUSINESS!
FIRE CRACKER POWDER
MEANWHILE...
LETTER FOR YOU, LIEUTENANT HOLMES --- FROM YOUR DOPEY PALS, THE STOOGES!
THANKS, MULLIGAN!
WANT
LIEUTENANT TRACY HOLMES
COPPERS GAZETTE
WHAT IN BLAZES?
HERE IS OUR BIT OF BOITHDAY NEWS-- TO CHEER YOU UP IF YOU GOT DA BLUES-- SO IF YOU GO AN LIGHT DA FUSE-- DERE'LL BE A BIG SURPRISE FOR YOUSE!
YER PALS, LARRY- MOE + SHEMP
3 STOOGES NATIONEL FIREKRAKER ROUTE 26, NEW
FISSSS
FISSSS
SSSSSS
FISSS SSSSSS
FOOSHHHHH
CREAKIN' CELL-BARS! IT CAN'T BE! BUT IF THAT AIN'T GOLD DUST, I'LL EAT MY BADGE!
I TELL YOU MR. BLINKS, I'M FAMOUS FOR MY HUNCHES --- AN' I'VE GOT A STRONG HUNCH THAT THIS GOLD IS FROM THE BIG ROBBERY!
WE-E-ELL -- I SUPPOSE IT IS POSSIBLE, AND WE DO HAVE TO LOOK INTO EVERY ANGLE!
BLINKS ARMORED CA
MR BLINKS
HMMM--- THE CULPRITS COULD BE GRINDING THE BULLION INTO GOLD DUST AND USING THE FIRECRACKERS AS A DISGUISE FOR SHIPPING IT OUT OF THE COUNTRY!
BACK AT THE FIRECRACKER FACTORY...
TRIGGER! DA BAGS OF GOLD DUST! THEY'RE GONE!
AND THE SAFE'S EMPTY! THOSE THREE MORONS MUST'VE... WHERE ARE THEY? I'LL MURDER 'EM! I'LL...
7

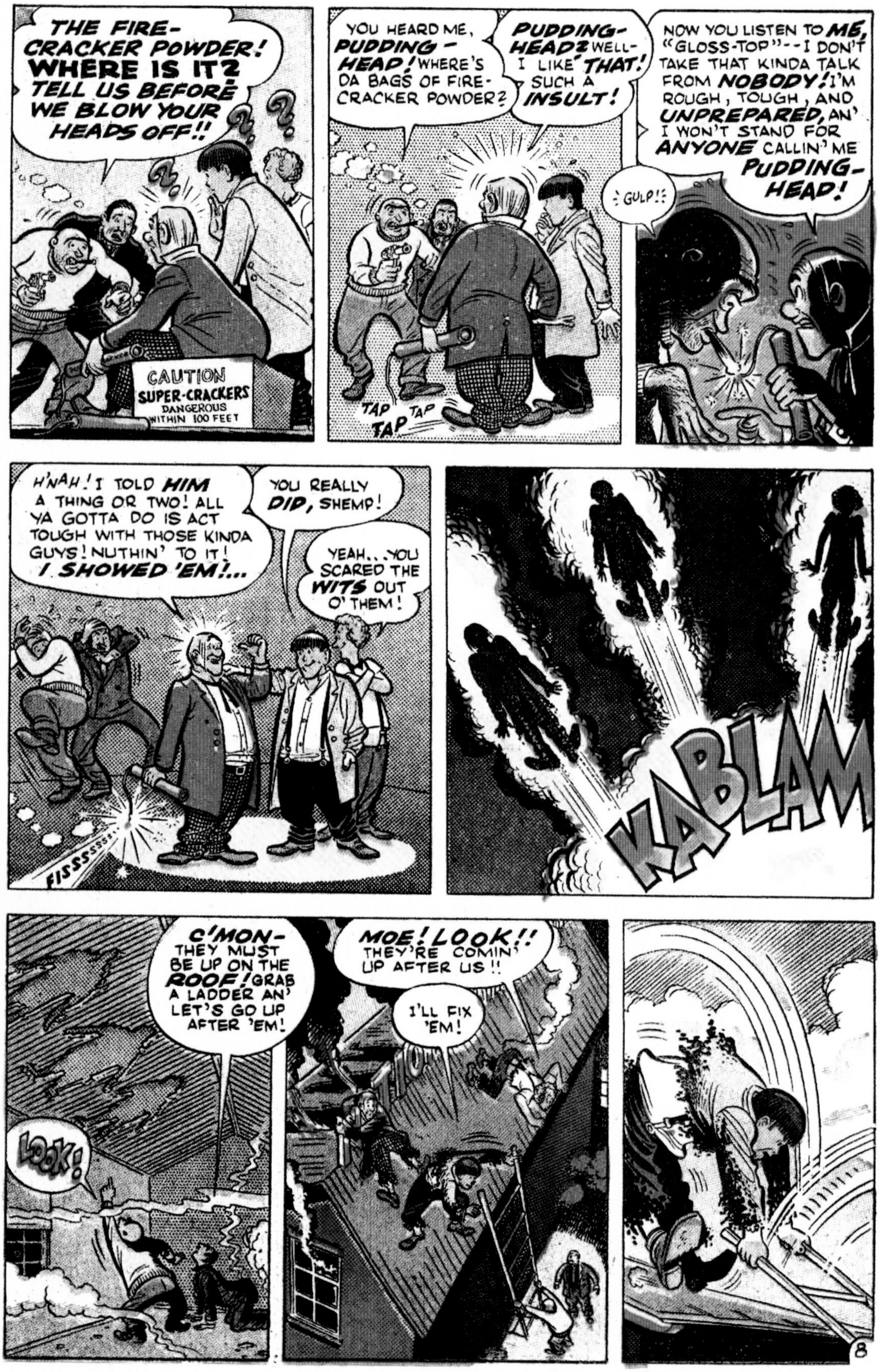
THE FIRE-CRACKER POWDER! WHERE IS IT? TELL US BEFORE WE BLOW YOUR HEADS OFF!!
CAUTION SUPER-CRACKERS DANGEROUS WITHIN 100 FEET
YOU HEARD ME, PUDDING-HEAD! WHERE'S DA BAGS OF FIRE-CRACKER POWDER?
PUDDING-HEAD? WELL-I LIKE THAT! SUCH A INSULT!
TAP TAP TAP
NOW YOU LISTEN TO ME, "GLOSS-TOP"--I DON'T TAKE THAT KINDA TALK FROM NOBODY! I'M ROUGH, TOUGH, AND UNPREPARED, AN' I WON'T STAND FOR ANYONE CALLIN' ME PUDDING-HEAD!
GULP!
H'NAH! I TOLD HIM A THING OR TWO! ALL YA GOTTA DO IS ACT TOUGH WITH THOSE KINDA GUYS! NUTHIN' TO IT! I SHOWED 'EM!...
YOU REALLY DID, SHEMP!
YEAH...YOU SCARED THE WITS OUT O' THEM!
FISSSSSSS
KABLAM
C'MON-THEY MUST BE UP ON THE ROOF! GRAB A LADDER AN' LET'S GO UP AFTER 'EM!
LOOK!
MOE! LOOK!! THEY'RE COMIN' UP AFTER US!!
I'LL FIX 'EM!
8

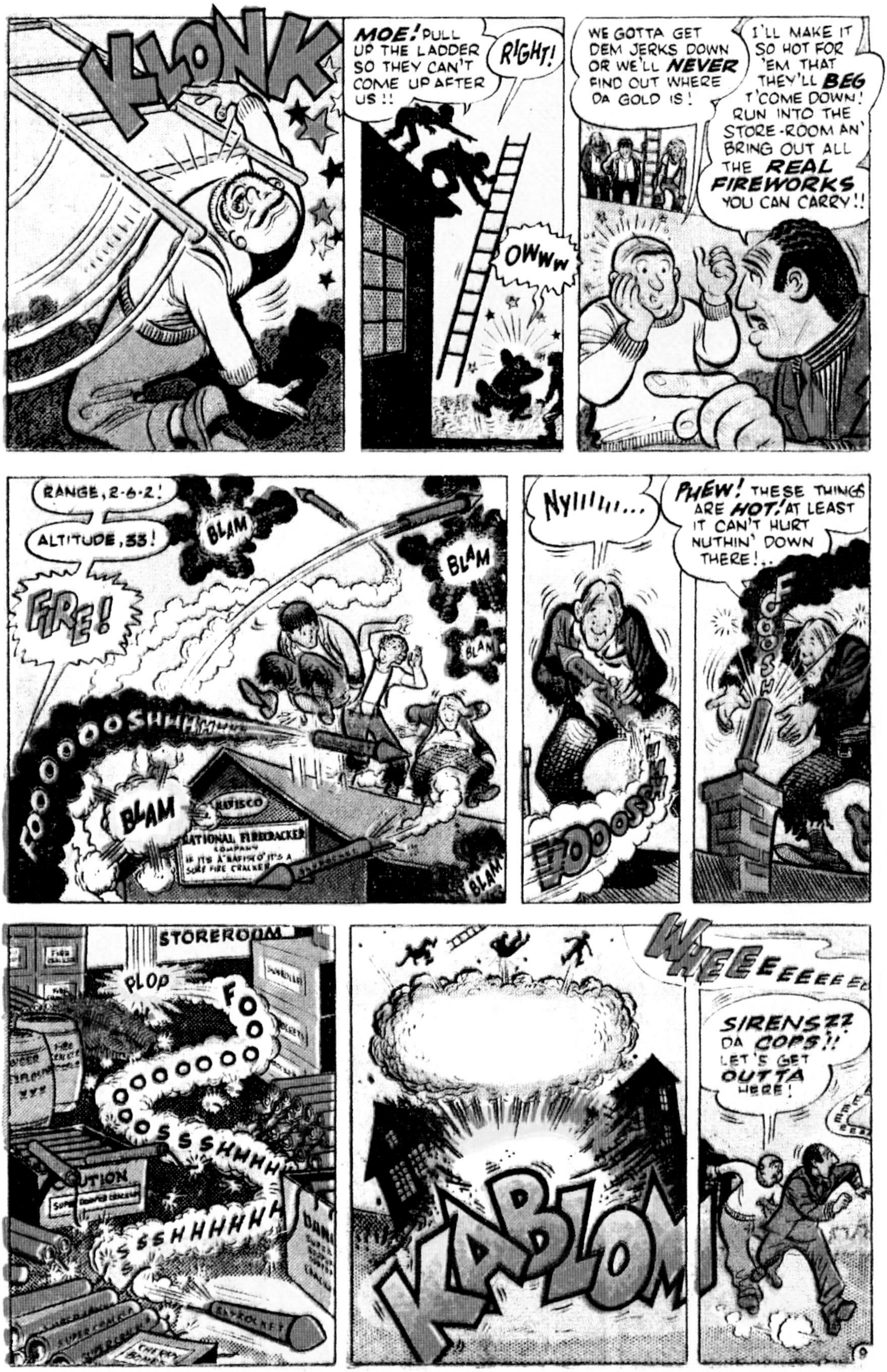
KLONK
MOE! PULL UP THE LADDER SO THEY CAN'T COME UP AFTER US!!
RIGHT!
OWWW
WE GOTTA GET DEM JERKS DOWN OR WE'LL NEVER FIND OUT WHERE DA GOLD IS!
I'LL MAKE IT SO HOT FOR 'EM THAT THEY'LL BEG T'COME DOWN! RUN INTO THE STORE-ROOM AN' BRING OUT ALL THE REAL FIREWORKS YOU CAN CARRY!!
RANGE, 2-6-2!
ALTITUDE, 33!
FIRE!
BLAM
BLAM
BLAM
FOOOOOOOSHHHH
BLAM
NATIONAL FIRECRACKER COMPANY
BLAM
NYIIIII...
PHEW! THESE THINGS ARE HOT! AT LEAST IT CAN'T HURT NUTHIN' DOWN THERE!..
STOREROOM
PLOP
FOOOOOOOOOOOSSSHHHH
SSSHHHHHH
CAUTION
SKYROCKET
WHEEEEEEEEE
SIRENS?? DA COPS!! LET'S GET OUTTA HERE!
KABLOOM

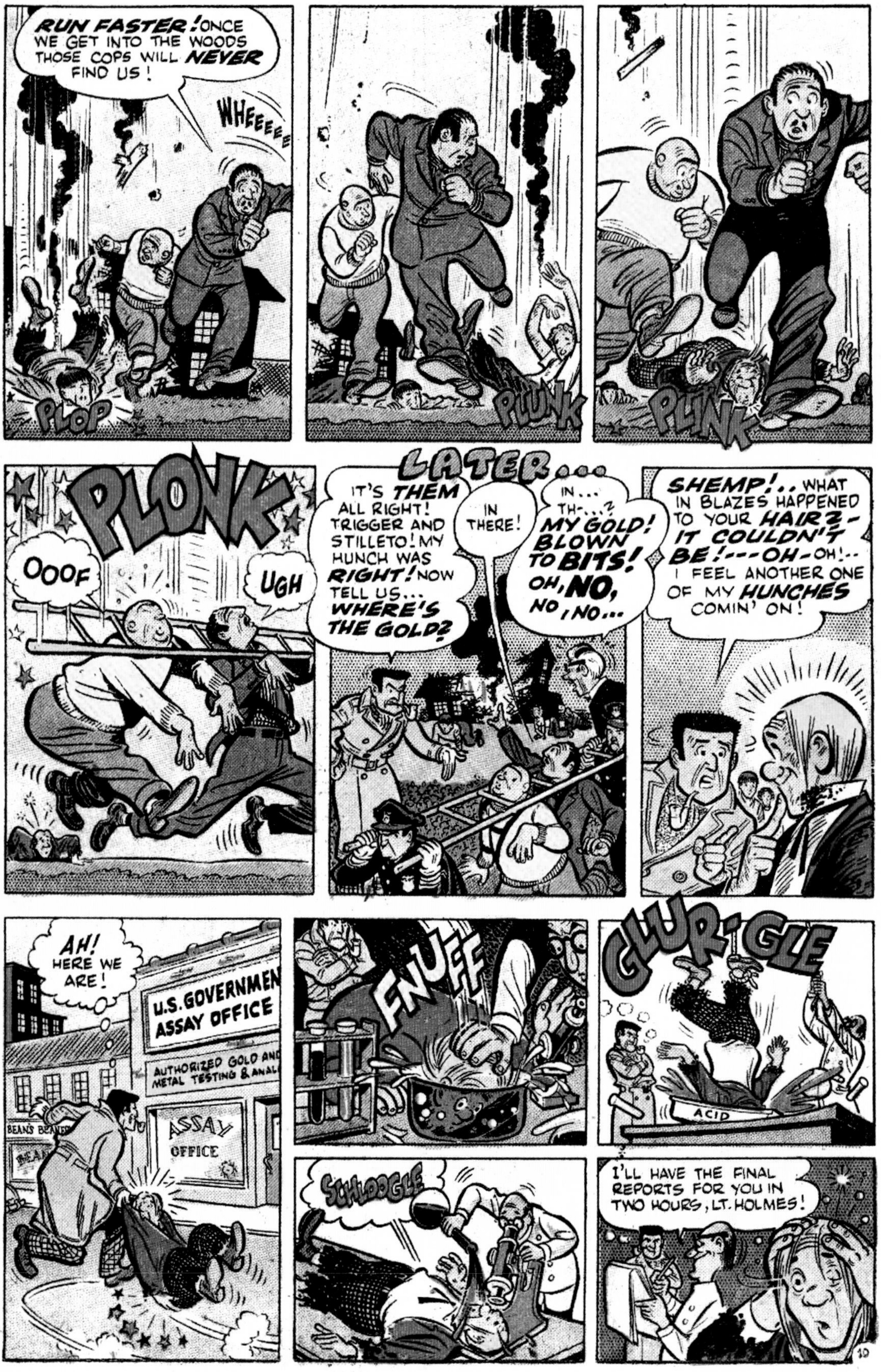
RUN FASTER! ONCE WE GET INTO THE WOODS THOSE COPS WILL NEVER FIND US!
WHEEEEEE
PLOP
PLUNK
PLINK
PLONK
OOOF
UGH
LATER...
IT'S THEM ALL RIGHT! TRIGGER AND STILLETO! MY HUNCH WAS RIGHT! NOW TELL US... WHERE'S THE GOLD?
IN THERE!
IN... TH-...? MY GOLD! BLOWN TO BITS! OH, NO, NO, NO...
SHEMP!.. WHAT IN BLAZES HAPPENED TO YOUR HAIR?- IT COULDN'T BE!---OH-OH!.. I FEEL ANOTHER ONE OF MY HUNCHES COMIN' ON!
AH! HERE WE ARE!
U.S. GOVERNMEN
ASSAY OFFICE
AUTHORIZED GOLD AND METAL TESTING & ANAL
BEAN'S BEAN
ASSAY OFFICE
FNUFF
GLUR-GLE
ACID
SCHLOOGLE
I'LL HAVE THE FINAL REPORTS FOR YOU IN TWO HOURS, LT. HOLMES!
10

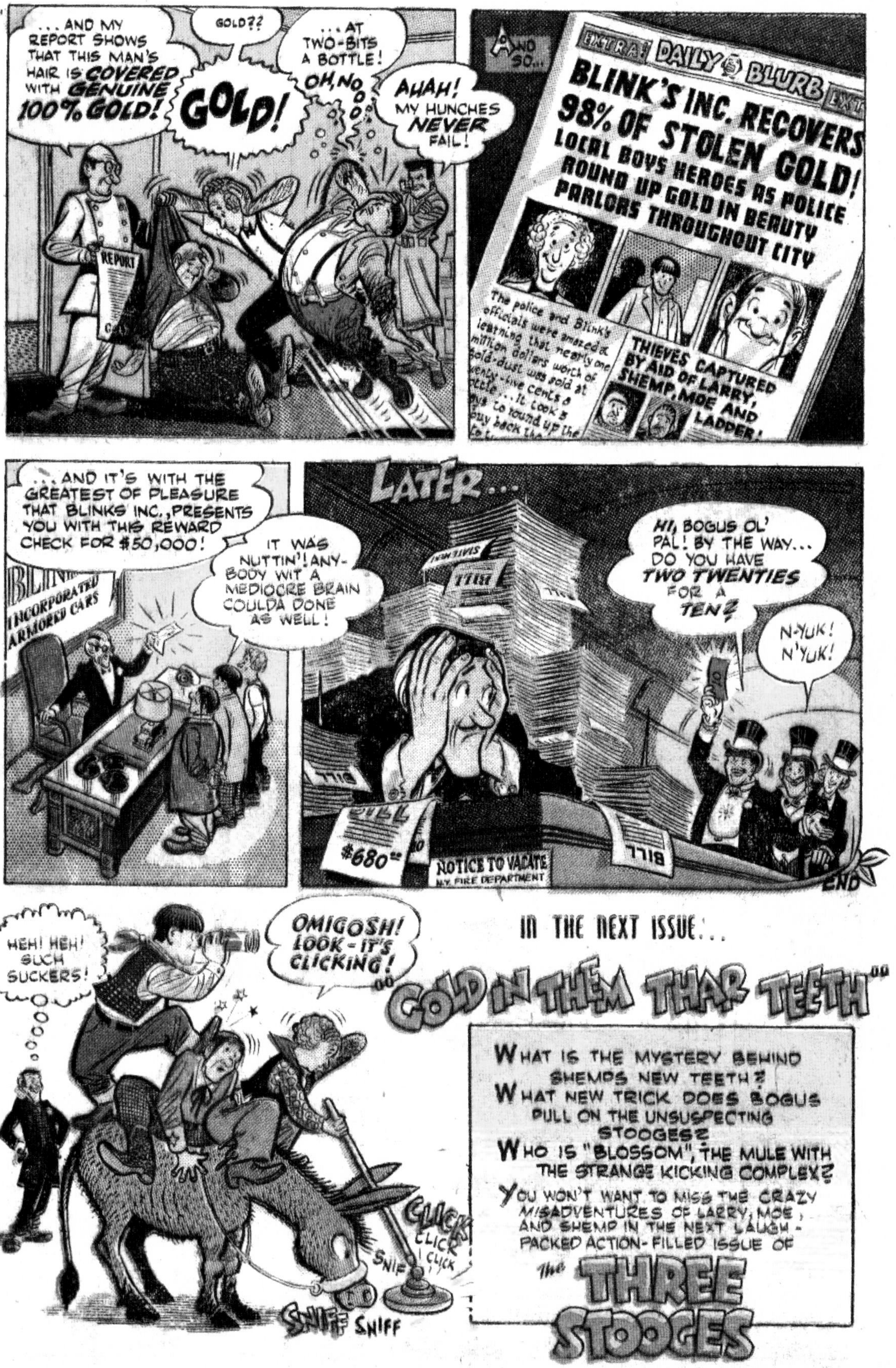
...AND MY REPORT SHOWS THAT THIS MAN'S HAIR IS COVERED WITH GENUINE 100% GOLD!
GOLD??
GOLD!
...AT TWO-BITS A BOTTLE!
OH, NOOOO!
AHAH! MY HUNCHES NEVER FAIL!
REPORT
AND SO...
EXTRA! DAILY BLURB EXTRA
BLINK'S INC. RECOVERS 98% OF STOLEN GOLD!
LOCAL BOYS HEROES AS POLICE ROUND UP GOLD IN BEAUTY PARLORS THROUGHOUT CITY
The police and Blink's officials were amazed at learning that nearly one million dollars worth of gold-dust was sold at twenty-five cents a bottle... it took 3 days to round up the...
THIEVES CAPTURED BY AID OF LARRY, SHEMP, MOE AND LADDER!
...AND IT'S WITH THE GREATEST OF PLEASURE THAT BLINKS INC., PRESENTS YOU WITH THIS REWARD CHECK FOR $50,000!
IT WAS NUTTIN'! ANYBODY WIT A MEDIOCRE BRAIN COULDA DONE AS WELL!
BLINKS INCORPORATED ARMORED CARS
LATER...
STATEMENT
BILL
HI, BOGUS OL' PAL! BY THE WAY... DO YOU HAVE TWO TWENTIES FOR A TEN?
N-YUK! N'YUK!
BILL
$680.00
NOTICE TO VACATE N.Y. FIRE DEPARTMENT
BILL
END
HEH! HEH! SUCH SUCKERS!
OMIGOSH! LOOK - IT'S CLICKING!
CLICK CLICK CLICK
SNIFF SNIFF SNIFF
IN THE NEXT ISSUE...
"GOLD IN THEM THAR TEETH"
WHAT IS THE MYSTERY BEHIND SHEMPS NEW TEETH?
WHAT NEW TRICK DOES BOGUS PULL ON THE UNSUSPECTING STOOGES?
WHO IS "BLOSSOM", THE MULE WITH THE STRANGE KICKING COMPLEX?
YOU WON'T WANT TO MISS THE CRAZY MISADVENTURES OF LARRY, MOE, AND SHEMP IN THE NEXT LAUGH-PACKED ACTION-FILLED ISSUE OF
The THREE STOOGES

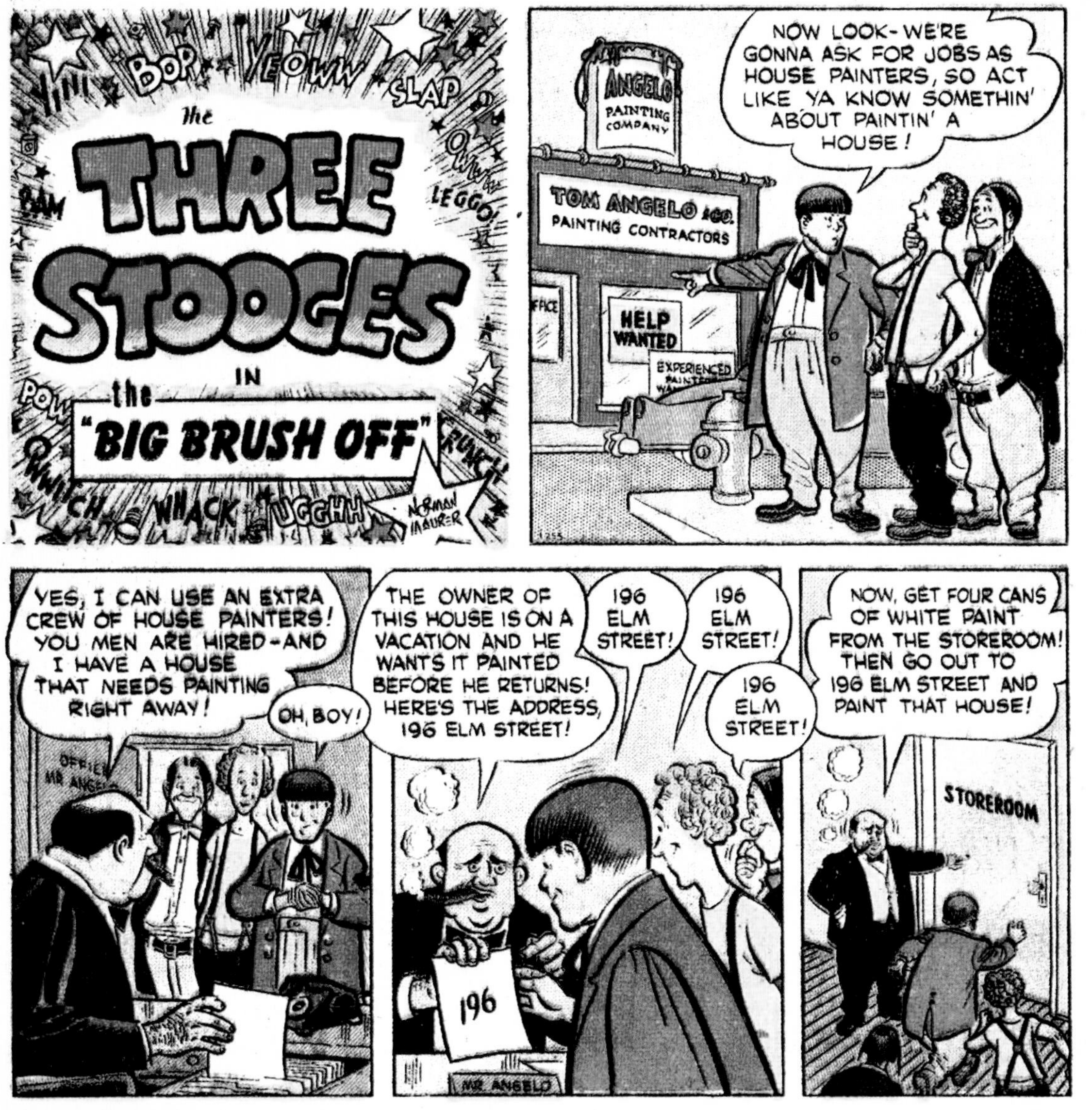

BOP
YEOWW
SLAP
the
THREE STOOGES
IN
the "BIG BRUSH OFF"
LEGGO
BAM
POW
WHACK
UGGHH
NORMAN MAURER
NOW LOOK- WE'RE GONNA ASK FOR JOBS AS HOUSE PAINTERS, SO ACT LIKE YA KNOW SOMETHIN' ABOUT PAINTIN' A HOUSE!
ANGELO PAINTING COMPANY
TOM ANGELO & CO. PAINTING CONTRACTORS
HELP WANTED
EXPERIENCED
YES, I CAN USE AN EXTRA CREW OF HOUSE PAINTERS! YOU MEN ARE HIRED - AND I HAVE A HOUSE THAT NEEDS PAINTING RIGHT AWAY!
OH, BOY!
THE OWNER OF THIS HOUSE IS ON A VACATION AND HE WANTS IT PAINTED BEFORE HE RETURNS! HERE'S THE ADDRESS, 196 ELM STREET!
196 ELM STREET!
196 ELM STREET!
196 ELM STREET!
196
MR ANGELO
NOW, GET FOUR CANS OF WHITE PAINT FROM THE STOREROOM! THEN GO OUT TO 196 ELM STREET AND PAINT THAT HOUSE!
STOREROOM
WHAT'S PAINT REMOVER?
GRAB DOSE WHITE PAINT CANS AND LET'S GO!
THAT MUST BE A GUY WHO STEALS PAINT!
WARNING PAINT REMOVER
MR ANGELO MUST'VE HAD A LOT OF PAINT STOLEN LATELY!
YEAH, HE'S EVEN GOT SIGNS ON THE PAINT CANS WARNING US ABOUT THE PAINT REMOVER THAT'S BEEN STEALING HIS PAINT!
MEANWHILE...
IMAGINE, YOU - MY OWN HUSBAND, OWNER OF A PAINT COMPANY AND I HAD TO WAIT 10 YEARS TO HAVE OUR OWN HOUSE PAINTED!
YES, DEAR, BUT THERE'S BEEN SO MUCH BUSINESS THAT I COULDN'T SPARE THE MEN UNTIL LAST WEEK!

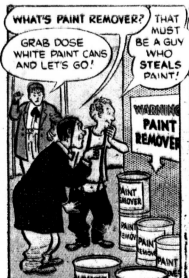

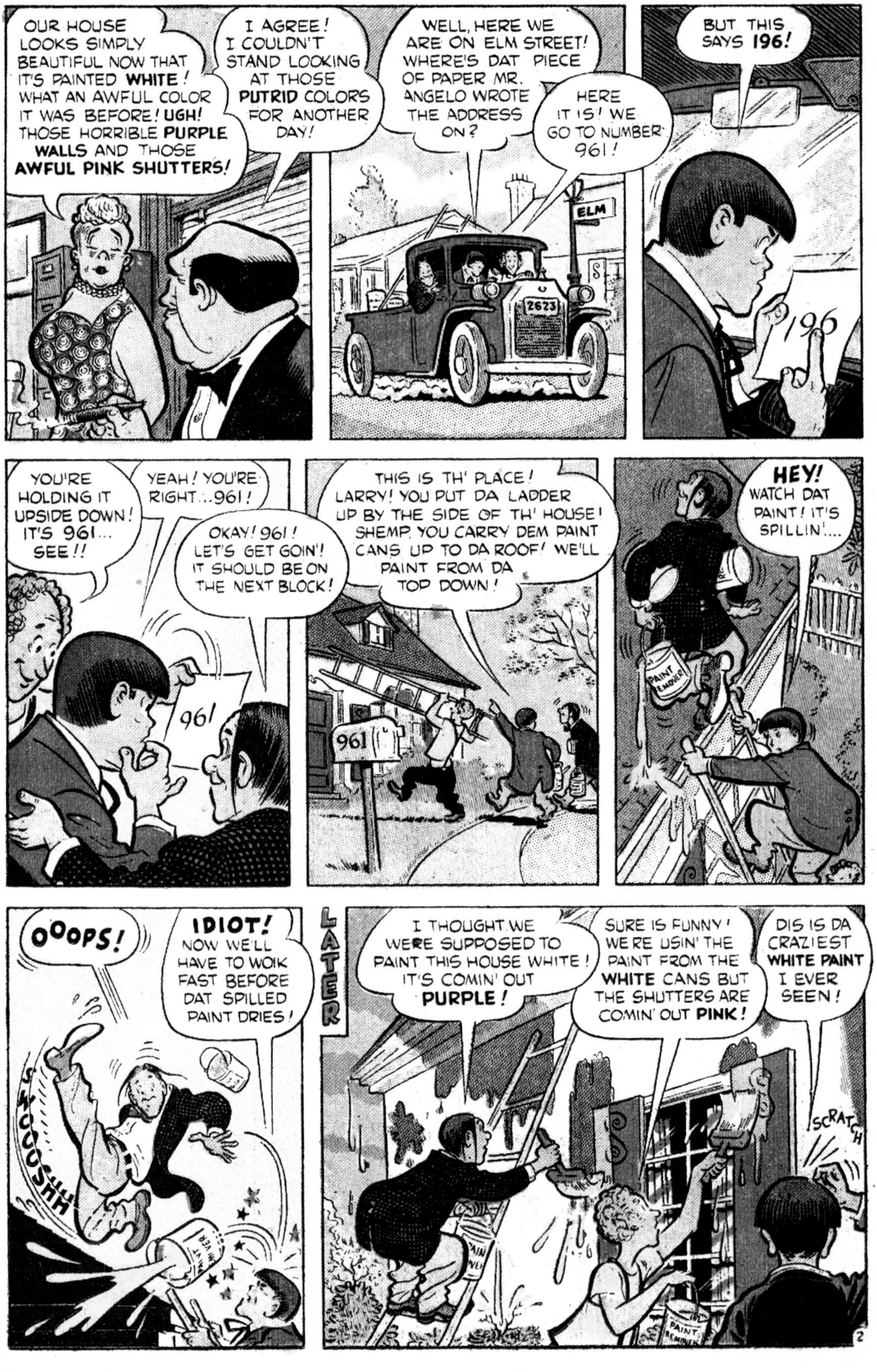
OUR HOUSE LOOKS SIMPLY BEAUTIFUL NOW THAT IT'S PAINTED **WHITE**! WHAT AN AWFUL COLOR IT WAS BEFORE! **UGH!** THOSE HORRIBLE **PURPLE WALLS** AND THOSE **AWFUL PINK SHUTTERS!**
I AGREE! I COULDN'T STAND LOOKING AT THOSE **PUTRID** COLORS FOR ANOTHER DAY!
WELL, HERE WE ARE ON ELM STREET! WHERE'S DAT PIECE OF PAPER MR. ANGELO WROTE THE ADDRESS ON?
HERE IT IS! WE GO TO NUMBER 961!
ELM
2623
BUT THIS SAYS **196!**
196
YOU'RE HOLDING IT UPSIDE DOWN! IT'S 961... SEE!!
YEAH! YOU'RE RIGHT...961!
OKAY! 961! LET'S GET GOIN'! IT SHOULD BE ON THE NEXT BLOCK!
961
THIS IS TH' PLACE! LARRY! YOU PUT DA LADDER UP BY THE SIDE OF TH' HOUSE! SHEMP, YOU CARRY DEM PAINT CANS UP TO DA ROOF! WE'LL PAINT FROM DA TOP DOWN!
961
HEY! WATCH DAT PAINT! IT'S SPILLIN'....
PAINT REMOVER
OOOPS!
IDIOT! NOW WE'LL HAVE TO WOIK FAST BEFORE DAT SPILLED PAINT DRIES!
SWOOOSHHH
LATER
I THOUGHT WE WERE SUPPOSED TO PAINT THIS HOUSE WHITE! IT'S COMIN' OUT **PURPLE!**
SURE IS FUNNY! WE'RE USIN' THE PAINT FROM THE **WHITE** CANS BUT THE SHUTTERS ARE COMIN' OUT **PINK!**
DIS IS DA CRAZIEST **WHITE PAINT** I EVER SEEN!
SCRATCH
PAINT REMOVER

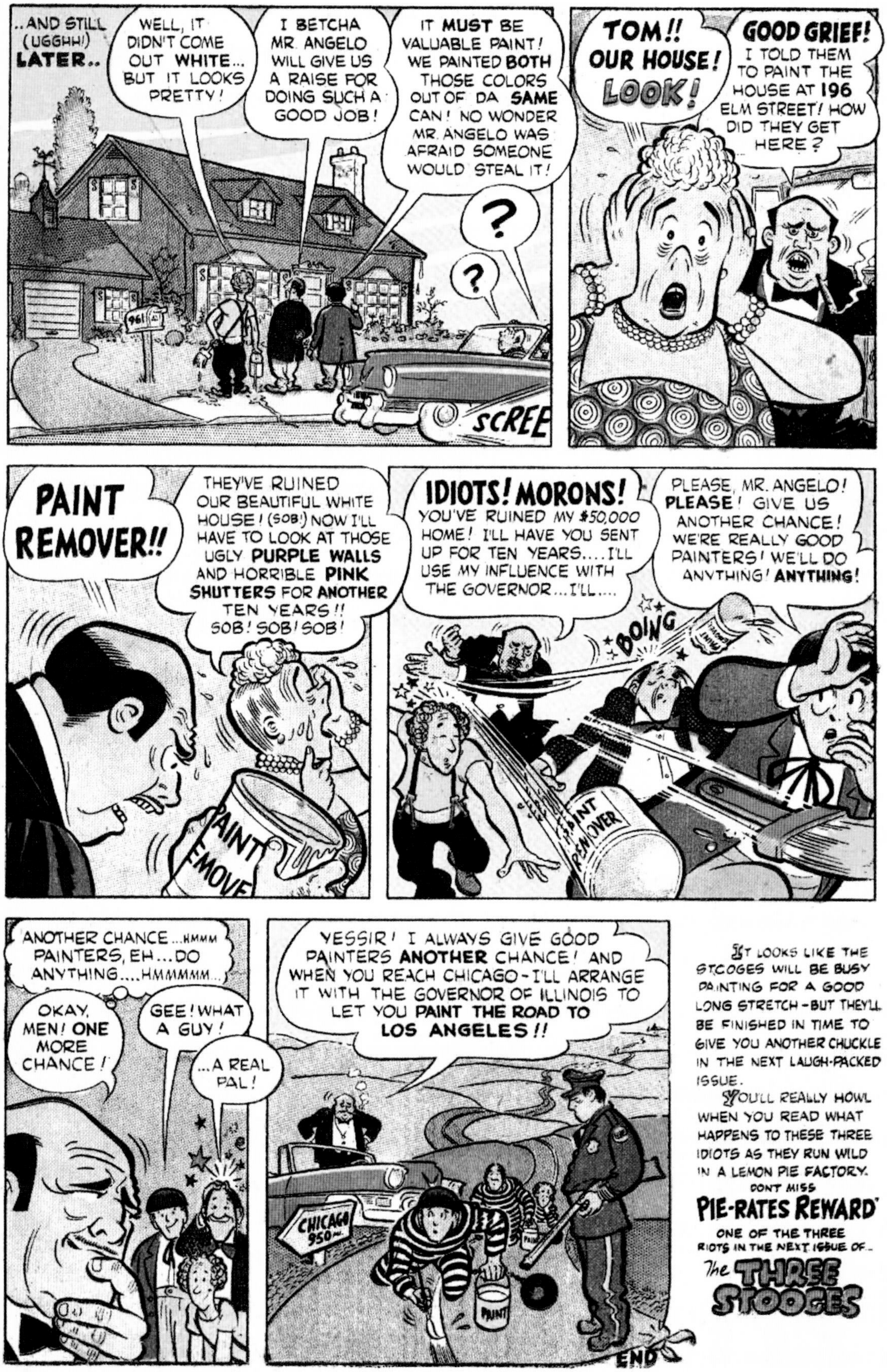
..AND STILL (UGGHH!) LATER..
WELL, IT DIDN'T COME OUT WHITE... BUT IT LOOKS PRETTY!
I BETCHA MR. ANGELO WILL GIVE US A RAISE FOR DOING SUCH A GOOD JOB!
IT MUST BE VALUABLE PAINT! WE PAINTED BOTH THOSE COLORS OUT OF DA SAME CAN! NO WONDER MR. ANGELO WAS AFRAID SOMEONE WOULD STEAL IT!
?
?
961
SCREE
TOM!! OUR HOUSE! LOOK!
GOOD GRIEF! I TOLD THEM TO PAINT THE HOUSE AT 196 ELM STREET! HOW DID THEY GET HERE?
PAINT REMOVER!!
THEY'VE RUINED OUR BEAUTIFUL WHITE HOUSE! (SOB!) NOW I'LL HAVE TO LOOK AT THOSE UGLY PURPLE WALLS AND HORRIBLE PINK SHUTTERS FOR ANOTHER TEN YEARS!! SOB! SOB! SOB!
PAINT REMOVE
IDIOTS! MORONS! YOU'VE RUINED MY $50,000 HOME! I'LL HAVE YOU SENT UP FOR TEN YEARS.... I'LL USE MY INFLUENCE WITH THE GOVERNOR... I'LL....
PLEASE, MR. ANGELO! PLEASE! GIVE US ANOTHER CHANCE! WE'RE REALLY GOOD PAINTERS! WE'LL DO ANYTHING! ANYTHING!
BOING
PAINT REMOVER
ANOTHER CHANCE...HMMM PAINTERS, EH... DO ANYTHING....HMMMMM...
OKAY, MEN! ONE MORE CHANCE!
GEE! WHAT A GUY!
...A REAL PAL!
YESSIR! I ALWAYS GIVE GOOD PAINTERS ANOTHER CHANCE! AND WHEN YOU REACH CHICAGO - I'LL ARRANGE IT WITH THE GOVERNOR OF ILLINOIS TO LET YOU PAINT THE ROAD TO LOS ANGELES!!
CHICAGO 950 MI.
PAINT
END
IT LOOKS LIKE THE STOOGES WILL BE BUSY PAINTING FOR A GOOD LONG STRETCH - BUT THEY'LL BE FINISHED IN TIME TO GIVE YOU ANOTHER CHUCKLE IN THE NEXT LAUGH-PACKED ISSUE.
YOU'LL REALLY HOWL WHEN YOU READ WHAT HAPPENS TO THESE THREE IDIOTS AS THEY RUN WILD IN A LEMON PIE FACTORY.
DONT MISS
PIE-RATES REWARD
ONE OF THE THREE RIOTS IN THE NEXT ISSUE OF...
The THREE STOOGES

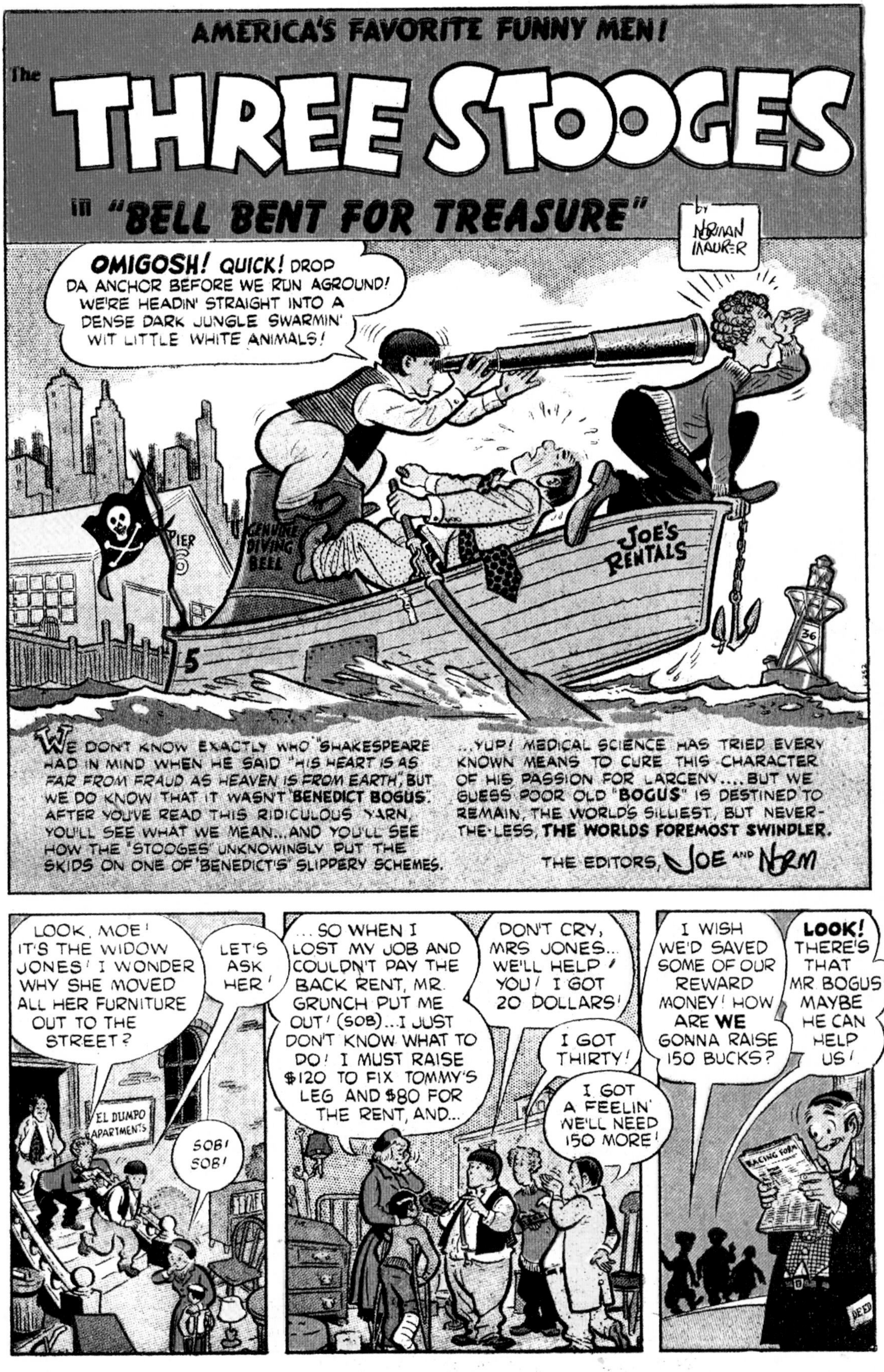
AMERICA'S FAVORITE FUNNY MEN!
The THREE STOOGES
in "BELL BENT FOR TREASURE"
by NORMAN MAURER
OMIGOSH! QUICK! DROP DA ANCHOR BEFORE WE RUN AGROUND! WE'RE HEADIN' STRAIGHT INTO A DENSE DARK JUNGLE SWARMIN' WIT LITTLE WHITE ANIMALS!
PIER
GENUINE DIVING BELL
JOE'S RENTALS
5
36
WE DON'T KNOW EXACTLY WHO "SHAKESPEARE" HAD IN MIND WHEN HE SAID "HIS HEART IS AS FAR FROM FRAUD AS HEAVEN IS FROM EARTH", BUT WE DO KNOW THAT IT WASN'T "BENEDICT BOGUS". AFTER YOU'VE READ THIS RIDICULOUS YARN, YOU'LL SEE WHAT WE MEAN...AND YOU'LL SEE HOW THE "STOOGES" UNKNOWINGLY PUT THE SKIDS ON ONE OF "BENEDICT'S" SLIPPERY SCHEMES.
...YUP! MEDICAL SCIENCE HAS TRIED EVERY KNOWN MEANS TO CURE THIS CHARACTER OF HIS PASSION FOR LARCENY.... BUT WE GUESS POOR OLD "BOGUS" IS DESTINED TO REMAIN, THE WORLD'S SILLIEST, BUT NEVER-THE-LESS, THE WORLDS FOREMOST SWINDLER.
THE EDITORS, JOE AND NORM
LOOK, MOE! IT'S THE WIDOW JONES! I WONDER WHY SHE MOVED ALL HER FURNITURE OUT TO THE STREET?
LET'S ASK HER!
EL DUMPO APARTMENTS
SOB! SOB!
...SO WHEN I LOST MY JOB AND COULDN'T PAY THE BACK RENT, MR. GRUNCH PUT ME OUT! (SOB)...I JUST DON'T KNOW WHAT TO DO! I MUST RAISE $120 TO FIX TOMMY'S LEG AND $80 FOR THE RENT, AND...
DON'T CRY, MRS JONES... WE'LL HELP! YOU! I GOT 20 DOLLARS!
I GOT THIRTY!
I GOT A FEELIN' WE'LL NEED 150 MORE!
I WISH WE'D SAVED SOME OF OUR REWARD MONEY! HOW ARE WE GONNA RAISE 150 BUCKS?
LOOK! THERE'S THAT MR BOGUS! MAYBE HE CAN HELP US!
RACING FORM

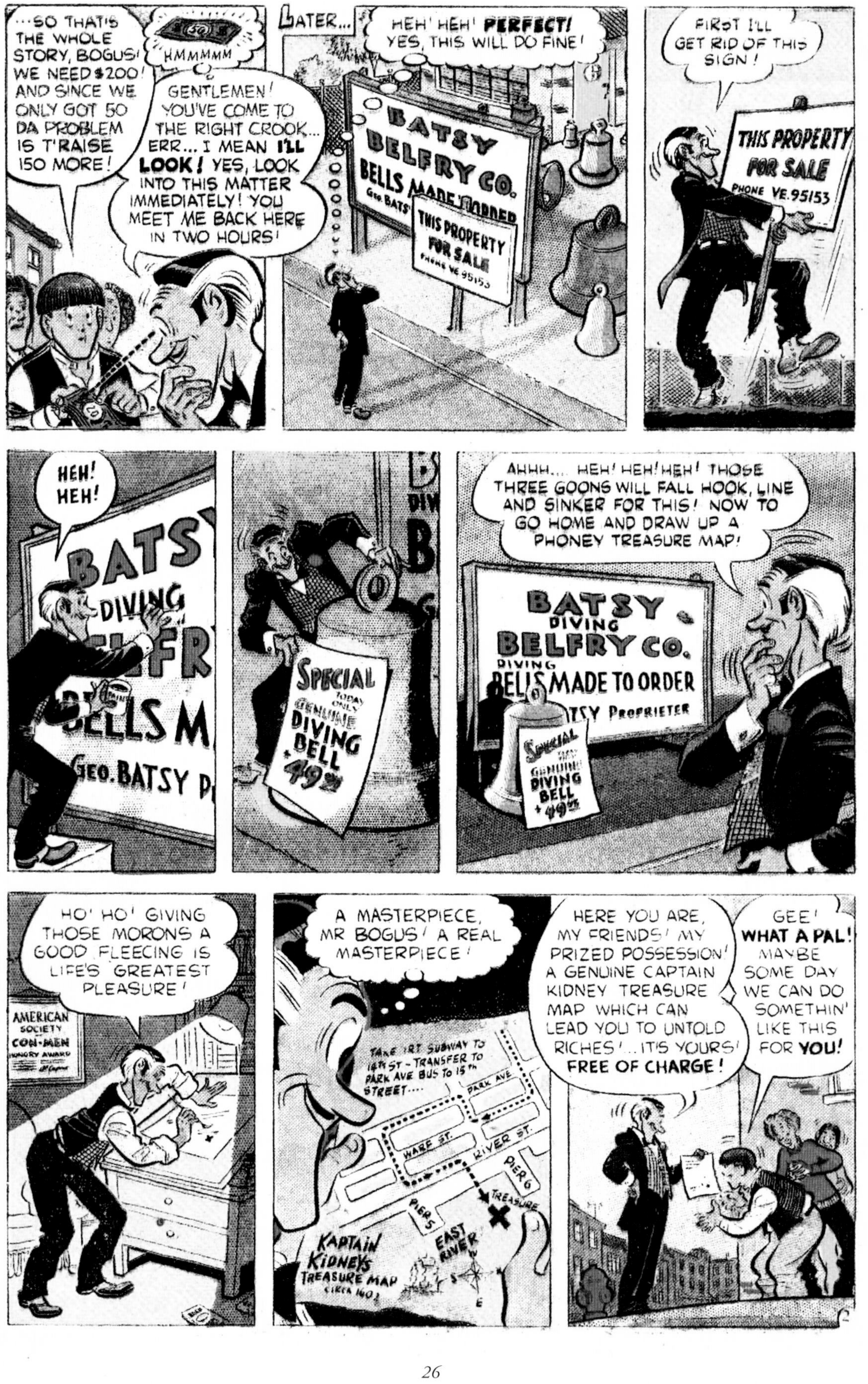
...SO THAT'S THE WHOLE STORY, BOGUS! WE NEED $200! AND SINCE WE ONLY GOT 50 DA PROBLEM IS T'RAISE 150 MORE!
HMMMMM
GENTLEMEN! YOU'VE COME TO THE RIGHT CROOK... ERR... I MEAN I'LL LOOK! YES, LOOK INTO THIS MATTER IMMEDIATELY! YOU MEET ME BACK HERE IN TWO HOURS!
LATER...
HEH! HEH! PERFECT! YES, THIS WILL DO FINE!
BATSY BELFRY CO.
BELLS MADE TO ORDER
THIS PROPERTY FOR SALE PHONE VE.95153
FIRST I'LL GET RID OF THIS SIGN!
THIS PROPERTY FOR SALE PHONE VE.95153
HEH! HEH!
BATSY DIVING BELFR
BELLS M
GEO. BATSY P
SPECIAL TODAY ONLY GENUINE DIVING BELL $49.95
AHHH... HEH! HEH! HEH! THOSE THREE GOONS WILL FALL HOOK, LINE AND SINKER FOR THIS! NOW TO GO HOME AND DRAW UP A PHONEY TREASURE MAP!
BATSY DIVING BELFRY CO.
DIVING BELLS MADE TO ORDER
TSY PROPRIETER
SPECIAL GENUINE DIVING BELL $49.95
HO! HO! GIVING THOSE MORONS A GOOD FLEECING IS LIFE'S GREATEST PLEASURE!
AMERICAN SOCIETY CON-MEN HONORY AWARD
A MASTERPIECE, MR BOGUS! A REAL MASTERPIECE!
TAKE IRT SUBWAY TO 14th ST - TRANSFER TO PARK AVE BUS TO 15th STREET....
PARK AVE
WARE ST.
RIVER ST.
PIER 6
PIER 5
TREASURE
EAST RIVER
KAPTAIN KIDNEY'S TREASURE MAP
HERE YOU ARE, MY FRIENDS! MY PRIZED POSSESSION! A GENUINE CAPTAIN KIDNEY TREASURE MAP WHICH CAN LEAD YOU TO UNTOLD RICHES! ...IT'S YOURS! FREE OF CHARGE!
GEE! WHAT A PAL! MAYBE SOME DAY WE CAN DO SOMETHIN' LIKE THIS FOR YOU!

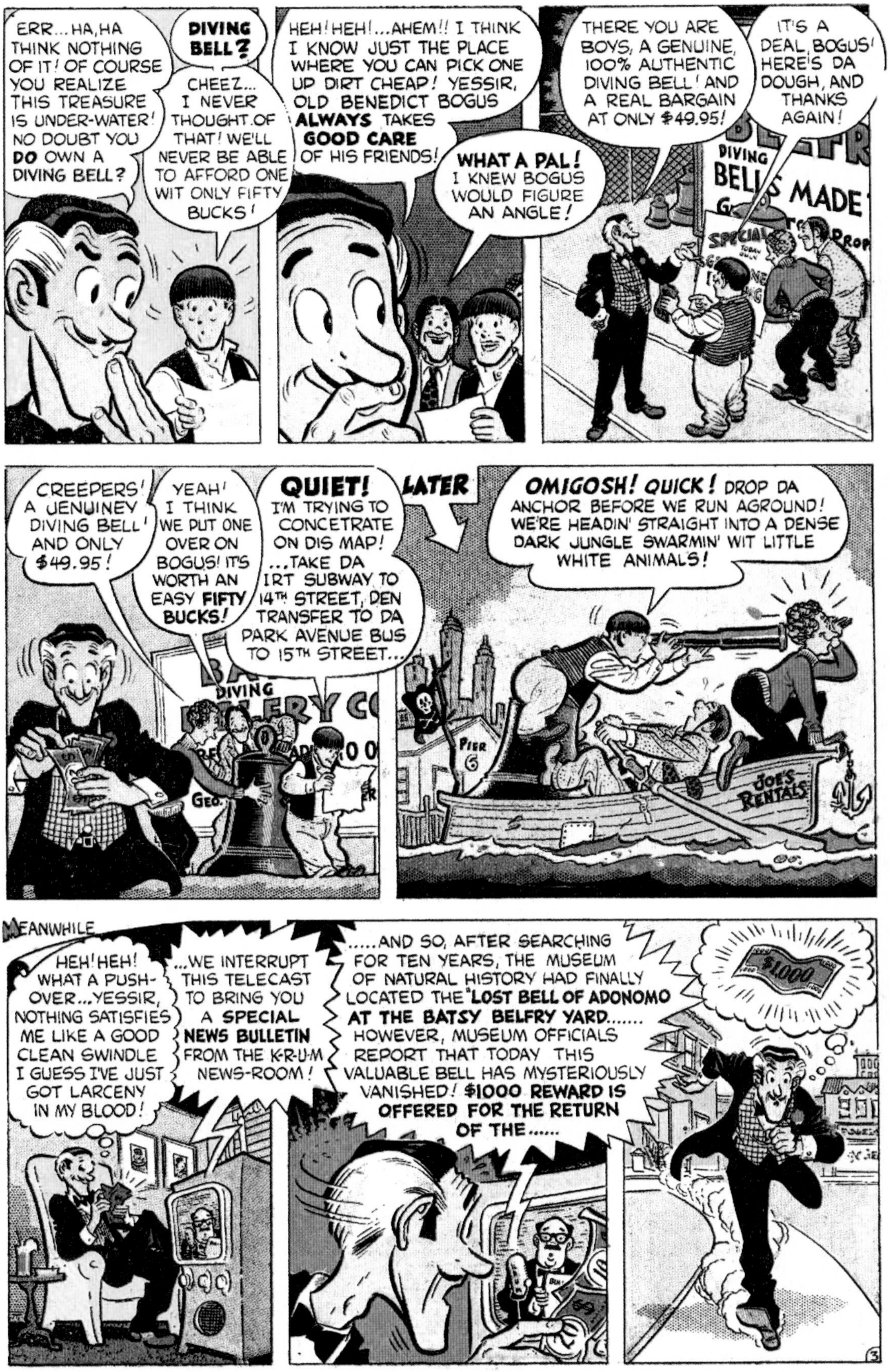
ERR... HA, HA THINK NOTHING OF IT! OF COURSE YOU REALIZE THIS TREASURE IS UNDER-WATER! NO DOUBT YOU DO OWN A DIVING BELL?
DIVING BELL?
CHEEZ... I NEVER THOUGHT OF THAT! WE'LL NEVER BE ABLE TO AFFORD ONE WIT ONLY FIFTY BUCKS!
HEH! HEH! ...AHEM!! I THINK I KNOW JUST THE PLACE WHERE YOU CAN PICK ONE UP DIRT CHEAP! YESSIR, OLD BENEDICT BOGUS ALWAYS TAKES GOOD CARE OF HIS FRIENDS!
WHAT A PAL! I KNEW BOGUS WOULD FIGURE AN ANGLE!
THERE YOU ARE BOYS, A GENUINE, 100% AUTHENTIC DIVING BELL! AND A REAL BARGAIN AT ONLY $49.95!
IT'S A DEAL, BOGUS! HERE'S DA DOUGH, AND THANKS AGAIN!
DIVING BELLS MADE
SPECIAL
CREEPERS! A JENUINEY DIVING BELL! AND ONLY $49.95!
YEAH! I THINK WE PUT ONE OVER ON BOGUS! IT'S WORTH AN EASY FIFTY BUCKS!
QUIET! I'M TRYING TO CONCETRATE ON DIS MAP! ...TAKE DA IRT SUBWAY TO 14TH STREET, DEN TRANSFER TO DA PARK AVENUE BUS TO 15TH STREET...
DIVING
LATER
OMIGOSH! QUICK! DROP DA ANCHOR BEFORE WE RUN AGROUND! WE'RE HEADIN' STRAIGHT INTO A DENSE DARK JUNGLE SWARMIN' WIT LITTLE WHITE ANIMALS!
PIER 6
JOE'S RENTALS
MEANWHILE
HEH! HEH! WHAT A PUSH-OVER... YESSIR, NOTHING SATISFIES ME LIKE A GOOD CLEAN SWINDLE I GUESS I'VE JUST GOT LARCENY IN MY BLOOD!
...WE INTERRUPT THIS TELECAST TO BRING YOU A SPECIAL NEWS BULLETIN FROM THE K-R-U-M NEWS-ROOM!
.....AND SO, AFTER SEARCHING FOR TEN YEARS, THE MUSEUM OF NATURAL HISTORY HAD FINALLY LOCATED THE "LOST BELL OF ADONOMO AT THE BATSY BELFRY YARD....... HOWEVER, MUSEUM OFFICIALS REPORT THAT TODAY THIS VALUABLE BELL HAS MYSTERIOUSLY VANISHED! $1000 REWARD IS OFFERED FOR THE RETURN OF THE......
$1,000
3

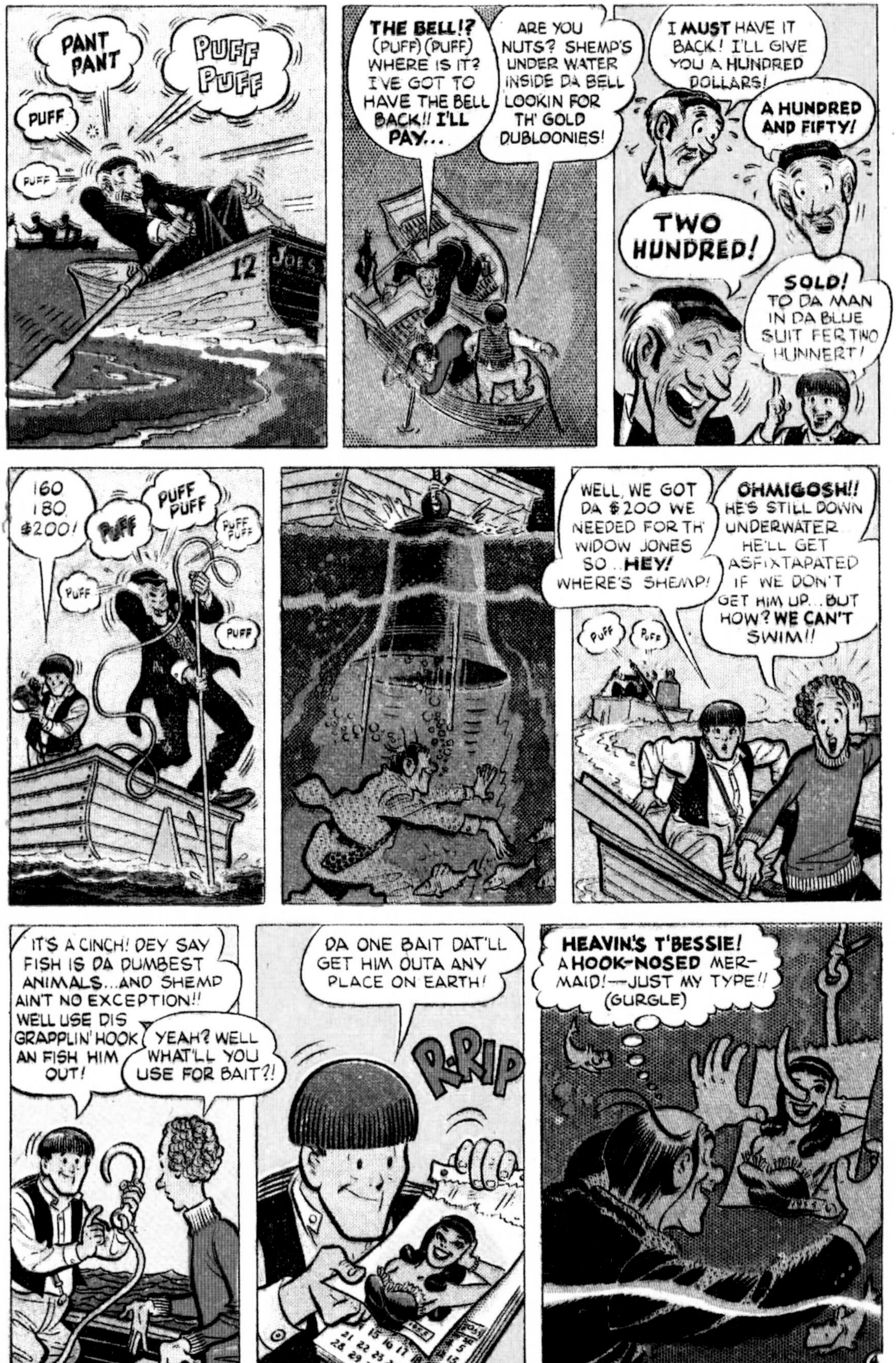
PANT PANT
PUFF PUFF
PUFF
PUFF
12 JOES
THE BELL!? (PUFF) (PUFF) WHERE IS IT? I'VE GOT TO HAVE THE BELL BACK!! I'LL PAY...
ARE YOU NUTS? SHEMP'S UNDER WATER INSIDE DA BELL LOOKIN FOR TH' GOLD DUBLOONIES!
I MUST HAVE IT BACK! I'LL GIVE YOU A HUNDRED DOLLARS!
A HUNDRED AND FIFTY!
TWO HUNDRED!
SOLD! TO DA MAN IN DA BLUE SUIT FER TWO HUNNERT!
160 180 $200!
PUFF
PUFF PUFF
PUFF PUFF
PUFF
PUFF
WELL, WE GOT DA $200 WE NEEDED FOR TH' WIDOW JONES SO...HEY! WHERE'S SHEMP!
OHMIGOSH!! HE'S STILL DOWN UNDERWATER... HE'LL GET ASFIXTAPATED IF WE DON'T GET HIM UP...BUT HOW? WE CAN'T SWIM!!
PUFF
PUFF
IT'S A CINCH! DEY SAY FISH IS DA DUMBEST ANIMALS...AND SHEMP AIN'T NO EXCEPTION!! WE'LL USE DIS GRAPPLIN' HOOK AN FISH HIM OUT!
YEAH? WELL WHAT'LL YOU USE FOR BAIT?!
DA ONE BAIT DAT'LL GET HIM OUTA ANY PLACE ON EARTH!
R-RIP
HEAVIN'S T'BESSIE! A HOOK-NOSED MER-MAID!—JUST MY TYPE!! (GURGLE)
4

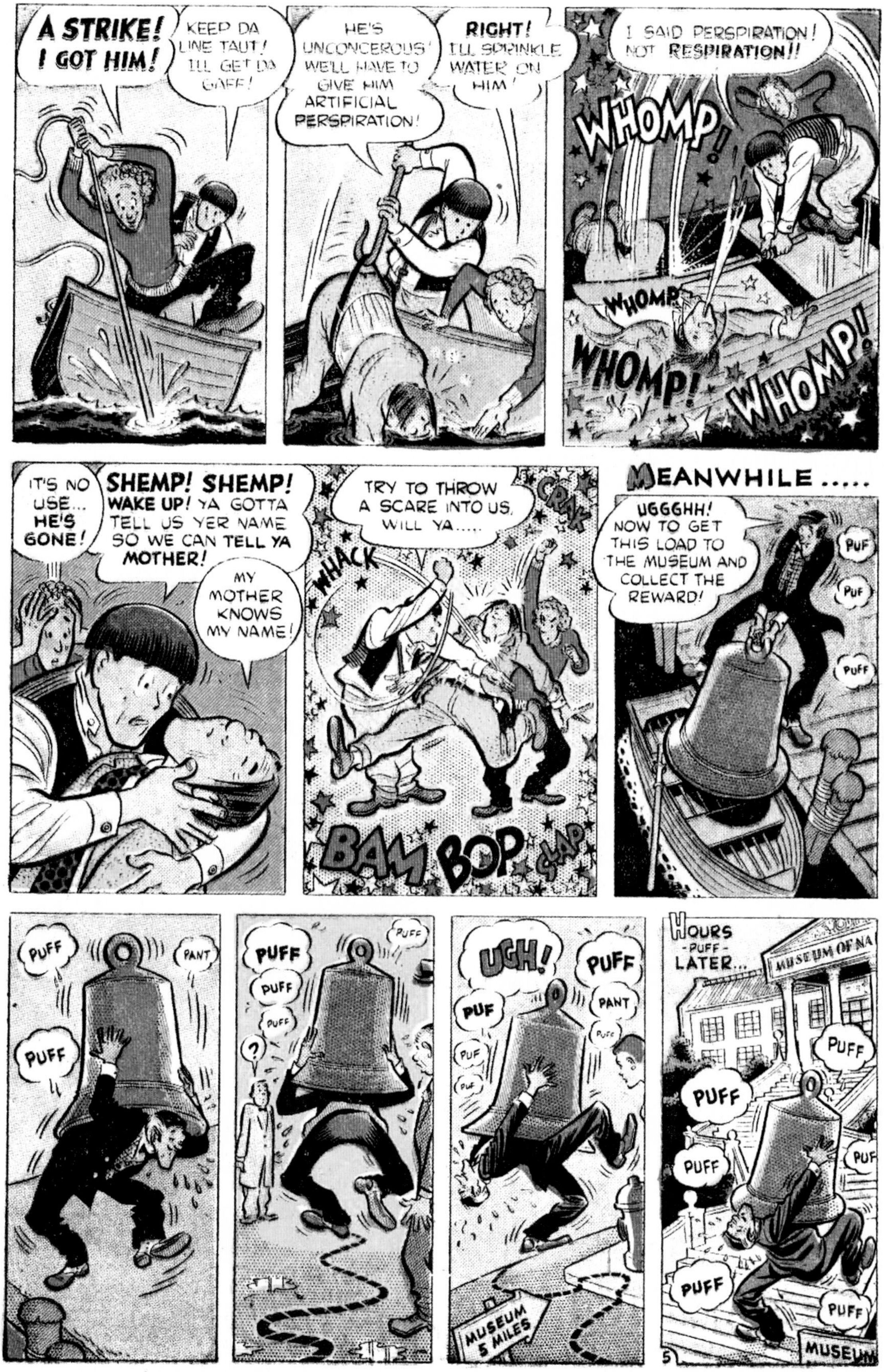
A STRIKE! I GOT HIM!
KEEP DA LINE TAUT! I'LL GET DA GAFF!
HE'S UNCONCEROUS! WE'LL HAVE TO GIVE HIM ARTIFICIAL PERSPIRATION!
RIGHT! I'LL SPRINKLE WATER ON HIM!
I SAID PERSPIRATION! NOT RESPIRATION!!
WHOMP!
WHOMP
WHOMP!
WHOMP!
IT'S NO USE... HE'S GONE!
SHEMP! SHEMP! WAKE UP! YA GOTTA TELL US YER NAME SO WE CAN TELL YA MOTHER!
MY MOTHER KNOWS MY NAME!
TRY TO THROW A SCARE INTO US, WILL YA.....
CRAK
WHACK
BAM
BOP
SLAP
MEANWHILE.....
UGGGHH! NOW TO GET THIS LOAD TO THE MUSEUM AND COLLECT THE REWARD!
PUF
PUF
PUFF
PUFF
PANT
PUFF
PUFF
PUFF
PUFF
PUFF
?
UGH!
PUFF
PUF
PANT
PUF
MUSEUM 5 MILES
HOURS -PUFF- LATER...
MUSEUM OF NA
PUFF
PUFF
PUFF
PUF
PUFF
PUFF
MUSEUM
5

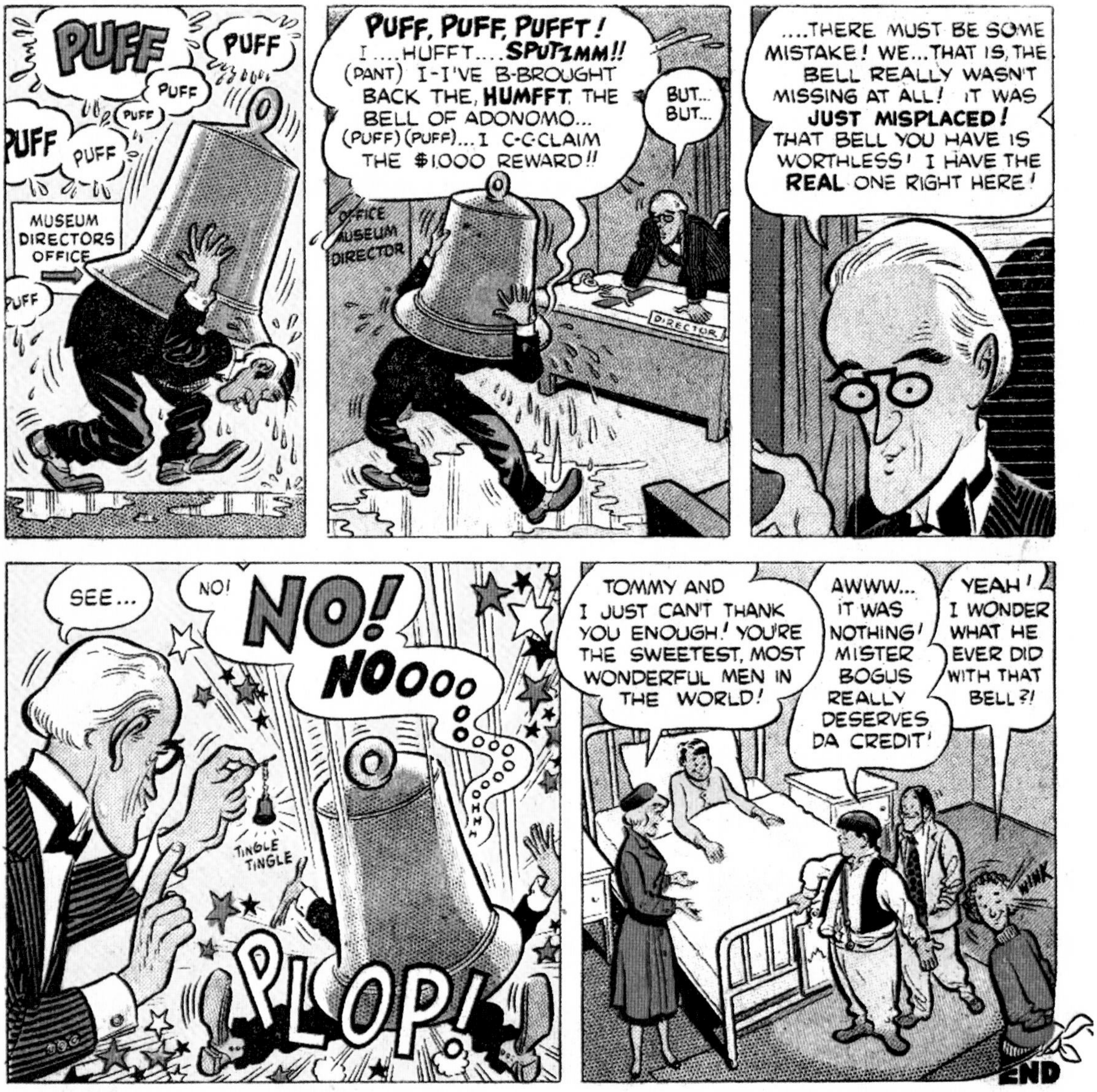
PUFF
PUFF
PUFF
PUFF
PUFF
PUFF
PUFF
MUSEUM DIRECTORS OFFICE
PUFF, PUFF, PUFFT! I....HUFFT....SPUTZMM!! (PANT) I-I'VE B-BROUGHT BACK THE, HUMFFT, THE BELL OF ADONOMO... (PUFF)(PUFF)...I C-C-CLAIM THE $1,000 REWARD!!
BUT... BUT...
OFFICE MUSEUM DIRECTOR
DIRECTOR
....THERE MUST BE SOME MISTAKE! WE...THAT IS, THE BELL REALLY WASN'T MISSING AT ALL! IT WAS JUST MISPLACED! THAT BELL YOU HAVE IS WORTHLESS! I HAVE THE REAL ONE RIGHT HERE!
SEE...
NO!
NO! NOOOO OOOOOOO
TINGLE TINGLE
PLOP!
TOMMY AND I JUST CAN'T THANK YOU ENOUGH! YOU'RE THE SWEETEST, MOST WONDERFUL MEN IN THE WORLD!
AWWW... IT WAS NOTHING! MISTER BOGUS REALLY DESERVES DA CREDIT!
YEAH! I WONDER WHAT HE EVER DID WITH THAT BELL?!
WINK
END

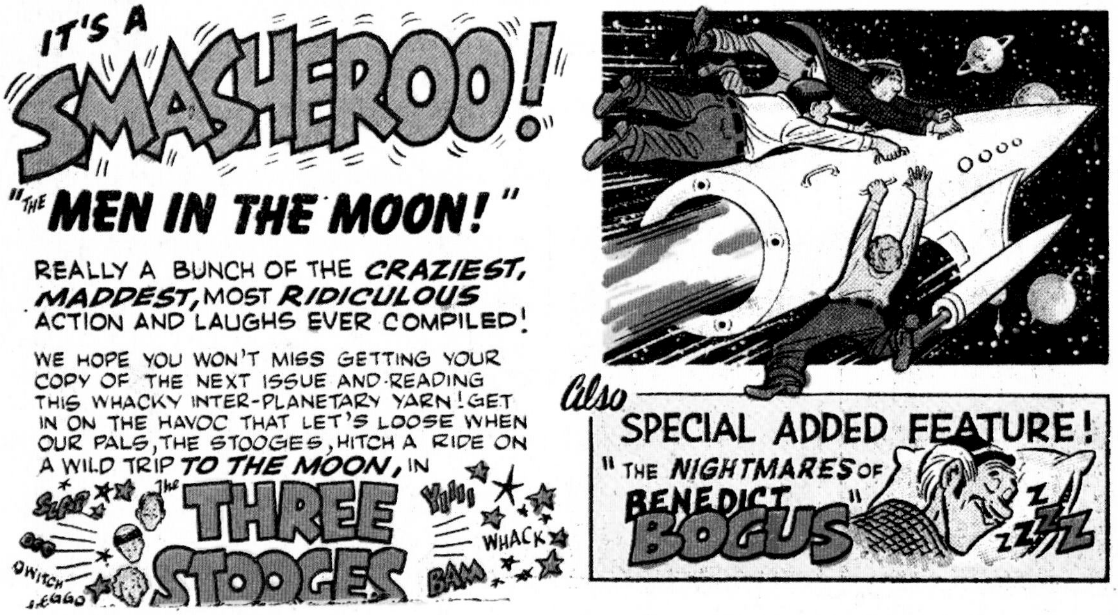
IT'S A SMASHEROO!
"THE MEN IN THE MOON!"
REALLY A BUNCH OF THE CRAZIEST, MADDEST, MOST RIDICULOUS ACTION AND LAUGHS EVER COMPILED!
WE HOPE YOU WON'T MISS GETTING YOUR COPY OF THE NEXT ISSUE AND READING THIS WHACKY INTER-PLANETARY YARN! GET IN ON THE HAVOC THAT LET'S LOOSE WHEN OUR PALS, THE STOOGES, HITCH A RIDE ON A WILD TRIP TO THE MOON, IN
The THREE STOOGES
WHACK
BAM
Also
SPECIAL ADDED FEATURE!
"THE NIGHTMARES OF BENEDICT BOGUS"
ZZZ

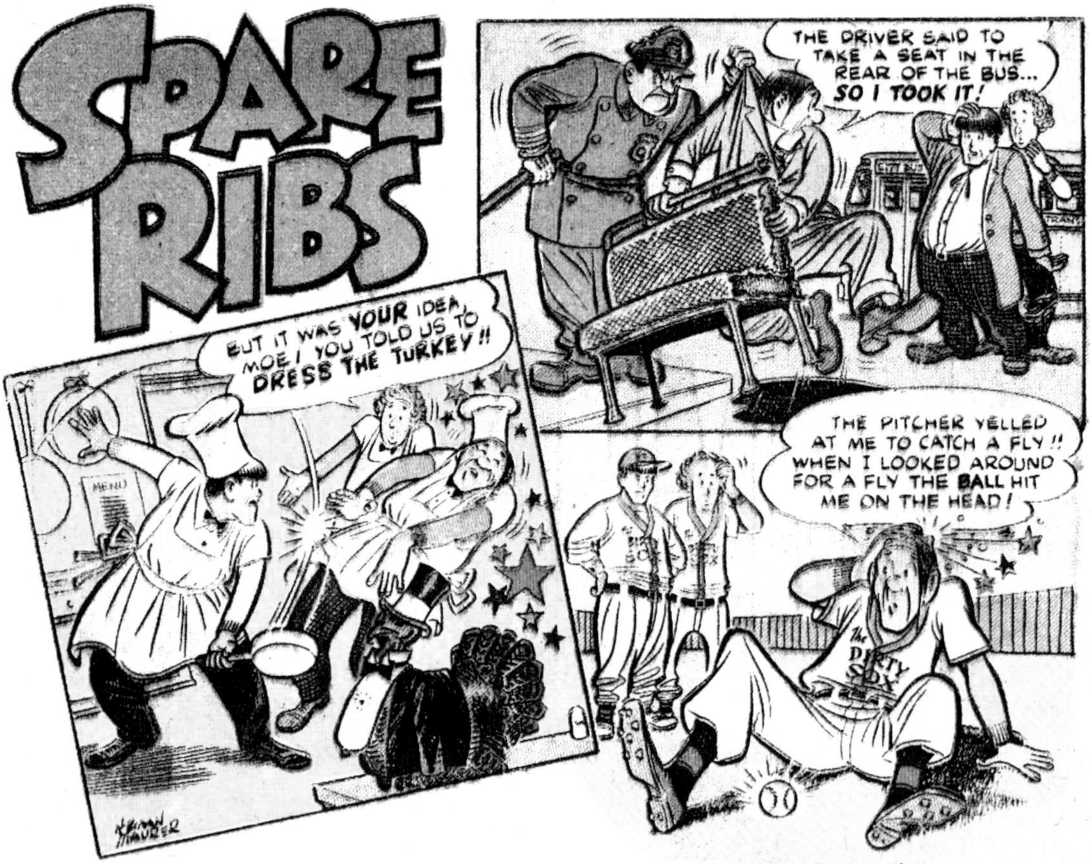
SPARE RIBS
THE DRIVER SAID TO TAKE A SEAT IN THE REAR OF THE BUS... SO I TOOK IT!
BUT IT WAS YOUR IDEA, MOE! YOU TOLD US TO DRESS THE TURKEY!!
MENU
THE PITCHER YELLED AT ME TO CATCH A FLY!! WHEN I LOOKED AROUND FOR A FLY THE BALL HIT ME ON THE HEAD!
The DIRTY SOX

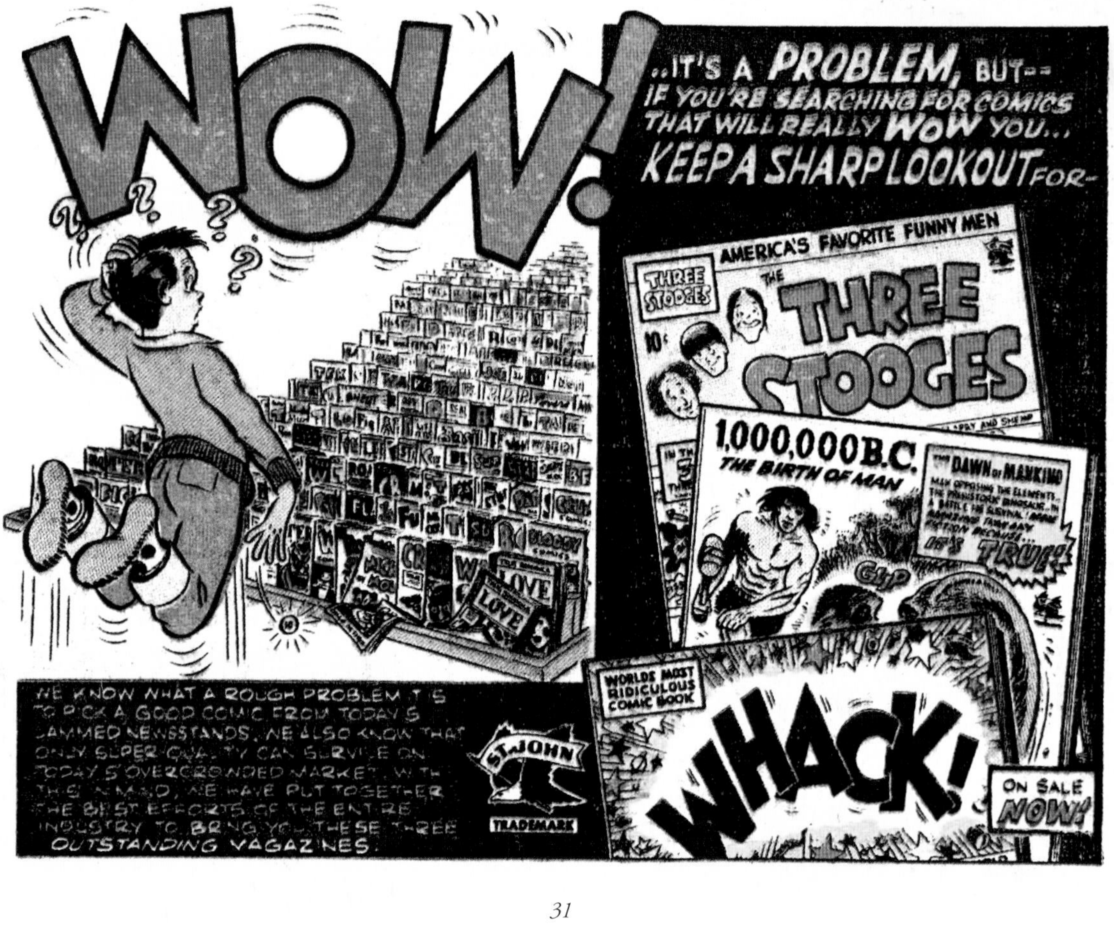
WOW!
..IT'S A PROBLEM, BUT-- IF YOU'RE SEARCHING FOR COMICS THAT WILL REALLY WOW YOU... KEEP A SHARP LOOKOUT FOR-
AMERICA'S FAVORITE FUNNY MEN
THE THREE STOOGES
10¢
1,000,000 B.C. THE BIRTH OF MAN
THE DAWN OF MANKIND
IT'S TRUE!
GULP
WORLDS MOST RIDICULOUS COMIC BOOK
WHACK!
ON SALE NOW!
LOVE
WE KNOW WHAT A ROUGH PROBLEM IT IS TO PICK A GOOD COMIC FROM TODAY'S JAMMED NEWSSTANDS. WE ALSO KNOW THAT ONLY SUPER-QUALITY CAN SURVIVE ON TODAY'S OVERCROWDED MARKET. WITH THIS IN MIND, WE HAVE PUT TOGETHER THE BEST EFFORTS OF THE ENTIRE INDUSTRY TO BRING YOU THESE THREE OUTSTANDING MAGAZINES.
ST. JOHN
TRADEMARK

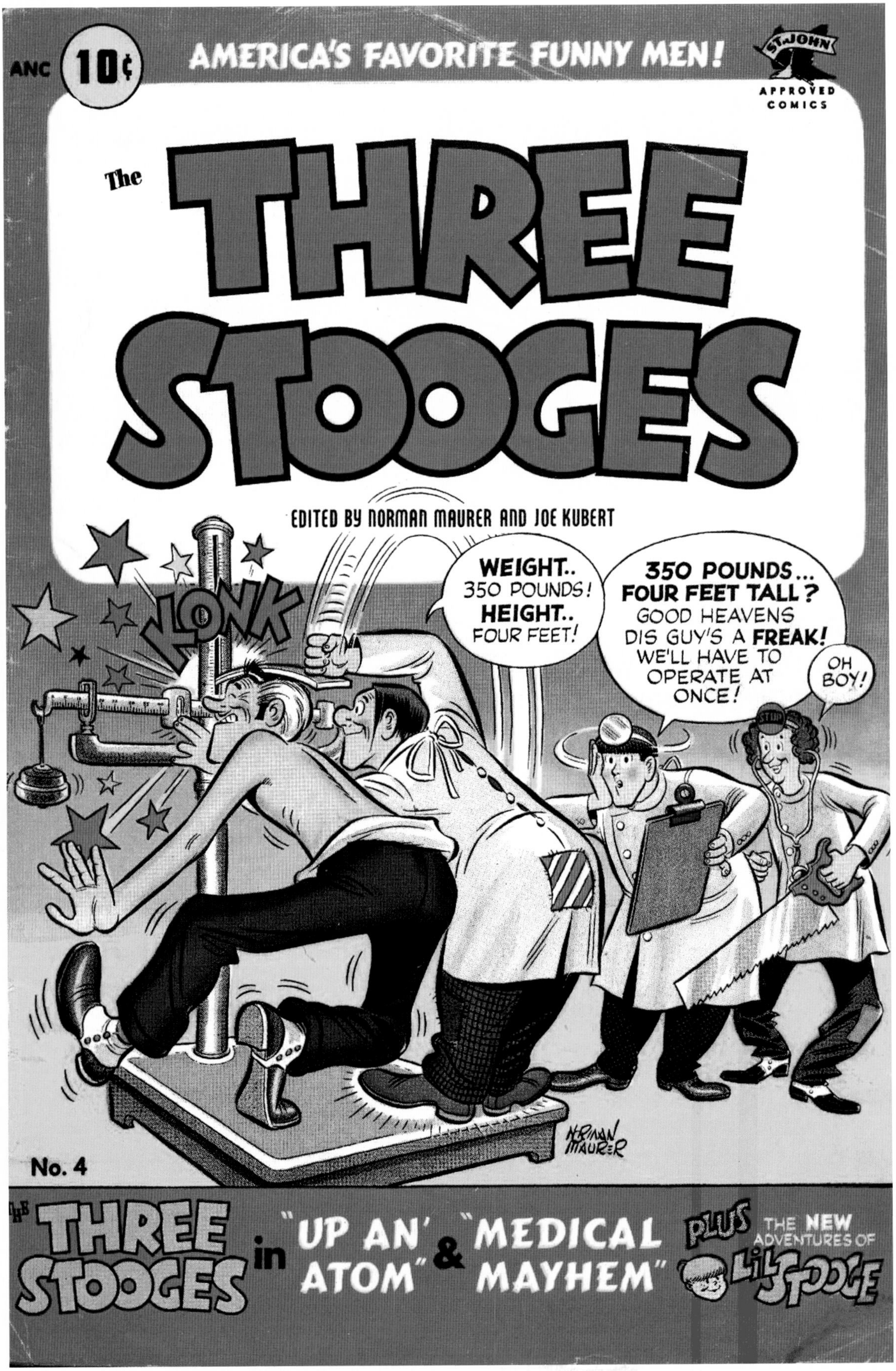
ANC 10¢
AMERICA'S FAVORITE FUNNY MEN!
ST. JOHN APPROVED COMICS
The THREE STOOGES
EDITED BY NORMAN MAURER AND JOE KUBERT
KLONK
WEIGHT.. 350 POUNDS! HEIGHT.. FOUR FEET!
350 POUNDS... FOUR FEET TALL? GOOD HEAVENS DIS GUY'S A FREAK! WE'LL HAVE TO OPERATE AT ONCE!
OH BOY!
NORMAN MAURER
No. 4
THE THREE STOOGES in "UP AN' ATOM" & "MEDICAL MAYHEM" PLUS THE NEW ADVENTURES OF LI'L STOOGE

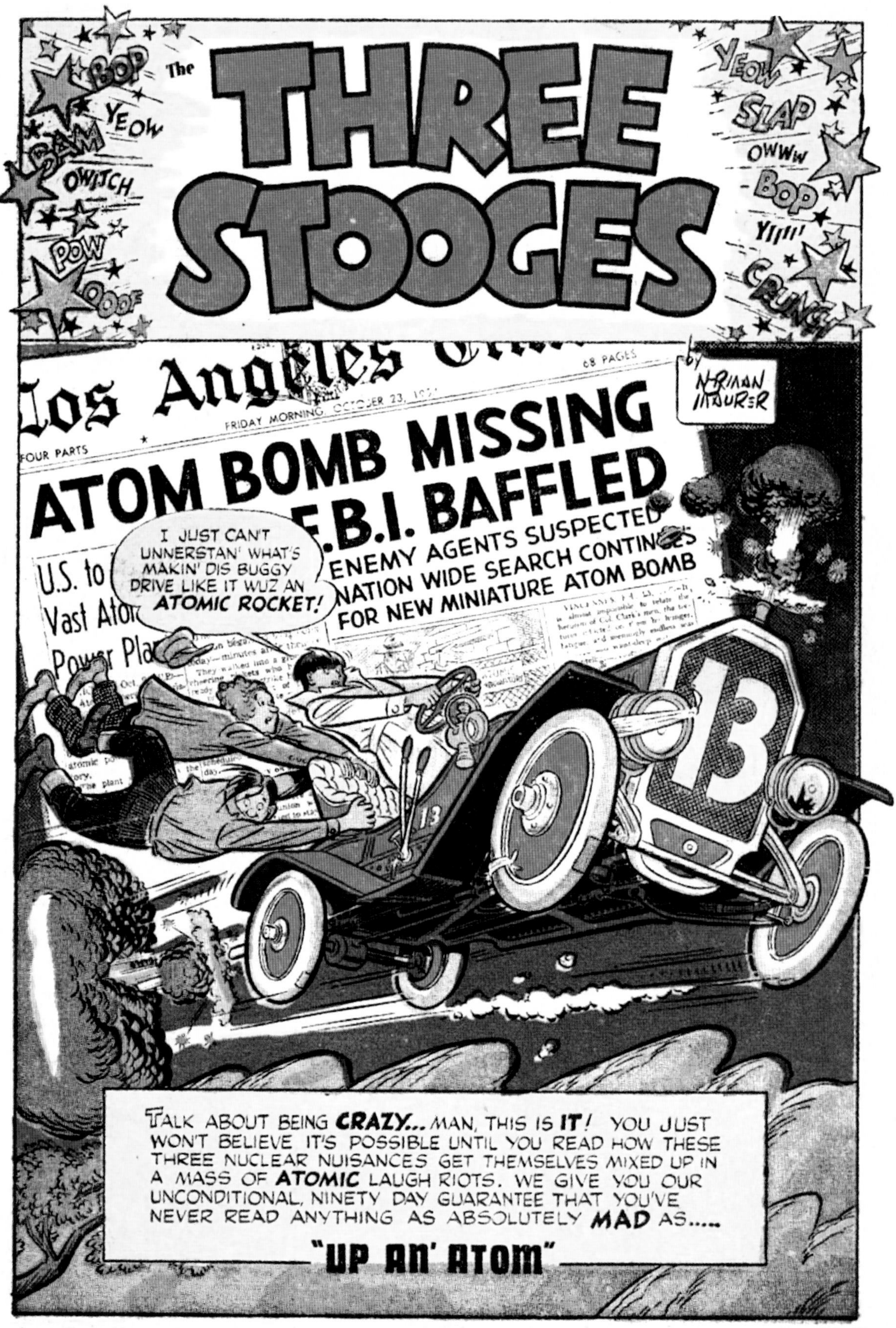
The THREE STOOGES
BOP
YEOW
BAM
OWITCH
POW
OOOF
YEOW
SLAP
OWWW
BOP
YIIII
CRUNCH
Los Angeles
68 PAGES
FRIDAY MORNING, OCTOBER 23,
FOUR PARTS
ATOM BOMB MISSING
F.B.I. BAFFLED
ENEMY AGENTS SUSPECTED
NATION WIDE SEARCH CONTINUES
FOR NEW MINIATURE ATOM BOMB
U.S. to
Vast Ato
Power Pla
by NORMAN MAURER
I JUST CAN'T UNNERSTAN' WHAT'S MAKIN' DIS BUGGY DRIVE LIKE IT WUZ AN ATOMIC ROCKET!
13
TALK ABOUT BEING CRAZY... MAN, THIS IS IT! YOU JUST WON'T BELIEVE IT'S POSSIBLE UNTIL YOU READ HOW THESE THREE NUCLEAR NUISANCES GET THEMSELVES MIXED UP IN A MASS OF ATOMIC LAUGH RIOTS. WE GIVE YOU OUR UNCONDITIONAL, NINETY DAY GUARANTEE THAT YOU'VE NEVER READ ANYTHING AS ABSOLUTELY MAD AS.....
"UP AN' ATOM"

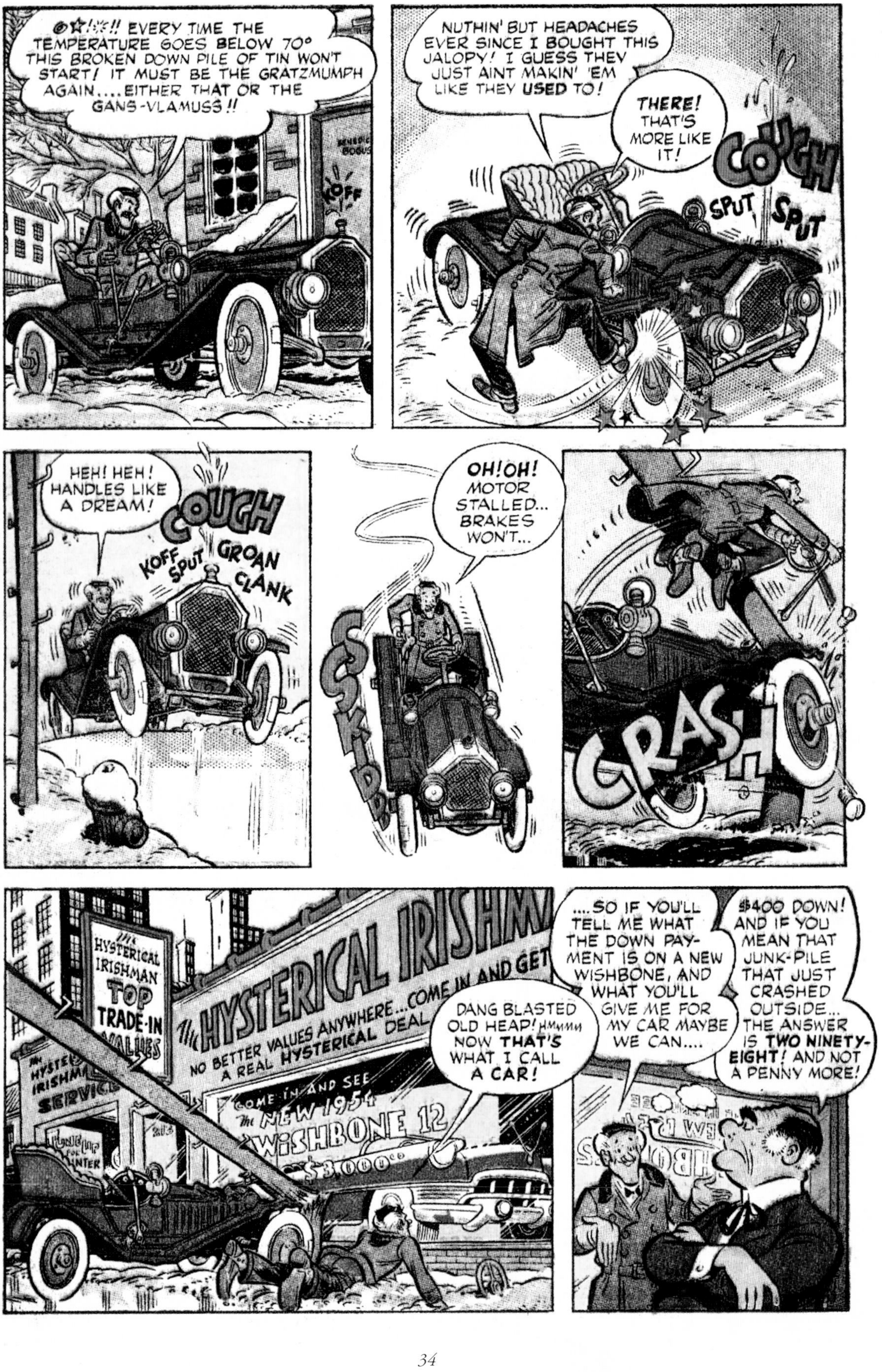
@☆!✲!! EVERY TIME THE TEMPERATURE GOES BELOW 70° THIS BROKEN DOWN PILE OF TIN WON'T START! IT MUST BE THE GRATZMUMPH AGAIN....EITHER THAT OR THE GANS-VLAMUSS!!
KOFF
NUTHIN' BUT HEADACHES EVER SINCE I BOUGHT THIS JALOPY! I GUESS THEY JUST AINT MAKIN' 'EM LIKE THEY USED TO!
THERE! THAT'S MORE LIKE IT!
COUGH
SPUT SPUT
HEH! HEH! HANDLES LIKE A DREAM!
COUGH
KOFF SPUT GROAN CLANK
OH! OH! MOTOR STALLED... BRAKES WON'T...
SKIDD
CRASH
HYSTERICAL IRISHMAN TOP TRADE-IN VALUES
HYSTERICAL IRISHMAN
NO BETTER VALUES ANYWHERE...COME IN AND GET A REAL HYSTERICAL DEAL
COME IN AND SEE THE NEW 1954 WISHBONE 12 $3,000.00
DANG BLASTED OLD HEAP! HMMMM NOW THAT'S WHAT I CALL A CAR!
....SO IF YOU'LL TELL ME WHAT THE DOWN PAYMENT IS ON A NEW WISHBONE, AND WHAT YOU'LL GIVE ME FOR MY CAR MAYBE WE CAN....
$400 DOWN! AND IF YOU MEAN THAT JUNK-PILE THAT JUST CRASHED OUTSIDE... THE ANSWER IS TWO NINETY-EIGHT! AND NOT A PENNY MORE!

TWO NINETY-EIGHT! *WONDERFUL!* WITH THE $102 I HAVE, IT'LL JUST COVER THE DOWN-PAYMENT!

EASY, BUSTER! I SAID TWO NINETY-EIGHT! TWO *DOLLARS*, NINETY-EIGHT CENTS, NOT TWO *HUNDRED* NINETY-EIGHT!

TWO DOLLARS NINETY-EIGHT CENTS? WHY....WHY THAT'S RIDICULOUS...YOU MUST BE...

OF COURSE, YOU MIGHT DO A LITTLE BETTER BY SELLING IT PRIVATELY!

$2.98...EH? I'LL SHOW 'EM! JUST WAIT'LL I FINISH WITH THIS JALOP.....ERRR LIMOUSINE!

LATER..

CLANK CLANK

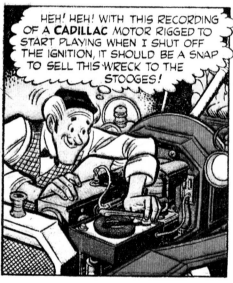

HEH! HEH! WITH THIS RECORDING OF A *CADILLAC* MOTOR RIGGED TO START PLAYING WHEN I SHUT OFF THE IGNITION, IT SHOULD BE A SNAP TO SELL THIS WRECK TO THE STOOGES!

LARRY! MOE! SHEMP! I'VE BEEN LOOKIN' ALL OVER FOR YOU GUYS!

BETTER CUT THE MOTOR NOW SO'S THE RECORD STARTS PLAYING!

COUGH COFF

HEY! LOOK! IT'S BOGUS!..GEE GET A LOAD OF DAT BUGGY!

HOW D'YA LIKE HER, BOYS? SHE'S A GENUINE *STRUTZ-CATBEAR*...WORTH $2,000! JUST LISTEN TO THAT MOTOR... *PURRS* LIKE A KITTEN! I COULD MAKE A FORTUNE RACING IT ONLY I CAN'T QUALIFY ON ACCOUNT OF MY BAD EYES!.....OF COURSE, I MIGHT CONSIDER SELLING IT IF....

PURRRR

GEE! YOU MEAN YOU'D SELL IT? *WOW!* WE COULD BE REAL RACING CHUMPS! HOW MUCH?

ERRRR.. SEEIN' AS HOW YOU GUYS ARE MY BUDDIES, HOW'S $200?

IT'S A BOGUS DEAL....I MEAN A DEAL, BOGUS! HERE'S DA DOUGH!

HO! HO! HEE! THESE GUYS ARE SUCH PUSHOVERS, THEY TAKE ALL THE PLEASURE OUT OF SWINDLING!

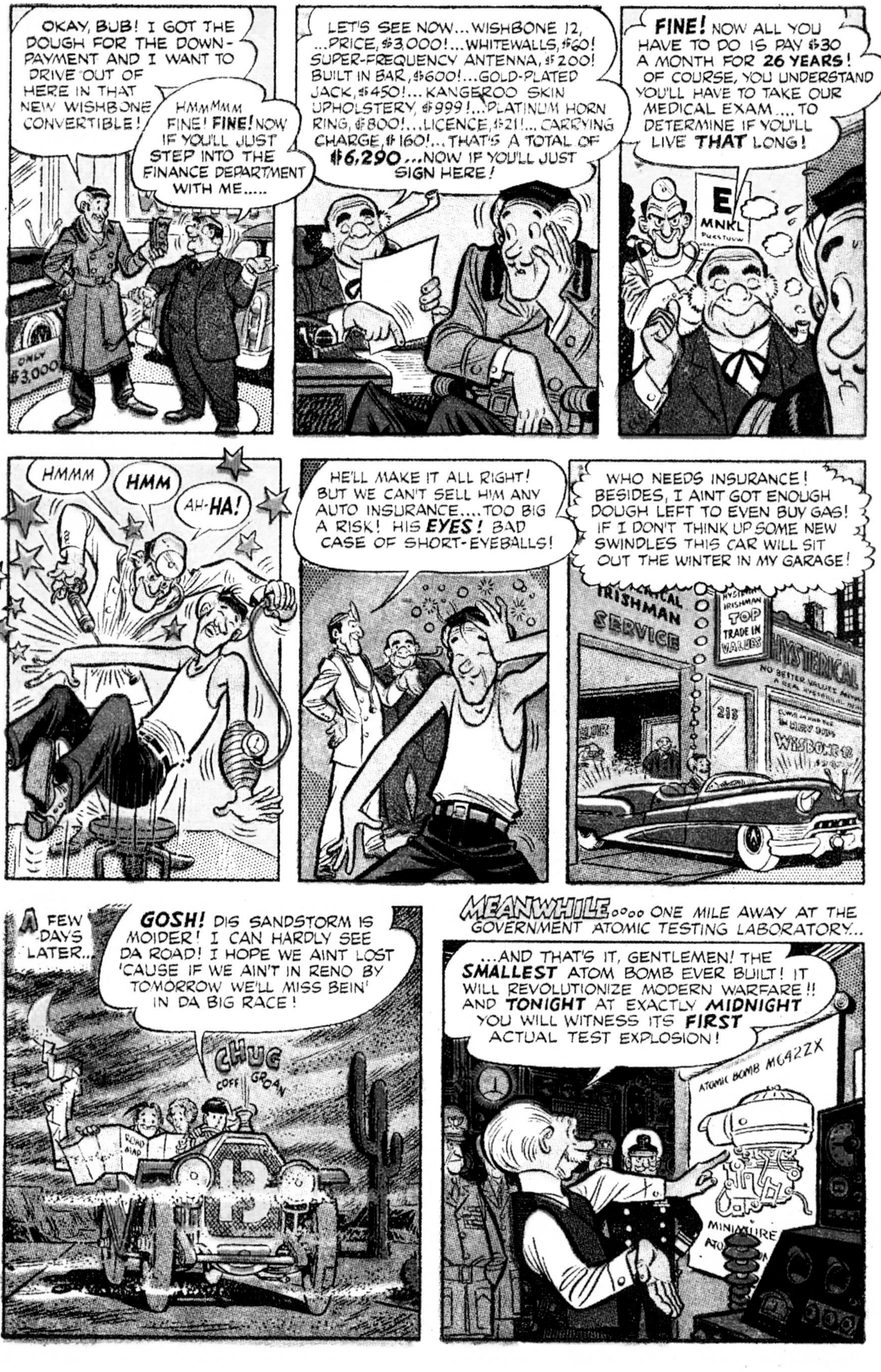
OKAY, BUB! I GOT THE DOUGH FOR THE DOWN-PAYMENT AND I WANT TO DRIVE OUT OF HERE IN THAT NEW WISHBONE CONVERTIBLE!
HMMMMM FINE! **FINE!** NOW IF YOU'LL JUST STEP INTO THE FINANCE DEPARTMENT WITH ME.....
ONLY $3,000
LET'S SEE NOW... WISHBONE 12, ...PRICE, $3,000!... WHITEWALLS, $60! SUPER-FREQUENCY ANTENNA, $200! BUILT IN BAR, $600!...GOLD-PLATED JACK, $450!... KANGEROO SKIN UPHOLSTERY, $999!...PLATINUM HORN RING, $800!...LICENCE, $21!... CARRYING CHARGE, $160!... THAT'S A TOTAL OF **$6,290**... NOW IF YOU'LL JUST SIGN HERE!
FINE! NOW ALL YOU HAVE TO DO IS PAY $30 A MONTH FOR **26 YEARS!** OF COURSE, YOU UNDERSTAND YOU'LL HAVE TO TAKE OUR MEDICAL EXAM.... TO DETERMINE IF YOU'LL LIVE **THAT** LONG!
E
MNKL
HMMM
HMM
AH-**HA!**
HE'LL MAKE IT ALL RIGHT! BUT WE CAN'T SELL HIM ANY AUTO INSURANCE.... TOO BIG A RISK! HIS **EYES!** BAD CASE OF SHORT-EYEBALLS!
WHO NEEDS INSURANCE! BESIDES, I AINT GOT ENOUGH DOUGH LEFT TO EVEN BUY GAS! IF I DON'T THINK UP SOME NEW SWINDLES THIS CAR WILL SIT OUT THE WINTER IN MY GARAGE!
IRISHMAN SERVICE
HYSTERICAL IRISHMAN TOP TRADE IN VALUES
HYSTERICAL
213
WISBONE 12
A FEW DAYS LATER..
GOSH! DIS SANDSTORM IS MOIDER! I CAN HARDLY SEE DA ROAD! I HOPE WE AINT LOST 'CAUSE IF WE AIN'T IN RENO BY TOMORROW WE'LL MISS BEIN' IN DA BIG RACE!
CHUG
COFF
GROAN
ROAD MAP
13
MEANWHILE.... ONE MILE AWAY AT THE GOVERNMENT ATOMIC TESTING LABORATORY...
...AND THAT'S IT, GENTLEMEN! THE **SMALLEST** ATOM BOMB EVER BUILT! IT WILL REVOLUTIONIZE MODERN WARFARE!! AND **TONIGHT** AT EXACTLY **MIDNIGHT** YOU WILL WITNESS ITS **FIRST** ACTUAL TEST EXPLOSION!
ATOMIC BOMB M642ZX
MINIATURE

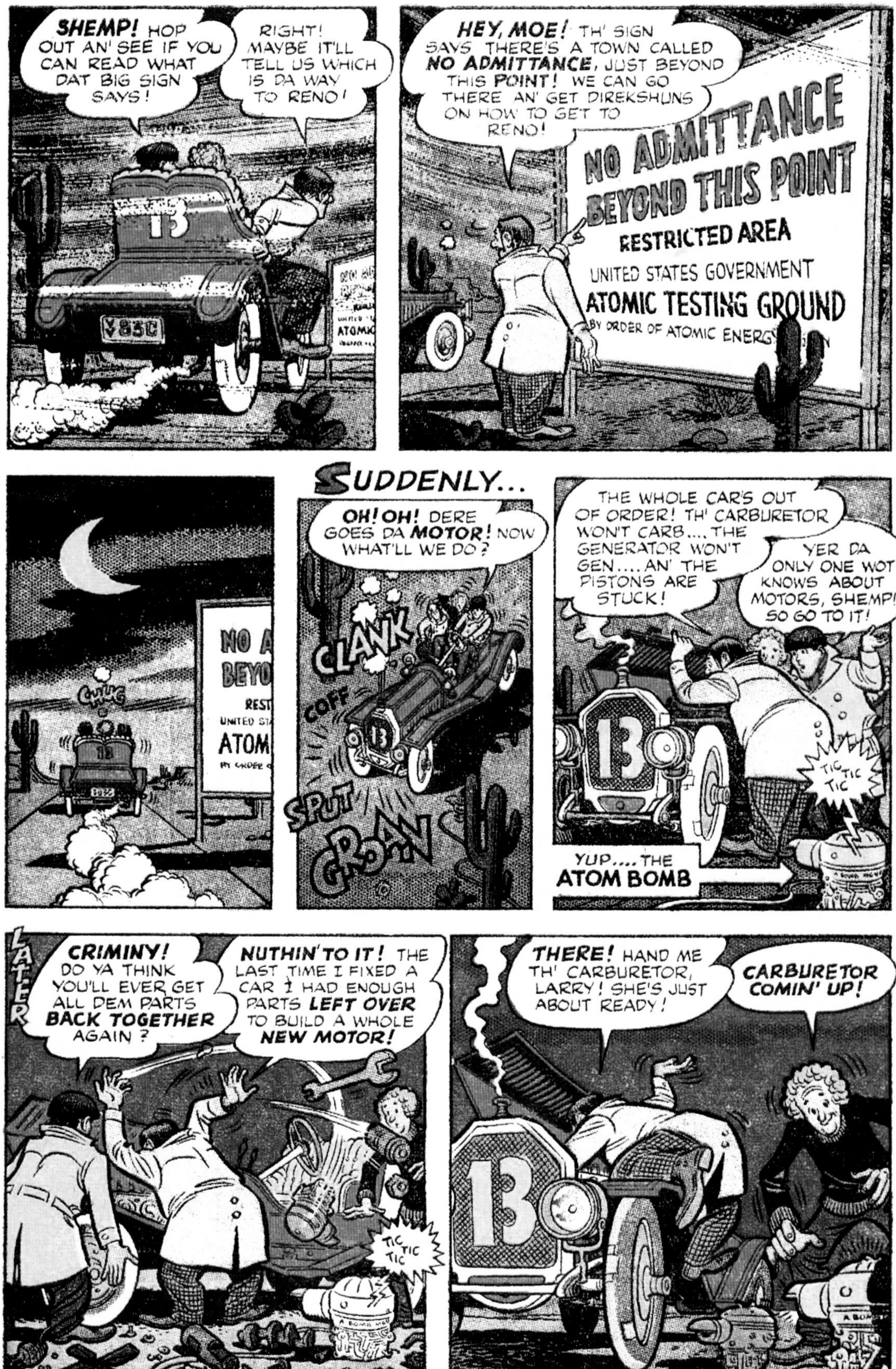
SHEMP! HOP OUT AN' SEE IF YOU CAN READ WHAT DAT BIG SIGN SAYS!
RIGHT! MAYBE IT'LL TELL US WHICH IS DA WAY TO RENO!
HEY, MOE! TH' SIGN SAYS THERE'S A TOWN CALLED NO ADMITTANCE, JUST BEYOND THIS POINT! WE CAN GO THERE AN' GET DIREKSHUNS ON HOW TO GET TO RENO!
NO ADMITTANCE BEYOND THIS POINT
RESTRICTED AREA
UNITED STATES GOVERNMENT
ATOMIC TESTING GROUND
SUDDENLY...
OH! OH! DERE GOES DA MOTOR! NOW WHAT'LL WE DO?
CLANK
COFF
SPUT
GROAN
THE WHOLE CAR'S OUT OF ORDER! TH' CARBURETOR WON'T CARB.... THE GENERATOR WON'T GEN.... AN' THE PISTONS ARE STUCK!
YER DA ONLY ONE WOT KNOWS ABOUT MOTORS, SHEMP! SO GO TO IT!
TIC TIC TIC
YUP.... THE ATOM BOMB
LATER
CRIMINY! DO YA THINK YOU'LL EVER GET ALL DEM PARTS BACK TOGETHER AGAIN?
NUTHIN' TO IT! THE LAST TIME I FIXED A CAR I HAD ENOUGH PARTS LEFT OVER TO BUILD A WHOLE NEW MOTOR!
TIC TIC TIC
THERE! HAND ME TH' CARBURETOR, LARRY! SHE'S JUST ABOUT READY!
CARBURETOR COMIN' UP!

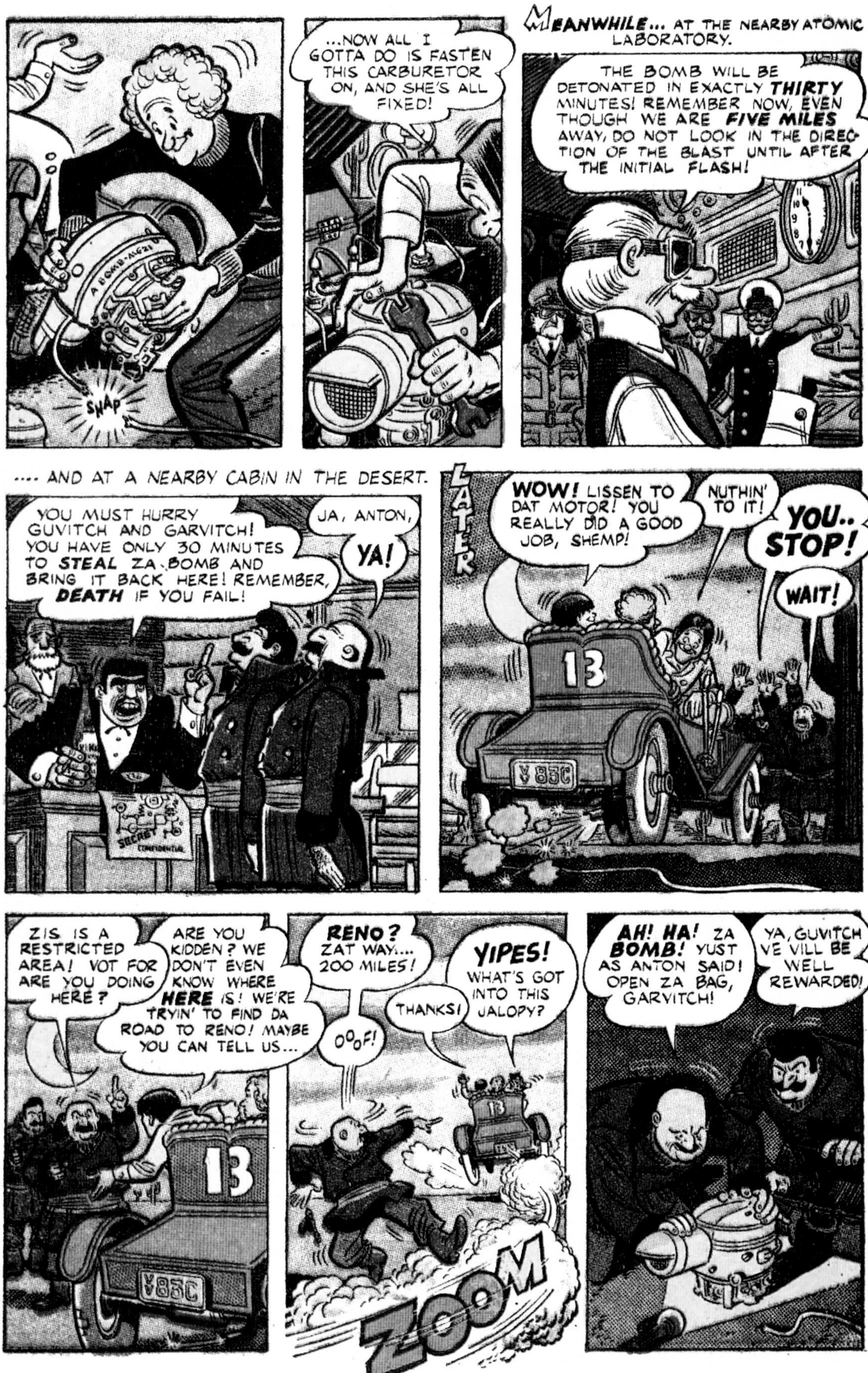
SNAP
...NOW ALL I GOTTA DO IS FASTEN THIS CARBURETOR ON, AND SHE'S ALL FIXED!
MEANWHILE... AT THE NEARBY ATOMIC LABORATORY.
THE BOMB WILL BE DETONATED IN EXACTLY THIRTY MINUTES! REMEMBER NOW, EVEN THOUGH WE ARE FIVE MILES AWAY, DO NOT LOOK IN THE DIRECTION OF THE BLAST UNTIL AFTER THE INITIAL FLASH!
.... AND AT A NEARBY CABIN IN THE DESERT.
YOU MUST HURRY GUVITCH AND GARVITCH! YOU HAVE ONLY 30 MINUTES TO STEAL ZA BOMB AND BRING IT BACK HERE! REMEMBER, DEATH IF YOU FAIL!
JA, ANTON,
YA!
LATER
WOW! LISSEN TO DAT MOTOR! YOU REALLY DID A GOOD JOB, SHEMP!
NUTHIN' TO IT!
YOU.. STOP!
WAIT!
ZIS IS A RESTRICTED AREA! VOT FOR ARE YOU DOING HERE?
ARE YOU KIDDEN? WE DON'T EVEN KNOW WHERE HERE IS! WE'RE TRYIN' TO FIND DA ROAD TO RENO! MAYBE YOU CAN TELL US...
RENO? ZAT WAY... 200 MILES!
THANKS!
OOOF!
YIPES! WHAT'S GOT INTO THIS JALOPY?
ZOOM
AH! HA! ZA BOMB! YUST AS ANTON SAID! OPEN ZA BAG, GARVITCH!
YA, GUVITCH VE VILL BE WELL REWARDED!

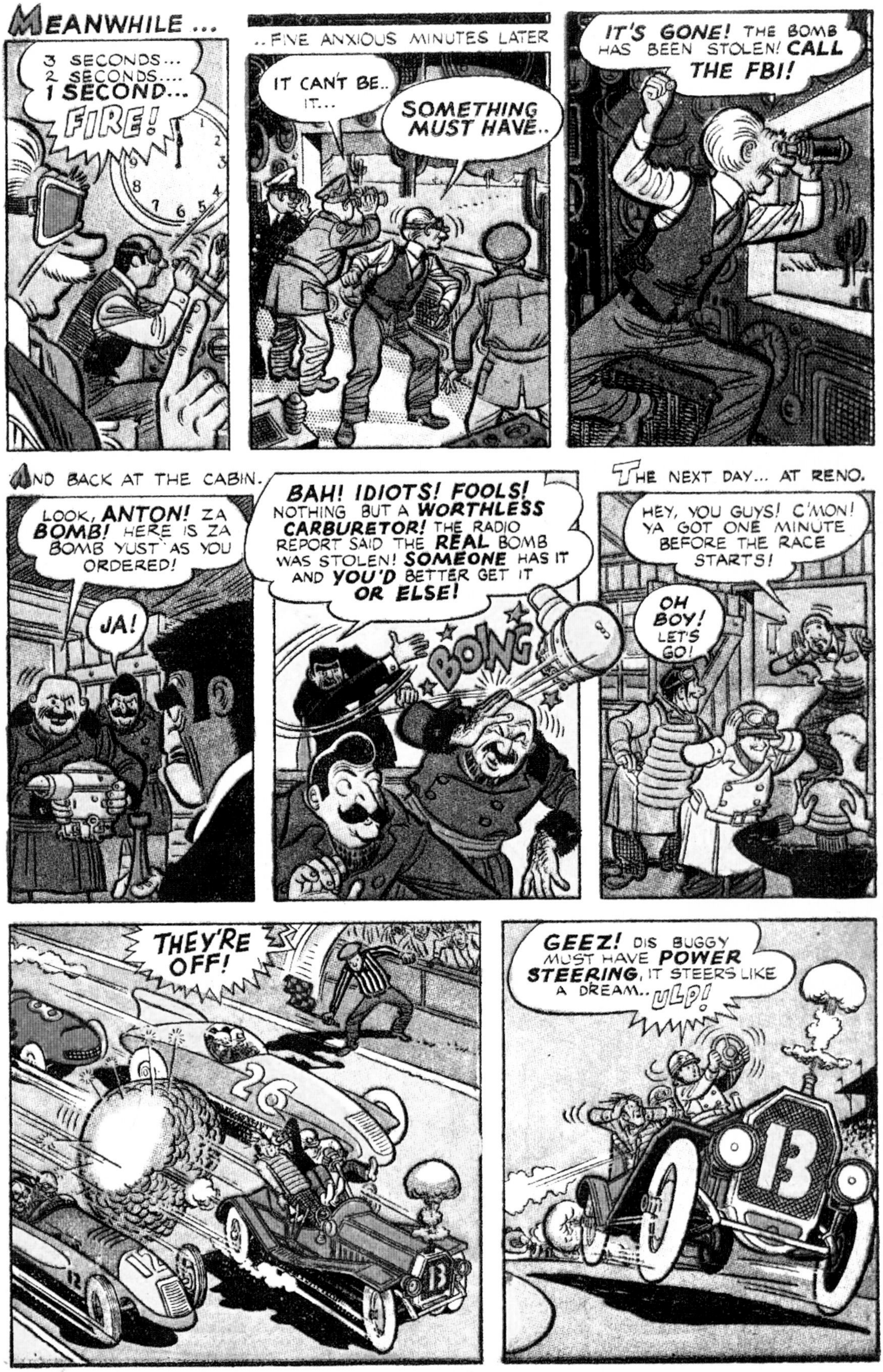
MEANWHILE ...
3 SECONDS... 2 SECONDS.... 1 SECOND... FIRE!
..FIVE ANXIOUS MINUTES LATER
IT CAN'T BE.. IT...
SOMETHING MUST HAVE..
IT'S GONE! THE BOMB HAS BEEN STOLEN! CALL THE FBI!
AND BACK AT THE CABIN.
LOOK, ANTON! ZA BOMB! HERE IS ZA BOMB YUST AS YOU ORDERED!
JA!
BAH! IDIOTS! FOOLS! NOTHING BUT A WORTHLESS CARBURETOR! THE RADIO REPORT SAID THE REAL BOMB WAS STOLEN! SOMEONE HAS IT AND YOU'D BETTER GET IT OR ELSE!
BOING
THE NEXT DAY... AT RENO.
HEY, YOU GUYS! C'MON! YA GOT ONE MINUTE BEFORE THE RACE STARTS!
OH BOY! LET'S GO!
THEY'RE OFF!
GEEZ! DIS BUGGY MUST HAVE POWER STEERING, IT STEERS LIKE A DREAM.. ULP!

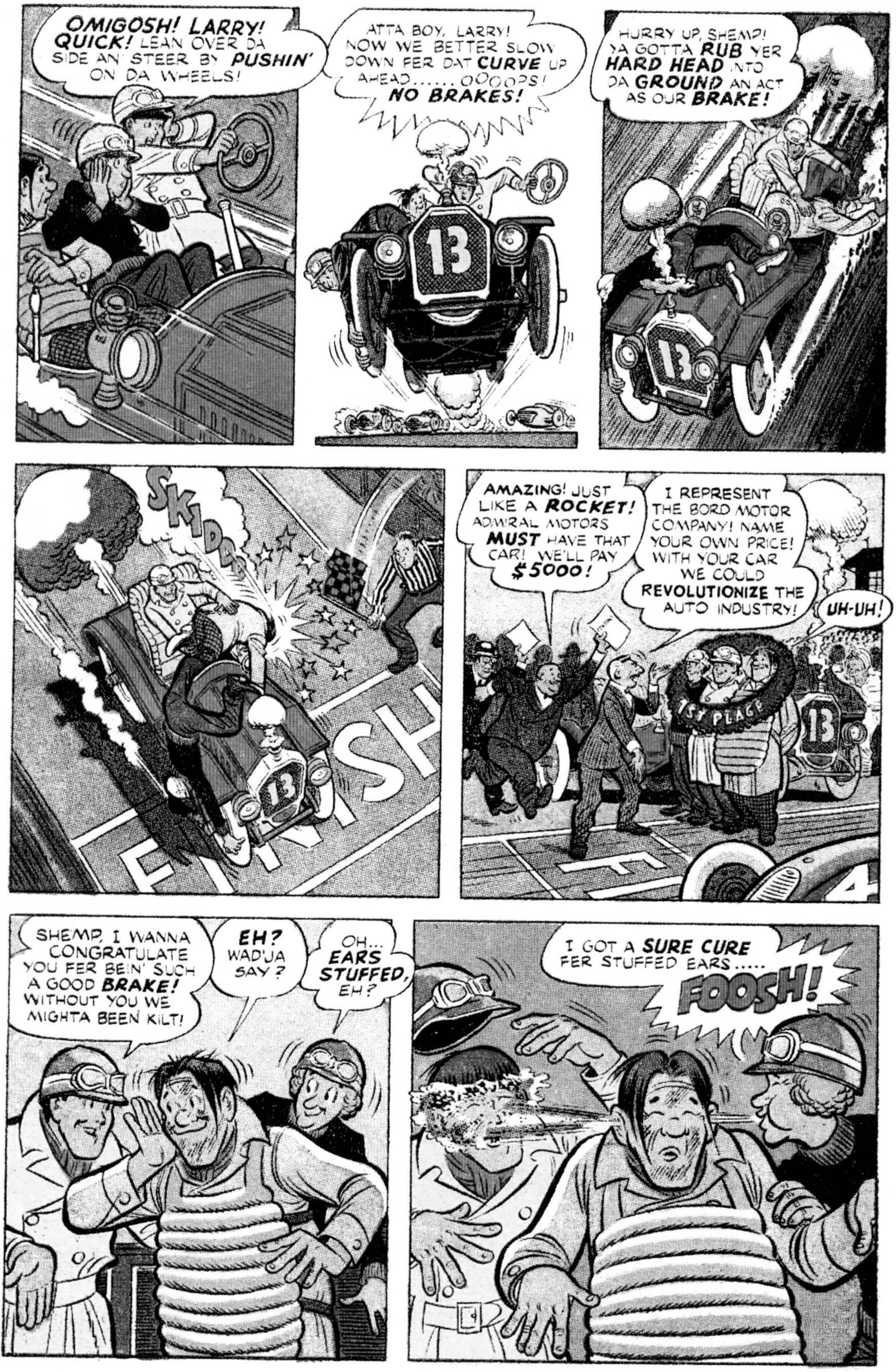
OMIGOSH! LARRY! QUICK! LEAN OVER DA SIDE AN' STEER BY PUSHIN' ON DA WHEELS!
ATTA BOY, LARRY! NOW WE BETTER SLOW DOWN FER DAT CURVE UP AHEAD...... OOOOPS! NO BRAKES!
HURRY UP, SHEMP! YA GOTTA RUB YER HARD HEAD INTO DA GROUND AN ACT AS OUR BRAKE!
SKIDD
AMAZING! JUST LIKE A ROCKET! ADMIRAL MOTORS MUST HAVE THAT CAR! WE'LL PAY $5000!
I REPRESENT THE BORD MOTOR COMPANY! NAME YOUR OWN PRICE! WITH YOUR CAR WE COULD REVOLUTIONIZE THE AUTO INDUSTRY!
UH-UH!
1ST PLACE
SHEMP, I WANNA CONGRATULATE YOU FER BEIN' SUCH A GOOD BRAKE! WITHOUT YOU WE MIGHTA BEEN KILT!
EH? WAD'JA SAY?
OH... EARS STUFFED, EH?
I GOT A SURE CURE FER STUFFED EARS.....
FOOSH!

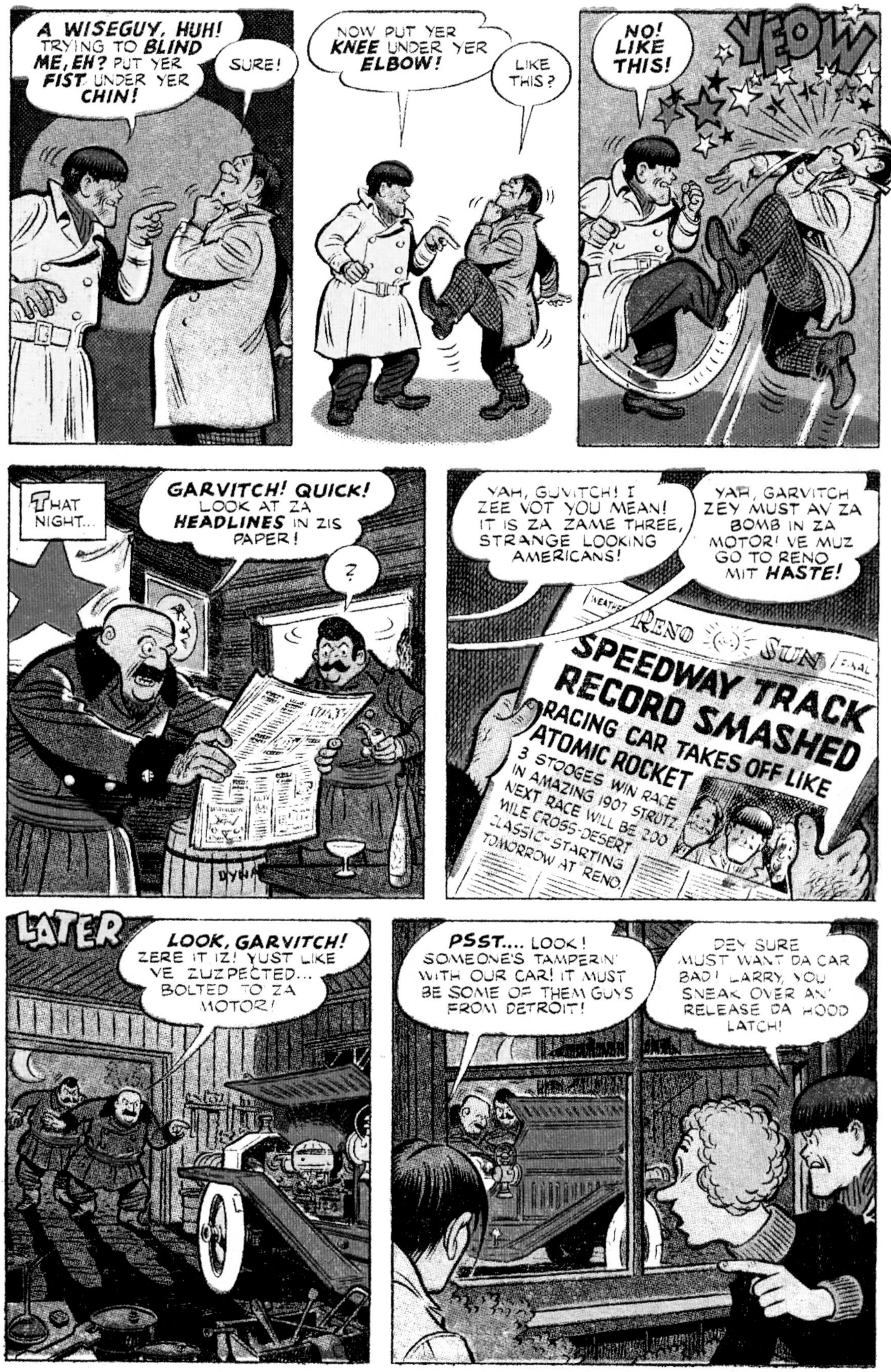
A WISEGUY, HUH! TRYING TO BLIND ME, EH? PUT YER FIST UNDER YER CHIN!
SURE!
NOW PUT YER KNEE UNDER YER ELBOW!
LIKE THIS?
NO! LIKE THIS!
YEOW
THAT NIGHT...
GARVITCH! QUICK! LOOK AT ZA HEADLINES IN ZIS PAPER!
?
YAH, GUVITCH! I ZEE VOT YOU MEAN! IT IS ZA ZAME THREE, STRANGE LOOKING AMERICANS!
YAH, GARVITCH ZEY MUST AV ZA BOMB IN ZA MOTOR! VE MUZ GO TO RENO MIT HASTE!
RENO SUN
FINAL
SPEEDWAY TRACK RECORD SMASHED
RACING CAR TAKES OFF LIKE ATOMIC ROCKET
3 STOOGES WIN RACE IN AMAZING 1907 STRUTZ
NEXT RACE WILL BE 200 MILE CROSS-DESERT CLASSIC-STARTING TOMORROW AT RENO.
LATER
LOOK, GARVITCH! ZERE IT IZ! YUST LIKE VE ZUZPECTED... BOLTED TO ZA MOTOR!
PSST.... LOOK! SOMEONE'S TAMPERIN' WITH OUR CAR! IT MUST BE SOME OF THEM GUYS FROM DETROIT!
DEY SURE MUST WANT DA CAR BAD! LARRY, YOU SNEAK OVER AN' RELEASE DA HOOD LATCH!

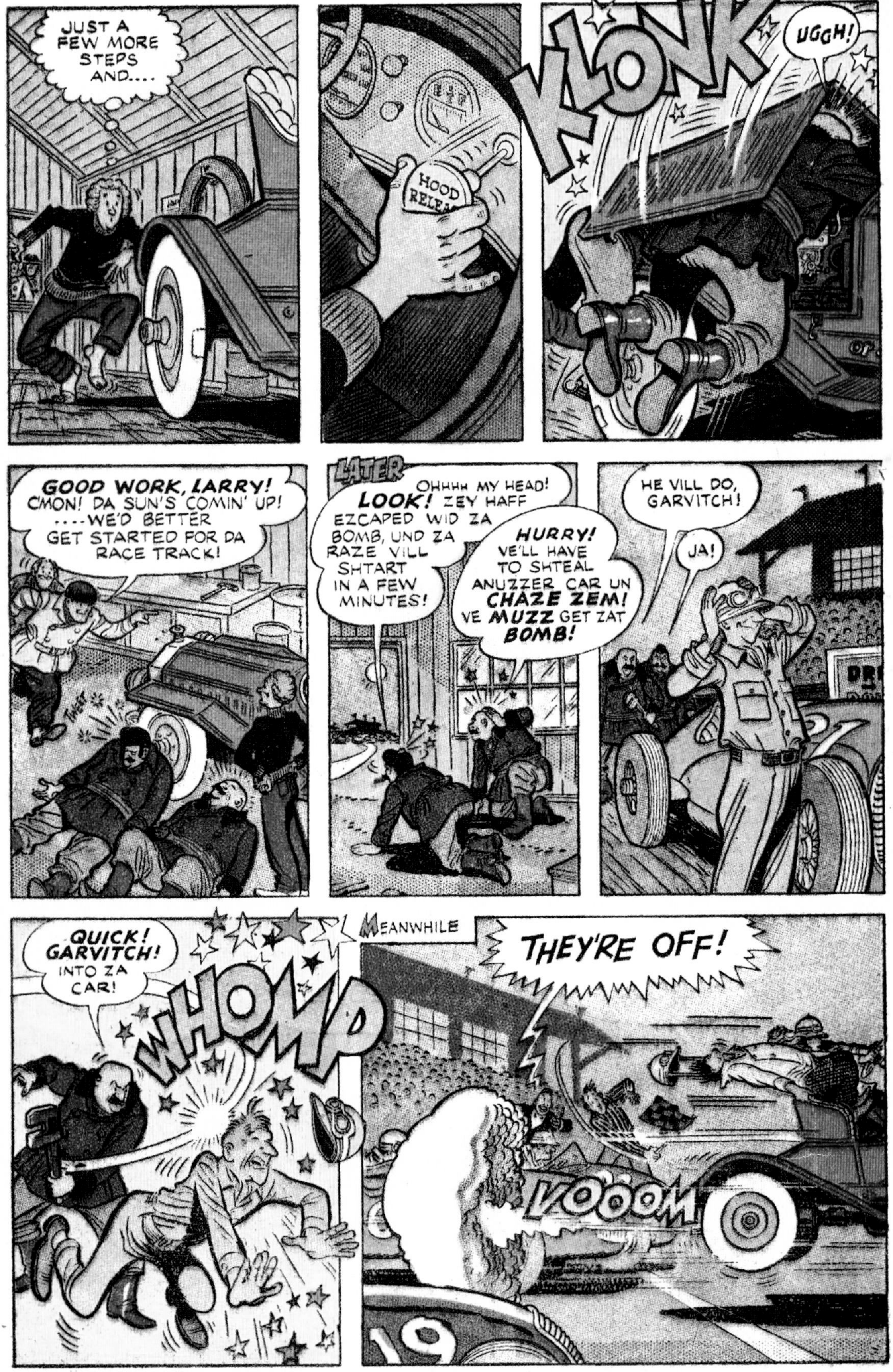
JUST A FEW MORE STEPS AND....
HOOD RELEA
KLONK
UGGH!
GOOD WORK, LARRY! C'MON! DA SUN'S COMIN' UP! ....WE'D BETTER GET STARTED FOR DA RACE TRACK!
LATER
OHHHH MY HEAD! LOOK! ZEY HAFF EZCAPED WID ZA BOMB, UND ZA RAZE VILL SHTART IN A FEW MINUTES!
HURRY! VE'LL HAVE TO SHTEAL ANUZZER CAR UN CHAZE ZEM! VE MUZZ GET ZAT BOMB!
HE VILL DO, GARVITCH!
JA!
QUICK! GARVITCH! INTO ZA CAR!
WHOMP
MEANWHILE
THEY'RE OFF!
VOOOM
19

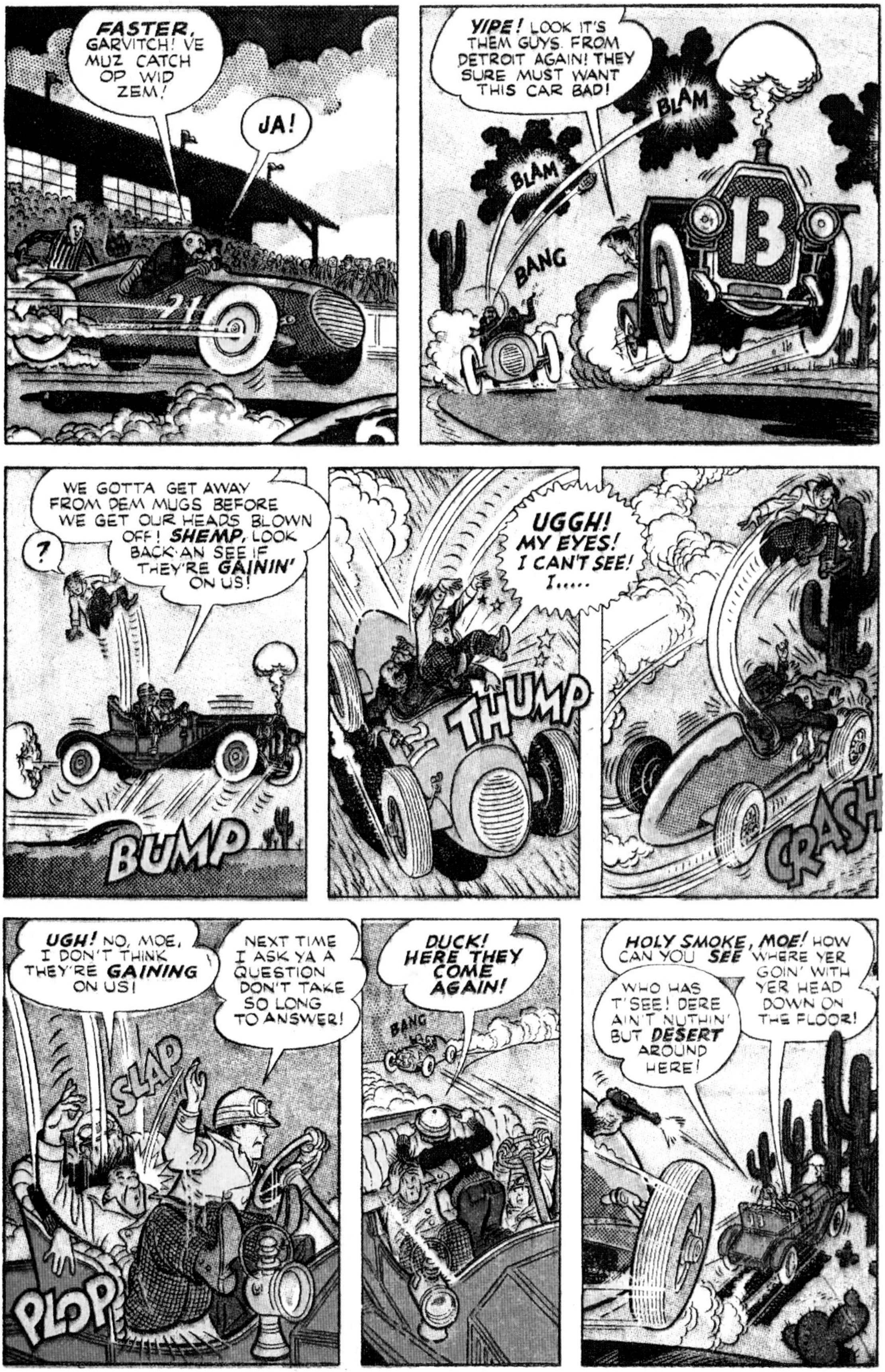
FASTER, GARVITCH! VE MUZ CATCH OP WID ZEM!
JA!
YIPE! LOOK IT'S THEM GUYS. FROM DETROIT AGAIN! THEY SURE MUST WANT THIS CAR BAD!
BLAM
BLAM
BANG
13
WE GOTTA GET AWAY FROM DEM MUGS BEFORE WE GET OUR HEADS BLOWN OFF! SHEMP, LOOK BACK AN SEE IF THEY'RE GAININ' ON US!
?
BUMP
UGGH! MY EYES! I CAN'T SEE! I.....
THUMP
CRASH
UGH! NO, MOE, I DON'T THINK THEY'RE GAINING ON US!
NEXT TIME I ASK YA A QUESTION DON'T TAKE SO LONG TO ANSWER!
SLAP
PLOP
DUCK! HERE THEY COME AGAIN!
BANG
HOLY SMOKE, MOE! HOW CAN YOU SEE WHERE YER GOIN' WITH YER HEAD DOWN ON THE FLOOR!
WHO HAS T'SEE! DERE AIN'T NUTHIN' BUT DESERT AROUND HERE!

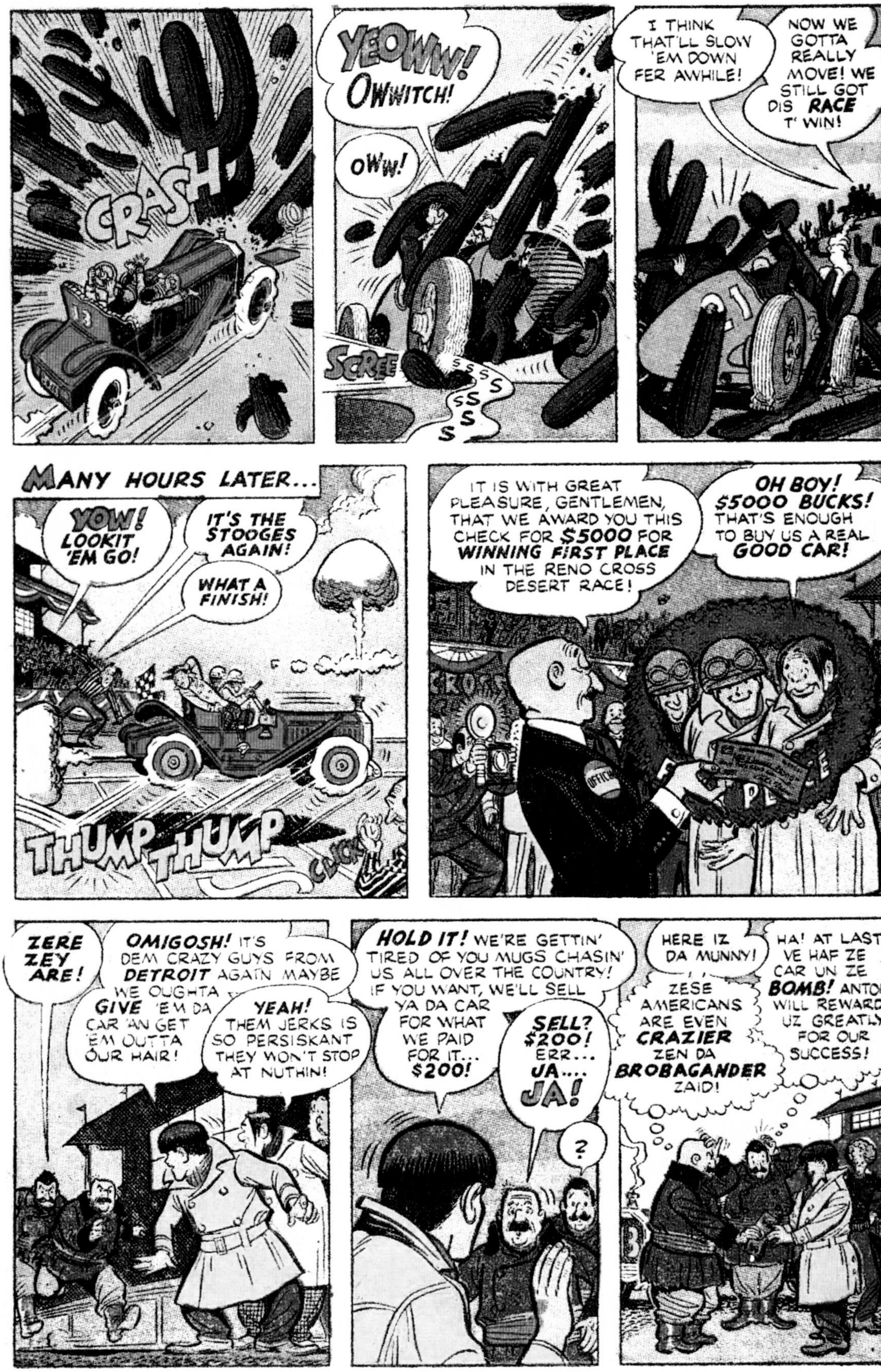
CRASH
YEOWW! OWWITCH!
OWW!
SCREE
SSSS
I THINK THAT'LL SLOW 'EM DOWN FER AWHILE!
NOW WE GOTTA REALLY MOVE! WE STILL GOT DIS RACE T' WIN!
MANY HOURS LATER...
YOW! LOOKIT 'EM GO!
IT'S THE STOOGES AGAIN!
WHAT A FINISH!
THUMP THUMP
CLICK
IT IS WITH GREAT PLEASURE, GENTLEMEN, THAT WE AWARD YOU THIS CHECK FOR $5000 FOR WINNING FIRST PLACE IN THE RENO CROSS DESERT RACE!
OH BOY! $5000 BUCKS! THAT'S ENOUGH TO BUY US A REAL GOOD CAR!
ZERE ZEY ARE!
OMIGOSH! IT'S DEM CRAZY GUYS FROM DETROIT AGAIN MAYBE WE OUGHTA GIVE 'EM DA CAR AN GET 'EM OUTTA OUR HAIR!
YEAH! THEM JERKS IS SO PERSISKANT THEY WON'T STOP AT NUTHIN!
HOLD IT! WE'RE GETTIN' TIRED OF YOU MUGS CHASIN' US ALL OVER THE COUNTRY! IF YOU WANT, WE'LL SELL YA DA CAR FOR WHAT WE PAID FOR IT... $200!
SELL? $200! ERR... JA.... JA!
?
HERE IZ DA MUNNY!
ZESE AMERICANS ARE EVEN CRAZIER ZEN DA BROBAGANDER ZAID!
HA! AT LAST VE HAF ZE CAR UN ZE BOMB! ANTON WILL REWARD UZ GREATLY FOR OUR SUCCESS!

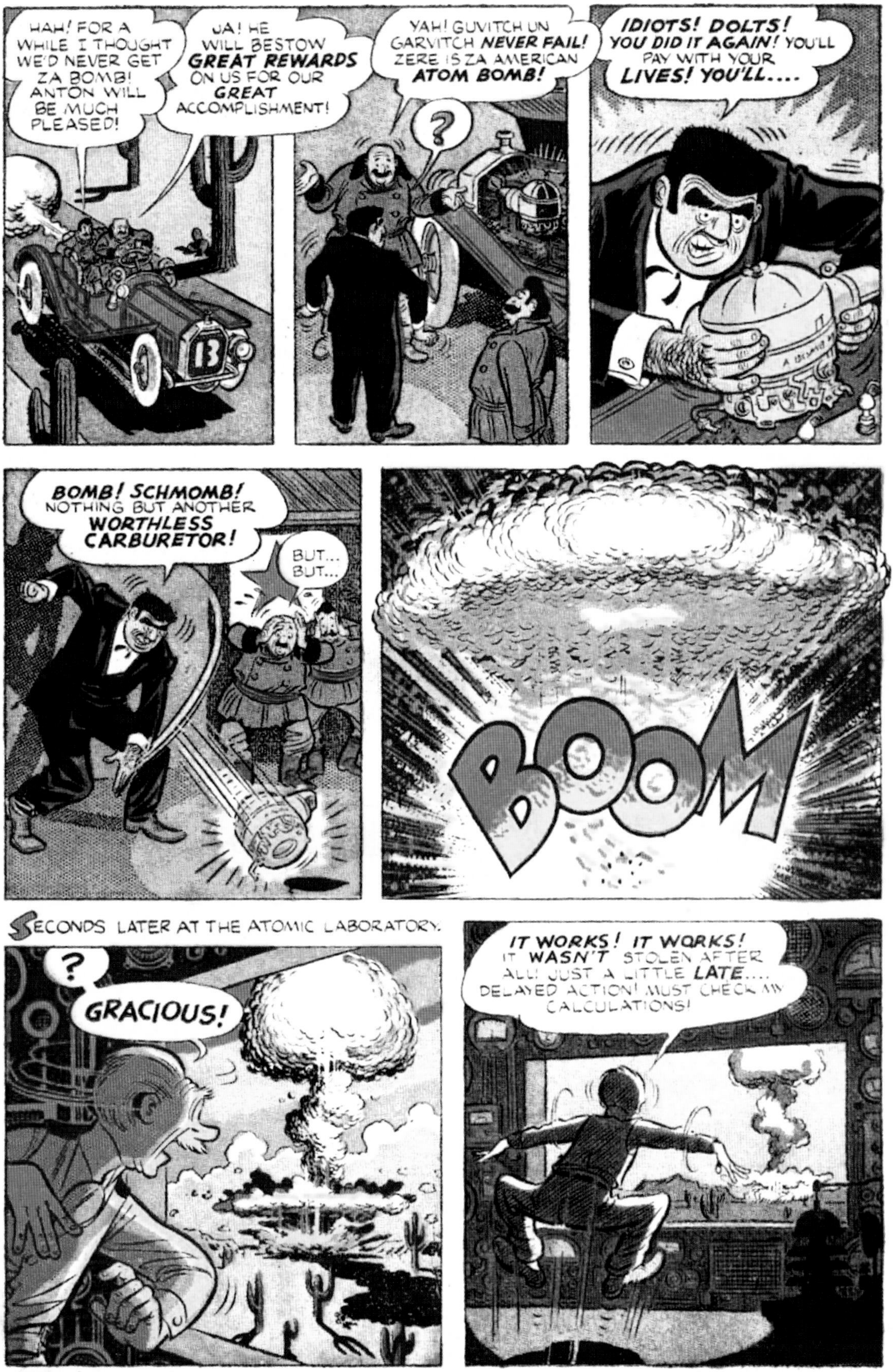
HAH! FOR A WHILE I THOUGHT WE'D NEVER GET ZA BOMB! ANTON WILL BE MUCH PLEASED!
JA! HE WILL BESTOW GREAT REWARDS ON US FOR OUR GREAT ACCOMPLISHMENT!
YAH! GUVITCH UN GARVITCH NEVER FAIL! ZERE IS ZA AMERICAN ATOM BOMB!
?
IDIOTS! DOLTS! YOU DID IT AGAIN! YOU'LL PAY WITH YOUR LIVES! YOU'LL....
13
BOMB! SCHMOMB! NOTHING BUT ANOTHER WORTHLESS CARBURETOR!
BUT... BUT...
BOOM
SECONDS LATER AT THE ATOMIC LABORATORY.
?
GRACIOUS!
IT WORKS! IT WORKS! IT WASN'T STOLEN AFTER ALL! JUST A LITTLE LATE.... DELAYED ACTION! MUST CHECK MY CALCULATIONS!

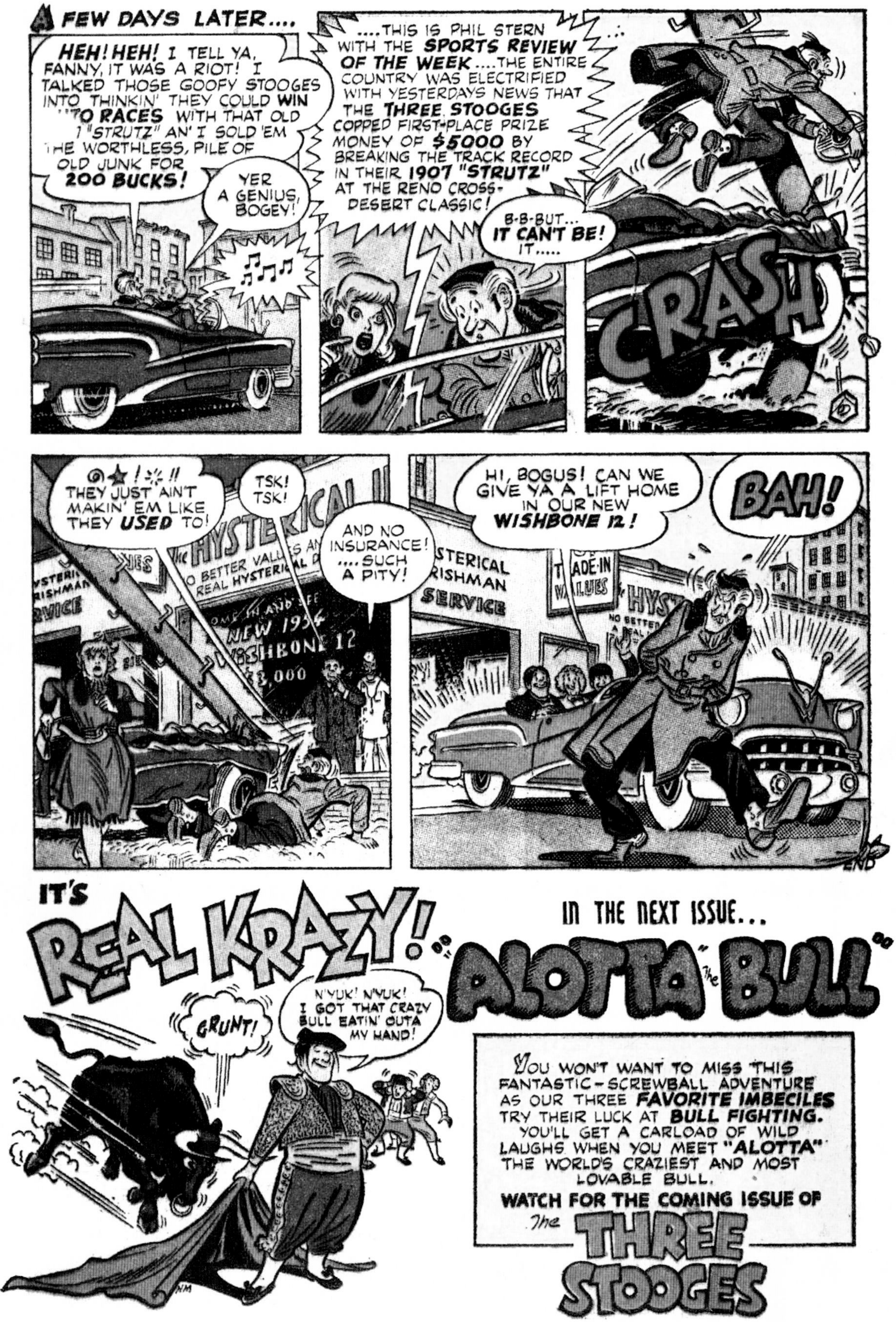
A FEW DAYS LATER....
HEH! HEH! I TELL YA, FANNY, IT WAS A RIOT! I TALKED THOSE GOOFY STOOGES INTO THINKIN' THEY COULD WIN ...O RACES WITH THAT OLD ..."STRUTZ" AN' I SOLD 'EM THE WORTHLESS, PILE OF OLD JUNK FOR 200 BUCKS!
YER A GENIUS, BOGEY!
....THIS IS PHIL STERN WITH THE SPORTS REVIEW OF THE WEEK....THE ENTIRE COUNTRY WAS ELECTRIFIED WITH YESTERDAYS NEWS THAT THE THREE STOOGES COPPED FIRST-PLACE PRIZE MONEY OF $5000 BY BREAKING THE TRACK RECORD IN THEIR 1907 "STRUTZ" AT THE RENO CROSS-DESERT CLASSIC!
B-B-BUT... IT CAN'T BE! IT.....
CRASH
@★!*!! THEY JUST AIN'T MAKIN' EM LIKE THEY USED TO!
TSK! TSK!
AND NO INSURANCE! ....SUCH A PITY!
HYSTERICAL
NO BETTER VALUES AN... REAL HYSTERICAL D...
NEW 1954 WISHBONE 12
HI, BOGUS! CAN WE GIVE YA A LIFT HOME IN OUR NEW WISHBONE 12!
BAH!
STERICAL RISHMAN SERVICE
TRADE-IN VALUES
END
IT'S REAL KRAZY!
GRUNT!
N'YUK! N'YUK! I GOT THAT CRAZY BULL EATIN' OUTA MY HAND!
IN THE NEXT ISSUE...
"ALOTTA" The "BULL"
YOU WON'T WANT TO MISS THIS FANTASTIC-SCREWBALL ADVENTURE AS OUR THREE FAVORITE IMBECILES TRY THEIR LUCK AT BULL FIGHTING. YOU'LL GET A CARLOAD OF WILD LAUGHS WHEN YOU MEET "ALOTTA" THE WORLD'S CRAZIEST AND MOST LOVABLE BULL.
WATCH FOR THE COMING ISSUE OF The THREE STOOGES

MAGIC PAGE
CONTEST WINNERS

IN THE LAST **3-D** ISSUE OF *The* **THREE STOOGES**, WE HELD A SPECIAL, **MAGIC PAGE** CONTEST... ALTHOUGH, THIS CONTEST WAS SPECIFICALLY DESIGNED FOR **3-D COMICS**, THE QUALITY OF THE TWO WINNING ENTRIES WAS SO GOOD THAT WE HAVE DECIDED TO PRINT THEM, ANYWAY, IN THIS TWO-DIMENSIONAL BOOK. WE WISH TO THANK ALL THE SWELL GUYS AND GIRLS WHO SENT IN ENTRIES AND WE HOPE THEY'LL BE WITH US AGAIN IN THE NEW, **SUPER-CONTEST** THAT WILL BE IN THE NEXT ISSUE.

The EDITORS

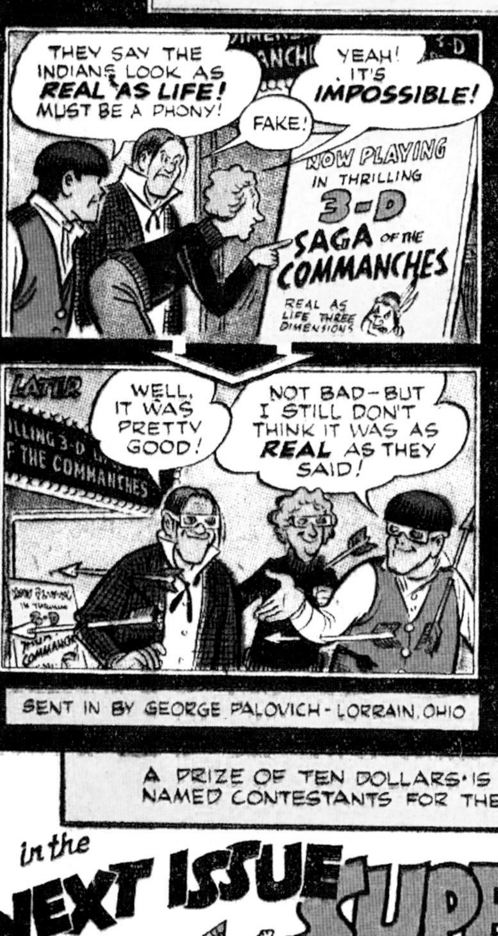
THEY SAY THE INDIANS LOOK AS REAL AS LIFE! MUST BE A PHONY!
YEAH! IT'S IMPOSSIBLE!
FAKE!
NOW PLAYING IN THRILLING 3-D SAGA OF THE COMMANCHES
REAL AS LIFE THREE DIMENSIONS
LATER
WELL, IT WAS PRETTY GOOD!
NOT BAD—BUT I STILL DON'T THINK IT WAS AS REAL AS THEY SAID!
F THE COMMANCHES

SENT IN BY GEORGE PALOVICH - LORRAIN, OHIO

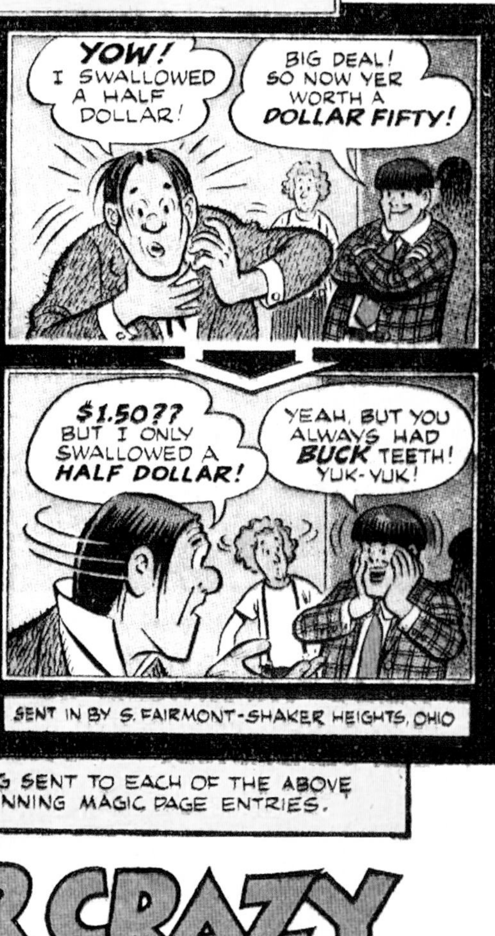
YOW! I SWALLOWED A HALF DOLLAR!
BIG DEAL! SO NOW YER WORTH A DOLLAR FIFTY!
$1.50?? BUT I ONLY SWALLOWED A HALF DOLLAR!
YEAH, BUT YOU ALWAYS HAD BUCK TEETH! YUK-YUK!

SENT IN BY S. FAIRMONT - SHAKER HEIGHTS, OHIO

A PRIZE OF TEN DOLLARS IS BEING SENT TO EACH OF THE ABOVE NAMED CONTESTANTS FOR THEIR WINNING MAGIC PAGE ENTRIES.

in the NEXT ISSUE SUPER CRAZY PUZZLE CONTEST

LOADS OF GRAND PRIZES IN A BIG CONTEST THAT'S DIFFERENT FROM ANY CONTEST EVER HELD IN ANY COMIC BOOK!

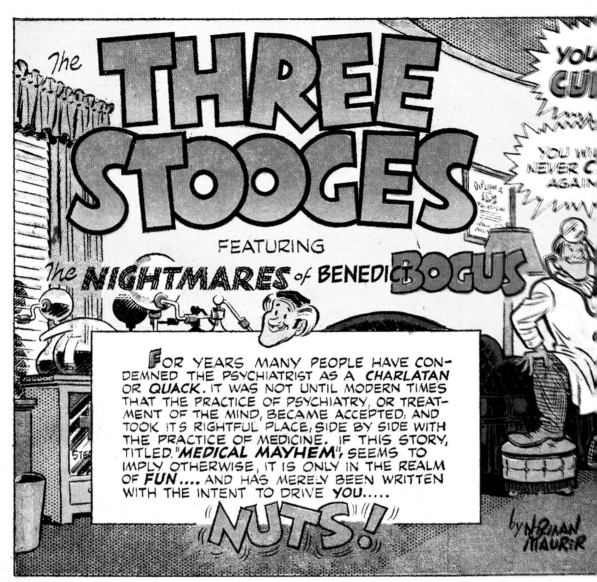

The THREE STOOGES
FEATURING
The NIGHTMARES of BENEDICT BOGUS
YOU CU
YOU WI NEVER C AGAI
FOR YEARS MANY PEOPLE HAVE CONDEMNED THE PSYCHIATRIST AS A CHARLATAN OR QUACK. IT WAS NOT UNTIL MODERN TIMES THAT THE PRACTICE OF PSYCHIATRY, OR TREATMENT OF THE MIND, BECAME ACCEPTED, AND TOOK ITS RIGHTFUL PLACE, SIDE BY SIDE WITH THE PRACTICE OF MEDICINE. IF THIS STORY, TITLED "MEDICAL MAYHEM", SEEMS TO IMPLY OTHERWISE, IT IS ONLY IN THE REALM OF FUN.... AND HAS MERELY BEEN WRITTEN WITH THE INTENT TO DRIVE YOU.....
NUTS!
by NORMAN MAURER
HMMM.... THIS LOOKS LIKE AN INTERESTING ARTICLE ..."AN ANALYSIS OF HABITUAL SWINDLERS AND SHOPLIFTERS"... HMMMMM
STRIFE
I'D WALK A FOOT FOR A...."BUCK"
AMERICA'S FAVORITE CIGARETTE
SWINDLERS AND SH
BY DR. B.B. SYCOSANE PHD.
AFTER YEARS OF INTENSE STUDY INTO THE HABITS OF HABITUAL SWINDLERS AND SHOPLIFTERS IT IS CLEARLY PROVEN THAT THESE POOR UNFORTUNATES KNOWN AS KLEPTO-SWINDLIACS SKEETZO-FRINNICS ARE DEFINITELY VICTIMS OF A GROTESQUE AND ALMOST INCURABLE MALADY OF THE MENTAL SYSTEM....
GOODNESS! KLEPTO-SWINDLIAC SKEETZO-FRINNIC? SOUNDS LIKE A DISEASE!
STRIFE

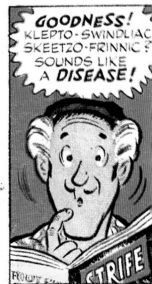

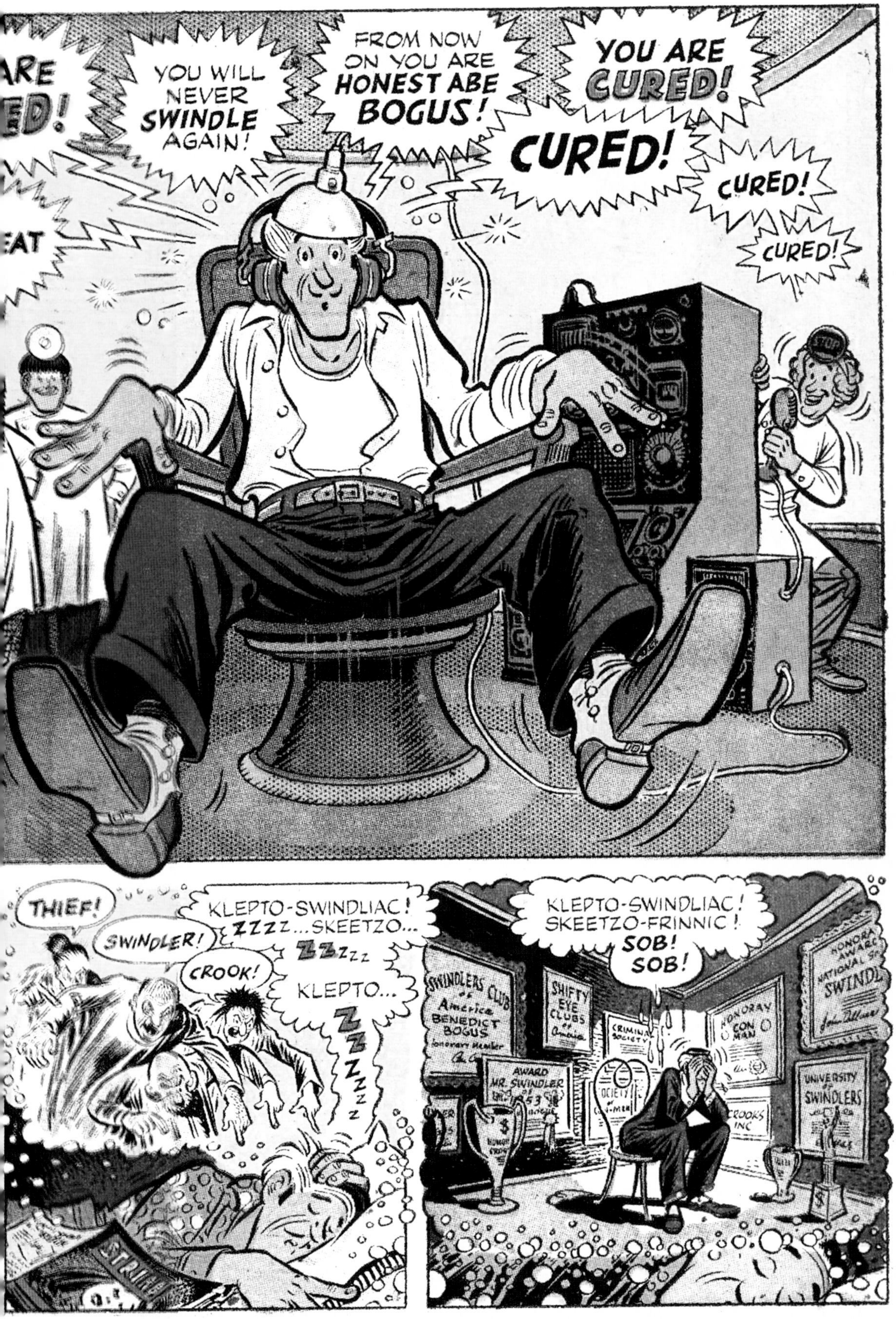
YOU WILL NEVER SWINDLE AGAIN!
FROM NOW ON YOU ARE HONEST ABE BOGUS!
YOU ARE CURED!
CURED!
CURED!
CURED!
THIEF!
SWINDLER!
CROOK!
KLEPTO-SWINDLIAC! ZZZz...SKEETZO... ZZzzz KLEPTO... ZZZzzz
KLEPTO-SWINDLIAC! SKEETZO-FRINNIC! SOB! SOB!
SWINDLERS CLUB of America BENEDICT BOGUS
SHIFTY EYE CLUBS of America
AWARD MR. SWINDLER
HONORARY CON MAN
UNIVERSITY of SWINDLERS
CROOKS INC

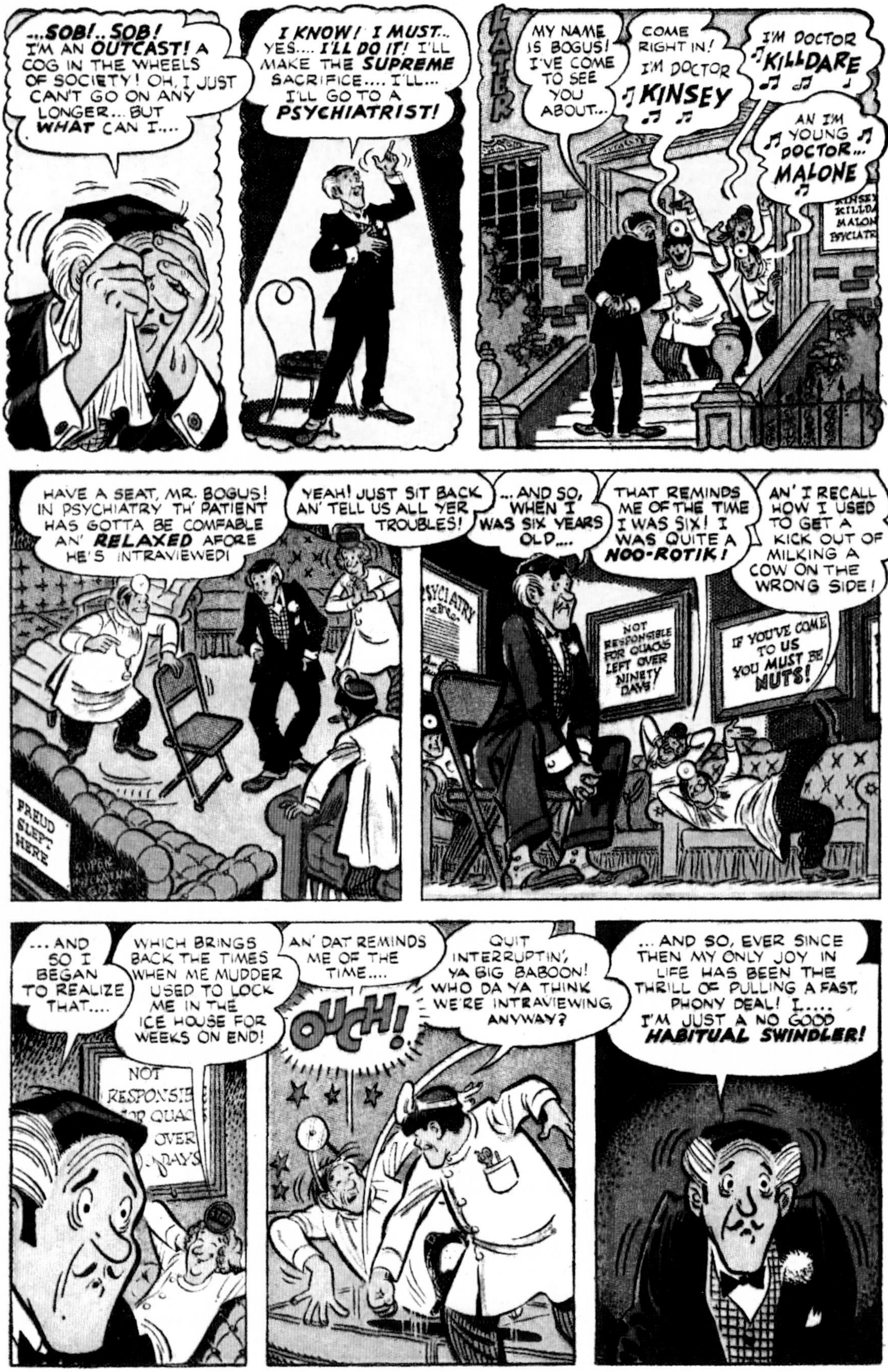
...SOB!..SOB! I'M AN OUTCAST! A COG IN THE WHEELS OF SOCIETY! OH, I JUST CAN'T GO ON ANY LONGER... BUT WHAT CAN I....
I KNOW! I MUST.. YES.... I'LL DO IT! I'LL MAKE THE SUPREME SACRIFICE.... I'LL... I'LL GO TO A PSYCHIATRIST!
LATER
MY NAME IS BOGUS! I'VE COME TO SEE YOU ABOUT...
COME RIGHT IN! I'M DOCTOR KINSEY
I'M DOCTOR KILLDARE
AN I'M YOUNG DOCTOR... MALONE
HAVE A SEAT, MR. BOGUS! IN PSYCHIATRY TH' PATIENT HAS GOTTA BE COMFABLE AN' RELAXED AFORE HE'S INTRAVIEWED!
YEAH! JUST SIT BACK AN' TELL US ALL YER TROUBLES!
FREUD SLEPT HERE
...AND SO, WHEN I WAS SIX YEARS OLD....
THAT REMINDS ME OF THE TIME I WAS SIX! I WAS QUITE A NOO-ROTIK!
AN' I RECALL HOW I USED TO GET A KICK OUT OF MILKING A COW ON THE WRONG SIDE!
NOT RESPONSIBLE FOR QUACKS LEFT OVER NINETY DAYS!
IF YOU'VE COME TO US YOU MUST BE NUTS!
...AND SO I BEGAN TO REALIZE THAT....
WHICH BRINGS BACK THE TIMES WHEN ME MUDDER USED TO LOCK ME IN THE ICE HOUSE FOR WEEKS ON END!
AN' DAT REMINDS ME OF THE TIME....
OUCH!
QUIT INTERRUPTIN', YA BIG BABOON! WHO DA YA THINK WE'RE INTRAVIEWING, ANYWAY?
...AND SO, EVER SINCE THEN MY ONLY JOY IN LIFE HAS BEEN THE THRILL OF PULLING A FAST, PHONY DEAL! I.... I'M JUST A NO GOOD HABITUAL SWINDLER!

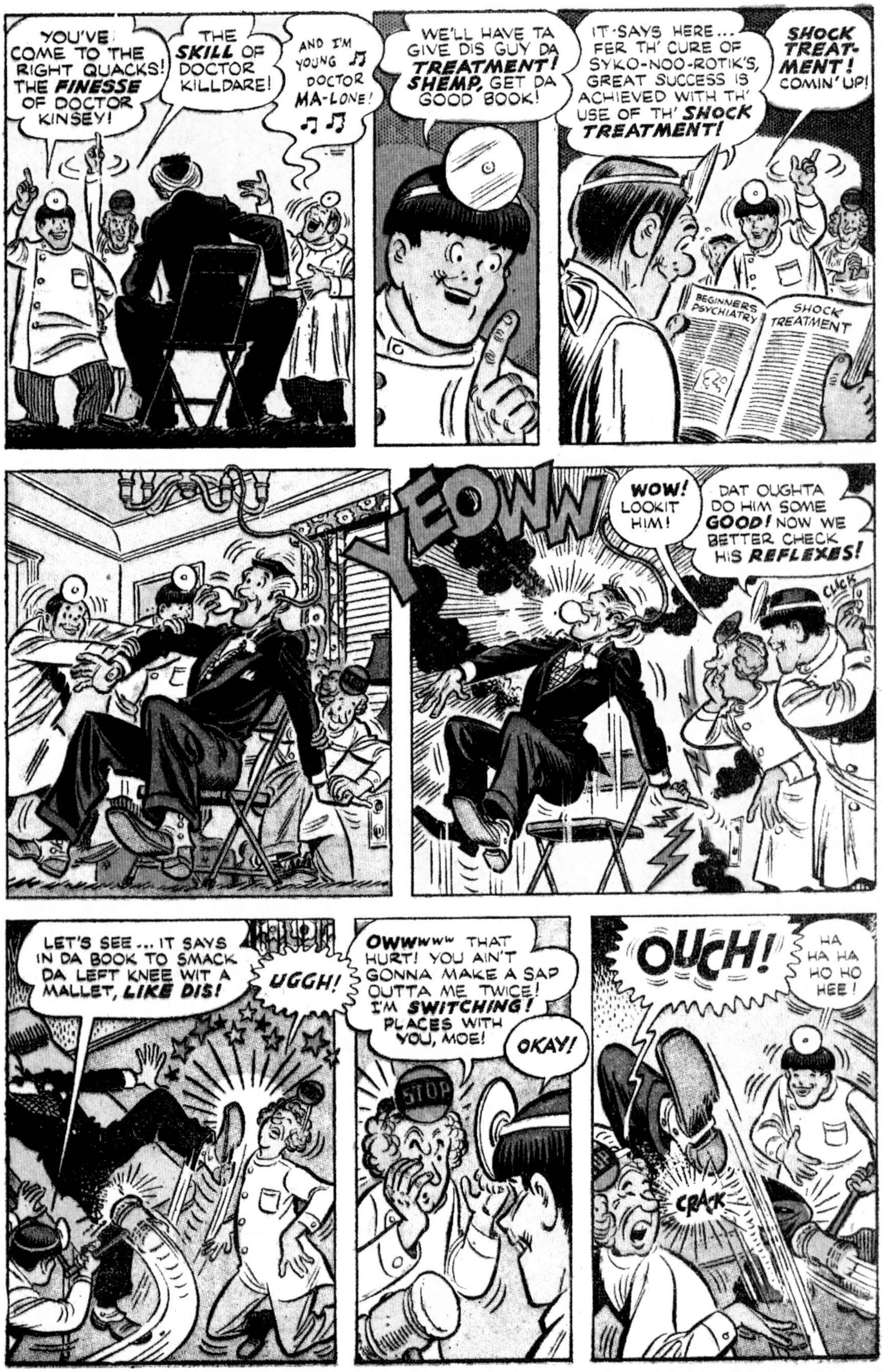
YOU'VE COME TO THE RIGHT QUACKS! THE FINESSE OF DOCTOR KINSEY!
THE SKILL OF DOCTOR KILLDARE!
AND I'M YOUNG DOCTOR MA-LONE!
WE'LL HAVE TA GIVE DIS GUY DA TREATMENT! SHEMP, GET DA GOOD BOOK!
IT SAYS HERE... FER TH' CURE OF SYKO-NOO-ROTIK'S, GREAT SUCCESS IS ACHIEVED WITH TH' USE OF TH' SHOCK TREATMENT!
SHOCK TREAT-MENT! COMIN' UP!
BEGINNERS PSYCHIATRY
SHOCK TREATMENT
YEOWW
WOW! LOOKIT HIM!
DAT OUGHTA DO HIM SOME GOOD! NOW WE BETTER CHECK HIS REFLEXES!
CLICK
LET'S SEE... IT SAYS IN DA BOOK TO SMACK DA LEFT KNEE WIT A MALLET, LIKE DIS!
UGGH!
OWWwww THAT HURT! YOU AIN'T GONNA MAKE A SAP OUTTA ME TWICE! I'M SWITCHING! PLACES WITH YOU, MOE!
OKAY!
STOP
OUCH!
HA HA HA HO HO HEE!
CRACK

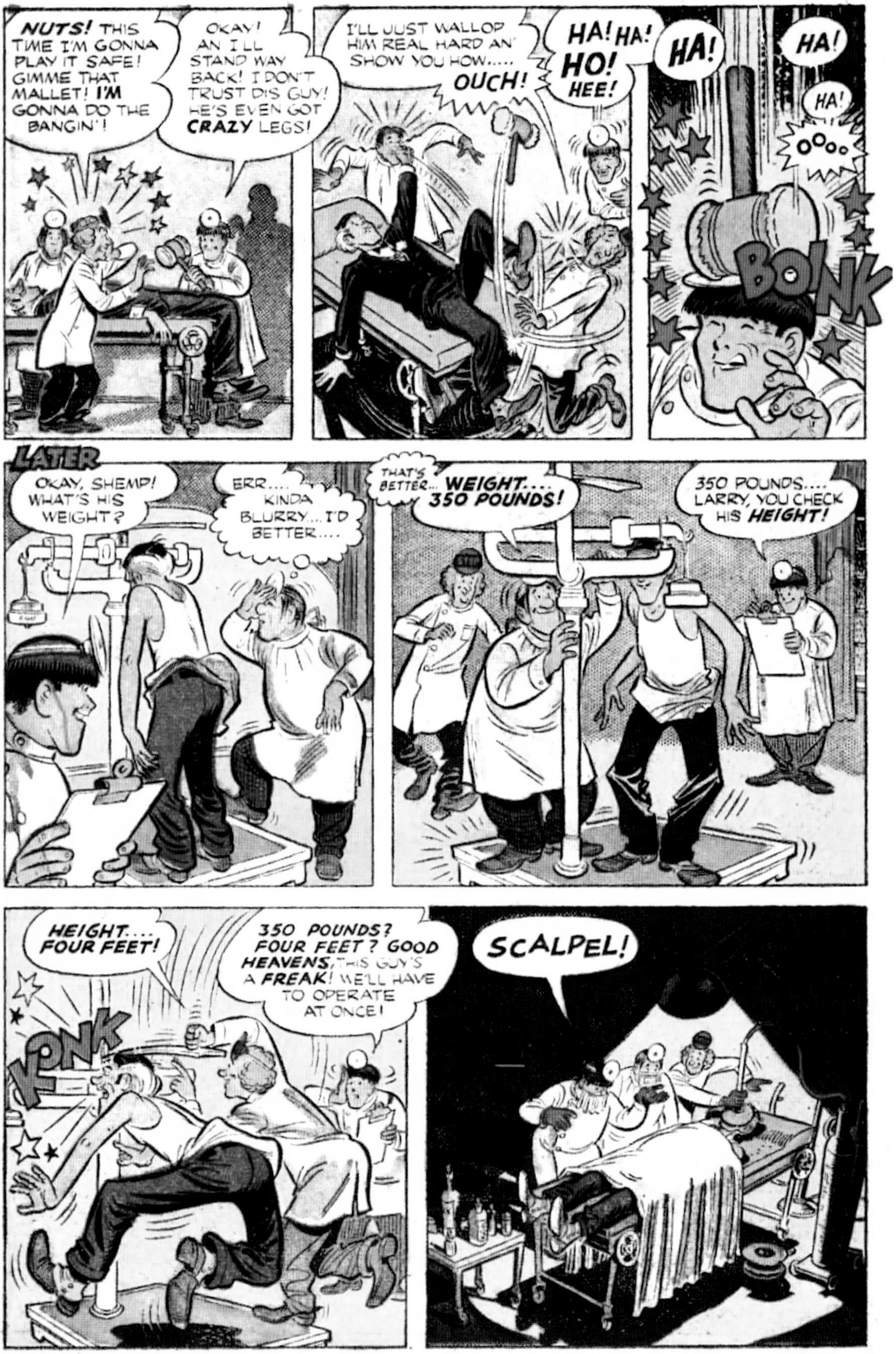
NUTS! THIS TIME I'M GONNA PLAY IT SAFE! GIMME THAT MALLET! I'M GONNA DO THE BANGIN'!
OKAY! AN I'LL STAND WAY BACK! I DON'T TRUST DIS GUY! HE'S EVEN GOT CRAZY LEGS!
I'LL JUST WALLOP HIM REAL HARD AN' SHOW YOU HOW.....
OUCH!
HA! HA! HO! HEE!
HA!
HA!
HA!
OOOo
BONK
LATER
OKAY, SHEMP! WHAT'S HIS WEIGHT?
ERR.... KINDA BLURRY...I'D BETTER....
THAT'S BETTER... WEIGHT.... 350 POUNDS!
350 POUNDS.... LARRY, YOU CHECK HIS HEIGHT!
HEIGHT.... FOUR FEET!
350 POUNDS? FOUR FEET? GOOD HEAVENS, THIS GUY'S A FREAK! WE'LL HAVE TO OPERATE AT ONCE!
KONK
SCALPEL!

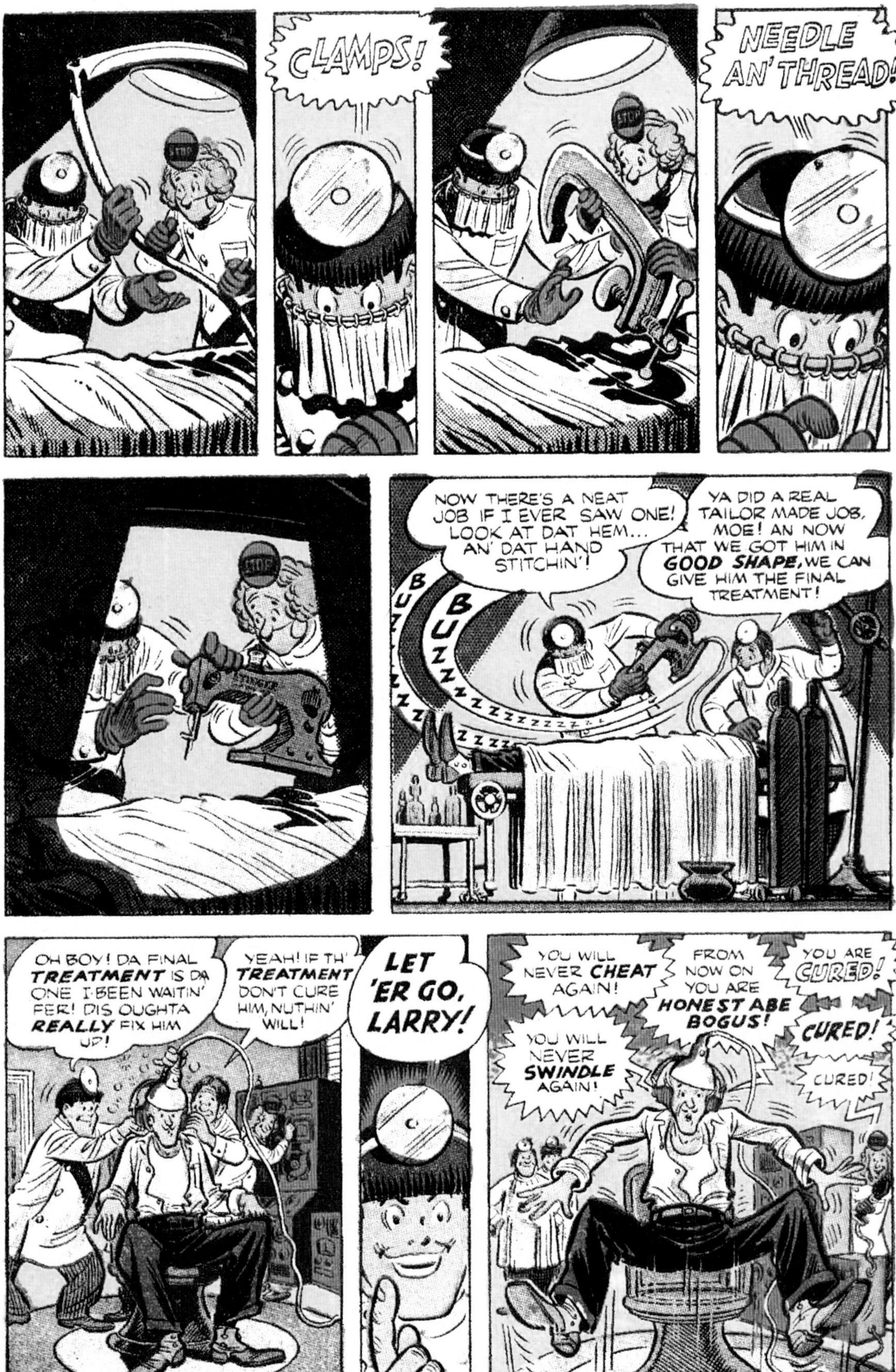
CLAMPS!
NEEDLE AN' THREAD!
NOW THERE'S A NEAT JOB IF I EVER SAW ONE! LOOK AT DAT HEM... AN' DAT HAND STITCHIN'!
YA DID A REAL TAILOR MADE JOB, MOE! AN NOW THAT WE GOT HIM IN GOOD SHAPE, WE CAN GIVE HIM THE FINAL TREATMENT!
BUZZZZZ
BUZZZZZZZZZZZZZZZ
OH BOY! DA FINAL TREATMENT IS DA ONE I BEEN WAITIN' FER! DIS OUGHTA REALLY FIX HIM UP!
YEAH! IF TH' TREATMENT DON'T CURE HIM, NUTHIN' WILL!
LET 'ER GO, LARRY!
YOU WILL NEVER CHEAT AGAIN!
FROM NOW ON YOU ARE HONEST ABE BOGUS!
YOU ARE CURED!
YOU WILL NEVER SWINDLE AGAIN!
CURED!
CURED!

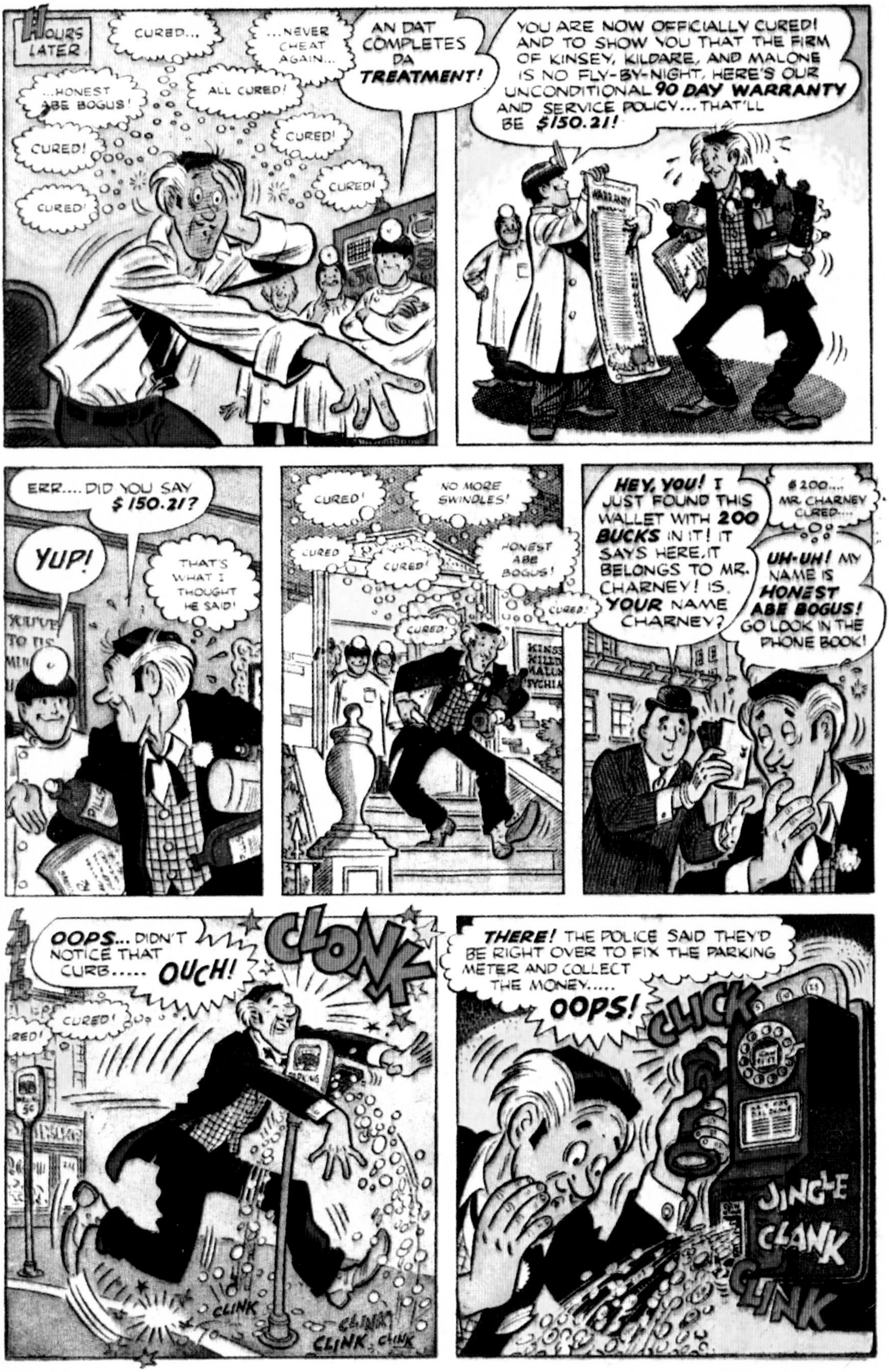
HOURS LATER
CURED...
...NEVER CHEAT AGAIN...
...HONEST ABE BOGUS!
ALL CURED!
CURED!
CURED!
CURED!
CURED!
AN DAT COMPLETES DA TREATMENT!
YOU ARE NOW OFFICIALLY CURED! AND TO SHOW YOU THAT THE FIRM OF KINSEY, KILDARE, AND MALONE IS NO FLY-BY-NIGHT, HERE'S OUR UNCONDITIONAL 90 DAY WARRANTY AND SERVICE POLICY... THAT'LL BE $150.21!
WARRANTY
ERR.... DID YOU SAY $ 150.21?
YUP!
THAT'S WHAT I THOUGHT HE SAID!
CURED!
NO MORE SWINDLES!
CURED
CURED!
HONEST ABE BOGUS!
CURED!
CURED!
HEY, YOU! I JUST FOUND THIS WALLET WITH 200 BUCKS IN IT! IT SAYS HERE, IT BELONGS TO MR. CHARNEY! IS YOUR NAME CHARNEY?
$200... MR. CHARNEY CURED....
UH-UH! MY NAME IS HONEST ABE BOGUS! GO LOOK IN THE PHONE BOOK!
OOPS... DIDN'T NOTICE THAT CURB..... OUCH!
CLONK
CURED!
CURED!
CLINK
CLINK
CLINK
CLINK
THERE! THE POLICE SAID THEY'D BE RIGHT OVER TO FIX THE PARKING METER AND COLLECT THE MONEY.....
OOPS!
CLICK
JINGLE
CLANK
CLINK

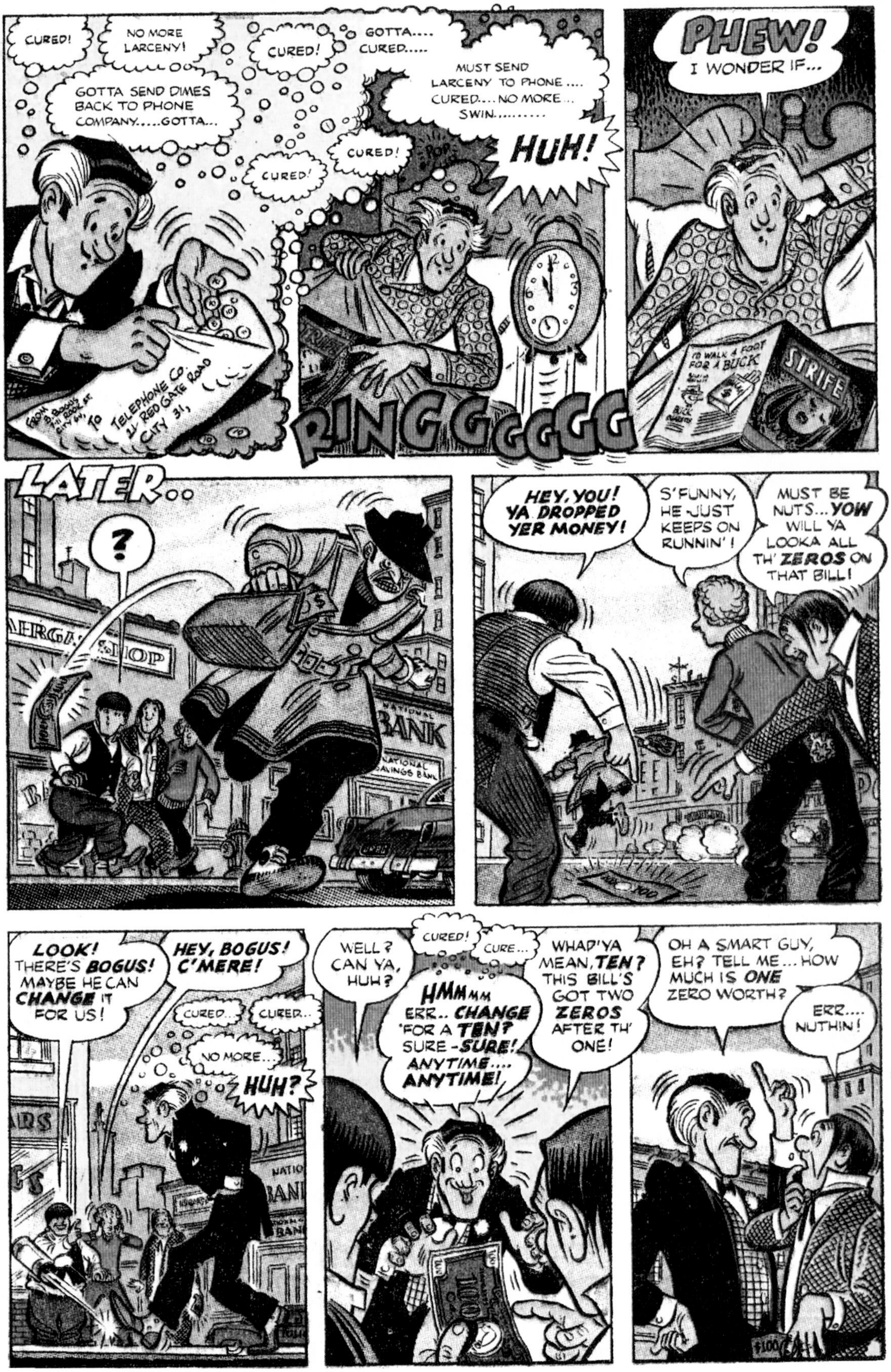
CURED!
NO MORE LARCENY!
GOTTA SEND DIMES BACK TO PHONE COMPANY.....GOTTA...
FROM B. BOGUS ... TO TELEPHONE CO. 21 RED GATE ROAD CITY 31,
CURED!
CURED!
GOTTA.... CURED.....
MUST SEND LARCENY TO PHONE.... CURED.... NO MORE... SWIN.........
CURED!
HUH!
RINGGGGGG
PHEW! I WONDER IF...
TO WALK A FOOT FOR A BUCK
STRIFE
LATER..
?
NATIONAL BANK
NATIONAL SAVINGS BANK
HEY, YOU! YA DROPPED YER MONEY!
S'FUNNY, HE JUST KEEPS ON RUNNIN'!
MUST BE NUTS... YOW WILL YA LOOKA ALL TH' ZEROS ON THAT BILL!
LOOK! THERE'S BOGUS! MAYBE HE CAN CHANGE IT FOR US!
HEY, BOGUS! C'MERE!
CURED..
CURED..
NO MORE...
HUH?
WELL? CAN YA, HUH?
CURED!
CURE...
HMMMM ERR.. CHANGE FOR A TEN? SURE-SURE! ANYTIME.... ANYTIME!
WHAD'YA MEAN, TEN? THIS BILL'S GOT TWO ZEROS AFTER TH' ONE!
OH A SMART GUY, EH? TELL ME... HOW MUCH IS ONE ZERO WORTH?
ERR.... NUTHIN!

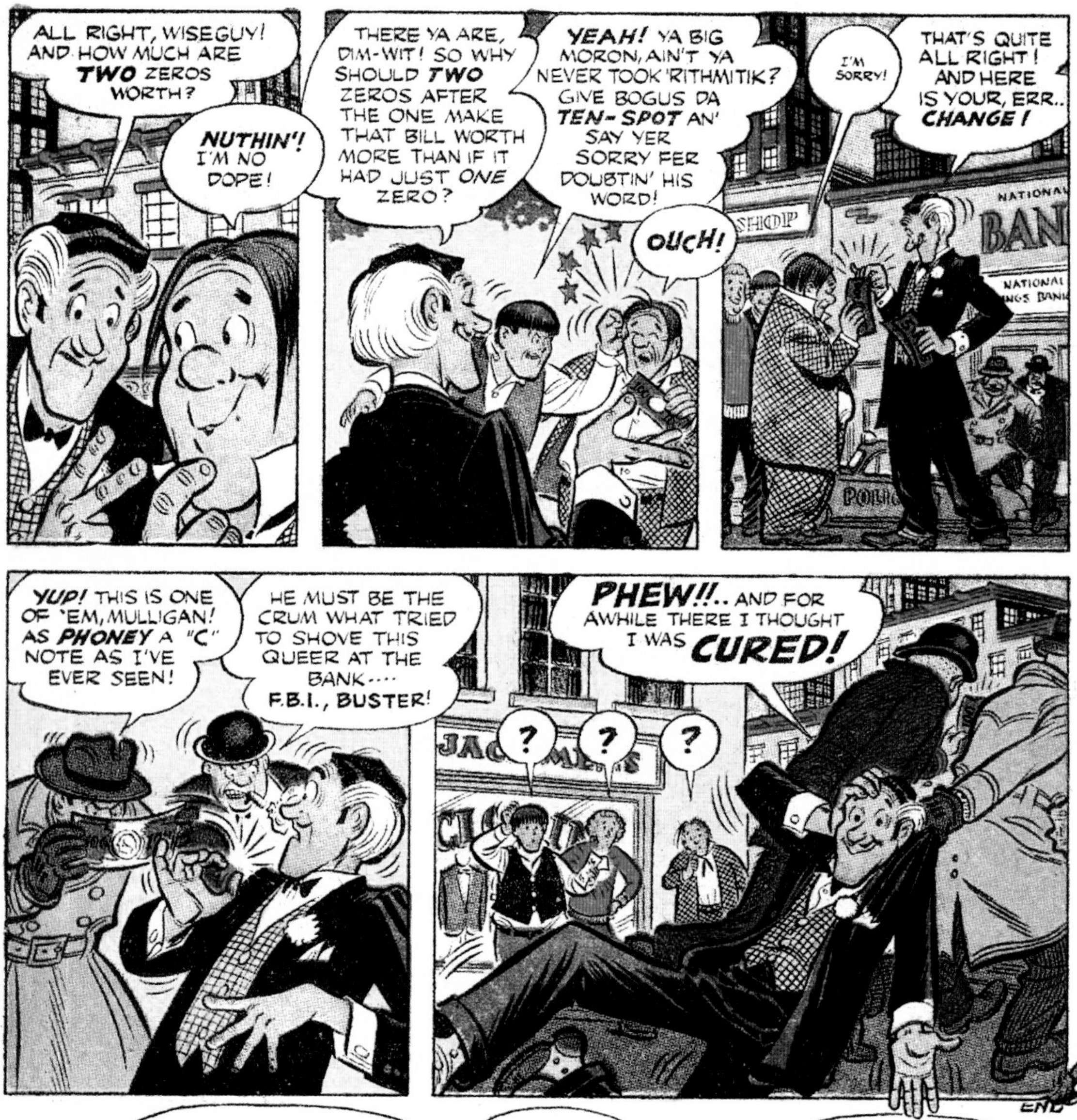
ALL RIGHT, WISEGUY! AND HOW MUCH ARE TWO ZEROS WORTH?
NUTHIN'! I'M NO DOPE!
THERE YA ARE, DIM-WIT! SO WHY SHOULD TWO ZEROS AFTER THE ONE MAKE THAT BILL WORTH MORE THAN IF IT HAD JUST ONE ZERO?
YEAH! YA BIG MORON, AIN'T YA NEVER TOOK 'RITHMITIK? GIVE BOGUS DA TEN-SPOT AN' SAY YER SORRY FER DOUBTIN' HIS WORD!
OUCH!
I'M SORRY!
THAT'S QUITE ALL RIGHT! AND HERE IS YOUR, ERR.. CHANGE!
YUP! THIS IS ONE OF 'EM, MULLIGAN! AS PHONEY A "C" NOTE AS I'VE EVER SEEN!
HE MUST BE THE CRUM WHAT TRIED TO SHOVE THIS QUEER AT THE BANK.... F.B.I., BUSTER!
PHEW!!.. AND FOR AWHILE THERE I THOUGHT I WAS CURED!
?
?
?
END

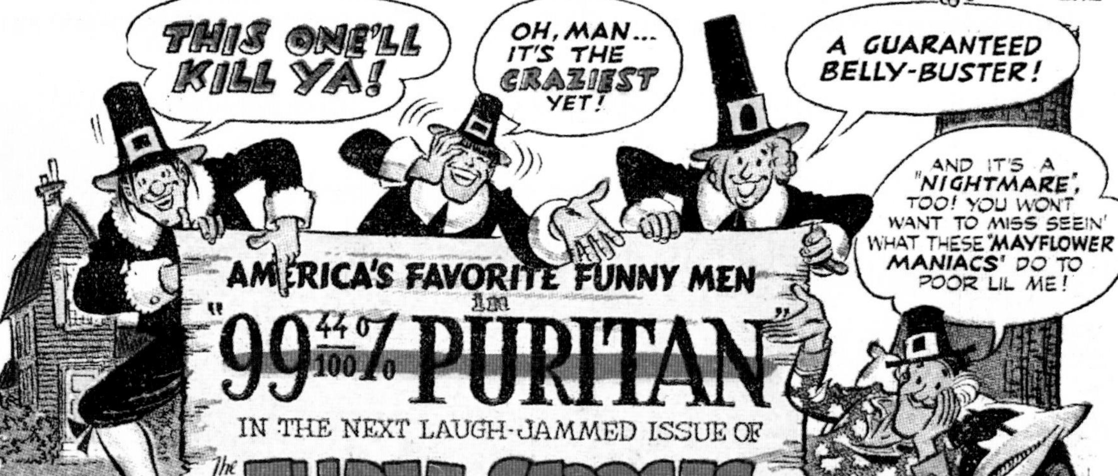
THIS ONE'LL KILL YA!
OH, MAN... IT'S THE CRAZIEST YET!
A GUARANTEED BELLY-BUSTER!
AND IT'S A "NIGHTMARE", TOO! YOU WON'T WANT TO MISS SEEIN' WHAT THESE "MAYFLOWER MANIACS" DO TO POOR LIL ME!
AMERICA'S FAVORITE FUNNY MEN
in
"99 44/100 % PURITAN"
IN THE NEXT LAUGH-JAMMED ISSUE OF
The THREE STOOGES

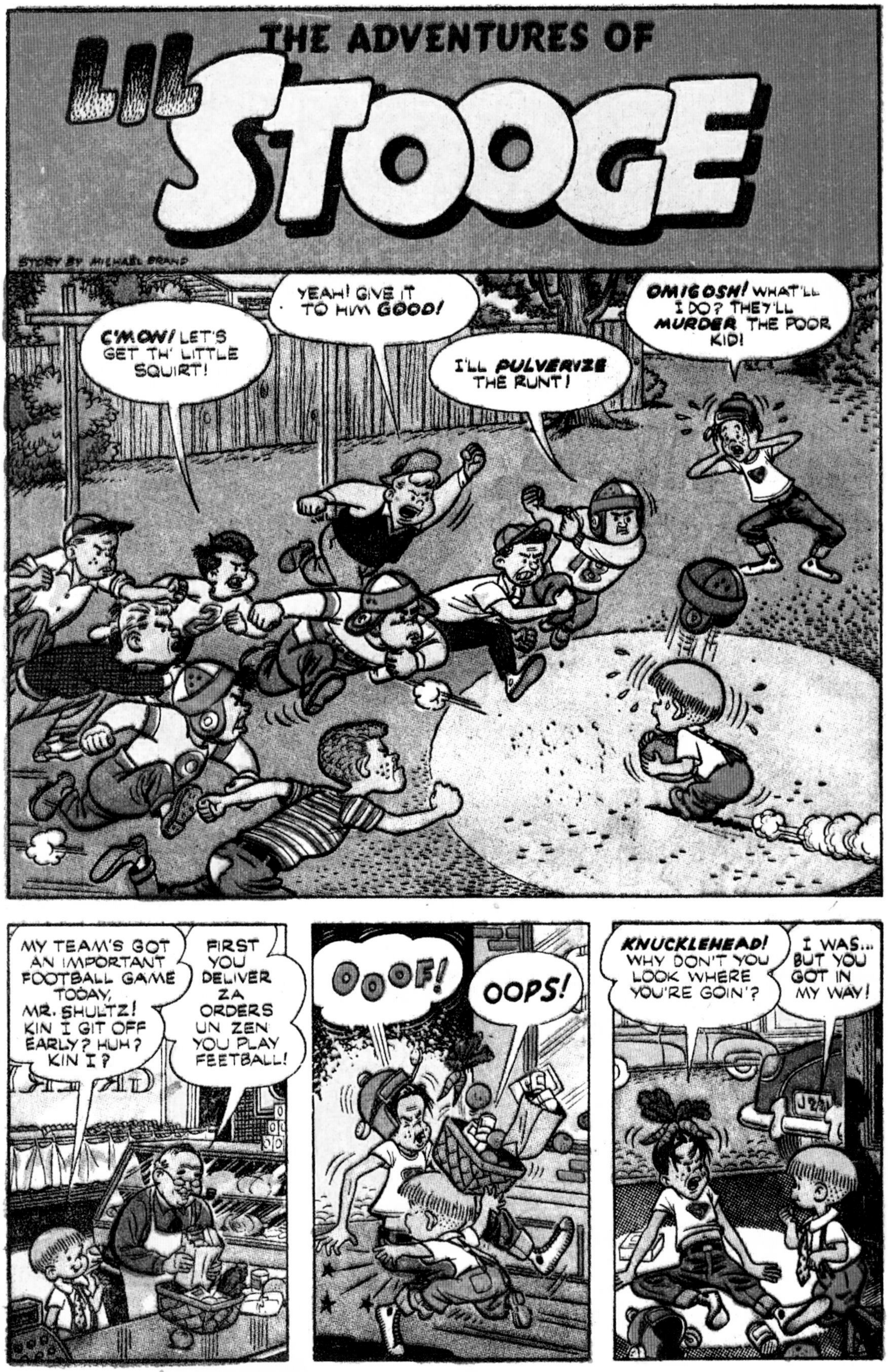
THE ADVENTURES OF
LI'L STOOGE
STORY BY MICHAEL BRAND
C'MON! LET'S GET TH' LITTLE SQUIRT!
YEAH! GIVE IT TO HIM GOOD!
I'LL PULVERIZE THE RUNT!
OMIGOSH! WHAT'LL I DO? THEY'LL MURDER THE POOR KID!
MY TEAM'S GOT AN IMPORTANT FOOTBALL GAME TODAY, MR. SHULTZ! KIN I GIT OFF EARLY? HUH? KIN I?
FIRST YOU DELIVER ZA ORDERS UN ZEN YOU PLAY FEETBALL!
OOOF!
OOPS!
KNUCKLEHEAD! WHY DON'T YOU LOOK WHERE YOU'RE GOIN'?
I WAS... BUT YOU GOT IN MY WAY!

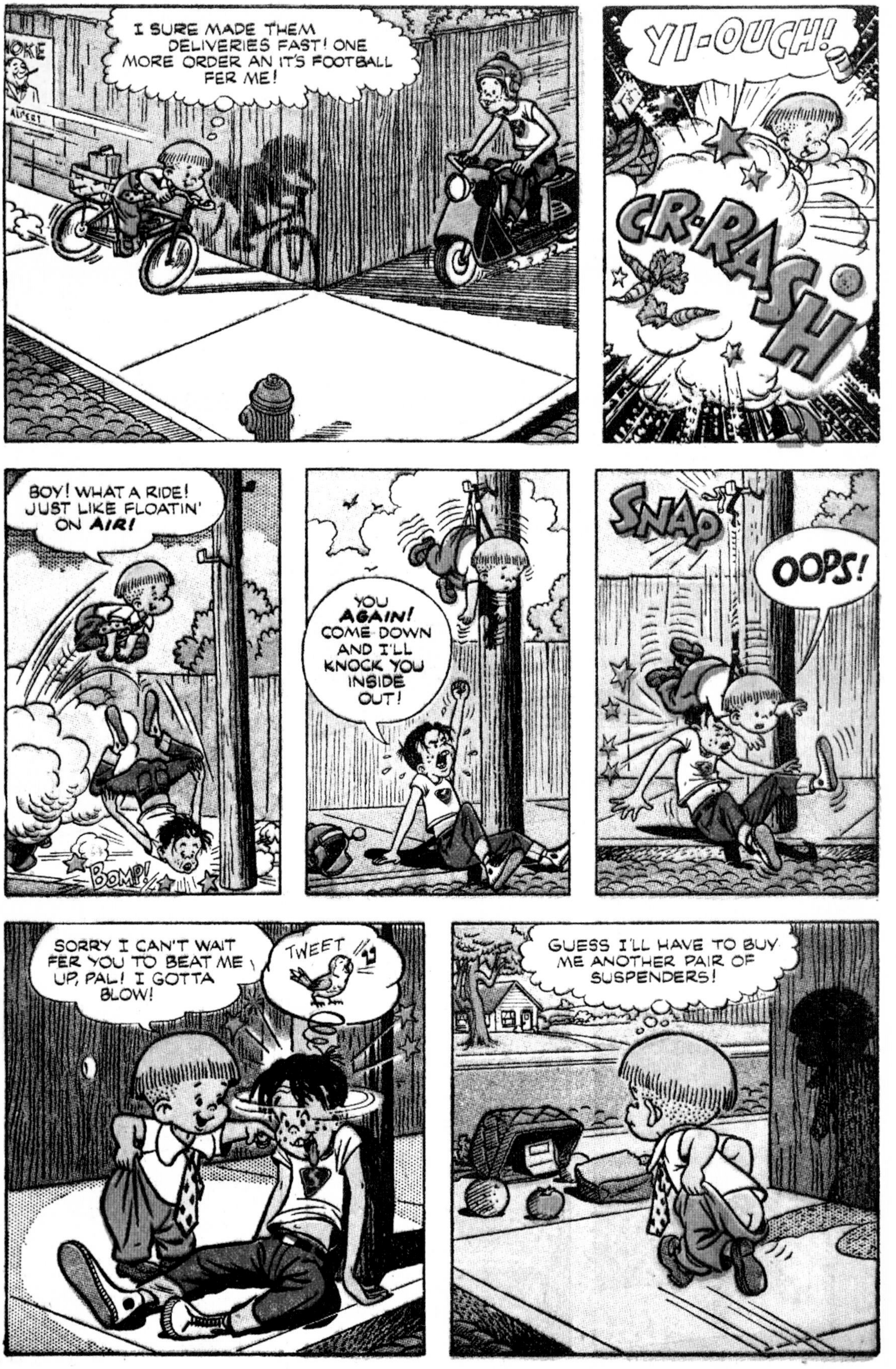
I SURE MADE THEM DELIVERIES FAST! ONE MORE ORDER AN IT'S FOOTBALL FER ME!
YI-OUCH!
CR-RASH
BOY! WHAT A RIDE! JUST LIKE FLOATIN' ON AIR!
BOMP!
YOU AGAIN! COME DOWN AND I'LL KNOCK YOU INSIDE OUT!
SNAP
OOPS!
SORRY I CAN'T WAIT FER YOU TO BEAT ME UP, PAL! I GOTTA BLOW!
TWEET
GUESS I'LL HAVE TO BUY ME ANOTHER PAIR OF SUSPENDERS!

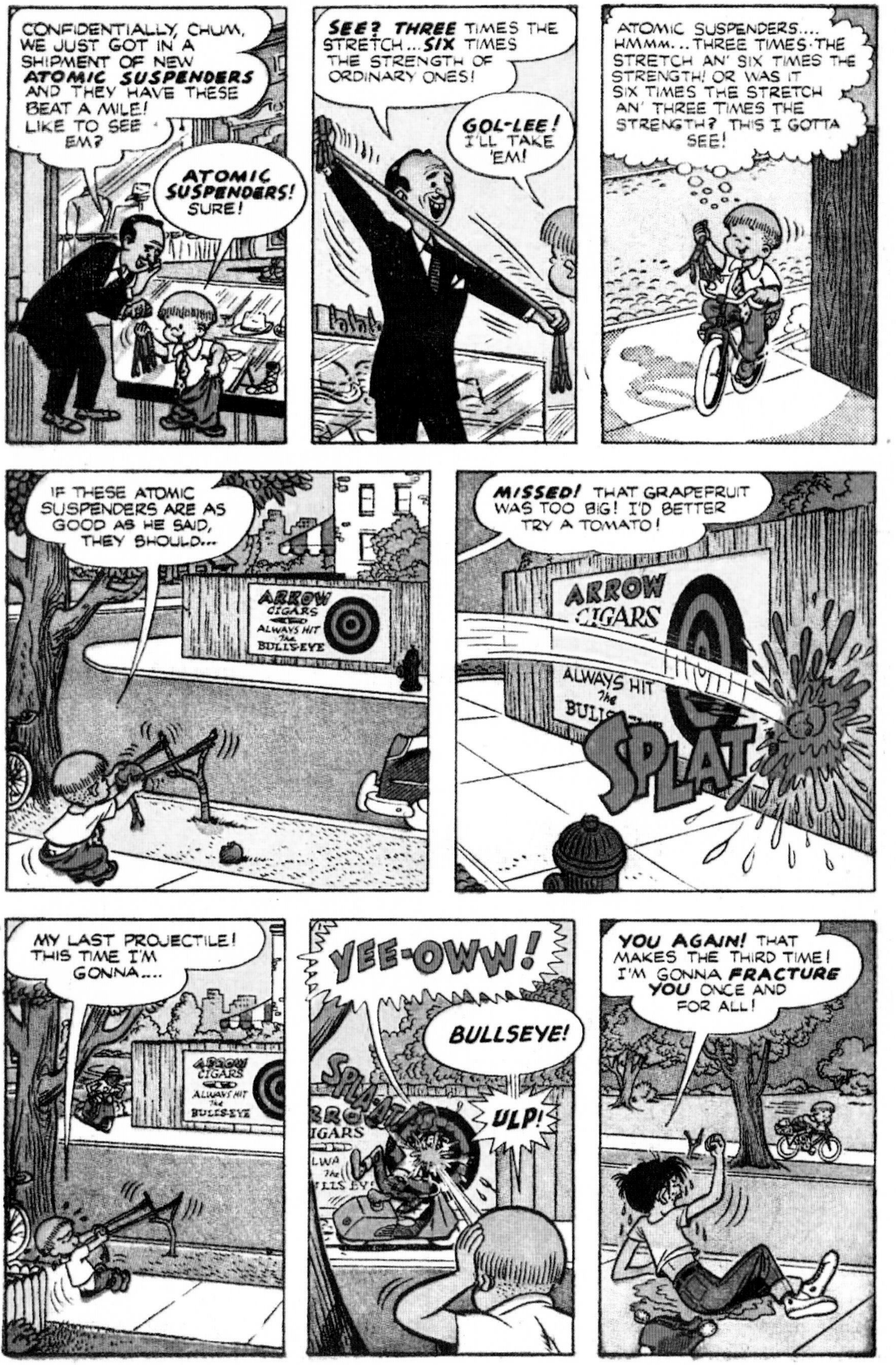
CONFIDENTIALLY, CHUM, WE JUST GOT IN A SHIPMENT OF NEW **ATOMIC SUSPENDERS** AND THEY HAVE THESE BEAT A MILE! LIKE TO SEE EM?
ATOMIC SUSPENDERS! SURE!
SEE? THREE TIMES THE STRETCH... **SIX** TIMES THE STRENGTH OF ORDINARY ONES!
GOL-LEE! I'LL TAKE 'EM!
ATOMIC SUSPENDERS.... HMMM... THREE TIMES THE STRETCH AN' SIX TIMES THE STRENGTH! OR WAS IT SIX TIMES THE STRETCH AN' THREE TIMES THE STRENGTH? THIS I GOTTA SEE!
IF THESE ATOMIC SUSPENDERS ARE AS GOOD AS HE SAID, THEY SHOULD...
ARROW CIGARS ALWAYS HIT The BULLS-EYE
MISSED! THAT GRAPEFRUIT WAS TOO BIG! I'D BETTER TRY A TOMATO!
ARROW CIGARS ALWAYS HIT The
SPLAT
MY LAST PROJECTILE! THIS TIME I'M GONNA....
ARROW CIGARS ALWAYS HIT The BULLS-EYE
YEE-OWW!
BULLSEYE!
ULP!
YOU AGAIN! THAT MAKES THE THIRD TIME! I'M GONNA **FRACTURE YOU** ONCE AND FOR ALL!

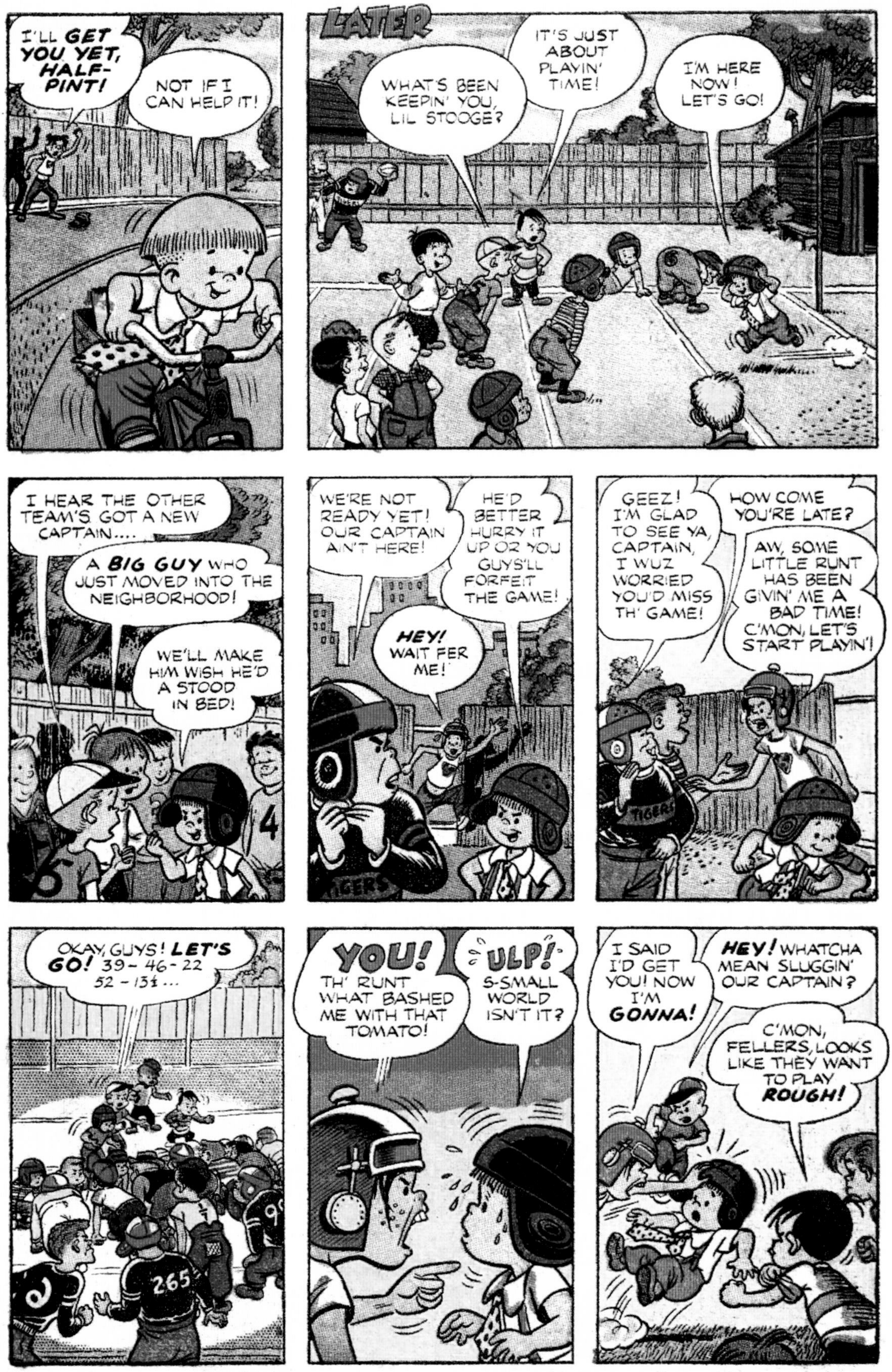
I'LL GET YOU YET, HALF-PINT!
NOT IF I CAN HELP IT!
LATER
WHAT'S BEEN KEEPIN' YOU, LIL STOOGE?
IT'S JUST ABOUT PLAYIN' TIME!
I'M HERE NOW! LET'S GO!
I HEAR THE OTHER TEAM'S GOT A NEW CAPTAIN....
A BIG GUY WHO JUST MOVED INTO THE NEIGHBORHOOD!
WE'LL MAKE HIM WISH HE'D A STOOD IN BED!
WE'RE NOT READY YET! OUR CAPTAIN AIN'T HERE!
HE'D BETTER HURRY IT UP OR YOU GUYS'LL FORFEIT THE GAME!
HEY! WAIT FER ME!
GEEZ! I'M GLAD TO SEE YA, CAPTAIN, I WUZ WORRIED YOU'D MISS TH' GAME!
HOW COME YOU'RE LATE?
AW, SOME LITTLE RUNT HAS BEEN GIVIN' ME A BAD TIME! C'MON, LET'S START PLAYIN'!
OKAY, GUYS! LET'S GO! 39 - 46 - 22 52 - 13½ ...
YOU! TH' RUNT WHAT BASHED ME WITH THAT TOMATO!
ULP! S-SMALL WORLD ISN'T IT?
I SAID I'D GET YOU! NOW I'M GONNA!
HEY! WHATCHA MEAN SLUGGIN' OUR CAPTAIN?
C'MON, FELLERS, LOOKS LIKE THEY WANT TO PLAY ROUGH!

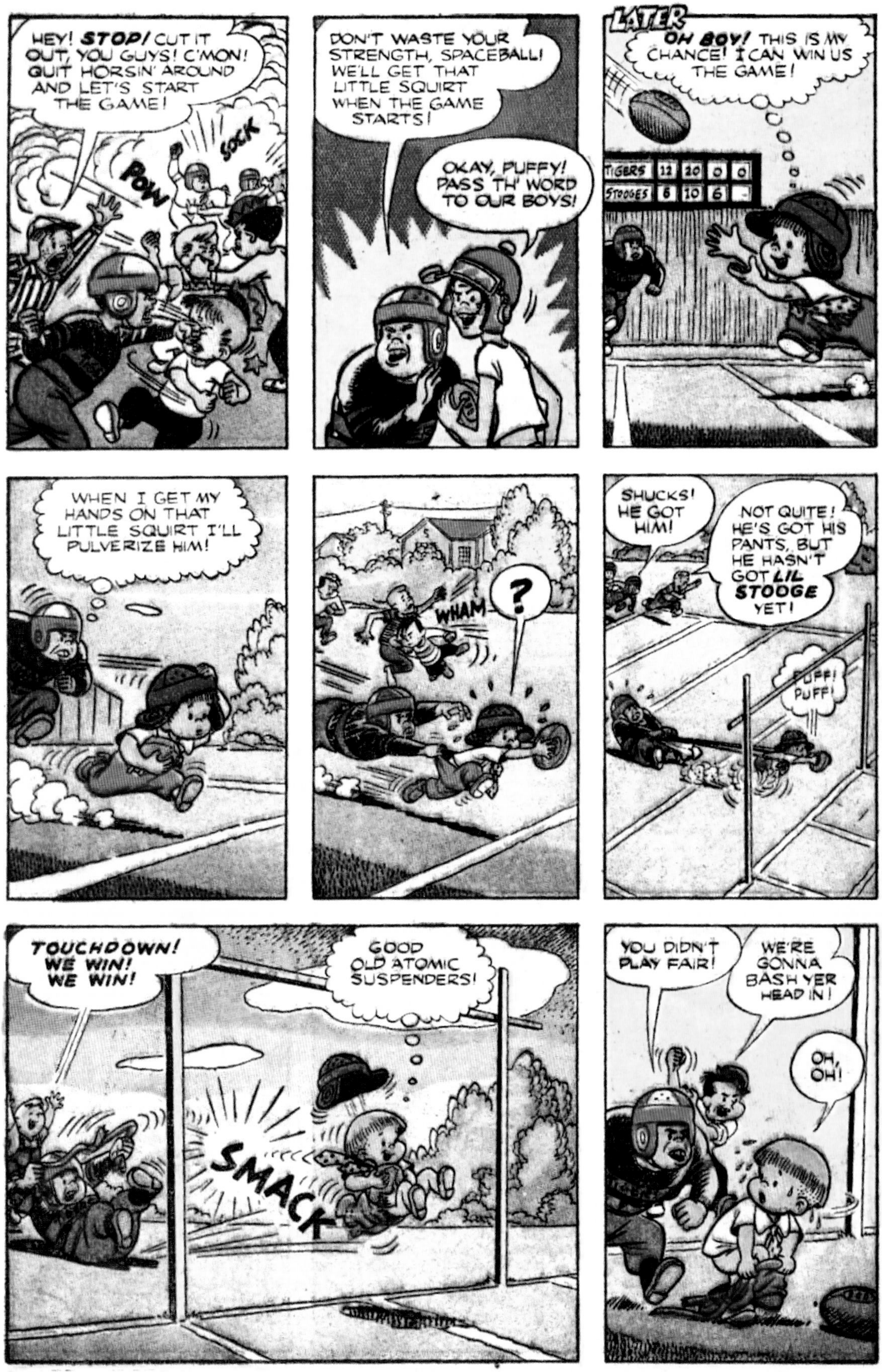
HEY! STOP! CUT IT OUT, YOU GUYS! C'MON! QUIT HORSIN' AROUND AND LET'S START THE GAME!
POW
SOCK
DON'T WASTE YOUR STRENGTH, SPACEBALL! WE'LL GET THAT LITTLE SQUIRT WHEN THE GAME STARTS!
OKAY, PUFFY! PASS TH' WORD TO OUR BOYS!
LATER
OH BOY! THIS IS MY CHANCE! I CAN WIN US THE GAME!
TIGERS 12 20 0 0
STOOGES 6 10 6
WHEN I GET MY HANDS ON THAT LITTLE SQUIRT I'LL PULVERIZE HIM!
WHAM
?
SHUCKS! HE GOT HIM!
NOT QUITE! HE'S GOT HIS PANTS, BUT HE HASN'T GOT LIL STOOGE YET!
PUFF! PUFF!
TOUCHDOWN! WE WIN! WE WIN!
GOOD OLD ATOMIC SUSPENDERS!
SMACK
YOU DIDN'T PLAY FAIR!
WE'RE GONNA BASH YER HEAD IN!
OH, OH!

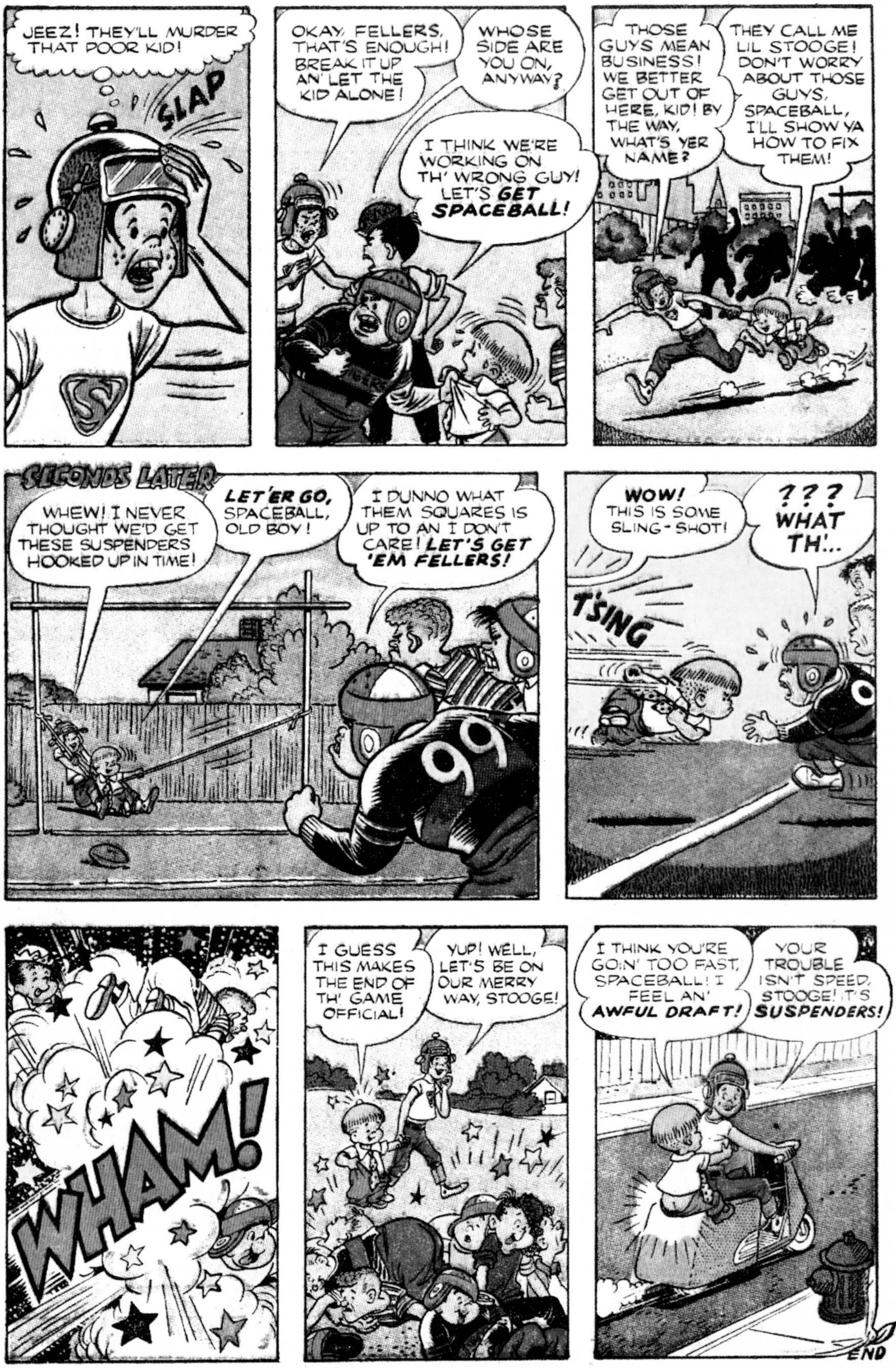
JEEZ! THEY'LL MURDER THAT POOR KID!
SLAP
OKAY, FELLERS, THAT'S ENOUGH! BREAK IT UP AN' LET THE KID ALONE!
WHOSE SIDE ARE YOU ON, ANYWAY?
I THINK WE'RE WORKING ON TH' WRONG GUY! LET'S GET SPACEBALL!
THOSE GUYS MEAN BUSINESS! WE BETTER GET OUT OF HERE, KID! BY THE WAY, WHAT'S YER NAME?
THEY CALL ME LIL STOOGE! DON'T WORRY ABOUT THOSE GUYS, SPACEBALL, I'LL SHOW YA HOW TO FIX THEM!
SECONDS LATER
WHEW! I NEVER THOUGHT WE'D GET THESE SUSPENDERS HOOKED UP IN TIME!
LET'ER GO, SPACEBALL, OLD BOY!
I DUNNO WHAT THEM SQUARES IS UP TO AN I DON'T CARE! LET'S GET 'EM FELLERS!
WOW! THIS IS SOME SLING-SHOT!
??? WHAT TH'...
T'SING
WHAM!
I GUESS THIS MAKES THE END OF TH' GAME OFFICIAL!
YUP! WELL, LET'S BE ON OUR MERRY WAY, STOOGE!
I THINK YOU'RE GOIN' TOO FAST, SPACEBALL! I FEEL AN' AWFUL DRAFT!
YOUR TROUBLE ISN'T SPEED, STOOGE! IT'S SUSPENDERS!
END

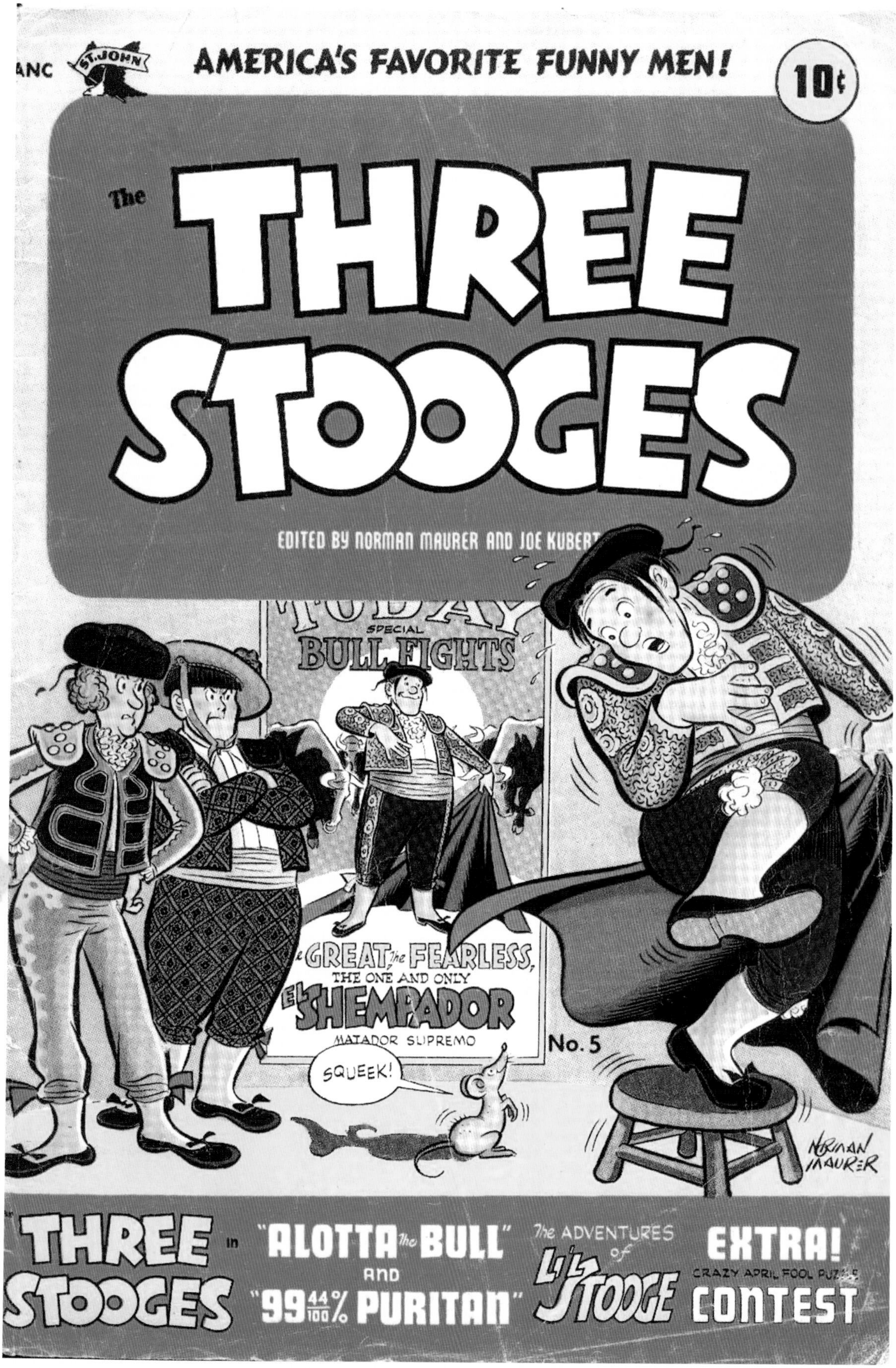
ANC
ST. JOHN
AMERICA'S FAVORITE FUNNY MEN!
10¢
The THREE STOOGES
EDITED BY NORMAN MAURER AND JOE KUBERT
TODAY
SPECIAL
BULL FIGHTS
THE GREAT, THE FEARLESS,
THE ONE AND ONLY
EL SHEMPADOR
MATADOR SUPREMO
No. 5
SQUEEK!
NORMAN MAURER
THREE STOOGES in "ALOTTA the BULL" AND "99 44/100% PURITAN"
The ADVENTURES of LI'L STOOGE
EXTRA! CRAZY APRIL FOOL PUZZLE CONTEST

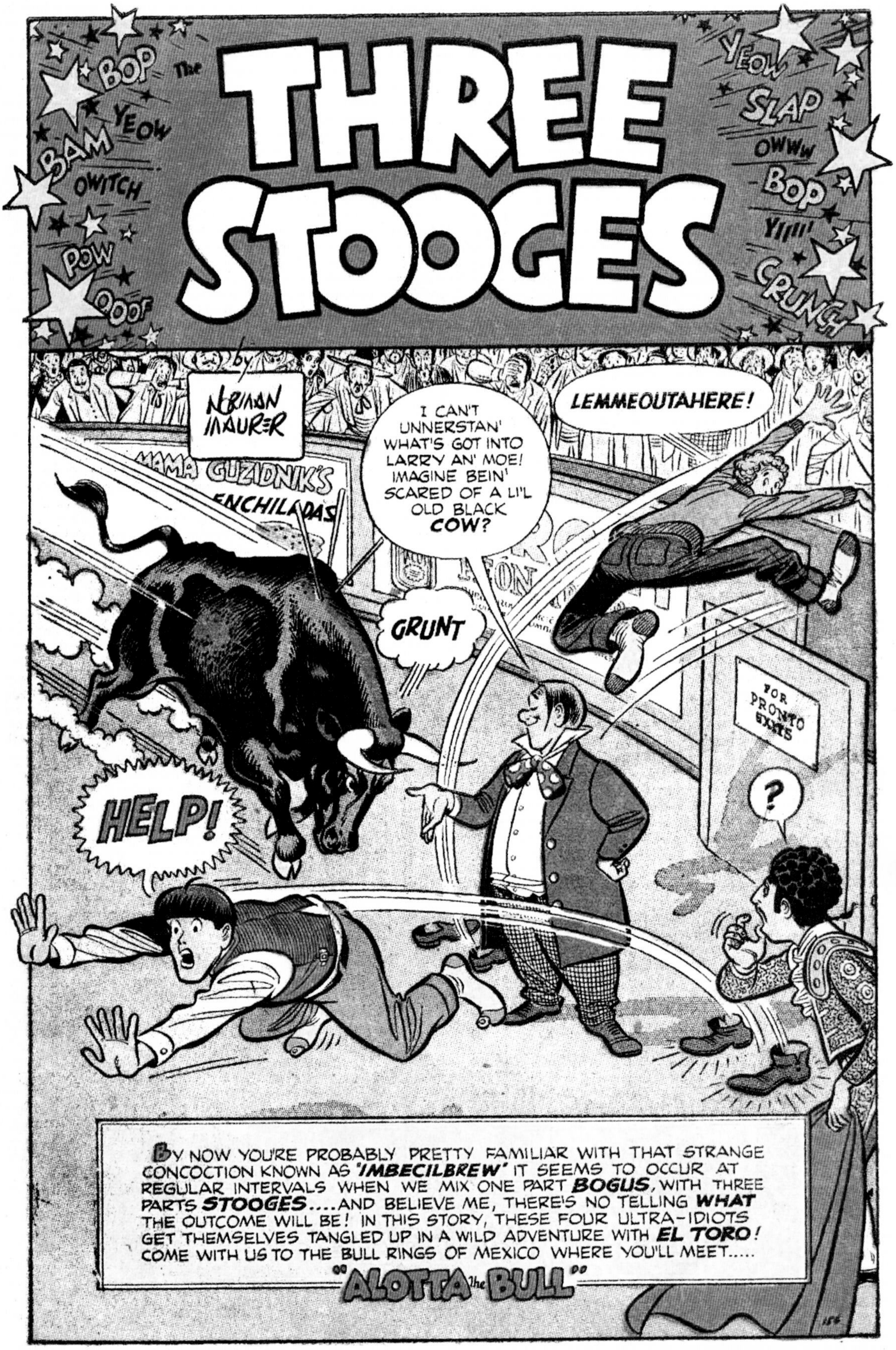

The THREE STOOGES
BOP YEOW BAM OWITCH POW OOOF
YEOW SLAP OWWW BOP YIII! CRUNCH
by NORMAN MAURER
MAMA GUZIDNIK'S ENCHILADAS
LEMMEOUTAHERE!
I CAN'T UNNERSTAN' WHAT'S GOT INTO LARRY AN' MOE! IMAGINE BEIN' SCARED OF A LI'L OLD BLACK COW?
GRUNT
HELP!
?
BY NOW YOU'RE PROBABLY PRETTY FAMILIAR WITH THAT STRANGE CONCOCTION KNOWN AS 'IMBECILBREW' IT SEEMS TO OCCUR AT REGULAR INTERVALS WHEN WE MIX ONE PART BOGUS, WITH THREE PARTS STOOGES....AND BELIEVE ME, THERE'S NO TELLING WHAT THE OUTCOME WILL BE! IN THIS STORY, THESE FOUR ULTRA-IDIOTS GET THEMSELVES TANGLED UP IN A WILD ADVENTURE WITH EL TORO! COME WITH US TO THE BULL RINGS OF MEXICO WHERE YOU'LL MEET.....
"ALOTTA the BULL"

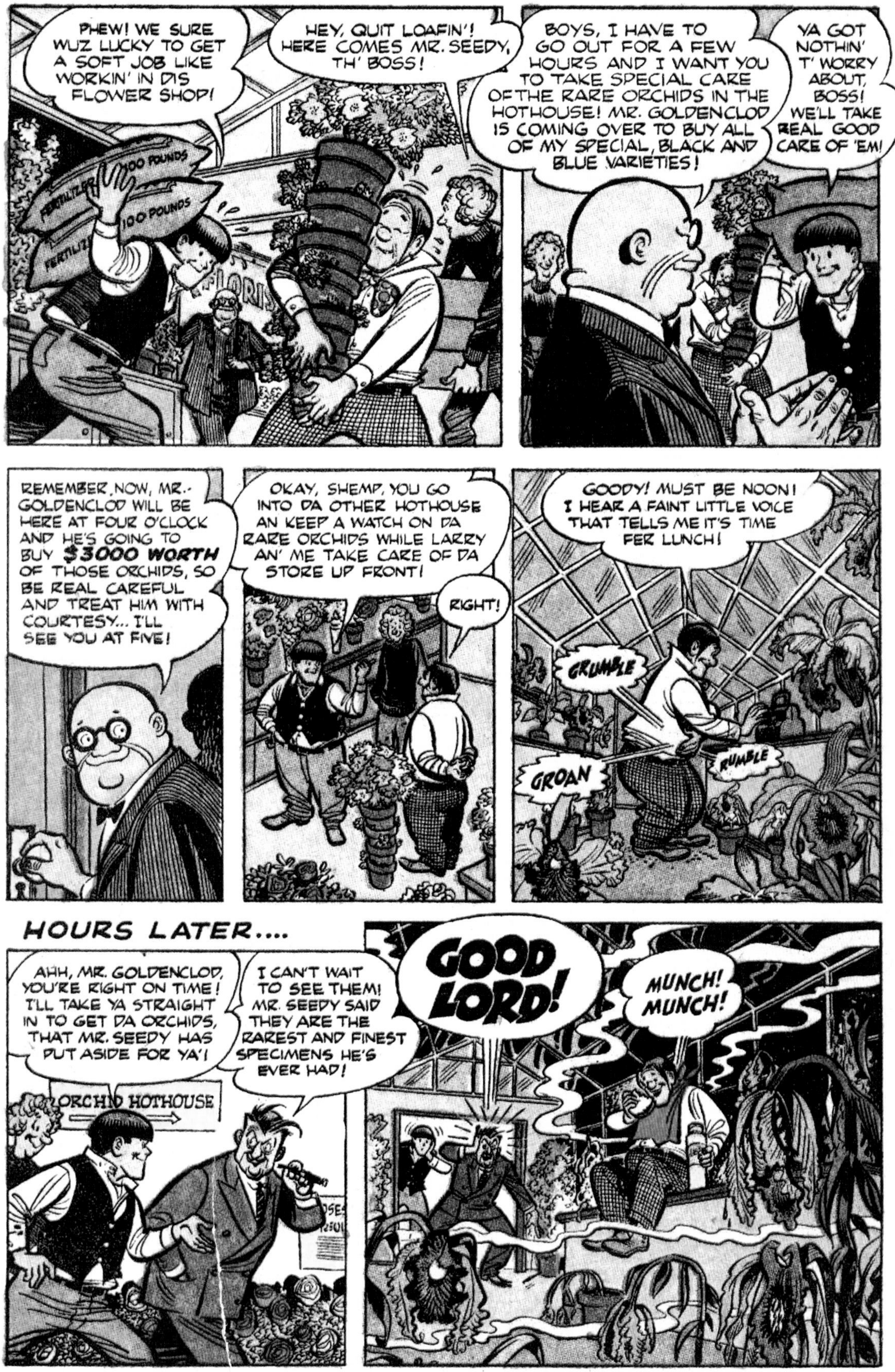
PHEW! WE SURE WUZ LUCKY TO GET A SOFT JOB LIKE WORKIN' IN DIS FLOWER SHOP!
HEY, QUIT LOAFIN'! HERE COMES MR. SEEDY, TH' BOSS!
FERTILIZER 100 POUNDS
FERTILIZER 100 POUNDS
BOYS, I HAVE TO GO OUT FOR A FEW HOURS AND I WANT YOU TO TAKE SPECIAL CARE OF THE RARE ORCHIDS IN THE HOTHOUSE! MR. GOLDENCLOD IS COMING OVER TO BUY ALL OF MY SPECIAL, BLACK AND BLUE VARIETIES!
YA GOT NOTHIN' T' WORRY ABOUT, BOSS! WE'LL TAKE REAL GOOD CARE OF 'EM!
REMEMBER NOW, MR. GOLDENCLOD WILL BE HERE AT FOUR O'CLOCK AND HE'S GOING TO BUY **$3000 WORTH** OF THOSE ORCHIDS, SO BE REAL CAREFUL AND TREAT HIM WITH COURTESY... I'LL SEE YOU AT FIVE!
OKAY, SHEMP, YOU GO INTO DA OTHER HOTHOUSE AN KEEP A WATCH ON DA RARE ORCHIDS WHILE LARRY AN' ME TAKE CARE OF DA STORE UP FRONT!
RIGHT!
GOODY! MUST BE NOON! I HEAR A FAINT LITTLE VOICE THAT TELLS ME IT'S TIME FER LUNCH!
GRUMBLE
GROAN
RUMBLE
HOURS LATER....
AHH, MR. GOLDENCLOD, YOU'RE RIGHT ON TIME! I'LL TAKE YA STRAIGHT IN TO GET DA ORCHIDS, THAT MR. SEEDY HAS PUT ASIDE FOR YA'!
I CAN'T WAIT TO SEE THEM! MR. SEEDY SAID THEY ARE THE RAREST AND FINEST SPECIMENS HE'S EVER HAD!
ORCHID HOTHOUSE
GOOD LORD!
MUNCH! MUNCH!

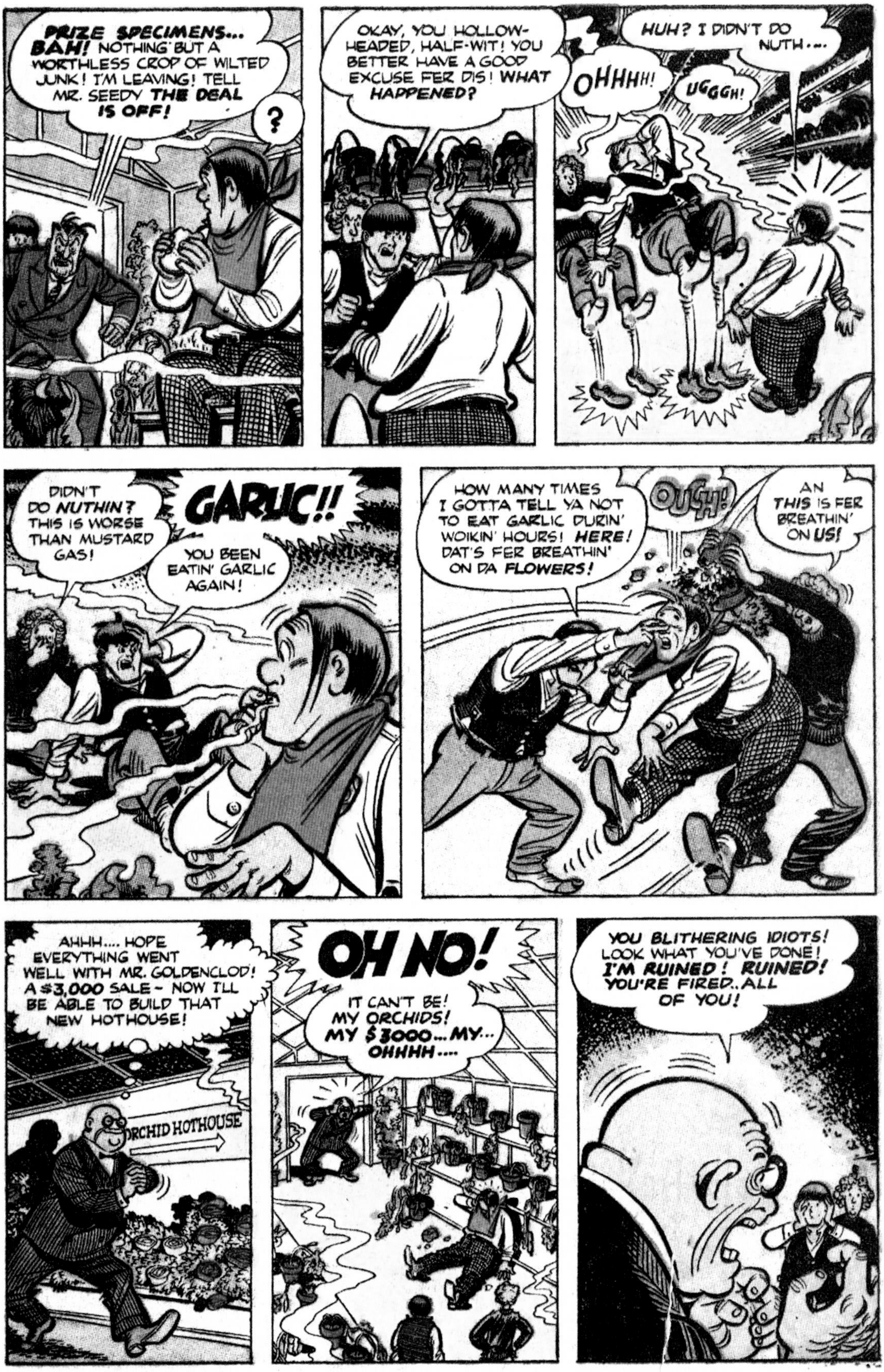
PRIZE SPECIMENS... BAH! NOTHING BUT A WORTHLESS CROP OF WILTED JUNK! I'M LEAVING! TELL MR. SEEDY THE DEAL IS OFF!
?
OKAY, YOU HOLLOW-HEADED, HALF-WIT! YOU BETTER HAVE A GOOD EXCUSE FER DIS! WHAT HAPPENED?
HUH? I DIDN'T DO NUTH...
OHHHH!
UGGGH!
DIDN'T DO NUTHIN? THIS IS WORSE THAN MUSTARD GAS!
GARLIC!!
YOU BEEN EATIN' GARLIC AGAIN!
HOW MANY TIMES I GOTTA TELL YA NOT TO EAT GARLIC DURIN' WOIKIN' HOURS! HERE! DAT'S FER BREATHIN' ON DA FLOWERS!
OUCH!
AN THIS IS FER BREATHIN' ON US!
AHHH.... HOPE EVERYTHING WENT WELL WITH MR. GOLDENCLOD! A $3,000 SALE - NOW I'LL BE ABLE TO BUILD THAT NEW HOTHOUSE!
ORCHID HOTHOUSE
OH NO!
IT CAN'T BE! MY ORCHIDS! MY $3000...MY... OHHHH....
YOU BLITHERING IDIOTS! LOOK WHAT YOU'VE DONE! I'M RUINED! RUINED! YOU'RE FIRED..ALL OF YOU!

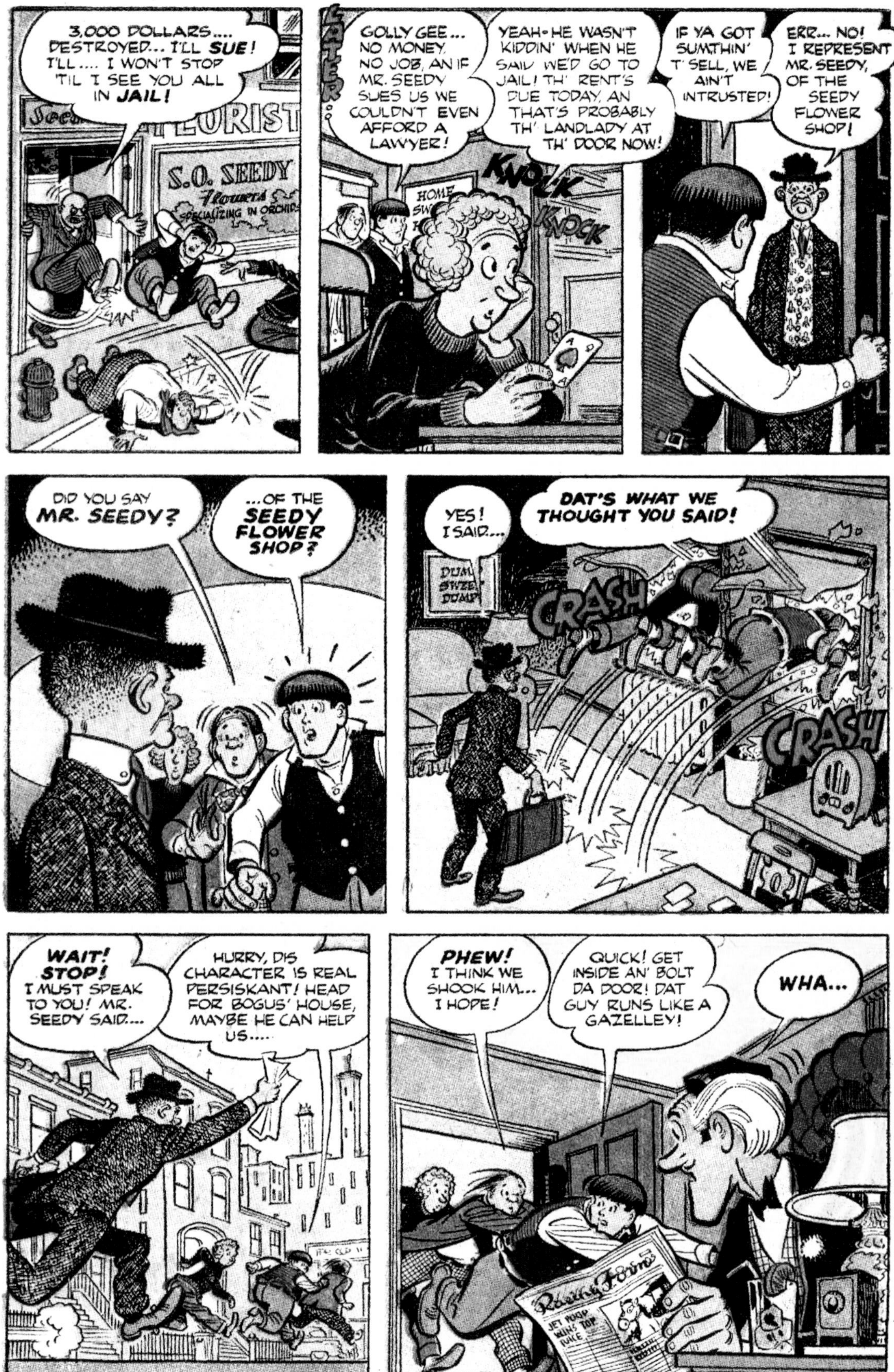
3,000 DOLLARS.... DESTROYED... I'LL SUE! I'LL.... I WON'T STOP 'TIL I SEE YOU ALL IN JAIL!
S.O. SEEDY FLOWERS SPECIALIZING IN ORCHIDS
LATER:
GOLLY GEE... NO MONEY, NO JOB, AN IF MR. SEEDY SUES US WE COULDN'T EVEN AFFORD A LAWYER!
YEAH- HE WASN'T KIDDIN' WHEN HE SAID WE'D GO TO JAIL! TH' RENT'S DUE TODAY, AN THAT'S PROBABLY TH' LANDLADY AT TH' DOOR NOW!
KNOCK
KNOCK
IF YA GOT SUMTHIN' T' SELL, WE AIN'T INTRUSTED!
ERR... NO! I REPRESENT MR. SEEDY, OF THE SEEDY FLOWER SHOP!
DID YOU SAY MR. SEEDY?
...OF THE SEEDY FLOWER SHOP?
YES! I SAID...
DAT'S WHAT WE THOUGHT YOU SAID!
CRASH
CRASH
WAIT! STOP! I MUST SPEAK TO YOU! MR. SEEDY SAID....
HURRY, DIS CHARACTER IS REAL PERSISKANT! HEAD FOR BOGUS' HOUSE, MAYBE HE CAN HELP US....
PHEW! I THINK WE SHOOK HIM... I HOPE!
QUICK! GET INSIDE AN' BOLT DA DOOR! DAT GUY RUNS LIKE A GAZELLEY!
WHA...
JET POOP WINS TOP PURSE

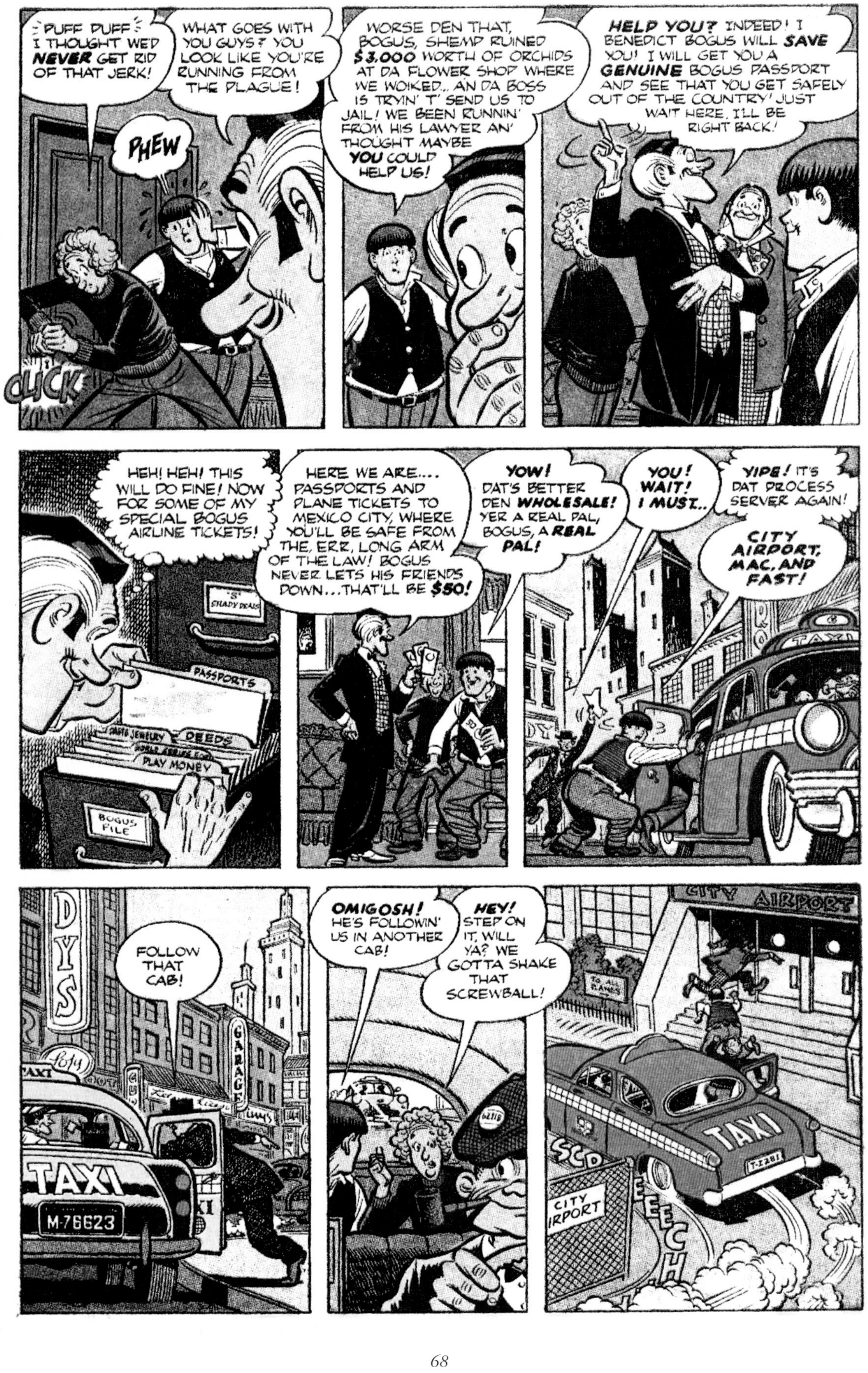
PUFF DUFF I THOUGHT WE'D **NEVER** GET RID OF THAT JERK!
WHAT GOES WITH YOU GUYS? YOU LOOK LIKE YOU'RE RUNNING FROM THE PLAGUE!
PHEW
CLICK
WORSE DEN THAT, BOGUS, SHEMP RUINED **$3,000** WORTH OF ORCHIDS AT DA FLOWER SHOP WHERE WE WOIKED.. AN DA BOSS IS TRYIN' T' SEND US TO JAIL! WE BEEN RUNNIN' FROM HIS LAWYER AN' THOUGHT MAYBE **YOU** COULD HELP US!
HELP YOU? INDEED! I BENEDICT BOGUS WILL **SAVE** YOU! I WILL GET YOU A **GENUINE** BOGUS PASSPORT AND SEE THAT YOU GET SAFELY OUT OF THE COUNTRY! JUST WAIT HERE. I'LL BE RIGHT BACK!
HEH! HEH! THIS WILL DO FINE! NOW FOR SOME OF MY SPECIAL BOGUS AIRLINE TICKETS!
"S" SHADY DEALS
PASSPORTS
DEEDS
PLAY MONEY
BOGUS FILE
HERE WE ARE.... PASSPORTS AND PLANE TICKETS TO MEXICO CITY, WHERE YOU'LL BE SAFE FROM THE, ERR, LONG ARM OF THE LAW! BOGUS NEVER LETS HIS FRIENDS DOWN...THAT'LL BE **$50!**
YOW! DAT'S BETTER DEN **WHOLESALE!** YER A REAL PAL, BOGUS, A **REAL PAL!**
YOU! WAIT! I MUST...
YIPE! IT'S DAT PROCESS SERVER AGAIN!
CITY AIRPORT, MAC, AND FAST!
TAXI
FOLLOW THAT CAB!
GARAGE
TAXI
M-76623
OMIGOSH! HE'S FOLLOWIN' US IN ANOTHER CAB!
HEY! STEP ON IT, WILL YA? WE GOTTA SHAKE THAT SCREWBALL!
CITY AIRPORT
TO ALL PLANES
TAXI
CITY AIRPORT
EEECH

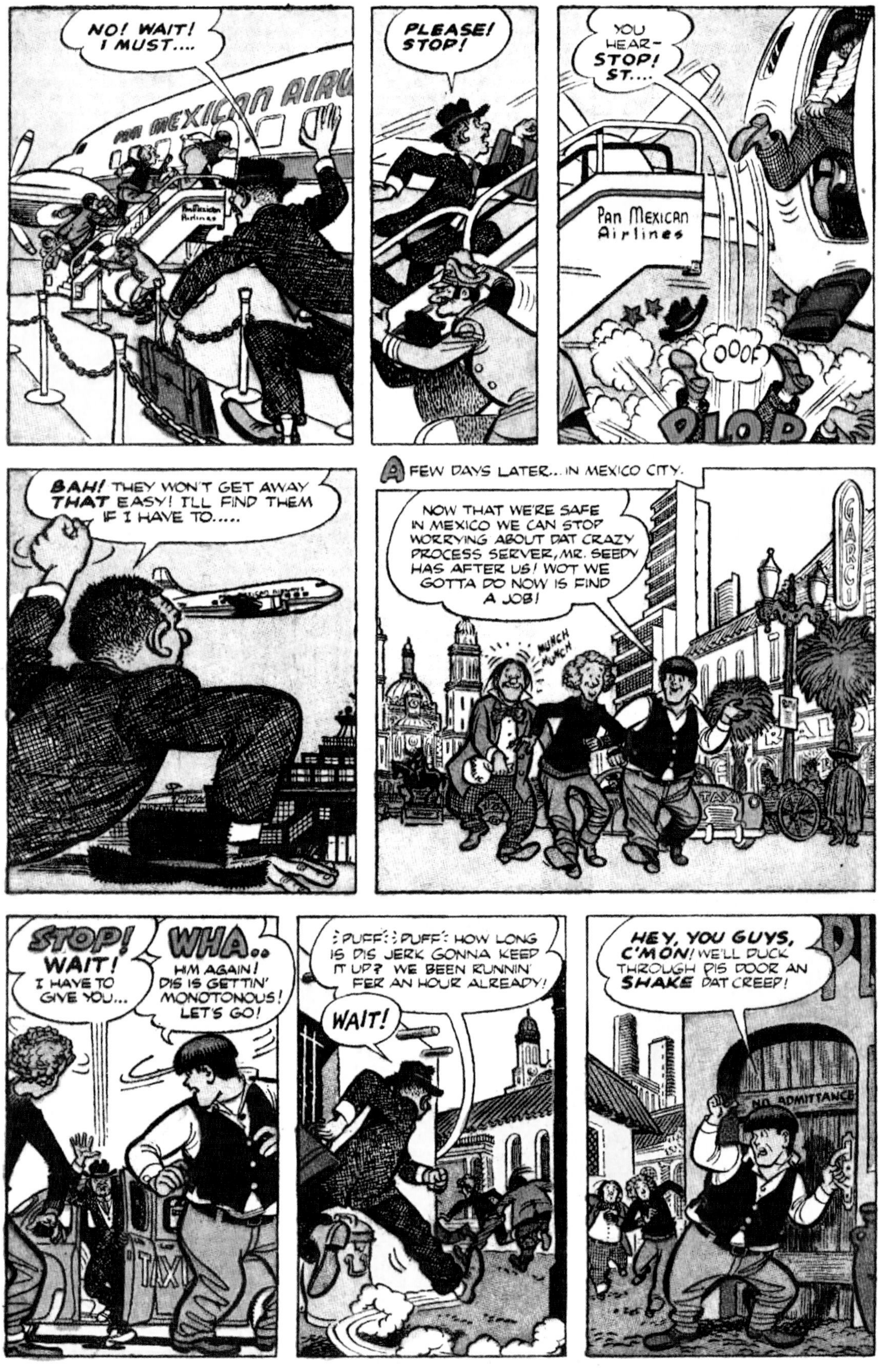
NO! WAIT! I MUST....
PAN MEXICAN AIRL
Pan Mexican Airlines
PLEASE! STOP!
YOU HEAR- STOP! ST....
Pan Mexican Airlines
OOOF
PLOP
BAH! THEY WON'T GET AWAY THAT EASY! I'LL FIND THEM IF I HAVE TO.....
A FEW DAYS LATER... IN MEXICO CITY.
NOW THAT WE'RE SAFE IN MEXICO WE CAN STOP WORRYING ABOUT DAT CRAZY PROCESS SERVER, MR. SEEDY HAS AFTER US! WOT WE GOTTA DO NOW IS FIND A JOB!
MUNCH MUNCH
GARCI
TAXI
STOP! WAIT! I HAVE TO GIVE YOU...
WHA.. HIM AGAIN! DIS IS GETTIN' MONOTONOUS! LET'S GO!
TAXI
PUFF PUFF HOW LONG IS DIS JERK GONNA KEEP IT UP? WE BEEN RUNNIN' FER AN HOUR ALREADY!
WAIT!
HEY, YOU GUYS, C'MON! WE'LL DUCK THROUGH DIS DOOR AN SHAKE DAT CREEP!
NO ADMITTANCE

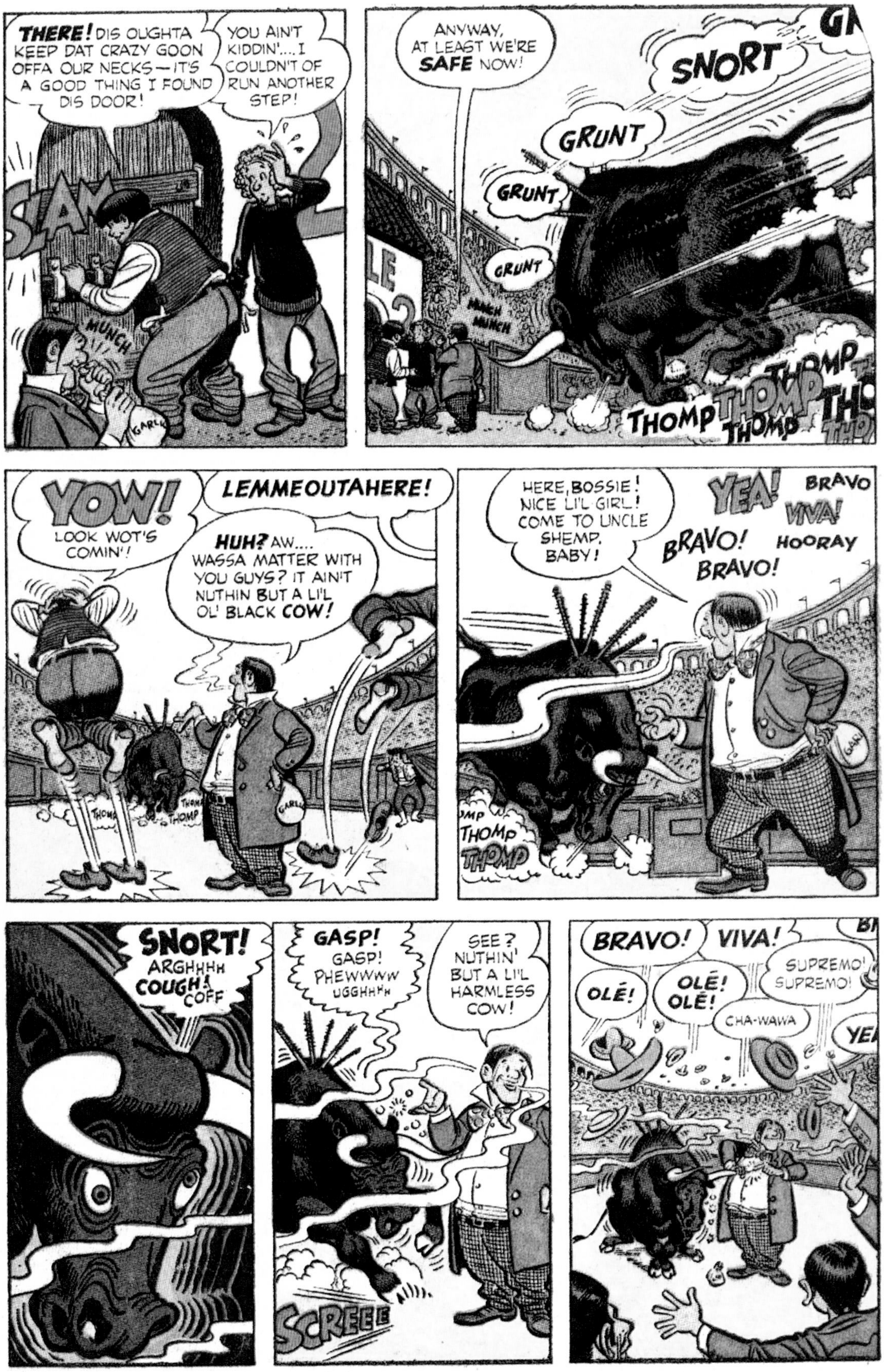
THERE! DIS OUGHTA KEEP DAT CRAZY GOON OFFA OUR NECKS—IT'S A GOOD THING I FOUND DIS DOOR!
YOU AIN'T KIDDIN'... I COULDN'T OF RUN ANOTHER STEP!
MUNCH
ANYWAY, AT LEAST WE'RE SAFE NOW!
SNORT
GRUNT
GRUNT
GRUNT
THOMP THOMP THOMP THOMP
YOW! LOOK WOT'S COMIN'!
LEMMEOUTAHERE!
HUH? AW.... WASSA MATTER WITH YOU GUYS? IT AIN'T NUTHIN BUT A LI'L OL' BLACK COW!
HERE, BOSSIE! NICE LI'L GIRL! COME TO UNCLE SHEMP, BABY!
YEA!
BRAVO
VIVA!
BRAVO!
HOORAY
BRAVO!
THOMP
SNORT! ARGHHHH COUGH! COFF
GASP! GASP! PHEWWWW UGGHHHH
SEE? NUTHIN' BUT A LI'L HARMLESS COW!
SCREEE
BRAVO!
VIVA!
SUPREMO! SUPREMO!
OLÉ!
OLÉ! OLÉ!
CHA-WAWA

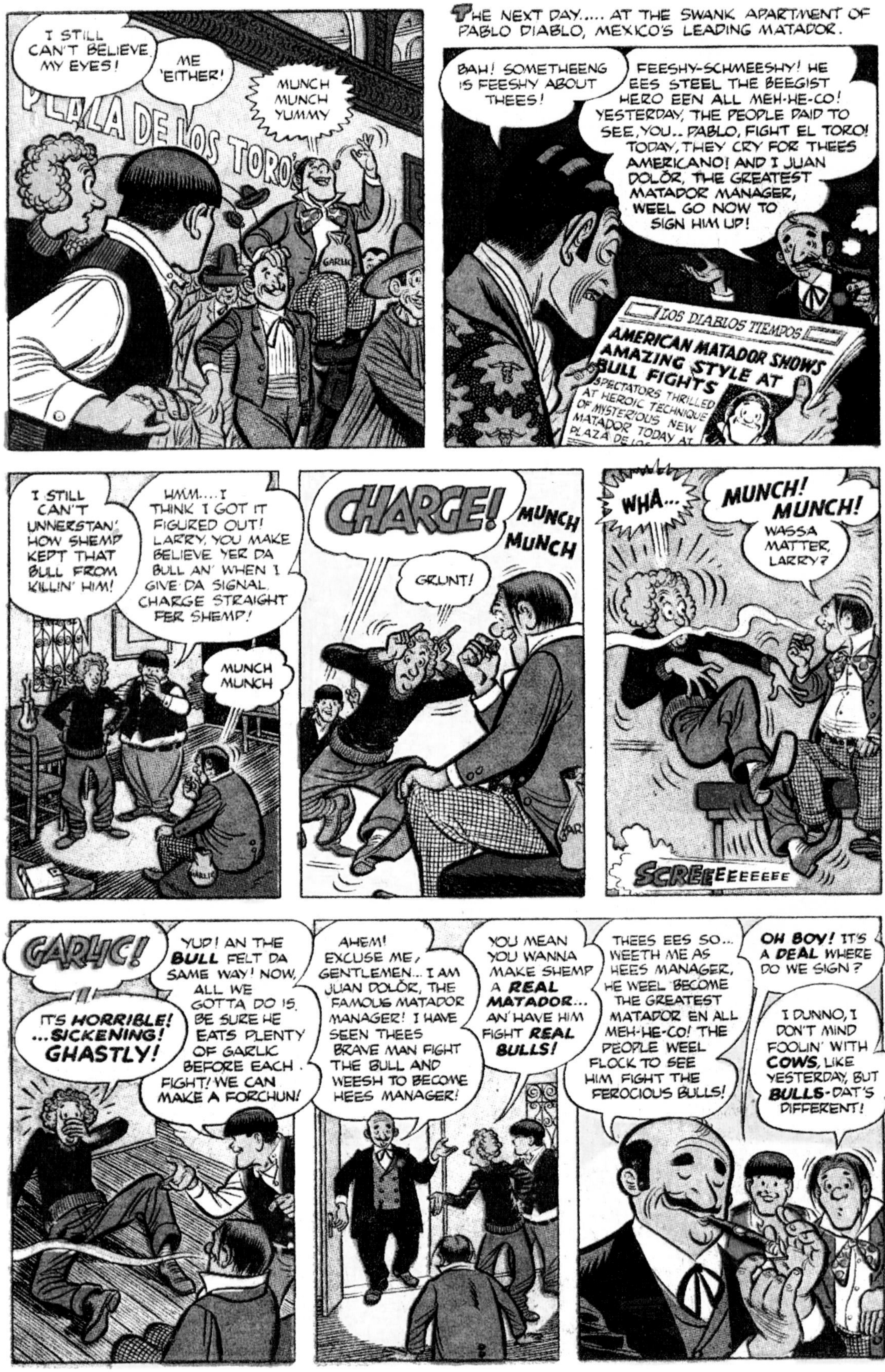

I STILL CAN'T BELIEVE MY EYES!
ME 'EITHER'!
MUNCH MUNCH YUMMY
PLAZA DE LOS TORO'
GARLIC
THE NEXT DAY.... AT THE SWANK APARTMENT OF PABLO DIABLO, MEXICO'S LEADING MATADOR.
BAH! SOMETHEENG IS FEESHY ABOUT THEES!
FEESHY-SCHMEESHY! HE EES STEEL THE BEEGIST HERO EEN ALL MEH-HE-CO! YESTERDAY, THE PEOPLE PAID TO SEE, YOU.. PABLO, FIGHT EL TORO! TODAY, THEY CRY FOR THEES AMERICANO! AND I JUAN DOLÖR, THE GREATEST MATADOR MANAGER, WEEL GO NOW TO SIGN HIM UP!
LOS DIABLOS TIEMPOS
AMERICAN MATADOR SHOWS AMAZING STYLE AT BULL FIGHTS
SPECTATORS THRILLED AT HEROIC TECHNIQUE OF MYSTERIOUS NEW MATADOR TODAY AT PLAZA DE LOS
I STILL CAN'T UNNERSTAN' HOW SHEMP KEPT THAT BULL FROM KILLIN' HIM!
HMM.... I THINK I GOT IT FIGURED OUT! LARRY, YOU MAKE BELIEVE YER DA BULL AN' WHEN I GIVE DA SIGNAL, CHARGE STRAIGHT FER SHEMP!
MUNCH MUNCH
CHARGE!
MUNCH MUNCH
GRUNT!
WHA...
MUNCH! MUNCH!
WASSA MATTER, LARRY?
SCREEEEEEEEE
GARLIC!
IT'S HORRIBLE! ...SICKENING! GHASTLY!
YUP! AN THE BULL FELT DA SAME WAY! NOW, ALL WE GOTTA DO IS BE SURE HE EATS PLENTY OF GARLIC BEFORE EACH FIGHT! WE CAN MAKE A FORCHUN!
AHEM! EXCUSE ME, GENTLEMEN... I AM JUAN DOLÖR, THE FAMOUS MATADOR MANAGER! I HAVE SEEN THEES BRAVE MAN FIGHT THE BULL AND WEESH TO BECOME HEES MANAGER!
YOU MEAN YOU WANNA MAKE SHEMP A REAL MATADOR... AN' HAVE HIM FIGHT REAL BULLS!
THEES EES SO... WEETH ME AS HEES MANAGER, HE WEEL BECOME THE GREATEST MATADOR EN ALL MEH-HE-CO! THE PEOPLE WEEL FLOCK TO SEE HIM FIGHT THE FEROCIOUS BULLS!
OH BOY! IT'S A DEAL WHERE DO WE SIGN?
I DUNNO, I DON'T MIND FOOLIN' WITH COWS, LIKE YESTERDAY, BUT BULLS-DAT'S DIFFERENT!

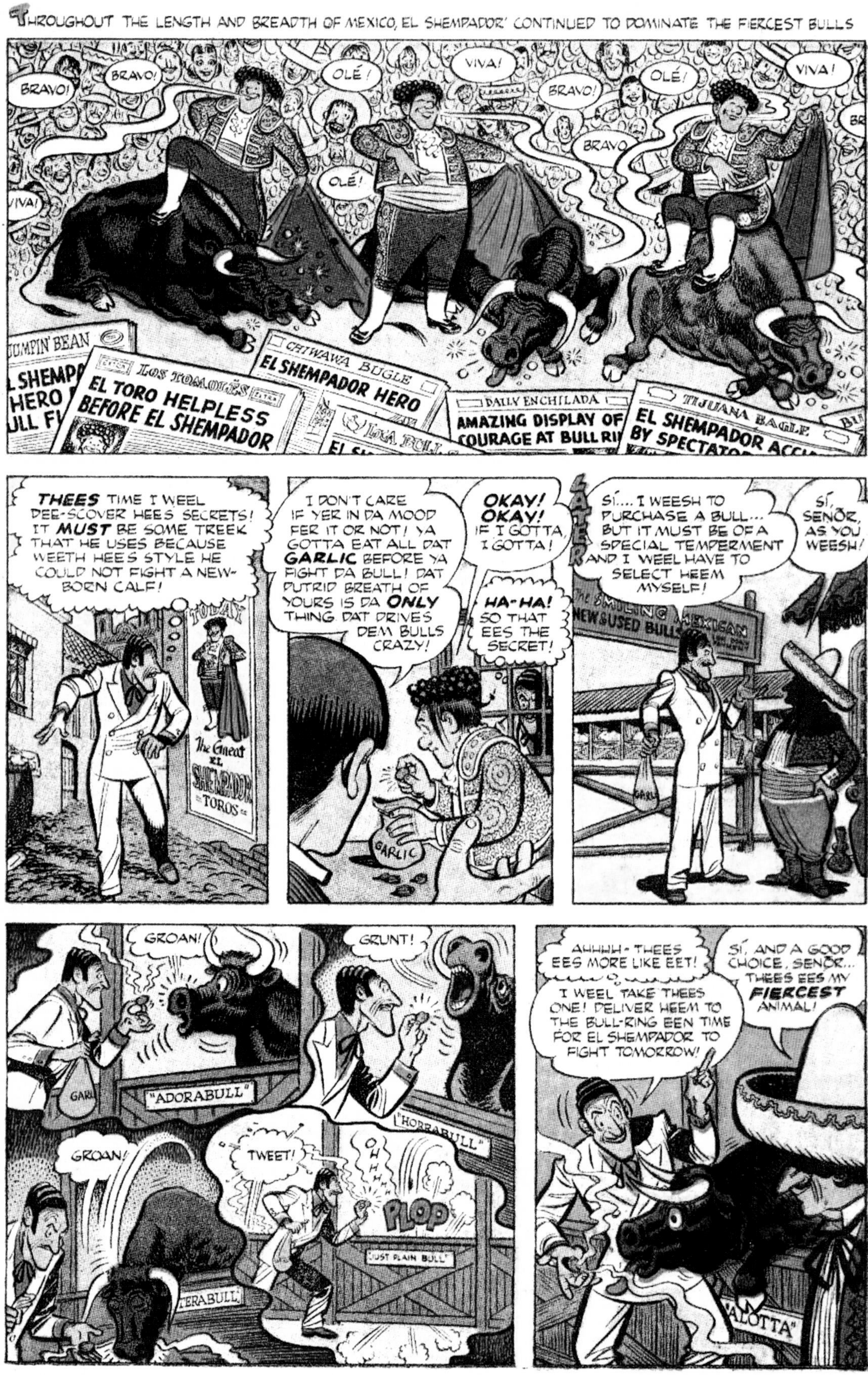
THROUGHOUT THE LENGTH AND BREADTH OF MEXICO, EL SHEMPADOR' CONTINUED TO DOMINATE THE FIERCEST BULLS
BRAVO!
BRAVO!
OLÉ!
VIVA!
BRAVO!
OLÉ!
VIVA!
VIVA!
OLÉ!
BRAVO
JUMPIN' BEAN
LOS TOMALES
EL TORO HELPLESS BEFORE EL SHEMPADOR
CHIWAWA BUGLE
EL SHEMPADOR HERO
DAILY ENCHILADA
AMAZING DISPLAY OF COURAGE AT BULL RI
TIJUANA BAGLE
EL SHEMPADOR BY SPECTATOR
THEES TIME I WEEL DEE-SCOVER HEES SECRETS! IT MUST BE SOME TREEK THAT HE USES BECAUSE WEETH HEE'S STYLE HE COULD NOT FIGHT A NEW-BORN CALF!
TODAY
The Great EL SHEMPADOR
TOROS
I DON'T CARE IF YER IN DA MOOD FER IT OR NOT! YA GOTTA EAT ALL DAT GARLIC BEFORE YA FIGHT DA BULL! DAT PUTRID BREATH OF YOURS IS DA ONLY THING DAT DRIVES DEM BULLS CRAZY!
OKAY! OKAY! IF I GOTTA, I GOTTA!
HA-HA! SO THAT EES THE SECRET!
GARLIC
LATER
SÍ.... I WEESH TO PURCHASE A BULL... BUT IT MUST BE OF A SPECIAL TEMPERMENT AND I WEEL HAVE TO SELECT HEEM MYSELF!
SÍ, SEÑOR, AS YOU WEESH!
THE SMILING MEXICAN
NEW & USED BULLS
GROAN!
GRUNT!
"ADORABULL"
"HORRABULL"
GROAN!
TWEET!
OHHHHH
PLOP
"JUST PLAIN BULL"
TERABULL
AHHHH - THEES EES MORE LIKE EET!
I WEEL TAKE THEES ONE! DELIVER HEEM TO THE BULL-RING EEN TIME FOR EL SHEMPADOR TO FIGHT TOMORROW!
SÍ, AND A GOOD CHOICE, SEÑOR... THEES EES MY FIERCEST ANIMAL!
"VALOTTA"

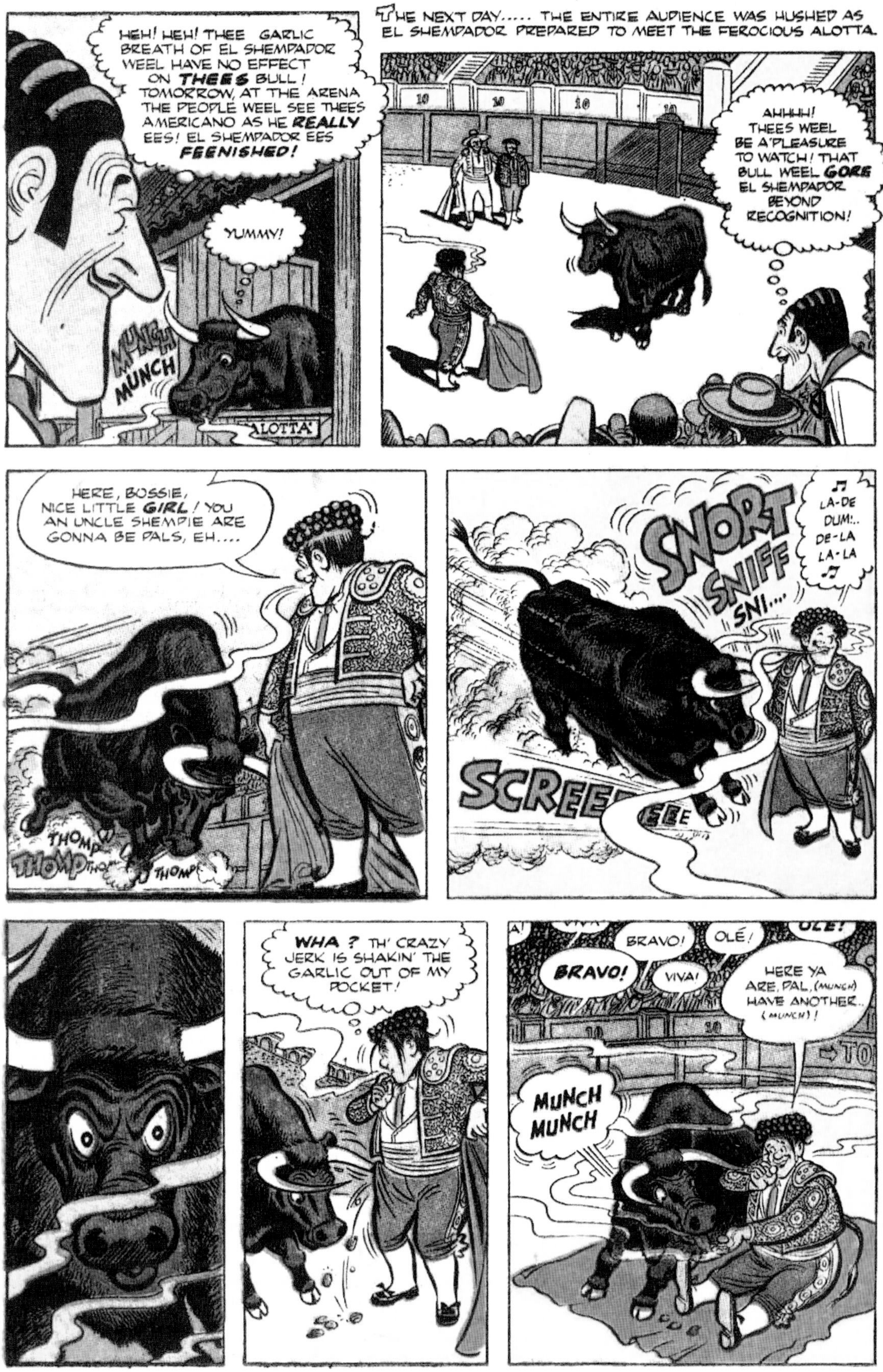
HEH! HEH! THEE GARLIC BREATH OF EL SHEMPADOR WEEL HAVE NO EFFECT ON THEES BULL! TOMORROW, AT THE ARENA THE PEOPLE WEEL SEE THEES AMERICANO AS HE REALLY EES! EL SHEMPADOR EES FEENISHED!
YUMMY!
MUNCH
MUNCH
ALOTTA
THE NEXT DAY..... THE ENTIRE AUDIENCE WAS HUSHED AS EL SHEMPADOR PREPARED TO MEET THE FEROCIOUS ALOTTA.
AHHHH! THEES WEEL BE A PLEASURE TO WATCH! THAT BULL WEEL GORE EL SHEMPADOR BEYOND RECOGNITION!
HERE, BOSSIE, NICE LITTLE GIRL! YOU AN UNCLE SHEMPIE ARE GONNA BE PALS, EH....
THOMP
THOMP
THOMP
SNORT
SNIFF
SNI....
LA-DE DUM!.. DE-LA LA-LA
SCREEEEEEE
WHA? TH' CRAZY JERK IS SHAKIN' THE GARLIC OUT OF MY POCKET!
BRAVO!
OLÉ!
OLÉ!
BRAVO!
VIVA!
HERE YA ARE, PAL, (MUNCH) HAVE ANOTHER.. (MUNCH)!
MUNCH MUNCH

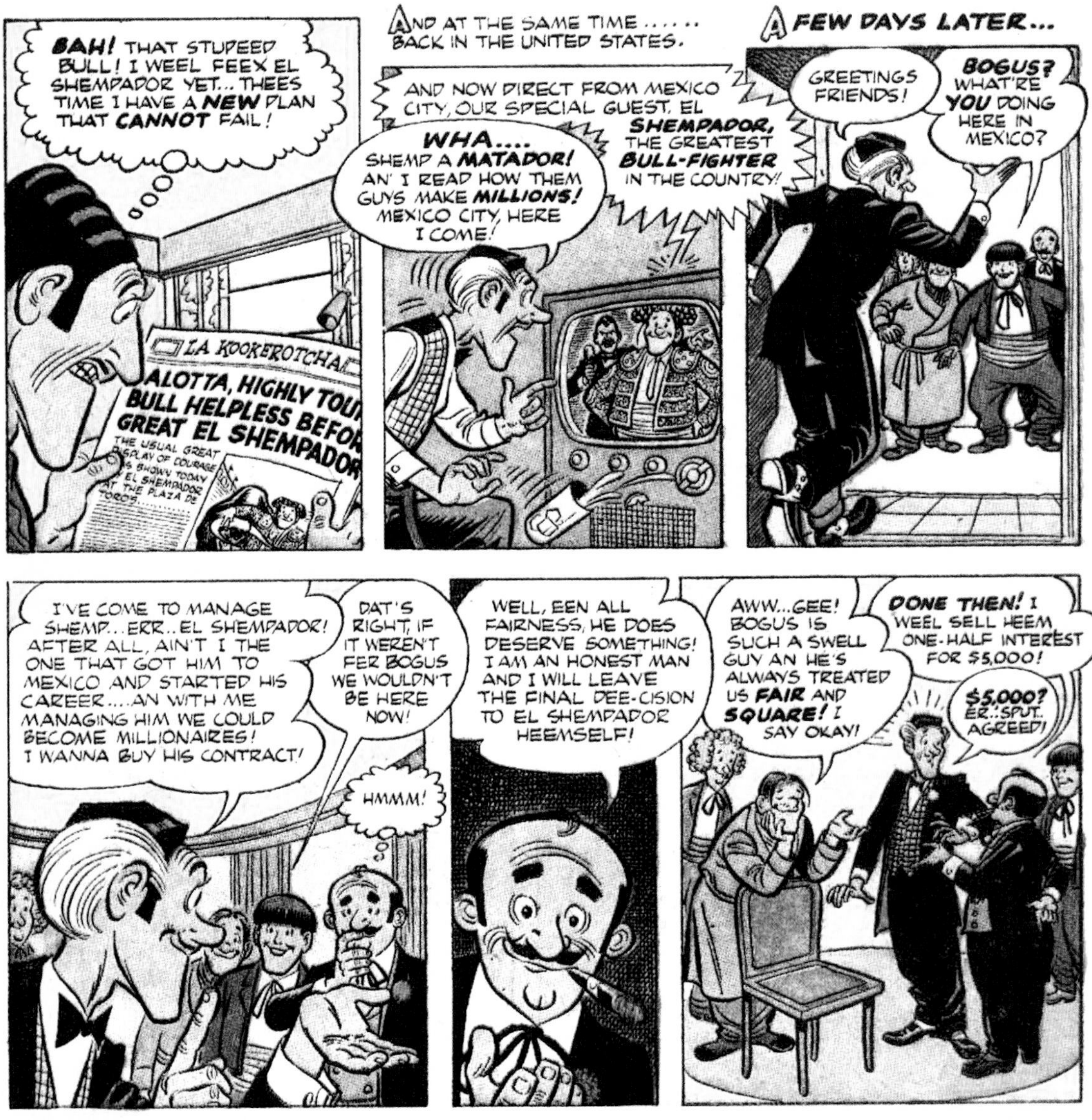
BAH! THAT STUPEED BULL! I WEEL FEEX EL SHEMPADOR YET... THEES TIME I HAVE A NEW PLAN THAT CANNOT FAIL!
LA KOOKEROTCHA
ALOTTA, HIGHLY TOU
BULL HELPLESS BEFOR
GREAT EL SHEMPADOR
THE USUAL GREAT DISPLAY OF COURAGE WAS SHOWN TODAY BY EL SHEMPADOR AT THE PLAZA DE TOROS...
AND AT THE SAME TIME...... BACK IN THE UNITED STATES.
AND NOW DIRECT FROM MEXICO CITY, OUR SPECIAL GUEST, EL SHEMPADOR, THE GREATEST BULL-FIGHTER IN THE COUNTRY!
WHA.... SHEMP A MATADOR! AN' I READ HOW THEM GUYS MAKE MILLIONS! MEXICO CITY, HERE I COME!
A FEW DAYS LATER...
GREETINGS FRIENDS!
BOGUS? WHAT'RE YOU DOING HERE IN MEXICO?
I'VE COME TO MANAGE SHEMP...ERR..EL SHEMPADOR! AFTER ALL, AIN'T I THE ONE THAT GOT HIM TO MEXICO AND STARTED HIS CAREER....AN WITH ME MANAGING HIM WE COULD BECOME MILLIONAIRES! I WANNA BUY HIS CONTRACT!
DAT'S RIGHT, IF IT WEREN'T FER BOGUS WE WOULDN'T BE HERE NOW!
HMMM!
WELL, EEN ALL FAIRNESS, HE DOES DESERVE SOMETHING! I AM AN HONEST MAN AND I WILL LEAVE THE FINAL DEE-CISION TO EL SHEMPADOR HEEMSELF!
AWW...GEE! BOGUS IS SUCH A SWELL GUY AN HE'S ALWAYS TREATED US FAIR AND SQUARE! I SAY OKAY!
DONE THEN! I WEEL SELL HEEM ONE-HALF INTEREST FOR $5,000!
$5,000? ER..SPUT.. AGREED!
LATER...
HEH! HEH! EL SHEMPADOR FIGHTS THEE BULL IN ONE HOUR...I MUST HURRY IF I AM TO FEEX EET SO EET IS HEES LAST BULLFIGHT!
DRESSING ROOM EL SHEMPA
AHHH... THERE EES HEES GARLIC! WEETH THEES, I WEEL RENDER IT AS HARMLESS AS BOBBLE GOM!
KEELER DEELE KING SIZE GARLIC
air-wi SPRAY KILLS ALL ODOR CONTAINS SUPER CHLOROPHYL
KEELER DEELE KING SIZE GARLIC

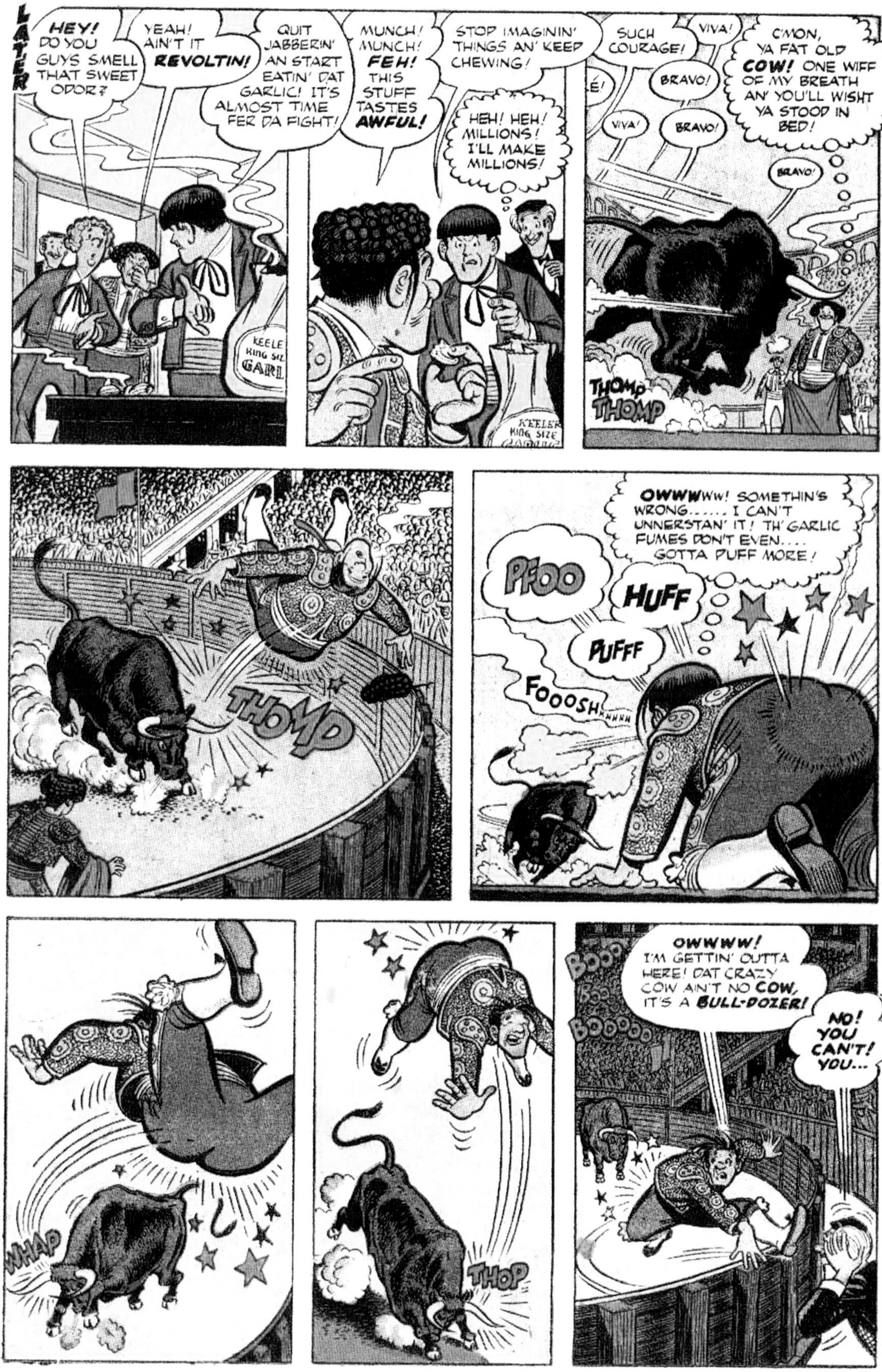
LATER
HEY! DO YOU GUYS SMELL THAT SWEET ODOR?
YEAH! AIN'T IT REVOLTIN!
QUIT JABBERIN' AN START EATIN' DAT GARLIC! IT'S ALMOST TIME FER DA FIGHT!
MUNCH! MUNCH! FEH! THIS STUFF TASTES AWFUL!
STOP IMAGININ' THINGS AN' KEEP CHEWING!
HEH! HEH! MILLIONS! I'LL MAKE MILLIONS!
KEELER KING SIZE
SUCH COURAGE!
VIVA!
BRAVO!
VIVA!
BRAVO!
BRAVO!
C'MON, YA FAT OLD COW! ONE WIFF OF MY BREATH AN' YOU'LL WISHT YA STOOD IN BED!
THOMP THOMP
THOMP
OWWWWW! SOMETHIN'S WRONG...... I CAN'T UNNERSTAN' IT! TH' GARLIC FUMES DON'T EVEN.... GOTTA PUFF MORE!
PFOO
HUFF
PUFFF
FOOOSHhhhhh
WHAP
THOP
BOOO BOO BOOOOOO
OWWWW! I'M GETTIN' OUTTA HERE! DAT CRAZY COW AIN'T NO COW, IT'S A BULL-DOZER!
NO! YOU CAN'T! YOU...

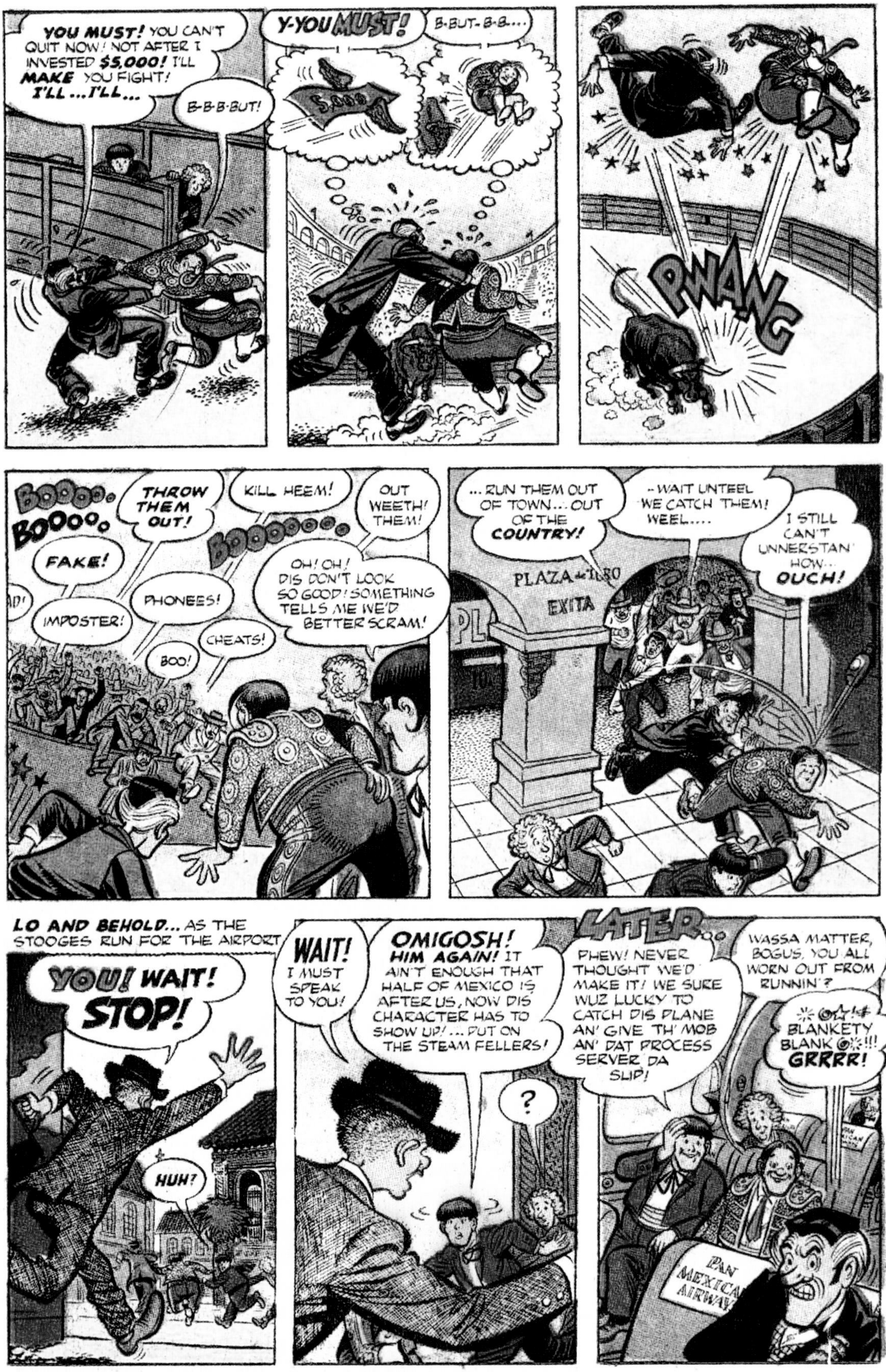
YOU MUST! YOU CAN'T QUIT NOW! NOT AFTER I INVESTED $5,000! I'LL MAKE YOU FIGHT! I'LL ...I'LL...
B-B-B-BUT!
Y-YOU MUST!
B-BUT-B-B...
PWANG
BOOOO
BOOOO
THROW THEM OUT!
KILL HEEM!
OUT WEETH! THEM!
BOOOOOO
FAKE!
IMPOSTER!
PHONEES!
BOO!
CHEATS!
OH! OH! DIS DON'T LOOK SO GOOD! SOMETHING TELLS ME WE'D BETTER SCRAM!
...RUN THEM OUT OF TOWN... OUT OF THE COUNTRY!
--WAIT UNTEEL WE CATCH THEM! WEEL....
I STILL CAN'T UNNERSTAN' HOW... OUCH!
PLAZA
EXITA
LO AND BEHOLD... AS THE STOOGES RUN FOR THE AIRPORT
YOU! WAIT! STOP!
HUH?
WAIT! I MUST SPEAK TO YOU!
OMIGOSH! HIM AGAIN! IT AIN'T ENOUGH THAT HALF OF MEXICO IS AFTER US, NOW DIS CHARACTER HAS TO SHOW UP! ...PUT ON THE STEAM FELLERS!
?
LATER
PHEW! NEVER THOUGHT WE'D MAKE IT! WE SURE WUZ LUCKY TO CATCH DIS PLANE AN' GIVE TH' MOB AN' DAT PROCESS SERVER DA SLIP!
WASSA MATTER, BOGUS, YOU ALL WORN OUT FROM RUNNIN'?
BLANKETY BLANK !!! GRRRR!
PAN

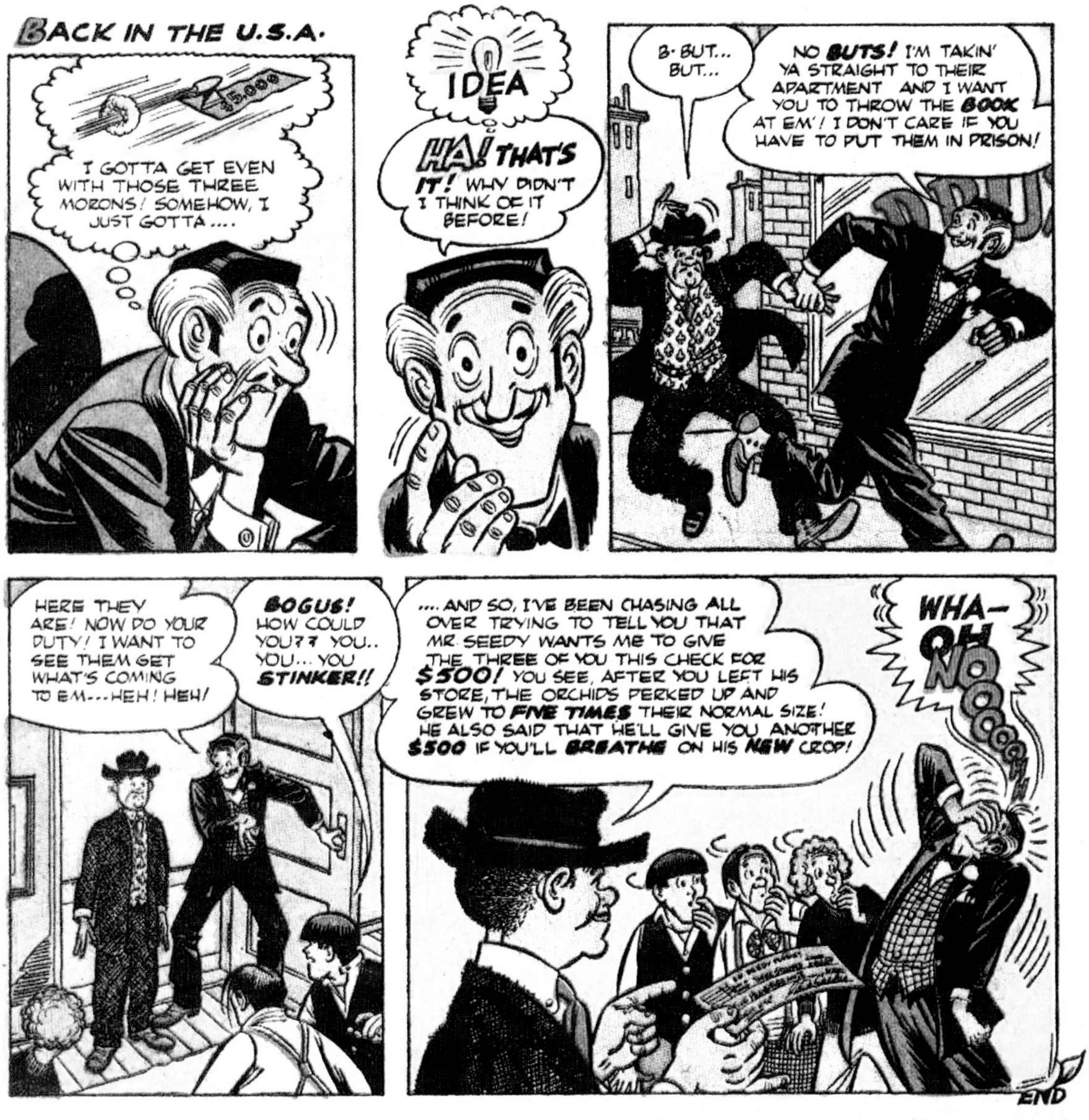
BACK IN THE U.S.A.
I GOTTA GET EVEN WITH THOSE THREE MORONS! SOMEHOW, I JUST GOTTA ....
IDEA
HA! THAT'S IT! WHY DIDN'T I THINK OF IT BEFORE!
B-BUT... BUT...
NO BUTS! I'M TAKIN' YA STRAIGHT TO THEIR APARTMENT AND I WANT YOU TO THROW THE BOOK AT EM'! I DON'T CARE IF YOU HAVE TO PUT THEM IN PRISON!
HERE THEY ARE! NOW DO YOUR DUTY! I WANT TO SEE THEM GET WHAT'S COMING TO EM---HEH! HEH!
BOGUS! HOW COULD YOU?? YOU.. YOU... YOU STINKER!!
....AND SO, I'VE BEEN CHASING ALL OVER TRYING TO TELL YOU THAT MR. SEEDY WANTS ME TO GIVE THE THREE OF YOU THIS CHECK FOR $500! YOU SEE, AFTER YOU LEFT HIS STORE, THE ORCHIDS PERKED UP AND GREW TO FIVE TIMES THEIR NORMAL SIZE! HE ALSO SAID THAT HE'LL GIVE YOU ANOTHER $500 IF YOU'LL BREATHE ON HIS NEW CROP!
WHA-OH NOOOOO
END

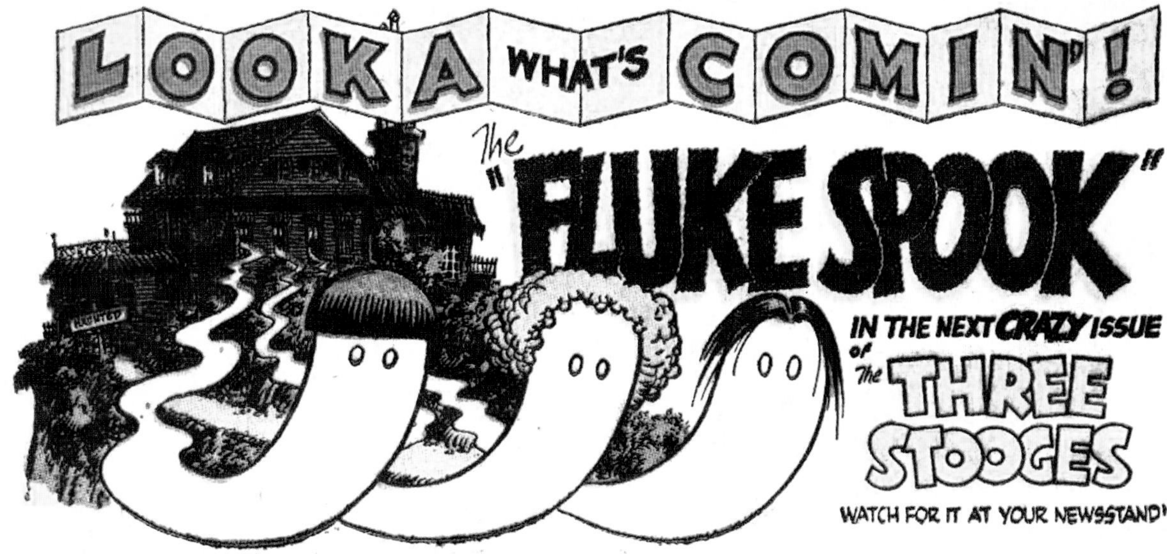
LOOKA WHAT'S COMIN'!
The "FLUKE SPOOK"
IN THE NEXT CRAZY ISSUE of The THREE STOOGES
WATCH FOR IT AT YOUR NEWSSTAND!

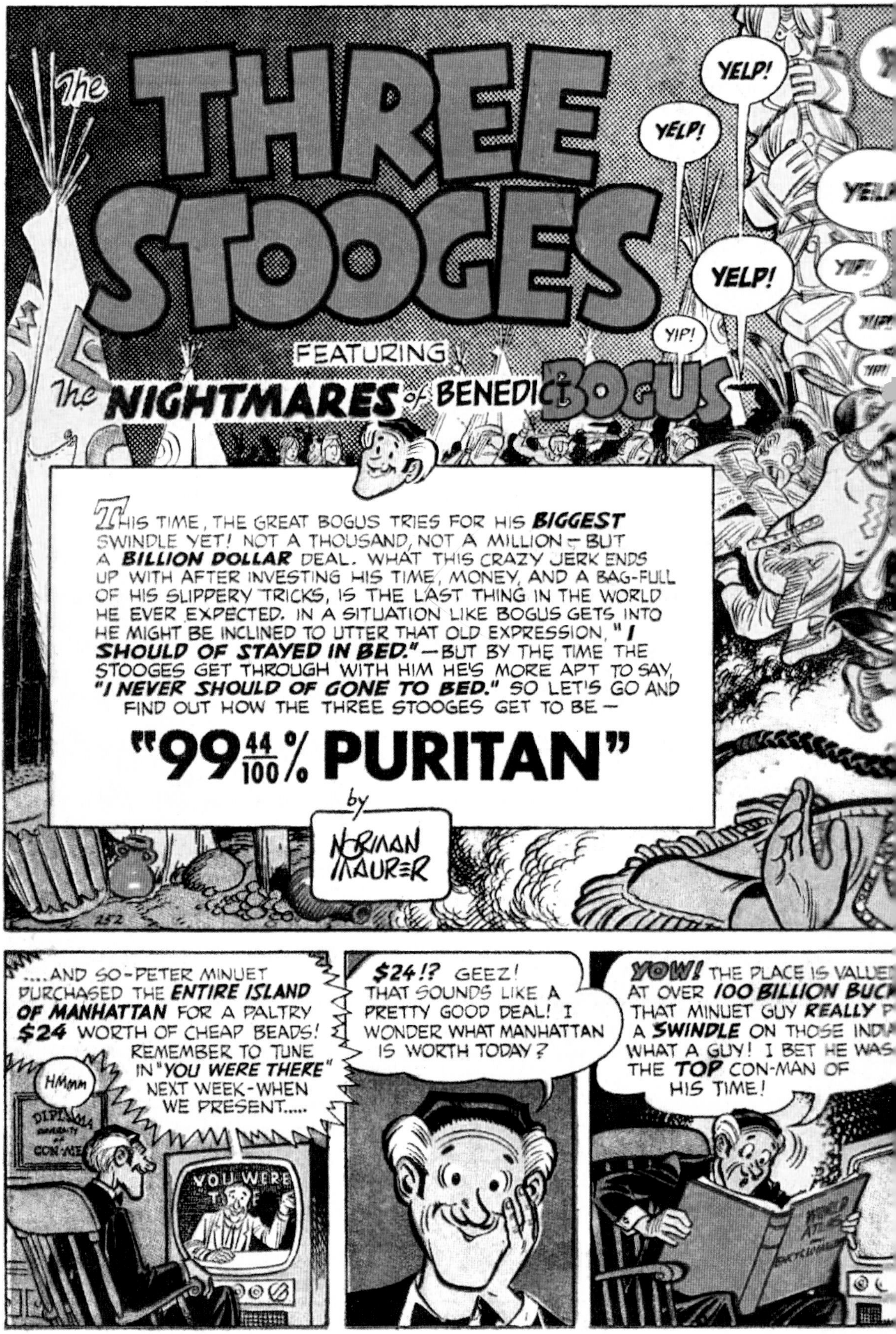

The THREE STOOGES
FEATURING
The NIGHTMARES of BENEDICT BOGUS
YELP!
YELP!
YELP!
YIP!
YIP!
THIS TIME, THE GREAT BOGUS TRIES FOR HIS **BIGGEST** SWINDLE YET! NOT A THOUSAND, NOT A MILLION — BUT A **BILLION DOLLAR** DEAL. WHAT THIS CRAZY JERK ENDS UP WITH AFTER INVESTING HIS TIME, MONEY, AND A BAG-FULL OF HIS SLIPPERY TRICKS, IS THE LAST THING IN THE WORLD HE EVER EXPECTED. IN A SITUATION LIKE BOGUS GETS INTO HE MIGHT BE INCLINED TO UTTER THAT OLD EXPRESSION, "**I SHOULD OF STAYED IN BED.**" — BUT BY THE TIME THE STOOGES GET THROUGH WITH HIM HE'S MORE APT TO SAY, "**I NEVER SHOULD OF GONE TO BED.**" SO LET'S GO AND FIND OUT HOW THE THREE STOOGES GET TO BE —
"99 44/100 % PURITAN"
by NORMAN MAURER
252
....AND SO-PETER MINUET PURCHASED THE **ENTIRE ISLAND OF MANHATTAN** FOR A PALTRY **$24** WORTH OF CHEAP BEADS! REMEMBER TO TUNE IN "**YOU WERE THERE**" NEXT WEEK-WHEN WE PRESENT.....
HMmm
DIPLOMA
CON-MEN
YOU WERE T
$24!? GEEZ! THAT SOUNDS LIKE A PRETTY GOOD DEAL! I WONDER WHAT MANHATTAN IS WORTH TODAY?
YOW! THE PLACE IS VALUE AT OVER **100 BILLION BUCK** THAT MINUET GUY **REALLY** P A **SWINDLE** ON THOSE INDIA WHAT A GUY! I BET HE WAS THE **TOP** CON-MAN OF HIS TIME!

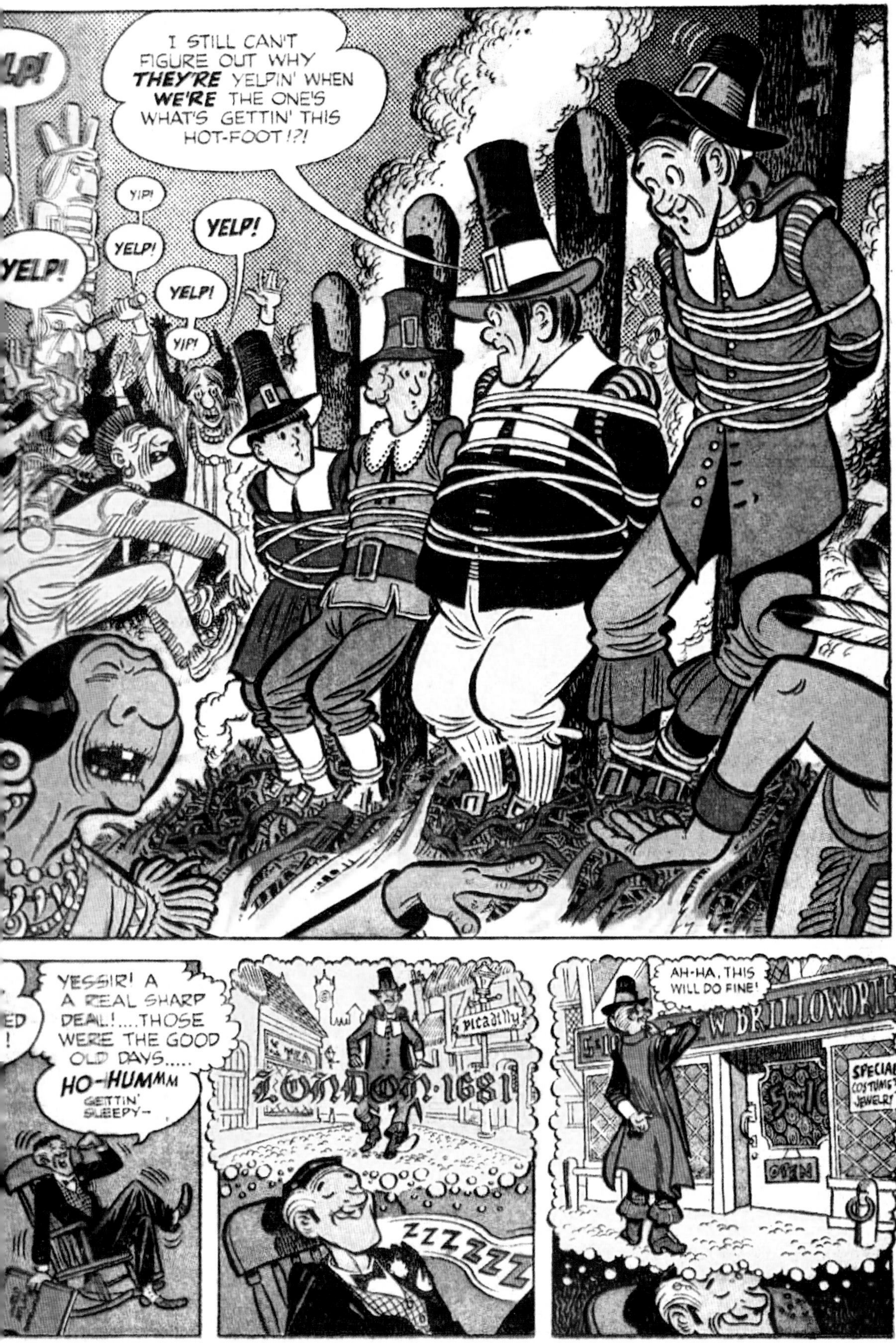
I STILL CAN'T FIGURE OUT WHY **THEY'RE** YELPIN' WHEN **WE'RE** THE ONE'S WHAT'S GETTIN' THIS HOT-FOOT!?!
YIP!
YELP!
YELP!
YELP!
YELP!
YIP!
YESSIR! A A REAL SHARP DEAL!....THOSE WERE THE GOOD OLD DAYS.....
HO-HUMMM
GETTIN' SLEEPY--
picadilly
LONDON 1681
ZZZZZZZ
AH-HA, THIS WILL DO FINE!
SPECIAL COSTUME JEWELRY!

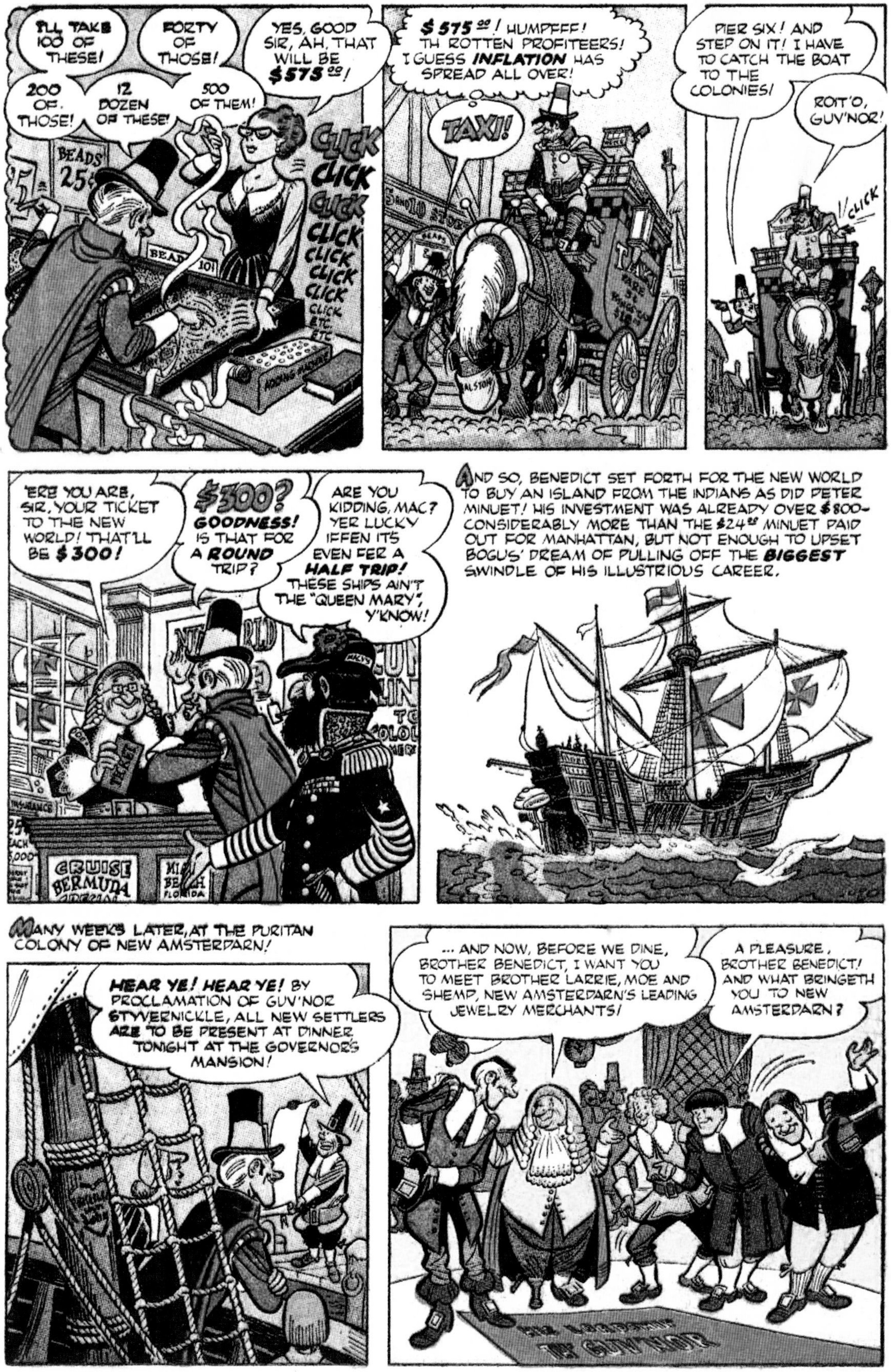
I'LL TAKE 100 OF THESE!
FORTY OF THOSE!
YES, GOOD SIR, AH, THAT WILL BE $575.00!
200 OF THOSE!
12 DOZEN OF THESE!
500 OF THEM!
BEADS 25¢
CLICK CLICK CLICK CLICK CLICK CLICK CLICK CLICK ETC. ETC.
$575.00! HUMPFFF! TH ROTTEN PROFITEERS! I GUESS INFLATION HAS SPREAD ALL OVER!
TAXI!
PIER SIX! AND STEP ON IT! I HAVE TO CATCH THE BOAT TO THE COLONIES!
ROIT'O, GUV'NOR!
CLICK
'ERE YOU ARE, SIR, YOUR TICKET TO THE NEW WORLD! THAT'LL BE $300!
$300? GOODNESS! IS THAT FOR A ROUND TRIP?
ARE YOU KIDDING, MAC? YER LUCKY IFFEN IT'S EVEN FER A HALF TRIP! THESE SHIPS AIN'T THE "QUEEN MARY", Y'KNOW!
CRUISE BERMUDA
AND SO, BENEDICT SET FORTH FOR THE NEW WORLD TO BUY AN ISLAND FROM THE INDIANS AS DID PETER MINUET! HIS INVESTMENT WAS ALREADY OVER $800 — CONSIDERABLY MORE THAN THE $24.00 MINUET PAID OUT FOR MANHATTAN, BUT NOT ENOUGH TO UPSET BOGUS' DREAM OF PULLING OFF THE BIGGEST SWINDLE OF HIS ILLUSTRIOUS CAREER.
MANY WEEKS LATER, AT THE PURITAN COLONY OF NEW AMSTERDARN!
HEAR YE! HEAR YE! BY PROCLAMATION OF GUV'NOR STYVERNICKLE, ALL NEW SETTLERS ARE TO BE PRESENT AT DINNER TONIGHT AT THE GOVERNOR'S MANSION!
... AND NOW, BEFORE WE DINE, BROTHER BENEDICT, I WANT YOU TO MEET BROTHER LARRIE, MOE AND SHEMP, NEW AMSTERDARN'S LEADING JEWELRY MERCHANTS!
A PLEASURE, BROTHER BENEDICT! AND WHAT BRINGETH YOU TO NEW AMSTERDARN?

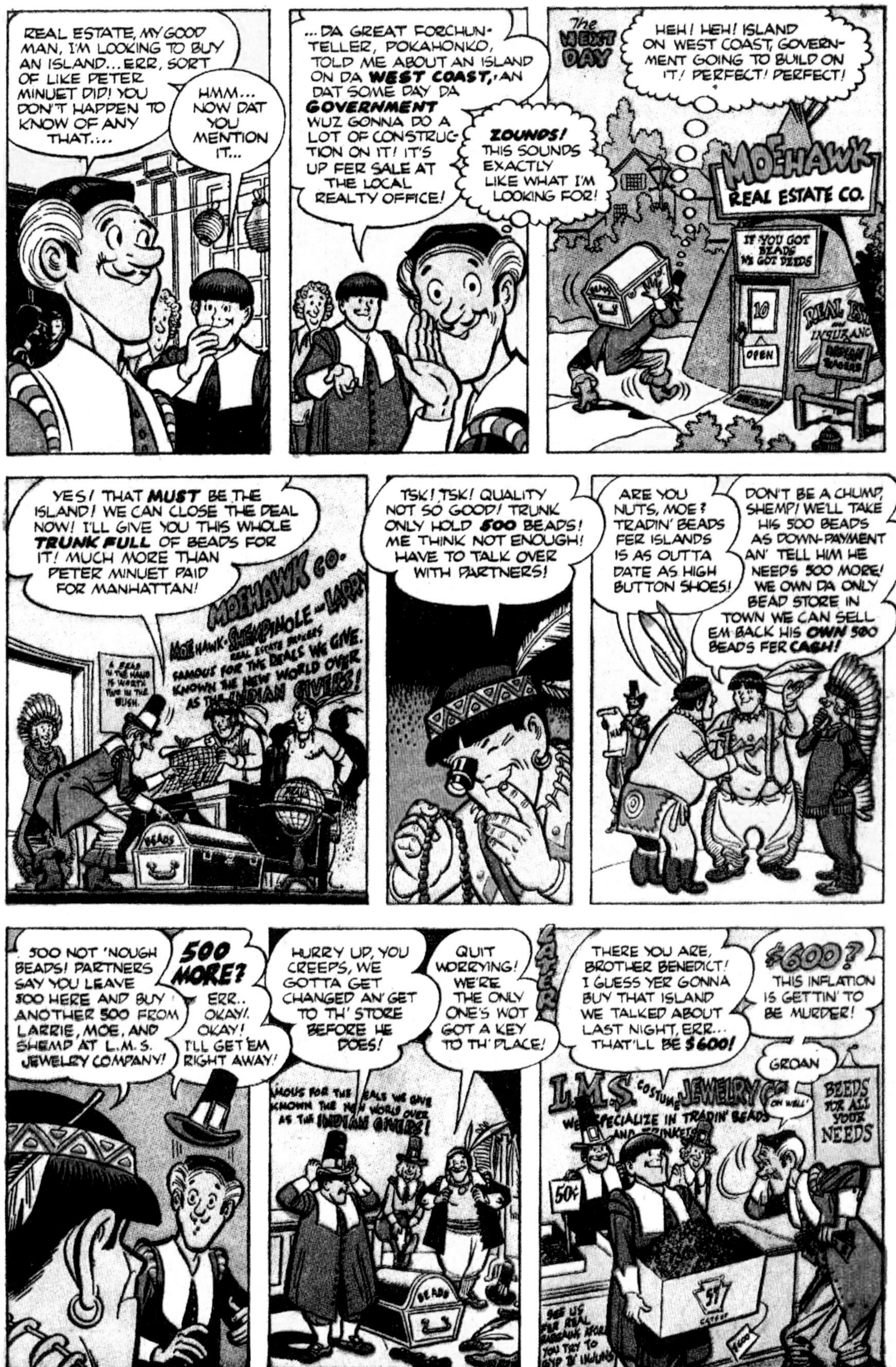

REAL ESTATE, MY GOOD MAN, I'M LOOKING TO BUY AN ISLAND... ERR, SORT OF LIKE PETER MINUET DID! YOU DON'T HAPPEN TO KNOW OF ANY THAT....
HMM... NOW DAT YOU MENTION IT...
...DA GREAT FORCHUN-TELLER, POKAHONKO, TOLD ME ABOUT AN ISLAND ON DA WEST COAST,- AN DAT SOME DAY DA GOVERNMENT WUZ GONNA DO A LOT OF CONSTRUC-TION ON IT! IT'S UP FER SALE AT THE LOCAL REALTY OFFICE!
ZOUNDS! THIS SOUNDS EXACTLY LIKE WHAT I'M LOOKING FOR!
The NEXT DAY
HEH! HEH! ISLAND ON WEST COAST, GOVERN-MENT GOING TO BUILD ON IT! PERFECT! PERFECT!
MOE-HAWK REAL ESTATE CO.
IF YOU GOT BEADS WE GOT DEEDS
10
OPEN
YES! THAT MUST BE THE ISLAND! WE CAN CLOSE THE DEAL NOW! I'LL GIVE YOU THIS WHOLE TRUNK FULL OF BEADS FOR IT! MUCH MORE THAN PETER MINUET PAID FOR MANHATTAN!
MOEHAWK CO.
SAMOUS FOR THE DEALS WE GIVE. KNOWN THE NEW WORLD OVER AS THE INDIAN GIVERS!
BEADS
TSK! TSK! QUALITY NOT SO GOOD! TRUNK ONLY HOLD 500 BEADS! ME THINK NOT ENOUGH! HAVE TO TALK OVER WITH PARTNERS!
ARE YOU NUTS, MOE? TRADIN' BEADS FER ISLANDS IS AS OUTTA DATE AS HIGH BUTTON SHOES!
DON'T BE A CHUMP, SHEMP! WE'LL TAKE HIS 500 BEADS AS DOWN-PAYMENT AN' TELL HIM HE NEEDS 500 MORE! WE OWN DA ONLY BEAD STORE IN TOWN WE CAN SELL EM BACK HIS OWN 500 BEADS FER CASH!
500 NOT 'NOUGH BEADS! PARTNERS SAY YOU LEAVE 500 HERE AND BUY ANOTHER 500 FROM LARRIE, MOE, AND SHEMP AT L.M.S. JEWELRY COMPANY!
500 MORE? ERR.. OKAY!. OKAY! I'LL GET 'EM RIGHT AWAY!
HURRY UP, YOU CREEPS, WE GOTTA GET CHANGED AN' GET TO TH' STORE BEFORE HE DOES!
QUIT WORRYING! WE'RE THE ONLY ONE'S WOT GOT A KEY TO TH' PLACE!
BEADS
THERE YOU ARE, BROTHER BENEDICT! I GUESS YER GONNA BUY THAT ISLAND WE TALKED ABOUT LAST NIGHT, ERR... THAT'LL BE $600!
$600? THIS INFLATION IS GETTIN' TO BE MURDER!
GROAN
L.M.S. COSTUME JEWELRY CO. WE SPECIALIZE IN TRADIN' BEADS AND TRINKETS
BEEDS FOR ALL YOUR NEEDS
50¢
57

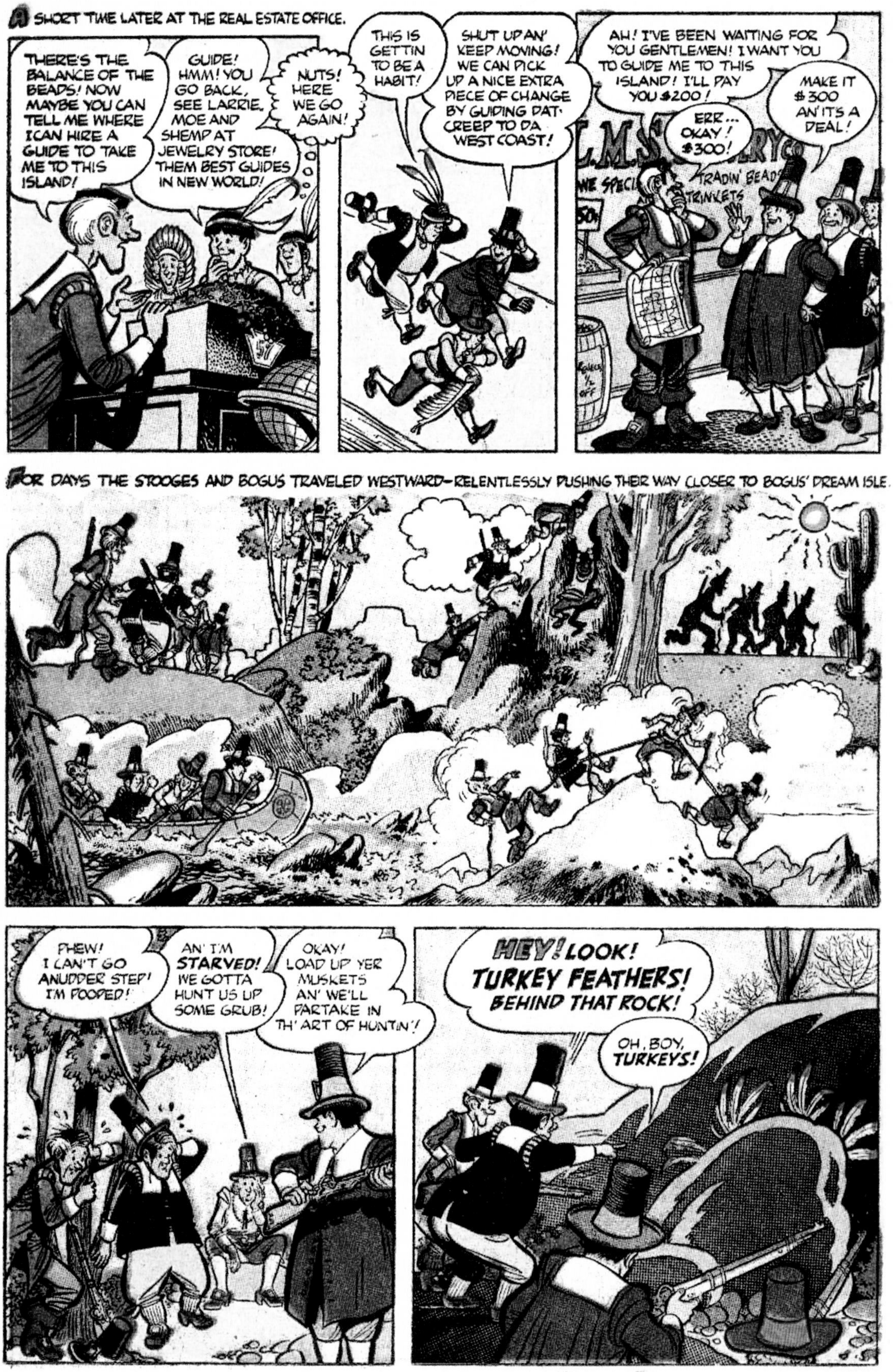
A SHORT TIME LATER AT THE REAL ESTATE OFFICE.
THERE'S THE BALANCE OF THE BEADS! NOW MAYBE YOU CAN TELL ME WHERE I CAN HIRE A GUIDE TO TAKE ME TO THIS ISLAND!
GUIDE! HMM! YOU GO BACK, SEE LARRIE, MOE AND SHEMP AT JEWELRY STORE! THEM BEST GUIDES IN NEW WORLD!
NUTS! HERE WE GO AGAIN!
THIS IS GETTIN TO BE A HABIT!
SHUT UP AN' KEEP MOVING! WE CAN PICK UP A NICE EXTRA PIECE OF CHANGE BY GUIDING DAT CREEP TO DA WEST COAST!
AH! I'VE BEEN WAITING FOR YOU GENTLEMEN! I WANT YOU TO GUIDE ME TO THIS ISLAND! I'LL PAY YOU $200!
MAKE IT $300 AN' IT'S A DEAL!
ERR... OKAY! $300!
TRADIN' BEADS TRINKETS
FOR DAYS THE STOOGES AND BOGUS TRAVELED WESTWARD—RELENTLESSLY PUSHING THEIR WAY CLOSER TO BOGUS' DREAM ISLE.
PHEW! I CAN'T GO ANUDDER STEP! I'M POOPED!
AN' I'M STARVED! WE GOTTA HUNT US UP SOME GRUB!
OKAY! LOAD UP YER MUSKETS AN' WE'LL PARTAKE IN TH' ART OF HUNTIN'!
HEY! LOOK! TURKEY FEATHERS! BEHIND THAT ROCK!
OH, BOY, TURKEYS!

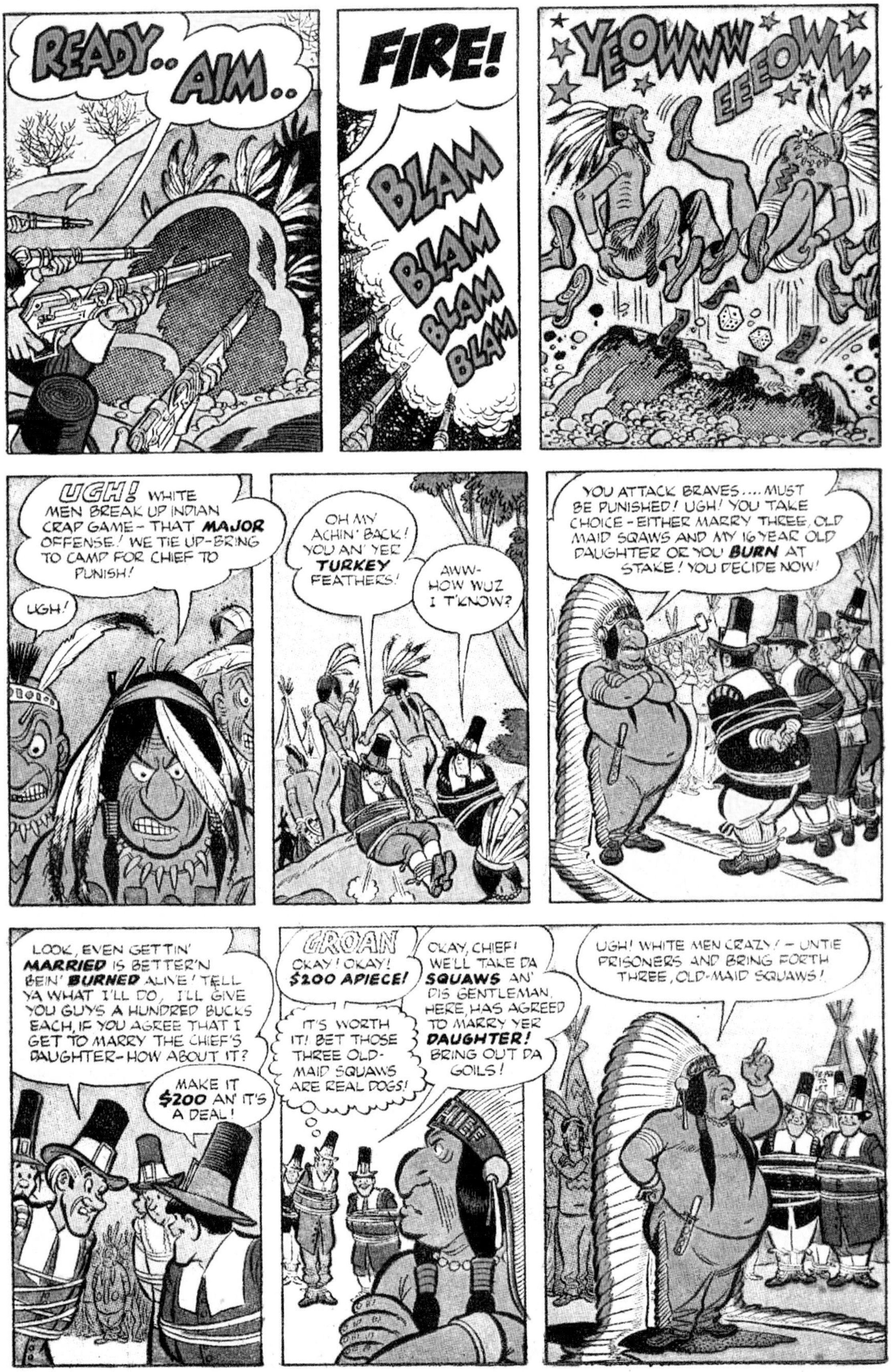
READY.. AIM..
FIRE!
BLAM BLAM BLAM BLAM
YEOWWW EEEOWW
UGH! WHITE MEN BREAK UP INDIAN CRAP GAME - THAT MAJOR OFFENSE! WE TIE UP-BRING TO CAMP FOR CHIEF TO PUNISH!
UGH!
OH MY ACHIN' BACK! YOU AN' YER TURKEY FEATHERS!
AWW- HOW WUZ I T'KNOW?
YOU ATTACK BRAVES.... MUST BE PUNISHED! UGH! YOU TAKE CHOICE - EITHER MARRY THREE, OLD MAID SQUAWS AND MY 16 YEAR OLD DAUGHTER OR YOU BURN AT STAKE! YOU DECIDE NOW!
LOOK, EVEN GETTIN' MARRIED IS BETTER'N BEIN' BURNED ALIVE! TELL YA WHAT I'LL DO, I'LL GIVE YOU GUYS A HUNDRED BUCKS EACH, IF YOU AGREE THAT I GET TO MARRY THE CHIEF'S DAUGHTER - HOW ABOUT IT?
MAKE IT $200 AN' IT'S A DEAL!
GROAN OKAY! OKAY! $200 APIECE!
IT'S WORTH IT! BET THOSE THREE OLD-MAID SQUAWS ARE REAL DOGS!
OKAY, CHIEF! WE'LL TAKE DA SQUAWS AN' DIS GENTLEMAN, HERE, HAS AGREED TO MARRY YER DAUGHTER! BRING OUT DA GOILS!
UGH! WHITE MEN CRAZY! - UNTIE PRISONERS AND BRING FORTH THREE, OLD-MAID SQUAWS!

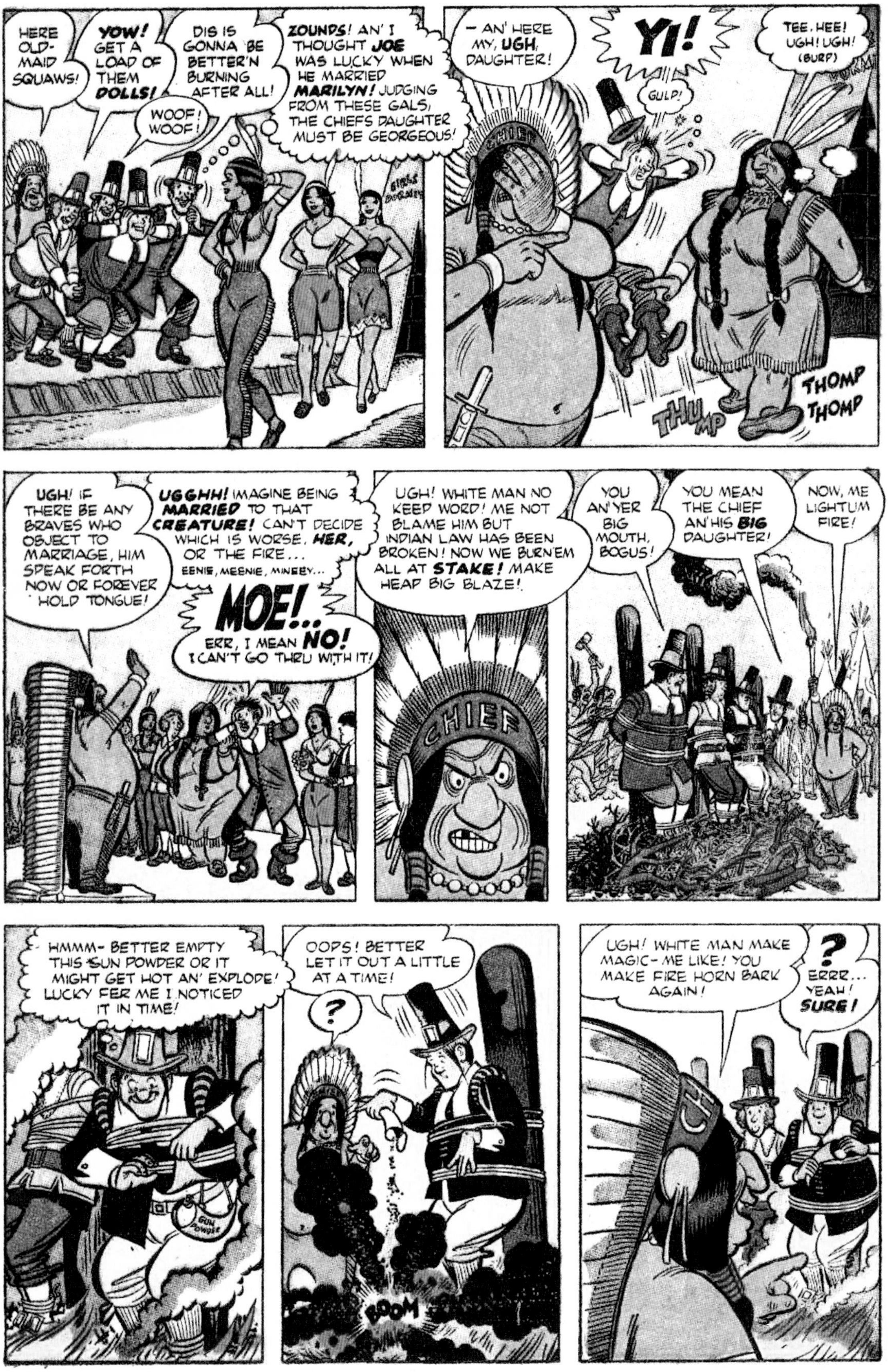
HERE OLD-MAID SQUAWS!
YOW! GET A LOAD OF THEM DOLLS!
DIS IS GONNA BE BETTER'N BURNING AFTER ALL!
WOOF! WOOF!
ZOUNDS! AN' I THOUGHT JOE WAS LUCKY WHEN HE MARRIED MARILYN! JUDGING FROM THESE GALS, THE CHIEF'S DAUGHTER MUST BE GEORGEOUS!
— AN' HERE MY, UGH, DAUGHTER!
CHIEF
YI!
GULP!
TEE. HEE! UGH! UGH! (BURP)
THUMP
THOMP THOMP
UGH! IF THERE BE ANY BRAVES WHO OBJECT TO MARRIAGE, HIM SPEAK FORTH NOW OR FOREVER HOLD TONGUE!
UGGHH! IMAGINE BEING MARRIED TO THAT CREATURE! CAN'T DECIDE WHICH IS WORSE, HER, OR THE FIRE... EENIE, MEENIE, MINEEY...
MOE!... ERR, I MEAN NO! I CAN'T GO THRU WITH IT!
UGH! WHITE MAN NO KEEP WORD! ME NOT BLAME HIM BUT INDIAN LAW HAS BEEN BROKEN! NOW WE BURN'EM ALL AT STAKE! MAKE HEAP BIG BLAZE!
CHIEF
YOU AN'YER BIG MOUTH, BOGUS!
YOU MEAN THE CHIEF AN'HIS BIG DAUGHTER!
NOW, ME LIGHTUM FIRE!
HMMM- BETTER EMPTY THIS GUN POWDER OR IT MIGHT GET HOT AN' EXPLODE! LUCKY FER ME I NOTICED IT IN TIME!
GUN POWDER
OOPS! BETTER LET IT OUT A LITTLE AT A TIME!
?
BOOM
UGH! WHITE MAN MAKE MAGIC- ME LIKE! YOU MAKE FIRE HORN BARK AGAIN!
? ERRR... YEAH! SURE!

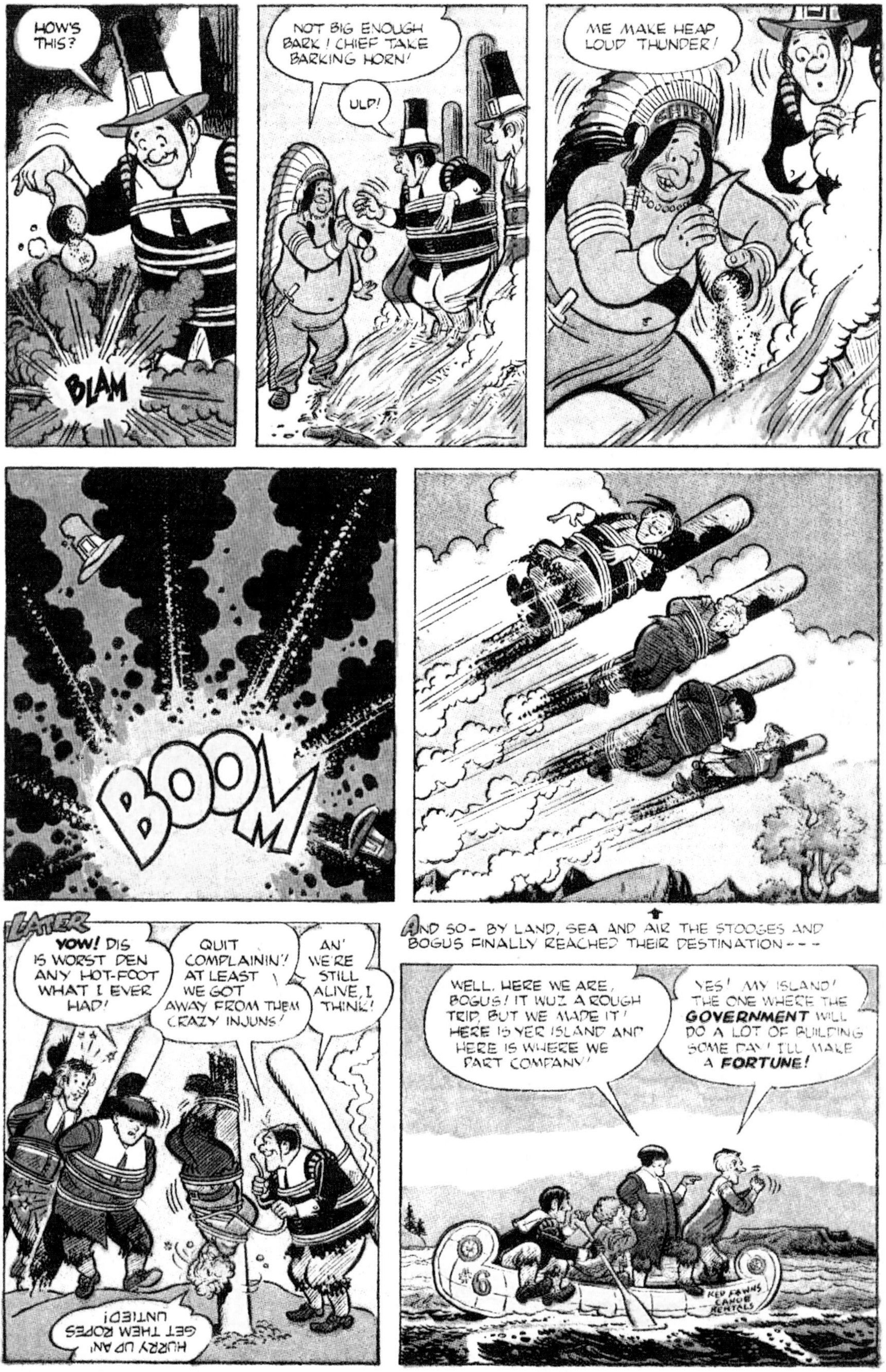
HOW'S THIS?
BLAM
NOT BIG ENOUGH BARK! CHIEF TAKE BARKING HORN!
ULP!
ME MAKE HEAP LOUD THUNDER!
CHIEF
BOOM
LATER
YOW! DIS IS WORST DEN ANY HOT-FOOT WHAT I EVER HAD!
QUIT COMPLAININ'! AT LEAST WE GOT AWAY FROM THEM CRAZY INJUNS!
AN' WE'RE STILL ALIVE, I THINK!
HURRY UP AN' GET THEM ROPES UNTIED!
AND SO- BY LAND, SEA AND AIR THE STOOGES AND BOGUS FINALLY REACHED THEIR DESTINATION---
WELL, HERE WE ARE, BOGUS! IT WUZ A ROUGH TRIP, BUT WE MADE IT! HERE IS YER ISLAND AND HERE IS WHERE WE PART COMPANY!
YES! MY ISLAND! THE ONE WHERE THE GOVERNMENT WILL DO A LOT OF BUILDING SOME DAY! I'LL MAKE A FORTUNE!
6
RED FAWNS CANOE RENTALS

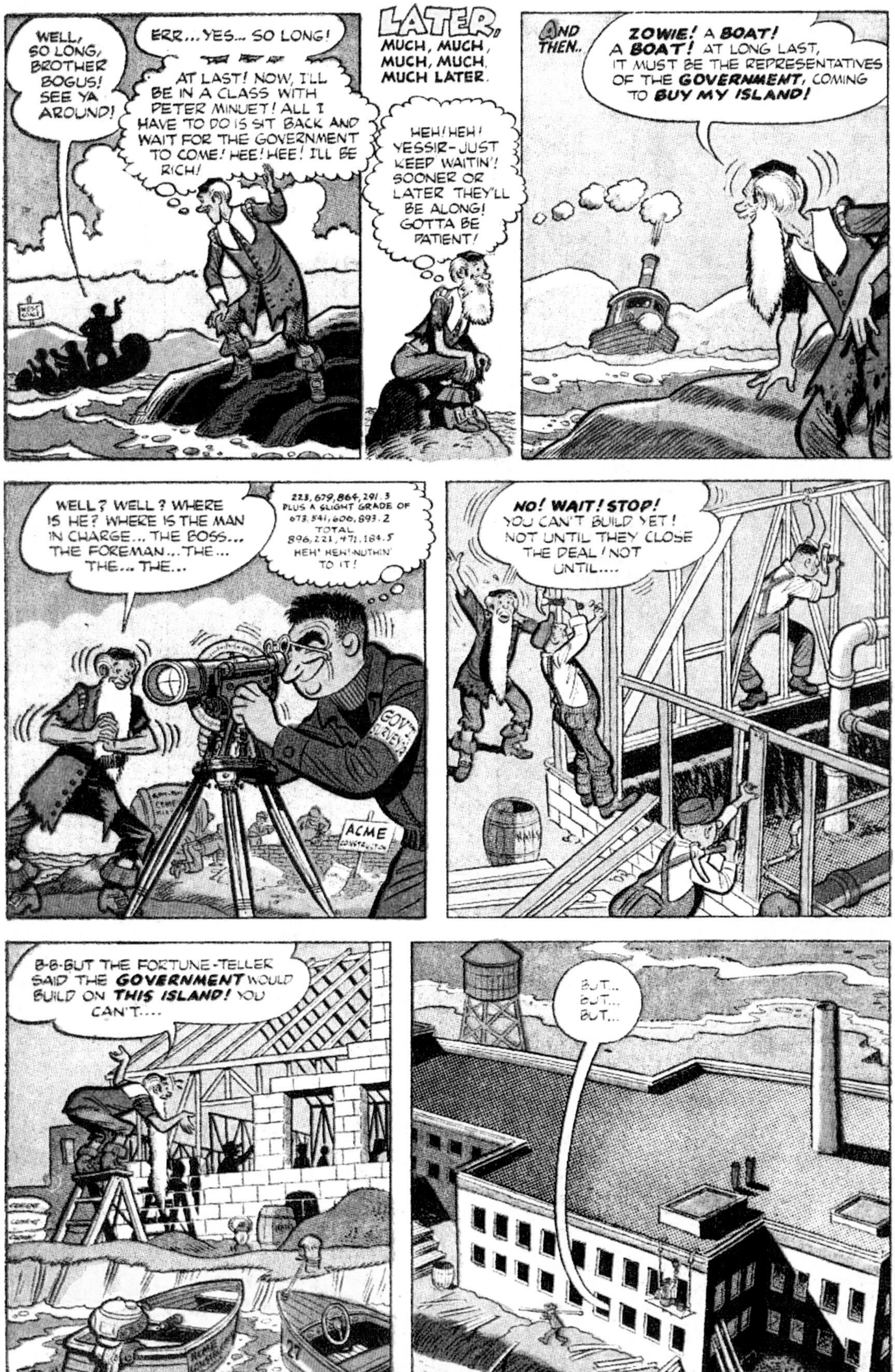
WELL, SO LONG, BROTHER BOGUS! SEE YA AROUND!
ERR... YES... SO LONG!
AT LAST! NOW, I'LL BE IN A CLASS WITH PETER MINUET! ALL I HAVE TO DO IS SIT BACK AND WAIT FOR THE GOVERNMENT TO COME! HEE! HEE! I'LL BE RICH!
LATER, MUCH, MUCH, MUCH, MUCH, MUCH LATER.
HEH! HEH! YESSIR- JUST KEEP WAITIN'! SOONER OR LATER THEY'LL BE ALONG! GOTTA BE PATIENT!
AND THEN..
ZOWIE! A BOAT! A BOAT! AT LONG LAST, IT MUST BE THE REPRESENTATIVES OF THE GOVERNMENT, COMING TO BUY MY ISLAND!
WELL? WELL? WHERE IS HE? WHERE IS THE MAN IN CHARGE... THE BOSS... THE FOREMAN... THE... THE... THE...
223,679,864,291.3 PLUS A SLIGHT GRADE OF 673,541,606,893.2 TOTAL 896,221,471,184.5 HEH' HEH'-NUTHIN' TO IT!
GOV'T SURVEYOR
ACME CONSTRUCTION
NO! WAIT! STOP! YOU CAN'T BUILD YET! NOT UNTIL THEY CLOSE THE DEAL! NOT UNTIL....
NAILS
B-B-BUT THE FORTUNE-TELLER SAID THE GOVERNMENT WOULD BUILD ON THIS ISLAND! YOU CAN'T....
BUT.. BUT... BUT...

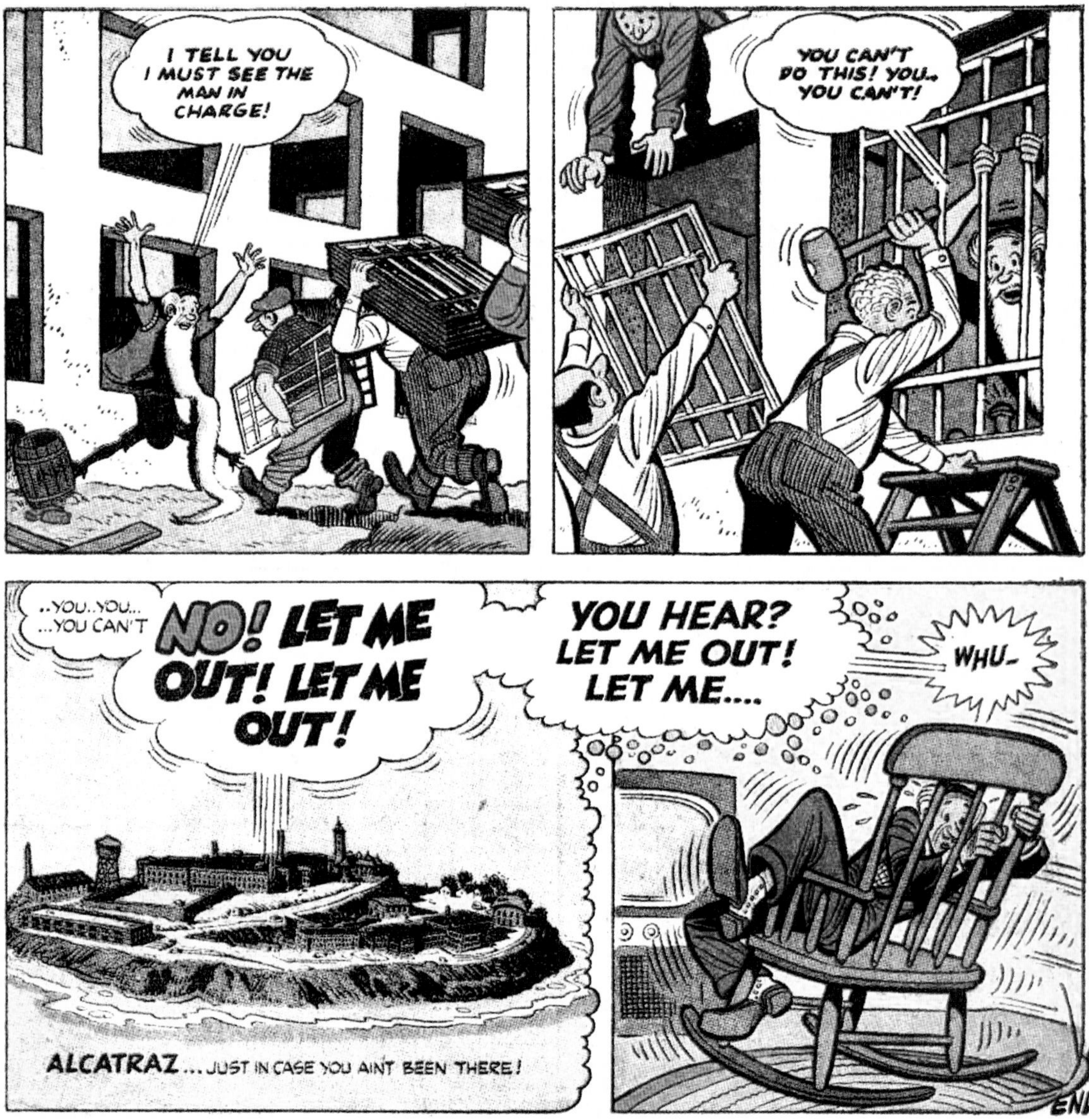
I TELL YOU I MUST SEE THE MAN IN CHARGE!
YOU CAN'T DO THIS! YOU.. YOU CAN'T!
..YOU..YOU... ...YOU CAN'T
NO! LET ME OUT! LET ME OUT!
YOU HEAR? LET ME OUT! LET ME....
WHU_
ALCATRAZ... JUST IN CASE YOU AIN'T BEEN THERE!
END

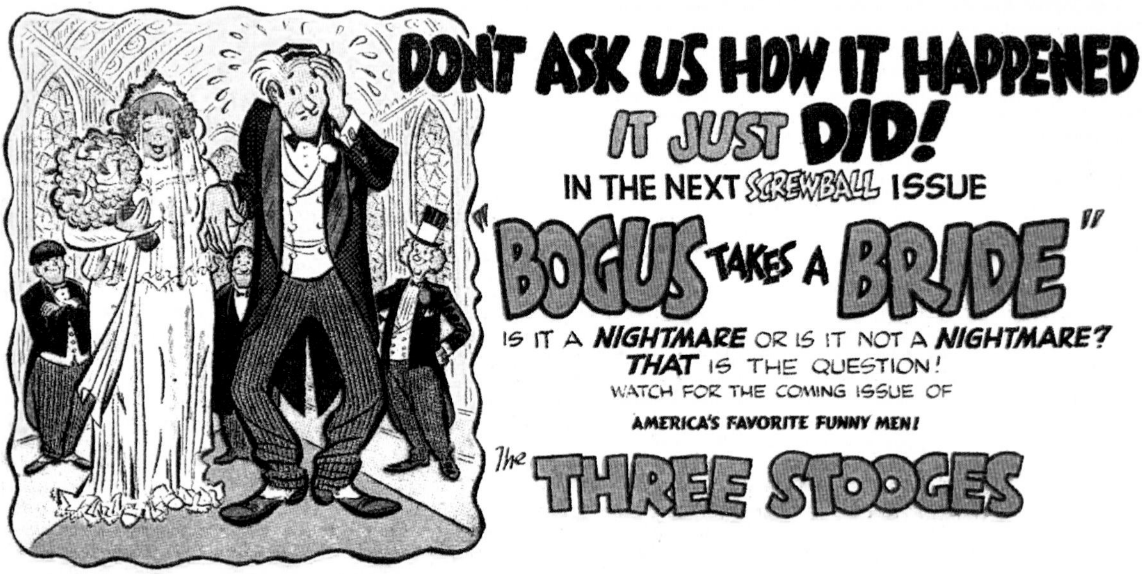
DON'T ASK US HOW IT HAPPENED
IT JUST DID!
IN THE NEXT SCREWBALL ISSUE
"BOGUS TAKES A BRIDE"
IS IT A NIGHTMARE OR IS IT NOT A NIGHTMARE?
THAT IS THE QUESTION!
WATCH FOR THE COMING ISSUE OF
AMERICA'S FAVORITE FUNNY MEN!
The THREE STOOGES

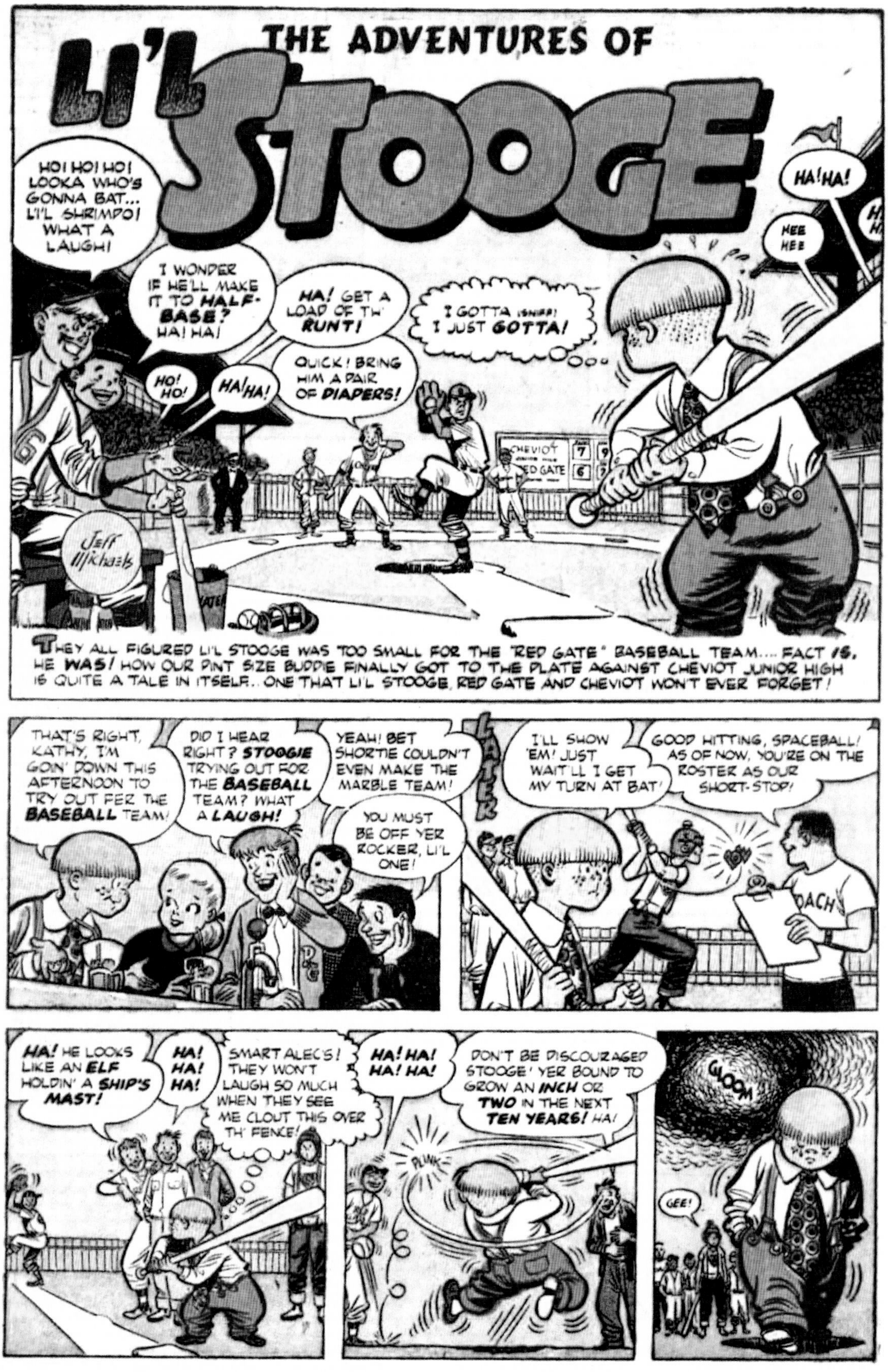
THE ADVENTURES OF
LI'L STOOGE
HO! HO! HO! LOOKA WHO'S GONNA BAT... LI'L SHRIMPO! WHAT A LAUGH!
I WONDER IF HE'LL MAKE IT TO HALF-BASE? HA! HA!
HA! GET A LOAD OF TH' RUNT!
HO! HO!
HA! HA!
QUICK! BRING HIM A PAIR OF DIAPERS!
I GOTTA (SNIFF) I JUST GOTTA!
HA! HA!
HEE HEE
CHEVIOT
RED GATE
Jeff Michaels
THEY ALL FIGURED LI'L STOOGE WAS TOO SMALL FOR THE "RED GATE" BASEBALL TEAM.... FACT IS, HE WAS! HOW OUR PINT SIZE BUDDIE FINALLY GOT TO THE PLATE AGAINST CHEVIOT JUNIOR HIGH IS QUITE A TALE IN ITSELF.. ONE THAT LI'L STOOGE, RED GATE AND CHEVIOT WON'T EVER FORGET!
THAT'S RIGHT, KATHY, I'M GOIN' DOWN THIS AFTERNOON TO TRY OUT FER THE BASEBALL TEAM!
DID I HEAR RIGHT? STOOGIE TRYING OUT FOR THE BASEBALL TEAM? WHAT A LAUGH!
YEAH! BET SHORTIE COULDN'T EVEN MAKE THE MARBLE TEAM!
YOU MUST BE OFF YER ROCKER, LI'L ONE!
LATER
I'LL SHOW 'EM! JUST WAIT'LL I GET MY TURN AT BAT!
GOOD HITTING, SPACEBALL! AS OF NOW, YOU'RE ON THE ROSTER AS OUR SHORT-STOP!
COACH
HA! HE LOOKS LIKE AN ELF HOLDIN' A SHIP'S MAST!
HA! HA! HA!
SMART ALEC'S! THEY WON'T LAUGH SO MUCH WHEN THEY SEE ME CLOUT THIS OVER TH' FENCE!
HA! HA! HA! HA!
DON'T BE DISCOURAGED STOOGE' YER BOUND TO GROW AN INCH OR TWO IN THE NEXT TEN YEARS! HA!
PLINK
GLOOM
GEE!

GEE WHIZ, STOOGIE, YOU BEEN SULKING ALL EVENING! YA SHOULDN'T TAKE IT SO HARD! THEY'LL GIVE YOU ANOTHER TRY-OUT NEXT SEASON... MAYBE THEN YOU..

YEAH! MAYBE I'LL GROW A FEW FEET, TOO... NUTS! I'M GOIN' FER A WALK IN THE PARK....ALONE!

FOOEY! KATHY MUST THINK I'M A REAL, GONE, SISSY! HOW'M I GONNA FACE HER AN'....

YOU HEARD ME! AN' KEEP 'EM UP!

HUH? HOLY SMOKE! A STICK-UP!

THUMP

OOF

?

THAT WAS MIGHTY QUICK THINKING, SON! AND QUICK ACTING, TOO — YOU KNOCKED THE ROTTEN CROOK COLD! FIRST, WE'LL GET A POLICEMAN AN' THEN I'M GONNA BUY YOU THE BIGGEST HAMBURGER IN TOWN!

TWEET

OKAY, SON, YOU MIGHT AS WELL TELL ME ALL ABOUT IT! I OFFER YOU A $50 REWARD BUY YOU 'BURGERS AND ALL YOU DO IS ACT LIKE YOU LOST YOUR BEST PAL! JUST WHAT IS IT THAT'S TROUBLING YOU? MAYBE I CAN HELP!

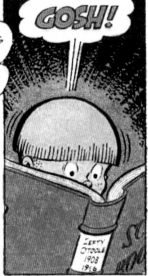

...AN' THAT'S THE WHOLE STORY, MISTER! I WANTED MORE THAN ANYTHING IN THE WORLD TO PLAY ON THE BASEBALL TEAM.. BUT IT'S NO USE! I'M JUST TOO SMALL TO MAKE THE GRADE! NO ONE CAN HELP ME!

HMMM.... YOU MAY BE MISTAKEN, LITTLE FELLER! I MIGHT! YOU COME OVER TO MY APARTMENT AND WE'LL SEE WHAT WE CAN FIGURE OUT!

THIS HERE'S A REAL NICE PLACE, BUT I STILL DON'T SEE HOW YOU CAN HELP ME!

WHEN I TOLD YOU MY NAME WAS LEFTY O'TOOLE, IT DIDN'T MEAN ANYTHING TO YOU! YOU'RE A BIT TOO YOUNG TO HAVE HEARD OF ME, SO I GUESS YOU'LL JUST HAVE TO TAKE A LOOK AT THIS!

GOSH!

LEFTY O'TOOLE 1908 1916

HOLY GEE!

O'TOOLE WINS WORLD SERIES WITH BUNT

LEFTY O'TOOLE HERO OF 1915 WORLD SERIES
Precision bunting pays dividends

O'TOOLE NAMED MOST VALUABLE PLAYER OF 1916
Bunting record proves importance of short hit

GIANTS W... PENNANT 1... Ninth inning bunt by O'Toole wins crucial game

FANS ASTOUNDED AS O'TOOLE CALLS SHOT AND BUNTS IN WINNING RUN

I CAN'T BLAME YOU FOR NOT HAVING HEARD OF ME.... I SUPPOSE IT WAS A BIT BEFORE *YOUR* TIME... BUT I HAVEN'T FORGOTTEN ALL THE TRICKS OF BUNTING AND I THINK I COULD TEACH 'EM TO *YOU!* HOW ABOUT IT?

GOLLY, WOULD YOU?

G'NIGHT, LI'L STOOGE! I'LL SEE YOU IN THE MORNING... THE FIELD NEAR THE ZOO! DON'T FORGET, NINE SHARP!

I WOULDN'T MISS IT FOR ANYTHING, MR. O'TOOLE, AND THANKS *MILLIONS!*

NO! NO! HIT IT HIGHER ON THE BAT!

BETTER, ONLY WATCH YOUR GRIP... GOTTA HOLD THE BAT FIRMLY!

PERFECT! PERFECT! THAT'S *SIX* IN A ROW! YOU'RE DOIN' *GREAT!*

IT'S BEEN FOUR WEEKS, LI'L STOOGE, AN NOW YOU'RE *REALLY* READY TO TRY OUT FOR YOUR TEAM AGAIN!

I'LL MAKE IT THIS TIME FER *SURE,* THANKS TO YOU, MR. O'TOOLE!

LATER

BUT, COACH, YA *GOTTA* GIVE ME ANOTHER CHANCE! JUST LET ME SHOW YA! I TELL YA IT'S DIFFERENT NOW! I CAN....

I'M SORRY, FELLA, BUT THERE ISN'T A CHANCE! YOU'RE JUST NOT BIG ENOUGH!

COACH

AW, DON'T TAKE IT SO HARD, PAL! LIKE I SAID.... MAYBE NEXT SEASON!

CUT IT, SPACEBALL, I JUST DON'T WANNA TALK ABOUT IT NO MORE!

GOSH, KID, HOW LONG YOU GONNA KEEP UP THIS MOPING AROUND? EVER SINCE THE COACH REFUSED YOU A TRY-OUT LAST WEEK, YOU'VE BEEN A REAL CRAB-APPLE! C'MON, TODAY'S THE BIG GAME WITH CHEVIOT JUNIOR HIGH, AN' YOU'RE GONNA WATCH IT!

AWW! OKAY!

GOLLY GEE! THEY'RE LEADING US **7** TO **6**! AN' ONLY *ONE* INNING TO GO! I SURE WISH I WUZ PLAYING!

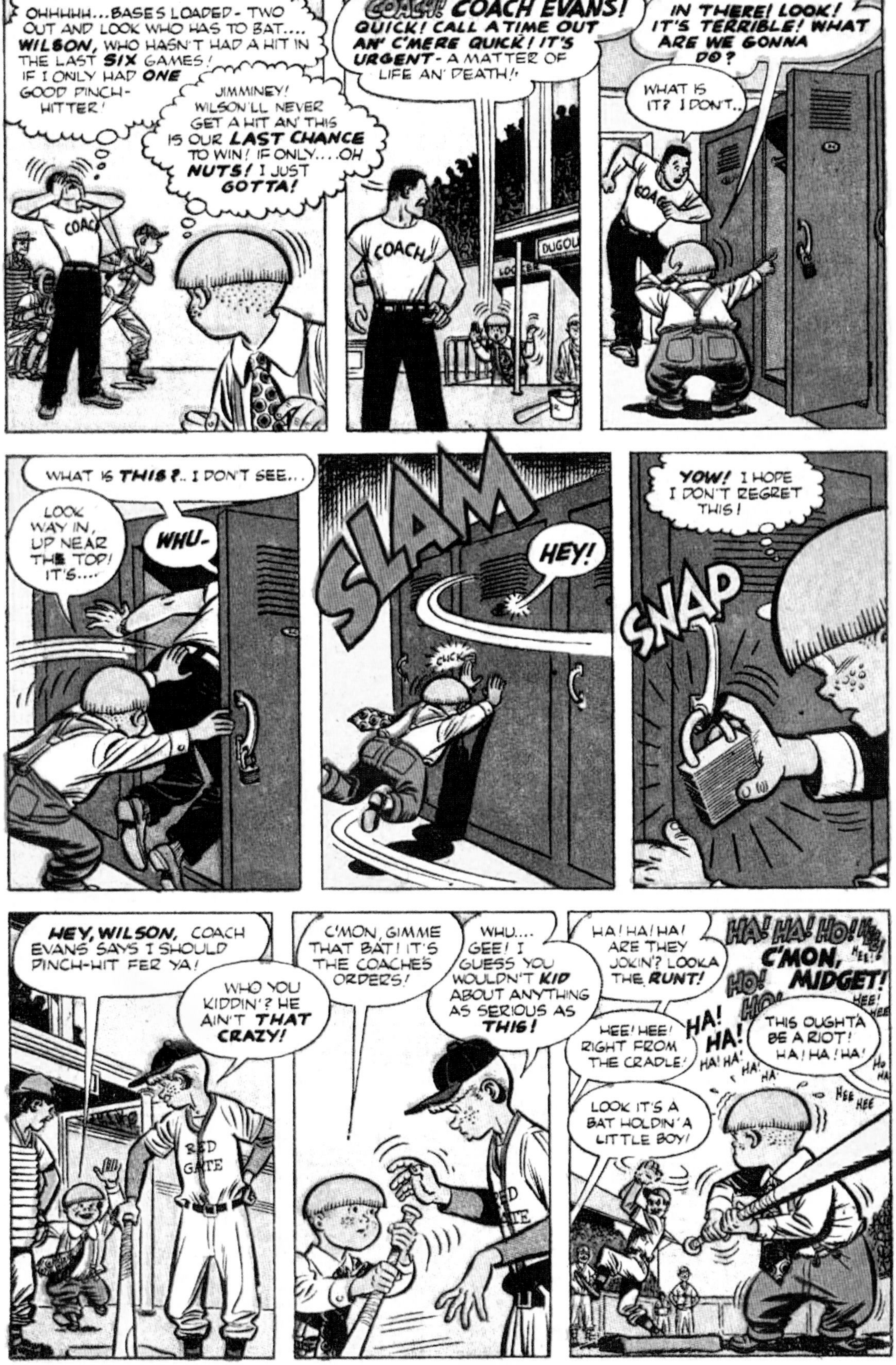
OHHHHH...BASES LOADED - TWO OUT AND LOOK WHO HAS TO BAT.... WILSON, WHO HASN'T HAD A HIT IN THE LAST SIX GAMES! IF I ONLY HAD ONE GOOD PINCH-HITTER!
JIMMINEY! WILSON'LL NEVER GET A HIT AN' THIS IS OUR LAST CHANCE TO WIN! IF ONLY....OH NUTS! I JUST GOTTA!
COACH
COACH! COACH EVANS! QUICK! CALL A TIME OUT AN' C'MERE QUICK! IT'S URGENT - A MATTER OF LIFE AN' DEATH!
COACH
DUGOU
LOCKER
IN THERE! LOOK! IT'S TERRIBLE! WHAT ARE WE GONNA DO?
WHAT IS IT? I DON'T..
COA
WHAT IS THIS?.. I DON'T SEE...
LOOK WAY IN, UP NEAR THE TOP! IT'S....
WHU-
SLAM
HEY!
CLICK
YOW! I HOPE I DON'T REGRET THIS!
SNAP
HEY, WILSON, COACH EVANS SAYS I SHOULD PINCH-HIT FER YA!
WHO YOU KIDDIN'? HE AIN'T THAT CRAZY!
RED GATE
C'MON, GIMME THAT BAT! IT'S THE COACHE'S ORDERS!
WHU.... GEE! I GUESS YOU WOULDN'T KID ABOUT ANYTHING AS SERIOUS AS THIS!
HA! HA! HA! ARE THEY JOKIN'? LOOKA THE RUNT!
HA! HA! HO! C'MON, MIDGET!
HEE! HEE! RIGHT FROM THE CRADLE!
HA! HA!
THIS OUGHTA BE A RIOT! HA! HA! HA!
LOOK IT'S A BAT HOLDIN' A LITTLE BOY!

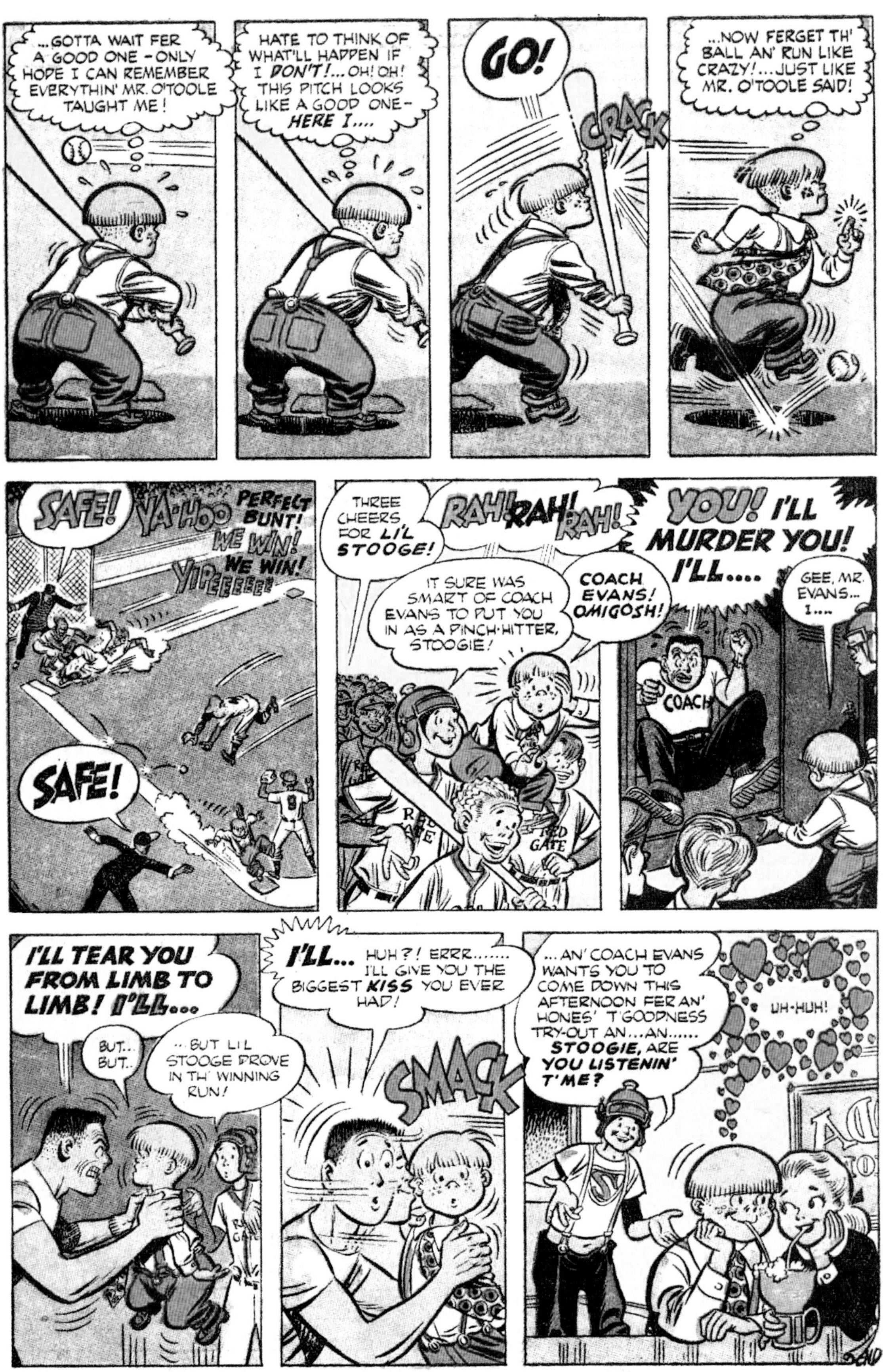
...GOTTA WAIT FER A GOOD ONE - ONLY HOPE I CAN REMEMBER EVERYTHIN' MR. O'TOOLE TAUGHT ME!
HATE TO THINK OF WHAT'LL HAPPEN IF I DON'T!... OH! OH! THIS PITCH LOOKS LIKE A GOOD ONE- HERE I....
GO!
CRACK
...NOW FERGET TH' BALL AN' RUN LIKE CRAZY!... JUST LIKE MR. O'TOOLE SAID!
SAFE!
YA-HOO
PERFECT BUNT!
WE WIN!
WE WIN!
YIPEEEEE!
SAFE!
THREE CHEERS FOR LI'L STOOGE!
RAH! RAH! RAH!
IT SURE WAS SMART OF COACH EVANS TO PUT YOU IN AS A PINCH-HITTER, STOOGIE!
COACH EVANS! OMIGOSH!
YOU! I'LL MURDER YOU! I'LL....
GEE, MR. EVANS... I....
COACH
I'LL TEAR YOU FROM LIMB TO LIMB! I'LL...
BUT... BUT..
...BUT LI'L STOOGE DROVE IN TH' WINNING RUN!
I'LL... HUH?! ERRR....... I'LL GIVE YOU THE BIGGEST KISS YOU EVER HAD!
SMACK
...AN' COACH EVANS WANTS YOU TO COME DOWN THIS AFTERNOON FER AN' HONES' T'GOODNESS TRY-OUT AN...AN...... STOOGIE, ARE YOU LISTENIN' T'ME?
UH-HUH!
END

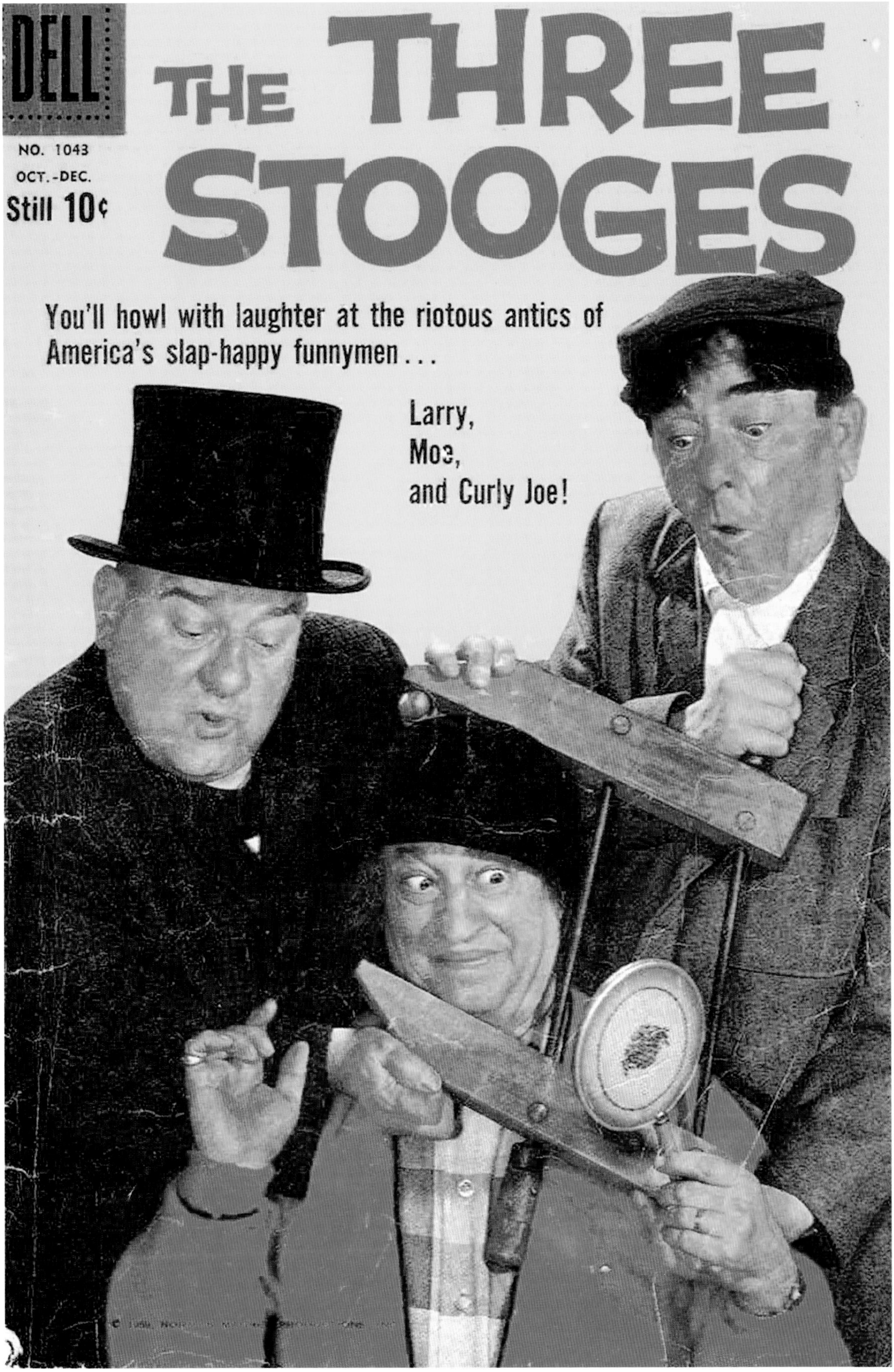
DELL
THE THREE STOOGES
NO. 1043
OCT.-DEC.
Still 10¢
You'll howl with laughter at the riotous antics of America's slap-happy funnymen...
Larry,
Moe,
and Curly Joe!

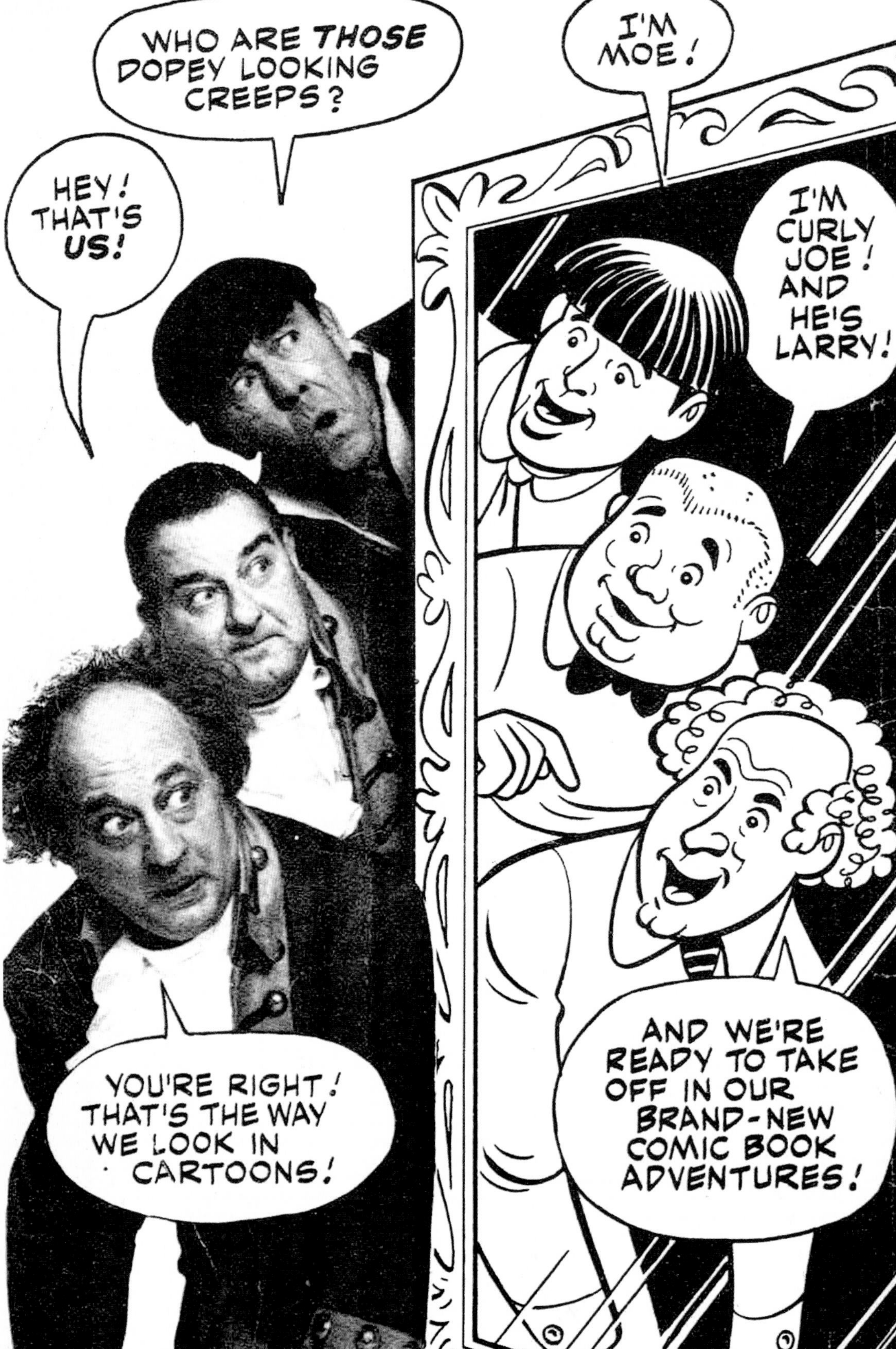
WHO ARE *THOSE* DOPEY LOOKING CREEPS?
I'M MOE!
HEY! THAT'S *US*!
I'M CURLY JOE! AND HE'S LARRY!
YOU'RE RIGHT! THAT'S THE WAY WE LOOK IN CARTOONS!
AND WE'RE READY TO TAKE OFF IN OUR BRAND-NEW COMIC BOOK ADVENTURES!

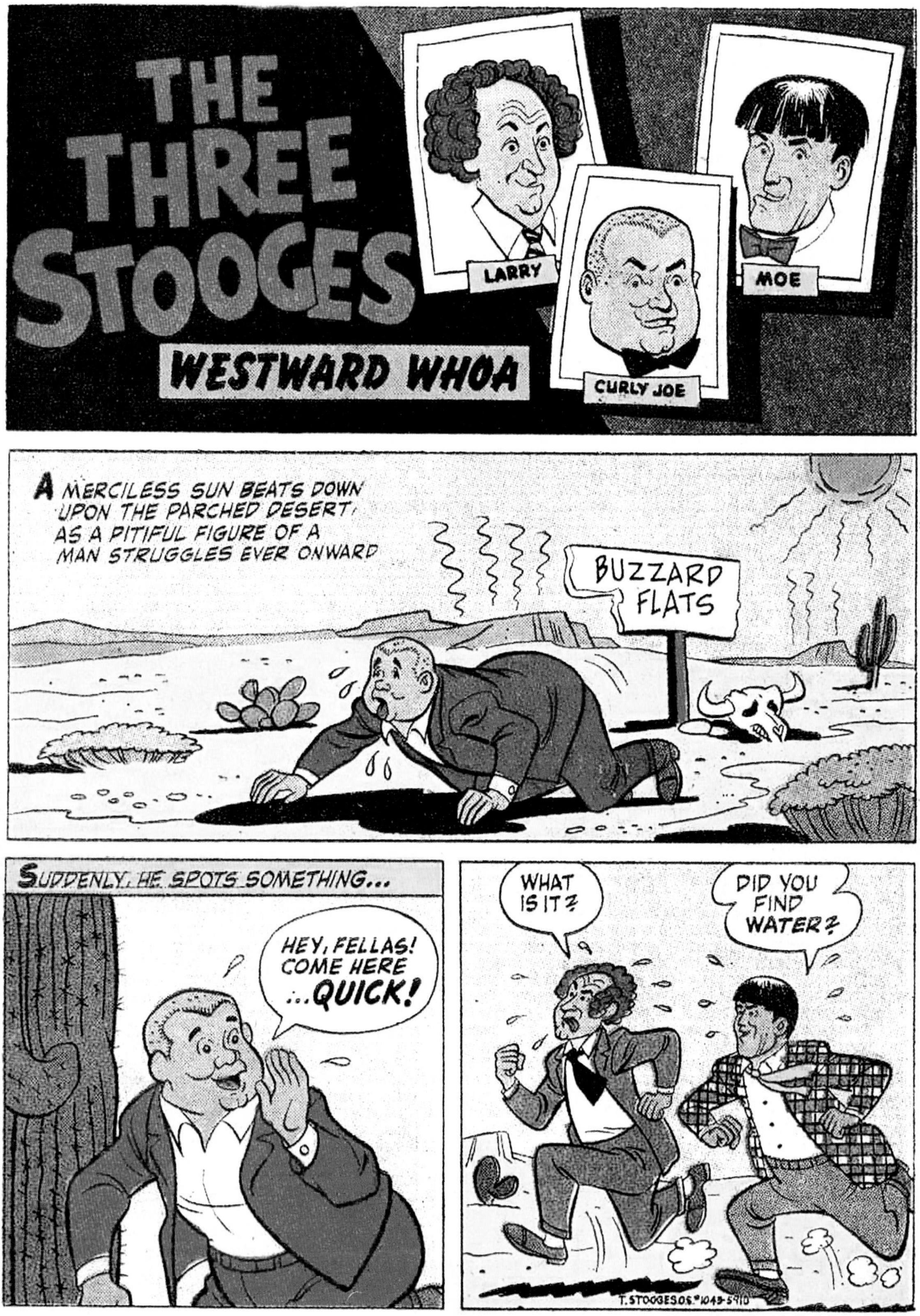
THE THREE STOOGES
LARRY
CURLY JOE
MOE
WESTWARD WHOA
A MERCILESS SUN BEATS DOWN UPON THE PARCHED DESERT, AS A PITIFUL FIGURE OF A MAN STRUGGLES EVER ONWARD
BUZZARD FLATS
SUDDENLY, HE SPOTS SOMETHING...
HEY, FELLAS! COME HERE ...QUICK!
WHAT IS IT?
DID YOU FIND WATER?

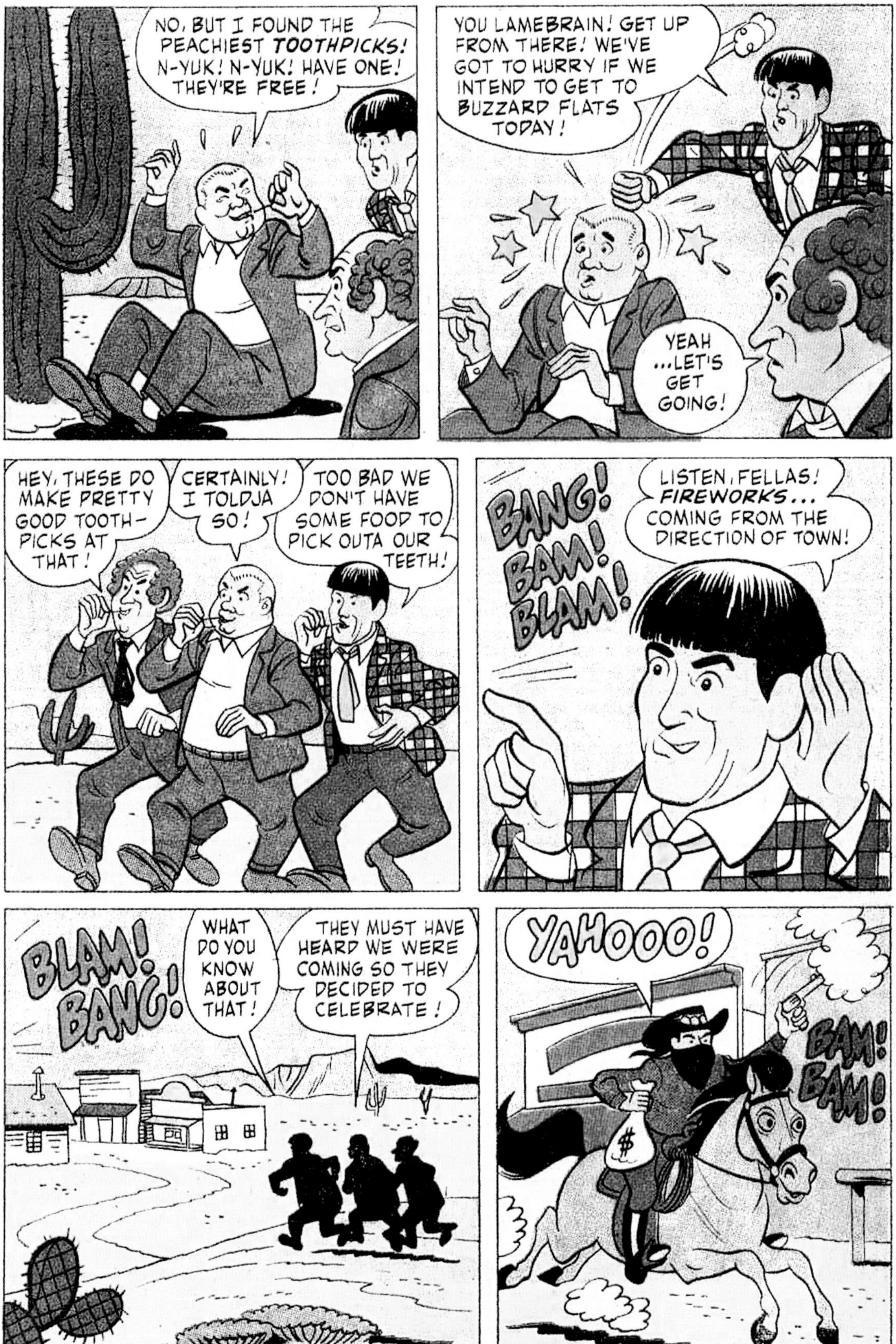

NO, BUT I FOUND THE PEACHIEST TOOTHPICKS! N-YUK! N-YUK! HAVE ONE! THEY'RE FREE!
YOU LAMEBRAIN! GET UP FROM THERE! WE'VE GOT TO HURRY IF WE INTEND TO GET TO BUZZARD FLATS TODAY!
YEAH ...LET'S GET GOING!
HEY, THESE DO MAKE PRETTY GOOD TOOTH-PICKS AT THAT!
CERTAINLY! I TOLDJA SO!
TOO BAD WE DON'T HAVE SOME FOOD TO PICK OUTA OUR TEETH!
BANG! BAM! BLAM!
LISTEN, FELLAS! FIREWORKS... COMING FROM THE DIRECTION OF TOWN!
BLAM! BANG!
WHAT DO YOU KNOW ABOUT THAT!
THEY MUST HAVE HEARD WE WERE COMING SO THEY DECIDED TO CELEBRATE!
YAHOOO!
BAM! BAM!

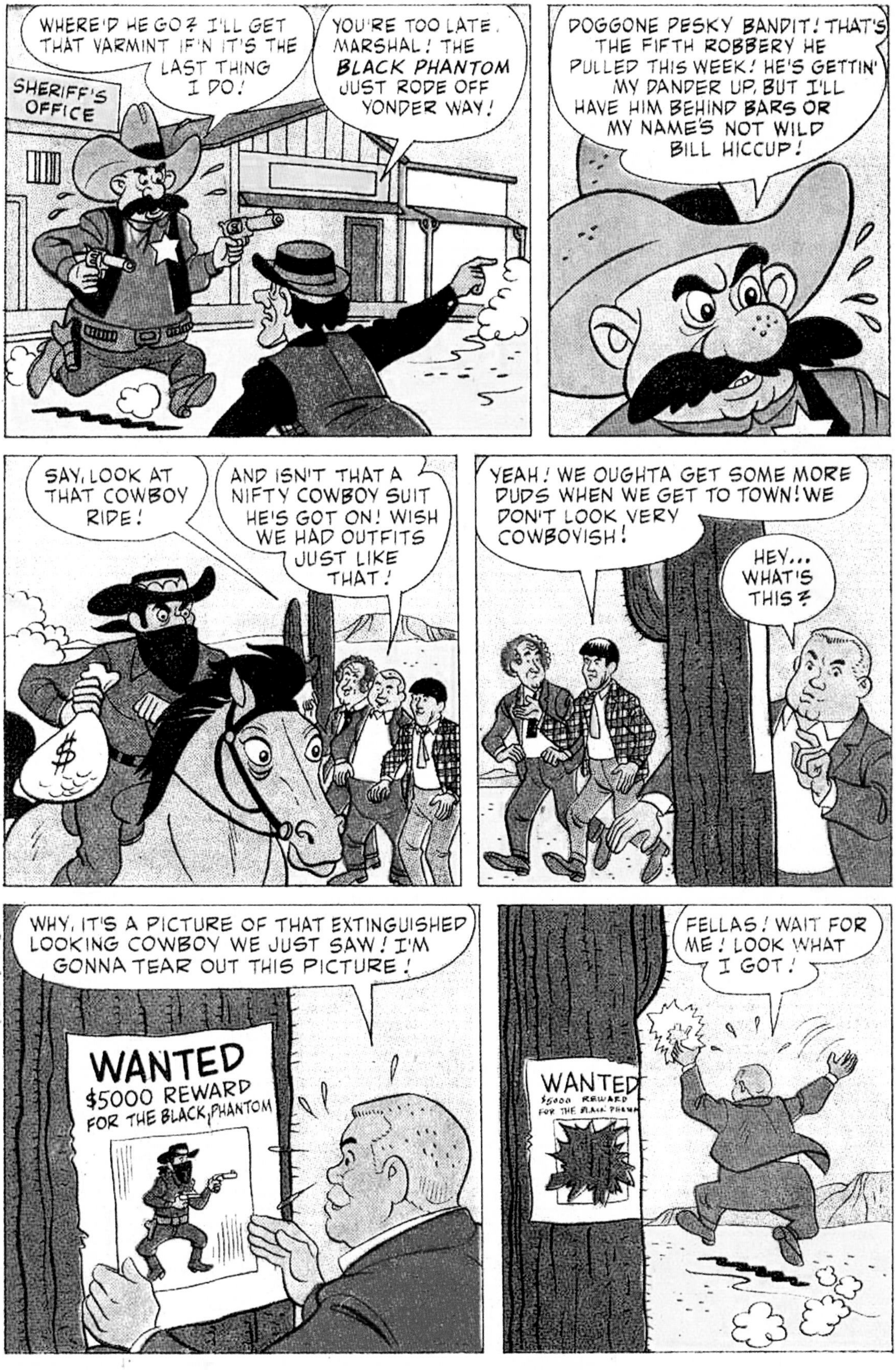
WHERE'D HE GO? I'LL GET THAT VARMINT IF'N IT'S THE LAST THING I DO!
SHERIFF'S OFFICE
YOU'RE TOO LATE, MARSHAL! THE BLACK PHANTOM JUST RODE OFF YONDER WAY!
DOGGONE PESKY BANDIT! THAT'S THE FIFTH ROBBERY HE PULLED THIS WEEK! HE'S GETTIN' MY DANDER UP, BUT I'LL HAVE HIM BEHIND BARS OR MY NAME'S NOT WILD BILL HICCUP!
SAY, LOOK AT THAT COWBOY RIDE!
AND ISN'T THAT A NIFTY COWBOY SUIT HE'S GOT ON! WISH WE HAD OUTFITS JUST LIKE THAT!
YEAH! WE OUGHTA GET SOME MORE DUDS WHEN WE GET TO TOWN! WE DON'T LOOK VERY COWBOYISH!
HEY... WHAT'S THIS?
WHY, IT'S A PICTURE OF THAT EXTINGUISHED LOOKING COWBOY WE JUST SAW! I'M GONNA TEAR OUT THIS PICTURE!
WANTED
$5000 REWARD
FOR THE BLACK PHANTOM
FELLAS! WAIT FOR ME! LOOK WHAT I GOT!
WANTED

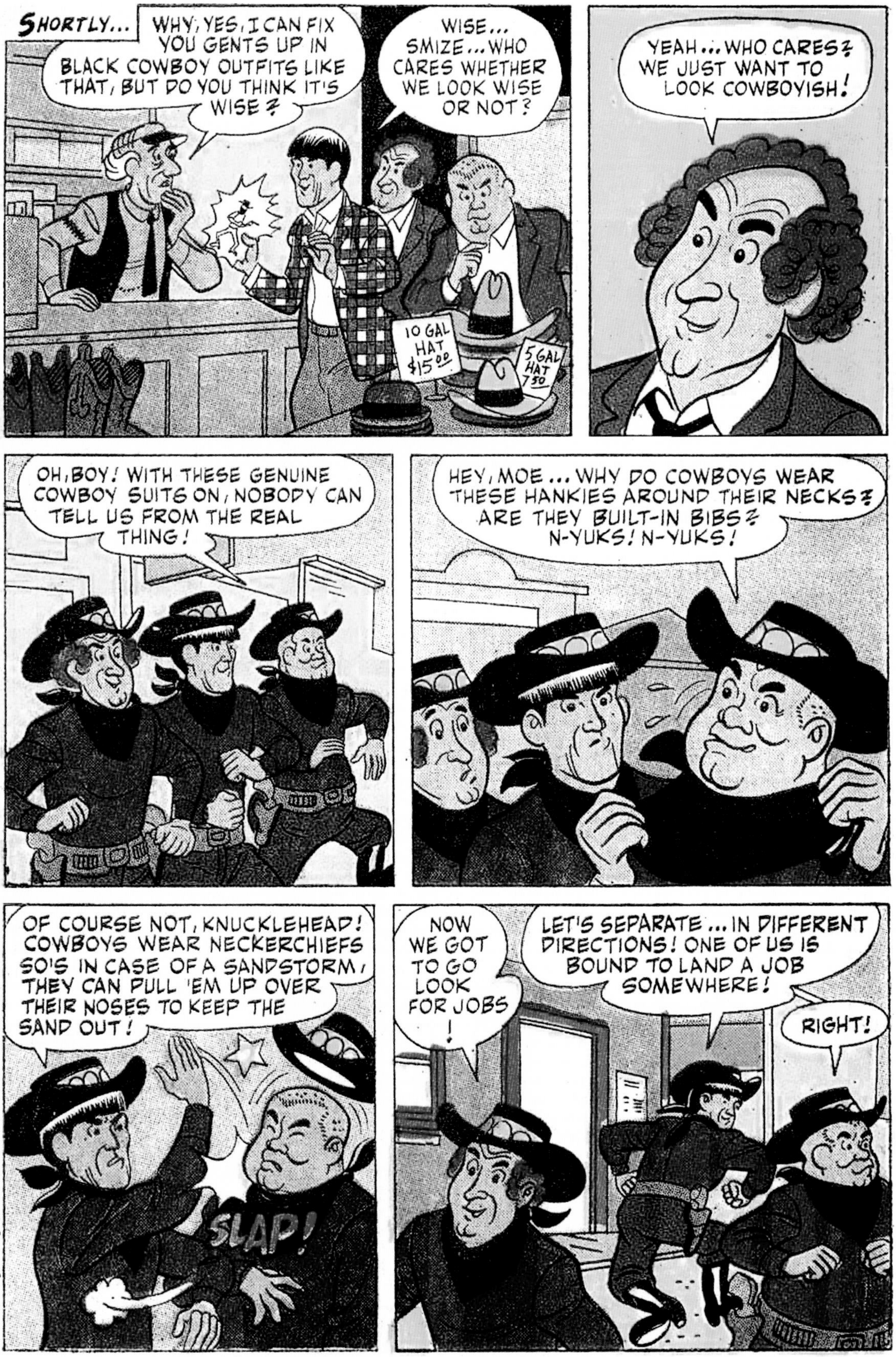
SHORTLY...
WHY, YES, I CAN FIX YOU GENTS UP IN BLACK COWBOY OUTFITS LIKE THAT, BUT DO YOU THINK IT'S WISE?
WISE... SMIZE... WHO CARES WHETHER WE LOOK WISE OR NOT?
10 GAL HAT $15.00
5 GAL HAT 7.50
YEAH... WHO CARES? WE JUST WANT TO LOOK COWBOYISH!
OH, BOY! WITH THESE GENUINE COWBOY SUITS ON, NOBODY CAN TELL US FROM THE REAL THING!
HEY, MOE... WHY DO COWBOYS WEAR THESE HANKIES AROUND THEIR NECKS? ARE THEY BUILT-IN BIBS? N-YUKS! N-YUKS!
OF COURSE NOT, KNUCKLEHEAD! COWBOYS WEAR NECKERCHIEFS SO'S IN CASE OF A SANDSTORM, THEY CAN PULL 'EM UP OVER THEIR NOSES TO KEEP THE SAND OUT!
SLAP!
NOW WE GOT TO GO LOOK FOR JOBS!
LET'S SEPARATE... IN DIFFERENT DIRECTIONS! ONE OF US IS BOUND TO LAND A JOB SOMEWHERE!
RIGHT!

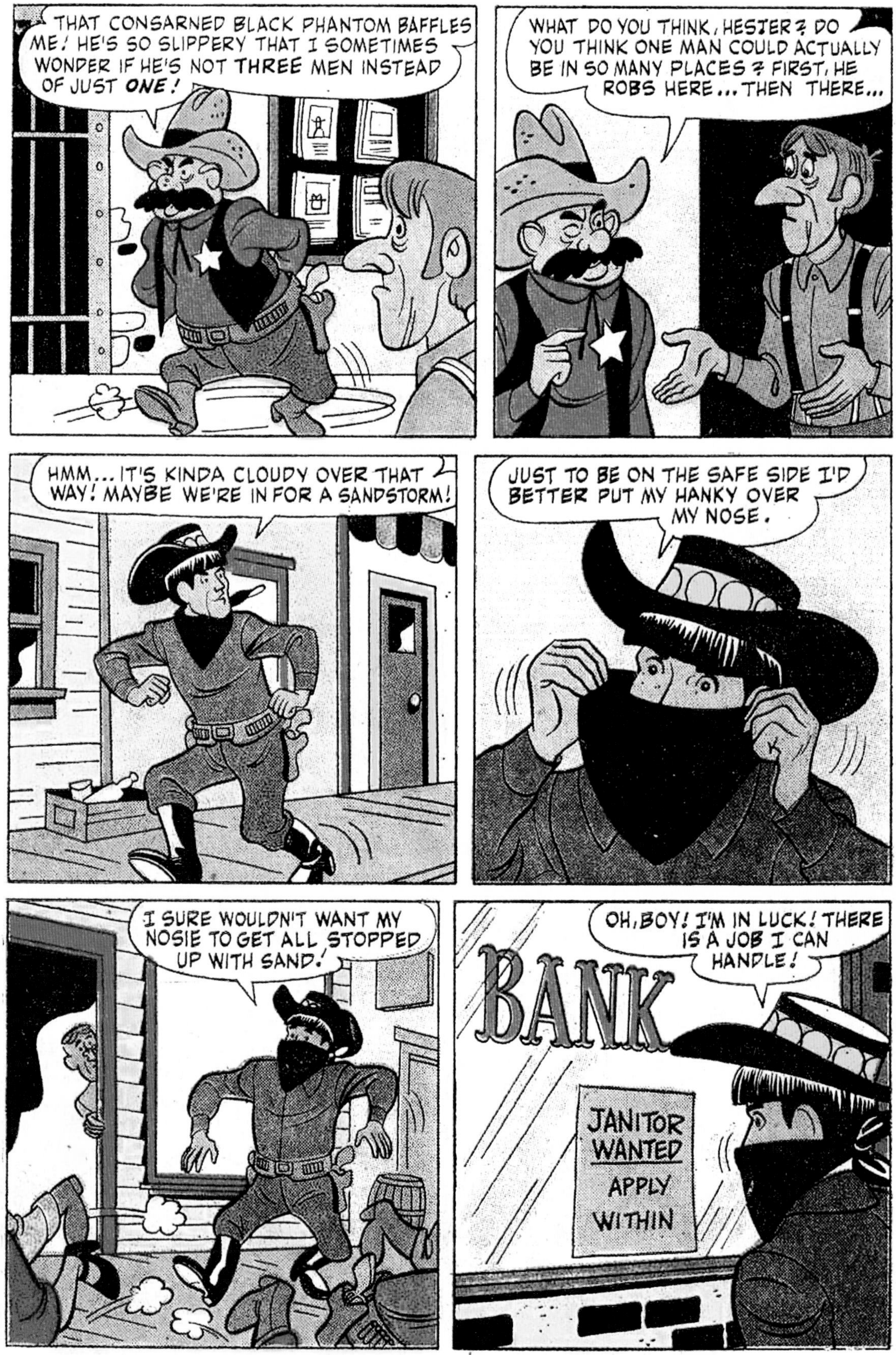
THAT CONSARNED BLACK PHANTOM BAFFLES ME! HE'S SO SLIPPERY THAT I SOMETIMES WONDER IF HE'S NOT THREE MEN INSTEAD OF JUST ONE!
WHAT DO YOU THINK, HESTER? DO YOU THINK ONE MAN COULD ACTUALLY BE IN SO MANY PLACES? FIRST, HE ROBS HERE... THEN THERE...
HMM... IT'S KINDA CLOUDY OVER THAT WAY! MAYBE WE'RE IN FOR A SANDSTORM!
JUST TO BE ON THE SAFE SIDE I'D BETTER PUT MY HANKY OVER MY NOSE.
I SURE WOULDN'T WANT MY NOSIE TO GET ALL STOPPED UP WITH SAND!
OH, BOY! I'M IN LUCK! THERE IS A JOB I CAN HANDLE!
BANK
JANITOR WANTED
APPLY WITHIN

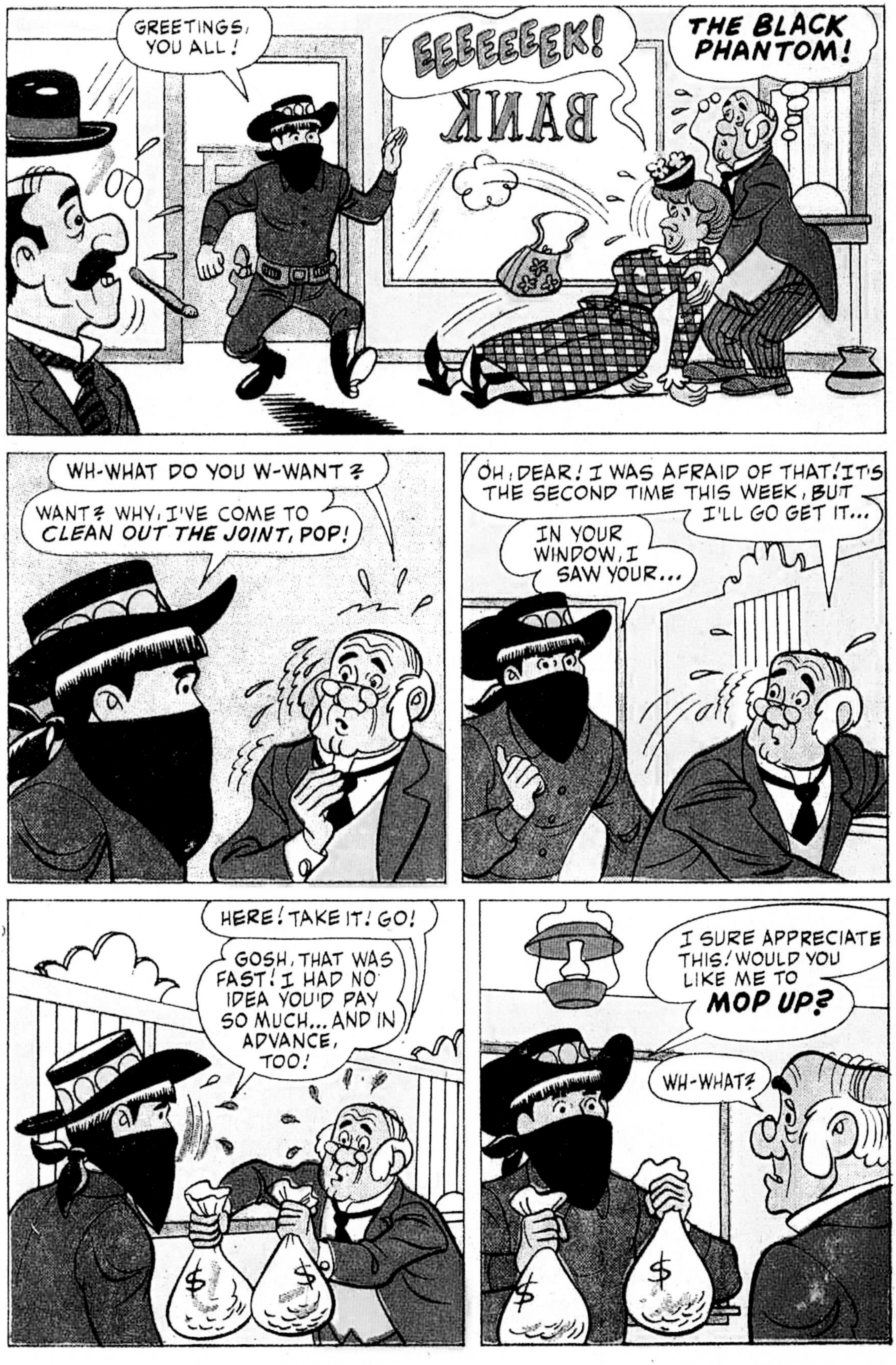
GREETINGS, YOU ALL!
EEEEEEEK!
BANK
THE BLACK PHANTOM!
WH-WHAT DO YOU W-WANT?
WANT? WHY, I'VE COME TO CLEAN OUT THE JOINT, POP!
OH, DEAR! I WAS AFRAID OF THAT! IT'S THE SECOND TIME THIS WEEK, BUT
IN YOUR WINDOW, I SAW YOUR...
I'LL GO GET IT...
HERE! TAKE IT! GO!
GOSH, THAT WAS FAST! I HAD NO IDEA YOU'D PAY SO MUCH... AND IN ADVANCE, TOO!
I SURE APPRECIATE THIS! WOULD YOU LIKE ME TO MOP UP?
WH-WHAT?

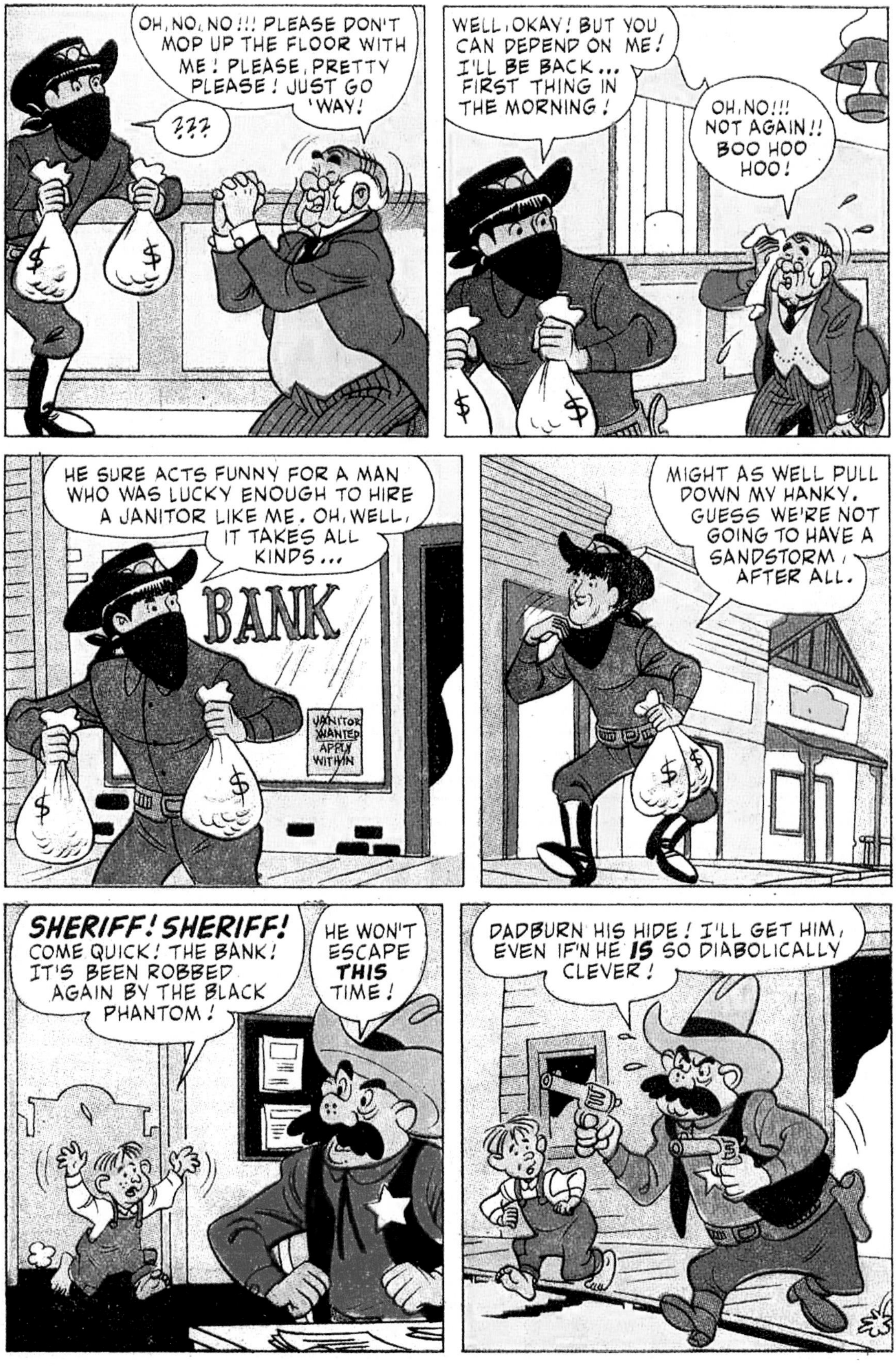
OH, NO, NO!!! PLEASE DON'T MOP UP THE FLOOR WITH ME! PLEASE, PRETTY PLEASE! JUST GO 'WAY!
???
WELL, OKAY! BUT YOU CAN DEPEND ON ME! I'LL BE BACK... FIRST THING IN THE MORNING!
OH, NO!!! NOT AGAIN!! BOO HOO HOO!
HE SURE ACTS FUNNY FOR A MAN WHO WAS LUCKY ENOUGH TO HIRE A JANITOR LIKE ME. OH, WELL, IT TAKES ALL KINDS...
BANK
JANITOR WANTED APPLY WITHIN
MIGHT AS WELL PULL DOWN MY HANKY. GUESS WE'RE NOT GOING TO HAVE A SANDSTORM, AFTER ALL.
SHERIFF! SHERIFF! COME QUICK! THE BANK! IT'S BEEN ROBBED AGAIN BY THE BLACK PHANTOM!
HE WON'T ESCAPE THIS TIME!
DADBURN HIS HIDE! I'LL GET HIM, EVEN IF'N HE IS SO DIABOLICALLY CLEVER!

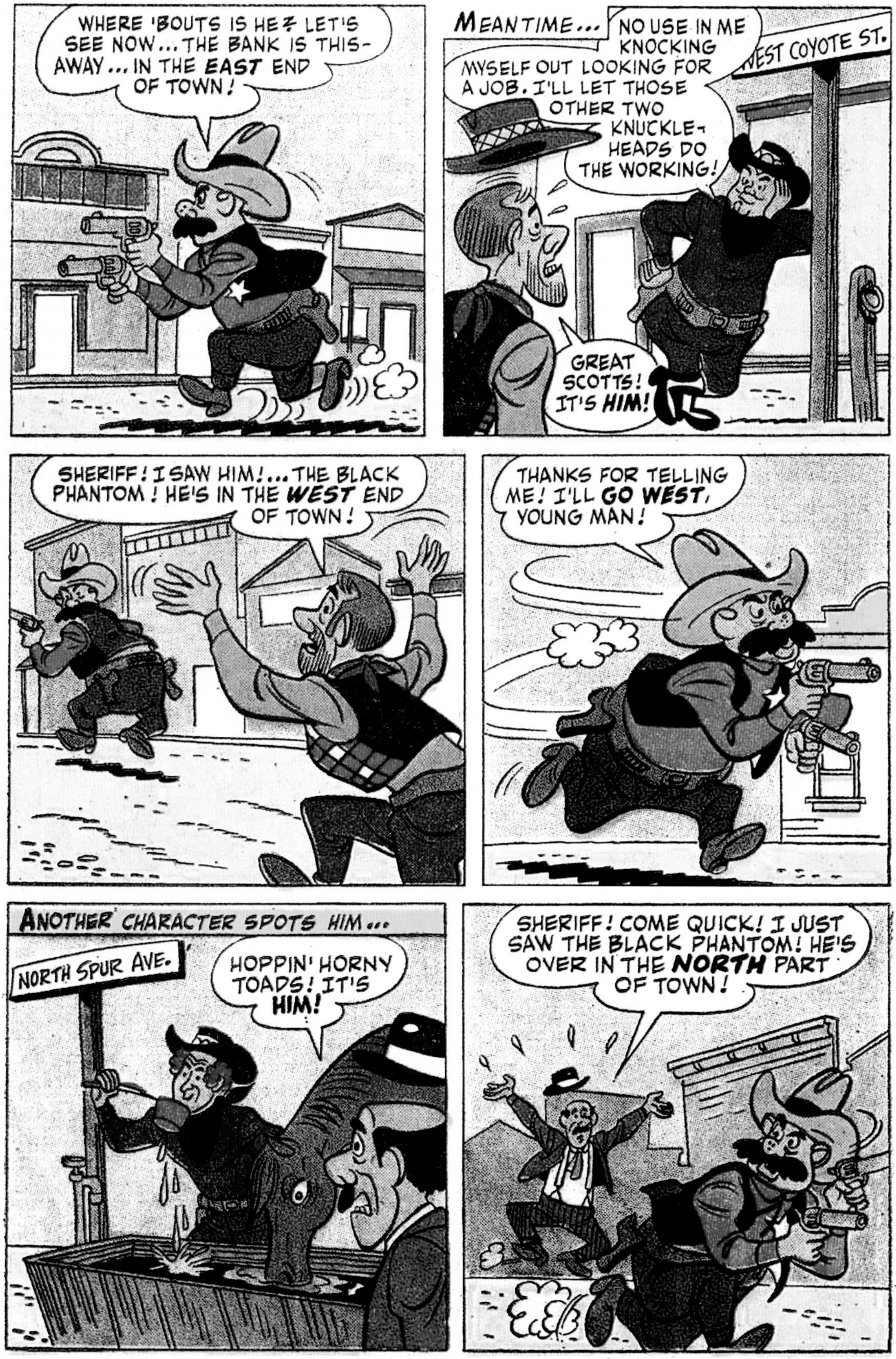
WHERE 'BOUTS IS HE? LET'S SEE NOW... THE BANK IS THIS-AWAY... IN THE EAST END OF TOWN!
MEANTIME...
NO USE IN ME KNOCKING MYSELF OUT LOOKING FOR A JOB. I'LL LET THOSE OTHER TWO KNUCKLE-HEADS DO THE WORKING!
WEST COYOTE ST.
GREAT SCOTTS! IT'S HIM!
SHERIFF! I SAW HIM!... THE BLACK PHANTOM! HE'S IN THE WEST END OF TOWN!
THANKS FOR TELLING ME! I'LL GO WEST, YOUNG MAN!
ANOTHER CHARACTER SPOTS HIM...
NORTH SPUR AVE.
HOPPIN' HORNY TOADS! IT'S HIM!
SHERIFF! COME QUICK! I JUST SAW THE BLACK PHANTOM! HE'S OVER IN THE NORTH PART OF TOWN!

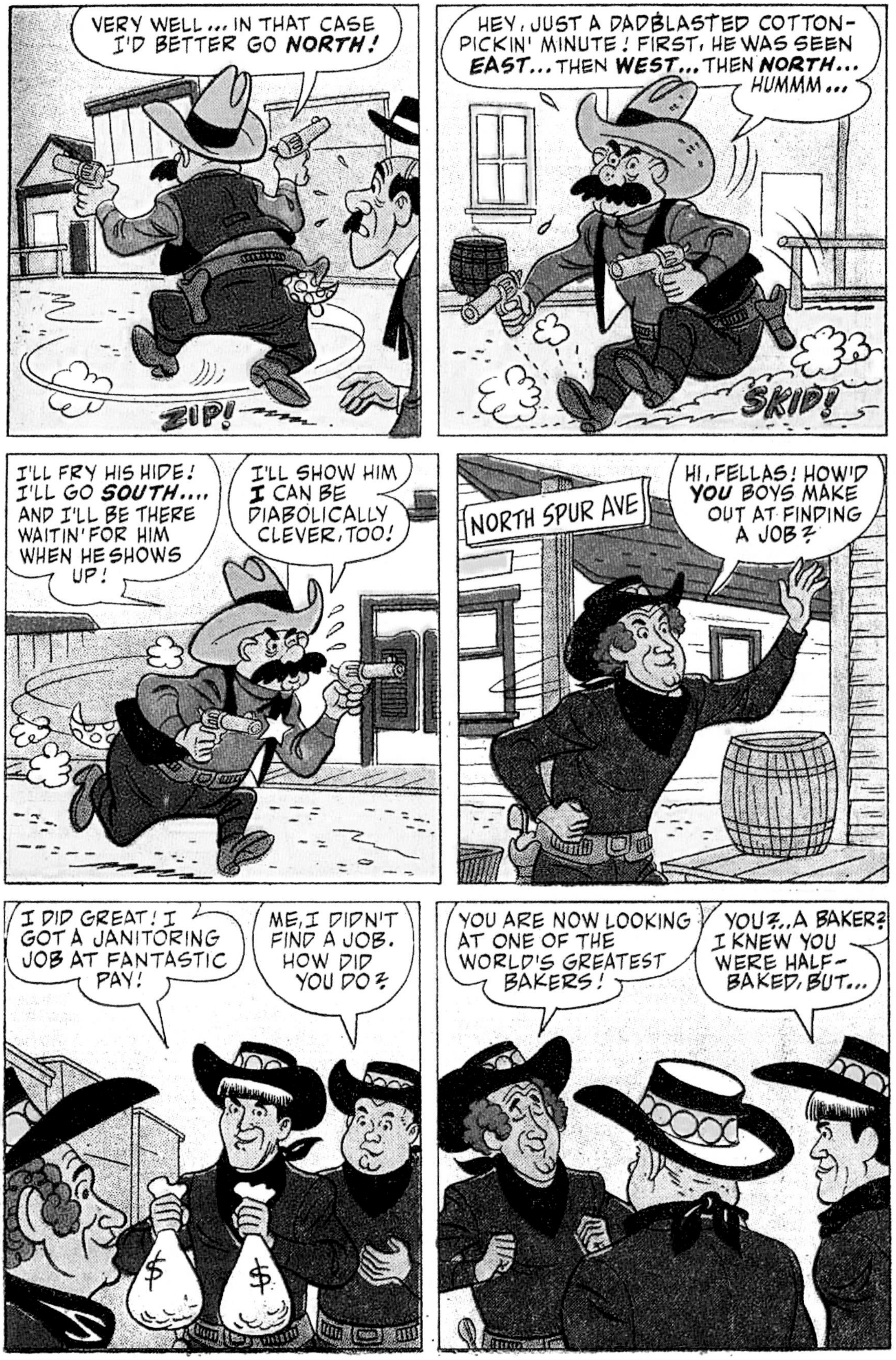
VERY WELL... IN THAT CASE I'D BETTER GO NORTH!
ZIP!
HEY, JUST A DADBLASTED COTTON-PICKIN' MINUTE! FIRST, HE WAS SEEN EAST... THEN WEST... THEN NORTH... HUMMM...
SKID!
I'LL FRY HIS HIDE! I'LL GO SOUTH.... AND I'LL BE THERE WAITIN' FOR HIM WHEN HE SHOWS UP!
I'LL SHOW HIM I CAN BE DIABOLICALLY CLEVER, TOO!
NORTH SPUR AVE
HI, FELLAS! HOW'D YOU BOYS MAKE OUT AT FINDING A JOB?
I DID GREAT! I GOT A JANITORING JOB AT FANTASTIC PAY!
ME, I DIDN'T FIND A JOB. HOW DID YOU DO?
$
$
YOU ARE NOW LOOKING AT ONE OF THE WORLD'S GREATEST BAKERS!
YOU?..A BAKER? I KNEW YOU WERE HALF-BAKED, BUT...

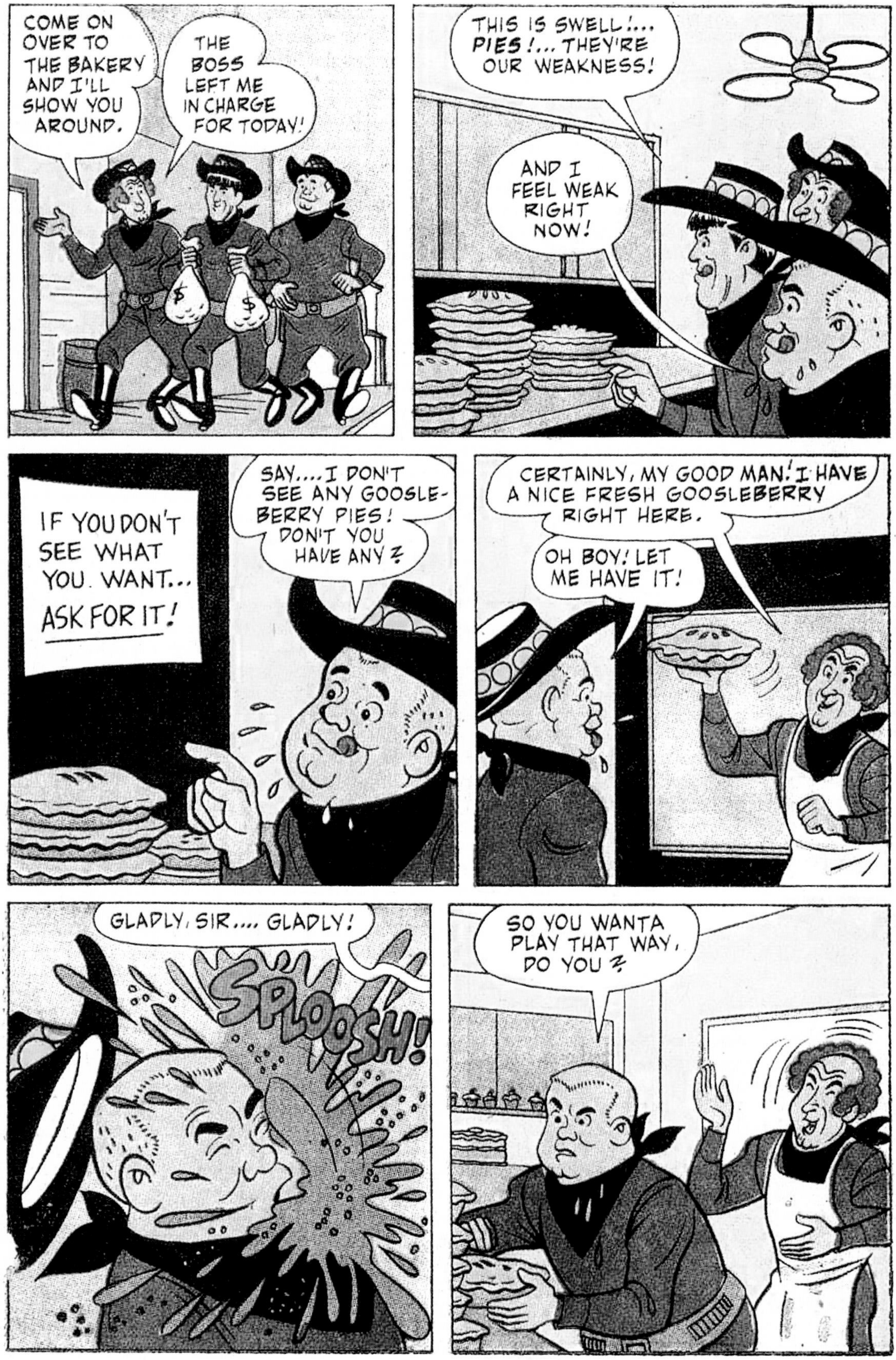
COME ON OVER TO THE BAKERY AND I'LL SHOW YOU AROUND.
THE BOSS LEFT ME IN CHARGE FOR TODAY!
THIS IS SWELL!... PIES!... THEY'RE OUR WEAKNESS!
AND I FEEL WEAK RIGHT NOW!
IF YOU DON'T SEE WHAT YOU. WANT... ASK FOR IT!
SAY.... I DON'T SEE ANY GOOSLEBERRY PIES! DON'T YOU HAVE ANY?
CERTAINLY, MY GOOD MAN! I HAVE A NICE FRESH GOOSLEBERRY RIGHT HERE.
OH BOY! LET ME HAVE IT!
GLADLY, SIR.... GLADLY!
SPLOOSH!
SO YOU WANTA PLAY THAT WAY, DO YOU?

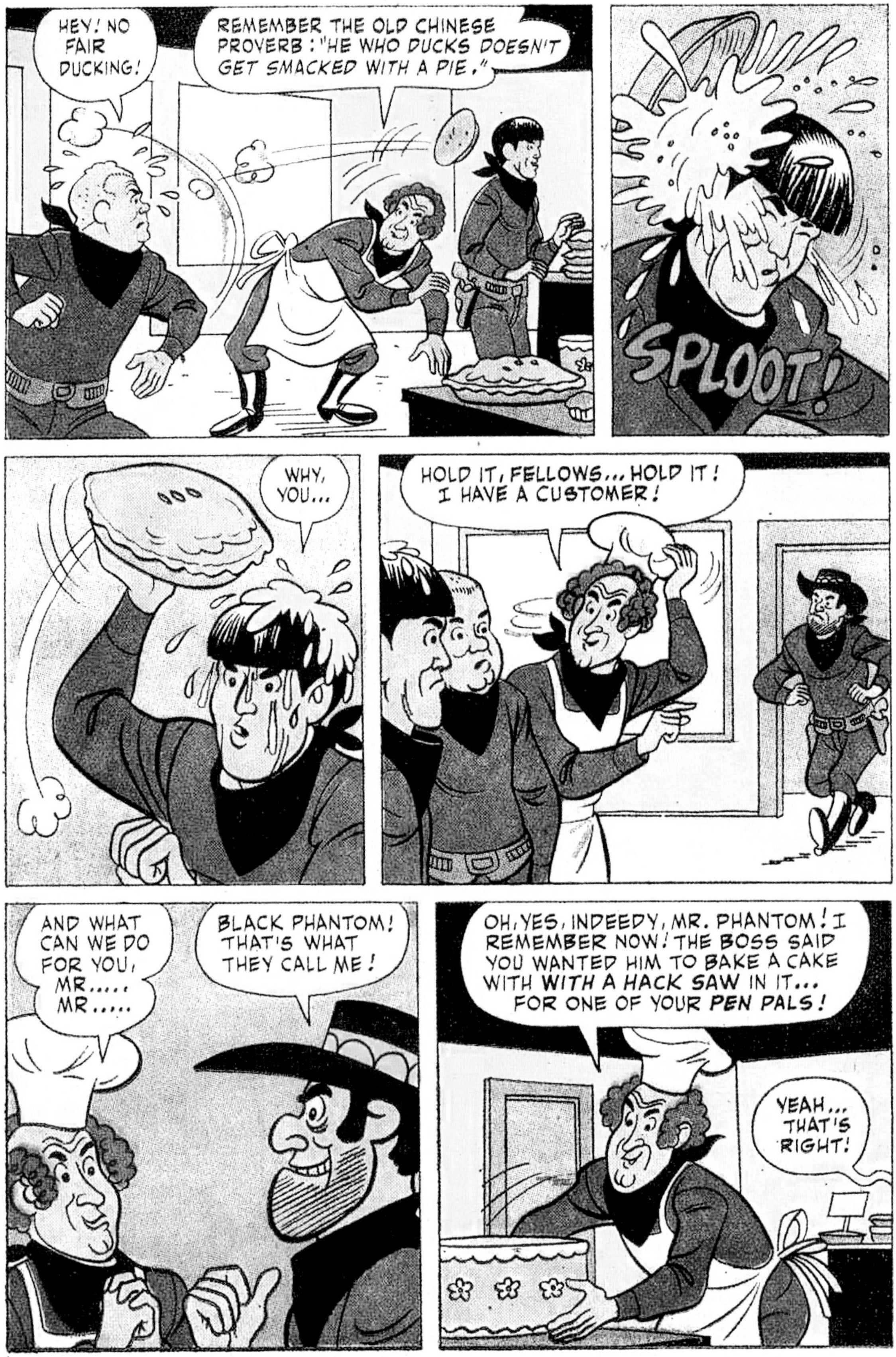
HEY! NO FAIR DUCKING!
REMEMBER THE OLD CHINESE PROVERB: "HE WHO DUCKS DOESN'T GET SMACKED WITH A PIE."
SPLOOT!
WHY, YOU...
HOLD IT, FELLOWS... HOLD IT! I HAVE A CUSTOMER!
AND WHAT CAN WE DO FOR YOU, MR..... MR.....
BLACK PHANTOM! THAT'S WHAT THEY CALL ME!
OH, YES, INDEEDY, MR. PHANTOM! I REMEMBER NOW! THE BOSS SAID YOU WANTED HIM TO BAKE A CAKE WITH WITH A HACK SAW IN IT... FOR ONE OF YOUR PEN PALS!
YEAH... THAT'S RIGHT!

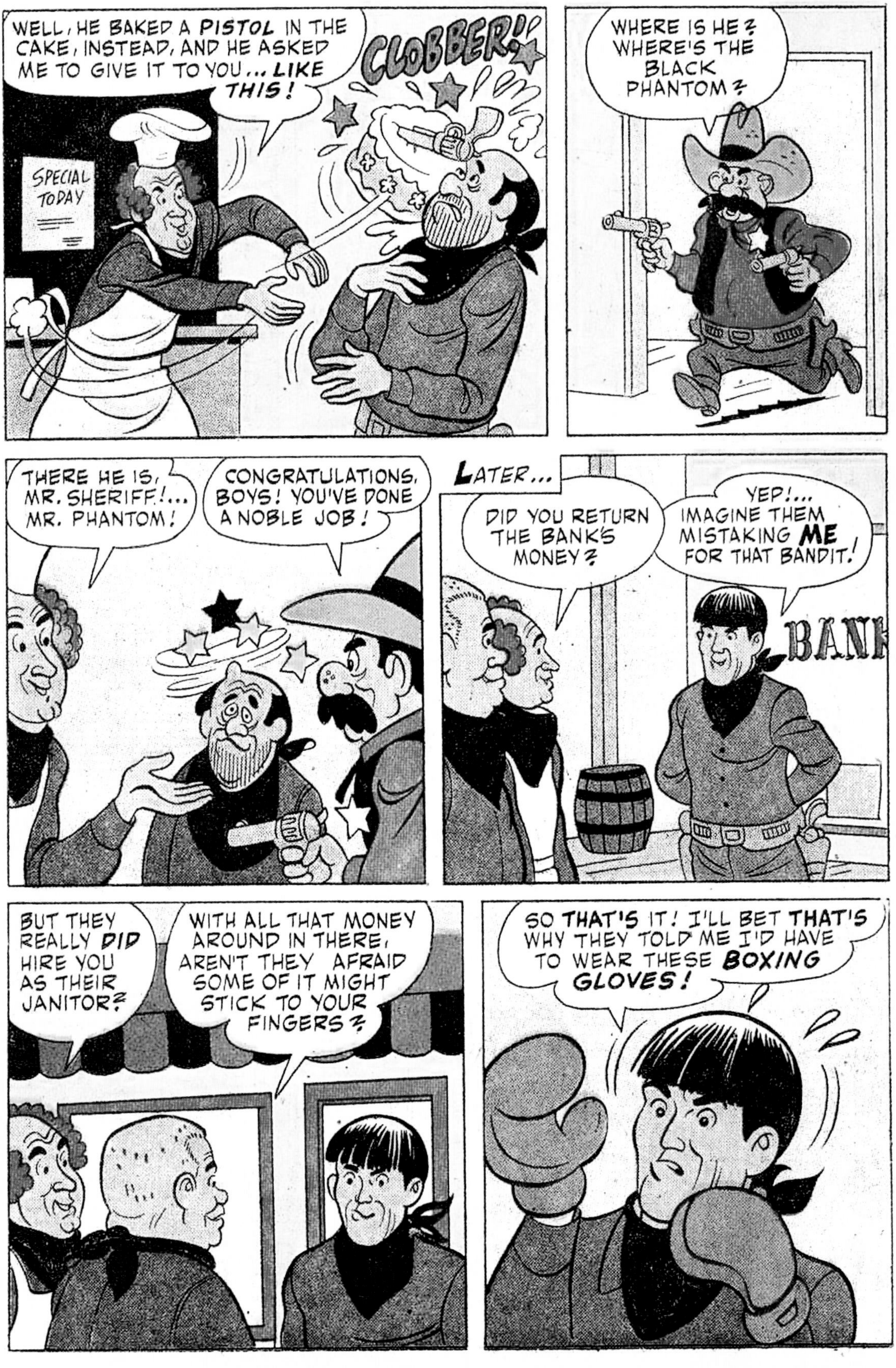

WELL, HE BAKED A PISTOL IN THE CAKE, INSTEAD, AND HE ASKED ME TO GIVE IT TO YOU... LIKE THIS!
CLOBBER!!
SPECIAL TODAY
WHERE IS HE? WHERE'S THE BLACK PHANTOM?
THERE HE IS, MR. SHERIFF!... MR. PHANTOM!
CONGRATULATIONS, BOYS! YOU'VE DONE A NOBLE JOB!
LATER...
DID YOU RETURN THE BANK'S MONEY?
YEP!... IMAGINE THEM MISTAKING ME FOR THAT BANDIT!
BANK
BUT THEY REALLY DID HIRE YOU AS THEIR JANITOR?
WITH ALL THAT MONEY AROUND IN THERE, AREN'T THEY AFRAID SOME OF IT MIGHT STICK TO YOUR FINGERS?
SO THAT'S IT! I'LL BET THAT'S WHY THEY TOLD ME I'D HAVE TO WEAR THESE BOXING GLOVES!

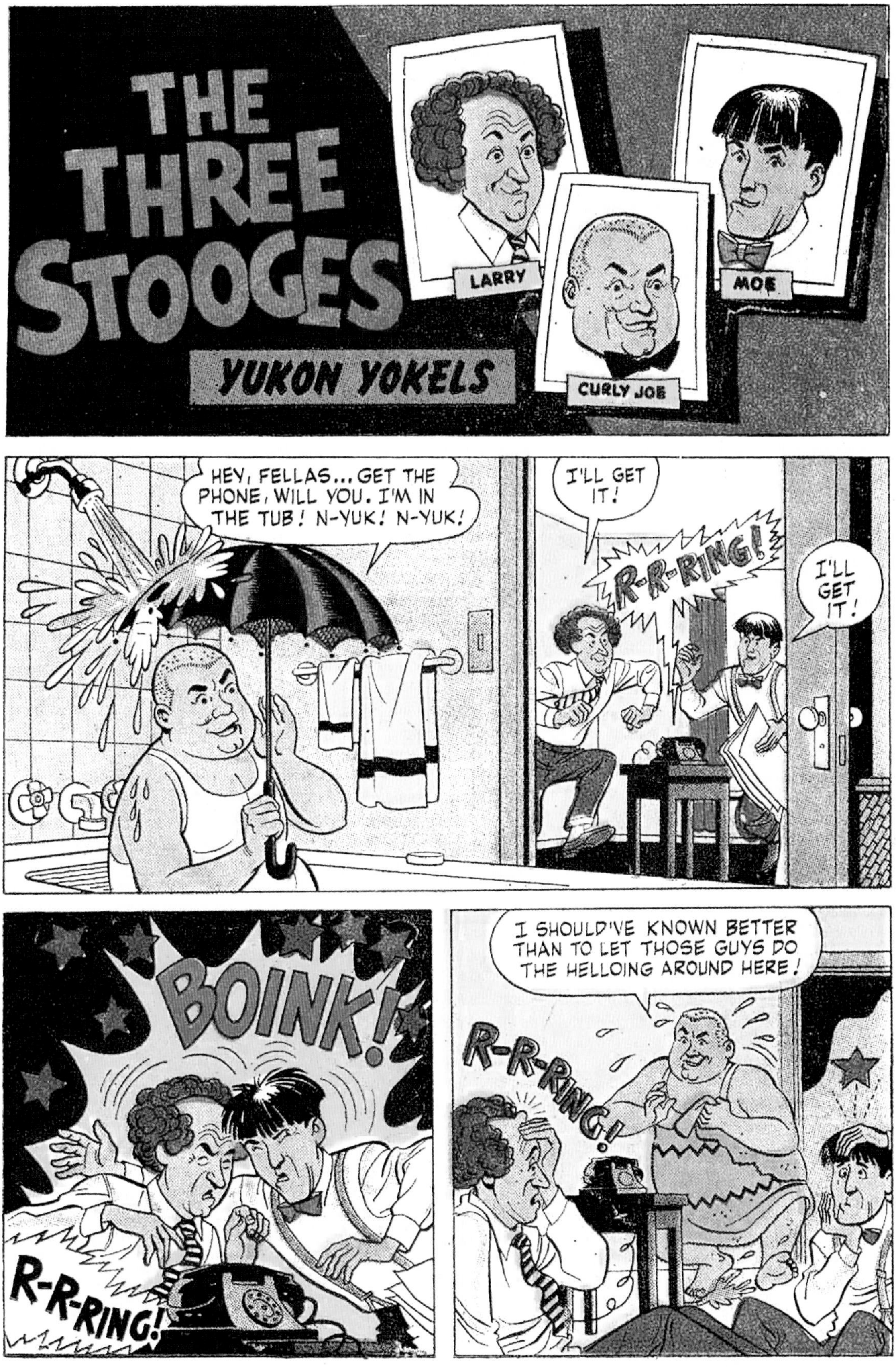
THE THREE STOOGES
LARRY
CURLY JOE
MOE
YUKON YOKELS
HEY, FELLAS... GET THE PHONE, WILL YOU. I'M IN THE TUB! N-YUK! N-YUK!
I'LL GET IT!
R-R-RING!
I'LL GET IT!
BOINK!
R-R-RING!
I SHOULD'VE KNOWN BETTER THAN TO LET THOSE GUYS DO THE HELLOING AROUND HERE!
R-R-RING!

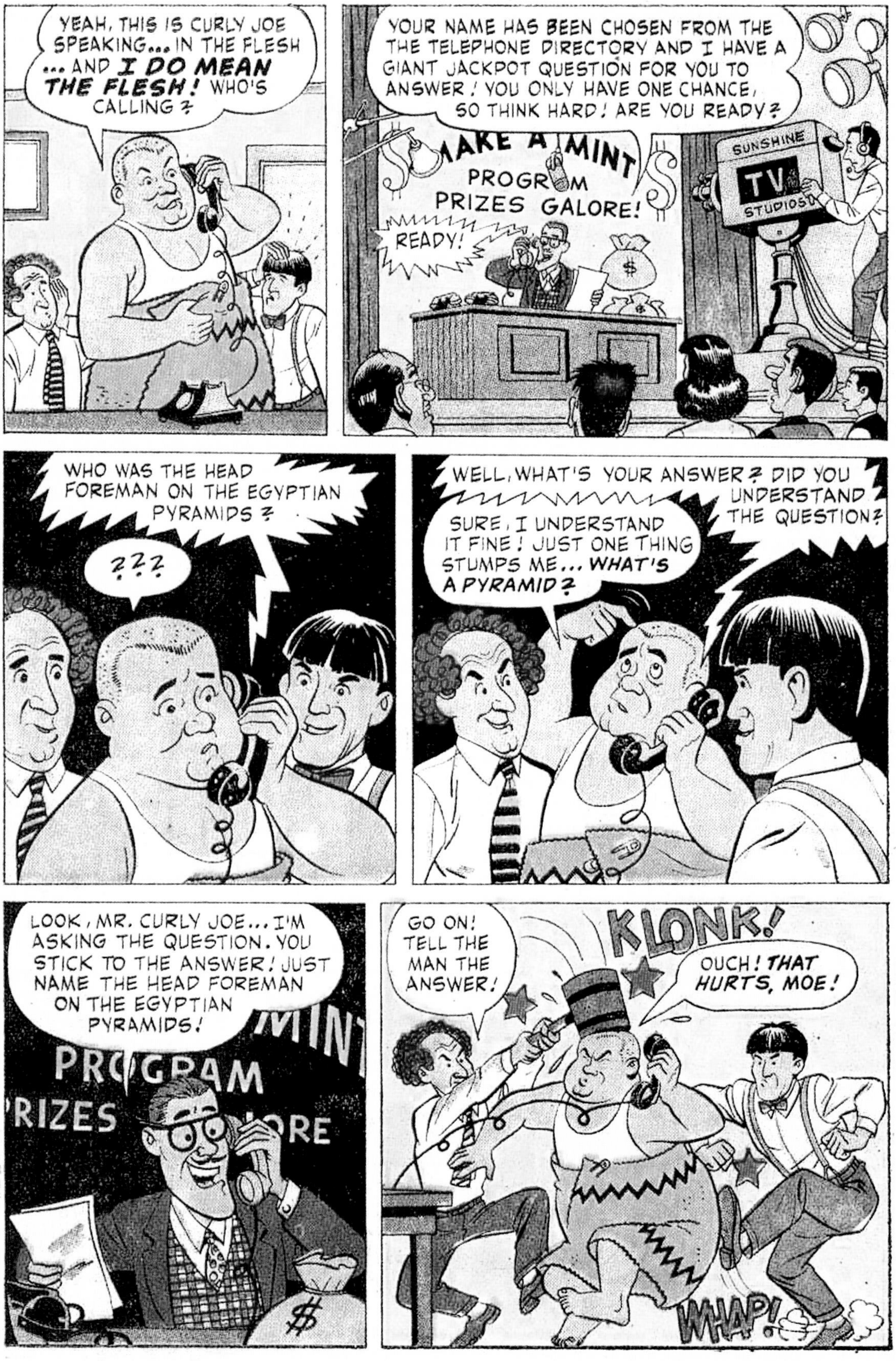
YEAH, THIS IS CURLY JOE SPEAKING... IN THE FLESH ... AND I DO MEAN THE FLESH! WHO'S CALLING?
YOUR NAME HAS BEEN CHOSEN FROM THE THE TELEPHONE DIRECTORY AND I HAVE A GIANT JACKPOT QUESTION FOR YOU TO ANSWER! YOU ONLY HAVE ONE CHANCE, SO THINK HARD! ARE YOU READY?
MAKE A MINT
PROGRAM
PRIZES GALORE!
SUNSHINE
TV
STUDIOS
READY!
WHO WAS THE HEAD FOREMAN ON THE EGYPTIAN PYRAMIDS?
???
WELL, WHAT'S YOUR ANSWER? DID YOU UNDERSTAND THE QUESTION?
SURE, I UNDERSTAND IT FINE! JUST ONE THING STUMPS ME... WHAT'S A PYRAMID?
LOOK, MR. CURLY JOE... I'M ASKING THE QUESTION. YOU STICK TO THE ANSWER! JUST NAME THE HEAD FOREMAN ON THE EGYPTIAN PYRAMIDS!
GO ON! TELL THE MAN THE ANSWER!
KLONK!
OUCH! THAT HURTS, MOE!
WHAP!

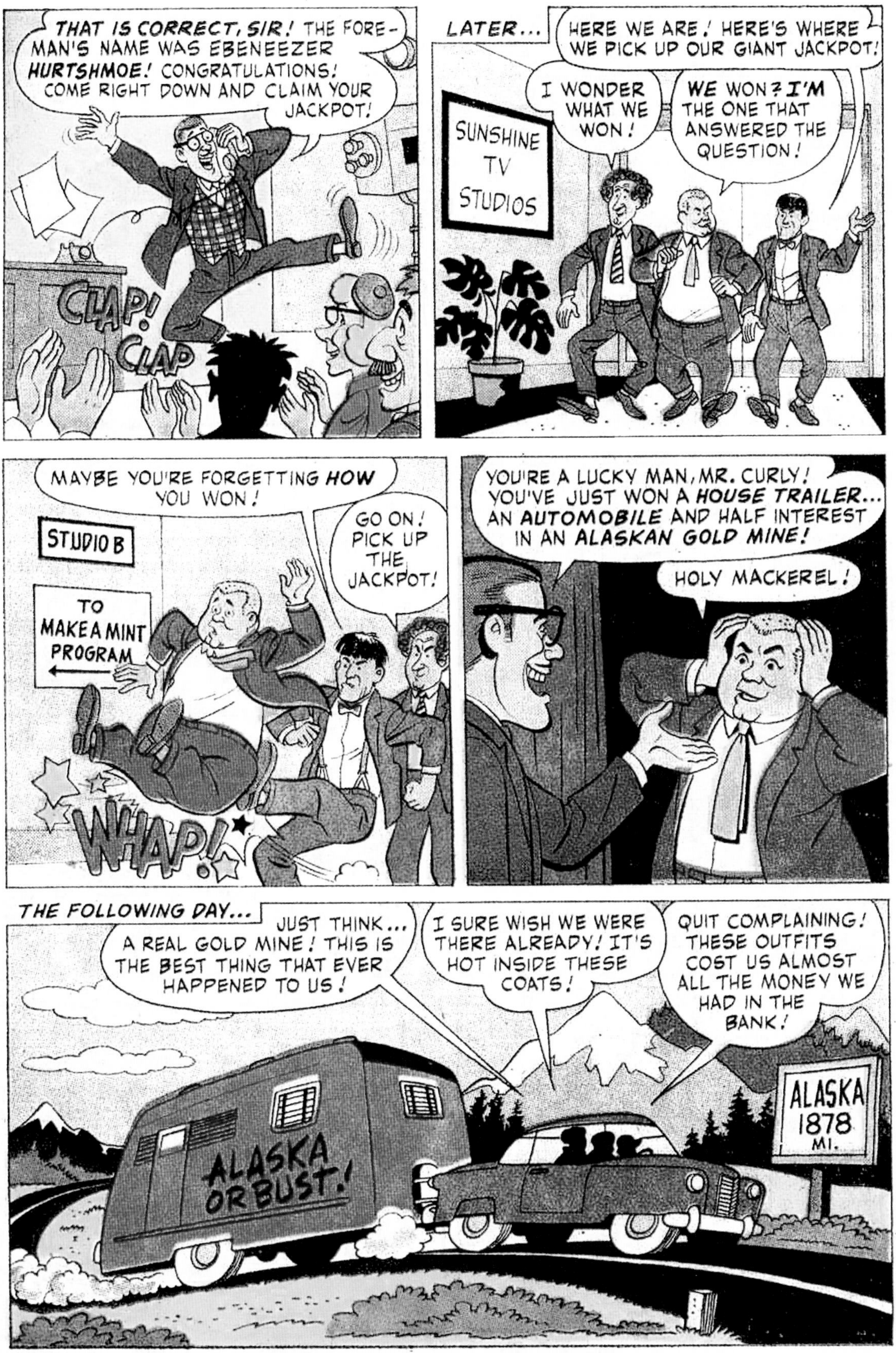
THAT IS CORRECT, SIR! THE FOREMAN'S NAME WAS EBENEEZER HURTSHMOE! CONGRATULATIONS! COME RIGHT DOWN AND CLAIM YOUR JACKPOT!
CLAP! CLAP
LATER...
HERE WE ARE! HERE'S WHERE WE PICK UP OUR GIANT JACKPOT!
I WONDER WHAT WE WON!
WE WON? I'M THE ONE THAT ANSWERED THE QUESTION!
SUNSHINE TV STUDIOS
MAYBE YOU'RE FORGETTING HOW YOU WON!
GO ON! PICK UP THE JACKPOT!
STUDIO B
TO MAKE A MINT PROGRAM
WHAP!
YOU'RE A LUCKY MAN, MR. CURLY! YOU'VE JUST WON A HOUSE TRAILER... AN AUTOMOBILE AND HALF INTEREST IN AN ALASKAN GOLD MINE!
HOLY MACKEREL!
THE FOLLOWING DAY...
JUST THINK... A REAL GOLD MINE! THIS IS THE BEST THING THAT EVER HAPPENED TO US!
I SURE WISH WE WERE THERE ALREADY! IT'S HOT INSIDE THESE COATS!
QUIT COMPLAINING! THESE OUTFITS COST US ALMOST ALL THE MONEY WE HAD IN THE BANK!
ALASKA OR BUST!
ALASKA 1878 MI.

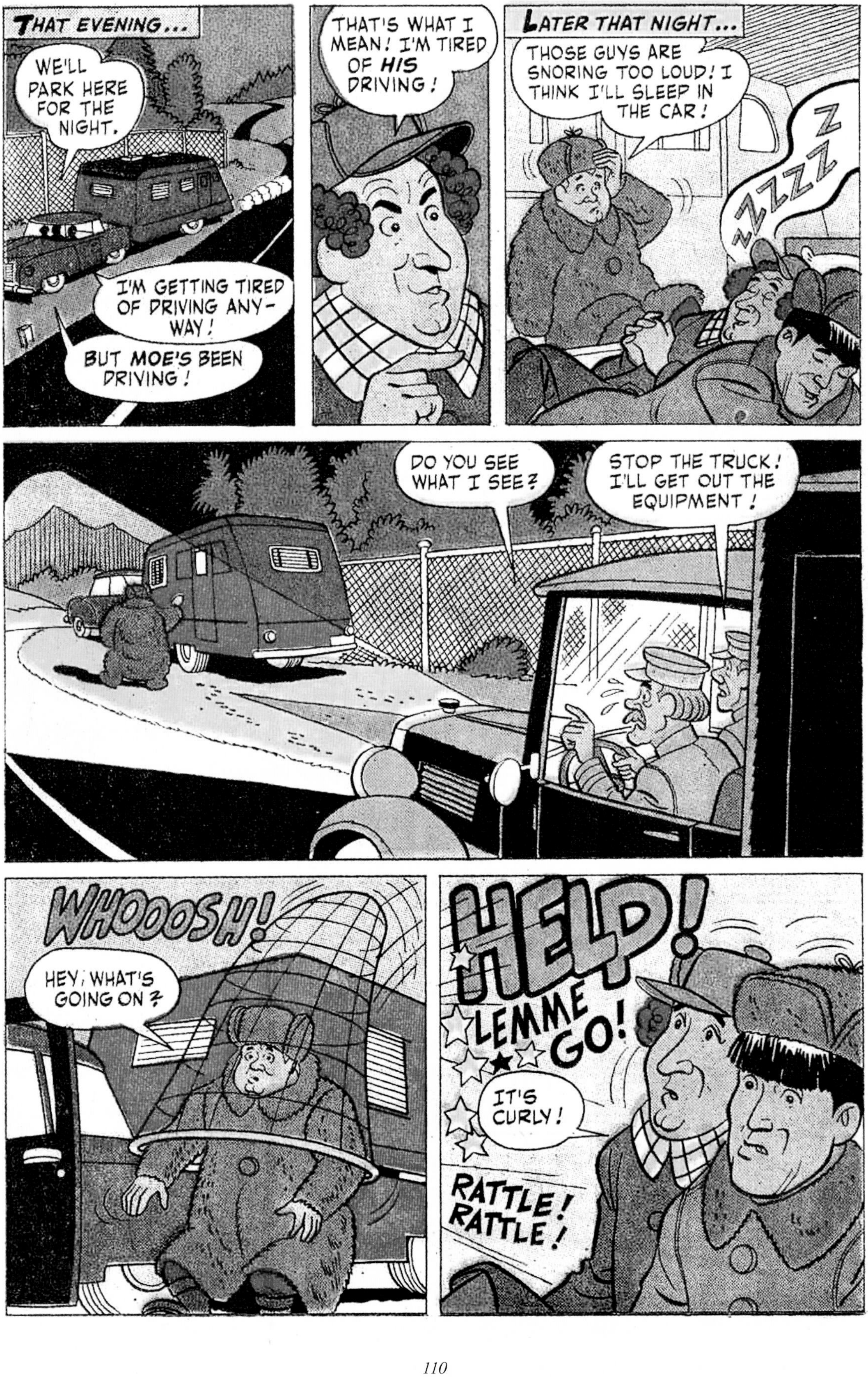
THAT EVENING...
WE'LL PARK HERE FOR THE NIGHT.
I'M GETTING TIRED OF DRIVING ANY-WAY!
BUT MOE'S BEEN DRIVING!
THAT'S WHAT I MEAN! I'M TIRED OF HIS DRIVING!
LATER THAT NIGHT...
THOSE GUYS ARE SNORING TOO LOUD! I THINK I'LL SLEEP IN THE CAR!
ZZZZZZ
DO YOU SEE WHAT I SEE?
STOP THE TRUCK! I'LL GET OUT THE EQUIPMENT!
WHOOOOSH!
HEY, WHAT'S GOING ON?
HELP!
LEMME GO!
IT'S CURLY!
RATTLE! RATTLE!

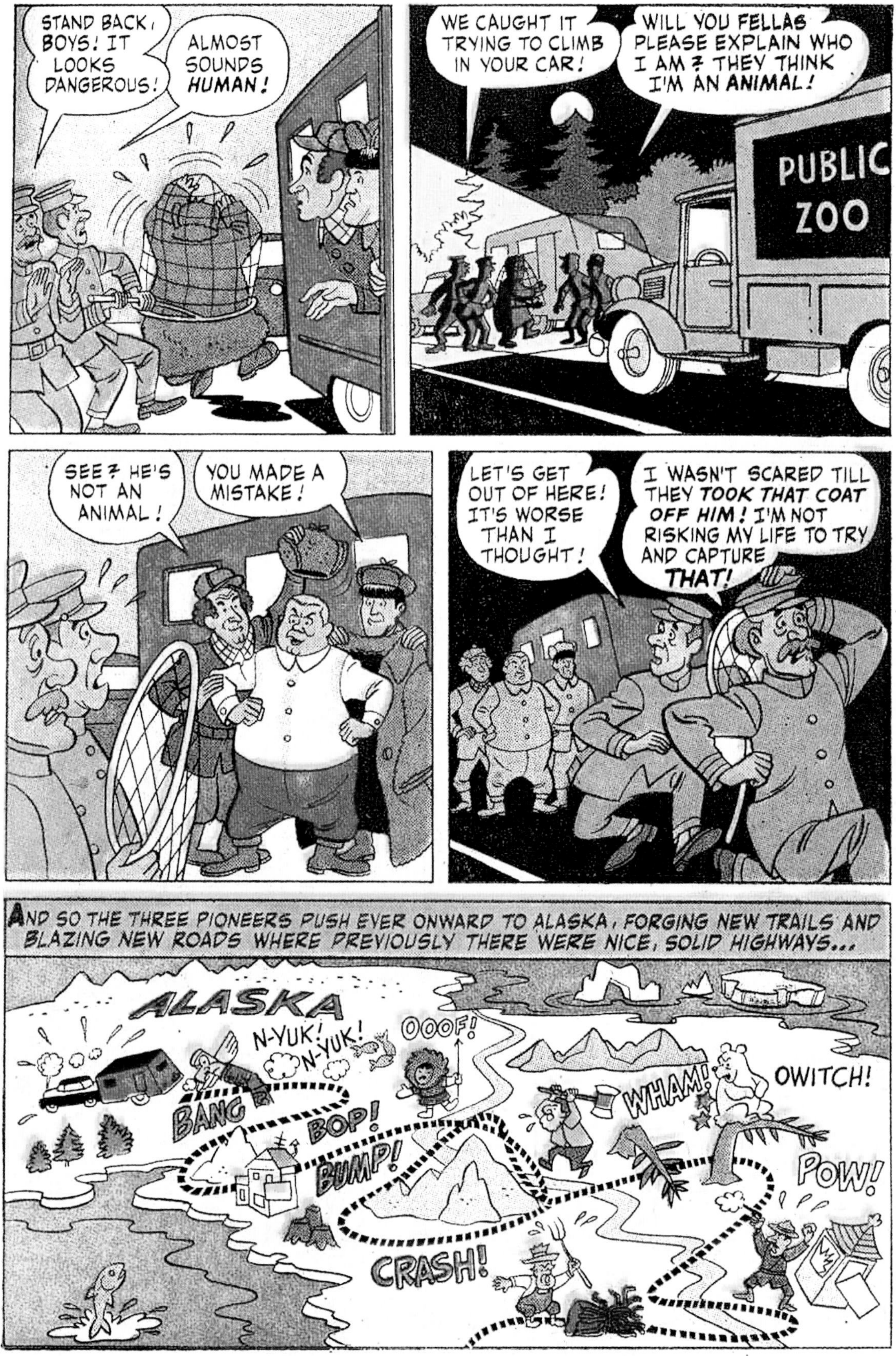
STAND BACK, BOYS! IT LOOKS DANGEROUS!
ALMOST SOUNDS HUMAN!
WE CAUGHT IT TRYING TO CLIMB IN YOUR CAR!
WILL YOU FELLAS PLEASE EXPLAIN WHO I AM? THEY THINK I'M AN ANIMAL!
PUBLIC ZOO
SEE? HE'S NOT AN ANIMAL!
YOU MADE A MISTAKE!
LET'S GET OUT OF HERE! IT'S WORSE THAN I THOUGHT!
I WASN'T SCARED TILL THEY TOOK THAT COAT OFF HIM! I'M NOT RISKING MY LIFE TO TRY AND CAPTURE THAT!
AND SO THE THREE PIONEERS PUSH EVER ONWARD TO ALASKA, FORGING NEW TRAILS AND BLAZING NEW ROADS WHERE PREVIOUSLY THERE WERE NICE, SOLID HIGHWAYS...
ALASKA
N-YUK! N-YUK!
OOOF!
OWITCH!
BANG
BOP!
BUMP!
WHAM!
POW!
CRASH!

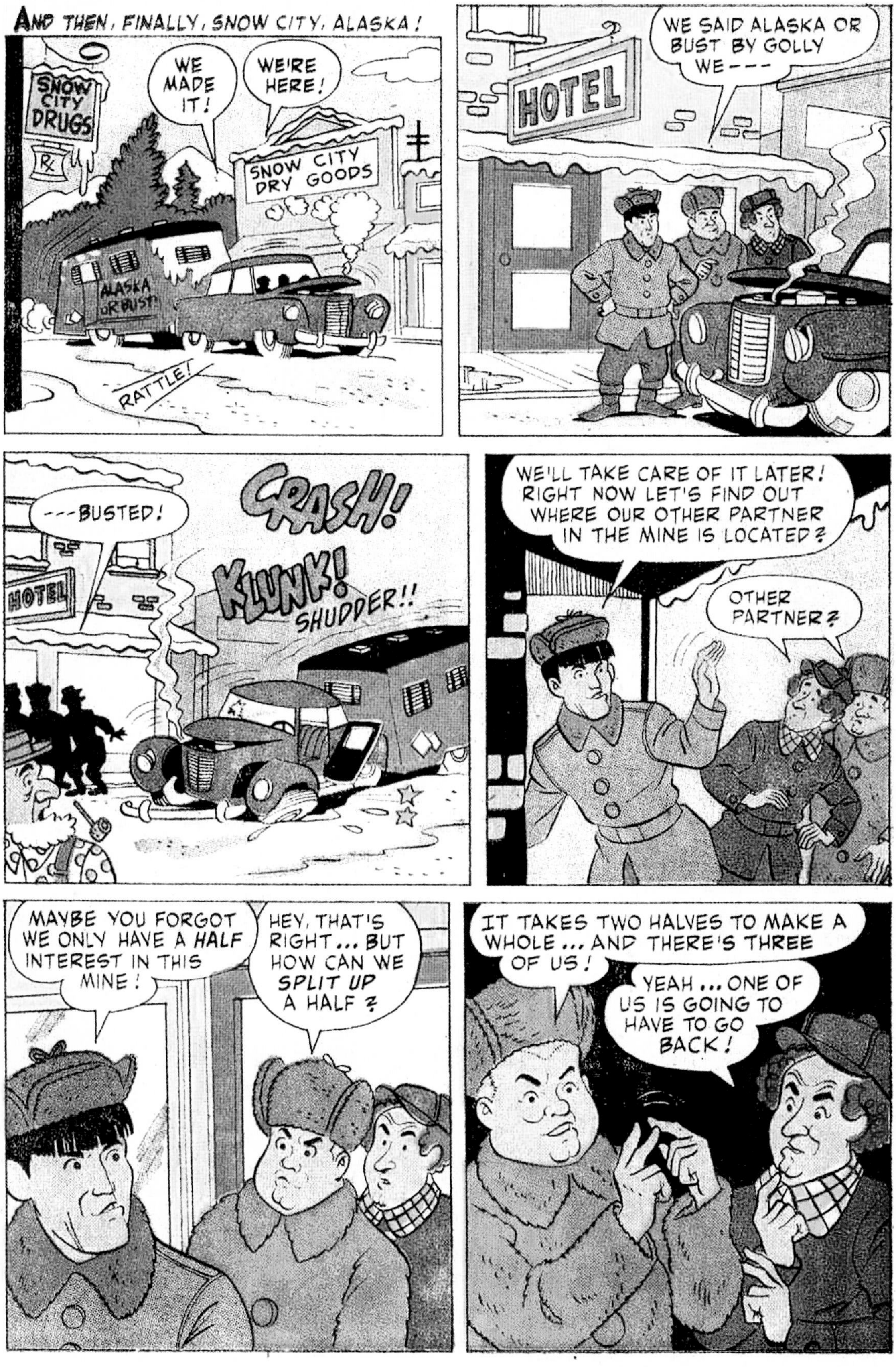
AND THEN, FINALLY, SNOW CITY, ALASKA!
SNOW CITY DRUGS
Rx
WE MADE IT!
WE'RE HERE!
SNOW CITY DRY GOODS
ALASKA OR BUST!
RATTLE!
WE SAID ALASKA OR BUST BY GOLLY WE---
HOTEL
---BUSTED!
HOTEL
CRASH!
KLUNK!
SHUDDER!!
WE'LL TAKE CARE OF IT LATER! RIGHT NOW LET'S FIND OUT WHERE OUR OTHER PARTNER IN THE MINE IS LOCATED?
OTHER PARTNER?
MAYBE YOU FORGOT WE ONLY HAVE A HALF INTEREST IN THIS MINE!
HEY, THAT'S RIGHT... BUT HOW CAN WE SPLIT UP A HALF?
IT TAKES TWO HALVES TO MAKE A WHOLE... AND THERE'S THREE OF US!
YEAH... ONE OF US IS GOING TO HAVE TO GO BACK!

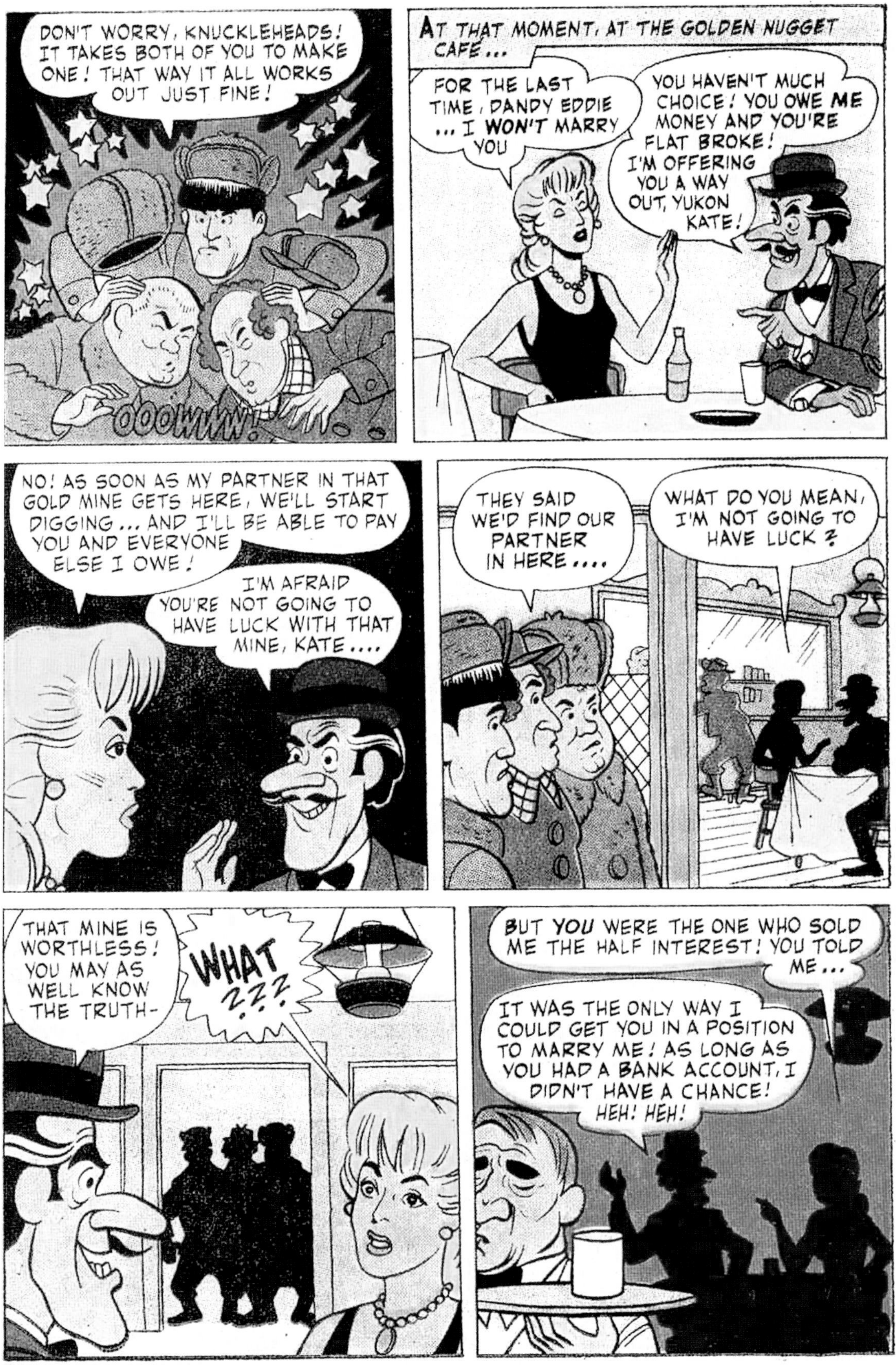
DON'T WORRY, KNUCKLEHEADS! IT TAKES BOTH OF YOU TO MAKE ONE! THAT WAY IT ALL WORKS OUT JUST FINE!
OOOWWW!
AT THAT MOMENT, AT THE GOLDEN NUGGET CAFÉ...
FOR THE LAST TIME, DANDY EDDIE ... I WON'T MARRY YOU
YOU HAVEN'T MUCH CHOICE! YOU OWE ME MONEY AND YOU'RE FLAT BROKE! I'M OFFERING YOU A WAY OUT, YUKON KATE!
NO! AS SOON AS MY PARTNER IN THAT GOLD MINE GETS HERE, WE'LL START DIGGING... AND I'LL BE ABLE TO PAY YOU AND EVERYONE ELSE I OWE!
I'M AFRAID YOU'RE NOT GOING TO HAVE LUCK WITH THAT MINE, KATE....
THEY SAID WE'D FIND OUR PARTNER IN HERE....
WHAT DO YOU MEAN, I'M NOT GOING TO HAVE LUCK ?
THAT MINE IS WORTHLESS! YOU MAY AS WELL KNOW THE TRUTH-
WHAT ???
BUT YOU WERE THE ONE WHO SOLD ME THE HALF INTEREST! YOU TOLD ME...
IT WAS THE ONLY WAY I COULD GET YOU IN A POSITION TO MARRY ME! AS LONG AS YOU HAD A BANK ACCOUNT, I DIDN'T HAVE A CHANCE! HEH! HEH!

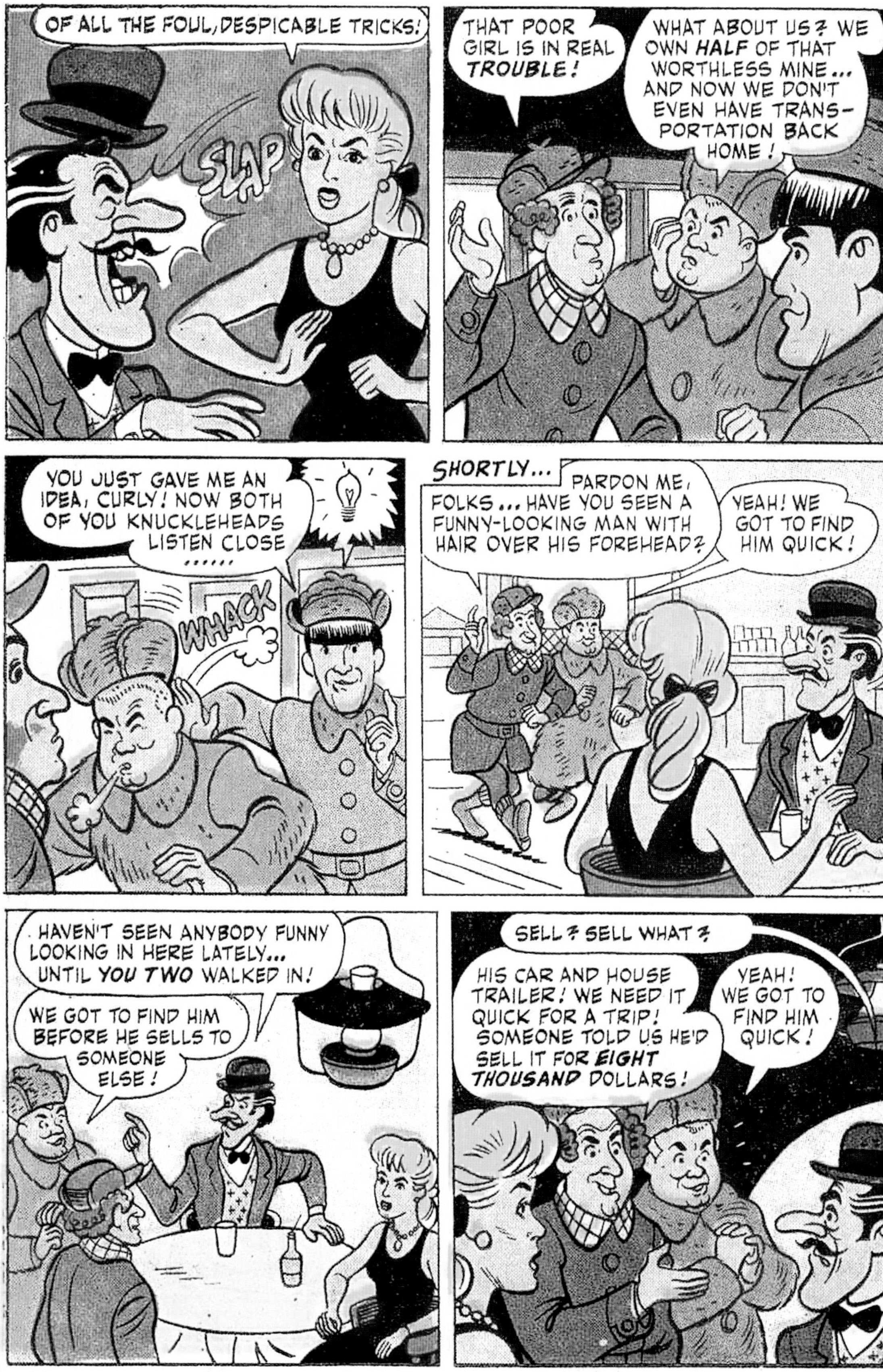
OF ALL THE FOUL, DESPICABLE TRICKS!
SLAP
THAT POOR GIRL IS IN REAL TROUBLE!
WHAT ABOUT US? WE OWN HALF OF THAT WORTHLESS MINE... AND NOW WE DON'T EVEN HAVE TRANS-PORTATION BACK HOME!
YOU JUST GAVE ME AN IDEA, CURLY! NOW BOTH OF YOU KNUCKLEHEADS LISTEN CLOSE ......
WHACK
SHORTLY...
PARDON ME, FOLKS... HAVE YOU SEEN A FUNNY-LOOKING MAN WITH HAIR OVER HIS FOREHEAD?
YEAH! WE GOT TO FIND HIM QUICK!
HAVEN'T SEEN ANYBODY FUNNY LOOKING IN HERE LATELY... UNTIL YOU TWO WALKED IN!
WE GOT TO FIND HIM BEFORE HE SELLS TO SOMEONE ELSE!
SELL? SELL WHAT?
HIS CAR AND HOUSE TRAILER! WE NEED IT QUICK FOR A TRIP! SOMEONE TOLD US HE'D SELL IT FOR EIGHT THOUSAND DOLLARS!
YEAH! WE GOT TO FIND HIM QUICK!

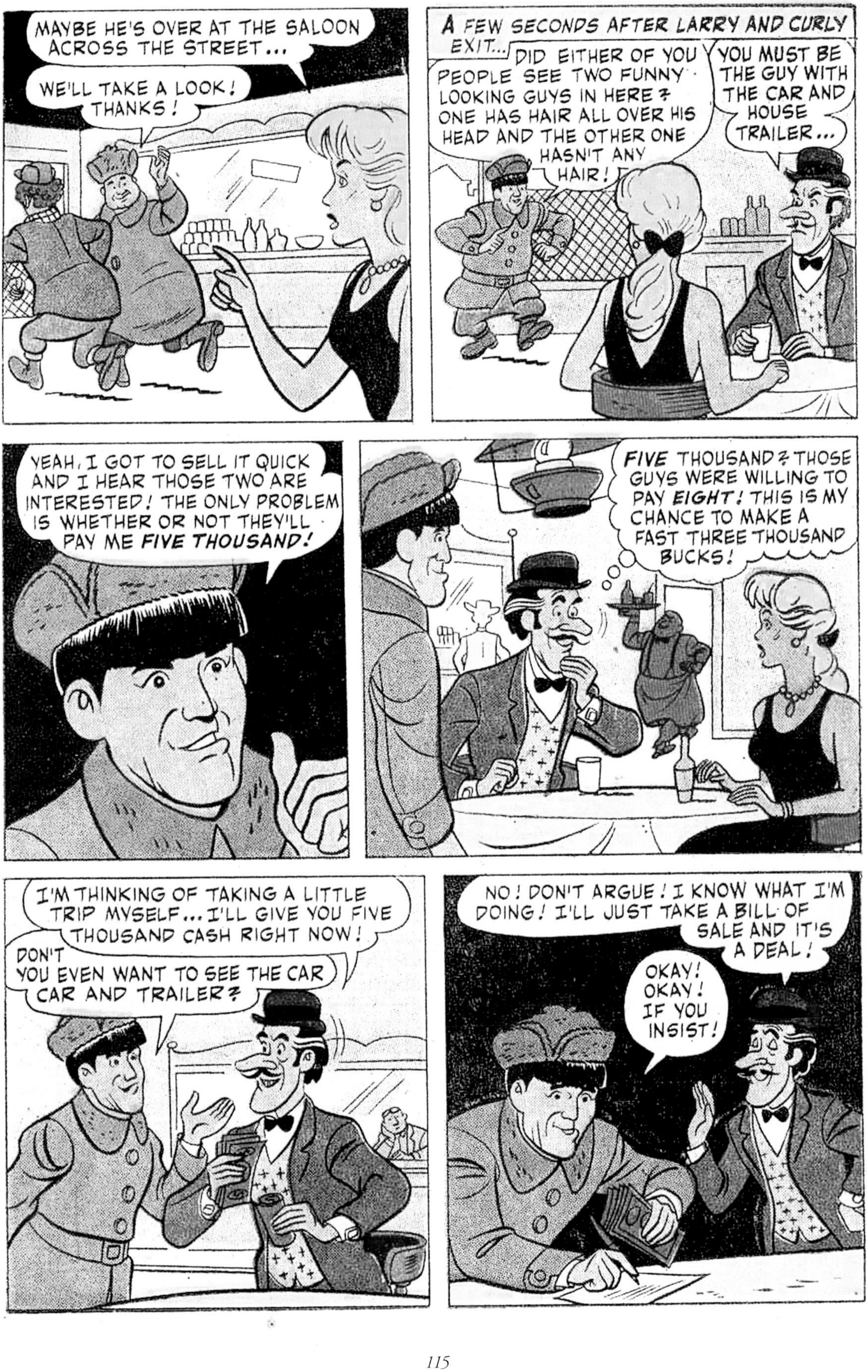

MAYBE HE'S OVER AT THE SALOON ACROSS THE STREET...
WE'LL TAKE A LOOK! THANKS!
A FEW SECONDS AFTER LARRY AND CURLY EXIT...
DID EITHER OF YOU PEOPLE SEE TWO FUNNY LOOKING GUYS IN HERE? ONE HAS HAIR ALL OVER HIS HEAD AND THE OTHER ONE HASN'T ANY HAIR!
YOU MUST BE THE GUY WITH THE CAR AND HOUSE TRAILER...
YEAH, I GOT TO SELL IT QUICK AND I HEAR THOSE TWO ARE INTERESTED! THE ONLY PROBLEM IS WHETHER OR NOT THEY'LL PAY ME **FIVE THOUSAND!**
FIVE THOUSAND? THOSE GUYS WERE WILLING TO PAY **EIGHT!** THIS IS MY CHANCE TO MAKE A FAST THREE THOUSAND BUCKS!
I'M THINKING OF TAKING A LITTLE TRIP MYSELF... I'LL GIVE YOU FIVE THOUSAND CASH RIGHT NOW!
DON'T YOU EVEN WANT TO SEE THE CAR CAR AND TRAILER?
NO! DON'T ARGUE! I KNOW WHAT I'M DOING! I'LL JUST TAKE A BILL OF SALE AND IT'S A DEAL!
OKAY! OKAY! IF YOU INSIST!

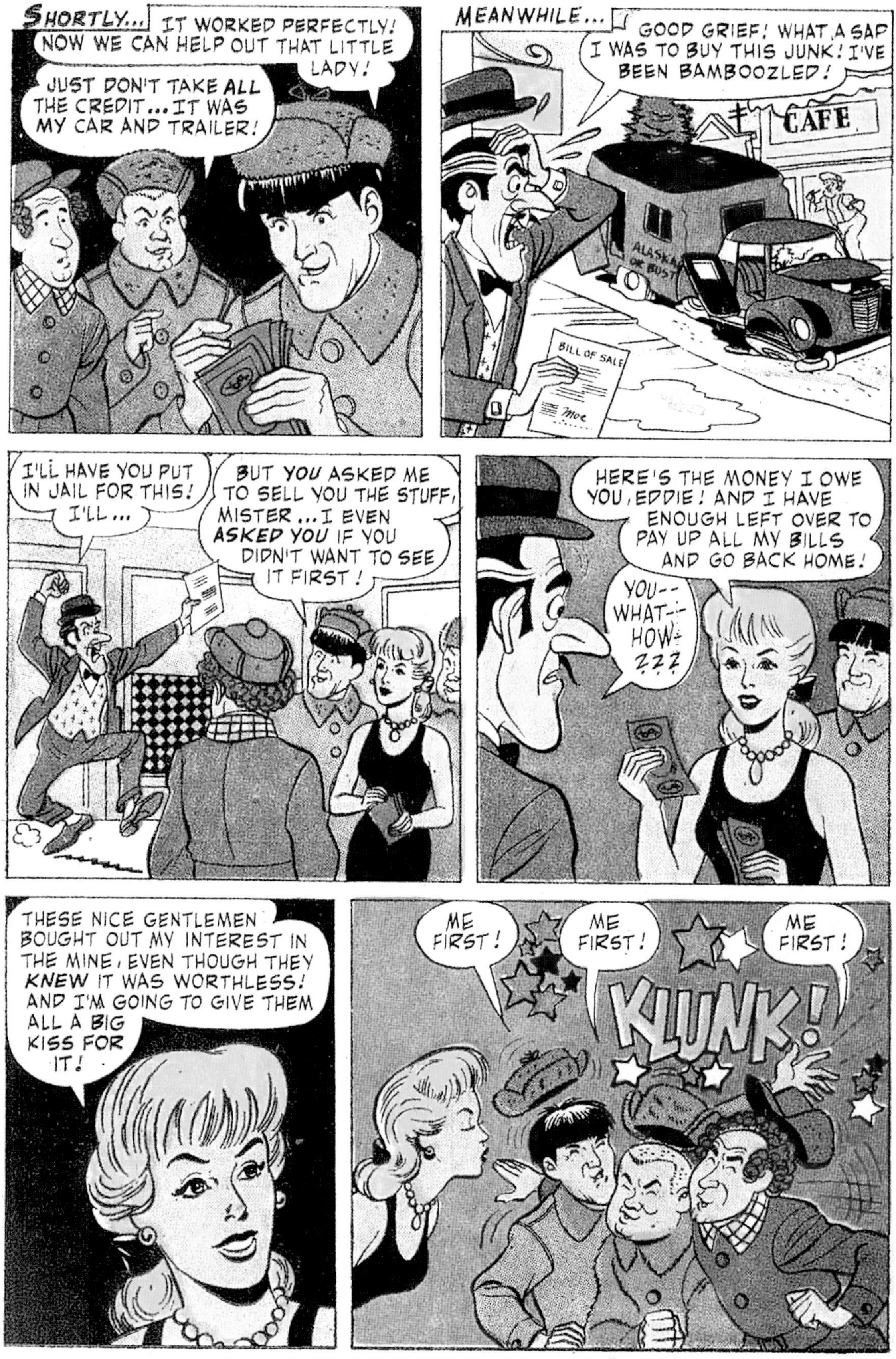
SHORTLY...
IT WORKED PERFECTLY! NOW WE CAN HELP OUT THAT LITTLE LADY!
JUST DON'T TAKE ALL THE CREDIT... IT WAS MY CAR AND TRAILER!
MEANWHILE...
GOOD GRIEF! WHAT A SAP I WAS TO BUY THIS JUNK! I'VE BEEN BAMBOOZLED!
CAFE
ALASKA OR BUST
BILL OF SALE
Moe
I'LL HAVE YOU PUT IN JAIL FOR THIS! I'LL...
BUT YOU ASKED ME TO SELL YOU THE STUFF, MISTER... I EVEN ASKED YOU IF YOU DIDN'T WANT TO SEE IT FIRST!
HERE'S THE MONEY I OWE YOU, EDDIE! AND I HAVE ENOUGH LEFT OVER TO PAY UP ALL MY BILLS AND GO BACK HOME!
YOU-- WHAT-- HOW- ???
THESE NICE GENTLEMEN BOUGHT OUT MY INTEREST IN THE MINE, EVEN THOUGH THEY KNEW IT WAS WORTHLESS! AND I'M GOING TO GIVE THEM ALL A BIG KISS FOR IT!
ME FIRST!
ME FIRST!
ME FIRST!
KLUNK!

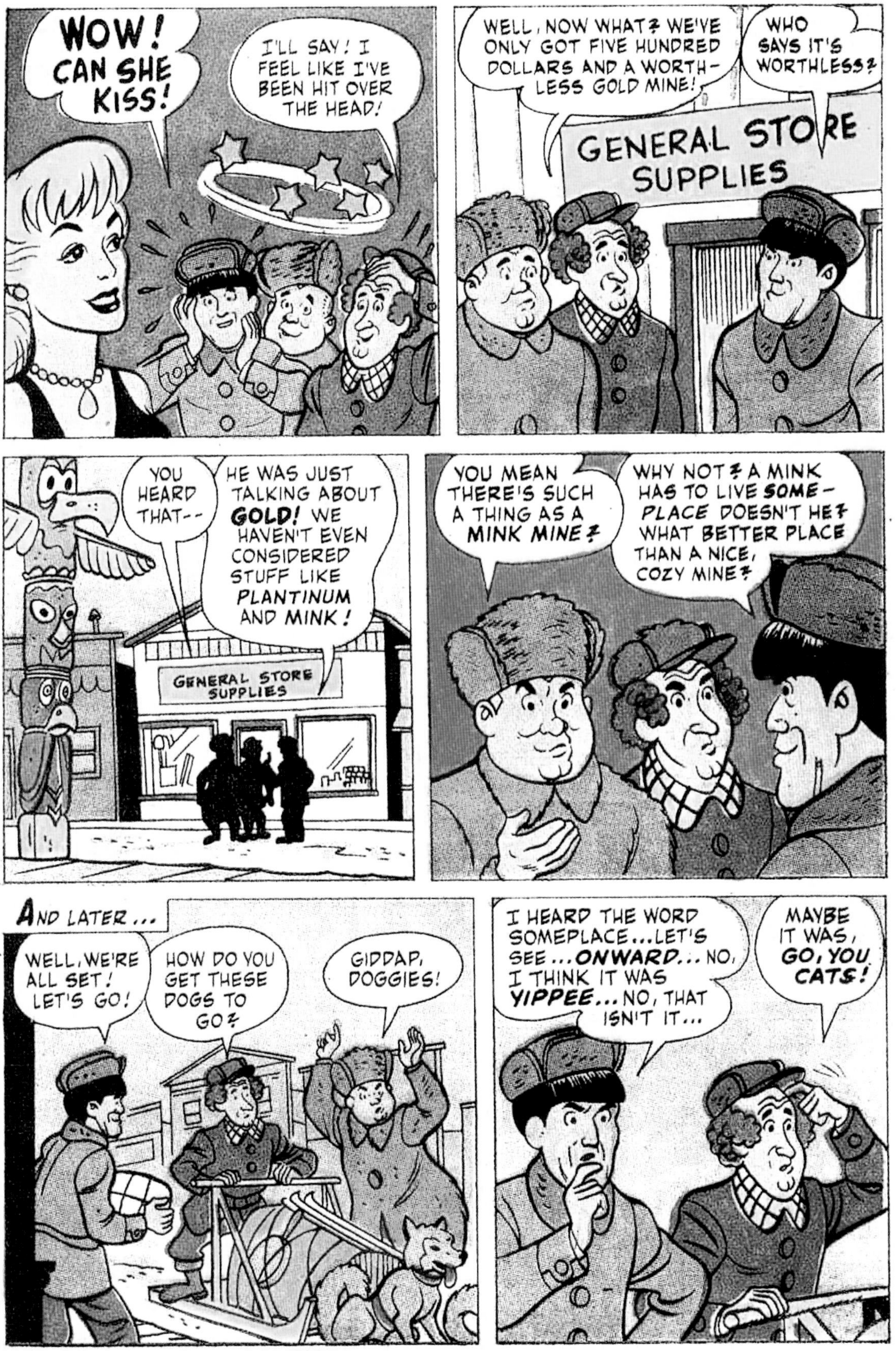
WOW! CAN SHE KISS!
I'LL SAY! I FEEL LIKE I'VE BEEN HIT OVER THE HEAD!
WELL, NOW WHAT? WE'VE ONLY GOT FIVE HUNDRED DOLLARS AND A WORTHLESS GOLD MINE!
WHO SAYS IT'S WORTHLESS?
GENERAL STORE SUPPLIES
YOU HEARD THAT--
HE WAS JUST TALKING ABOUT GOLD! WE HAVEN'T EVEN CONSIDERED STUFF LIKE PLANTINUM AND MINK!
GENERAL STORE SUPPLIES
YOU MEAN THERE'S SUCH A THING AS A MINK MINE?
WHY NOT? A MINK HAS TO LIVE SOME-PLACE DOESN'T HE? WHAT BETTER PLACE THAN A NICE, COZY MINE?
AND LATER...
WELL, WE'RE ALL SET! LET'S GO!
HOW DO YOU GET THESE DOGS TO GO?
GIDDAP, DOGGIES!
I HEARD THE WORD SOMEPLACE...LET'S SEE...ONWARD... NO, I THINK IT WAS YIPPEE... NO, THAT ISN'T IT...
MAYBE IT WAS, GO, YOU CATS!

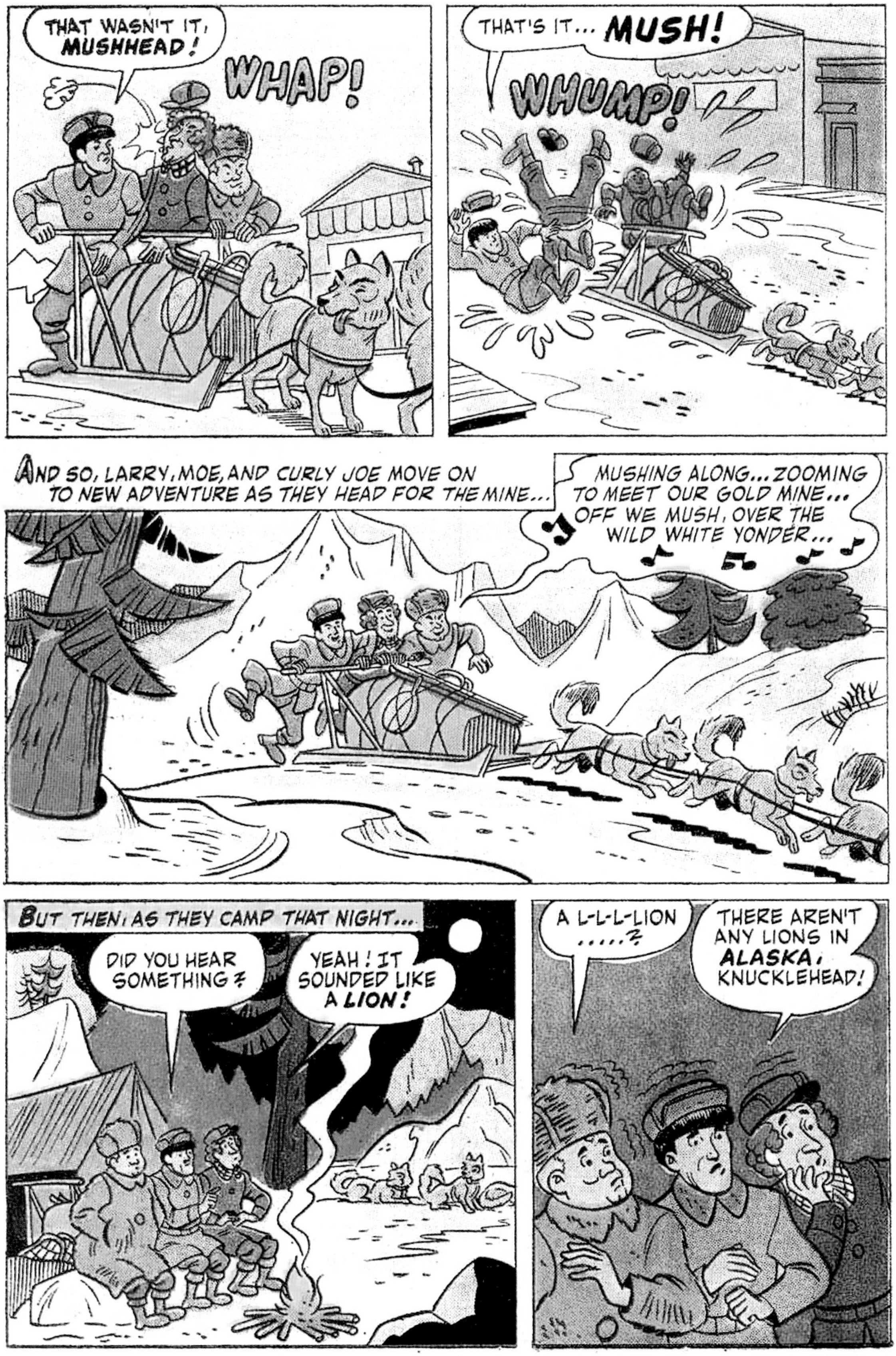
THAT WASN'T IT, MUSHHEAD!
WHAP!
THAT'S IT... MUSH!
WHUMP!
AND SO, LARRY, MOE, AND CURLY JOE MOVE ON TO NEW ADVENTURE AS THEY HEAD FOR THE MINE...
MUSHING ALONG...ZOOMING TO MEET OUR GOLD MINE... OFF WE MUSH, OVER THE WILD WHITE YONDER...
BUT THEN, AS THEY CAMP THAT NIGHT...
DID YOU HEAR SOMETHING?
YEAH! IT SOUNDED LIKE A LION!
A L-L-L-LION .....?
THERE AREN'T ANY LIONS IN ALASKA, KNUCKLEHEAD!

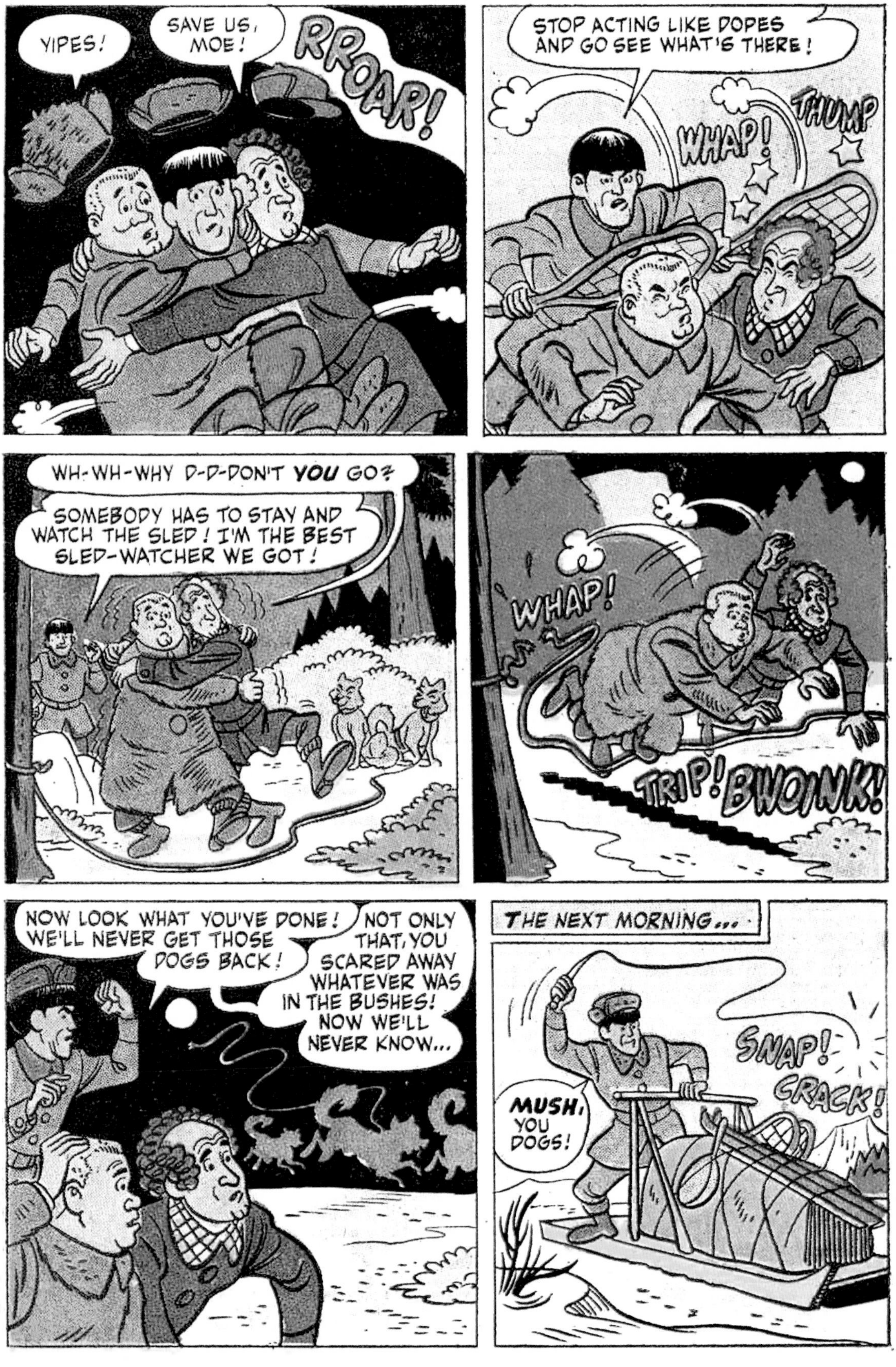
YIPES!
SAVE US, MOE!
RROAR!
STOP ACTING LIKE DOPES AND GO SEE WHAT'S THERE!
WHAP!
THUMP
WH-WH-WHY D-D-DON'T YOU GO?
SOMEBODY HAS TO STAY AND WATCH THE SLED! I'M THE BEST SLED-WATCHER WE GOT!
WHAP!
TRIP!
BWOINK!
NOW LOOK WHAT YOU'VE DONE! WE'LL NEVER GET THOSE DOGS BACK!
NOT ONLY THAT, YOU SCARED AWAY WHATEVER WAS IN THE BUSHES! NOW WE'LL NEVER KNOW...
THE NEXT MORNING...
SNAP!
CRACK!
MUSH, YOU DOGS!

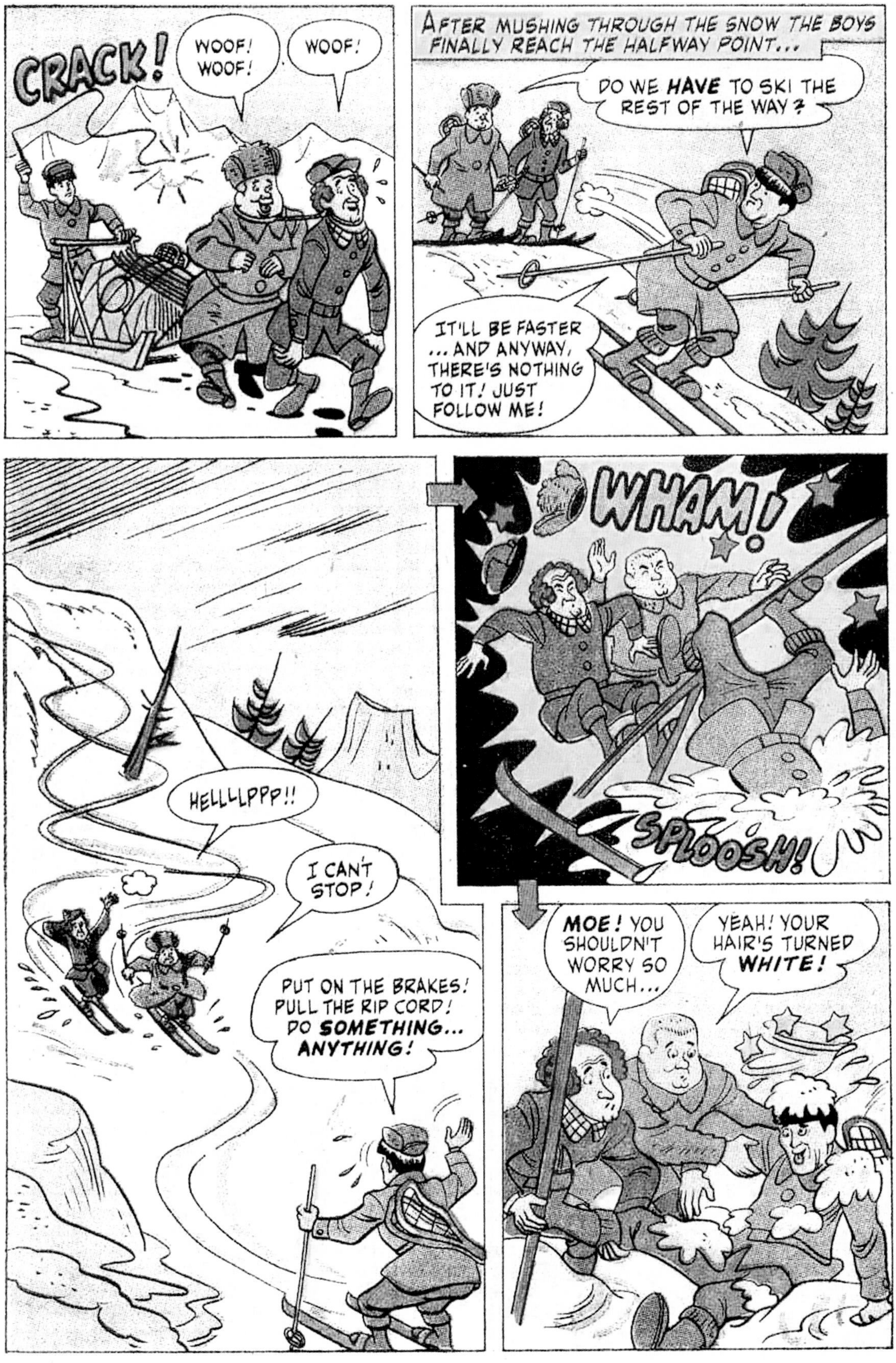
CRACK!
WOOF! WOOF!
WOOF!
AFTER MUSHING THROUGH THE SNOW THE BOYS FINALLY REACH THE HALFWAY POINT...
DO WE HAVE TO SKI THE REST OF THE WAY?
IT'LL BE FASTER ... AND ANYWAY, THERE'S NOTHING TO IT! JUST FOLLOW ME!
HELLLLPPP!!
I CAN'T STOP!
PUT ON THE BRAKES! PULL THE RIP CORD! DO SOMETHING... ANYTHING!
WHAM!
SPLOOSH!
MOE! YOU SHOULDN'T WORRY SO MUCH...
YEAH! YOUR HAIR'S TURNED WHITE!

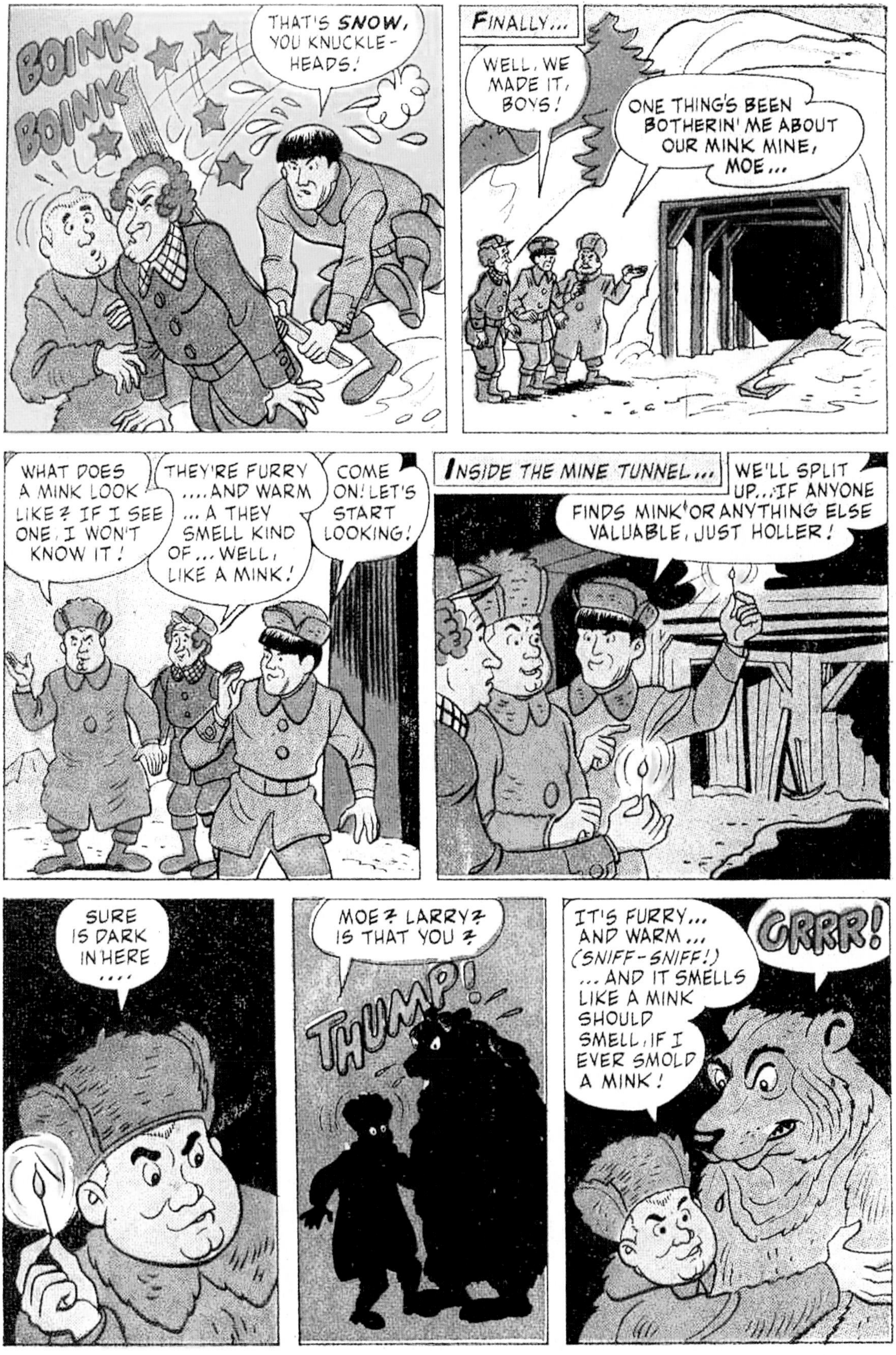

BOINK
BOINK
BOINK
THAT'S SNOW, YOU KNUCKLE-HEADS!
FINALLY...
WELL, WE MADE IT, BOYS!
ONE THING'S BEEN BOTHERIN' ME ABOUT OUR MINK MINE, MOE...
WHAT DOES A MINK LOOK LIKE? IF I SEE ONE, I WON'T KNOW IT!
THEY'RE FURRY ....AND WARM ... A THEY SMELL KIND OF ... WELL, LIKE A MINK!
COME ON! LET'S START LOOKING!
INSIDE THE MINE TUNNEL...
WE'LL SPLIT UP...IF ANYONE FINDS MINK OR ANYTHING ELSE VALUABLE, JUST HOLLER!
SURE IS DARK IN HERE ....
MOE? LARRY? IS THAT YOU?
THUMP!
IT'S FURRY... AND WARM... (SNIFF-SNIFF!) ... AND IT SMELLS LIKE A MINK SHOULD SMELL, IF I EVER SMOLD A MINK!
GRRR!

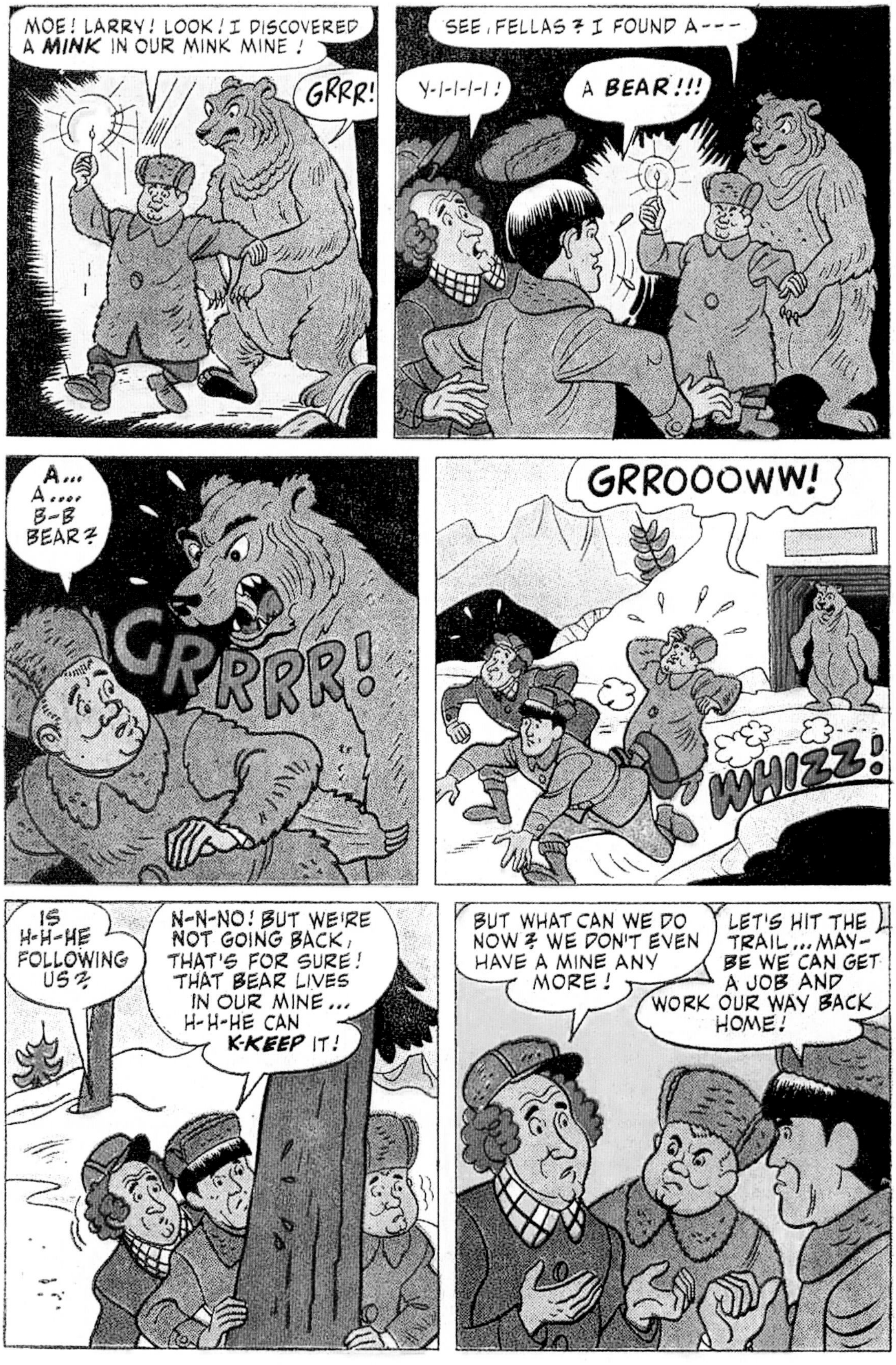
MOE! LARRY! LOOK! I DISCOVERED A MINK IN OUR MINK MINE!
GRRR!
SEE, FELLAS? I FOUND A---
Y-I-I-I-I!
A BEAR!!!
A... A.... B-B BEAR?
GRRRR!
GRROOOWW!
WHIZZ!
IS H-H-HE FOLLOWING US?
N-N-NO! BUT WE'RE NOT GOING BACK, THAT'S FOR SURE! THAT BEAR LIVES IN OUR MINE... H-H-HE CAN K-KEEP IT!
BUT WHAT CAN WE DO NOW? WE DON'T EVEN HAVE A MINE ANY MORE!
LET'S HIT THE TRAIL... MAY-BE WE CAN GET A JOB AND WORK OUR WAY BACK HOME!

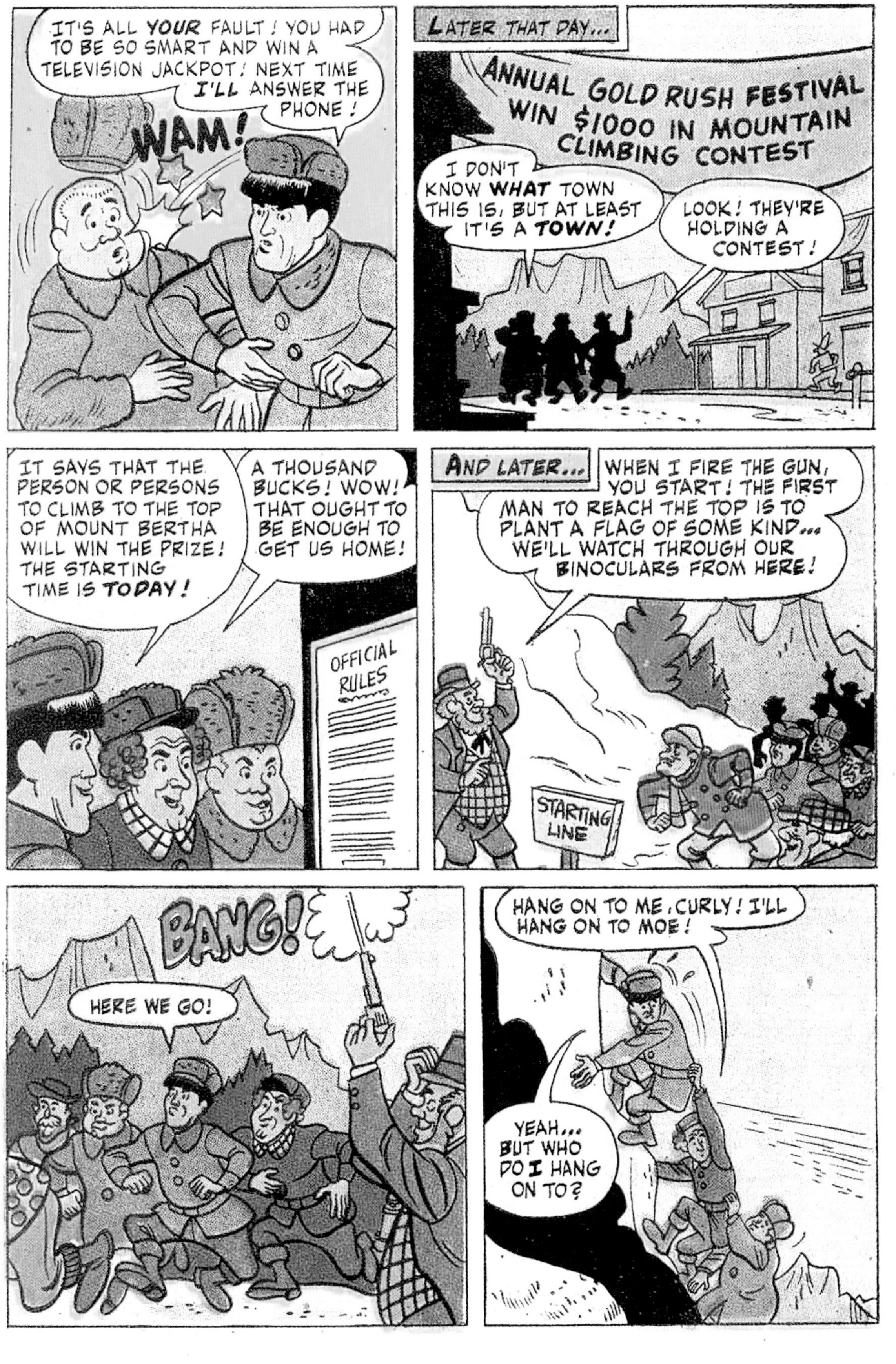
IT'S ALL YOUR FAULT! YOU HAD TO BE SO SMART AND WIN A TELEVISION JACKPOT! NEXT TIME I'LL ANSWER THE PHONE!
WAM!
LATER THAT DAY...
ANNUAL GOLD RUSH FESTIVAL WIN $1000 IN MOUNTAIN CLIMBING CONTEST
I DON'T KNOW WHAT TOWN THIS IS, BUT AT LEAST IT'S A TOWN!
LOOK! THEY'RE HOLDING A CONTEST!
IT SAYS THAT THE PERSON OR PERSONS TO CLIMB TO THE TOP OF MOUNT BERTHA WILL WIN THE PRIZE! THE STARTING TIME IS TODAY!
A THOUSAND BUCKS! WOW! THAT OUGHT TO BE ENOUGH TO GET US HOME!
OFFICIAL RULES
AND LATER...
WHEN I FIRE THE GUN, YOU START! THE FIRST MAN TO REACH THE TOP IS TO PLANT A FLAG OF SOME KIND... WE'LL WATCH THROUGH OUR BINOCULARS FROM HERE!
STARTING LINE
BANG!
HERE WE GO!
HANG ON TO ME, CURLY! I'LL HANG ON TO MOE!
YEAH... BUT WHO DO I HANG ON TO?

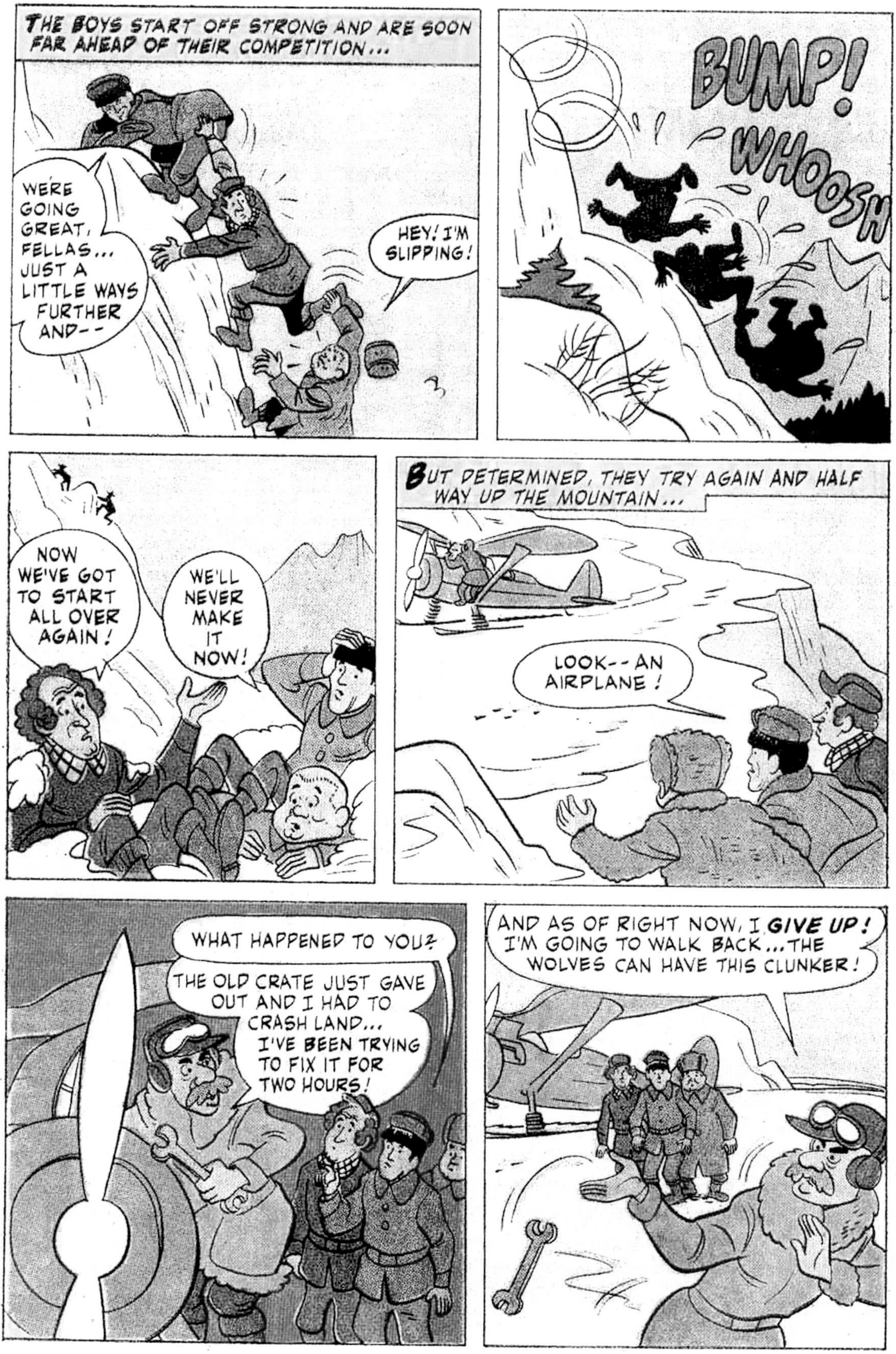
THE BOYS START OFF STRONG AND ARE SOON FAR AHEAD OF THEIR COMPETITION...
WE'RE GOING GREAT, FELLAS... JUST A LITTLE WAYS FURTHER AND--
HEY! I'M SLIPPING!
BUMP!
WHOOSH
NOW WE'VE GOT TO START ALL OVER AGAIN!
WE'LL NEVER MAKE IT NOW!
BUT DETERMINED, THEY TRY AGAIN AND HALF WAY UP THE MOUNTAIN...
LOOK--AN AIRPLANE!
WHAT HAPPENED TO YOU?
THE OLD CRATE JUST GAVE OUT AND I HAD TO CRASH LAND... I'VE BEEN TRYING TO FIX IT FOR TWO HOURS!
AND AS OF RIGHT NOW, I GIVE UP! I'M GOING TO WALK BACK... THE WOLVES CAN HAVE THIS CLUNKER!

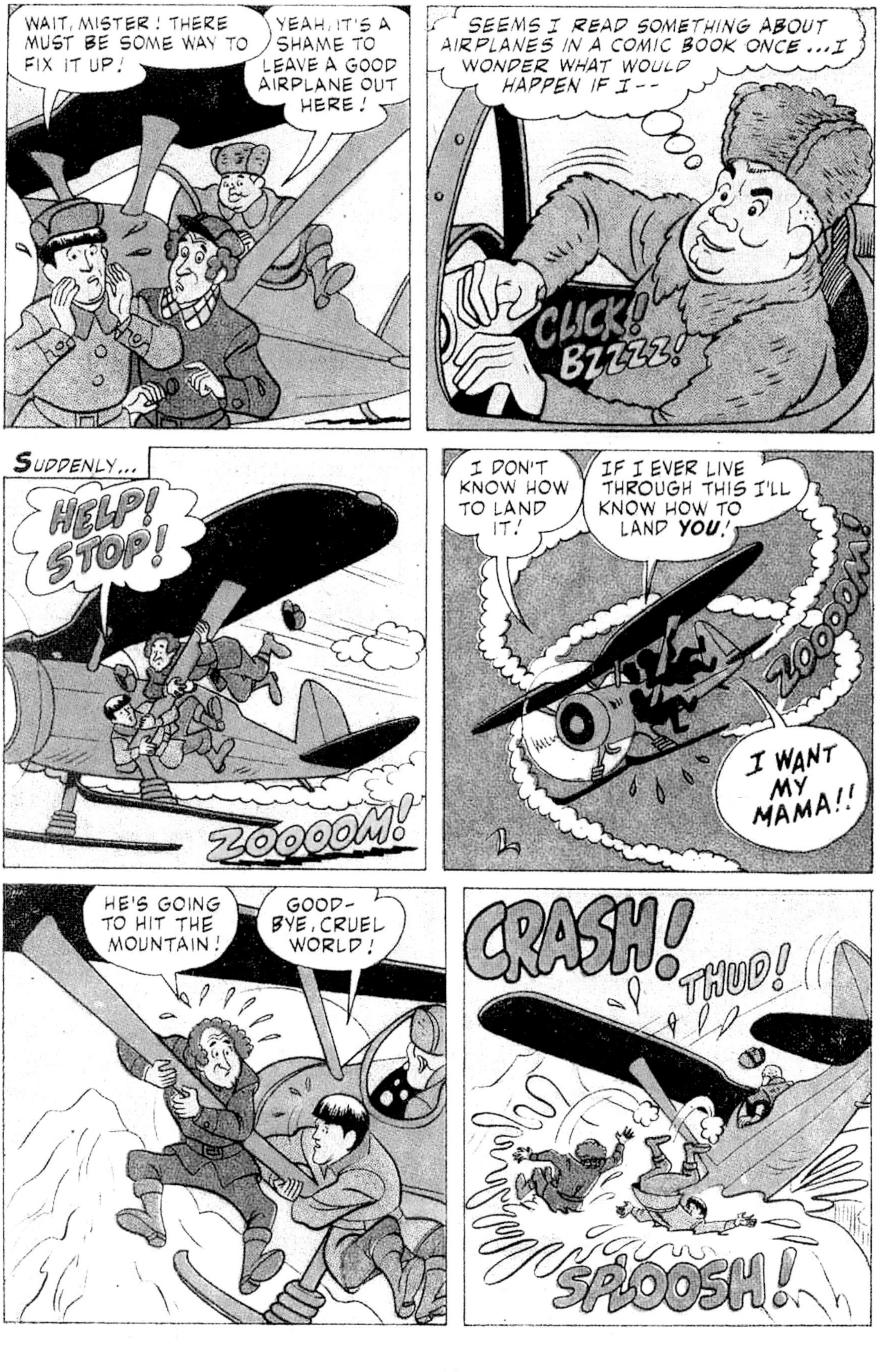
WAIT, MISTER! THERE MUST BE SOME WAY TO FIX IT UP!
YEAH, IT'S A SHAME TO LEAVE A GOOD AIRPLANE OUT HERE!
SEEMS I READ SOMETHING ABOUT AIRPLANES IN A COMIC BOOK ONCE ... I WONDER WHAT WOULD HAPPEN IF I--
CLICK! BZZZZ!
SUDDENLY...
HELP! STOP!
ZOOOOOM!
I DON'T KNOW HOW TO LAND IT!
IF I EVER LIVE THROUGH THIS I'LL KNOW HOW TO LAND YOU!
ZOOOOM!
I WANT MY MAMA!!
HE'S GOING TO HIT THE MOUNTAIN!
GOOD-BYE, CRUEL WORLD!
CRASH!
THUD!
SPLOOSH!

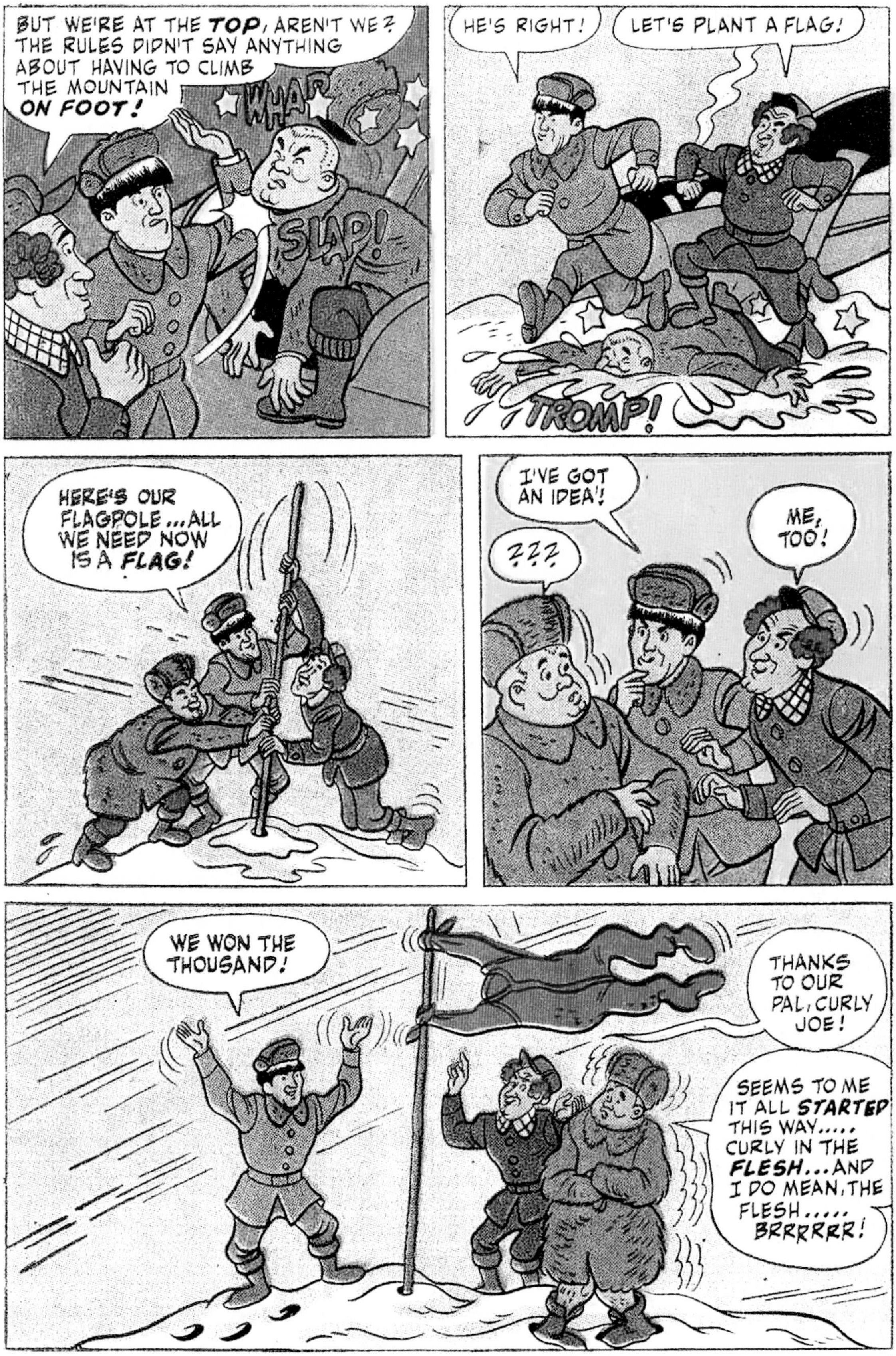
BUT WE'RE AT THE TOP, AREN'T WE? THE RULES DIDN'T SAY ANYTHING ABOUT HAVING TO CLIMB THE MOUNTAIN ON FOOT!
WHAP
SLAP!
HE'S RIGHT!
LET'S PLANT A FLAG!
TROMP!
HERE'S OUR FLAGPOLE ... ALL WE NEED NOW IS A FLAG!
I'VE GOT AN IDEA!
???
ME, TOO!
WE WON THE THOUSAND!
THANKS TO OUR PAL, CURLY JOE!
SEEMS TO ME IT ALL STARTED THIS WAY..... CURLY IN THE FLESH... AND I DO MEAN, THE FLESH..... BRRRRRR!

LARRY *tries to* FOLD IT!

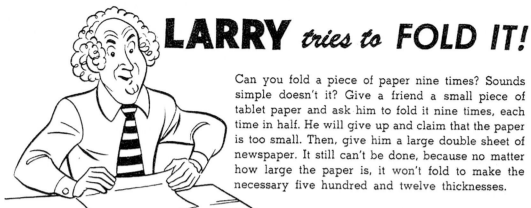

Can you fold a piece of paper nine times? Sounds simple doesn't it? Give a friend a small piece of tablet paper and ask him to fold it nine times, each time in half. He will give up and claim that the paper is too small. Then, give him a large double sheet of newspaper. It still can't be done, because no matter how large the paper is, it won't fold to make the necessary five hundred and twelve thicknesses.

MOE *tries to* PICK IT UP!

There is a dollar bill on the floor, but Moe can't bend over and pick it up while keeping his heels against the wall. Challenge a friend to try this stunt without bending his knees or moving his feet. Anything you put on the floor before him will be safe.

CURLY JOE
tries to MOVE IT!

Curly Joe has three empty glasses and three glasses filled with water arranged as in picture (A). He wants to change them so that they will alternate, one filled, one empty, and so on, as shown in picture (B). He can move only one glass. Before reading on, see if you can do it. To accomplish this trick, simply lift glass number four and pour its contents into glass number one, then replace the glass. Test the wits of your friends with these "Stooge Stunts."

(A)   (B)

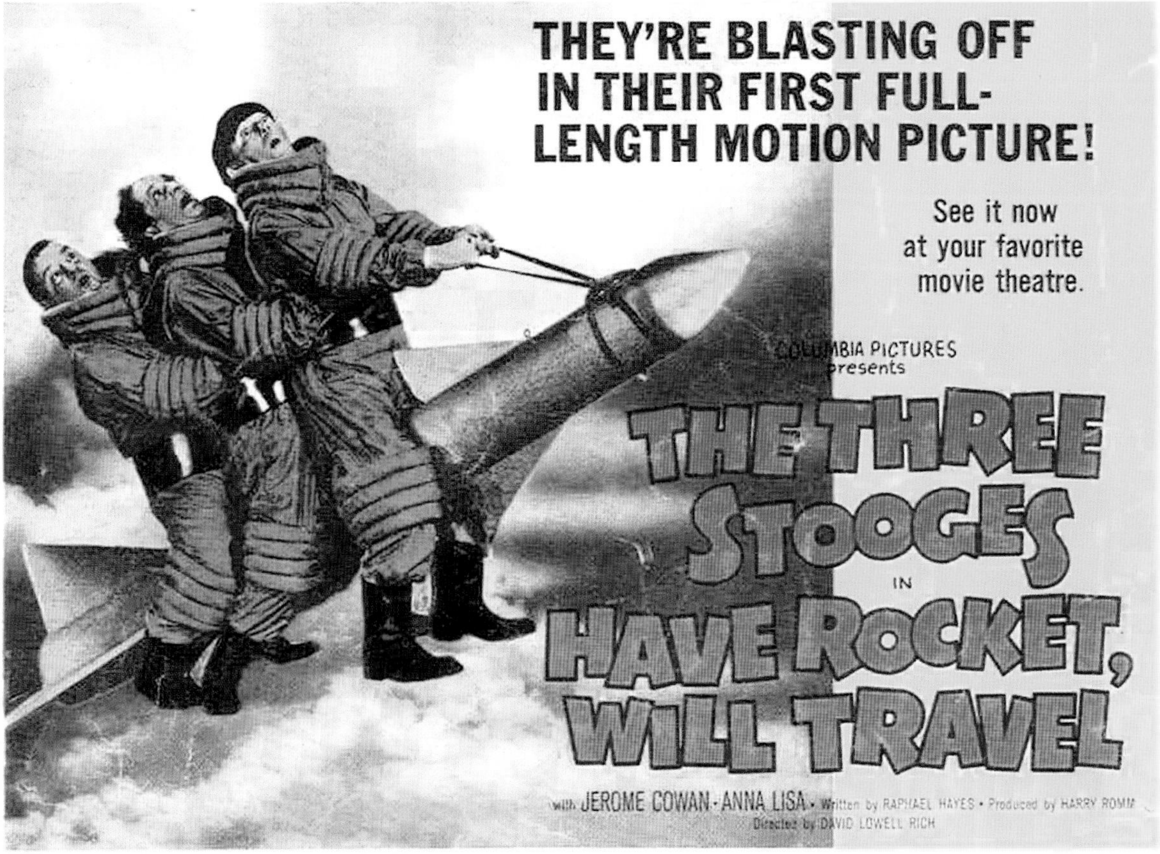
THEY'RE BLASTING OFF IN THEIR FIRST FULL-LENGTH MOTION PICTURE!
See it now at your favorite movie theatre.
COLUMBIA PICTURES presents
THE THREE STOOGES IN HAVE ROCKET, WILL TRAVEL
with JEROME COWAN · ANNA LISA · Written by RAPHAEL HAYES · Produced by HARRY ROMM
Directed by DAVID LOWELL RICH

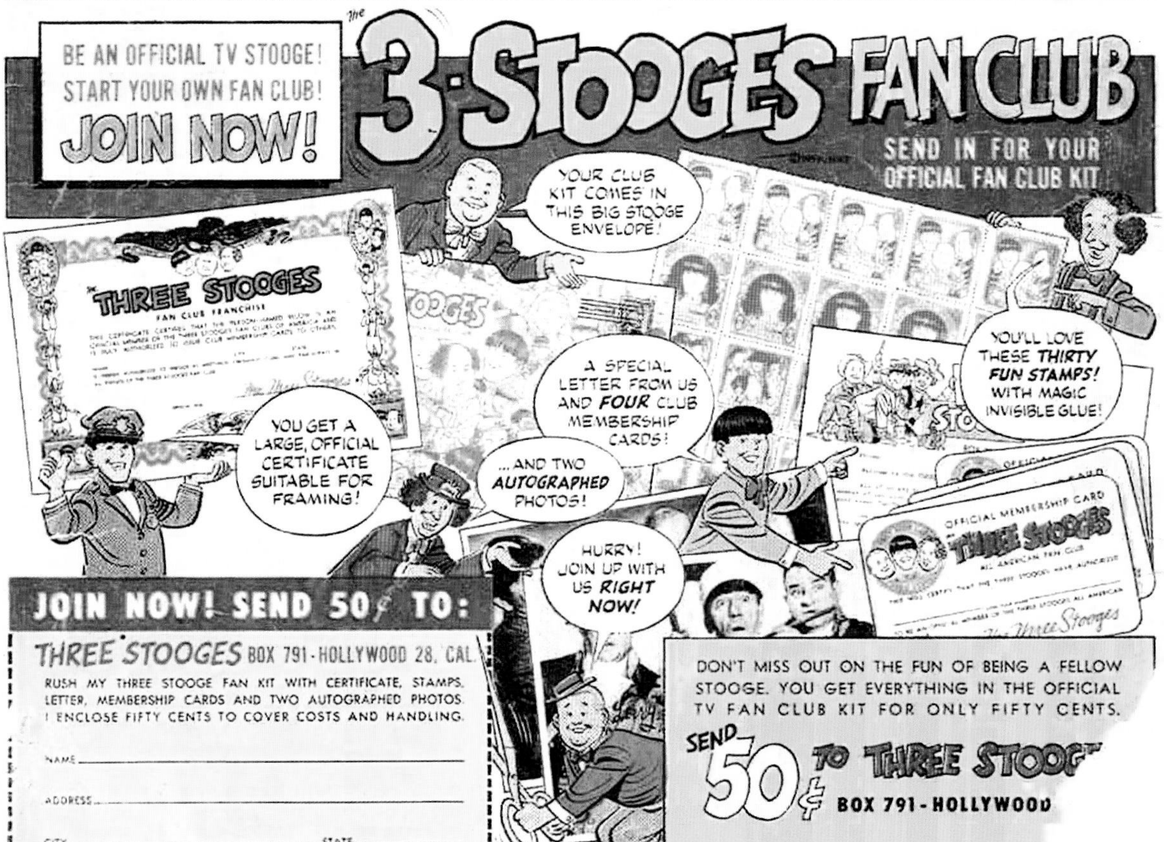
BE AN OFFICIAL TV STOOGE! START YOUR OWN FAN CLUB! JOIN NOW!
The 3-STOOGES FAN CLUB
SEND IN FOR YOUR OFFICIAL FAN CLUB KIT
YOUR CLUB KIT COMES IN THIS BIG STOOGE ENVELOPE!
THREE STOOGES FAN CLUB FRANCHISE
YOU'LL LOVE THESE THIRTY FUN STAMPS! WITH MAGIC INVISIBLE GLUE!
A SPECIAL LETTER FROM US AND FOUR CLUB MEMBERSHIP CARDS!
YOU GET A LARGE, OFFICIAL CERTIFICATE SUITABLE FOR FRAMING!
...AND TWO AUTOGRAPHED PHOTOS!
HURRY! JOIN UP WITH US RIGHT NOW!
OFFICIAL MEMBERSHIP CARD THREE STOOGES ALL AMERICAN FAN CLUB
JOIN NOW! SEND 50¢ TO:
THREE STOOGES BOX 791 - HOLLYWOOD 28, CAL.
RUSH MY THREE STOOGE FAN KIT WITH CERTIFICATE, STAMPS, LETTER, MEMBERSHIP CARDS AND TWO AUTOGRAPHED PHOTOS. I ENCLOSE FIFTY CENTS TO COVER COSTS AND HANDLING.
NAME
ADDRESS
CITY STATE
DON'T MISS OUT ON THE FUN OF BEING A FELLOW STOOGE. YOU GET EVERYTHING IN THE OFFICIAL TV FAN CLUB KIT FOR ONLY FIFTY CENTS.
SEND 50¢ TO THREE STOOG
BOX 791 - HOLLYWOOD

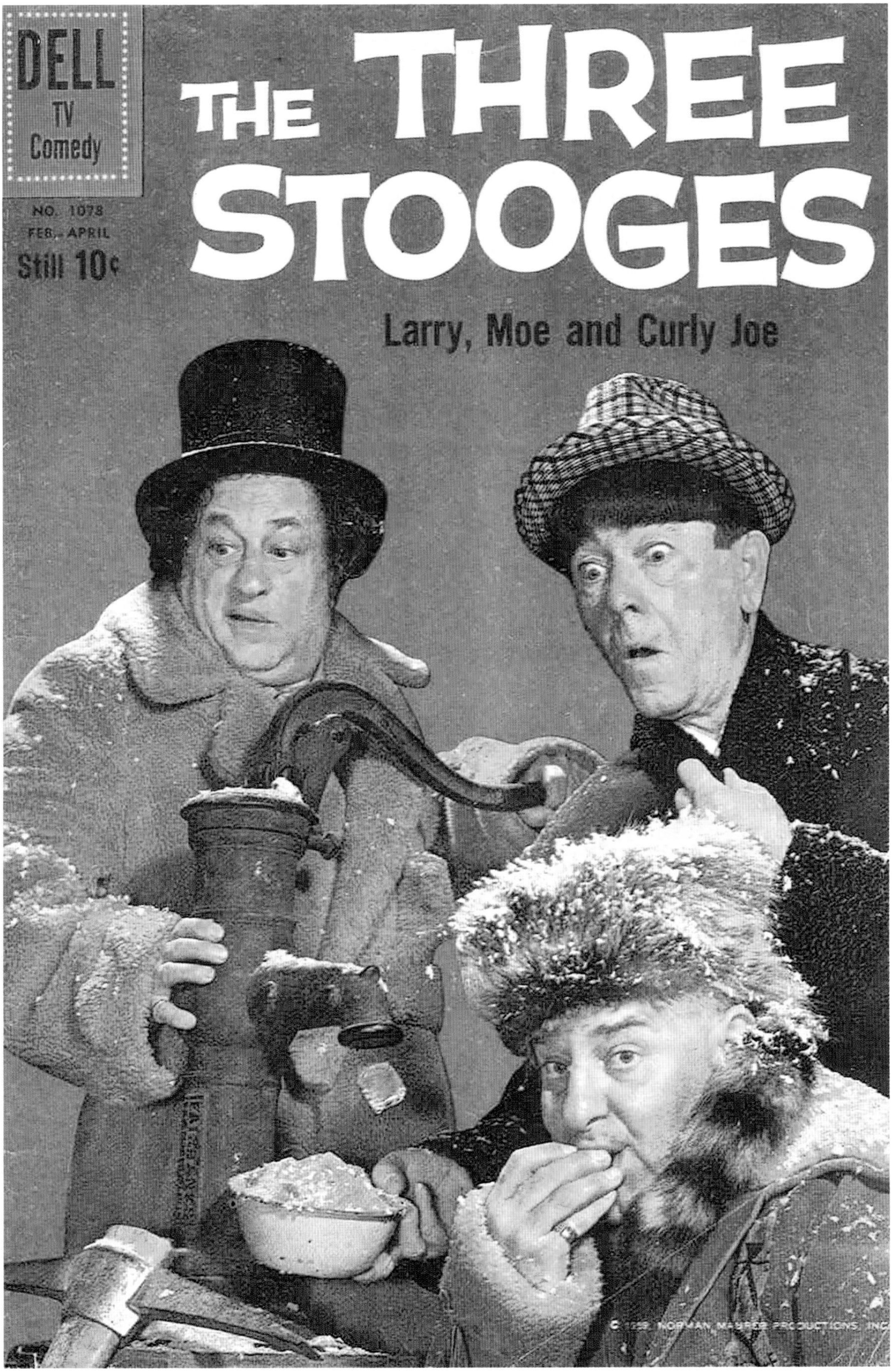
DELL
TV
Comedy
NO. 1078
FEB.-APRIL
Still 10¢
THE THREE STOOGES
Larry, Moe and Curly Joe

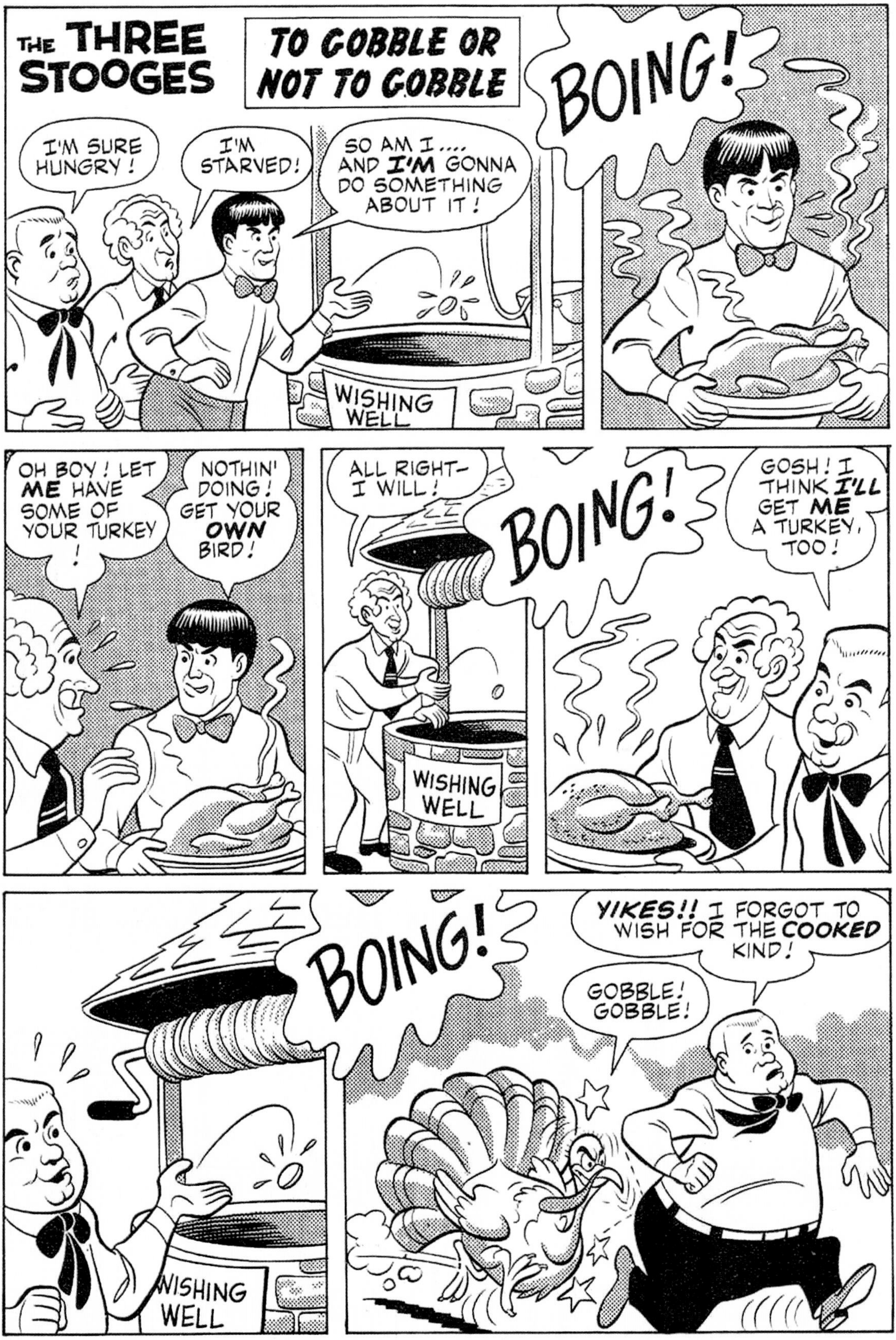

THE THREE STOOGES
TO GOBBLE OR NOT TO GOBBLE
I'M SURE HUNGRY!
I'M STARVED!
SO AM I.... AND I'M GONNA DO SOMETHING ABOUT IT!
WISHING WELL
BOING!
OH BOY! LET ME HAVE SOME OF YOUR TURKEY!
NOTHIN' DOING! GET YOUR OWN BIRD!
ALL RIGHT- I WILL!
WISHING WELL
BOING!
GOSH! I THINK I'LL GET ME A TURKEY, TOO!
BOING!
WISHING WELL
YIKES!! I FORGOT TO WISH FOR THE COOKED KIND!
GOBBLE! GOBBLE!

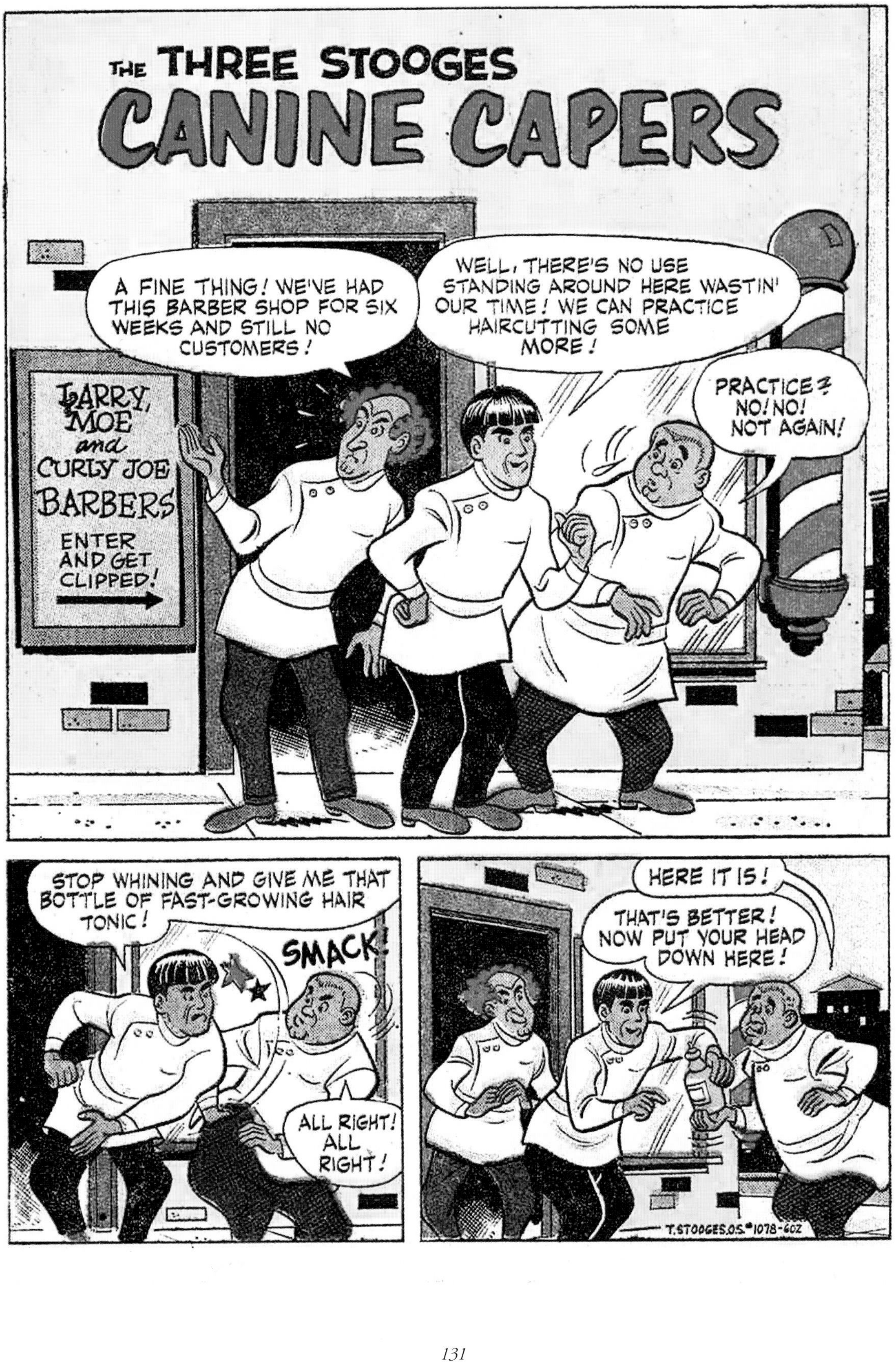
THE THREE STOOGES
CANINE CAPERS
A FINE THING! WE'VE HAD THIS BARBER SHOP FOR SIX WEEKS AND STILL NO CUSTOMERS!
WELL, THERE'S NO USE STANDING AROUND HERE WASTIN' OUR TIME! WE CAN PRACTICE HAIRCUTTING SOME MORE!
PRACTICE? NO! NO! NOT AGAIN!
LARRY, MOE and CURLY JOE BARBERS
ENTER AND GET CLIPPED!
STOP WHINING AND GIVE ME THAT BOTTLE OF FAST-GROWING HAIR TONIC!
SMACK!
ALL RIGHT! ALL RIGHT!
HERE IT IS!
THAT'S BETTER! NOW PUT YOUR HEAD DOWN HERE!
T.STOOGES.O.S.#1078-602

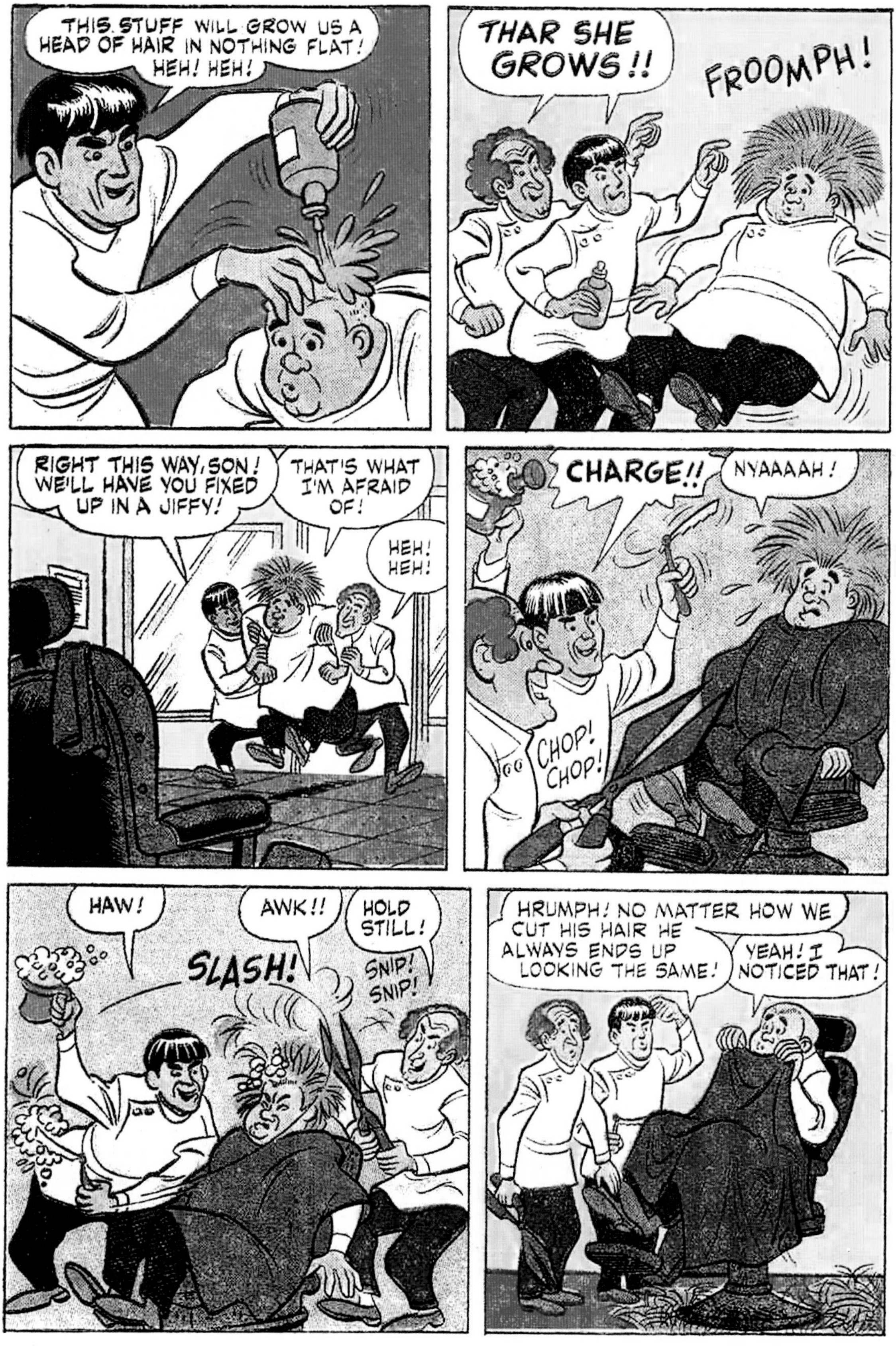
THIS STUFF WILL GROW US A HEAD OF HAIR IN NOTHING FLAT! HEH! HEH!
THAR SHE GROWS!!
FROOMPH!
RIGHT THIS WAY, SON! WE'LL HAVE YOU FIXED UP IN A JIFFY!
THAT'S WHAT I'M AFRAID OF!
HEH! HEH!
CHARGE!!
NYAAAAH!
CHOP! CHOP!
HAW!
SLASH!
AWK!!
HOLD STILL!
SNIP! SNIP!
HRUMPH! NO MATTER HOW WE CUT HIS HAIR HE ALWAYS ENDS UP LOOKING THE SAME!
YEAH! I NOTICED THAT!

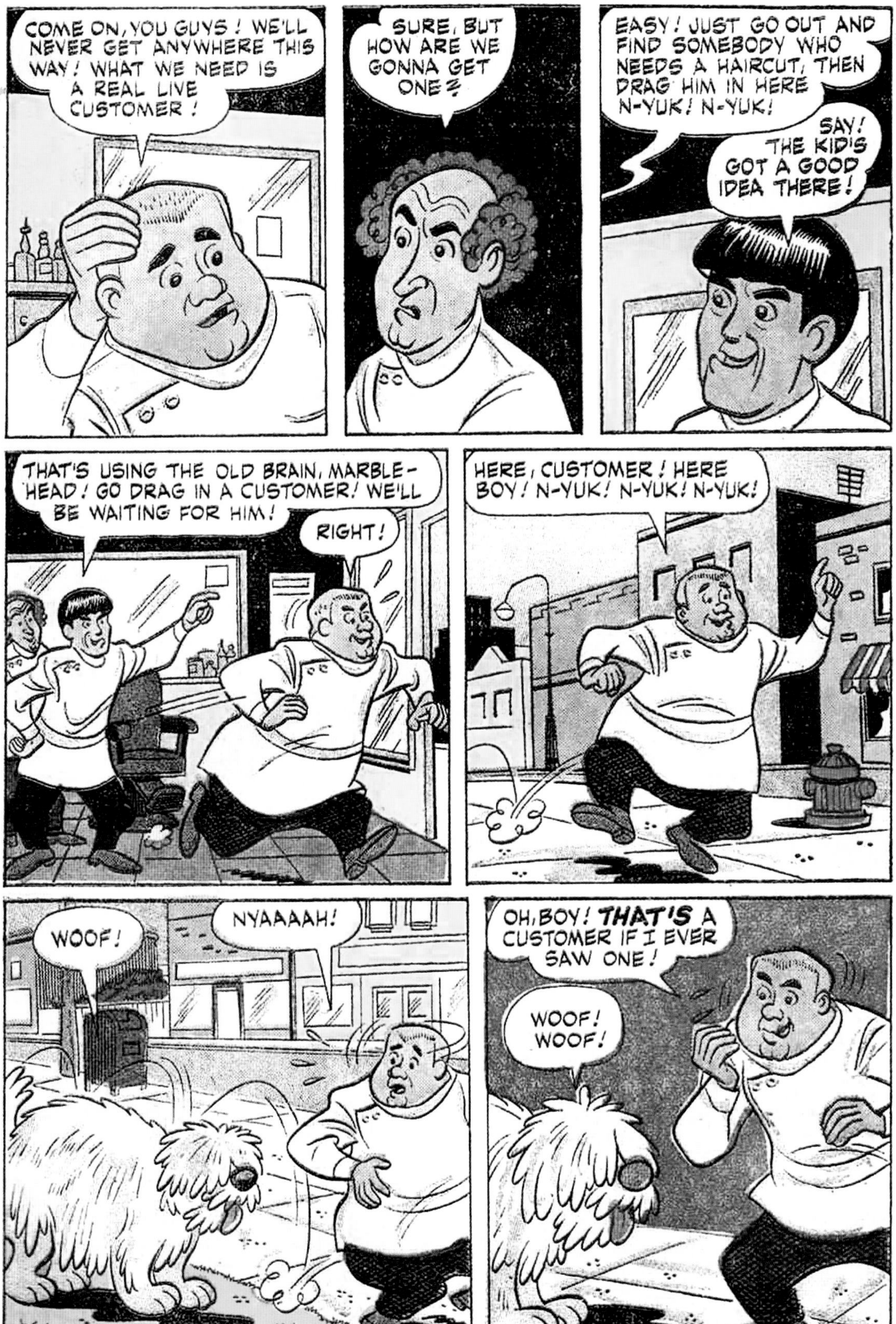
COME ON, YOU GUYS! WE'LL NEVER GET ANYWHERE THIS WAY! WHAT WE NEED IS A REAL LIVE CUSTOMER!
SURE, BUT HOW ARE WE GONNA GET ONE?
EASY! JUST GO OUT AND FIND SOMEBODY WHO NEEDS A HAIRCUT, THEN DRAG HIM IN HERE N-YUK! N-YUK!
SAY! THE KID'S GOT A GOOD IDEA THERE!
THAT'S USING THE OLD BRAIN, MARBLE-HEAD! GO DRAG IN A CUSTOMER! WE'LL BE WAITING FOR HIM!
RIGHT!
HERE, CUSTOMER! HERE BOY! N-YUK! N-YUK! N-YUK!
WOOF!
NYAAAAH!
OH, BOY! THAT'S A CUSTOMER IF I EVER SAW ONE!
WOOF! WOOF!

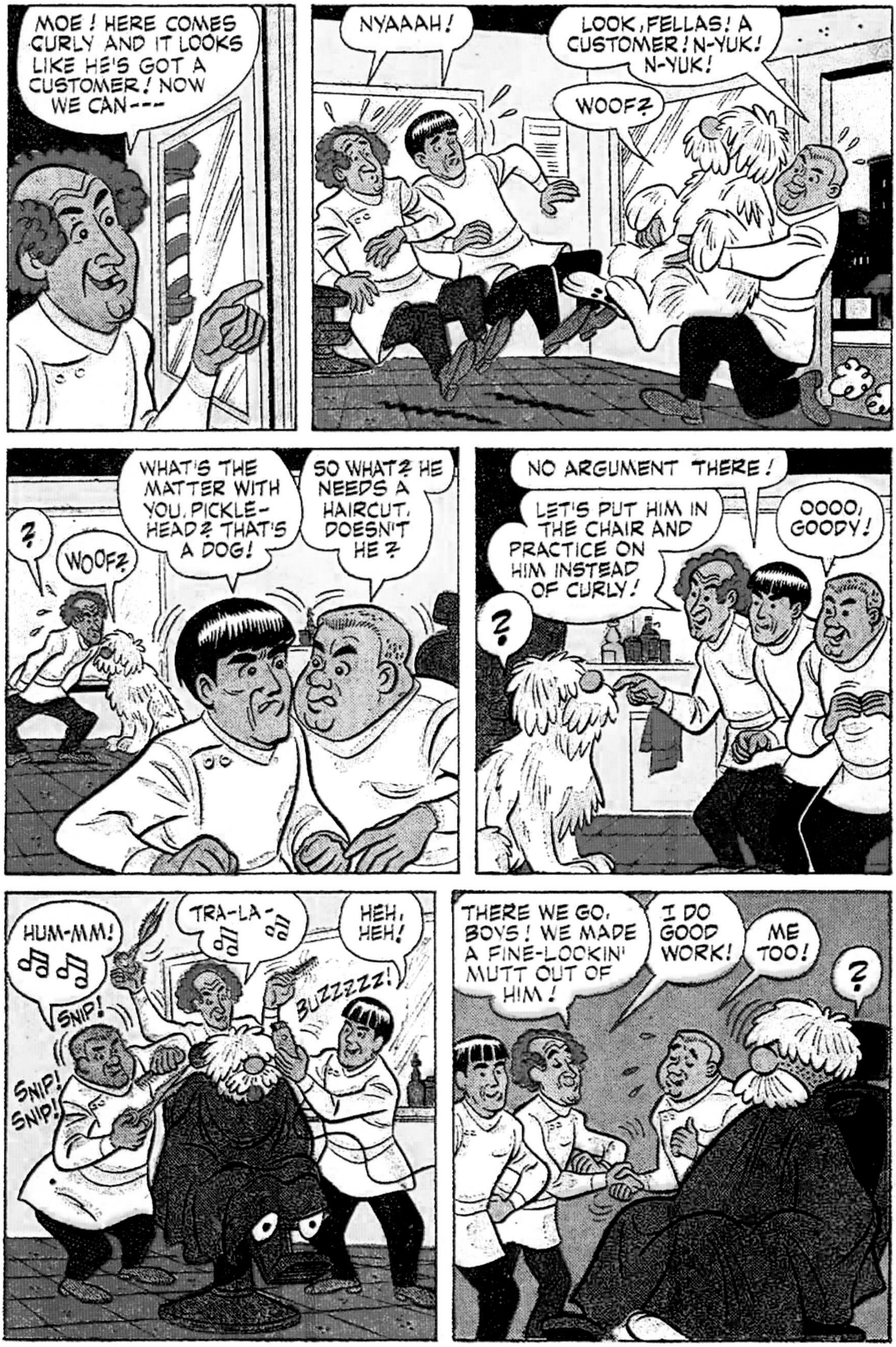
MOE! HERE COMES CURLY AND IT LOOKS LIKE HE'S GOT A CUSTOMER! NOW WE CAN---
NYAAAH!
LOOK, FELLAS! A CUSTOMER! N-YUK! N-YUK!
WOOF?
?
WOOF?
WHAT'S THE MATTER WITH YOU, PICKLE-HEAD? THAT'S A DOG!
SO WHAT? HE NEEDS A HAIRCUT, DOESN'T HE?
NO ARGUMENT THERE!
LET'S PUT HIM IN THE CHAIR AND PRACTICE ON HIM INSTEAD OF CURLY!
OOOO, GOODY!
?
HUM-MM!
TRA-LA-
HEH, HEH!
SNIP!
SNIP! SNIP!
BUZZZZZ!
THERE WE GO, BOYS! WE MADE A FINE-LOOKIN' MUTT OUT OF HIM!
I DO GOOD WORK!
ME TOO!
?

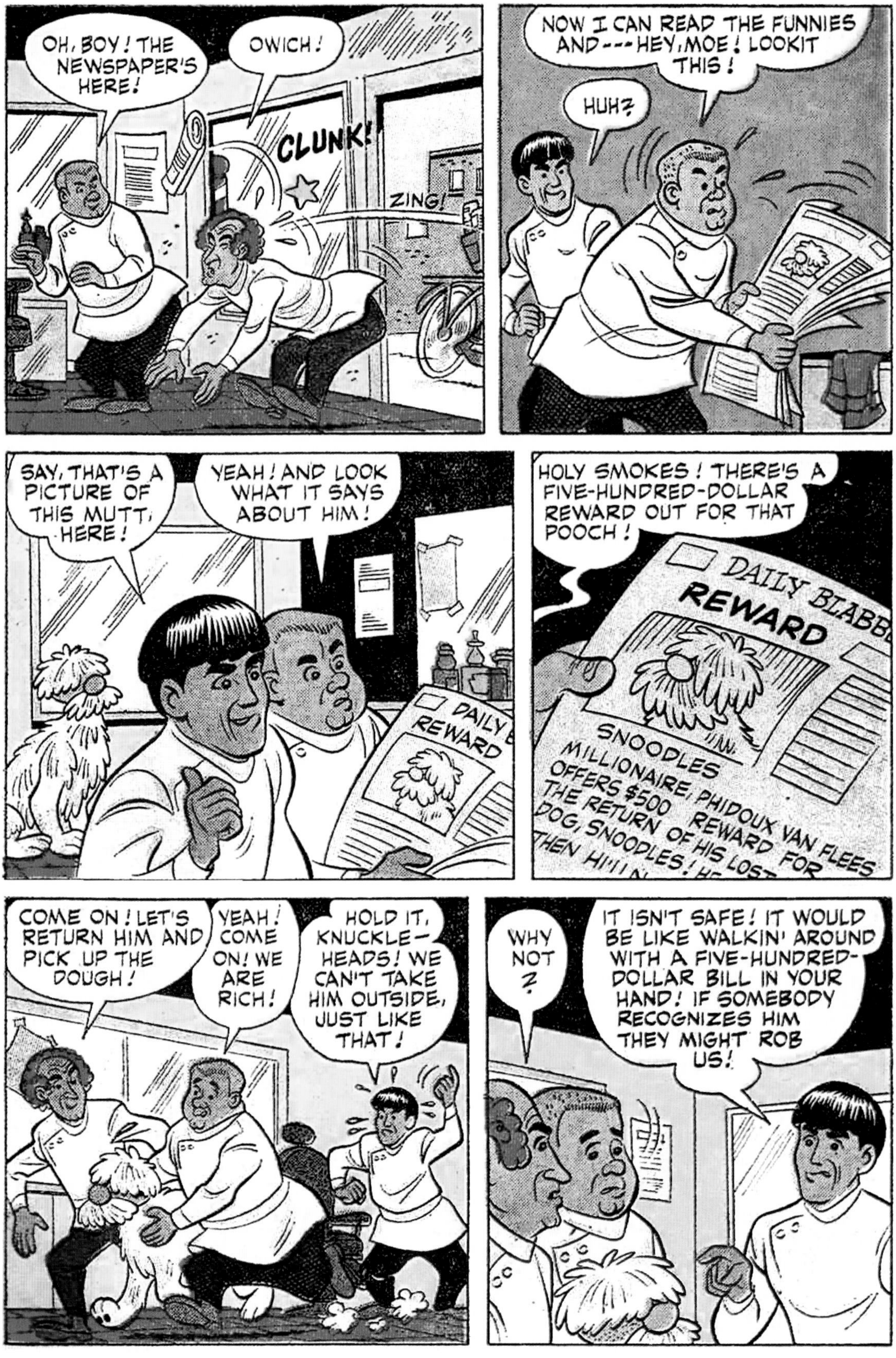
OH, BOY! THE NEWSPAPER'S HERE!
OWICH!
CLUNK!
ZING!
NOW I CAN READ THE FUNNIES AND---HEY, MOE! LOOKIT THIS!
HUH?
SAY, THAT'S A PICTURE OF THIS MUTT, HERE!
YEAH! AND LOOK WHAT IT SAYS ABOUT HIM!
DAILY
REWARD
HOLY SMOKES! THERE'S A FIVE-HUNDRED-DOLLAR REWARD OUT FOR THAT POOCH!
DAILY BLABB
REWARD
SNOODLES
MILLIONAIRE, PHIDOUX VAN FLEES
OFFERS $500 REWARD FOR
THE RETURN OF HIS LOST
DOG, SNOODLES!
COME ON! LET'S RETURN HIM AND PICK UP THE DOUGH!
YEAH! COME ON! WE ARE RICH!
HOLD IT, KNUCKLE-HEADS! WE CAN'T TAKE HIM OUTSIDE, JUST LIKE THAT!
WHY NOT?
IT ISN'T SAFE! IT WOULD BE LIKE WALKIN' AROUND WITH A FIVE-HUNDRED-DOLLAR BILL IN YOUR HAND! IF SOMEBODY RECOGNIZES HIM THEY MIGHT ROB US!

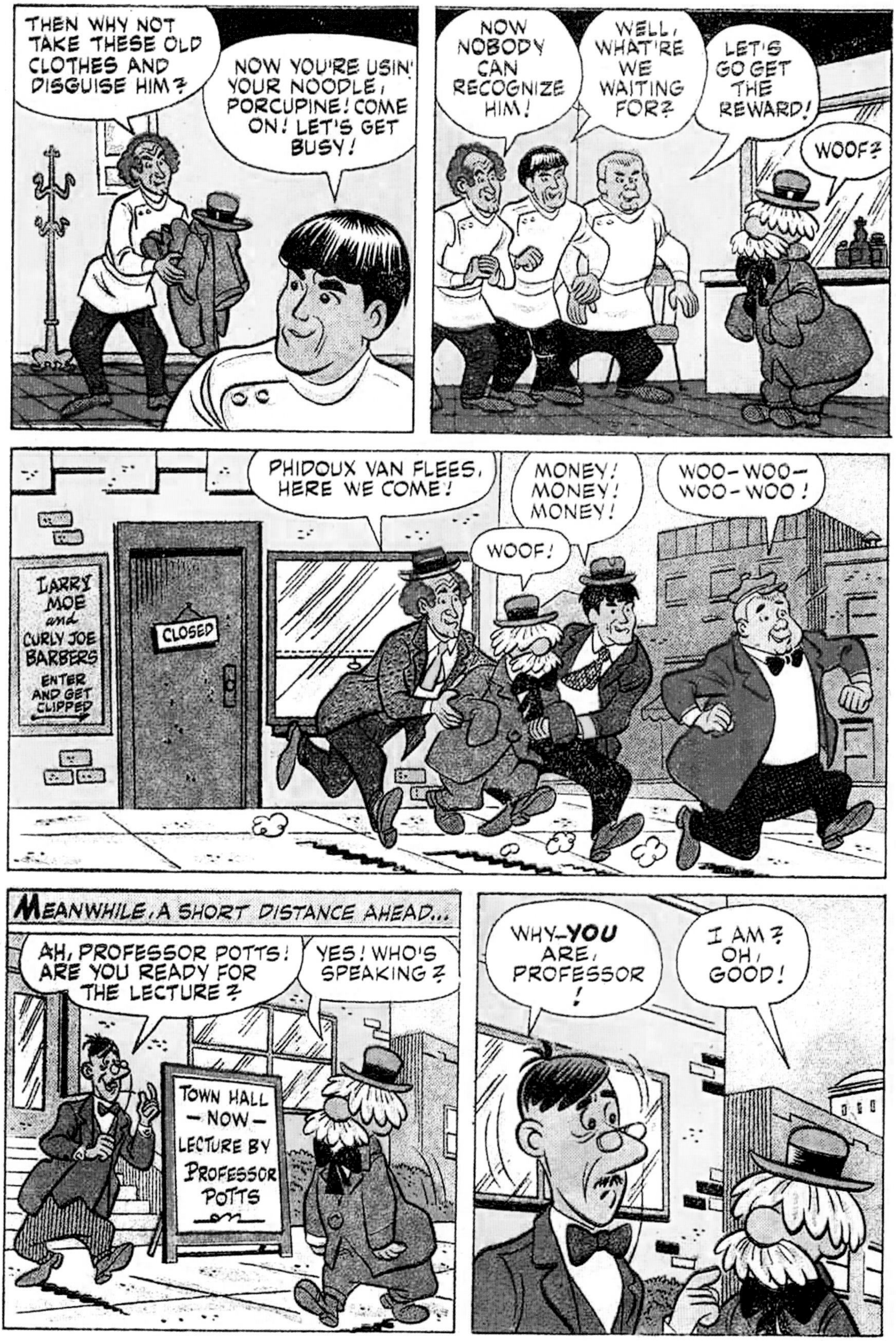
THEN WHY NOT TAKE THESE OLD CLOTHES AND DISGUISE HIM?
NOW YOU'RE USIN' YOUR NOODLE, PORCUPINE! COME ON! LET'S GET BUSY!
NOW NOBODY CAN RECOGNIZE HIM!
WELL, WHAT'RE WE WAITING FOR?
LET'S GO GET THE REWARD!
WOOF?
PHIDOUX VAN FLEES, HERE WE COME!
WOOF!
MONEY! MONEY! MONEY!
WOO-WOO-WOO-WOO!
LARRY MOE and CURLY JOE BARBERS ENTER AND GET CLIPPED
CLOSED
MEANWHILE, A SHORT DISTANCE AHEAD...
AH, PROFESSOR POTTS! ARE YOU READY FOR THE LECTURE?
YES! WHO'S SPEAKING?
TOWN HALL —NOW— LECTURE BY PROFESSOR POTTS
WHY—YOU ARE, PROFESSOR!
I AM? OH, GOOD!

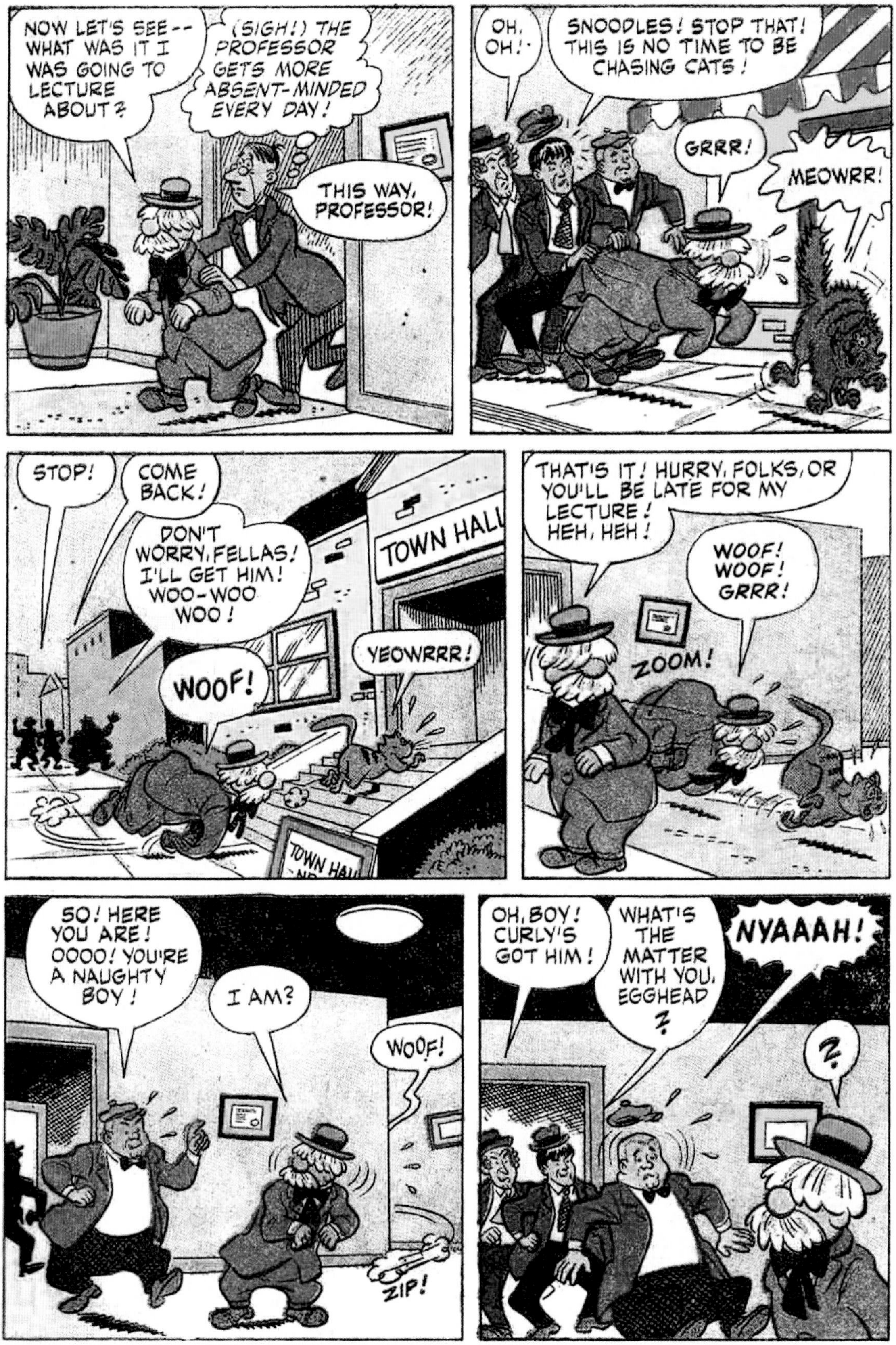
NOW LET'S SEE-- WHAT WAS IT I WAS GOING TO LECTURE ABOUT?
(SIGH!) THE PROFESSOR GETS MORE ABSENT-MINDED EVERY DAY!
THIS WAY, PROFESSOR!
OH, OH!
SNOODLES! STOP THAT! THIS IS NO TIME TO BE CHASING CATS!
GRRR!
MEOWRR!
STOP!
COME BACK!
DON'T WORRY, FELLAS! I'LL GET HIM! WOO-WOO WOO!
TOWN HALL
WOOF!
YEOWRRR!
THAT'S IT! HURRY, FOLKS, OR YOU'LL BE LATE FOR MY LECTURE! HEH, HEH!
WOOF! WOOF! GRRR!
ZOOM!
SO! HERE YOU ARE! OOOO! YOU'RE A NAUGHTY BOY!
I AM?
WOOF!
ZIP!
OH, BOY! CURLY'S GOT HIM!
WHAT'S THE MATTER WITH YOU, EGGHEAD?
NYAAAH!
?

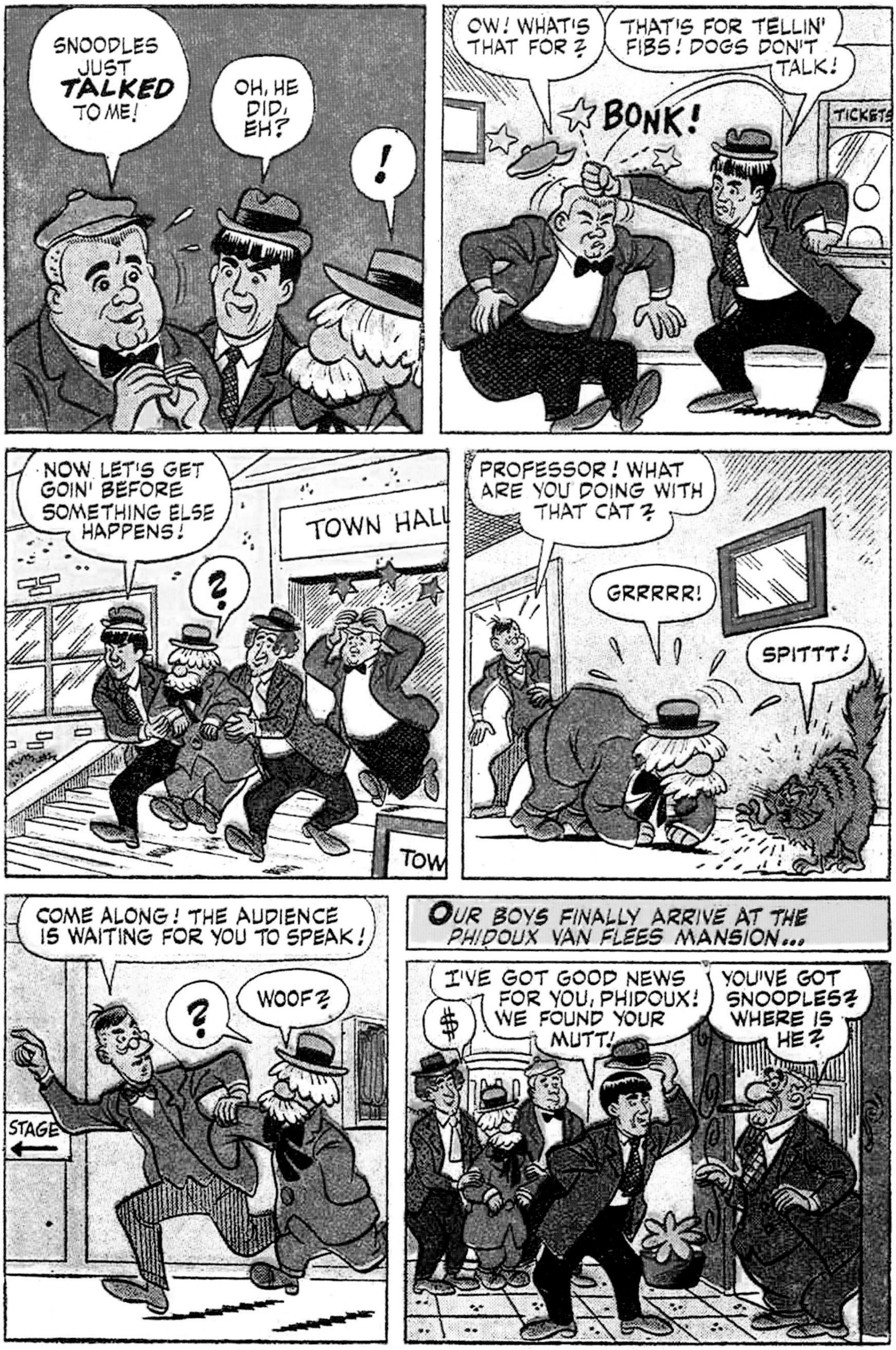

SNOODLES JUST TALKED TO ME!
OH, HE DID, EH?
!
OW! WHAT'S THAT FOR?
THAT'S FOR TELLIN' FIBS! DOGS DON'T TALK!
BONK!
TICKETS
NOW LET'S GET GOIN' BEFORE SOMETHING ELSE HAPPENS!
TOWN HALL
?
TOW
PROFESSOR! WHAT ARE YOU DOING WITH THAT CAT?
GRRRRR!
SPITTT!
COME ALONG! THE AUDIENCE IS WAITING FOR YOU TO SPEAK!
?
WOOF?
STAGE
OUR BOYS FINALLY ARRIVE AT THE PHIDOUX VAN FLEES MANSION...
I'VE GOT GOOD NEWS FOR YOU, PHIDOUX! WE FOUND YOUR MUTT!
$
YOU'VE GOT SNOODLES? WHERE IS HE?

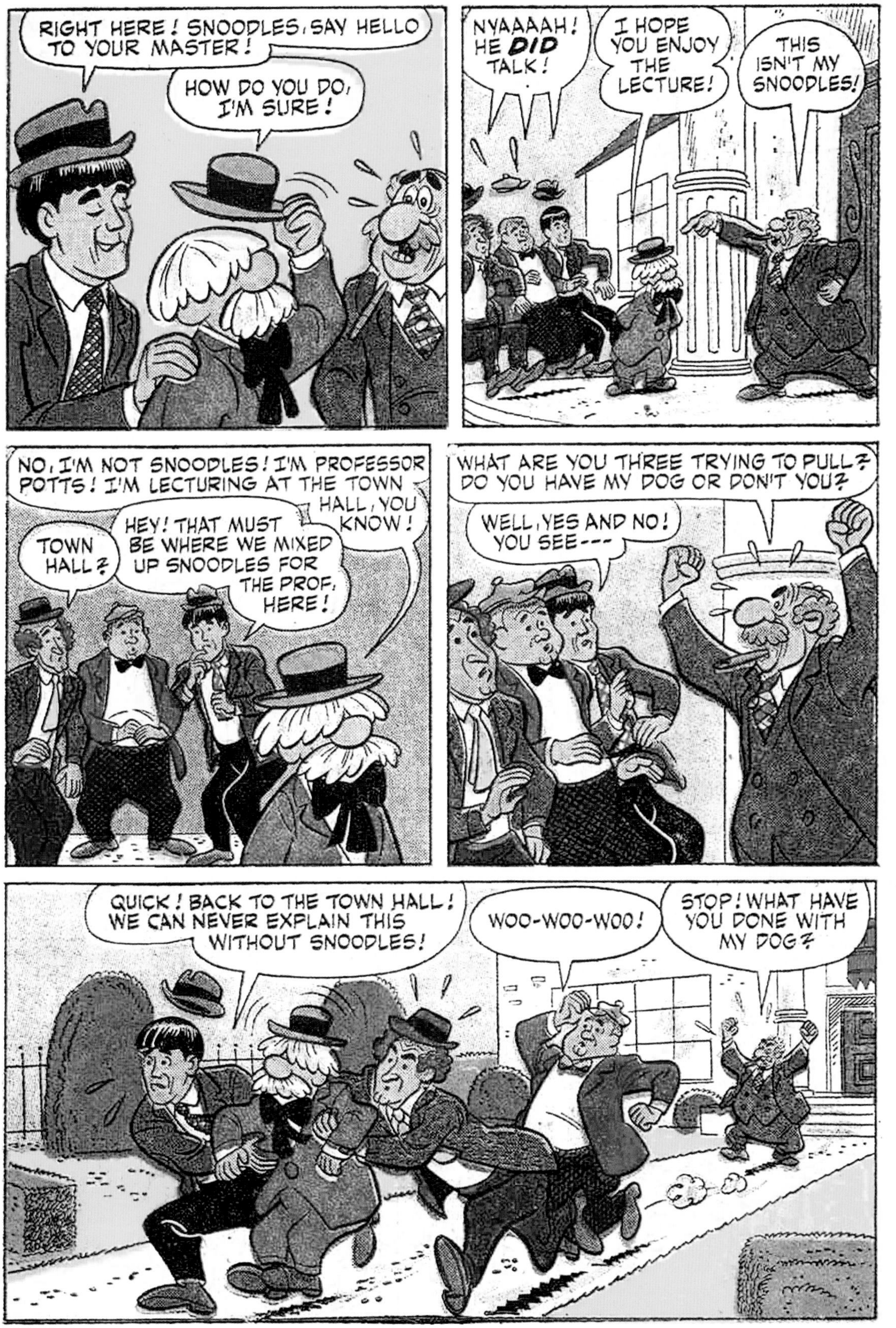
RIGHT HERE! SNOODLES, SAY HELLO TO YOUR MASTER!
HOW DO YOU DO, I'M SURE!
NYAAAAH! HE DID TALK!
I HOPE YOU ENJOY THE LECTURE!
THIS ISN'T MY SNOODLES!
NO, I'M NOT SNOODLES! I'M PROFESSOR POTTS! I'M LECTURING AT THE TOWN HALL, YOU KNOW!
TOWN HALL?
HEY! THAT MUST BE WHERE WE MIXED UP SNOODLES FOR THE PROF, HERE!
WHAT ARE YOU THREE TRYING TO PULL? DO YOU HAVE MY DOG OR DON'T YOU?
WELL, YES AND NO! YOU SEE---
QUICK! BACK TO THE TOWN HALL! WE CAN NEVER EXPLAIN THIS WITHOUT SNOODLES!
WOO-WOO-WOO!
STOP! WHAT HAVE YOU DONE WITH MY DOG?

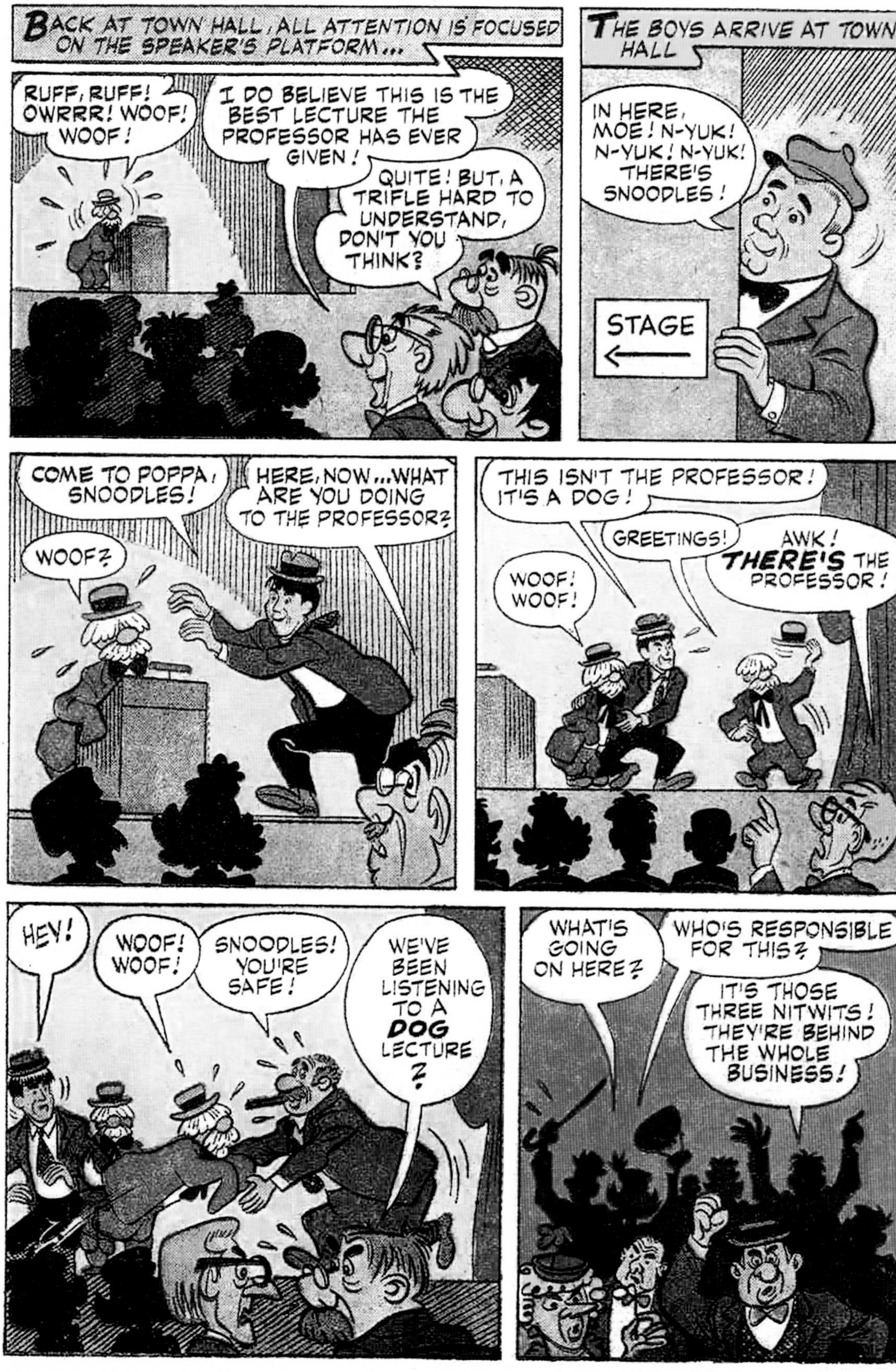
BACK AT TOWN HALL, ALL ATTENTION IS FOCUSED ON THE SPEAKER'S PLATFORM...
RUFF, RUFF! OWRRR! WOOF! WOOF!
I DO BELIEVE THIS IS THE BEST LECTURE THE PROFESSOR HAS EVER GIVEN!
QUITE! BUT, A TRIFLE HARD TO UNDERSTAND, DON'T YOU THINK?
THE BOYS ARRIVE AT TOWN HALL
IN HERE, MOE! N-YUK! N-YUK! N-YUK! THERE'S SNOODLES!
STAGE
COME TO POPPA, SNOODLES!
WOOF?
HERE, NOW... WHAT ARE YOU DOING TO THE PROFESSOR?
THIS ISN'T THE PROFESSOR! IT'S A DOG!
WOOF! WOOF!
GREETINGS!
AWK! THERE'S THE PROFESSOR!
HEY!
WOOF! WOOF!
SNOODLES! YOU'RE SAFE!
WE'VE BEEN LISTENING TO A DOG LECTURE?
WHAT'S GOING ON HERE?
WHO'S RESPONSIBLE FOR THIS?
IT'S THOSE THREE NITWITS! THEY'RE BEHIND THE WHOLE BUSINESS!

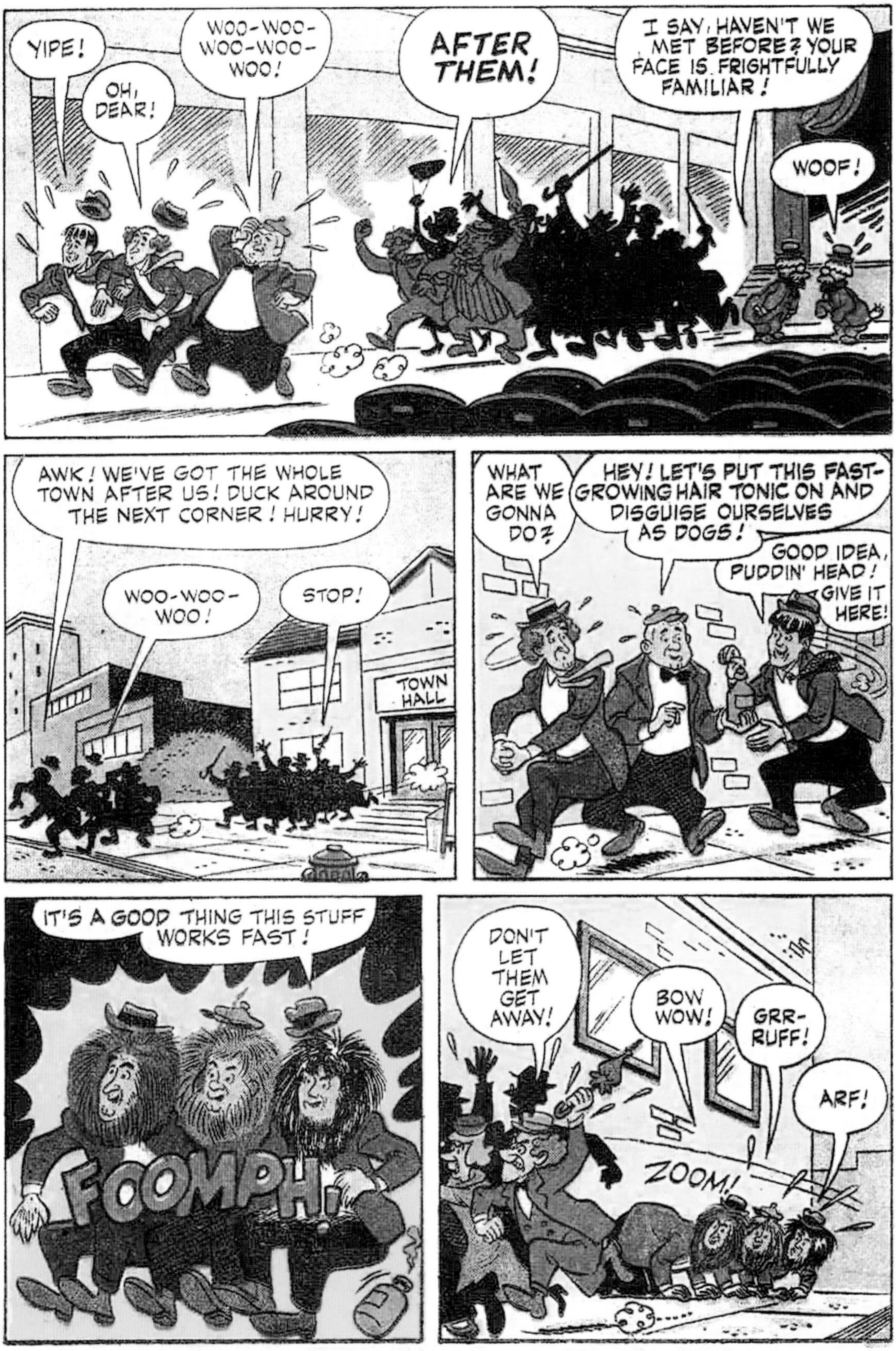
YIPE!
OH, DEAR!
WOO-WOO-WOO-WOO-WOO!
AFTER THEM!
I SAY, HAVEN'T WE MET BEFORE? YOUR FACE IS FRIGHTFULLY FAMILIAR!
WOOF!
AWK! WE'VE GOT THE WHOLE TOWN AFTER US! DUCK AROUND THE NEXT CORNER! HURRY!
WOO-WOO-WOO!
STOP!
TOWN HALL
WHAT ARE WE GONNA DO?
HEY! LET'S PUT THIS FAST-GROWING HAIR TONIC ON AND DISGUISE OURSELVES AS DOGS!
GOOD IDEA, PUDDIN' HEAD! GIVE IT HERE!
IT'S A GOOD THING THIS STUFF WORKS FAST!
FOOMPH!
DON'T LET THEM GET AWAY!
BOW WOW!
GRR-RUFF!
ARF!
ZOOM!

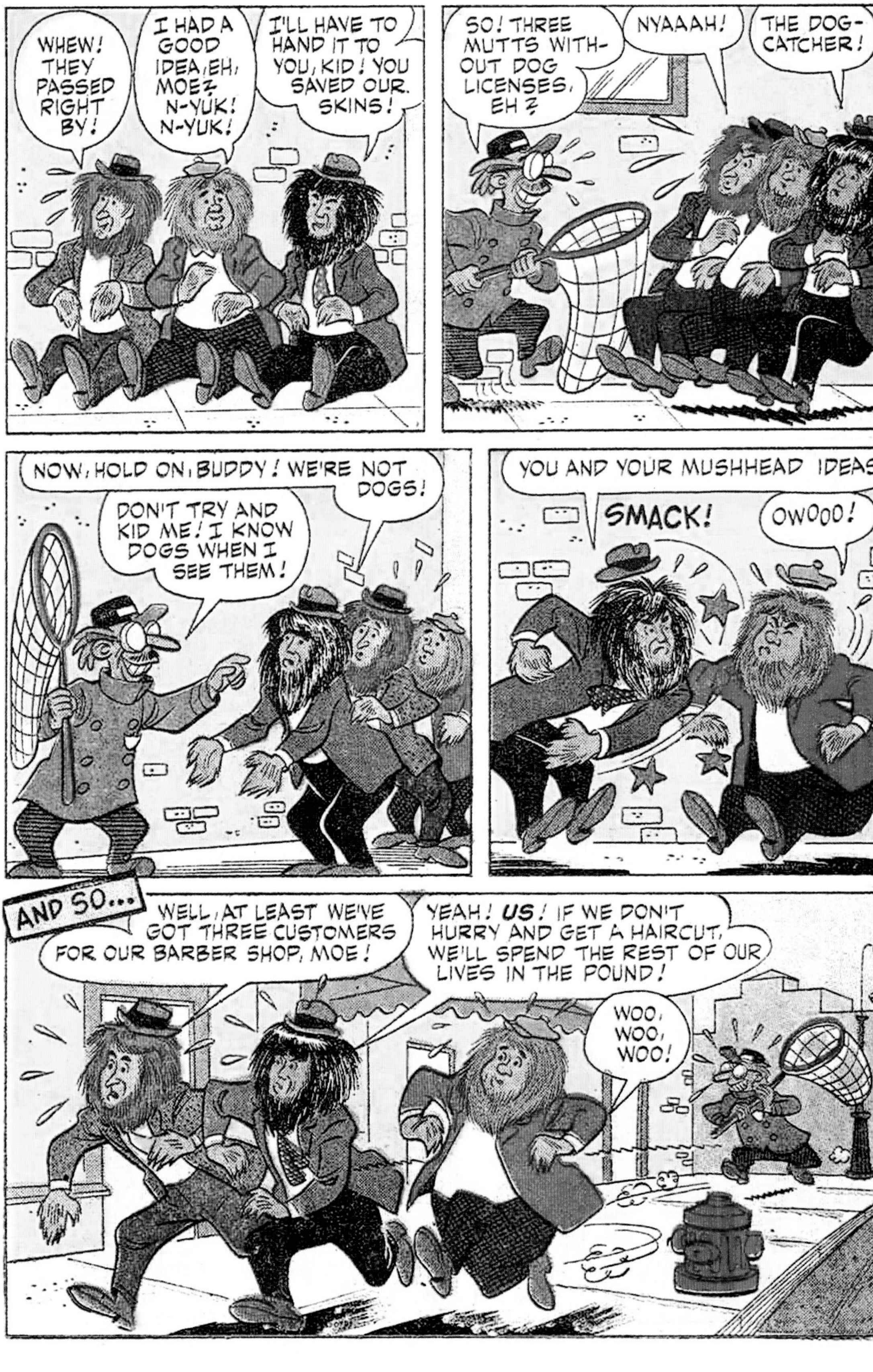
WHEW! THEY PASSED RIGHT BY!
I HAD A GOOD IDEA, EH, MOE? N-YUK! N-YUK!
I'LL HAVE TO HAND IT TO YOU, KID! YOU SAVED OUR SKINS!
SO! THREE MUTTS WITHOUT DOG LICENSES, EH?
NYAAAH!
THE DOG-CATCHER!
NOW, HOLD ON, BUDDY! WE'RE NOT DOGS!
DON'T TRY AND KID ME! I KNOW DOGS WHEN I SEE THEM!
YOU AND YOUR MUSHHEAD IDEAS!
SMACK!
OWOOO!
AND SO...
WELL, AT LEAST WE'VE GOT THREE CUSTOMERS FOR OUR BARBER SHOP, MOE!
YEAH! US! IF WE DON'T HURRY AND GET A HAIRCUT, WE'LL SPEND THE REST OF OUR LIVES IN THE POUND!
WOO, WOO, WOO!

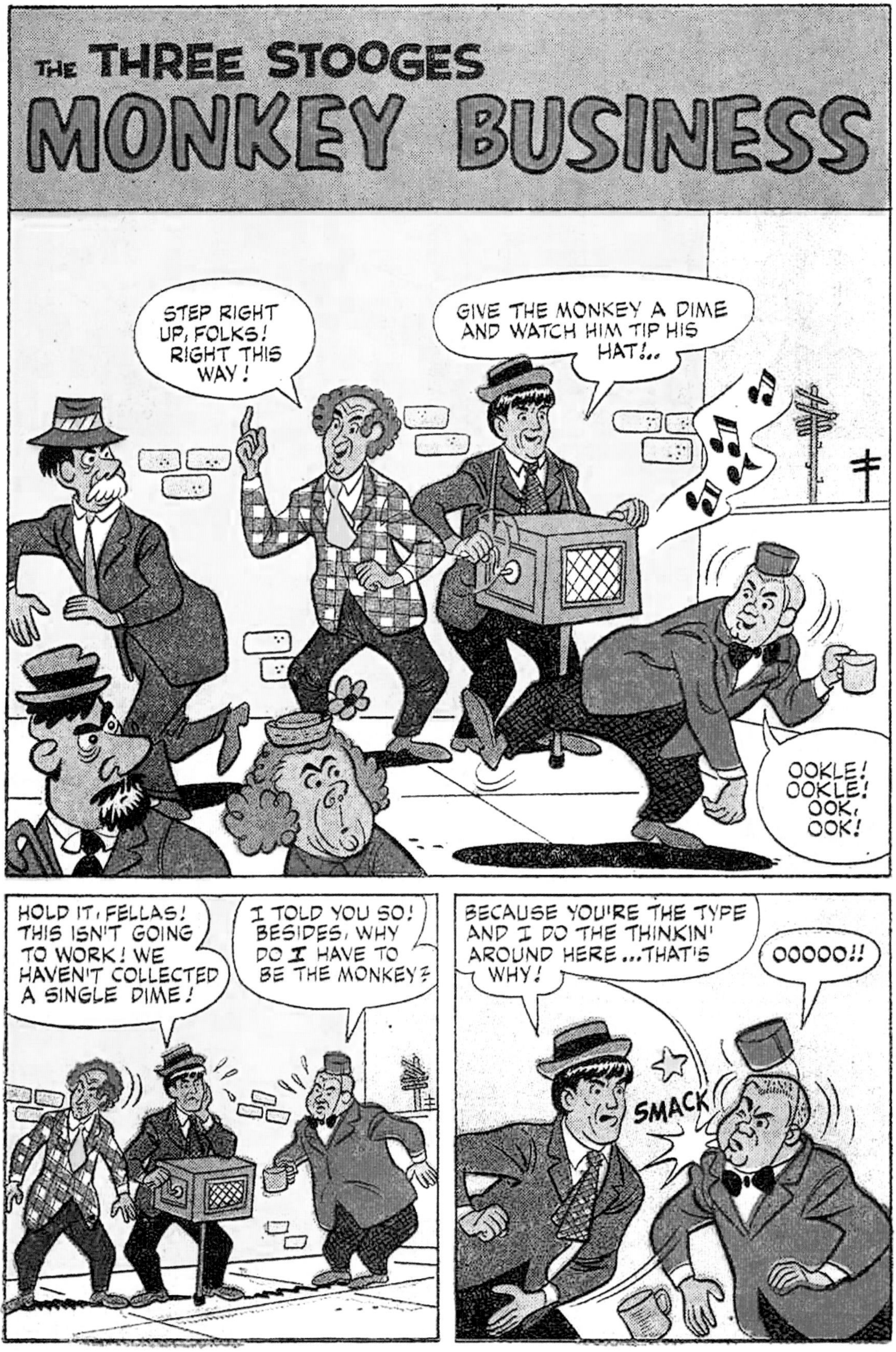
THE THREE STOOGES
MONKEY BUSINESS
STEP RIGHT UP, FOLKS! RIGHT THIS WAY!
GIVE THE MONKEY A DIME AND WATCH HIM TIP HIS HAT!..
OOKLE! OOKLE! OOK, OOK!
HOLD IT, FELLAS! THIS ISN'T GOING TO WORK! WE HAVEN'T COLLECTED A SINGLE DIME!
I TOLD YOU SO! BESIDES, WHY DO I HAVE TO BE THE MONKEY?
BECAUSE YOU'RE THE TYPE AND I DO THE THINKIN' AROUND HERE ...THAT'S WHY!
OOOOO!!
SMACK

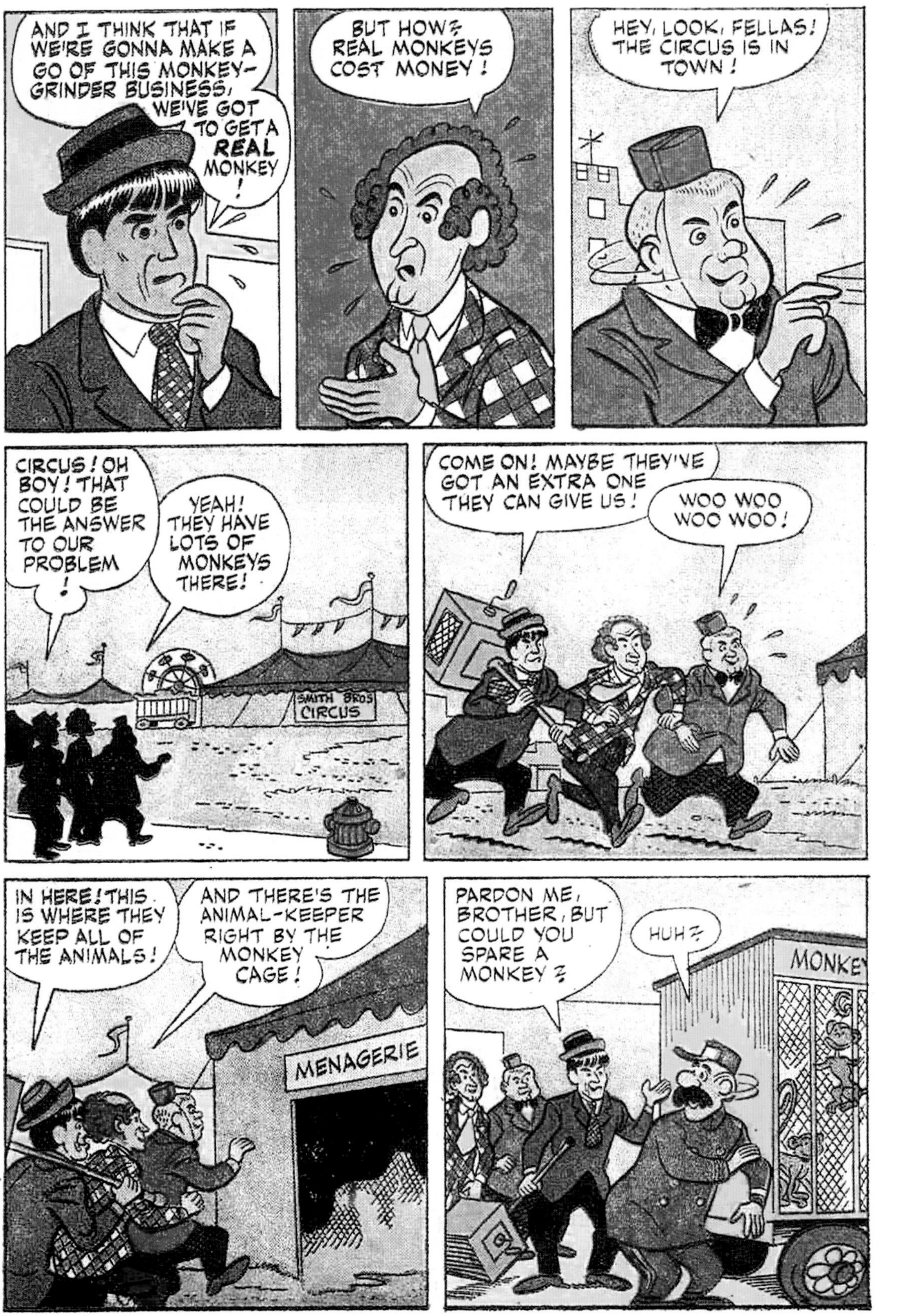
AND I THINK THAT IF WE'RE GONNA MAKE A GO OF THIS MONKEY-GRINDER BUSINESS,
WE'VE GOT TO GET A REAL MONKEY!
BUT HOW? REAL MONKEYS COST MONEY!
HEY, LOOK, FELLAS! THE CIRCUS IS IN TOWN!
CIRCUS! OH BOY! THAT COULD BE THE ANSWER TO OUR PROBLEM!
YEAH! THEY HAVE LOTS OF MONKEYS THERE!
SMITH BROS CIRCUS
COME ON! MAYBE THEY'VE GOT AN EXTRA ONE THEY CAN GIVE US!
WOO WOO WOO WOO!
IN HERE! THIS IS WHERE THEY KEEP ALL OF THE ANIMALS!
AND THERE'S THE ANIMAL-KEEPER RIGHT BY THE MONKEY CAGE!
MENAGERIE
PARDON ME, BROTHER, BUT COULD YOU SPARE A MONKEY?
HUH?
MONKEY

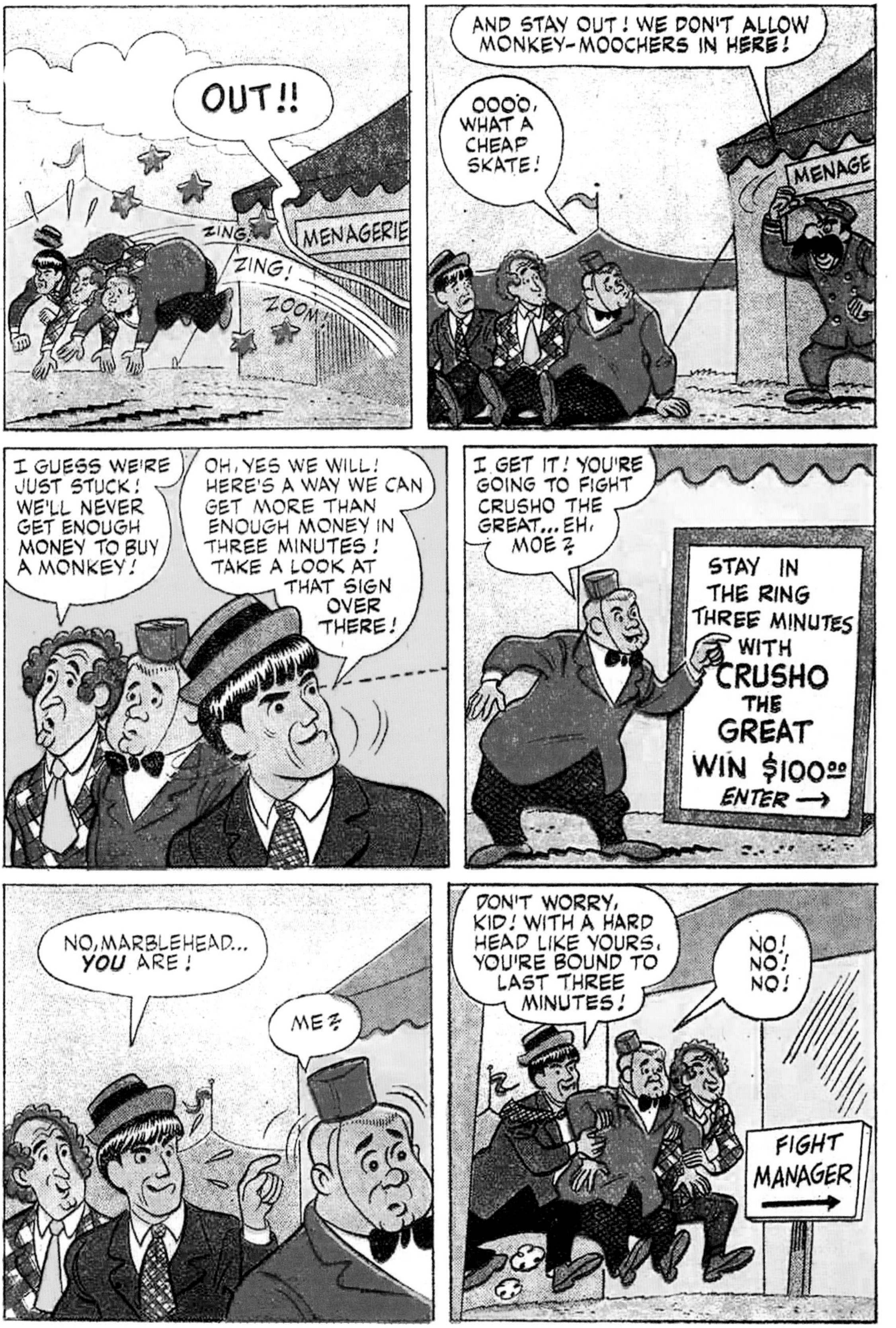

OUT!!
ZING!
ZING!
ZOOM!
MENAGERIE
AND STAY OUT! WE DON'T ALLOW MONKEY-MOOCHERS IN HERE!
OOOO, WHAT A CHEAP SKATE!
MENAGE
I GUESS WE'RE JUST STUCK! WE'LL NEVER GET ENOUGH MONEY TO BUY A MONKEY!
OH, YES WE WILL! HERE'S A WAY WE CAN GET MORE THAN ENOUGH MONEY IN THREE MINUTES! TAKE A LOOK AT THAT SIGN OVER THERE!
I GET IT! YOU'RE GOING TO FIGHT CRUSHO THE GREAT... EH, MOE?
STAY IN THE RING THREE MINUTES WITH CRUSHO THE GREAT WIN $100.00 ENTER →
NO, MARBLEHEAD... YOU ARE!
ME?
DON'T WORRY, KID! WITH A HARD HEAD LIKE YOURS, YOU'RE BOUND TO LAST THREE MINUTES!
NO! NO! NO!
FIGHT MANAGER →

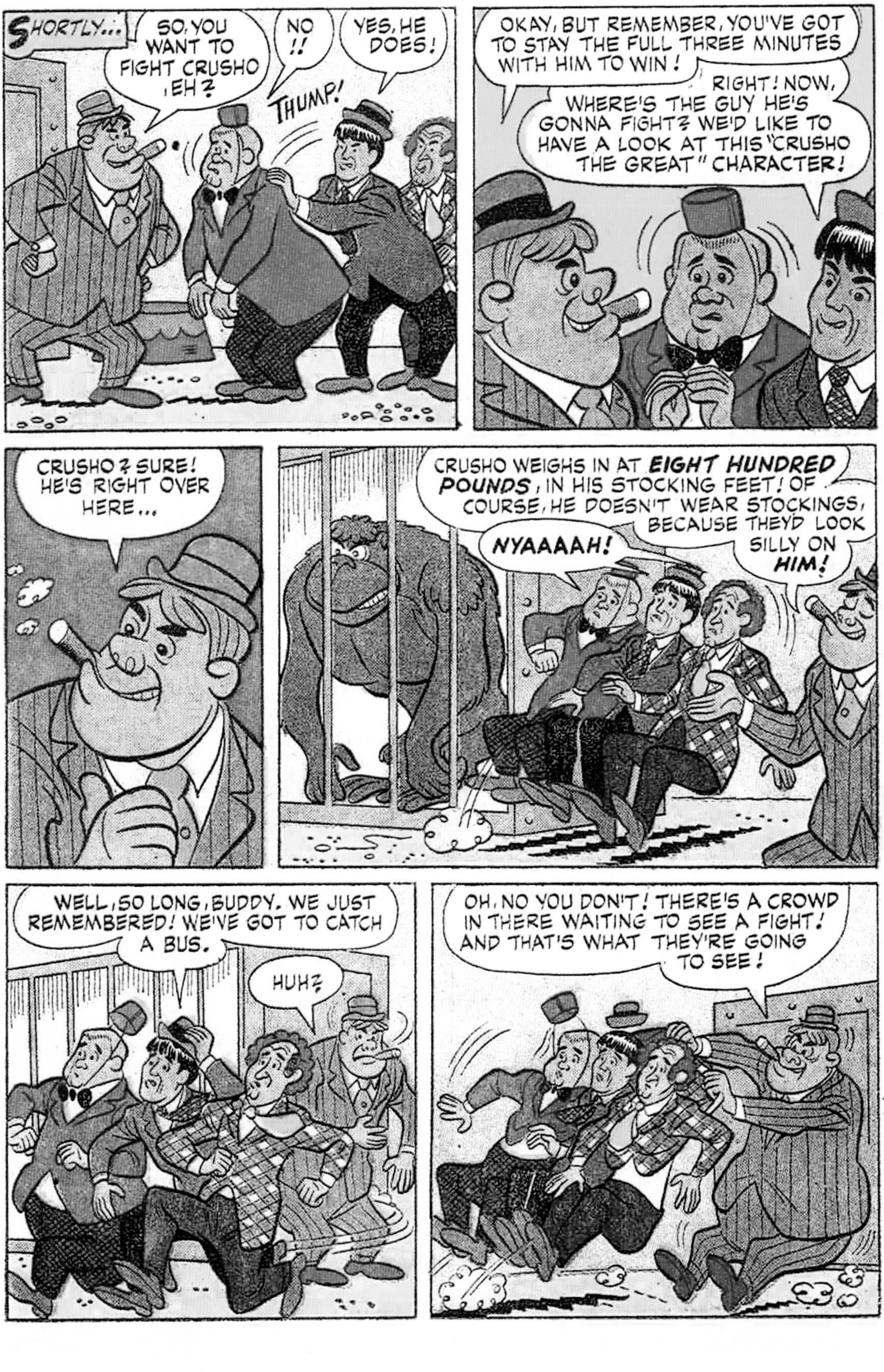
SHORTLY...
SO, YOU WANT TO FIGHT CRUSHO, EH?
NO !!
YES, HE DOES!
THUMP!
OKAY, BUT REMEMBER, YOU'VE GOT TO STAY THE FULL THREE MINUTES WITH HIM TO WIN!
RIGHT! NOW, WHERE'S THE GUY HE'S GONNA FIGHT? WE'D LIKE TO HAVE A LOOK AT THIS "CRUSHO THE GREAT" CHARACTER!
CRUSHO? SURE! HE'S RIGHT OVER HERE...
CRUSHO WEIGHS IN AT EIGHT HUNDRED POUNDS, IN HIS STOCKING FEET! OF COURSE, HE DOESN'T WEAR STOCKINGS, BECAUSE THEY'D LOOK SILLY ON HIM!
NYAAAAH!
WELL, SO LONG, BUDDY. WE JUST REMEMBERED! WE'VE GOT TO CATCH A BUS.
HUH?
OH, NO YOU DON'T! THERE'S A CROWD IN THERE WAITING TO SEE A FIGHT! AND THAT'S WHAT THEY'RE GOING TO SEE!

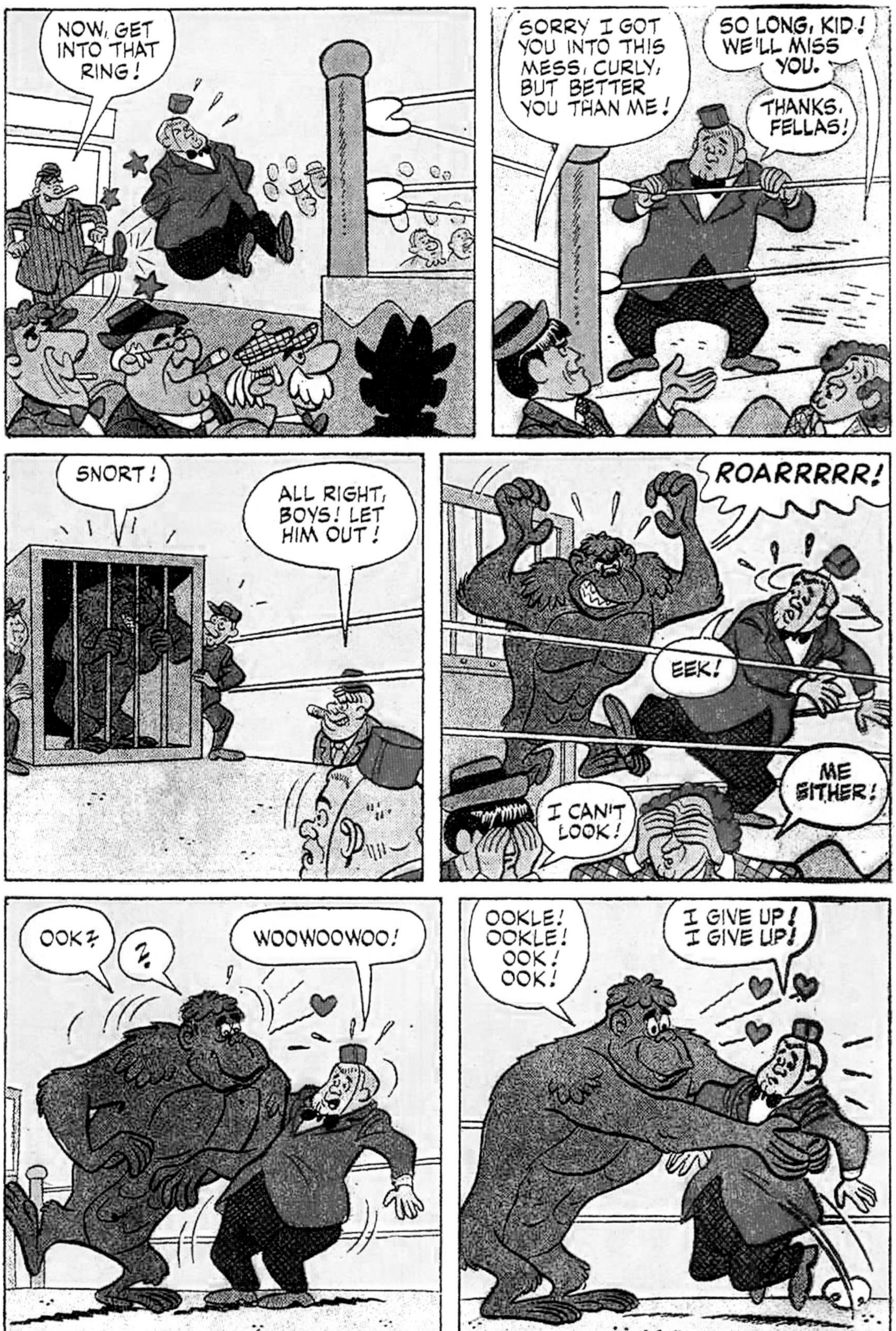
NOW, GET INTO THAT RING!
SORRY I GOT YOU INTO THIS MESS, CURLY, BUT BETTER YOU THAN ME!
SO LONG, KID! WE'LL MISS YOU.
THANKS, FELLAS!
SNORT!
ALL RIGHT, BOYS! LET HIM OUT!
ROARRRRR!
EEK!
I CAN'T LOOK!
ME EITHER!
OOK?
?
WOOWOOWOO!
OOKLE! OOKLE! OOK! OOK!
I GIVE UP! I GIVE UP!

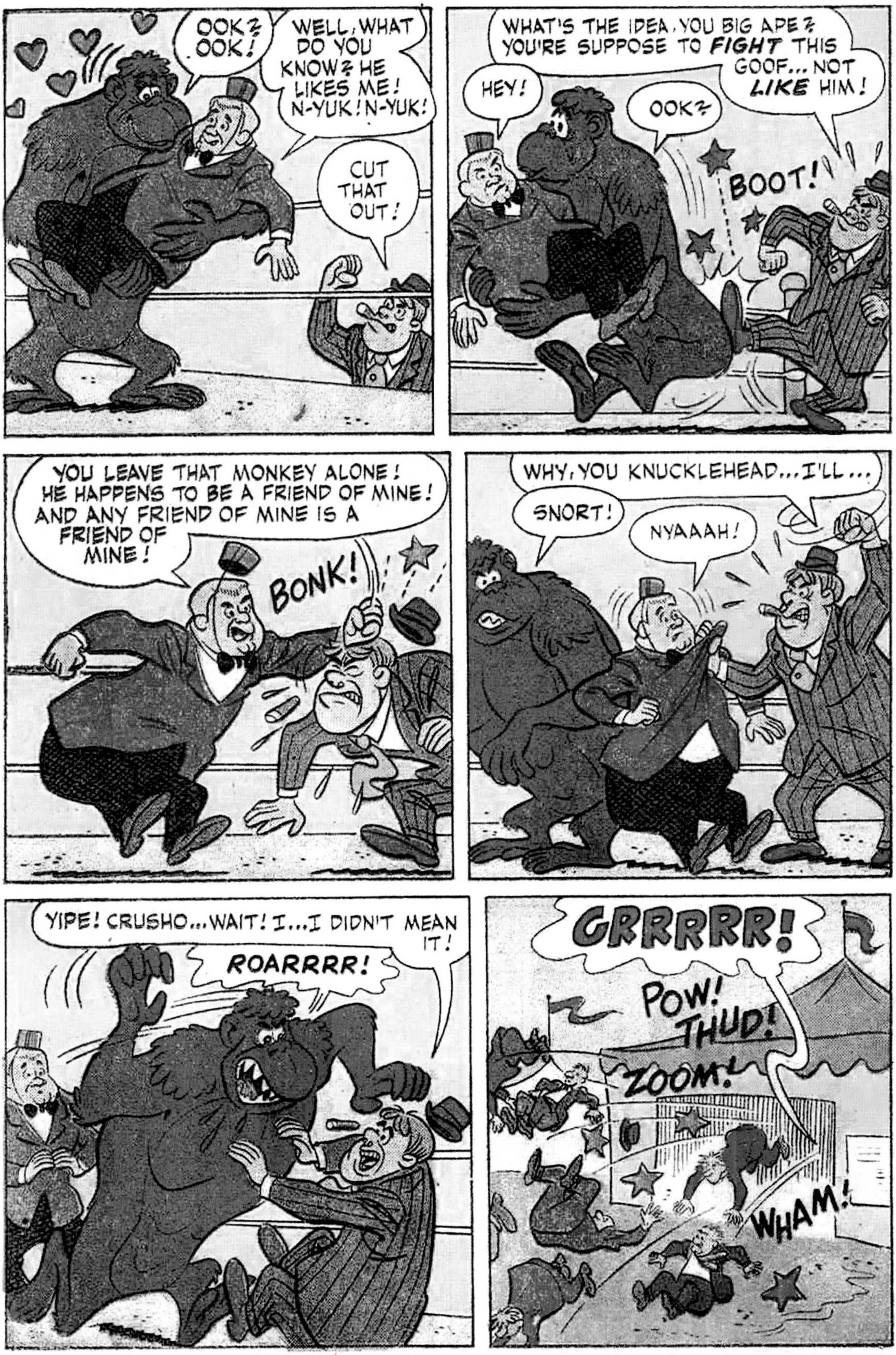
OOK? OOK!
WELL, WHAT DO YOU KNOW? HE LIKES ME! N-YUK! N-YUK!
CUT THAT OUT!
WHAT'S THE IDEA, YOU BIG APE? YOU'RE SUPPOSE TO FIGHT THIS GOOF... NOT LIKE HIM!
HEY!
OOK?
BOOT!
YOU LEAVE THAT MONKEY ALONE! HE HAPPENS TO BE A FRIEND OF MINE! AND ANY FRIEND OF MINE IS A FRIEND OF MINE!
BONK!
WHY, YOU KNUCKLEHEAD... I'LL...
SNORT!
NYAAAH!
YIPE! CRUSHO... WAIT! I... I DIDN'T MEAN IT!
ROARRRR!
GRRRRR!
POW!
THUD!
ZOOM!
WHAM!

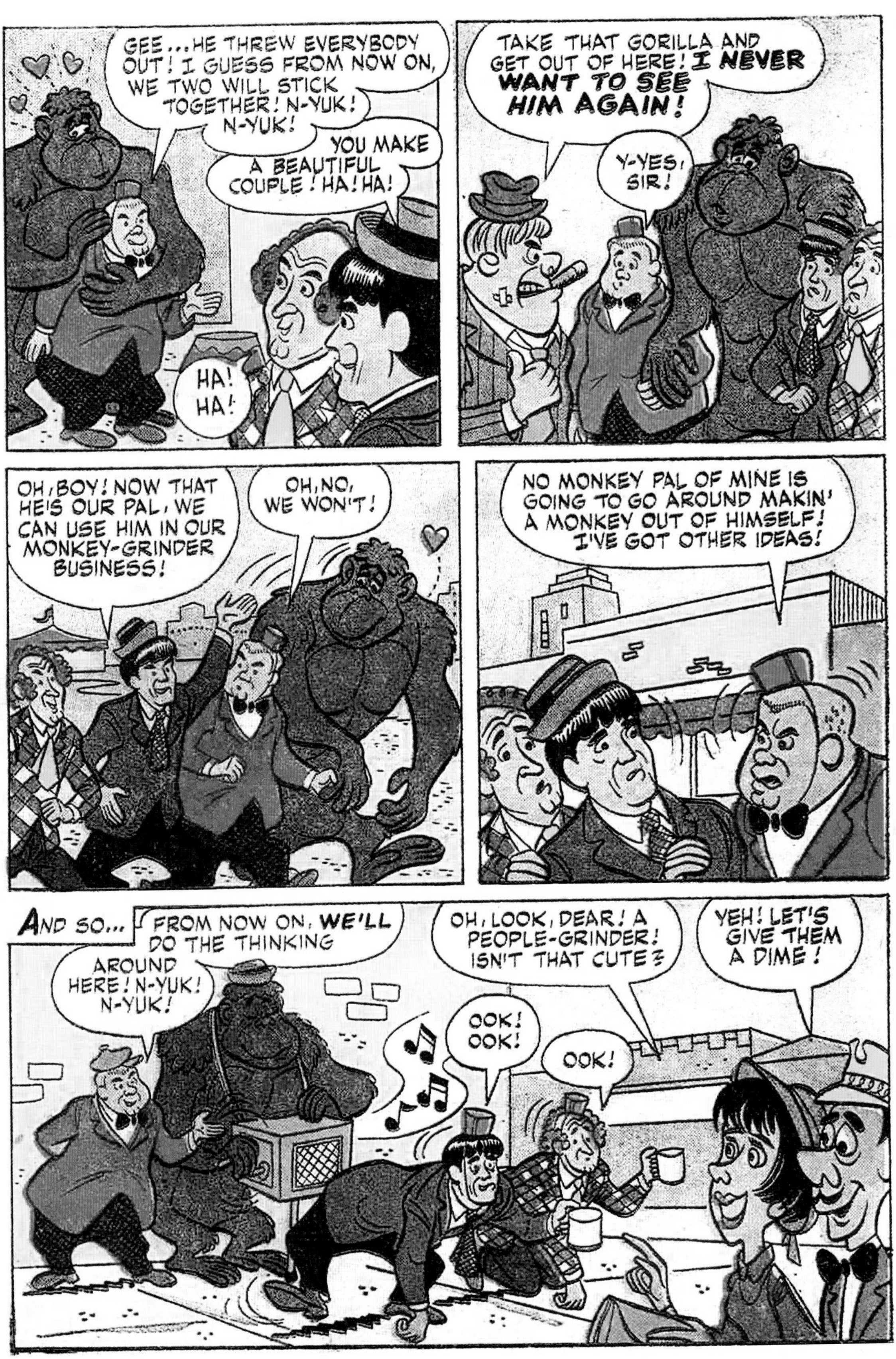
GEE...HE THREW EVERYBODY OUT! I GUESS FROM NOW ON, WE TWO WILL STICK TOGETHER! N-YUK! N-YUK!
YOU MAKE A BEAUTIFUL COUPLE! HA! HA!
HA! HA!
TAKE THAT GORILLA AND GET OUT OF HERE! I NEVER WANT TO SEE HIM AGAIN!
Y-YES, SIR!
OH, BOY! NOW THAT HE'S OUR PAL, WE CAN USE HIM IN OUR MONKEY-GRINDER BUSINESS!
OH, NO, WE WON'T!
NO MONKEY PAL OF MINE IS GOING TO GO AROUND MAKIN' A MONKEY OUT OF HIMSELF! I'VE GOT OTHER IDEAS!
AND SO...
FROM NOW ON, WE'LL DO THE THINKING AROUND HERE! N-YUK! N-YUK!
OH, LOOK, DEAR! A PEOPLE-GRINDER! ISN'T THAT CUTE?
YEH! LET'S GIVE THEM A DIME!
OOK! OOK!
OOK!

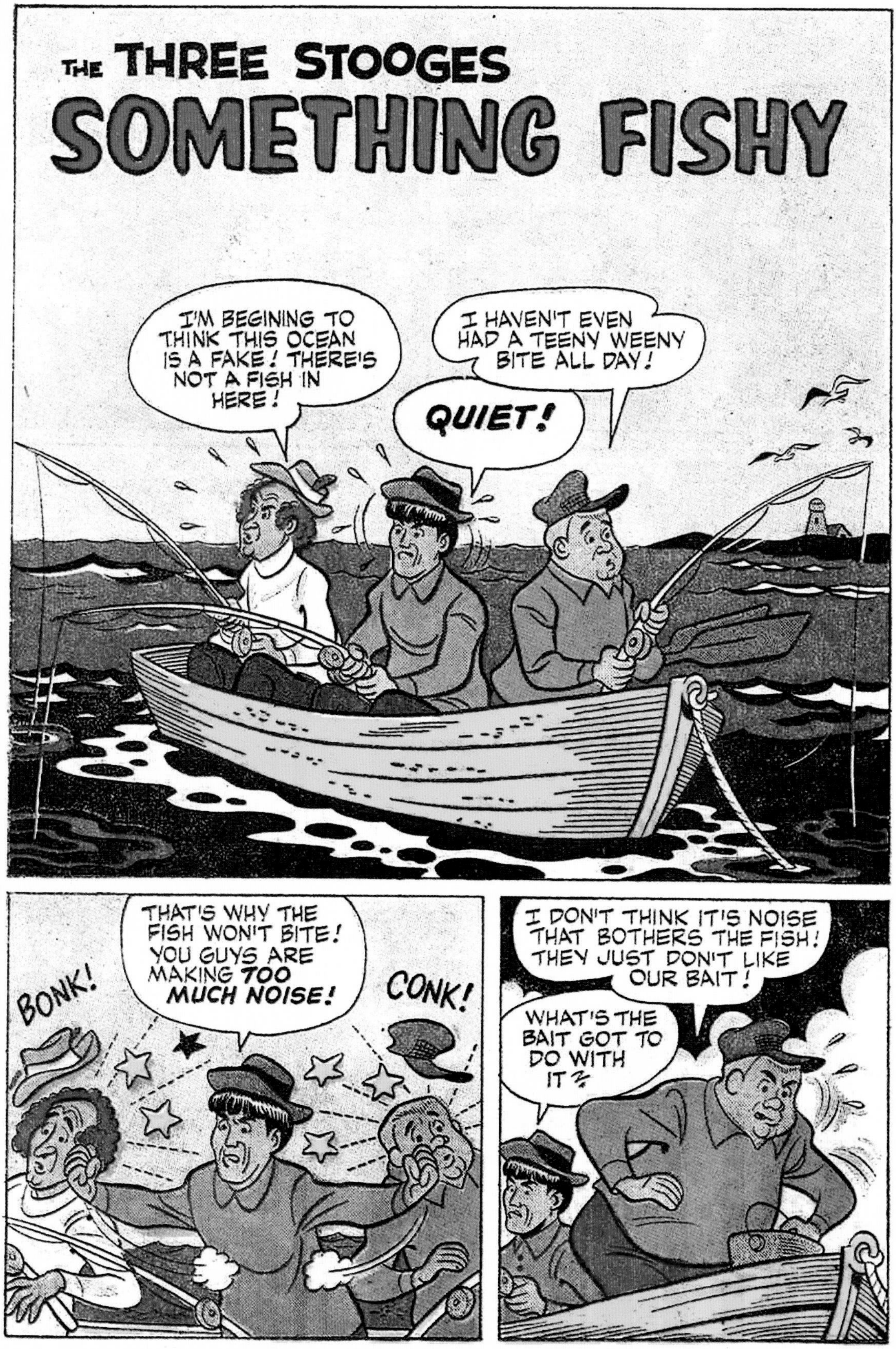
THE THREE STOOGES
SOMETHING FISHY
I'M BEGINING TO THINK THIS OCEAN IS A FAKE! THERE'S NOT A FISH IN HERE!
I HAVEN'T EVEN HAD A TEENY WEENY BITE ALL DAY!
QUIET!
BONK!
THAT'S WHY THE FISH WON'T BITE! YOU GUYS ARE MAKING TOO MUCH NOISE!
CONK!
I DON'T THINK IT'S NOISE THAT BOTHERS THE FISH! THEY JUST DON'T LIKE OUR BAIT!
WHAT'S THE BAIT GOT TO DO WITH IT?

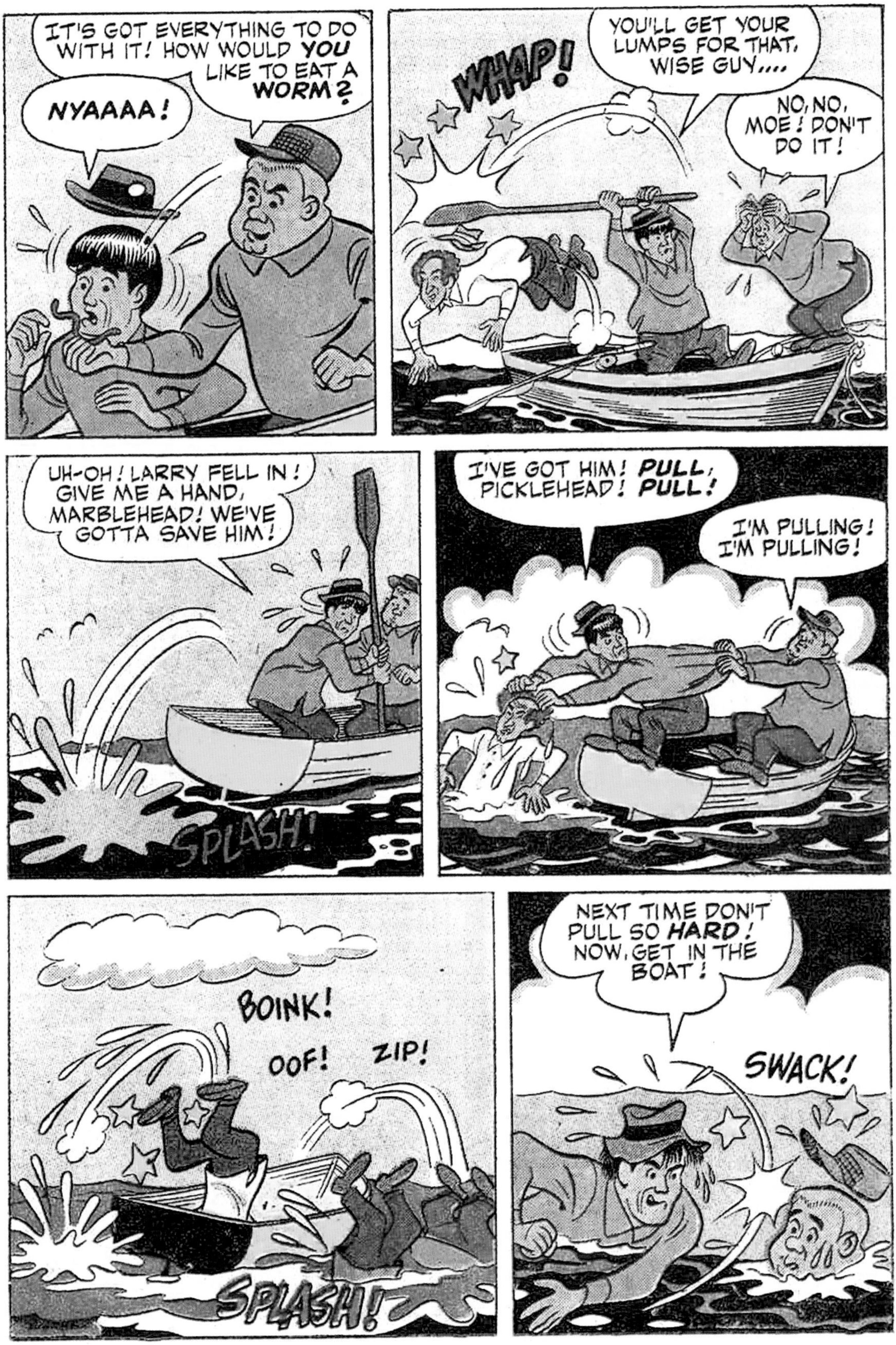
IT'S GOT EVERYTHING TO DO WITH IT! HOW WOULD **YOU** LIKE TO EAT A **WORM**?
NYAAAA!
WHAP!
YOU'LL GET YOUR LUMPS FOR THAT, WISE GUY....
NO, NO, MOE! DON'T DO IT!
UH-OH! LARRY FELL IN! GIVE ME A HAND, MARBLEHEAD! WE'VE GOTTA SAVE HIM!
SPLASH!
I'VE GOT HIM! **PULL**, PICKLEHEAD! **PULL**!
I'M PULLING! I'M PULLING!
BOINK!
OOF!
ZIP!
SPLASH!
NEXT TIME DON'T PULL SO **HARD**! NOW, GET IN THE BOAT!
SWACK!

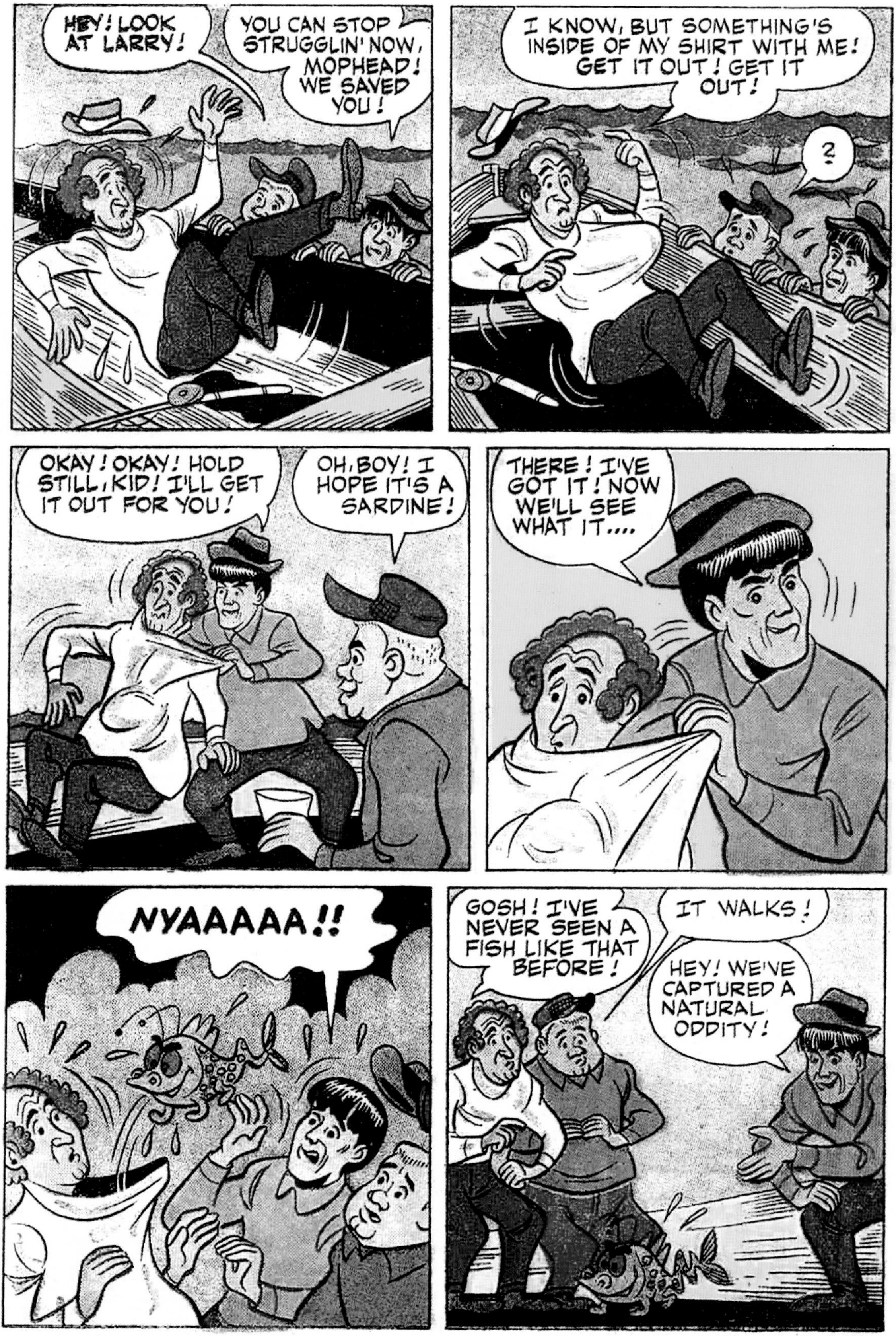
HEY! LOOK AT LARRY!
YOU CAN STOP STRUGGLIN' NOW, MOPHEAD! WE SAVED YOU!
I KNOW, BUT SOMETHING'S INSIDE OF MY SHIRT WITH ME! GET IT OUT! GET IT OUT!
?
OKAY! OKAY! HOLD STILL, KID! I'LL GET IT OUT FOR YOU!
OH, BOY! I HOPE IT'S A SARDINE!
THERE! I'VE GOT IT! NOW WE'LL SEE WHAT IT....
NYAAAAA!!
GOSH! I'VE NEVER SEEN A FISH LIKE THAT BEFORE!
IT WALKS!
HEY! WE'VE CAPTURED A NATURAL ODDITY!

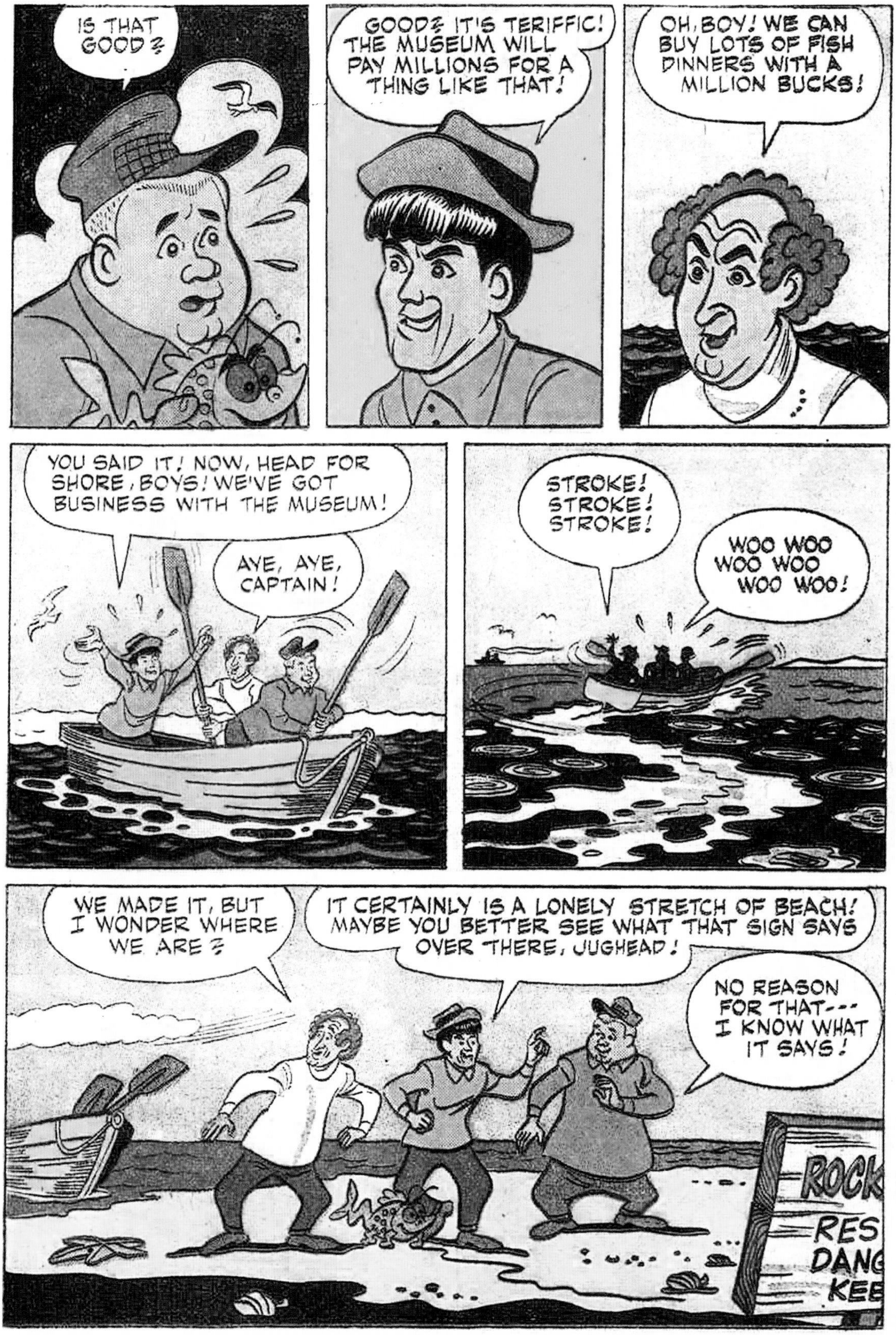
IS THAT GOOD ?
GOOD? IT'S TERIFFIC! THE MUSEUM WILL PAY MILLIONS FOR A THING LIKE THAT!
OH, BOY! WE CAN BUY LOTS OF FISH DINNERS WITH A MILLION BUCKS!
YOU SAID IT! NOW, HEAD FOR SHORE, BOYS! WE'VE GOT BUSINESS WITH THE MUSEUM!
AYE, AYE, CAPTAIN!
STROKE! STROKE! STROKE!
WOO WOO WOO WOO WOO WOO!
WE MADE IT, BUT I WONDER WHERE WE ARE ?
IT CERTAINLY IS A LONELY STRETCH OF BEACH! MAYBE YOU BETTER SEE WHAT THAT SIGN SAYS OVER THERE, JUGHEAD!
NO REASON FOR THAT--- I KNOW WHAT IT SAYS!
ROCK
RES
DANG
KEE

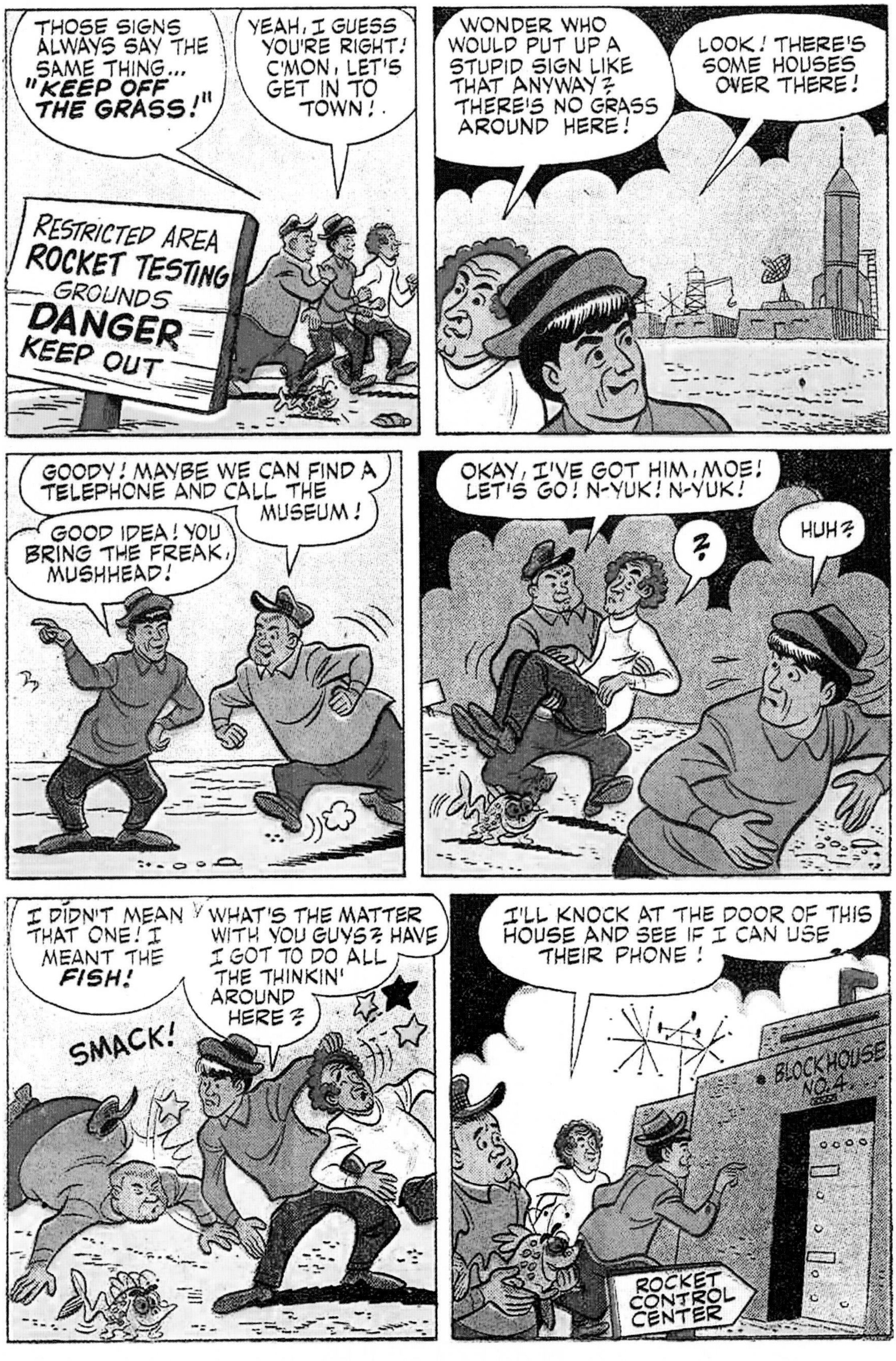
THOSE SIGNS ALWAYS SAY THE SAME THING... "KEEP OFF THE GRASS!"
YEAH, I GUESS YOU'RE RIGHT! C'MON, LET'S GET IN TO TOWN!
RESTRICTED AREA ROCKET TESTING GROUNDS DANGER KEEP OUT
WONDER WHO WOULD PUT UP A STUPID SIGN LIKE THAT ANYWAY? THERE'S NO GRASS AROUND HERE!
LOOK! THERE'S SOME HOUSES OVER THERE!
GOODY! MAYBE WE CAN FIND A TELEPHONE AND CALL THE MUSEUM!
GOOD IDEA! YOU BRING THE FREAK, MUSHHEAD!
OKAY, I'VE GOT HIM, MOE! LET'S GO! N-YUK! N-YUK!
?
HUH?
I DIDN'T MEAN THAT ONE! I MEANT THE FISH!
WHAT'S THE MATTER WITH YOU GUYS? HAVE I GOT TO DO ALL THE THINKIN' AROUND HERE?
SMACK!
I'LL KNOCK AT THE DOOR OF THIS HOUSE AND SEE IF I CAN USE THEIR PHONE!
BLOCKHOUSE NO. 4
ROCKET CONTROL CENTER

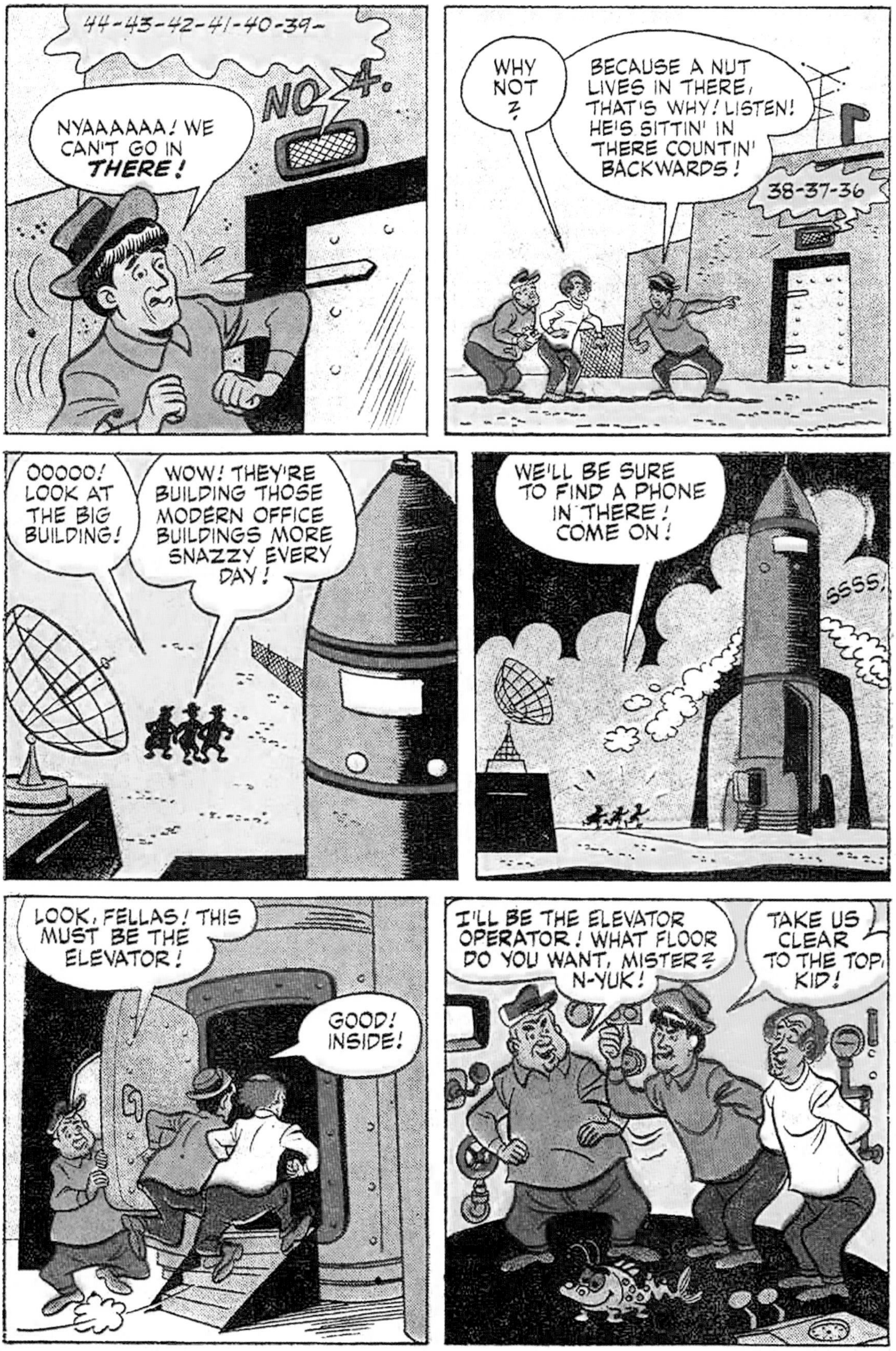
44-43-42-41-40-39-
NO. 4.
NYAAAAAA! WE CAN'T GO IN THERE!
WHY NOT ?
BECAUSE A NUT LIVES IN THERE, THAT'S WHY! LISTEN! HE'S SITTIN' IN THERE COUNTIN' BACKWARDS!
38-37-36
OOOOO! LOOK AT THE BIG BUILDING!
WOW! THEY'RE BUILDING THOSE MODERN OFFICE BUILDINGS MORE SNAZZY EVERY DAY!
WE'LL BE SURE TO FIND A PHONE IN THERE! COME ON!
SSSS!
LOOK, FELLAS! THIS MUST BE THE ELEVATOR!
GOOD! INSIDE!
I'LL BE THE ELEVATOR OPERATOR! WHAT FLOOR DO YOU WANT, MISTER? N-YUK!
TAKE US CLEAR TO THE TOP, KID!

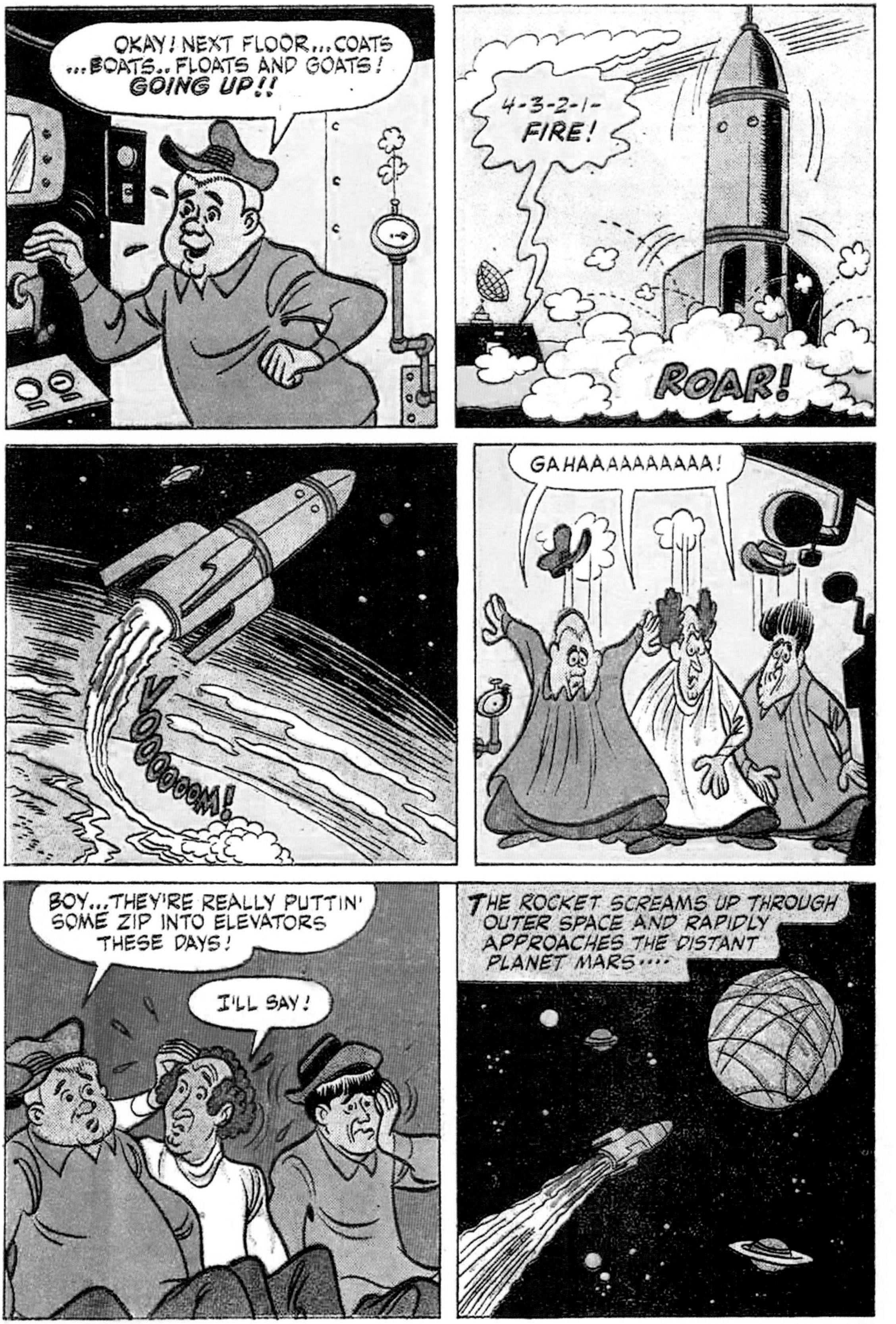
OKAY! NEXT FLOOR...COATS ...BOATS..FLOATS AND GOATS! GOING UP!!
4-3-2-1- FIRE!
ROAR!
VOOOOOOOM!
GAHAAAAAAAAAA!
BOY...THEY'RE REALLY PUTTIN' SOME ZIP INTO ELEVATORS THESE DAYS!
I'LL SAY!
THE ROCKET SCREAMS UP THROUGH OUTER SPACE AND RAPIDLY APPROACHES THE DISTANT PLANET MARS....

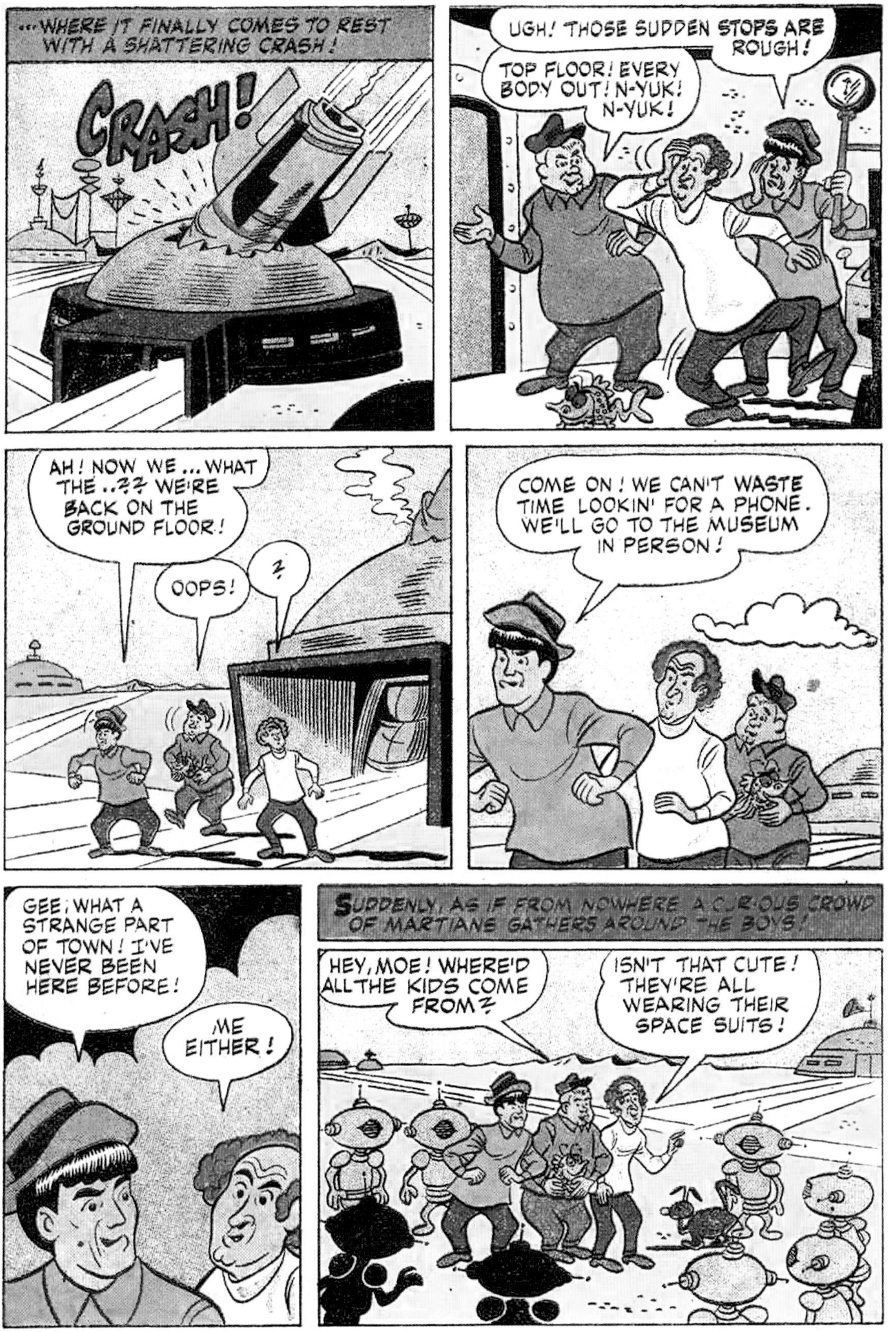

...WHERE IT FINALLY COMES TO REST WITH A SHATTERING CRASH!
CRASH!
UGH! THOSE SUDDEN STOPS ARE ROUGH!
TOP FLOOR! EVERY BODY OUT! N-YUK! N-YUK!
AH! NOW WE ... WHAT THE ..?? WE'RE BACK ON THE GROUND FLOOR!
OOPS!
?
COME ON! WE CAN'T WASTE TIME LOOKIN' FOR A PHONE. WE'LL GO TO THE MUSEUM IN PERSON!
GEE, WHAT A STRANGE PART OF TOWN! I'VE NEVER BEEN HERE BEFORE!
ME EITHER!
SUDDENLY, AS IF FROM NOWHERE A CURIOUS CROWD OF MARTIANS GATHERS AROUND THE BOYS!
HEY, MOE! WHERE'D ALL THE KIDS COME FROM?
ISN'T THAT CUTE! THEY'RE ALL WEARING THEIR SPACE SUITS!

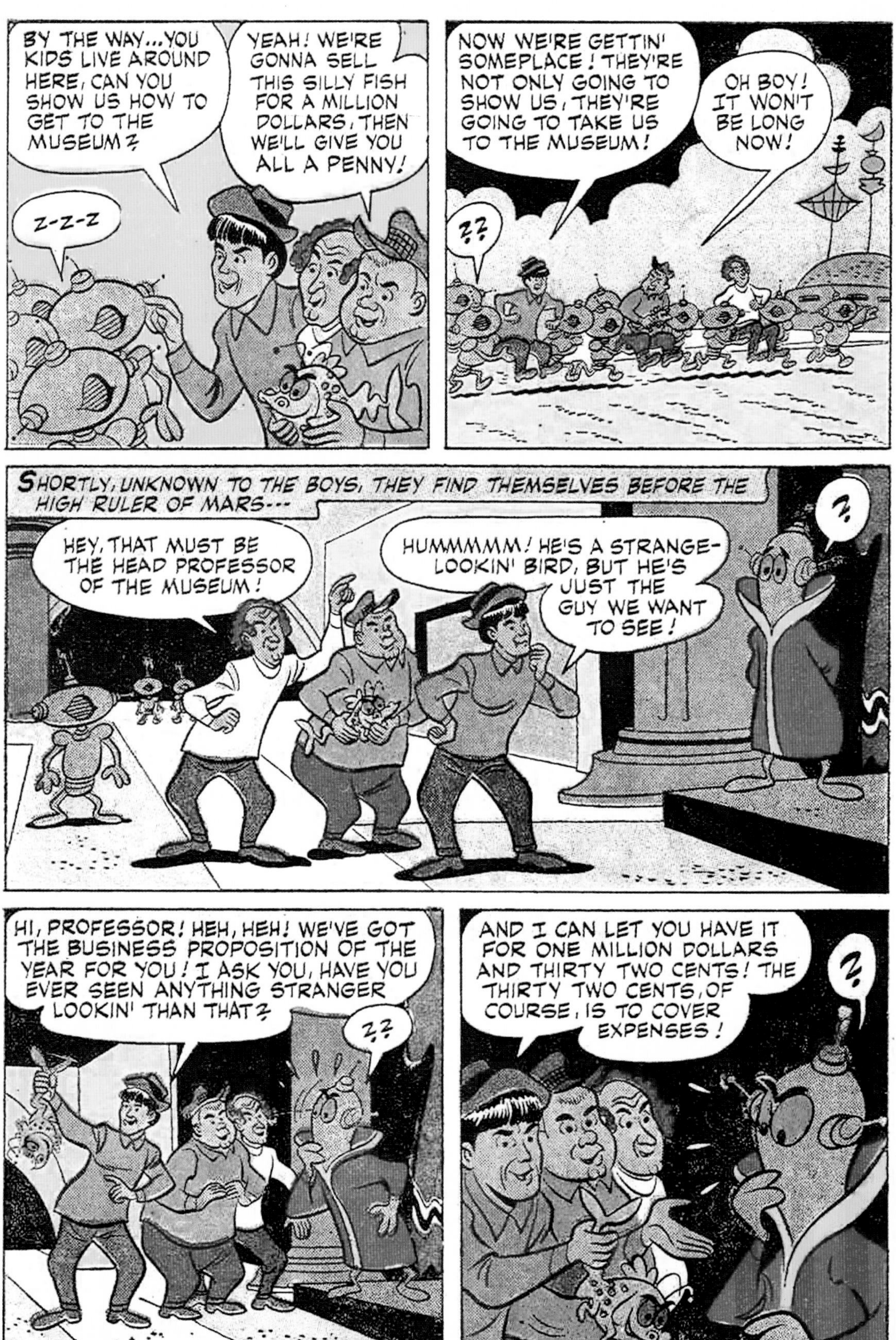
BY THE WAY...YOU KIDS LIVE AROUND HERE, CAN YOU SHOW US HOW TO GET TO THE MUSEUM?
YEAH! WE'RE GONNA SELL THIS SILLY FISH FOR A MILLION DOLLARS, THEN WE'LL GIVE YOU ALL A PENNY!
Z-Z-Z
NOW WE'RE GETTIN' SOMEPLACE! THEY'RE NOT ONLY GOING TO SHOW US, THEY'RE GOING TO TAKE US TO THE MUSEUM!
OH BOY! IT WON'T BE LONG NOW!
??
SHORTLY, UNKNOWN TO THE BOYS, THEY FIND THEMSELVES BEFORE THE HIGH RULER OF MARS---
HEY, THAT MUST BE THE HEAD PROFESSOR OF THE MUSEUM!
HUMMMMM! HE'S A STRANGE-LOOKIN' BIRD, BUT HE'S JUST THE GUY WE WANT TO SEE!
?
HI, PROFESSOR! HEH, HEH! WE'VE GOT THE BUSINESS PROPOSITION OF THE YEAR FOR YOU! I ASK YOU, HAVE YOU EVER SEEN ANYTHING STRANGER LOOKIN' THAN THAT?
??
AND I CAN LET YOU HAVE IT FOR ONE MILLION DOLLARS AND THIRTY TWO CENTS! THE THIRTY TWO CENTS, OF COURSE, IS TO COVER EXPENSES!
?

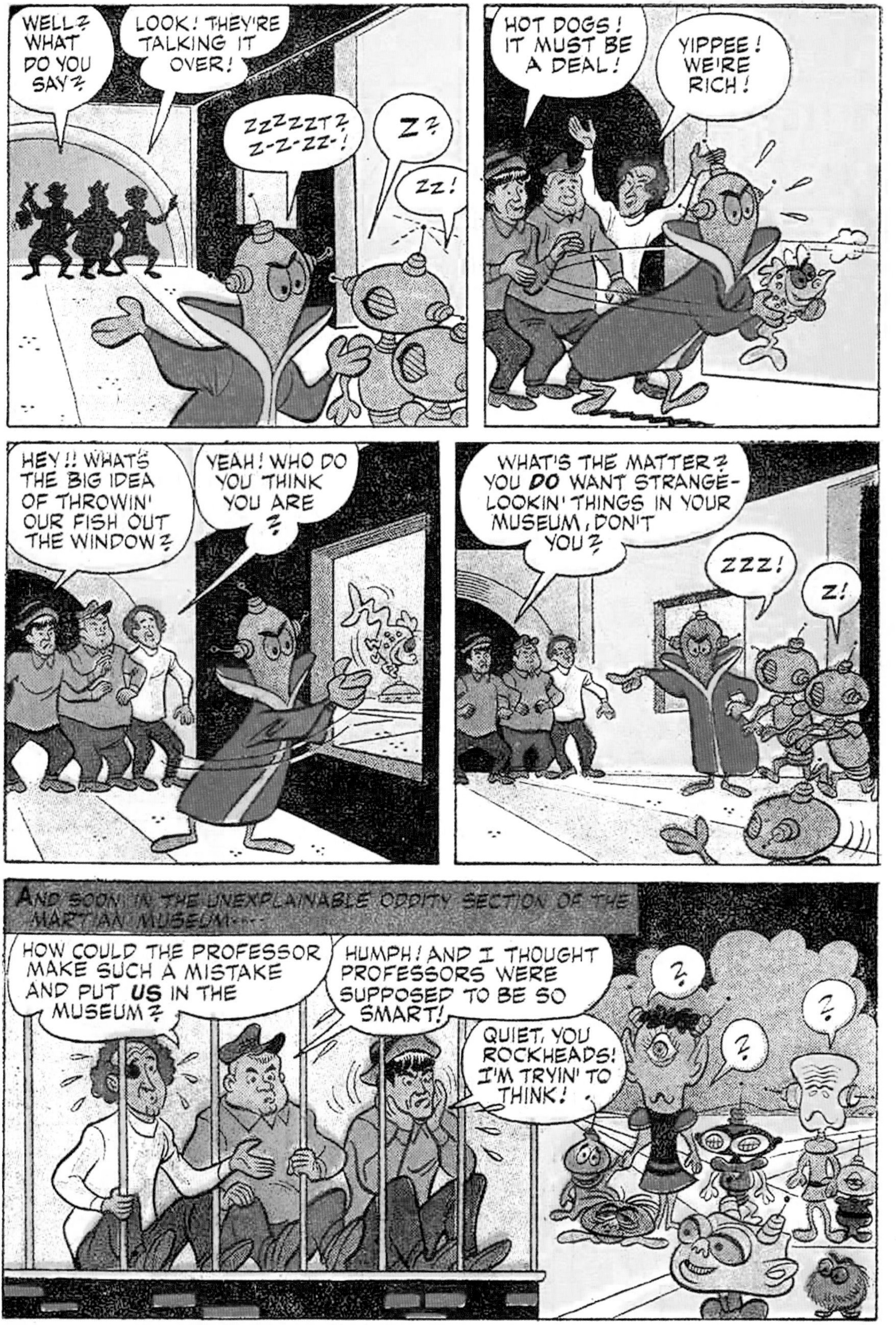
WELL? WHAT DO YOU SAY?
LOOK! THEY'RE TALKING IT OVER!
ZZZZZT Z Z-Z-ZZ-!
Z?
ZZ!
HOT DOGS! IT MUST BE A DEAL!
YIPPEE! WE'RE RICH!
HEY!! WHAT'S THE BIG IDEA OF THROWIN' OUR FISH OUT THE WINDOW?
YEAH! WHO DO YOU THINK YOU ARE ?
WHAT'S THE MATTER? YOU DO WANT STRANGE-LOOKIN' THINGS IN YOUR MUSEUM, DON'T YOU?
ZZZ!
Z!
AND SOON IN THE UNEXPLAINABLE ODDITY SECTION OF THE MARTIAN MUSEUM---
HOW COULD THE PROFESSOR MAKE SUCH A MISTAKE AND PUT US IN THE MUSEUM?
HUMPH! AND I THOUGHT PROFESSORS WERE SUPPOSED TO BE SO SMART!
QUIET, YOU ROCKHEADS! I'M TRYIN' TO THINK!
?
?
?

THE THREE STOOGES
HOME, SWEET HOME

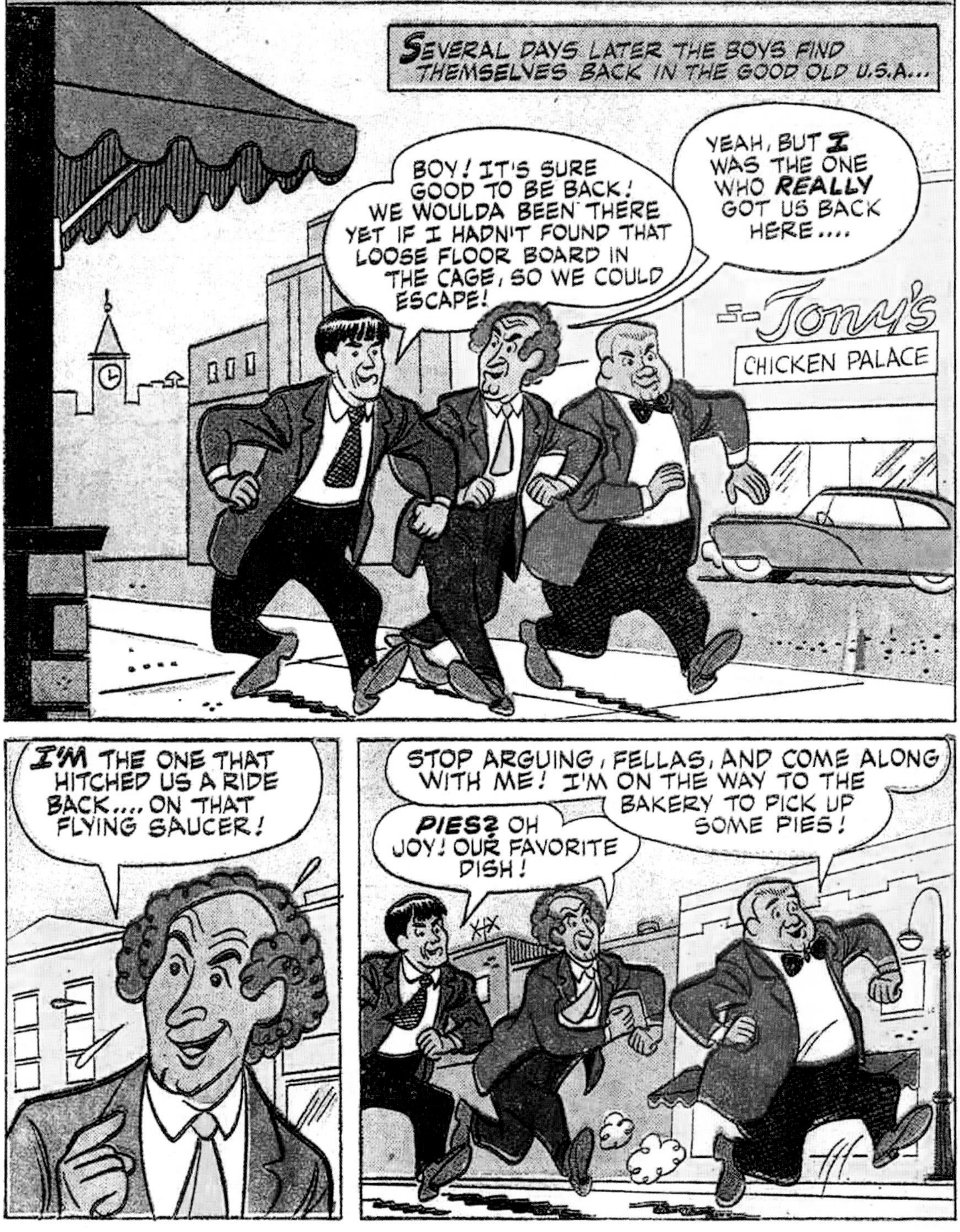
SEVERAL DAYS LATER THE BOYS FIND THEMSELVES BACK IN THE GOOD OLD U.S.A...
BOY! IT'S SURE GOOD TO BE BACK! WE WOULDA BEEN THERE YET IF I HADN'T FOUND THAT LOOSE FLOOR BOARD IN THE CAGE, SO WE COULD ESCAPE!
YEAH, BUT I WAS THE ONE WHO REALLY GOT US BACK HERE....
Tony's
CHICKEN PALACE
I'M THE ONE THAT HITCHED US A RIDE BACK.... ON THAT FLYING SAUCER!
STOP ARGUING, FELLAS, AND COME ALONG WITH ME! I'M ON THE WAY TO THE BAKERY TO PICK UP SOME PIES!
PIES? OH JOY! OUR FAVORITE DISH!

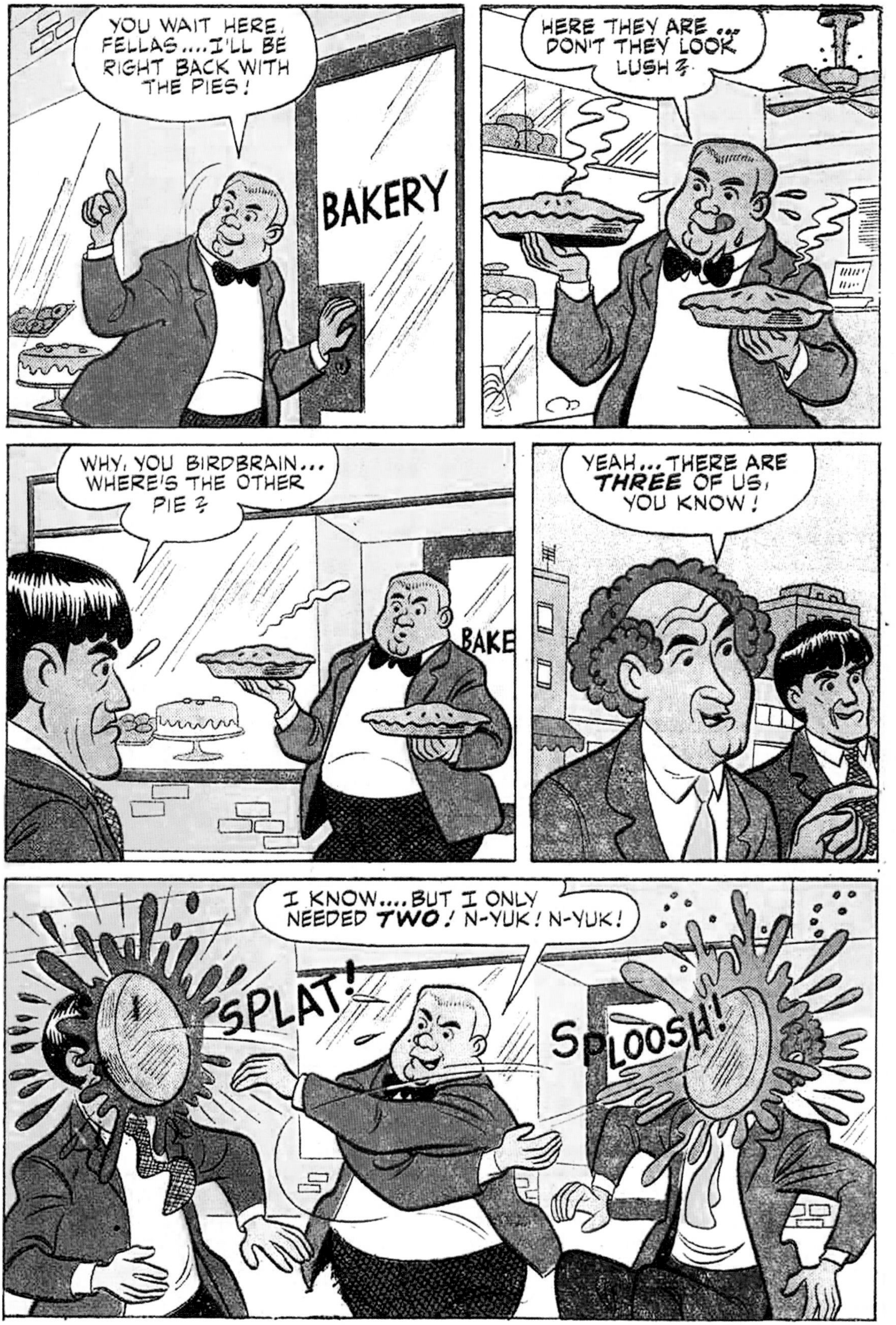
YOU WAIT HERE, FELLAS....I'LL BE RIGHT BACK WITH THE PIES!
BAKERY
HERE THEY ARE ... DON'T THEY LOOK LUSH?
WHY, YOU BIRDBRAIN... WHERE'S THE OTHER PIE?
BAKE
YEAH... THERE ARE THREE OF US, YOU KNOW!
I KNOW.... BUT I ONLY NEEDED TWO! N-YUK! N-YUK!
SPLAT!
SPLOOSH!

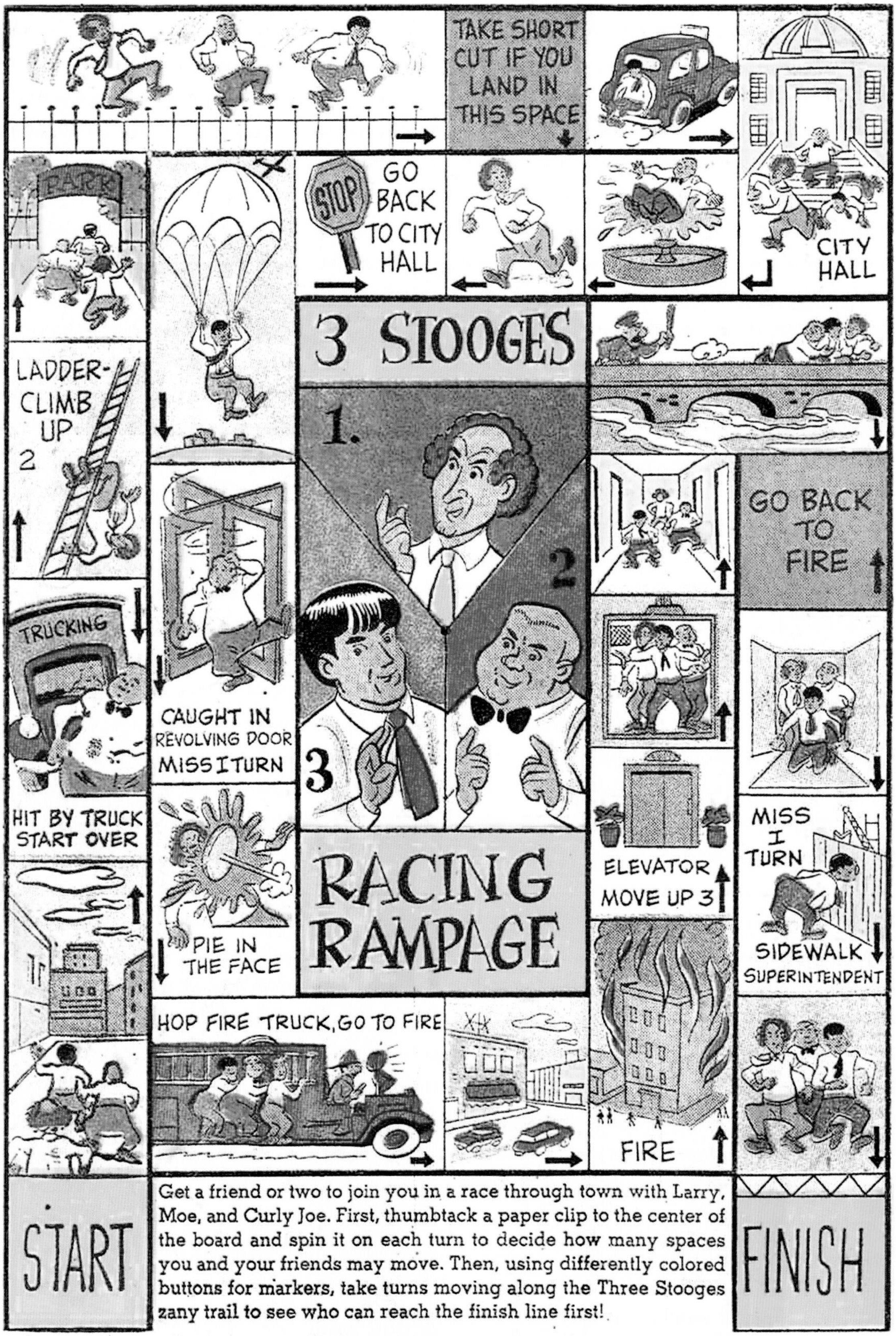
TAKE SHORT CUT IF YOU LAND IN THIS SPACE
CITY HALL
STOP
GO BACK TO CITY HALL
PARK
LADDER-CLIMB UP 2
TRUCKING
HIT BY TRUCK START OVER
CAUGHT IN REVOLVING DOOR MISS I TURN
PIE IN THE FACE
3 STOOGES
1.
2
3
RACING RAMPAGE
GO BACK TO FIRE
ELEVATOR MOVE UP 3
MISS I TURN
SIDEWALK SUPERINTENDENT
HOP FIRE TRUCK, GO TO FIRE
FIRE
START
FINISH
Get a friend or two to join you in a race through town with Larry, Moe, and Curly Joe. First, thumbtack a paper clip to the center of the board and spin it on each turn to decide how many spaces you and your friends may move. Then, using differently colored buttons for markers, take turns moving along the Three Stooges zany trail to see who can reach the finish line first!

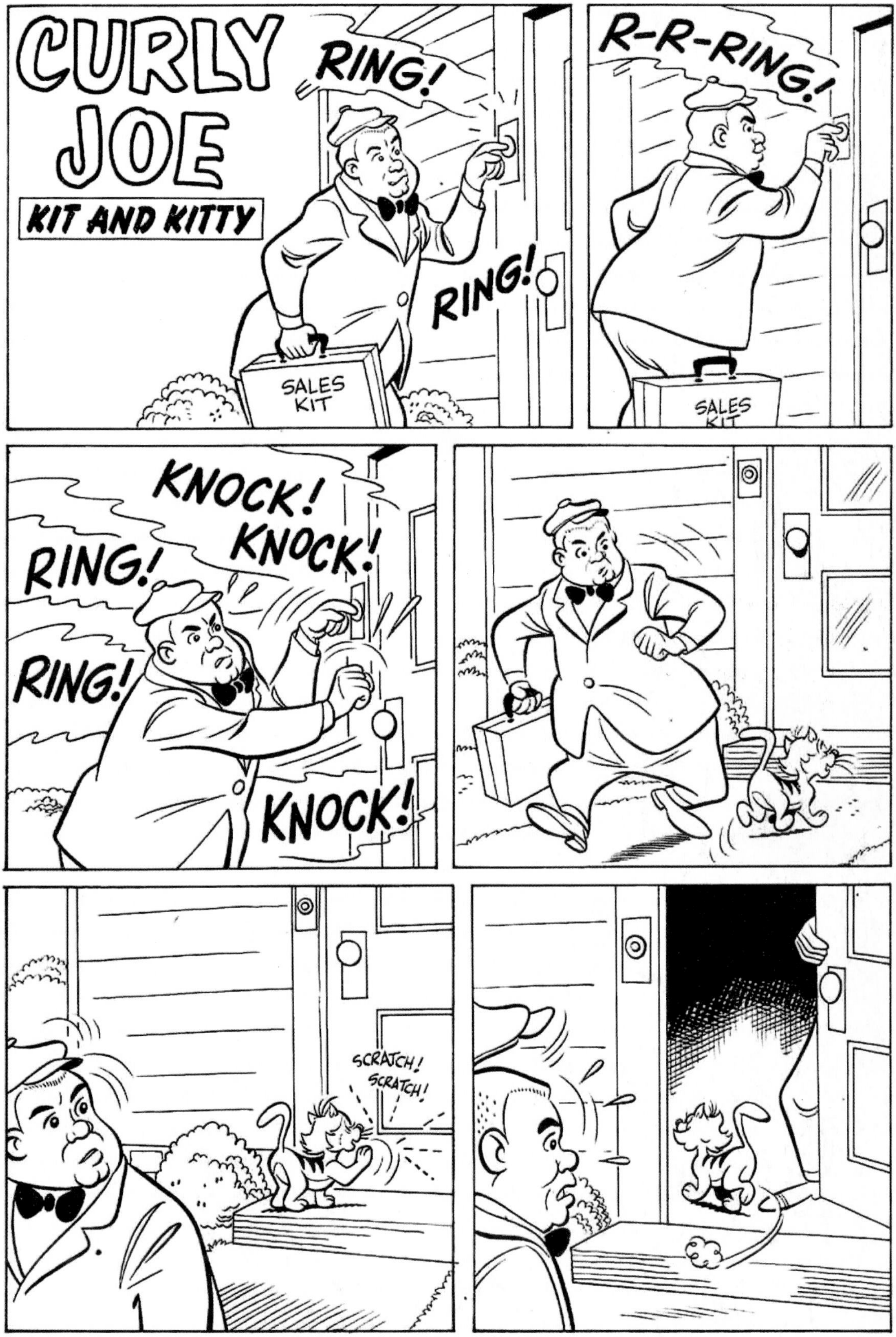
CURLY JOE
KIT AND KITTY
RING!
RING!
SALES KIT
R-R-RING!
SALES KIT
KNOCK!
KNOCK!
RING!
RING!
KNOCK!
SCRATCH!
SCRATCH!

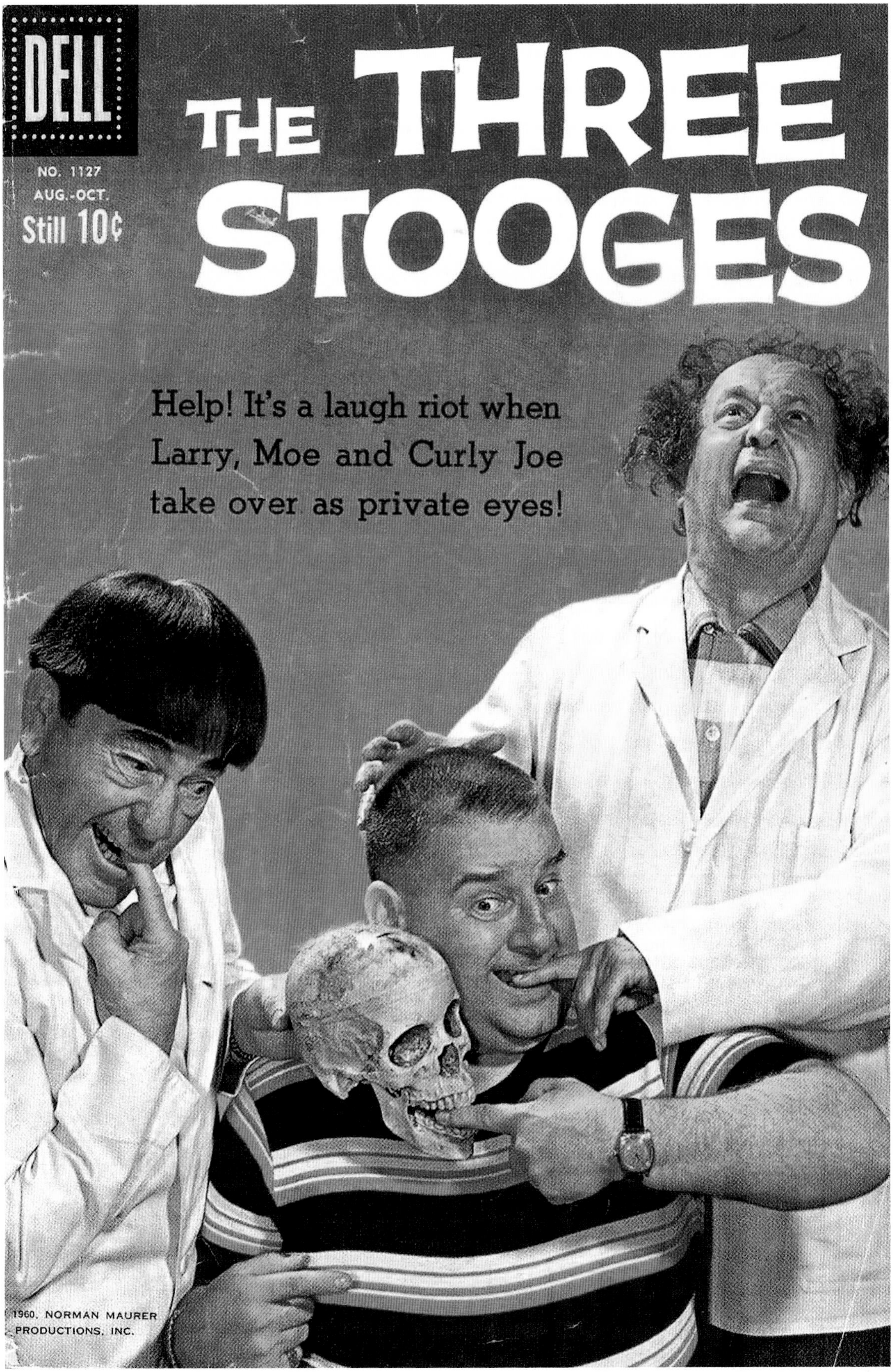
DELL
THE THREE STOOGES
NO. 1127
AUG.-OCT.
Still 10¢
Help! It's a laugh riot when Larry, Moe and Curly Joe take over as private eyes!
1960, NORMAN MAURER PRODUCTIONS, INC.

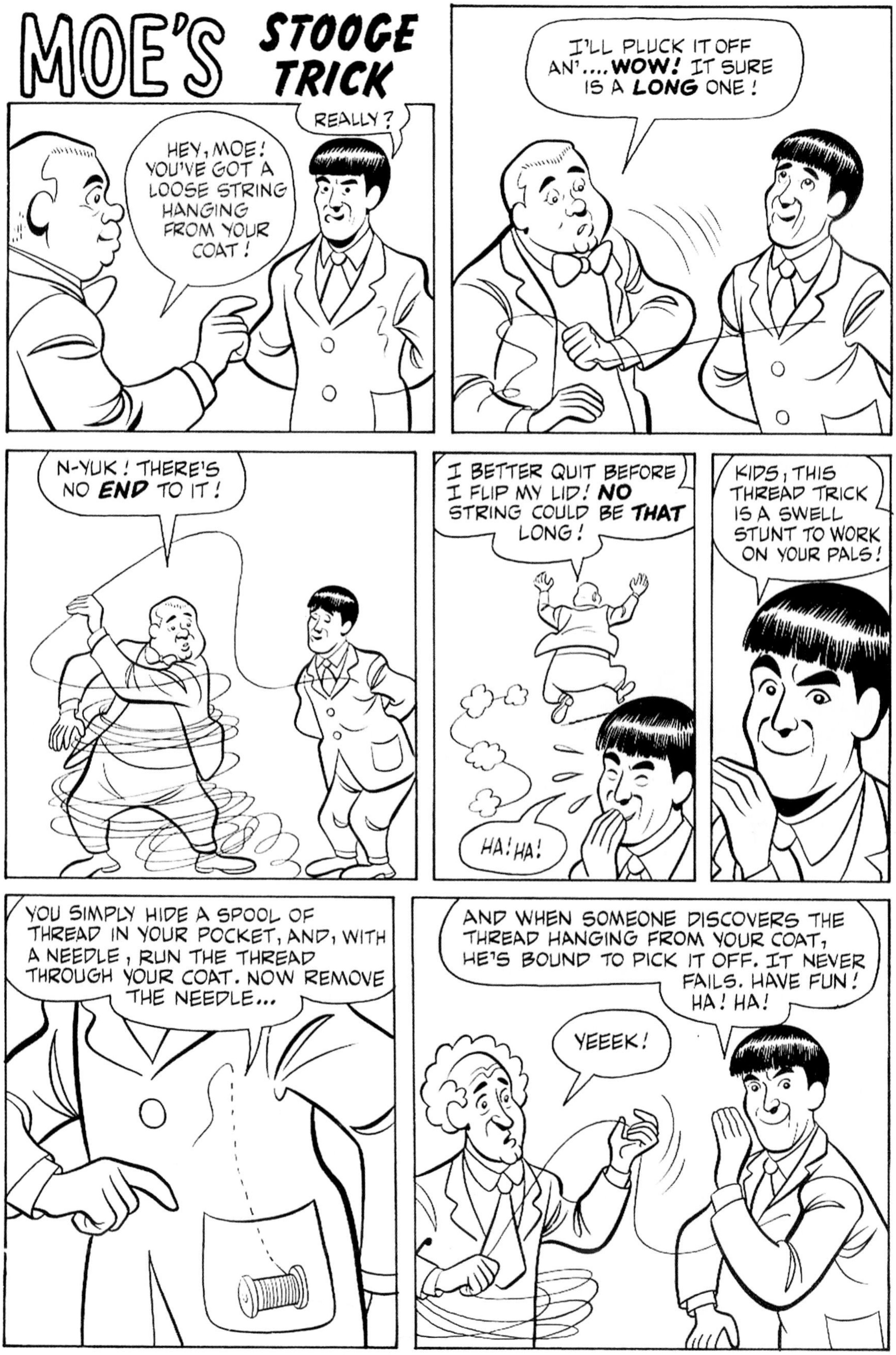
MOE'S STOOGE TRICK
HEY, MOE! YOU'VE GOT A LOOSE STRING HANGING FROM YOUR COAT!
REALLY?
I'LL PLUCK IT OFF AN'....**WOW!** IT SURE IS A **LONG** ONE!
N-YUK! THERE'S NO **END** TO IT!
I BETTER QUIT BEFORE I FLIP MY LID! **NO** STRING COULD BE **THAT** LONG!
HA! HA!
KIDS, THIS THREAD TRICK IS A SWELL STUNT TO WORK ON YOUR PALS!
YOU SIMPLY HIDE A SPOOL OF THREAD IN YOUR POCKET, AND, WITH A NEEDLE, RUN THE THREAD THROUGH YOUR COAT. NOW REMOVE THE NEEDLE...
AND WHEN SOMEONE DISCOVERS THE THREAD HANGING FROM YOUR COAT, HE'S BOUND TO PICK IT OFF. IT NEVER FAILS. HAVE FUN! HA! HA!
YEEEK!

THE THREE STOOGES
THE PRIVATE EYE-BALLS

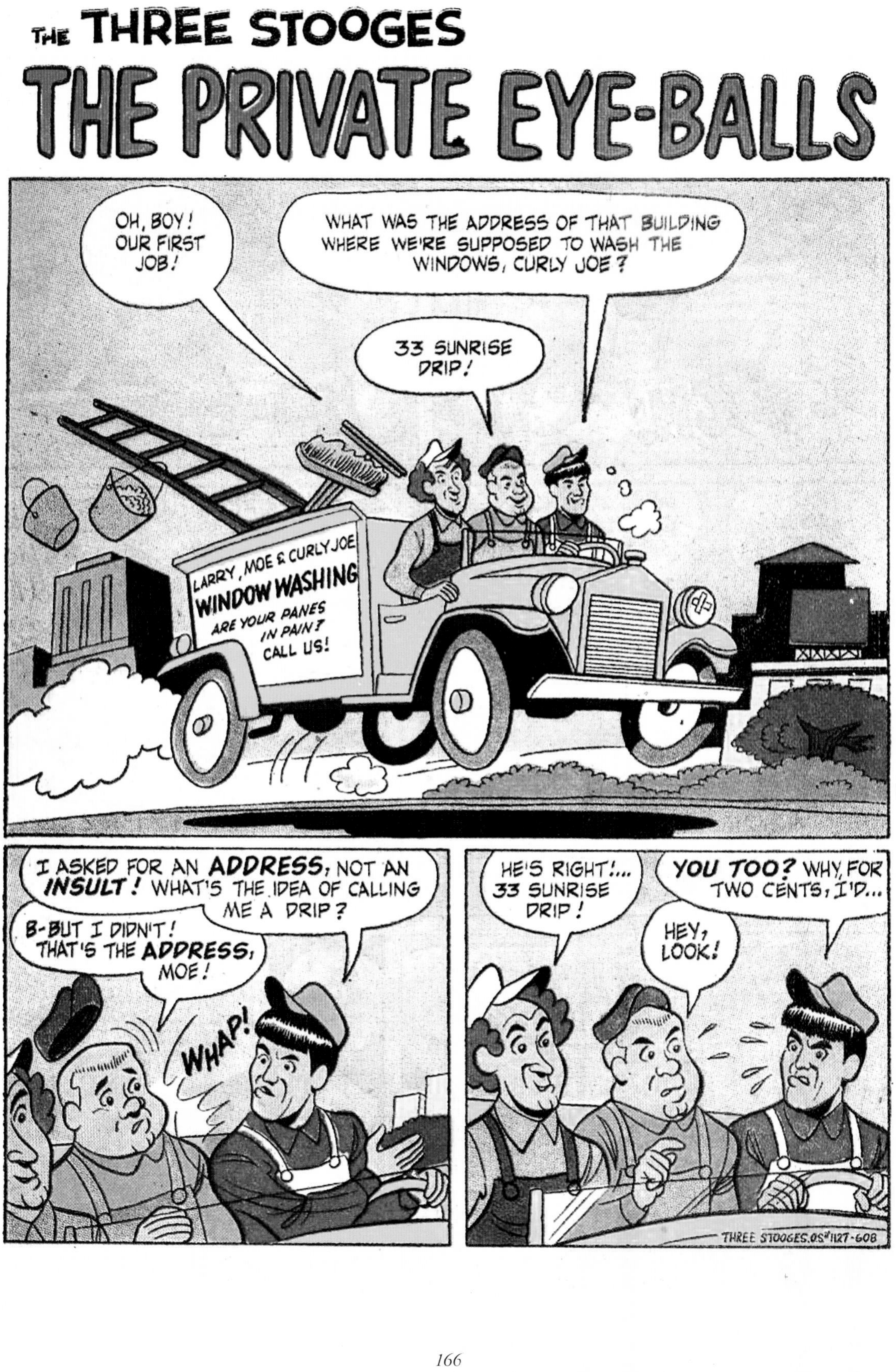

OH, BOY! OUR FIRST JOB!
WHAT WAS THE ADDRESS OF THAT BUILDING WHERE WE'RE SUPPOSED TO WASH THE WINDOWS, CURLY JOE?
33 SUNRISE DRIP!
LARRY, MOE & CURLY JOE
WINDOW WASHING
ARE YOUR PANES IN PAIN? CALL US!
I ASKED FOR AN ADDRESS, NOT AN INSULT! WHAT'S THE IDEA OF CALLING ME A DRIP?
B-BUT I DIDN'T! THAT'S THE ADDRESS, MOE!
WHAP!
HE'S RIGHT!... 33 SUNRISE DRIP!
YOU TOO? WHY, FOR TWO CENTS, I'D...
HEY, LOOK!
THREE STOOGES.OS#1127-608

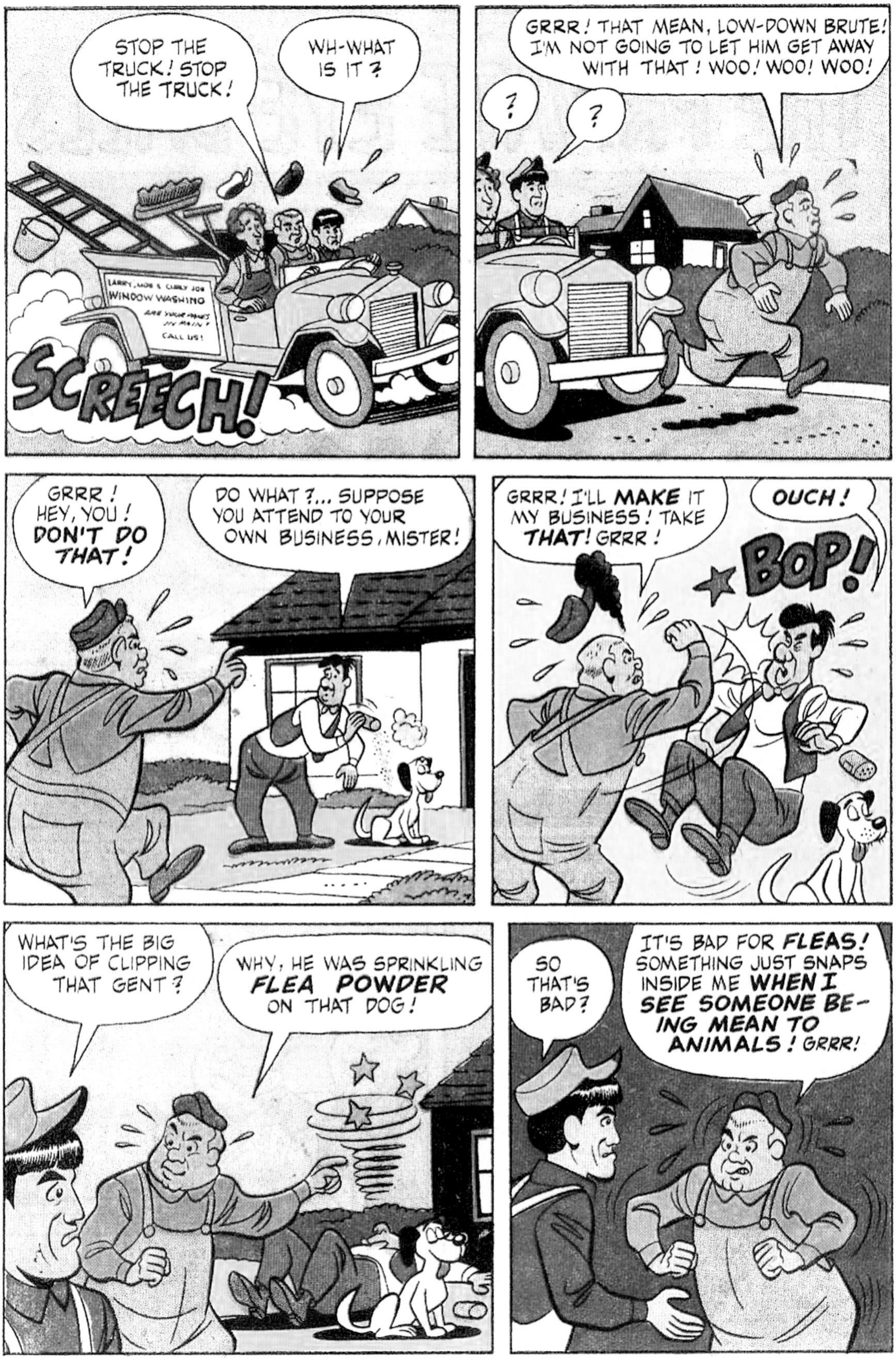
STOP THE TRUCK! STOP THE TRUCK!
WH-WHAT IS IT?
WINDOW WASHING
CALL US!
SCREECH!
GRRR! THAT MEAN, LOW-DOWN BRUTE! I'M NOT GOING TO LET HIM GET AWAY WITH THAT! WOO! WOO! WOO!
?
?
GRRR! HEY, YOU! DON'T DO THAT!
DO WHAT?... SUPPOSE YOU ATTEND TO YOUR OWN BUSINESS, MISTER!
GRRR! I'LL MAKE IT MY BUSINESS! TAKE THAT! GRRR!
OUCH!
BOP!
WHAT'S THE BIG IDEA OF CLIPPING THAT GENT?
WHY, HE WAS SPRINKLING FLEA POWDER ON THAT DOG!
SO THAT'S BAD?
IT'S BAD FOR FLEAS! SOMETHING JUST SNAPS INSIDE ME WHEN I SEE SOMEONE BEING MEAN TO ANIMALS! GRRR!

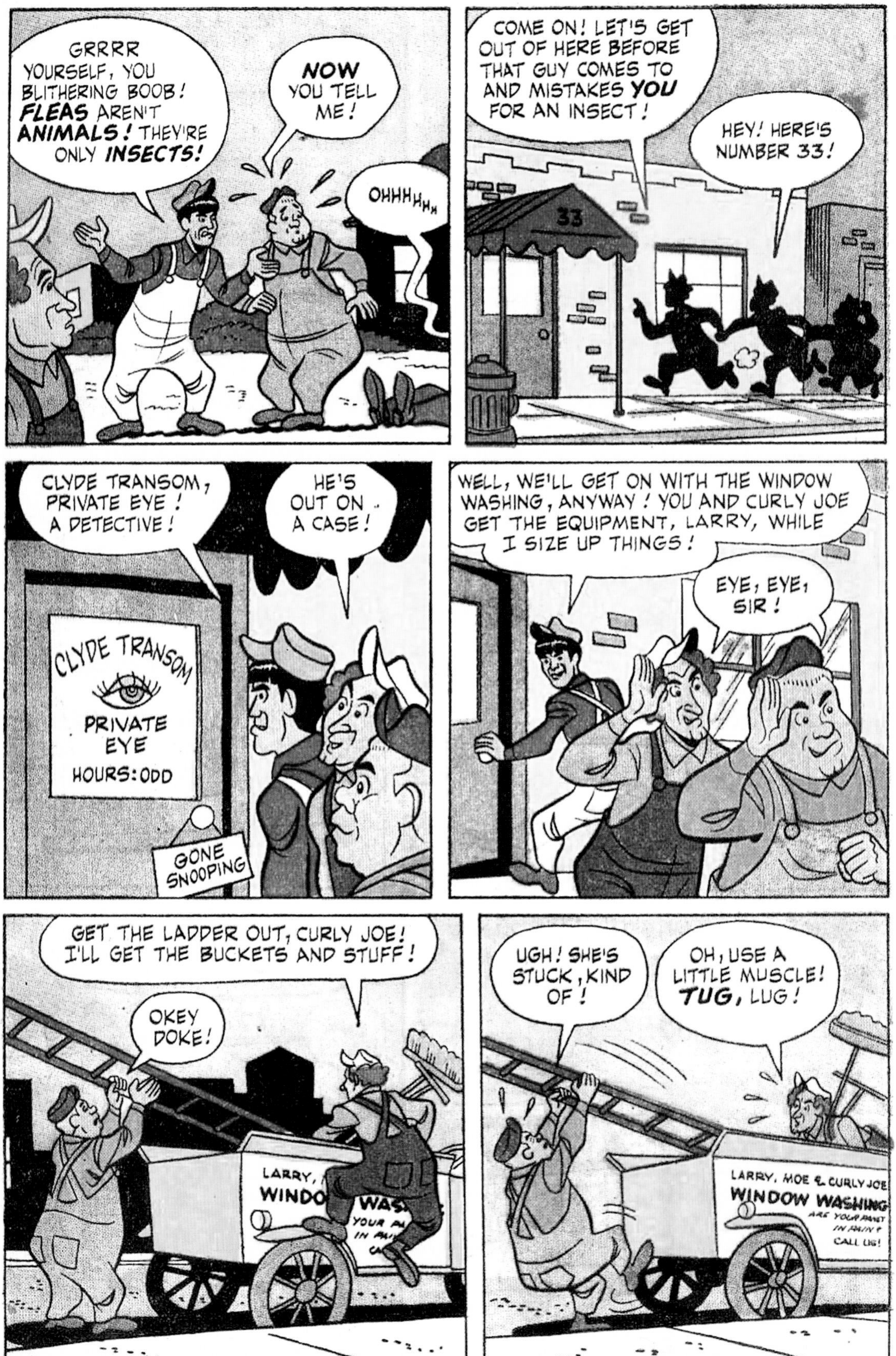
GRRRR YOURSELF, YOU BLITHERING BOOB! FLEAS AREN'T ANIMALS! THEY'RE ONLY INSECTS!
NOW YOU TELL ME!
OHHHHHH
COME ON! LET'S GET OUT OF HERE BEFORE THAT GUY COMES TO AND MISTAKES YOU FOR AN INSECT!
HEY! HERE'S NUMBER 33!
33
CLYDE TRANSOM, PRIVATE EYE! A DETECTIVE!
HE'S OUT ON A CASE!
CLYDE TRANSOM
PRIVATE EYE
HOURS: ODD
GONE SNOOPING
WELL, WE'LL GET ON WITH THE WINDOW WASHING, ANYWAY! YOU AND CURLY JOE GET THE EQUIPMENT, LARRY, WHILE I SIZE UP THINGS!
EYE, EYE, SIR!
GET THE LADDER OUT, CURLY JOE! I'LL GET THE BUCKETS AND STUFF!
OKEY DOKE!
UGH! SHE'S STUCK, KIND OF!
OH, USE A LITTLE MUSCLE! TUG, LUG!
LARRY, MOE & CURLY JOE
WINDOW WASHING
CALL US!

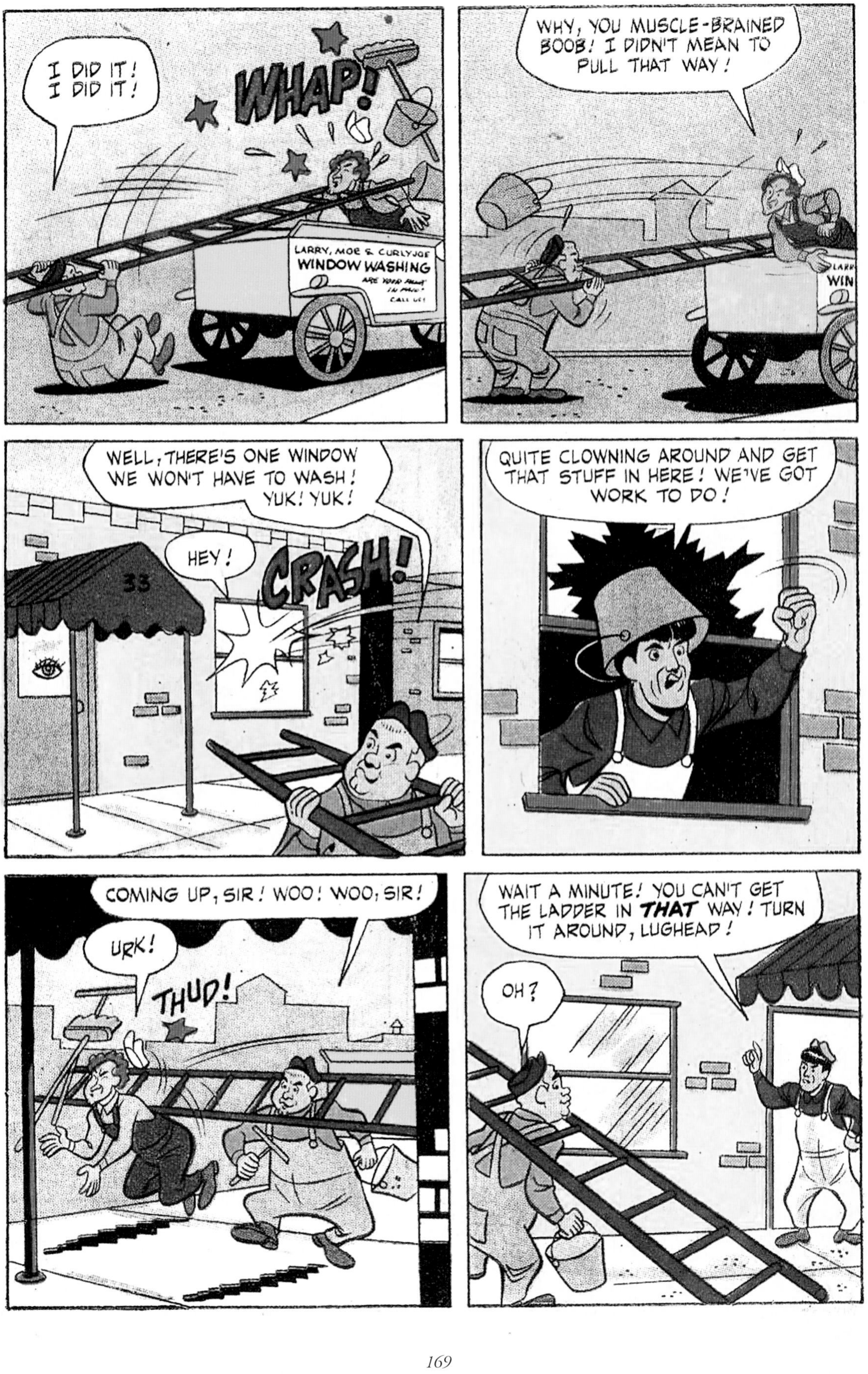
I DID IT! I DID IT!
WHAP!
LARRY, MOE & CURLYJOE
WINDOW WASHING
WHY, YOU MUSCLE-BRAINED BOOB! I DIDN'T MEAN TO PULL THAT WAY!
WELL, THERE'S ONE WINDOW WE WON'T HAVE TO WASH! YUK! YUK!
HEY!
33
CRASH!
QUITE CLOWNING AROUND AND GET THAT STUFF IN HERE! WE'VE GOT WORK TO DO!
COMING UP, SIR! WOO! WOO, SIR!
URK!
THUD!
WAIT A MINUTE! YOU CAN'T GET THE LADDER IN THAT WAY! TURN IT AROUND, LUGHEAD!
OH?

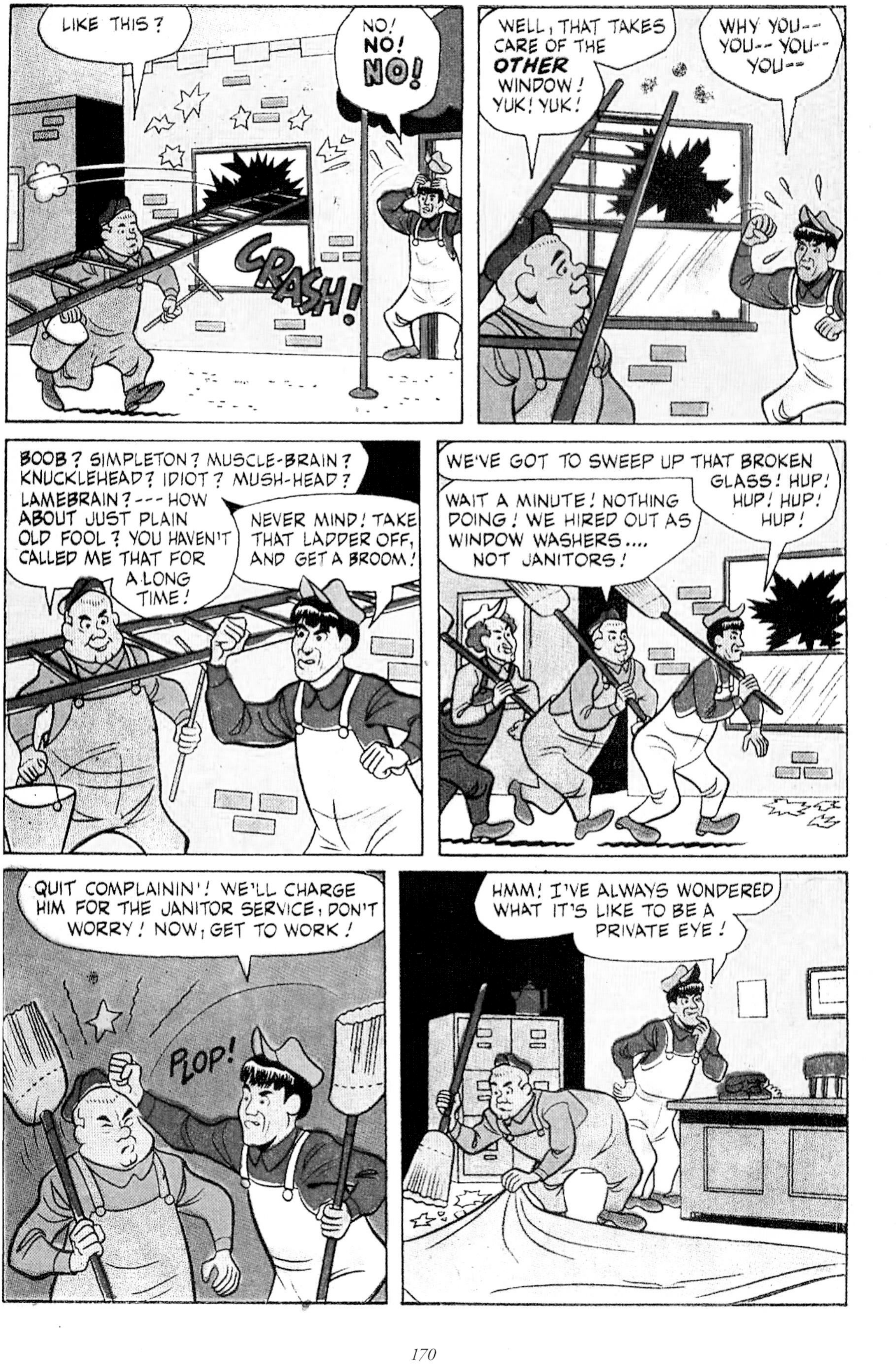
LIKE THIS?
NO! NO! NO!
CRASH!
WELL, THAT TAKES CARE OF THE OTHER WINDOW! YUK! YUK!
WHY YOU-- YOU-- YOU-- YOU--
BOOB? SIMPLETON? MUSCLE-BRAIN? KNUCKLEHEAD? IDIOT? MUSH-HEAD? LAMEBRAIN?--- HOW ABOUT JUST PLAIN OLD FOOL? YOU HAVEN'T CALLED ME THAT FOR A LONG TIME!
NEVER MIND! TAKE THAT LADDER OFF, AND GET A BROOM!
WE'VE GOT TO SWEEP UP THAT BROKEN GLASS! HUP! HUP! HUP! HUP!
WAIT A MINUTE! NOTHING DOING! WE HIRED OUT AS WINDOW WASHERS.... NOT JANITORS!
QUIT COMPLAININ'! WE'LL CHARGE HIM FOR THE JANITOR SERVICE; DON'T WORRY! NOW, GET TO WORK!
PLOP!
HMM! I'VE ALWAYS WONDERED WHAT IT'S LIKE TO BE A PRIVATE EYE!

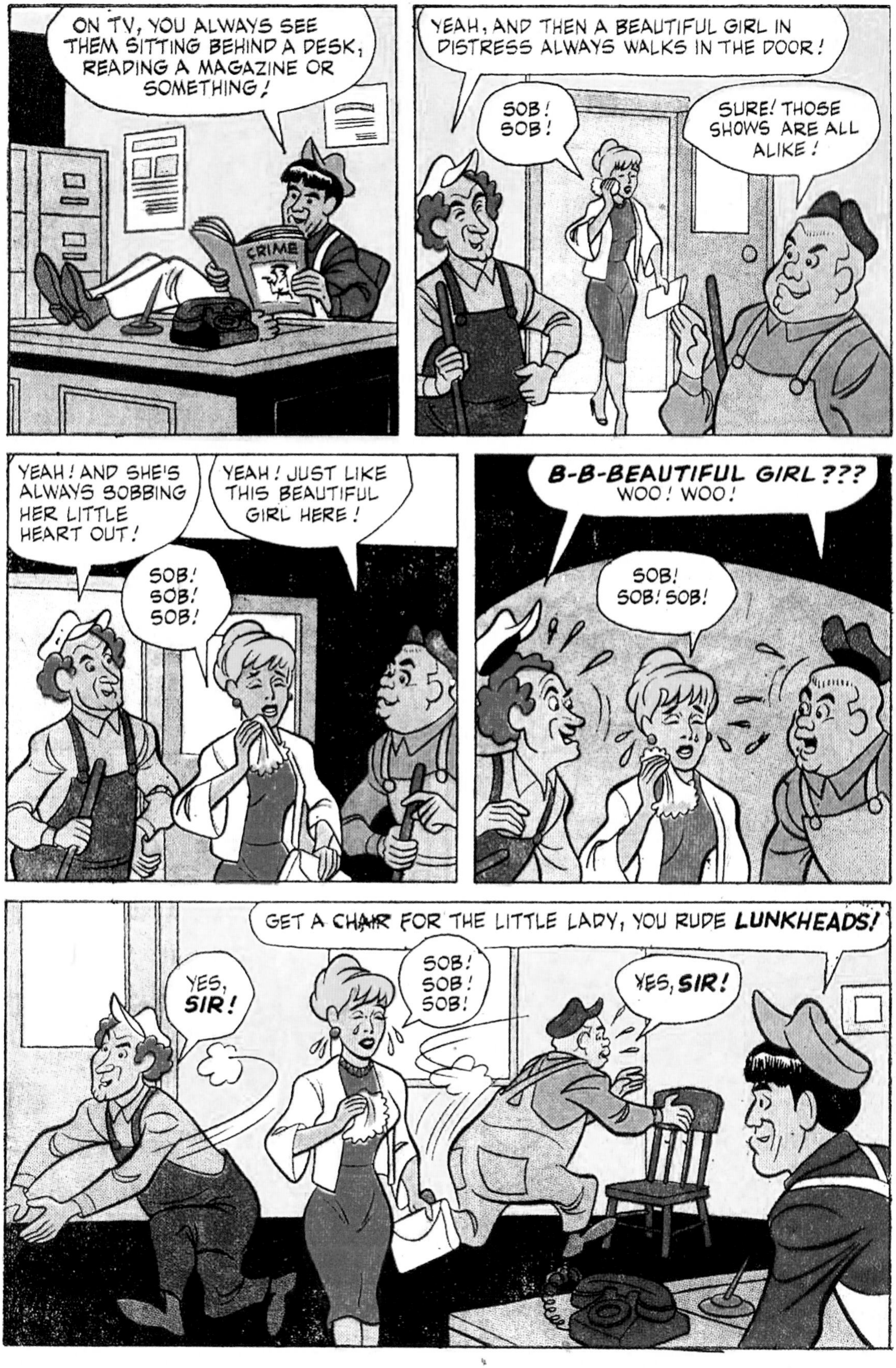
ON TV, YOU ALWAYS SEE THEM SITTING BEHIND A DESK, READING A MAGAZINE OR SOMETHING!
CRIME
YEAH, AND THEN A BEAUTIFUL GIRL IN DISTRESS ALWAYS WALKS IN THE DOOR!
SOB! SOB!
SURE! THOSE SHOWS ARE ALL ALIKE!
YEAH! AND SHE'S ALWAYS SOBBING HER LITTLE HEART OUT!
YEAH! JUST LIKE THIS BEAUTIFUL GIRL HERE!
SOB! SOB! SOB!
B-B-BEAUTIFUL GIRL??? WOO! WOO!
SOB! SOB! SOB!
GET A CHAIR FOR THE LITTLE LADY, YOU RUDE LUNKHEADS!
YES, SIR!
SOB! SOB! SOB!
YES, SIR!

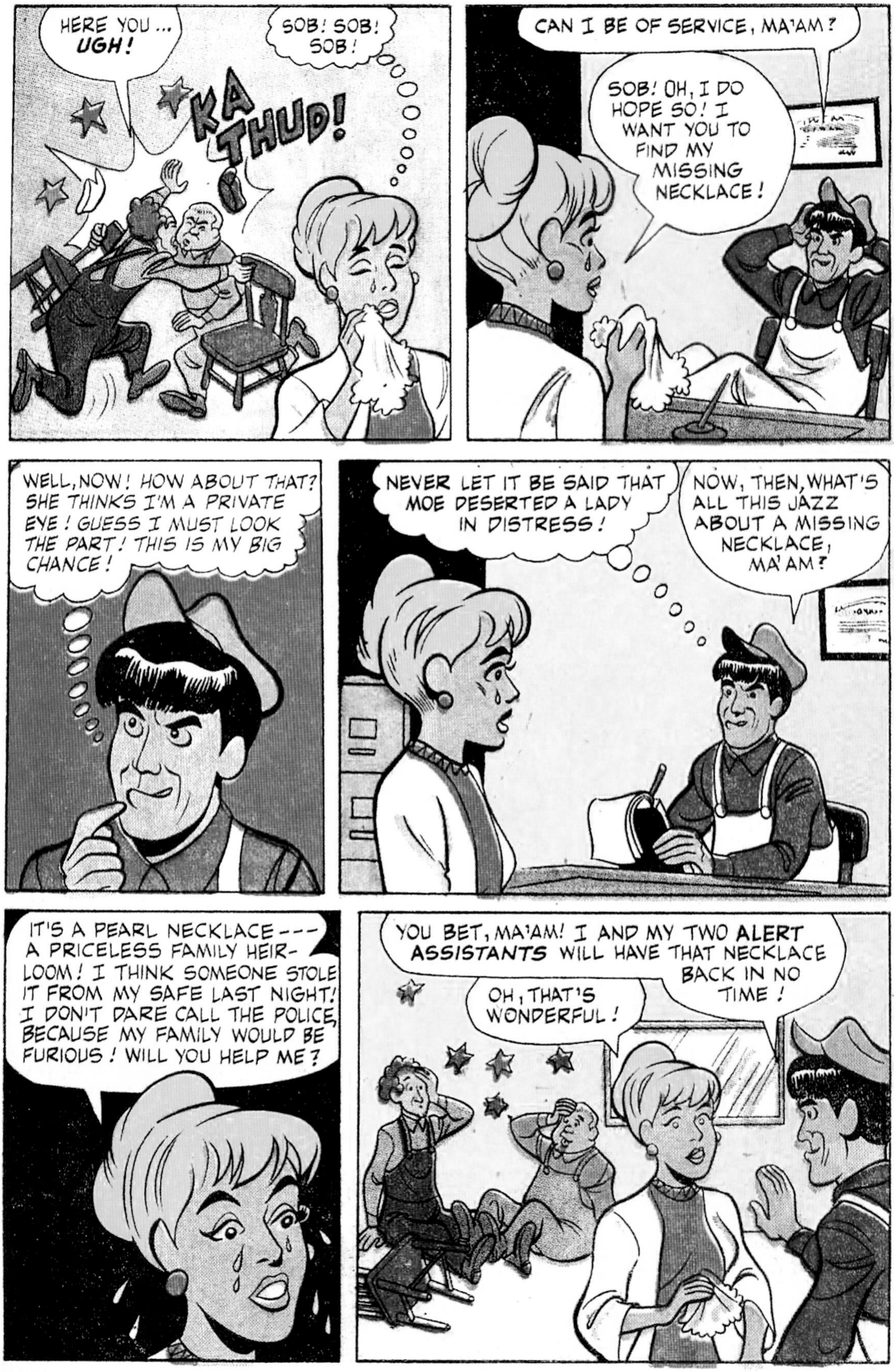
HERE YOU ... UGH!
SOB! SOB! SOB!
KA THUD!
CAN I BE OF SERVICE, MA'AM?
SOB! OH, I DO HOPE SO! I WANT YOU TO FIND MY MISSING NECKLACE!
WELL, NOW! HOW ABOUT THAT? SHE THINKS I'M A PRIVATE EYE! GUESS I MUST LOOK THE PART! THIS IS MY BIG CHANCE!
NEVER LET IT BE SAID THAT MOE DESERTED A LADY IN DISTRESS!
NOW, THEN, WHAT'S ALL THIS JAZZ ABOUT A MISSING NECKLACE, MA'AM?
IT'S A PEARL NECKLACE--- A PRICELESS FAMILY HEIR-LOOM! I THINK SOMEONE STOLE IT FROM MY SAFE LAST NIGHT! I DON'T DARE CALL THE POLICE, BECAUSE MY FAMILY WOULD BE FURIOUS! WILL YOU HELP ME?
YOU BET, MA'AM! I AND MY TWO ALERT ASSISTANTS WILL HAVE THAT NECKLACE BACK IN NO TIME!
OH, THAT'S WONDERFUL!

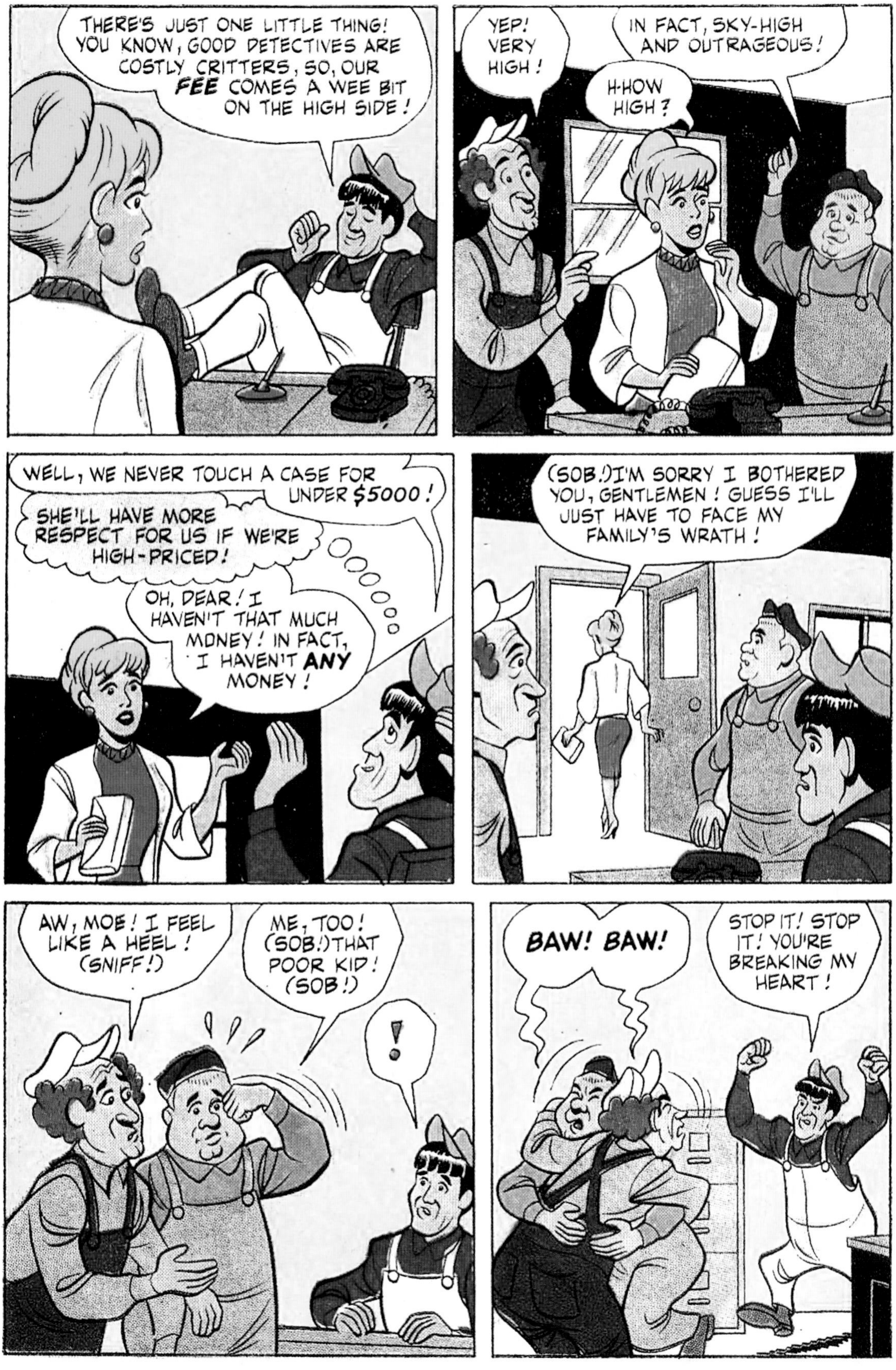
THERE'S JUST ONE LITTLE THING! YOU KNOW, GOOD DETECTIVES ARE COSTLY CRITTERS, SO, OUR FEE COMES A WEE BIT ON THE HIGH SIDE!
YEP! VERY HIGH!
IN FACT, SKY-HIGH AND OUTRAGEOUS!
H-HOW HIGH?
WELL, WE NEVER TOUCH A CASE FOR UNDER $5000!
SHE'LL HAVE MORE RESPECT FOR US IF WE'RE HIGH-PRICED!
OH, DEAR! I HAVEN'T THAT MUCH MONEY! IN FACT, I HAVEN'T ANY MONEY!
(SOB!) I'M SORRY I BOTHERED YOU, GENTLEMEN! GUESS I'LL JUST HAVE TO FACE MY FAMILY'S WRATH!
AW, MOE! I FEEL LIKE A HEEL! (SNIFF!)
ME, TOO! (SOB!) THAT POOR KID! (SOB!)
!
BAW! BAW!
STOP IT! STOP IT! YOU'RE BREAKING MY HEART!

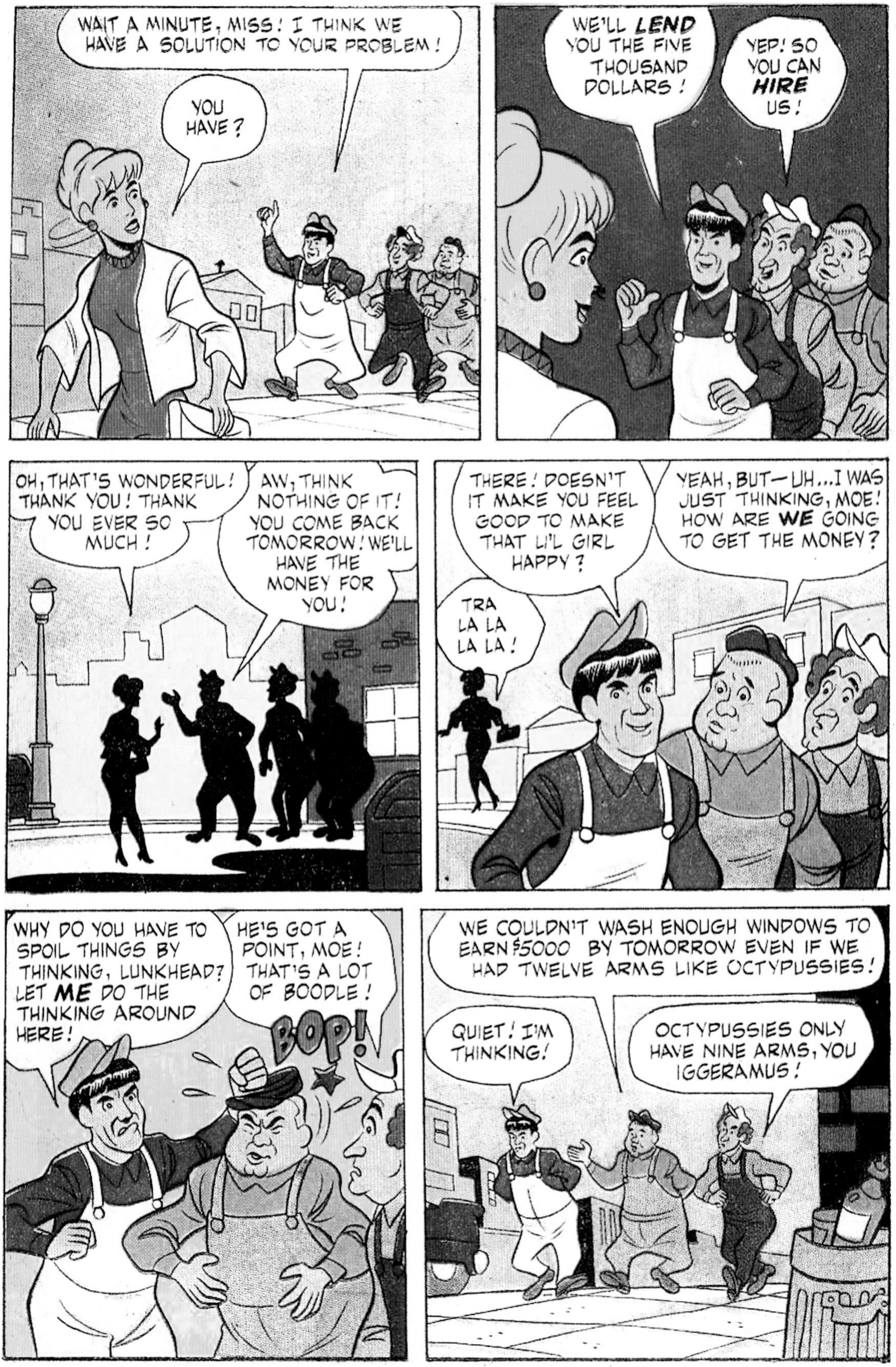
WAIT A MINUTE, MISS! I THINK WE HAVE A SOLUTION TO YOUR PROBLEM!
YOU HAVE?
WE'LL **LEND** YOU THE FIVE THOUSAND DOLLARS!
YEP! SO YOU CAN **HIRE** US!
OH, THAT'S WONDERFUL! THANK YOU! THANK YOU EVER SO MUCH!
AW, THINK NOTHING OF IT! YOU COME BACK TOMORROW! WE'LL HAVE THE MONEY FOR YOU!
THERE! DOESN'T IT MAKE YOU FEEL GOOD TO MAKE THAT LI'L GIRL HAPPY?
YEAH, BUT—UH...I WAS JUST THINKING, MOE! HOW ARE **WE** GOING TO GET THE MONEY?
TRA LA LA LA LA!
WHY DO YOU HAVE TO SPOIL THINGS BY THINKING, LUNKHEAD? LET **ME** DO THE THINKING AROUND HERE!
HE'S GOT A POINT, MOE! THAT'S A LOT OF BOODLE!
BOP!
WE COULDN'T WASH ENOUGH WINDOWS TO EARN $5000 BY TOMORROW EVEN IF WE HAD TWELVE ARMS LIKE OCTYPUSSIES!
QUIET! I'M THINKING!
OCTYPUSSIES ONLY HAVE NINE ARMS, YOU IGGERAMUS!

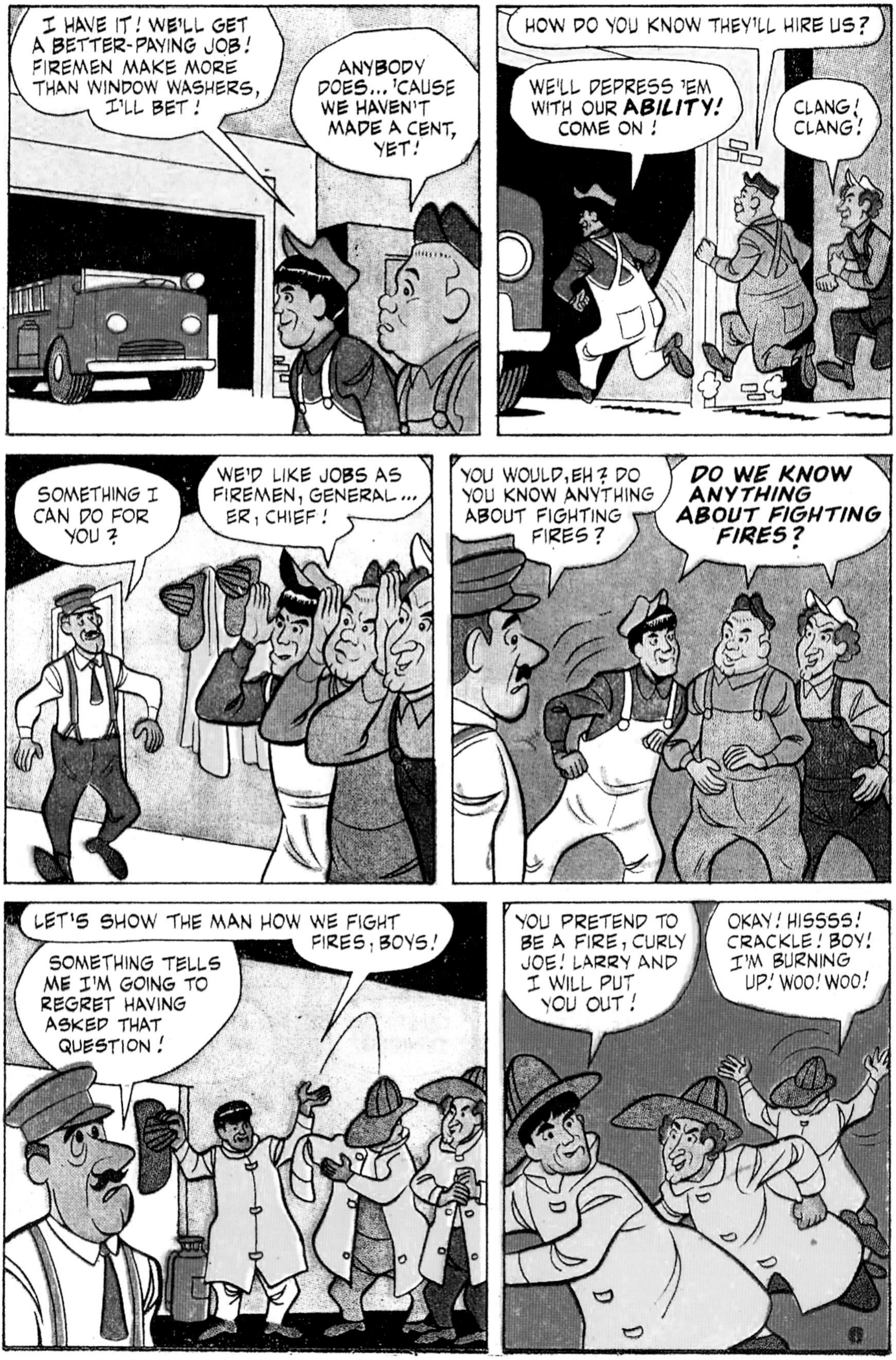
I HAVE IT! WE'LL GET A BETTER-PAYING JOB! FIREMEN MAKE MORE THAN WINDOW WASHERS, I'LL BET!
ANYBODY DOES... 'CAUSE WE HAVEN'T MADE A CENT, YET!
HOW DO YOU KNOW THEY'LL HIRE US?
WE'LL DEPRESS 'EM WITH OUR ABILITY! COME ON!
CLANG! CLANG!
SOMETHING I CAN DO FOR YOU?
WE'D LIKE JOBS AS FIREMEN, GENERAL... ER, CHIEF!
YOU WOULD, EH? DO YOU KNOW ANYTHING ABOUT FIGHTING FIRES?
DO WE KNOW ANYTHING ABOUT FIGHTING FIRES?
LET'S SHOW THE MAN HOW WE FIGHT FIRES, BOYS!
SOMETHING TELLS ME I'M GOING TO REGRET HAVING ASKED THAT QUESTION!
YOU PRETEND TO BE A FIRE, CURLY JOE! LARRY AND I WILL PUT YOU OUT!
OKAY! HISSSS! CRACKLE! BOY! I'M BURNING UP! WOO! WOO!

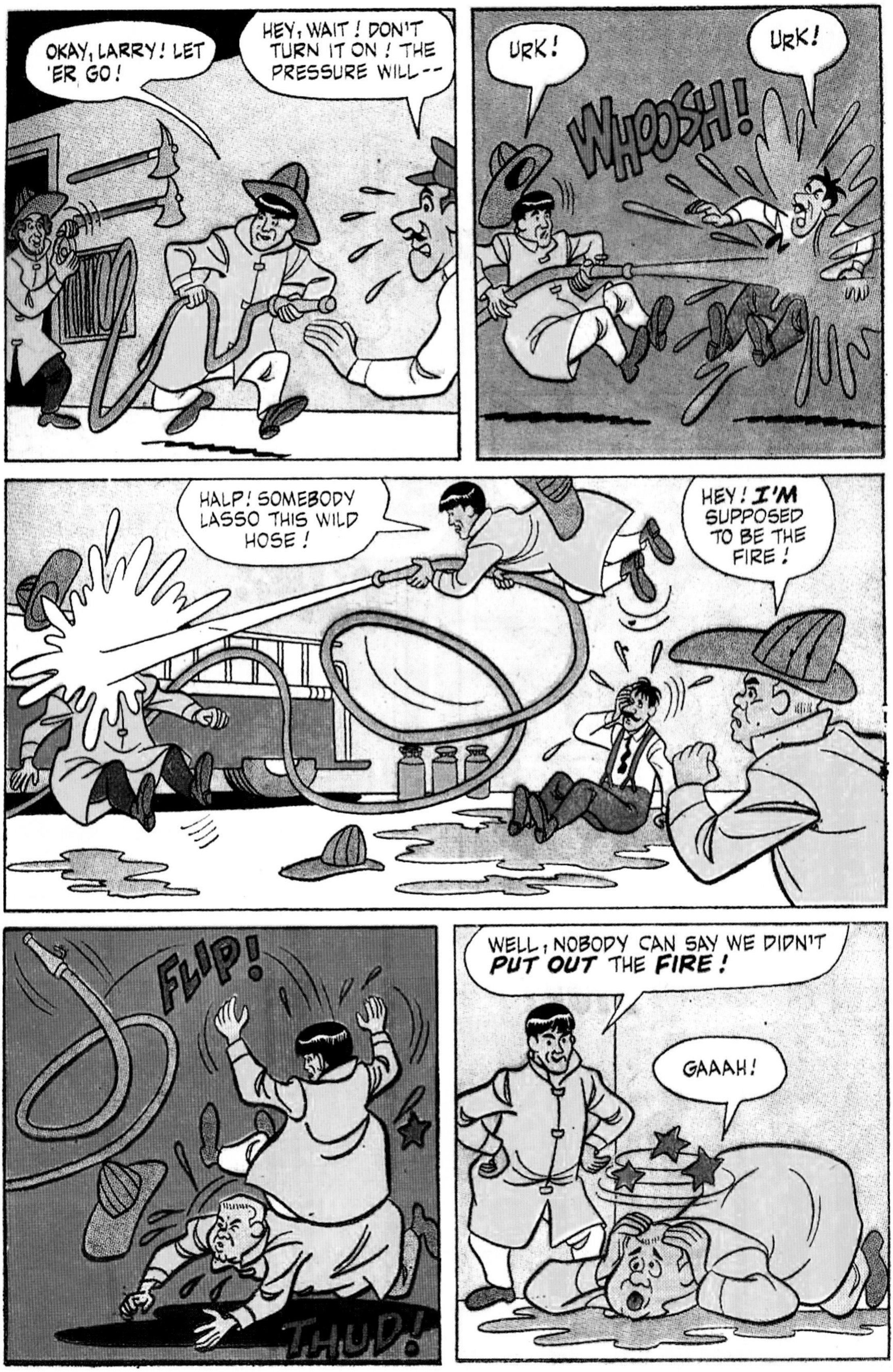
OKAY, LARRY! LET 'ER GO!
HEY, WAIT! DON'T TURN IT ON! THE PRESSURE WILL--
URK!
URK!
WHOOSH!
HALP! SOMEBODY LASSO THIS WILD HOSE!
HEY! I'M SUPPOSED TO BE THE FIRE!
FLIP!
THUD!
WELL, NOBODY CAN SAY WE DIDN'T PUT OUT THE FIRE!
GAAAH!

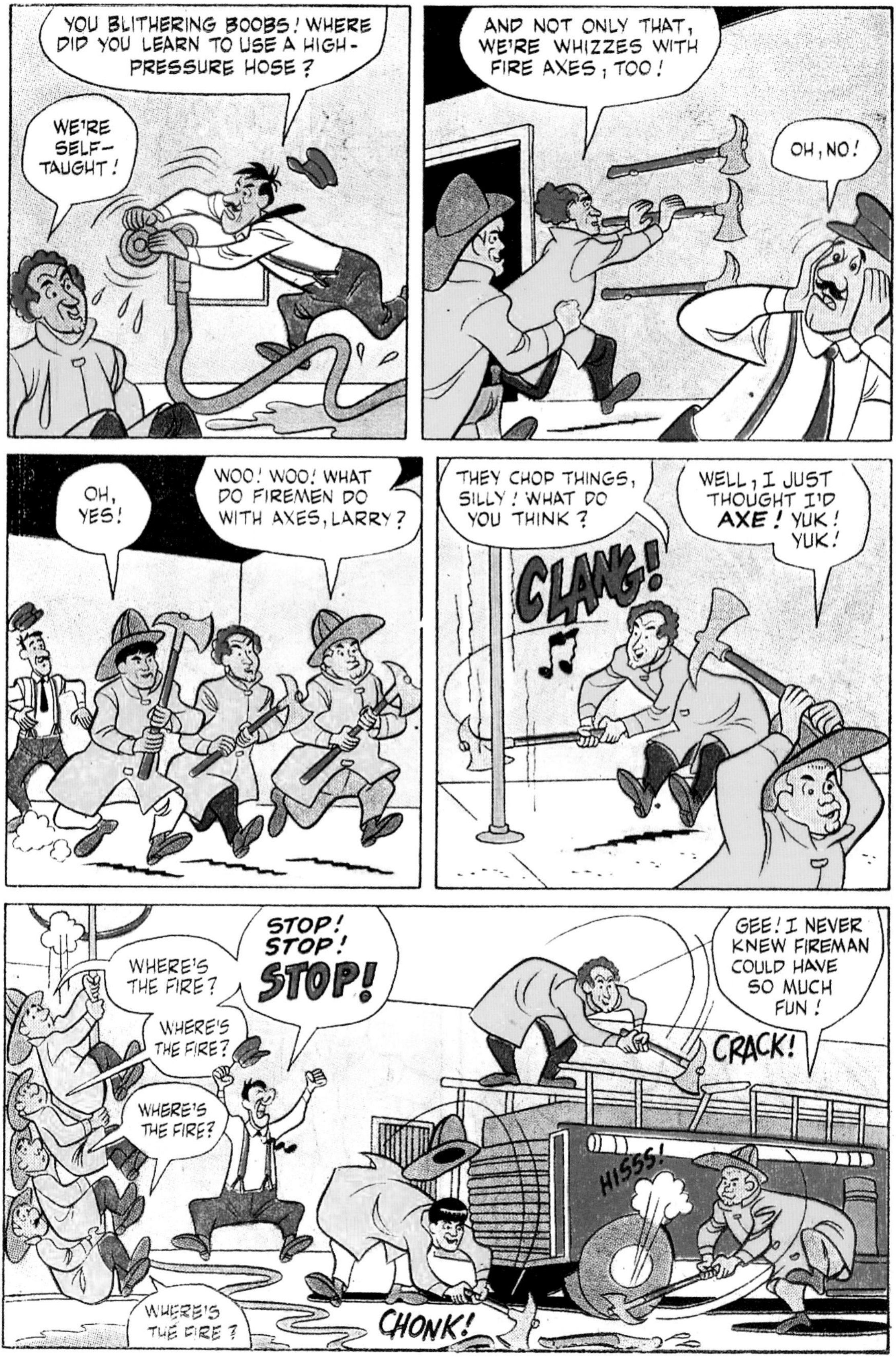
YOU BLITHERING BOOBS! WHERE DID YOU LEARN TO USE A HIGH-PRESSURE HOSE?
WE'RE SELF-TAUGHT!
AND NOT ONLY THAT, WE'RE WHIZZES WITH FIRE AXES, TOO!
OH, NO!
OH, YES!
WOO! WOO! WHAT DO FIREMEN DO WITH AXES, LARRY?
THEY CHOP THINGS, SILLY! WHAT DO YOU THINK?
WELL, I JUST THOUGHT I'D AXE! YUK! YUK!
CLANG!
WHERE'S THE FIRE?
STOP! STOP! STOP!
WHERE'S THE FIRE?
WHERE'S THE FIRE?
GEE! I NEVER KNEW FIREMAN COULD HAVE SO MUCH FUN!
CRACK!
HISSS!
WHERE'S THE FIRE?
CHONK!

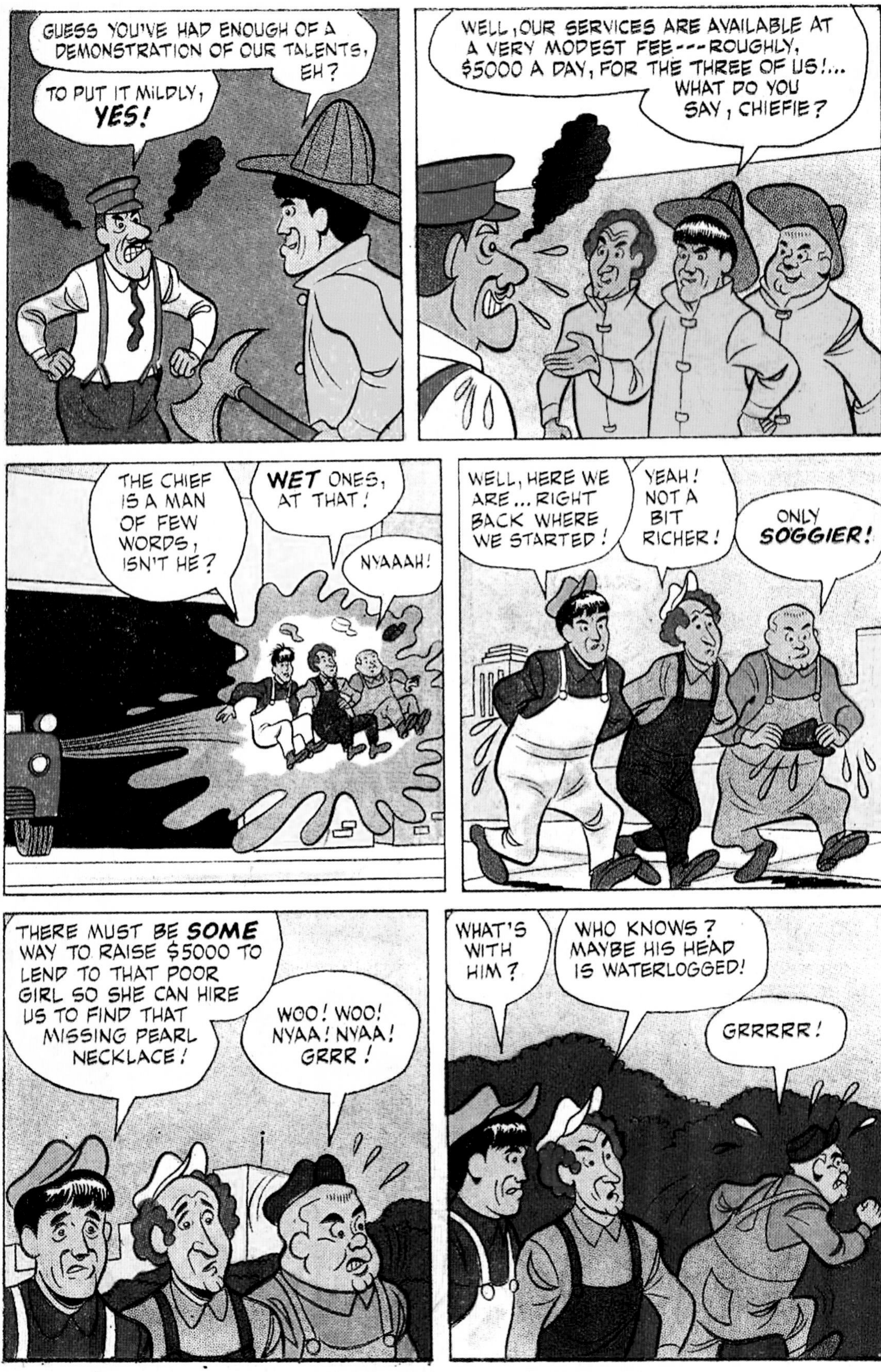
GUESS YOU'VE HAD ENOUGH OF A DEMONSTRATION OF OUR TALENTS, EH?
TO PUT IT MILDLY, YES!
WELL, OUR SERVICES ARE AVAILABLE AT A VERY MODEST FEE---ROUGHLY, $5000 A DAY, FOR THE THREE OF US!... WHAT DO YOU SAY, CHIEFIE?
THE CHIEF IS A MAN OF FEW WORDS, ISN'T HE?
WET ONES, AT THAT!
NYAAAH!
WELL, HERE WE ARE... RIGHT BACK WHERE WE STARTED!
YEAH! NOT A BIT RICHER!
ONLY SOGGIER!
THERE MUST BE SOME WAY TO RAISE $5000 TO LEND TO THAT POOR GIRL SO SHE CAN HIRE US TO FIND THAT MISSING PEARL NECKLACE!
WOO! WOO! NYAA! NYAA! GRRR!
WHAT'S WITH HIM?
WHO KNOWS? MAYBE HIS HEAD IS WATERLOGGED!
GRRRRR!

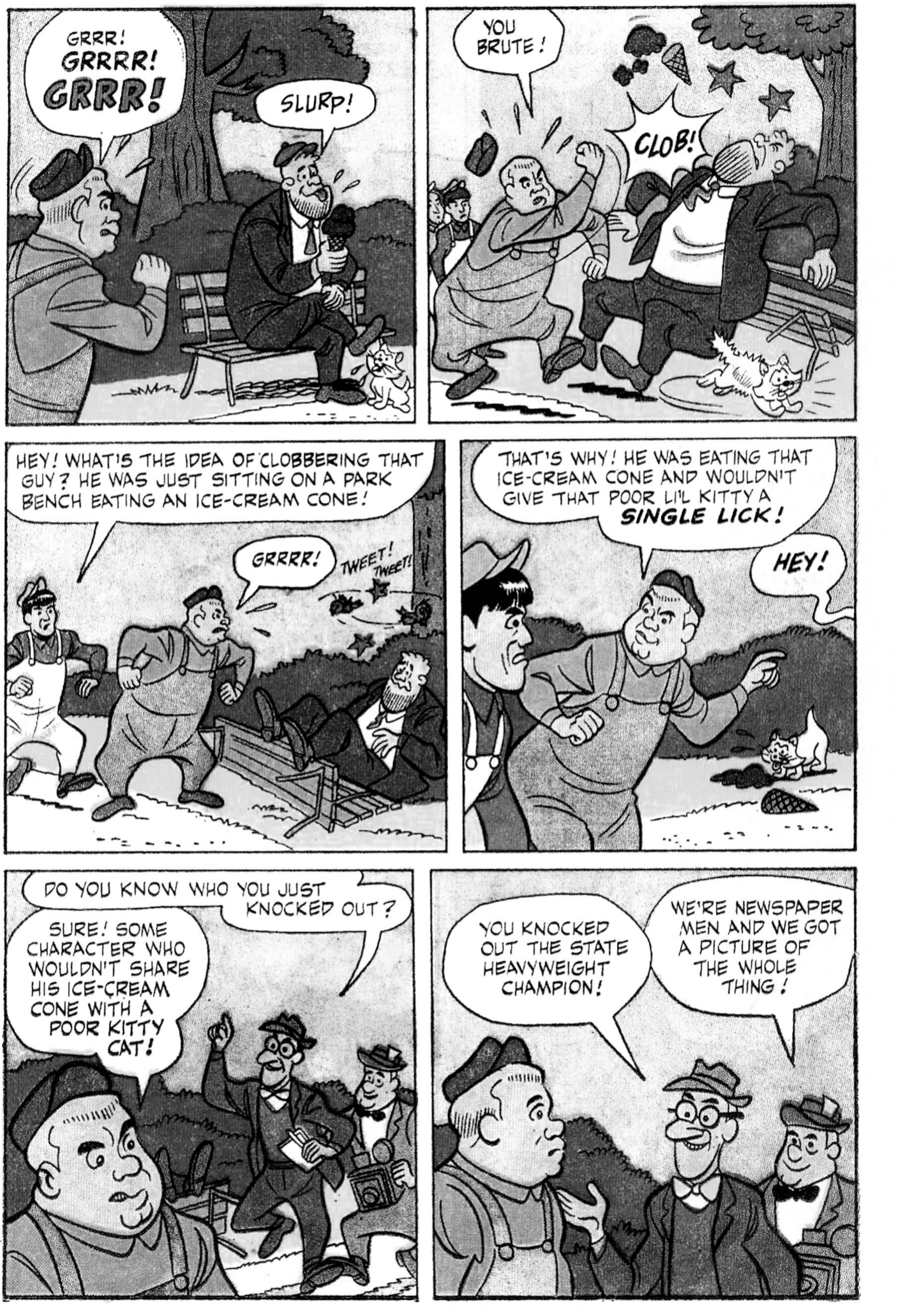
GRRR! GRRRR! GRRR!
SLURP!
YOU BRUTE!
CLOB!
HEY! WHAT'S THE IDEA OF CLOBBERING THAT GUY? HE WAS JUST SITTING ON A PARK BENCH EATING AN ICE-CREAM CONE!
GRRRR!
TWEET! TWEET!
THAT'S WHY! HE WAS EATING THAT ICE-CREAM CONE AND WOULDN'T GIVE THAT POOR LI'L KITTY A SINGLE LICK!
HEY!
DO YOU KNOW WHO YOU JUST KNOCKED OUT?
SURE! SOME CHARACTER WHO WOULDN'T SHARE HIS ICE-CREAM CONE WITH A POOR KITTY CAT!
YOU KNOCKED OUT THE STATE HEAVYWEIGHT CHAMPION!
WE'RE NEWSPAPER MEN AND WE GOT A PICTURE OF THE WHOLE THING!

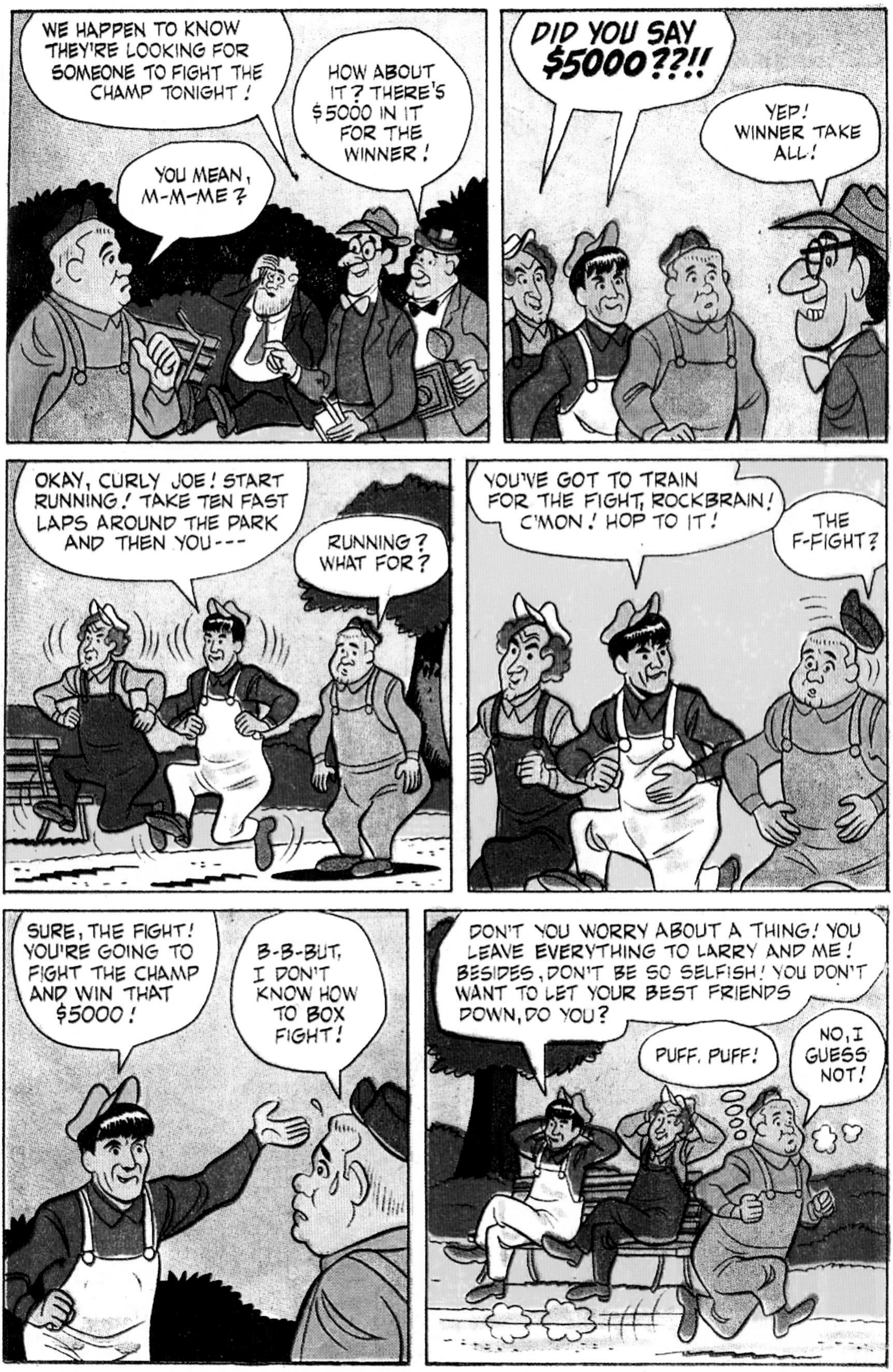
WE HAPPEN TO KNOW THEY'RE LOOKING FOR SOMEONE TO FIGHT THE CHAMP TONIGHT!
HOW ABOUT IT? THERE'S $5000 IN IT FOR THE WINNER!
YOU MEAN, M-M-ME?
DID YOU SAY $5000??!!
YEP! WINNER TAKE ALL!
OKAY, CURLY JOE! START RUNNING! TAKE TEN FAST LAPS AROUND THE PARK AND THEN YOU---
RUNNING? WHAT FOR?
YOU'VE GOT TO TRAIN FOR THE FIGHT, ROCKBRAIN! C'MON! HOP TO IT!
THE F-FIGHT?
SURE, THE FIGHT! YOU'RE GOING TO FIGHT THE CHAMP AND WIN THAT $5000!
B-B-BUT, I DON'T KNOW HOW TO BOX FIGHT!
DON'T YOU WORRY ABOUT A THING! YOU LEAVE EVERYTHING TO LARRY AND ME! BESIDES, DON'T BE SO SELFISH! YOU DON'T WANT TO LET YOUR BEST FRIENDS DOWN, DO YOU?
PUFF. PUFF!
NO, I GUESS NOT!

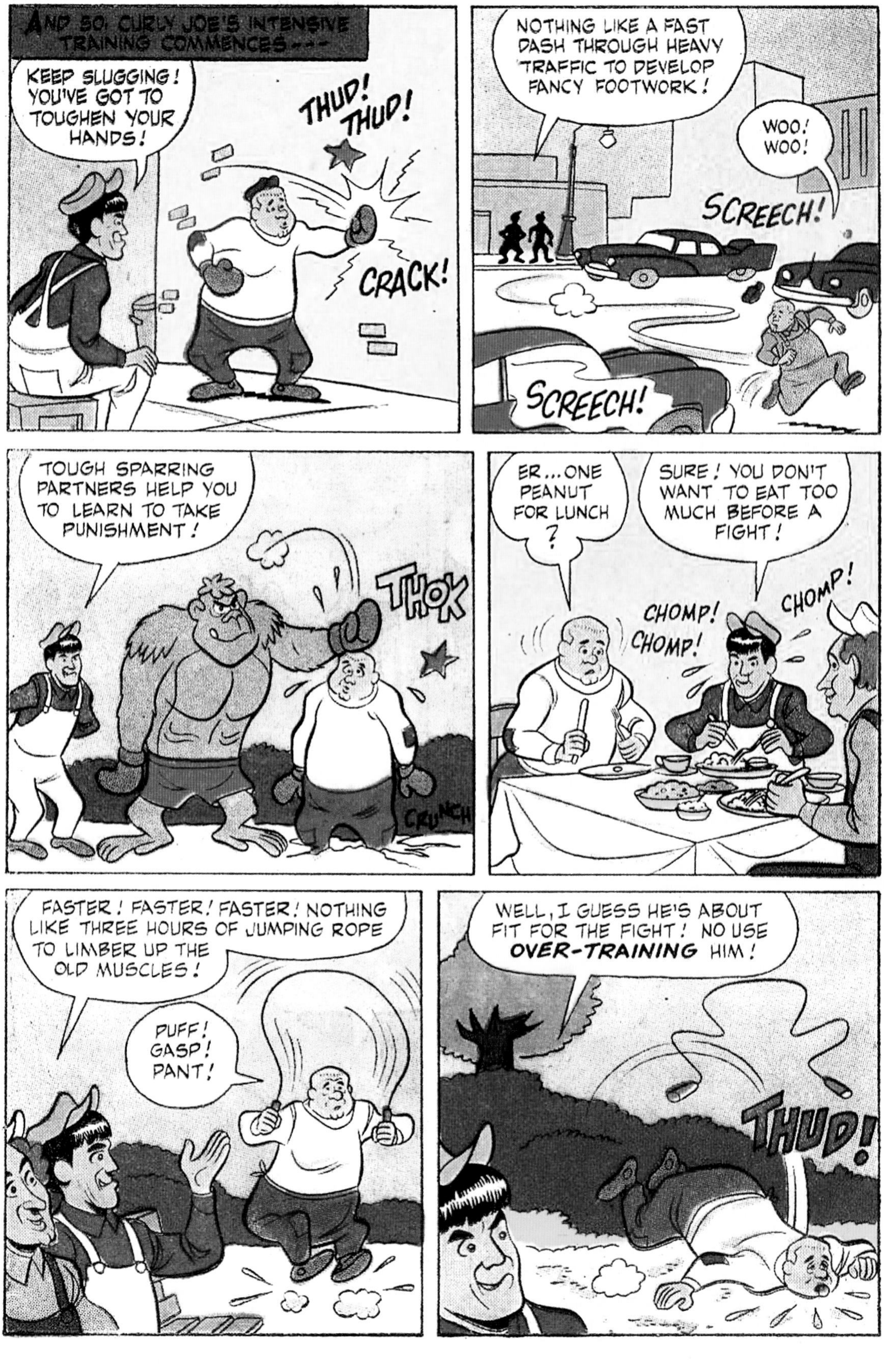
AND SO, CURLY JOE'S INTENSIVE TRAINING COMMENCES---
KEEP SLUGGING! YOU'VE GOT TO TOUGHEN YOUR HANDS!
THUD! THUD!
CRACK!
NOTHING LIKE A FAST DASH THROUGH HEAVY TRAFFIC TO DEVELOP FANCY FOOTWORK!
WOO! WOO!
SCREECH!
SCREECH!
TOUGH SPARRING PARTNERS HELP YOU TO LEARN TO TAKE PUNISHMENT!
THOK
CRUNCH
ER...ONE PEANUT FOR LUNCH ?
SURE! YOU DON'T WANT TO EAT TOO MUCH BEFORE A FIGHT!
CHOMP!
CHOMP!
CHOMP!
FASTER! FASTER! FASTER! NOTHING LIKE THREE HOURS OF JUMPING ROPE TO LIMBER UP THE OLD MUSCLES!
PUFF! GASP! PANT!
WELL, I GUESS HE'S ABOUT FIT FOR THE FIGHT! NO USE OVER-TRAINING HIM!
THUD!

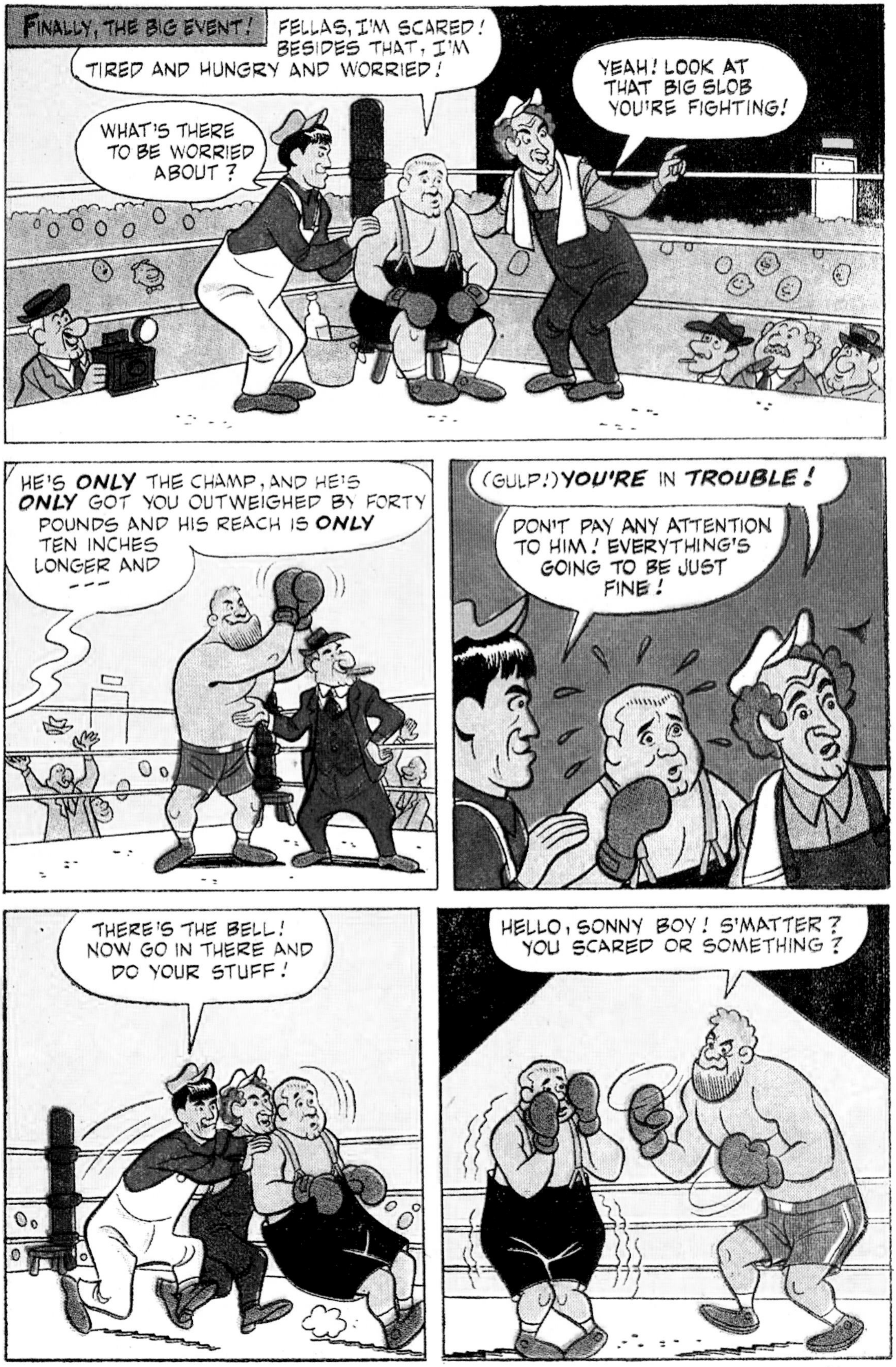
FINALLY, THE BIG EVENT!
FELLAS, I'M SCARED! BESIDES THAT, I'M TIRED AND HUNGRY AND WORRIED!
WHAT'S THERE TO BE WORRIED ABOUT?
YEAH! LOOK AT THAT BIG SLOB YOU'RE FIGHTING!
HE'S ONLY THE CHAMP, AND HE'S ONLY GOT YOU OUTWEIGHED BY FORTY POUNDS AND HIS REACH IS ONLY TEN INCHES LONGER AND ---
(GULP!) YOU'RE IN TROUBLE!
DON'T PAY ANY ATTENTION TO HIM! EVERYTHING'S GOING TO BE JUST FINE!
THERE'S THE BELL! NOW GO IN THERE AND DO YOUR STUFF!
HELLO, SONNY BOY! S'MATTER? YOU SCARED OR SOMETHING?

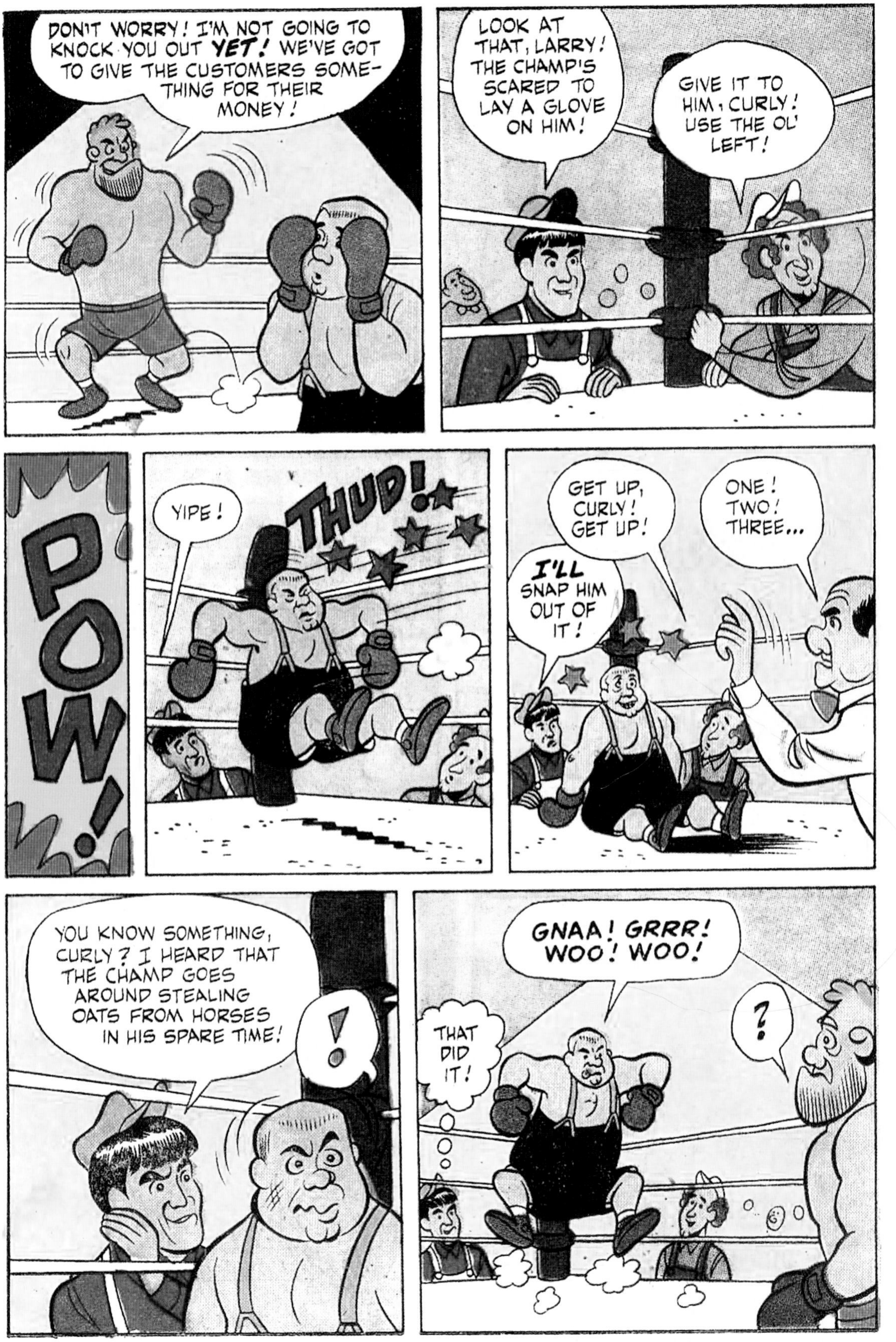
DON'T WORRY! I'M NOT GOING TO KNOCK YOU OUT YET! WE'VE GOT TO GIVE THE CUSTOMERS SOME-THING FOR THEIR MONEY!
LOOK AT THAT, LARRY! THE CHAMP'S SCARED TO LAY A GLOVE ON HIM!
GIVE IT TO HIM, CURLY! USE THE OL' LEFT!
POW!
YIPE!
THUD!
GET UP, CURLY! GET UP!
ONE! TWO! THREE...
I'LL SNAP HIM OUT OF IT!
YOU KNOW SOMETHING, CURLY? I HEARD THAT THE CHAMP GOES AROUND STEALING OATS FROM HORSES IN HIS SPARE TIME!
!
GNAA! GRRR! WOO! WOO!
THAT DID IT!
?

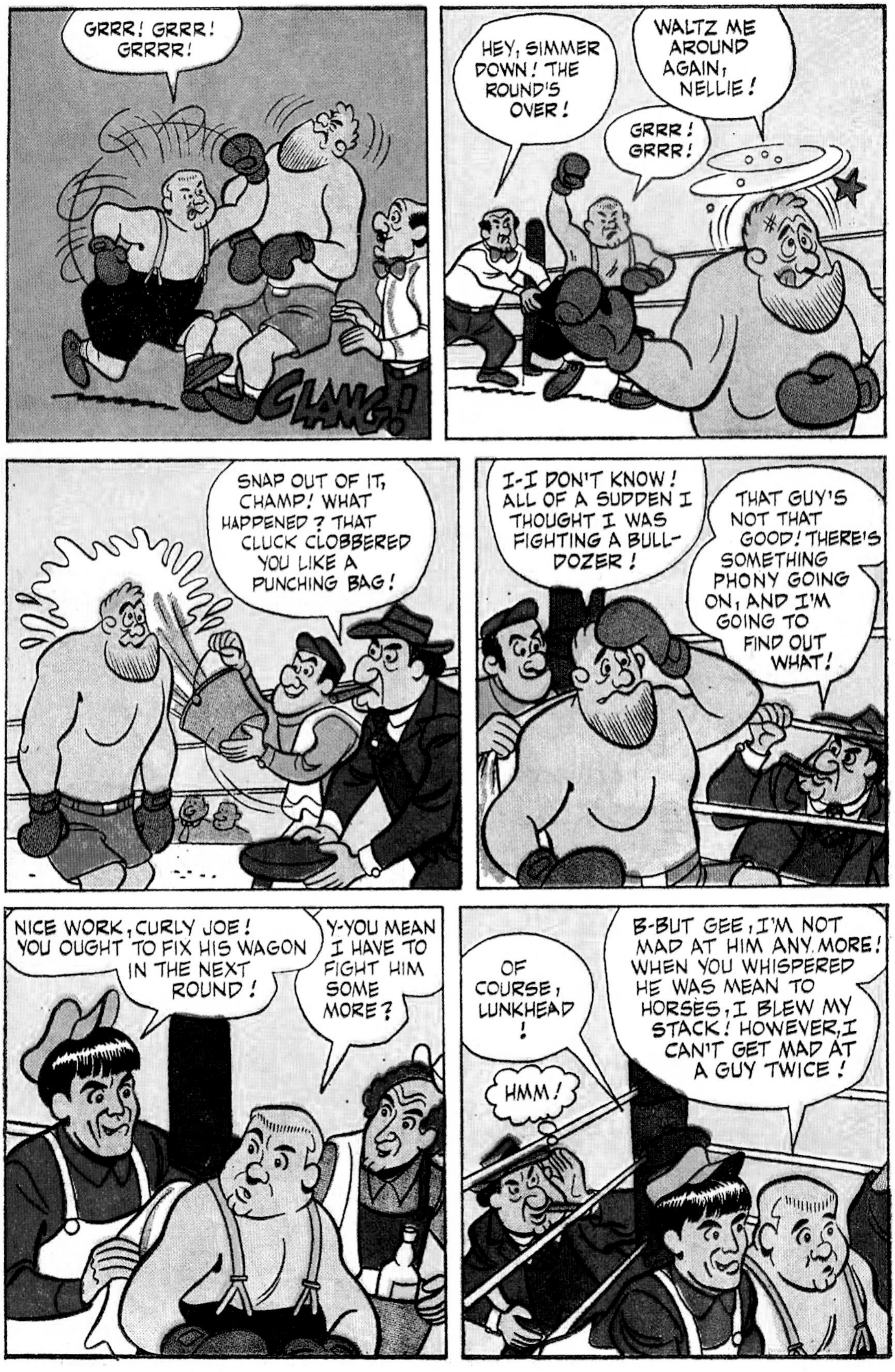
GRRR! GRRR! GRRRR!
CLANG!
HEY, SIMMER DOWN! THE ROUND'S OVER!
WALTZ ME AROUND AGAIN, NELLIE!
GRRR! GRRR!
SNAP OUT OF IT, CHAMP! WHAT HAPPENED? THAT CLUCK CLOBBERED YOU LIKE A PUNCHING BAG!
I-I DON'T KNOW! ALL OF A SUDDEN I THOUGHT I WAS FIGHTING A BULL-DOZER!
THAT GUY'S NOT THAT GOOD! THERE'S SOMETHING PHONY GOING ON, AND I'M GOING TO FIND OUT WHAT!
NICE WORK, CURLY JOE! YOU OUGHT TO FIX HIS WAGON IN THE NEXT ROUND!
Y-YOU MEAN I HAVE TO FIGHT HIM SOME MORE?
OF COURSE, LUNKHEAD!
B-BUT GEE, I'M NOT MAD AT HIM ANY MORE! WHEN YOU WHISPERED HE WAS MEAN TO HORSES, I BLEW MY STACK! HOWEVER, I CAN'T GET MAD AT A GUY TWICE!
HMM!

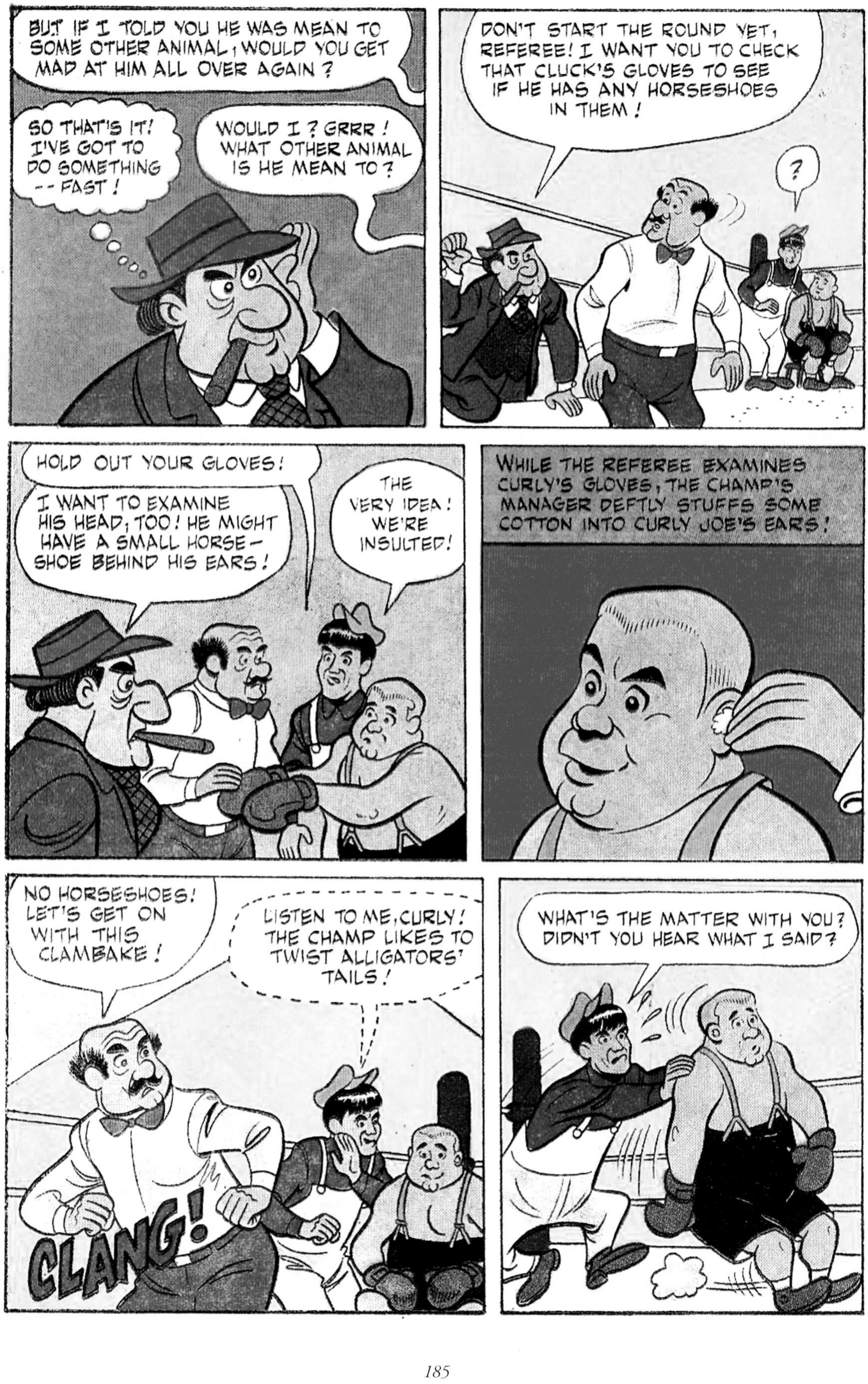
BUT IF I TOLD YOU HE WAS MEAN TO SOME OTHER ANIMAL, WOULD YOU GET MAD AT HIM ALL OVER AGAIN ?
SO THAT'S IT! I'VE GOT TO DO SOMETHING -- FAST !
WOULD I ? GRRR ! WHAT OTHER ANIMAL IS HE MEAN TO ?
DON'T START THE ROUND YET, REFEREE! I WANT YOU TO CHECK THAT CLUCK'S GLOVES TO SEE IF HE HAS ANY HORSESHOES IN THEM !
?
HOLD OUT YOUR GLOVES!
I WANT TO EXAMINE HIS HEAD, TOO! HE MIGHT HAVE A SMALL HORSE-SHOE BEHIND HIS EARS!
THE VERY IDEA! WE'RE INSULTED!
WHILE THE REFEREE EXAMINES CURLY'S GLOVES, THE CHAMP'S MANAGER DEFTLY STUFFS SOME COTTON INTO CURLY JOE'S EARS!
NO HORSESHOES! LET'S GET ON WITH THIS CLAMBAKE!
LISTEN TO ME, CURLY! THE CHAMP LIKES TO TWIST ALLIGATORS' TAILS!
CLANG!
WHAT'S THE MATTER WITH YOU? DIDN'T YOU HEAR WHAT I SAID?

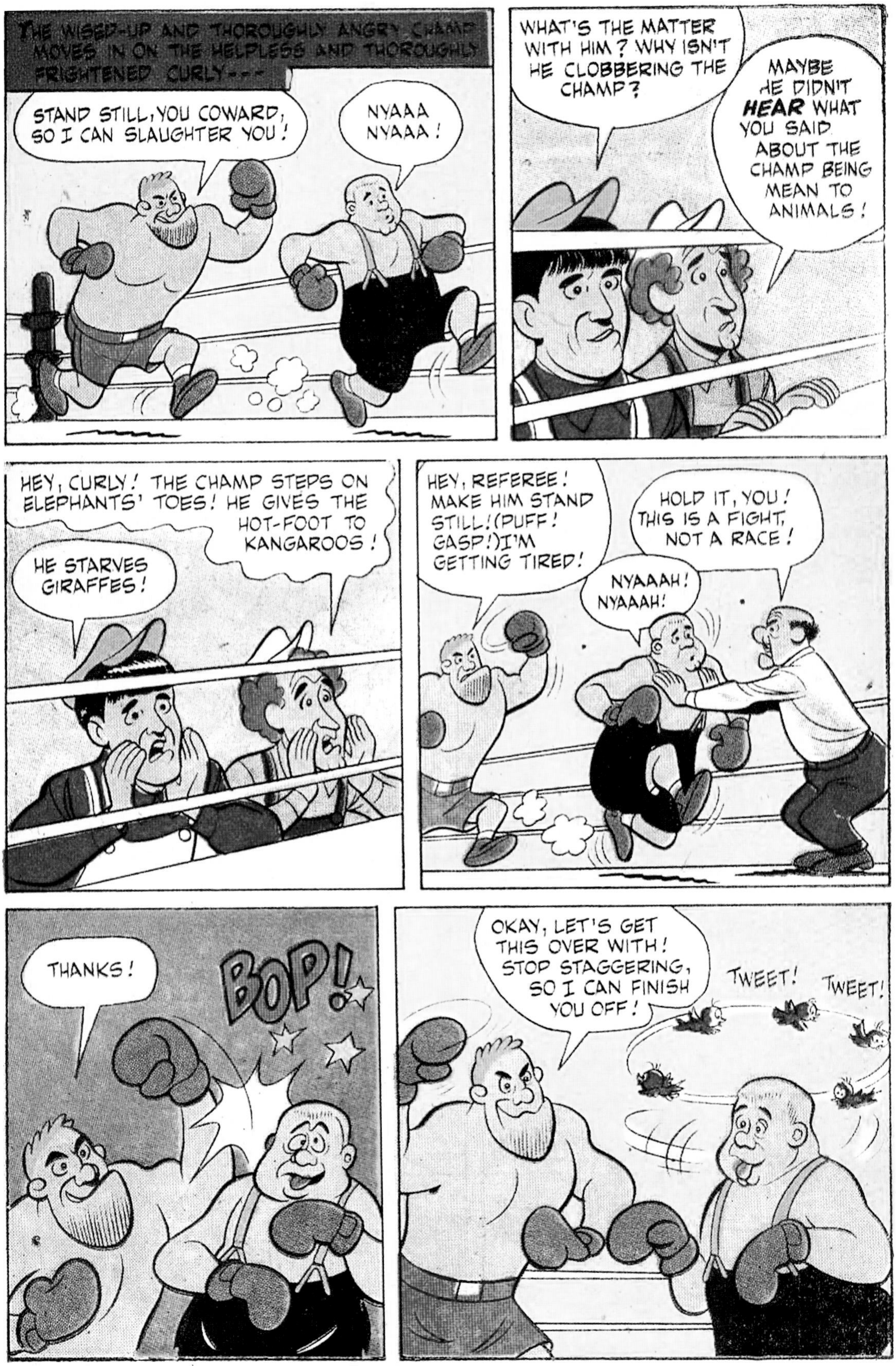
THE WISED-UP AND THOROUGHLY ANGRY CHAMP MOVES IN ON THE HELPLESS AND THOROUGHLY FRIGHTENED CURLY---
STAND STILL, YOU COWARD, SO I CAN SLAUGHTER YOU!
NYAAA NYAAA!
WHAT'S THE MATTER WITH HIM? WHY ISN'T HE CLOBBERING THE CHAMP?
MAYBE HE DIDN'T **HEAR** WHAT YOU SAID ABOUT THE CHAMP BEING MEAN TO ANIMALS!
HEY, CURLY! THE CHAMP STEPS ON ELEPHANTS' TOES! HE GIVES THE HOT-FOOT TO KANGAROOS!
HE STARVES GIRAFFES!
HEY, REFEREE! MAKE HIM STAND STILL! (PUFF! GASP!) I'M GETTING TIRED!
HOLD IT, YOU! THIS IS A FIGHT, NOT A RACE!
NYAAAH! NYAAAH!
THANKS!
BOP!
OKAY, LET'S GET THIS OVER WITH! STOP STAGGERING, SO I CAN FINISH YOU OFF!
TWEET!
TWEET!

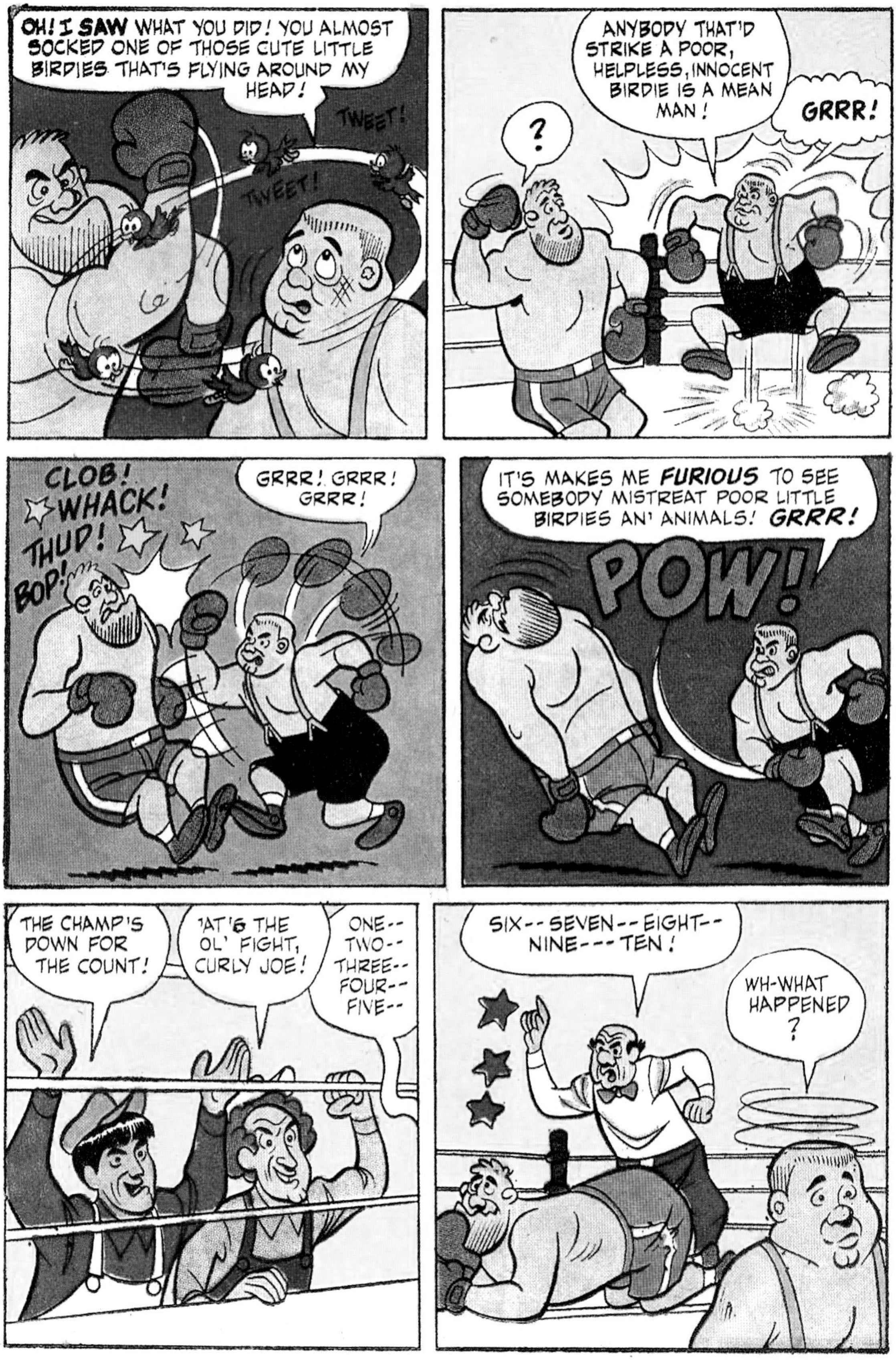
OH! I SAW WHAT YOU DID! YOU ALMOST SOCKED ONE OF THOSE CUTE LITTLE BIRDIES THAT'S FLYING AROUND MY HEAD!
TWEET!
TWEET!
?
ANYBODY THAT'D STRIKE A POOR, HELPLESS, INNOCENT BIRDIE IS A MEAN MAN!
GRRR!
CLOB! WHACK! THUD! BOP!
GRRR! GRRR! GRRR!
IT'S MAKES ME FURIOUS TO SEE SOMEBODY MISTREAT POOR LITTLE BIRDIES AN' ANIMALS! GRRR!
POW!
THE CHAMP'S DOWN FOR THE COUNT!
'AT'S THE OL' FIGHT, CURLY JOE!
ONE-- TWO-- THREE-- FOUR-- FIVE--
SIX-- SEVEN-- EIGHT-- NINE--- TEN!
WH-WHAT HAPPENED?

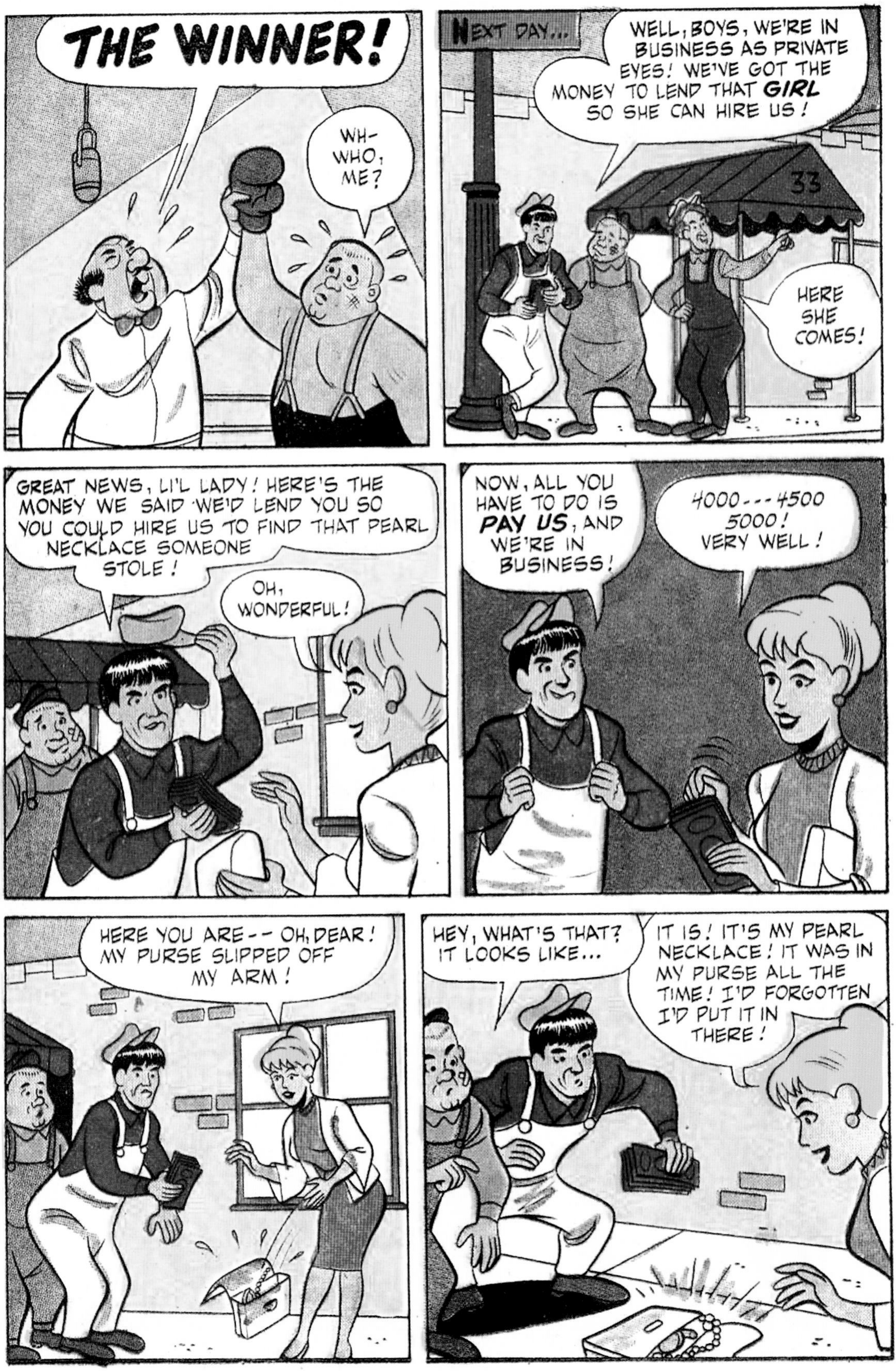
THE WINNER!
WH-WHO, ME?
NEXT DAY...
WELL, BOYS, WE'RE IN BUSINESS AS PRIVATE EYES! WE'VE GOT THE MONEY TO LEND THAT GIRL SO SHE CAN HIRE US!
33
HERE SHE COMES!
GREAT NEWS, LI'L LADY! HERE'S THE MONEY WE SAID WE'D LEND YOU SO YOU COULD HIRE US TO FIND THAT PEARL NECKLACE SOMEONE STOLE!
OH, WONDERFUL!
NOW, ALL YOU HAVE TO DO IS PAY US, AND WE'RE IN BUSINESS!
4000---4500 5000! VERY WELL!
HERE YOU ARE-- OH, DEAR! MY PURSE SLIPPED OFF MY ARM!
HEY, WHAT'S THAT? IT LOOKS LIKE...
IT IS! IT'S MY PEARL NECKLACE! IT WAS IN MY PURSE ALL THE TIME! I'D FORGOTTEN I'D PUT IT IN THERE!

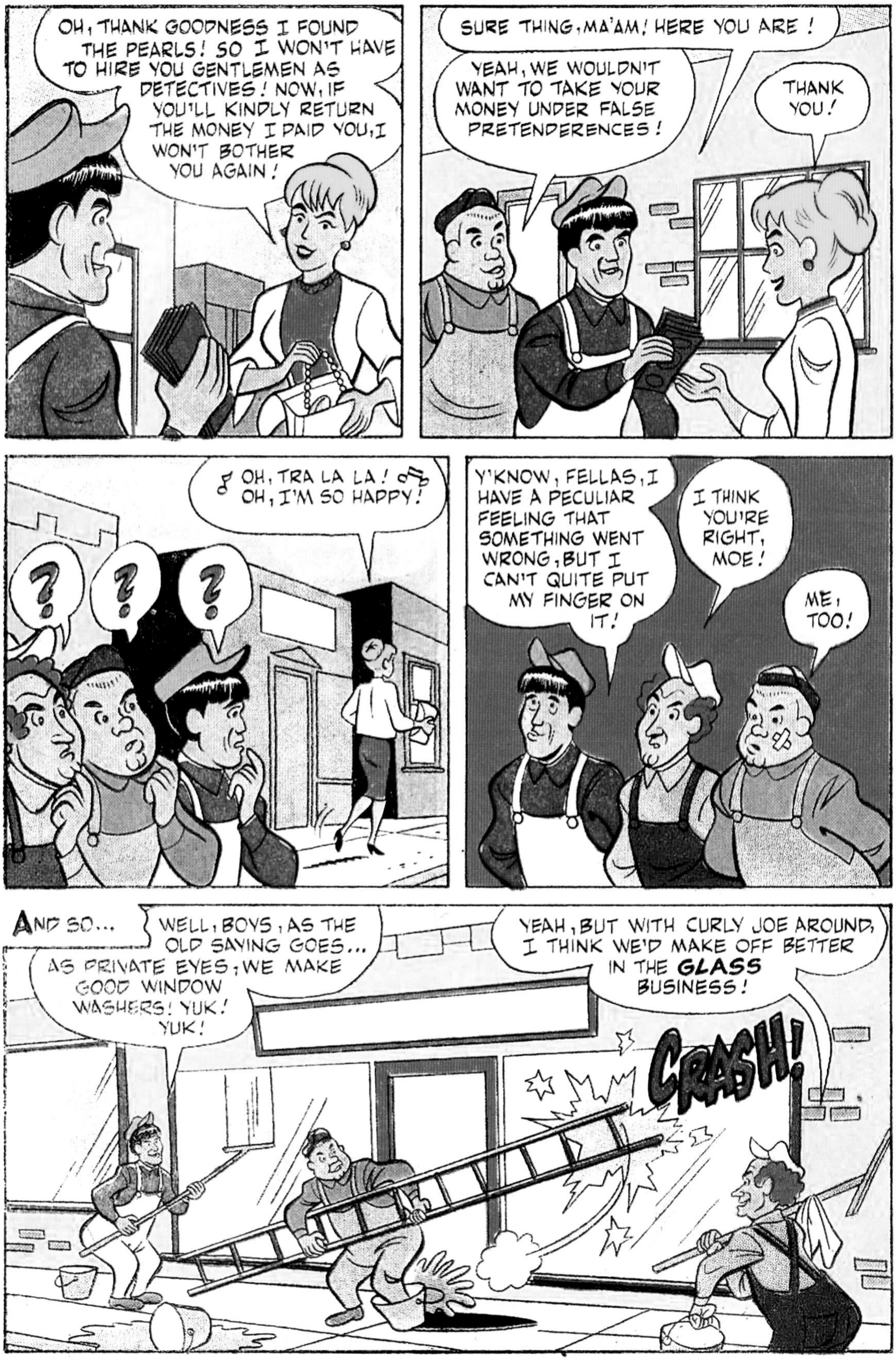
OH, THANK GOODNESS I FOUND THE PEARLS! SO I WON'T HAVE TO HIRE YOU GENTLEMEN AS DETECTIVES! NOW, IF YOU'LL KINDLY RETURN THE MONEY I PAID YOU, I WON'T BOTHER YOU AGAIN!
SURE THING, MA'AM! HERE YOU ARE!
YEAH, WE WOULDN'T WANT TO TAKE YOUR MONEY UNDER FALSE PRETENDERENCES!
THANK YOU!
OH, TRA LA LA! OH, I'M SO HAPPY!
?
?
?
Y'KNOW, FELLAS, I HAVE A PECULIAR FEELING THAT SOMETHING WENT WRONG, BUT I CAN'T QUITE PUT MY FINGER ON IT!
I THINK YOU'RE RIGHT, MOE!
ME, TOO!
AND SO...
WELL, BOYS, AS THE OLD SAYING GOES... AS PRIVATE EYES, WE MAKE GOOD WINDOW WASHERS! YUK! YUK!
YEAH, BUT WITH CURLY JOE AROUND, I THINK WE'D MAKE OFF BETTER IN THE GLASS BUSINESS!
CRASH!

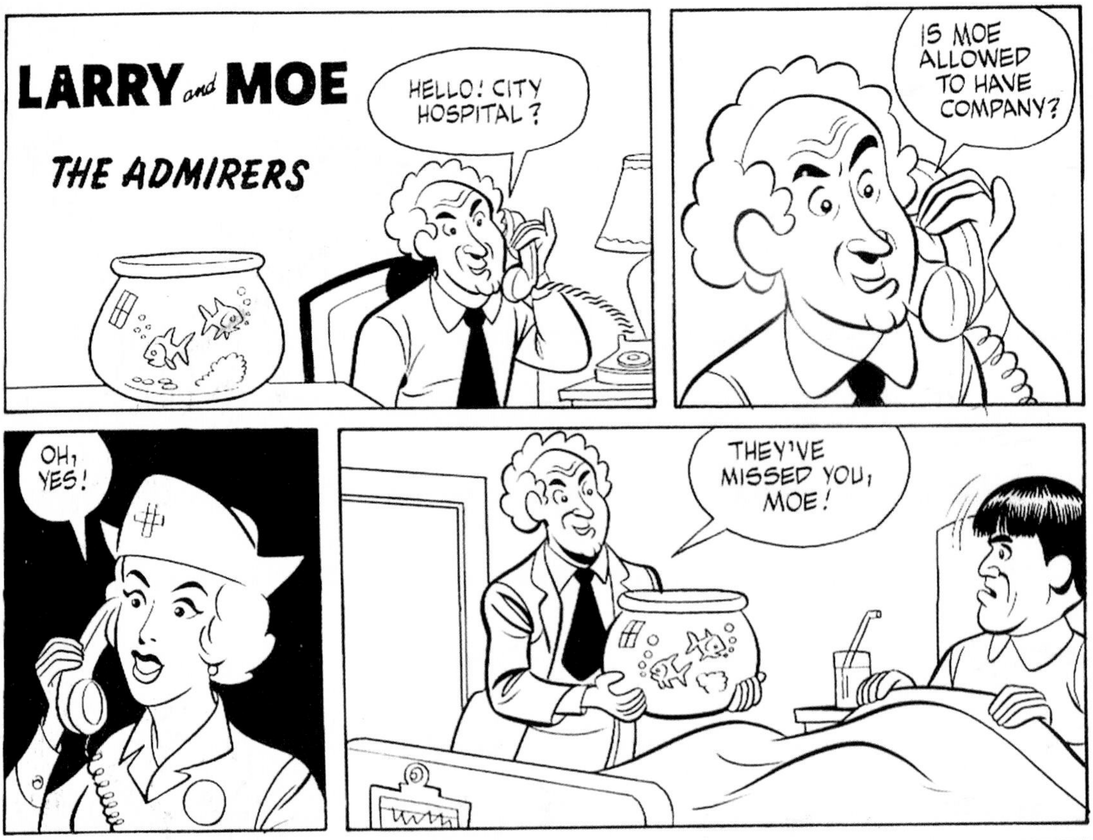
LARRY and MOE
THE ADMIRERS
HELLO! CITY HOSPITAL?
IS MOE ALLOWED TO HAVE COMPANY?
OH, YES!
THEY'VE MISSED YOU, MOE!

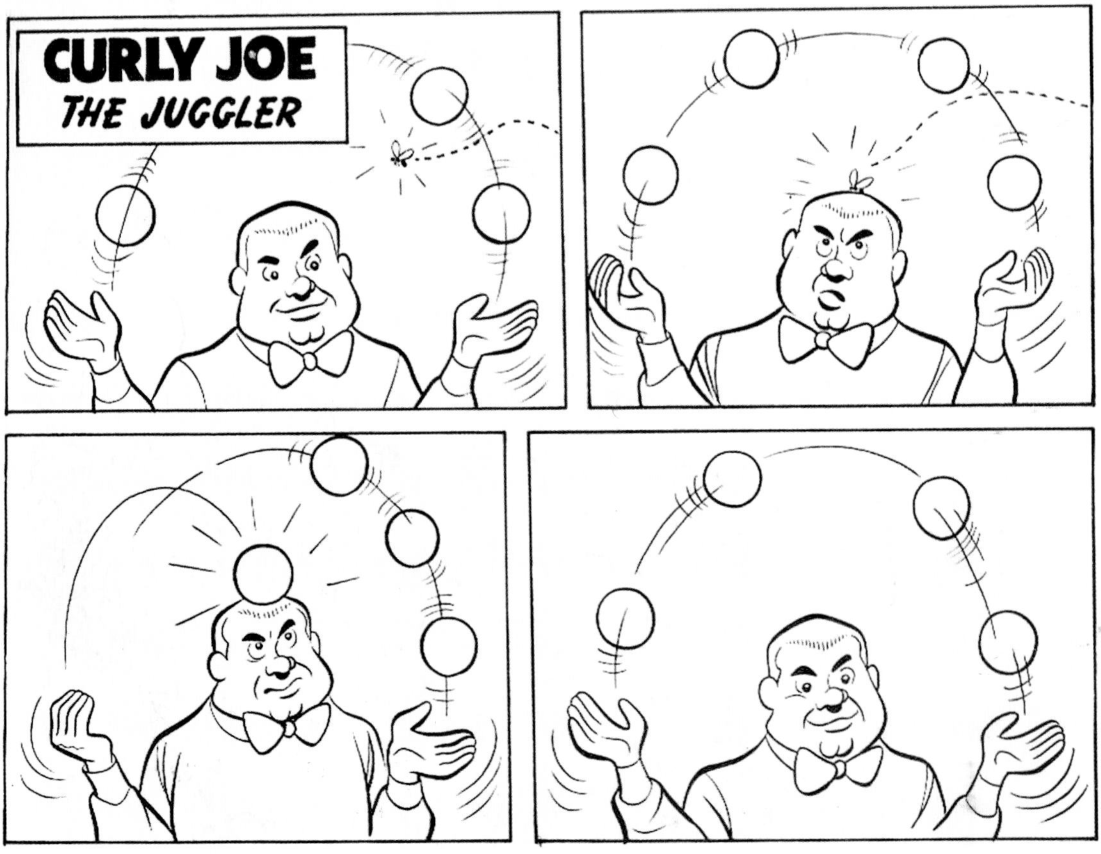
CURLY JOE
THE JUGGLER

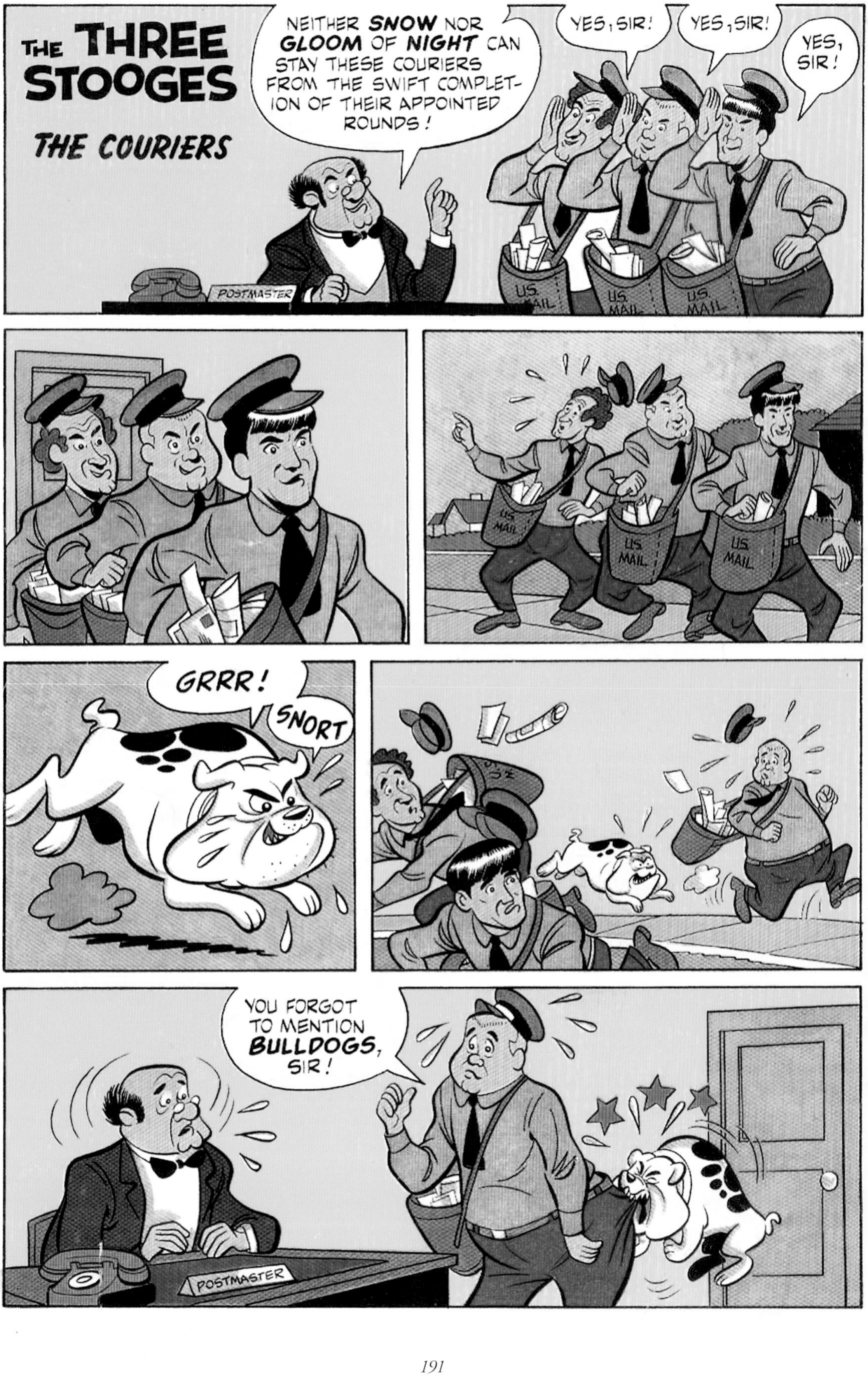
THE THREE STOOGES
THE COURIERS
NEITHER SNOW NOR GLOOM OF NIGHT CAN STAY THESE COURIERS FROM THE SWIFT COMPLETION OF THEIR APPOINTED ROUNDS!
YES, SIR!
YES, SIR!
YES, SIR!
POSTMASTER
U.S. MAIL
U.S. MAIL
U.S. MAIL
GRRR!
SNORT
YOU FORGOT TO MENTION BULLDOGS, SIR!
POSTMASTER

AFTERWORD

by Jim Salicrup

If you're a comicbook fan, chances are at some point you stumbled upon a batch of old, well-read comicbooks and it was like uncovering buried treasure. With the release of a new *Three Stooges* film from C3 Entertainment, Inc. and the Farrelly brothers, it seems like the perfect time to dig up some of the original Three Stooges comicbooks and present them to both their longtime baby-boomer fans, as well as their all-new films fans.

Just like real old comicbooks, the comics presented in this premiere collection are well-worn and show signs of wear and tear—the result of countless re-reading, no doubt. Besides old comics were printed on newsprint which tends to yellow with age, and old comics are famous for the color printing to routinely be off register. But despite all these flaws, the charm old the material always manages to show through.

And about those comics… there has always been a strong relationship (even literally) between the THE THREE STOOGES and comics. Their very first movie, 1930's "Soup to Nuts" was written by the famous cartoonist Rube Goldberg (The National Cartoonists Society's "Oscar" is named the "Reuben" after Goldberg). Near the end of World War II, when, as Stooge Moe Howard wrote in his 1977 autobiography, "my daughter fell in love with a sailor, Norman Maurer, a photographer stationed at the Long Beach Navy base. He was a comicbook cartoonist and a very handsome and likable fellow. After a two year courtship, they were married."

Moe proved to be very perceptive, and noted "in Norman's work as a comicbook cartoonist, a close parallel to the movie industry. He wrote the stories and dialogue, directed his characters, cast them, created their wardrobe, etc. Years later, when we finally did our features for Columbia, Norman was assigned the job of writing and producing them, and he directed our last two features." Indeed, Norman Maurer, an incredibly talented cartoonist drew the first THE THREE STOOGES comics in 1949 as well as many of the later ones, entitled THE LITTLE STOOGES, in 1972-74.

Another unique aspect about the relationship between the Stooges and comics, is that unlike when other real-life stars were featured in comicbooks and publicity photos or stills from TV or movies adorned their comicbook covers, the Stooges themselves posed for the photo-covers used on many of their comics.

Within this collection, we're featuring three THREE STOOGES comics originally published by St. John, that we're all written and drawn by Norman Maurer. Even the Li'l Stooge stories credited to Michael Brand and Jeff Michael is really by Norman—Michael and Jeffrey are his sons' names.

We're also proudly featuring three THREE STOOGES comics originally published by Dell and illustrated by Pete Avalrado and edited by Chase Craig. (Despite our best efforts we're unable to name the writers for these stories.) Pete, like Norman, was also involved in both Hollywood and comics. Pete Alvarado had a long and distinguished career in both animation and comics. Two 1949 Warner Bros. shorts Pete was involved with, "For Scent-imental Reasons," as a background artist, and "So Much, for So Little," as layout and background artist, won the Academy Award for Best Short Subject Cartoon and Best Short Subject Documentary. As an animator he worked for Disney, Warner Bros. (the legendary Termite Terrace), and for many TV animation studios, especially Hanna-Barbera. He drew the comicbook adventures of many of those same studios' famous cartoon characters.

Just as the line-up for the new film features new actors, the Three Stooges themselves went through various incarnations, with the Moe, Larry, and Curly being the most popular. Surprisingly, that configuration only appeared in two comics in 1949 (not counting the comics in 1986 -87 that redrew Shemp as Curly), and in the all-new THREE STOOGES graphic novel, by George Gladir, Stan Goldberg (no relation to Rube), and me, that's available now from Papercutz. Most of the comics featured either Moe, Larry, and Shemp or Moe, Larry, and "Curly" Joe. We hope to feature the two very first THREE STOOGES comics, with Curly, and by Norman Maurer, in an upcoming volume of THE BEST OF THE THREE STOOGES COMICBOOKS, as well as the two stories we dropped from this volume for space reasons.

We hope you enjoyed this collection of THREE STOOGES comicbooks and hope you'll return for Volume Two featuring more wonderful comics by Norman Maurer and Peter Alvarado. Just as the humor of the Three Stooges, from the original short films to today's new movie, is timeless, so is the appeal of these beautifully drawn comics. So, come back—we've got more!

—Jim Salicrup
Editor-in-Chief
PAPERCUTZ